A Hole in the World

White Harbor: Book 3

Carlos E. Rivera

Copyright © 2024 by Carlos E. Rivera

All rights reserved.

No portion of this book may be reproduced in any form without written permission from the publisher or author, except as permitted by U.S. copyright law.

ISBN-13: 978-0-9756380-7-1

Interior design and Edited by David-Jack Fletcher

Cover by Greg Chapman

Praise for White Harbor

"White Harbor is a brilliantly haunting tale of a small town's deadly and cursed history."
– Eric Woods, author of *This is How He Collects Them*

"Rivera weaves a tale that is reminiscent of early King, using foreshadowing to great effect. This author's work is a delight to read if you're all about horror!"
– Eryn McConnell, author of *Death by Sugar*

"Where *The Local Truth* set the stage, *Blackout* gives us the play, the drama, the horror, everything we've been waiting for, and it does not disappoint. Rivera has a way of writing that takes us further than merely reading a book. These pages feel like memories of our own hometown, our own childhood, our own nightmares. Mark my words, Carlos E. Rivera is a master of his craft and will be talked about for many years to come."
– Chisto Healy, author of *The Gateway in Apartment 8* and *The Pit*

"Rivera delivers prose that is both elegant and engrossing. His characterization is top notch, creating characters that are shades of light and dark, providing authenticity and complexity."
– Mark Allan Gunnells, author of *Haunted Places and Other Stories* and *Before He Wakes*

"White Harbor is small town horror, coming of age, and demonic cosmic horror told over the course of many years and many characters. I personally love this narrative choice as it gives you a look at the town, it's dark secrets, and the lives of the characters that affect the evils they face in the present day."
– Horror Reads, Goodreads Reviewer

"Carlos has an amazing talent at creating nightmares. Some of the creatures and body horror within this book are legendary."
– Jacy Morris, author of *This Rotten World*

Preface

I'm saving my actual notes for the very end. I just had two very important things to say before you dive back into White Harbor.

1) If you're here, you've read two fairly large books already, trusting it will all be worth it. I take that trust seriously. So, I'd like to thank you and tell you it will be worth it.

2) You're about to read horrible things; people doing, saying, or being subjected to reprehensible events. You might be tempted to stop or rage-quit. I urge you to press on to the very end. Don't skip the prologue, don't skip scenes, don't skip the epilogue. It will all make sense. I've lovingly crafted this story in a way that each scene helps balance another, everything counts, and missing part of it, down to the very last written word before "THE END", will make it feel incomplete. You'll see what I mean.

Talk to you more after that.

PROLOGUE
THE CAVE

From the files of Callum Baker

Account of the first colonial party arriving in the zone later named "White Harbor", led by a builder and a trader, respectively named Gideon McClemont and Amias Vanek.

The following letter recounts the unusual storm that assailed the expedition shortly after crossing the southern Crescent Mountains, upon first setting foot on this land in the winter of 1866. It was the first of four consecutive blizzards, burying the land under snow for over a month and a half—an event never recorded in the area again.

Few details survive of how the party reached the cave referenced below, but there would be one famous account of the horrors they experienced upon reaching the land they had hoped would become their new home: the letter of one Zephaniah Emmit, which would be entrusted from one person to another until it reached Emmit's sister, Rosanna Crane, long after his death. Books on the history of White Harbor often cite and translate Emmit's letter from Early Modern English into Contemporary English, as presented here, for the understanding of present-day eyes.

November 1966.

Dearest Rosanna,

I write this in hopes it reaches you, for my beautiful Clarice cannot read, and she must learn of my fate, so she be spared from a life spent in mourning. It was an evil fate that compelled me to join this doomed party. The relentless wind and snow make it impossible to sustain fire, and our flesh craves heat, as our bellies ache for food, which is scarce in this merciless winter.

The fruits we carried have shriveled and burned with frost, and the salted meat has become so hard it's inedible, likely to shatter our teeth. We don't even have our horses with us. Their meat and fat would have sustained us as we waited for this Devil's cold to subside.

It is as if the land itself rejects us, forcing us to flee or perish for our hubris. In my darkest dreams, I fear it's something more than mere nature. I dare not put it in writing, lest my words manifest as a curse. Mother always warned us, "Do not speak evil into existence, for words hold power." God keep her in His peace. Her wisdom meant to keep us from unwittingly invoking wicked influences.

The land hates us.

Day and night, the wind howls like the voices of the damned, and out of one hundred and forty-six souls who set foot on this accursed land, only eighty-one remain, taking refuge inside a dark cave, once home to a bear, which did not take kindly to eviction. It mauled Simon Ramsey and tore out Asa Pennel's throat before the beast was brought low. The bear was the last fresh meat we ate. At first with ravenous joy, as we savored the flesh and blood, then with sadness, as the last of it became a thin bone stew, boiled slowly with melted snow and a feeble fire.

The Sterrett family, who were once so dear to us, have all

perished. First the children: Ann, Theodosia, Amiel, Patience, Francis, Georgine, and the eldest, Amos, all between the ages of three and eleven. Then, their mother, Emeline, once blessed with God's joy and great beauty, died in grief.

Her last moments were spent first screaming, then mumbling her children's names amidst ramblings of demons whispering from the bowels of the cave, telling her that her children's souls were not at peace. Last was my dear friend, Bartholomew Sterrett, gone mad with grief and horror, seeing his entire family perish, their bodies tossed onto the growing pile of corpses outside, as holy interment is impossible in such unholy weather.

Bartholomew, naked and raving as a man possessed, threw him-self onto his Emeline's cold remains, as his children were buried too deep beneath the many frozen dead. I am ashamed to say none of us dared to pull him back into the cave, fearing the cold and his madness, which had eroded all signs of self-preservation.

Seeing Barty clutching the frozen husk of his wife, then becoming stuck to her with ice, will be an image etched into my memory until my last breath.

At one point, sanity returning ever so briefly, he realized his predicament. He attempted to release her, but their frozen skin was fused together in a terrible embrace. When he pulled his cheek from hers, his flesh tore away, sticking to her icy corpse. Blood flowed briefly before freezing into red streaks on both their faces.

His death was a grim spectacle. He howled, bound to his dead wife; howled louder than the wind. We covered our ears to block out his cries, but the cold numbed our hands, forcing us to hide them under our armpits for warmth. So, we were forced to listen as he cursed God with blasphemies too terrible to repeat, words I dare not write here, lest dear Mother berate me from Heaven. He screamed until his voice gave out, and even then, I saw him struggle to move, gradually being buried under the snow.

I fear the same fate awaits us all.

The leaders of our party, Gideon McClemont and Amias Vanek, the men who lured us here with promises of paradise, ventured deeper into the cave five days ago. They took with them a portion of what little remained: scraps of salted meat, sticks, rags, oil, and three of the stronger men who could still walk. They claimed they would search for a source of underground water, hoping it would lead to an exit in an area less ravaged by the storm. Strangely, John Ellis, known as "The Long-Lived", refused to join them. Despite his age, Ellis remains as strong and big as an ox, seeming untouched by hunger or cold.

"It is a fool's errand," Long-Lived John said, waving them off, and speaking no more.

Ellis is a strange, solitary widower, but he is wise with age. If he, with his size, strength, and vitality, declared the expedition foolish, I agree with his assessment.

Underground water doesn't always lead to the surface, and even if it did, we lack the strength to follow it.

Food is what we need, not false hope in that merciless darkness. Some whisper they have abandoned us, fled, fearing our wrath for having brought us here, so near the cold end of autumn.

They speculate our leaders knew some of us would decide there was nothing left for us but vengeance for our wasted lives. I do not think this way. I know Amias Vanek. He is an honorable, godly man. Wise and kind. I believe he and McClemont genuinely believed this journey would bring prosperity for us all.

Our quest may have been doomed from the start, but I blame misfortune and the Devil's hand, not ill intent from either man. If they haven't returned, I believe it's because death found them, perhaps a cave-in, or a tumble down a hidden chasm. An easier end than what awaits us. Thank God for small mercies.

My toes harden and blacken as I write, but my suffering is small compared to what Sarah Criswell endured. I watched her baby turn purple and black in her arms as the days passed, as if turning into stone and bark.

She steadfastly refused to let go of her dead babe until Eleazer Sinkler slapped some sense into her and pried the dead thing from her hands. Onto the pile it went, falling on top of where Bartholomew Sterrett still hugged his frozen wife.

I swear I saw Barty move, ever so slightly. Perhaps, my eyes deceived me, but I think not. He remains there, frozen alive, still clutching his dead wife, his face coated with icy blood.

Now, a dead baby rests on top of them, a grotesque addition to this ghastly tableau. Madness also possessed Robert Crummey, who proposed we eat from the newly dead, while the flesh is still tender.

"To survive," he insisted, but none agreed to such a desecration of a friend or loved one.

Crummey, in his absolute insanity, slit his own throat. He said he preferred a coward's death to slow starvation. He gave us his permission to feast on him, should the hunger become too unbearable.

None took him at his word, though there were some glances exchanged, which spoke of a possible change of heart later.

I do not expect to survive this storm. For all my regrets, I am glad I left Clarice and the twins back home. Tell her that her husband may have been a fool to leave her side, but he did so with love in his heart, seeking a better life for our family, even if, in the end, he was thwarted by nature's forces. To Peter and Joseph, tell them their father saw them in his dreams as good men, married and thriving.

I wish for either of them, perhaps Joseph, who loves books and knowledge, to take up my mantle as a scholar. However, if they choose a different path upon reaching adulthood, they have my blessing. Tell them their father's love endures, even as he stares into death's icy face.

You too, dear sister, know that I love you. Pray when death comes for me, it finds me in my sleep, and that my body is not defiled by those who, in desperation, would become like animals.

Love,

Zephaniah Emmit.

By the time the storm subsided, only thirty-two settlers remained, weak, scared, and nearly witless with grief and loss. No child was left alive and, of the elderly who came with the party—either by the stubbornness of their families or their own—only one remained: a man named John Ellis, mentioned in Emmit's letter. One account described Ellis as "an old, husky pig rancher with callused hands, a muscled body wrapped in a thick layer of fat, and skin that looked like old tree bark; a man likely to outlive them all and give God a run for his money."

According to later accounts, the long blizzard ended suddenly, approximately a week after Vanek and McClemont left the group. Below is a transcription from a journal entry by a man named Elbert Giffen, an ancestor of my old friend, Barry Giffen, and one of those thirty-two survivors (pity Barry didn't inherit his ease with words):

"The sun peered through the clouds, as if the storm had never happened. It was a milky, gauzy light. The kind that shines on most winter days, foggy and ephemeral, which, for most of our superstitious minds, was reason enough to wonder if perhaps we had died, and this was Heaven.

The pile of frozen corpses right outside was quick to dispel such a notion.

Something otherworldly had happened, however. We could all sense it.

At first, the horror had been too fresh, and the hundred and nine frozen, snow-covered bodies near the cave exit greeted us as grim reminders death might still lurk all too near.

From the moment we walked out of the cave, it appeared as if the land had changed its mind about us, would-be invaders. The rest of the winter was pleasant, not lacking in fire for warmth, and fish, meat, and fruit for nourishment.

The dead from the cave were finally given a holy burial. A large cairn was set over the mass grave, both for the hundred and nine buried there, and the five that ventured into the depths of the cave, who were never seen again. Long-Lived John himself set the stones that made up the cairn.

Little by little, our settlement grew into a town, started a fair distance away from that evil cave; superstitions, after all, are not easy to dispel. Houses and barns were erected, wells were dug up, fields were tilled, our living relatives immigrated into this brand-new land to join us, and soon there was the sound of work and the laughter of children. A small pier was built, and that, too, grew into a harbor.

The town was officially named White Harbor in 1867.

Memory would fade of the corpses' sunken, cloudy, hardened eyes like those of cooked fish: white, gray, doughy; under shriveled, peeled eyelids. Eyes staring up at those that would soon shovel dirt on them, filled with scorn for the ones granted survival. For all but a few of us, however, that memory would become a mere concept, a formless tale, not attached to the tangible, grisly images of the frailty of the human body and the price of hubris.

It was as if the land itself wanted us to forget we should fear it."

CHAPTER ONE

THE END IS THE BEGINNING IS THE END

1991

"Whoever grabs the railing is a big, clucking chicken," Leroy Howe said, resting his arms on the guardrail while standing on the safe side. Standing beside him on the gravel parking area of the Blue Overlook were his brother Royce, Callum Baker, Nadine Schaefer, Jess Cunningham, Bobby Novak, and Freddie Parham, staring with excitement at the two boys standing past the railing, at the edge of the overlook, where a steep drop led to nothing but ocean and crashing waves.

In the distance, to the left, was the town of White Harbor and the Crescent Mountains—the mountain range that nestled their hometown, and the bay across which they gazed. The clouds crawling across the sky were gray and pregnant with what would soon be rain.

"I don't think I want to do this anymore," Peter Lange said with a tremor in his voice. He was shorter and skinnier than most of his friends and looked like the wind flying up from the sea was likely to carry him up into the sky and drop him a mile away. Strands of black hair in his head fluttered this way and that, looking like a black spider was trying to crawl off his scalp.

"Guys, it *is* actually getting really windy," Bobby said. "Maybe we can come back some other—"

"Don't be such a pussy!" Freddie shouted over the sound of the wind and pointed a finger at Callum. "Even Droopy did it!"

"I certainly did," Callum said, confirming this with pride. He held his glasses in place with one hand, as if they were likely to be blown away.

Below, an enormous wave crashed into the cliff wall. Its impact could almost be felt all the way to the top of the overlook. The salty water sprayed in the air, drops swirling in a spiral before being carried away.

"You know what?" Barry Giffen said, standing to the right of Peter. "Fuck this! I ain't doin' this!" Barry looked like the opposite of Peter in every way. He was tall, wide, muscular (for his age), and bulky. His brown hair was cut short, so it barely bristled in the wind. He reached a large hand toward the railing—

"Ah-ah-ah-ahh!" Royce waggled a finger in the air toward him. "Seriously? Barry 'The Brickhouse' Giffen? Risking being forever known as a big clucking chicken just coz he was too afraid to do something even Droopy Baker did?"

Callum grimaced. "I'm beginning to take offense with the way you keep making me the lowest common denominator."

"You hear that shit?" Leroy said, picking up what his brother was throwing, grinning with mocking glee. "He talks like *that*, and he actually did this."

"The way I speak is perfectly adequate," Callum said. "Also, eat shit, Leroy."

Barry's hand stopped short from grabbing the railing, hesitated, glanced at Callum, then his eyes found Nadine and Jess. "I'm not gonna pull my dick out when there are girls present. That's like illegal, or somethin'."

"Oh, fuck off, Barr," Jess said with a huff as her fluffy, red perm swayed back and forth in the wind. "Don't make *us* your excuse for being a pussy. Also, it's probably so tiny we wouldn't see it from here."

"You'd be shocked, Ginger Bitch," he answered, then, catching himself, swallowed hard, looking embarrassed as Jess gave him a furious look. "Sorry. Fine. I'll do it."

Barry and Peter glanced down at the ocean below, then exchanged a look. Peter was still trembling, either from cold or pure terror.

Barry gave him a reassuring smile. "You'll be fine."

The smaller kid stared back. Dark-blue eyes, looking into Barry's baby blues. "Thanks."

"Eyes forward and just go for it."

Peter clenched his jaw and nodded.

Almost in unison, they unzipped, stared ahead, and urinated off the edge. Both streams curved in the wind to the left a short way down, drops and spray flying in the direction of the distant town.

A minute later, they emerged on the other side of the guardrail to cheers and pats in the back.

"You stepped beyond the railing as boys..." Royce said with an ample grin.

"You return to us as men!" Leroy said, completing his brother's sentence.

"Hold up for a second," Nadine interjected. "How come you guys get to do this and we can't?"

Every boy present exchanged an uncomfortable look.

"W-well..." Leroy stammered.

"We thought..." Royce continued.

"It's like..." Bobby said.

"It's because you're girls," Callum said, and got a gawking stare from all present. "I don't mean it in a misogynist, macho-posturing way."

Leroy raised an eyebrow. "Miso-what?"

"It's because it's mechanically impossible for you to do it," Callum continued, ignoring him. "It wouldn't work."

Nadine pressed her lips tight in a straight line and turned her head to Jess. "Jess, could you come with me for a minute?"

Jess gave her a mischievous smile.

Nadine took her hand, and they both ducked under the railing and stood side by side on the edge of the cliff. They looked down as another wave crashed at the bottom. Their expressions lost some of their resolve for a moment; particularly Nadine's, since, beside Barry, she was the tallest of the group, which made her vertical posture feel a little awkward. However, undeterred, Nadine turned her head and eyed Leroy. "So, as long as the person peeing doesn't grab the railing, it's fine, right?"

Leroy and Royce nodded in unison, eyes round with uncertainty.

Bobby looked over the railing with apprehension. "Um… Girls, look, I think you proved your point. We can, maybe, find something less dangerous for you to do. I mean, we don't want anyone dying here, right?"

Without answering, Nadine nodded at Jess, who grabbed the railing with a firm grip. Still holding Jess's hand, she pulled down her leggings from under her skirt and squatted just off the edge of the cliff, eliciting cries of shock from a group of suddenly blushing pre-teens who didn't know whether to look away. Before the gasps and murmurs subsided, from under her skirt came a stream of urine that, like those of Barry and Peter, got carried away by the wind in a thin mist. Once she was done, she hiked up her leggings with expert-level swiftness and grabbed the railing.

It was Jess's turn. She took Nadine's hand, then pulled down her cargo pants and squatted. Soon, another stream of urine poured down, its particles perhaps being carried into town to be breathed in by some unsuspecting townie.

Once done, her pants pulled up, both passed under the railing once more and stood triumphantly at the other end, following that with a high five.

"Um," Callum said. "You didn't wipe."

Nadine squinted at him and smiled. "We'll survive."

"Should we head to the Vanek House?" Freddie asked, grabbing his bike, and standing it upright. "It's still early, and"—he looked up at the gray clouds—"it looks like it's about to rain. Would be nice to have a roof over our heads when the rain hits."

"I can't," Bobby said. "Need to finish my homework for Monday or I won't be able to go with you guys to the Vanek House tomorrow." He smiled wide, a sudden idea shining through his expression. "But how about this? We've all passed the Blue Overlook trial now, so why don't we come up with like, a name or something? Like a group name? For all of us?"

"You mean like the Justice League, or the Avengers? Something like that?" Leroy asked.

Bobby nodded with enthusiasm. "Yeah! We just did something really brave—"

"Or really fucking stupid," Jess interjected.

"Really brave," Bobby repeated. "And we took the town's most infamous haunted house and made it our clubhouse! We're like superheroes or something!" Another idea appeared to have popped up in Bobby's head, and he swiveled his head toward Peter. "Peter was the one that brought us all together and brought us into the Vanek House. Why don't we let him choose the name?"

Peter seemed put on the spot. "I didn't bring us all together," he said with a shy smile. "You all just kinda started talking to me after that day in The Pines."

"Who's in favor of letting Peter name the group?" Bobby asked, raising his hand.

Barry was the first of the others to put his hand up, followed by Nadine. One by one, some with more enthusiasm than others, they all had their hands up. Bobby turned to Peter. "It's settled then, Pete. What's going to be our name?"

"Uh..." Peter fidgeted. His eyes flitted from one face to the other, considering, then he took a breath. "How about..."

1992

"And that's how we ended up with the stupidest fucking team name in history," Jess said, as they all sat around a long table, a spread of hot dogs, nachos, and soda in front of them.

They were enjoying a fun Saturday afternoon at the Seaside Amusement Park, a lofty name for what were basically a few small rides and game kiosks crammed together in a small fairground—one of the town's many failed attempts at becoming a tourist draw. Granted, it was surrounded by a large, beautiful park with trees and benches looking out toward the beach and had a small boardwalk that led to the pier; however, its humble size and simple presentation kept it as nothing more than a local attraction.

Raymond Chang and Sylvia Nguyen, the last two additions to The Vigilantes, stared at her in confusion.

"Okay." Ray tilted his head to one side. "You had sort of given me the cliffs notes before, so I thought there'd be at least a bit more to it."

"So," Sylvia said, "you literally just pissed off the edge of the Blue Overlook and then went, 'Hey, how about we let Peter give us a dumb name and not debate him on it?' I overestimated you guys."

"I'm sorry," Peter said in a meek voice.

"Well, if anything, it's Droopy's fault." Royce tilted his nose toward Callum.

"He was supposed to be the team's encyclopedia until you joined," Leroy finished, finger pointed at Sylvia.

She stuck her middle finger up. "I'm not your encyclopedia." She turned to Callum. "And, seriously, Cal, shame on you!"

He let his head fall in disappointment. "I'm sorry I wasn't able to curtail the group's ignorance."

"See?" Leroy pointed at him. "'Curtail'…"

"Who the fuck talks like that?" Royce finished.

"How in the world did you not know 'vigilantes' didn't mean 'superheroes'?" Leroy berated him.

Callum shrugged. "Batman, Green Arrow, The Punisher, Nightwing, Black Canary, Spider Man, Rorschach, Daredevil, Batgirl, arguably, all the X-Men, they're all vigilantes, so I…assumed!"

"That's right, Droopy, you *assumed*!" Leroy said, his voice accusatory.

"And you know what they say about assuming," Royce continued.

"Yeah…" Leroy said. "It's, like, shitty and stuff."

"I am so disappointed in you," Royce finished.

Ray raised his hand. "I have an unrelated question."

All gazes converged on him. Going around to his left were Barry, Bobby, Peter, and Nadine; then across from her were Royce, Callum, Sylvia, Jess, Leroy, and finally, Freddie on a folding chair at the head of the table.

"I know The Pines is this sacred place to us students, right?" Ray noted the scattered nods around the group. "Why?" He looked around. "From the very first day I went there, before Barry introduced me to the group, the first thing anyone told me was, 'This is a safe place. You can't start fights. No bullying. No insults. No discrimination. If you do any of those things, you'll be cursed.' And I was like, 'Cool!' I wasn't planning on doing any of that stuff, but it's cool there's a safe place right next to the school. Though, no matter how much I ask, no one tells me what the actual curse is."

A chilly wind blew through the concession stands, accentuating the awkward silence that followed.

Ray looked up at the sky and it seemed to have grown a little darker, the clouds moving a lot faster. "Alright." His gaze flitted from one nervous face to the next. "What's with the faces?"

"We can't talk about that," Barry said.

Ray squinted, regarded his best friend as if what he'd said made no sense.

Barry glanced at him, sighed, seemed to put his ideas together in his mind. "It's one of the rules of The Pines. You don't talk about what the curse is. We know there's a curse. We know what has happened to the people that broke the rules. We can't talk about it."

Ray's eyebrows arched, the intrigue eating up at his insides, wanting to ask more, though not knowing if he should.

"Oh, fuck all of that, Brickhouse." Freddie gave Ray a conceited smile. "Ignore your boyfriend, Plus-One—"

Barry bristled at this. "I'm not his b—"

"Oh, blah, blah, blah! I'm just messing with you, man." He turned to Ray again. "My whole family's cursed, anyway, so—"

"Freddie," Bobby cut in. "Don't."

Freddie ignored him outright. "I'm pretty sure the Curse of the Parhams trumps the Curse of the Pines. What's it gonna do? Extra-curse me?"

The wind kept blowing, its sound going from a soft, continuous rustling in the nearby trees to an eerie whistle and moan.

Blight Harbor, Ray thought, keenly aware the spirit—the other side—of White Harbor was always listening. He'd been in town for less than a year, and even if he still had his reservations about the tallest tales regarding White Harbor, he'd felt Blight Harbor from time to time, peering from the dark corners of his bedroom closet, and in the eyes of people who still saw him and his family as interchangeable, out-of-towner Asians who took over the old Chinese restaurant in town and turned it Korean—not that most people in town would know the difference.

"What you need to hear"—Freddie's voice pulled him from his creepy musings—"is what happened to Cody Mason."

"Freddie, shut the fuck up!" Barry said.

Freddie made a sad face and stuck his lower lip out. "Oh, I'm sowwy, Brickhouse. I forgot he was your buddy."

Ray flinched at this. "Was?"

Freddie let out that creepy hyena giggle that had earned him his nickname and affirmed, "Was."

CHAPTER TWO
THE CURSE OF THE PINES

Freddie regarded the disapproving looks with a self-satisfied smirk, his gaze gliding over his surrounding friends. "Cody was an asshole and a bully. Maybe not one as prominent as your reformed buddy, over there,"—he motioned with his head toward Barry, who sneered at him—"but a bully all the same. Do you see this?" He put his left hand forward to show Ray a small, barely visible, blackish dot in his palm. It was under his skin, faint, and clearly not a natural part of Freddie's body.

"What *is* that?" Ray asked, frowning.

"Pencil tip," Freddie spat. "Cody saw me at one of the school-yard tables with my drawing block, just minding my own business. He came out of nowhere, grabbed my wrist, curled my fingers around the tip of one of my pencils, and slammed it on the table. The pencil tip broke, and before I could scream, Cody grabbed my shirt, punched me once, and told me I was forbidden from taking it out. He said he'd check my hand every day, and if he saw I had pulled it out, he'd kick me in the balls before putting another pencil tip in my hand. So, every single day, he passed me in the hallway, or at lunch, and said,"—he raised his voice to sound loud, like a drill sergeant—"'Palms up!'"—Freddie put his palm forward again—"And he'd check, day after day, for three weeks, until the skin had grown over it. So, now, it's a part of me."

"That's awful, man." Ray pulled air through his teeth.

Freddie shrugged. "That's okay. It's a little bit of a reminder, you know? 'Never forgive. Never forget.'" He cast a glance in Barry's direction. "You know, it's cool that Brickhouse is such a success story in turning over a new leaf. He was standing there with Cody. Laughing while he did this to me. Like Cody was his apprentice and was learning the right way to make me hate his guts."

Ray's eyes flitted toward Barry, then back toward Freddie.

"I'm sorry about that." Barry lowered his gaze. Freddie knew the old Barry would've never apologized to him, which maybe did point to a genuine change in the huge troll.

Freddie kept his eyes on him for a moment that stretched and stretched and stretched, then he shrugged again. "That's okay, Brickhouse. The past is in the past. You're a good guy now. I already forgave you. I swear!"

As if sensing the discomfort radiating from Barry, Ray intervened. "Anyway, you were going to tell me about Cody and the Curse of The Pines. What happened?"

Freddie gave him a wide, crooked grin. "Right. See, there was this girl. A sixth grader named Aatiya, who came to The Pines every day. She had a little brother, a second grader named Jaban. He was one of these kids in special ed, not dumb or retarded, you know, those kids that only talk to themselves and make weird moans during the day?"

"My mom said the right word to call them was like 'O-tistic', or something like that?" Ray said.

"Not the point, Plus-One." Freddie waved a dismissive hand. "Let me tell the story, alright?"

"My name's Ray, man."

"Okay, Rain Man, sure." He continued without pausing for comment. "So, Aatiya always took Jaban with her during lunch to The Pines, right? That way, she could help him if he found something wrong with his food or needed help with anything. Now, Brickhouse, he'd always been there after school. Nobody wanted him there, but he was always there. Never at lunch, though. You never saw his other buddies there, either. So, this day, it was like a Tuesday—no, Wednesday—we're all shocked to see Cody Mason coming down the steps from the school to The Pines, and he has this grin on his face..."—he put on the most vile and evil grin he could muster; a wayward canine poking into his lower lip—"Bobby and I were like, 'What the fuck?' We would've never expected Cody at The Pines, so it's kinda freaky he's suddenly there, evil grin and all."

He stopped to glance around. Some kids from nearby tables had joined them to listen to the story. Freddie smiled with satisfaction. Disturbing people was what he loved. When he published his future award-winning graphic novel, he'd tell of this day as an example of where he filed his teeth as a storyteller.

To catch the new listeners' attention, he shouted, "'HEY! SAND NIG—'"

"Whoa!" Royce and Leroy interrupted at the same time.

A loud gasp erupted from the surrounding kids.

"What?" The smile on Freddie's face denoted he knew exactly what.

"Dude, what the fuck?" Leroy said.

Scandalized eyes. Horrified glances. All directed toward the grinning boy with the snaggletooth sticking out. "What?" he repeated with a shrug, acting all surprised.

"Don't play stupid, you fucking hyena!" Royce said.

"Dude, that's what Cody said!" Freddie raised his palms with a shrug. "You were there! You heard him! As soon as he reached The Pines! He shouted, 'Hey, sand n—'"

"Freddie, quit it!" Bobby interjected in a firm voice.

Freddie's smile faded. "Fine!" He huffed, resigned. "I'm just tryin' to be accurate, that's all!"

"We get it already," Nadine said. "There's no need to repeat it."

"Anyway," Freddie continued, "Cody stood right in front of Aatiya and Jaban, who were having their lunch with some of Aatiya's classmates, and that's when I noticed Cody focused his entire attention on Jaban's lunch box. The moment I saw that, it hit me. Couple months back, I was in The Pines when Jaban had a freakout during lunch. One of Aatiya's friends told me they have to arrange his food and vegetables in a specific way so he will eat them. If he doesn't find them in the order he expects to find them, he will freak out, and worse yet, if there's missing food, or if things aren't clean, he'll go nuclear!"

Ray pulled air through his teeth. "Oh, shit."

"'Oh, shit' is right, Ray Liotta, but here's the bad part. Cody started taunting the kid, calling him a san..."—he eyed Bobby—"something bad...and insulting his sister when she tried to step in. By then, everyone at The Pines was losing their shit! Everyone shouted: 'Dude, you can't do that here!', 'Cody, stop!', 'Cody, the Curse!', but he wasn't gonna stop. He'd come there with a purpose. He bent down and picked up Jaban's little lunch box. The little kid was already reaching up, grasping with his hands toward his food. Aatiya tried to take the lunch box back, but he slapped her away so hard, she stumbled back and tripped over a rock at the edge of the clearing, and she rolled down the hill a short way until the back of her head hit another rock, and she knocked herself out."

Ray shook his head. "You're making this up."

"No." Barry gave him a grave, regretful look. "He's not."

"Meanwhile, the kid is already letting out this low moan, going, 'Oooooh-Aaaaah! Oooooh-Aaaaah! Oooooh-Aaaaah!' and instead of making Cody take mercy on the kid, this just makes his meanness boner rock-hard. He flips the lunch box over and its contents hit the dirt. There are carrots, green beans, fruit, some kind of flat bread, bunch of other stuff, lying on the ground, and the kid's now moaning louder, 'Oooooh-Aaaaah! Oooooh-Aaaaah!' Cody ain't done, though—not even close—he crouches down, holding the lunch box upright with one hand, then with the other he starts rolling the rest of the food in the dirt, *really* making sure he gets it right in there, then picks everything up and puts it back in the lunch box, just like it was before, and he puts the lunch box on Jaban's lap, and says, 'Eat!'"

There was this look on Freddie's face as he reached this point in the story. An almost sadistic expression. Savoring the deathly silence around the table.

"Jaban isn't listening, though," he continued. "'Oooooh-Aaaaah! Oooooh-Aaaaah! Oooooh-Aaaaah!' That's all that's coming out of him, louder each time. Everyone's afraid of Cody, so no one's moving. 'Oooooh-Aaaaah! Oooooh-Aaaaah! Oooooh-Aaaaah!' We're also horrified, because by now, we know... We know Cody has just fucked up. He's doing this at The Pines. He's fucked! 'Oooooh-Aaaaah! Oooooh-Aaaaah! Oooooh-Aaaaah!'

"'Eat!' Cody says again. 'Oooooh-Aaaaah! Oooooh-Aaaaah! Oooooh-Aaaaah!' Jaban ain't listening. Then, suddenly, he starts shouting, 'Eat! Eat! Eat! Eat!' and Jaban goes louder, 'Oooooh-Aaaaah! Oooooh-Aaaaah! Oooooh-Aaaaah!' and Cody shouts, 'EAT, YOU FUCKING RETARD!' and he takes a handful of carrots and green beans, and *shoves them* into Jaban's mouth!"

The surrounding kids gasped again. Ray's expression was overcome with disgust.

Freddie continued, undaunted. "Jaban is now wailing, 'OOOOOH-AAAAAH! OOOOOH-AAAAAH!' and Cody is laughing his ass off, like he's just done the most entertaining thing ever. Nobody does anything coz everyone's afraid to come close to Cody because we know he's cursed now. Even if he's too stupid to realize it, we don't know if touching him transmits it. Then, just like that, he stops laughing. He's had his fun, he's bored now. He flashes this smug look at all of us, and turns and walks back up the hill, leaving the kid wailing like a car alarm, and Aatiya hurrying toward him, with blood running down her face."

"God." Ray sounded out of breath. "Why would anyone do something like that?"

"No, no, no, Sugar Ray Leonard." Freddie wagged a finger in his face. "That's not the question you should be asking. You see, Cody hadn't been to The Pines during the first freakout a month earlier. He didn't see it. He didn't talk to any of Aatiya's friends, so he couldn't have known the details. Sure, he could've found out somehow, but then, why wait a month to act like a psychotic shitball?" He pointed a finger toward Ray. "No, my innocent little Ray-of-Sunshine, somebody *told* him that day, maybe as an anecdote, maybe as a rumor—you know, one of those that crawl out of Blight Harbor right when they can do the most damage?—so, guess, who *was* at The Pines the day of the first freakout, even though he never goes there at lunch?" Freddie turned to Barry and if his grin had stretched any further, it would've cut a bloody line all the way past his ears.

Ray eyed Barry, who had his head down.

"What happened, Brickhouse?" Freddie's words oozed malevolence. "Did the pupil surpass the master?"

"Shut up," Barry said, sounding embarrassed. "I didn't know he was gonna do that. I would've never done something that messed up. I'm not like Cody. There was something really fucked up with him. I had limits. He didn't. Shoving heads in toilets and throwing people out of the locker room is one thing,"—he glanced at Peter with regret—"what Cody did was something else." He swiveled his eyes toward Ray, looking embarrassed. "If I'd known he was gonna do that, I would've stopped him."

"That's so inspiring, Brickhouse," Freddie said with sarcasm. "Glad to see I'm friends with someone who's just short of a sociopath."

"Hey," Ray intervened. "Stop that."

His voice was firm enough to let Freddie know he'd crossed too many lines already, and he should back off.

Freddie knew. He'd noticed the way Chang sometimes looked at the big brute. What Chang might not have noticed were the times Brickhouse looked at him the same way. But Freddie was "friends" with him now, "friends" with one of his worst tormentors. The group liked their banter, and he enjoyed taking jabs at Barry Giffen, but now that they were "friends", he had to hide how much he despised the giant turd. Seeing him act like he wasn't a piece of shit anymore made him want to puke his guts out. He had to rein it in, though. He liked the rest of the Vigilantes—yes, even Brickhouse's little boyfriend, a little. Telling the rest these two were gay for each other would cross a line, so he kept his mouth shut.

"What happened to Cody?" Ray asked.

"He got suspended for a week." Freddie rolled his eyes, then made a long pause.

Ray stared at him; a huge question mark drawn on his face.

Freddie shrugged.

"He got suspended? Is that all?"

"Yeah." Freddie grinned.

"Are you freaking joking, man?"

"No. He got suspended for a week."

Ray sighed, rolled his eyes, letting his shoulders droop in disappointment.

"Of course, then he came back from his suspension...and there was this gross, red rash covering his hands and his mouth, with hundreds of yellow blisters all over."

Ray eyed Freddie with surprise.

"He stepped through the front doors, and everyone stopped cold and stared as he walked in. Just gawking, as this guy that made our lives hell for such a long time walked quietly through the hallway. He pulled his hoodie over his head and tried to look down, and hid his hands under his armpits, but it didn't matter. We'd already seen him. And most importantly, Aatiya and Jaban saw him."

Freddie studied Ray's eyes, already wide with shock, but he wasn't done. "When one of the teachers noticed the rash, they sent Cody to the school nurse, afraid it might be contagious. He was sent home, and here's where things get crazy. Now, this comes from various sources; some you'd call rumors from Blight Harbor. Cody's parents took him to the hospital, thinking it was some kind of infection, but nothing came up—no known diseases, no aggressive bacteria, nothing. He was in and out of the hospital, and the rash only got worse. People who saw him said the rash had spread all over his body. The blisters got bigger, oozing pus, and it even soaked through his clothes. His nose, his lips, and his fingers started turning black.

"The last time anyone saw him was in one of the rooms at Clarendon Hospital. Summer Fletcher caught a glimpse through the window to his room. She said he looked like a naked, rotten zombie. He had no nose, just a hanging piece of cartilage, lips completely gone, teeth exposed, like a sick grin. His hands? Just stumps. And the creepiest part? His eyelids had fallen off. He had two dry, open eyeballs, just staring into space. There was a closed casket funeral for Cody about a week after that. Who the fuck knows what was left of him by the time he died?" Freddie sat back straight, shrugged. "So, you wanted to know what the Curse of The Pines does. Now you know."

Ray turned again to look at Barry. "Is all of that true?"

Barry gave a grim nod. "Yeah. I went to see him a couple times. It went just like he said. It wasn't only blisters. There were holes. And worms. They couldn't put bandages over the rash, coz for some reason, the moment they did, he'd start howlin' like he was on fire, and it wouldn't stop until they took them off, so by the end, he was lyin' naked in a hospital bed, rotting away...while still alive."

Ray paused, as if trying to put his thoughts in order. "Why do you think that happens there?"

Freddie shrugged.

Peter's thin voice rose out of nowhere. "There are events that sour a place. Turn it into a hole in the world." He glanced around at the crowd of children. "That's what my mother said about the

Vanek House. Maybe..." He paused for a moment. "Maybe there are events that do the opposite? Instead of 'souring' a place, they..."

"Make it hallowed?" Callum Baker said. "Like, holy?"

Peter nodded.

"That kind of makes sense," Nadine said. "It's like when someone dies, some people avoid the place where they died completely, while other people actually make a little shrine there to remember them? Act all nice and respectful around it? You know what I mean? Same tragedy, two different reactions, one negative, one positive?"

"Yes," Peter said. "Kinda like that."

CHAPTER THREE
MIST GIVEN SHAPE

2022

02:55a.m.
15 hours before Callum Baker's death

The beginning of the dream was a confusing fast series of images of Jenny, jabbed into his brain like knives. Images of their lives together, of their son, of a million moments crammed into seconds—birthdays, anniversaries, arguments, trips, hospital stays, movies, dinners, lazy afternoons together—ending in her bloodcurdling screams as she burned alive, her legs crushed under the fiery debris of their home.

Then he was back. Back in bed as if he'd awakened, eyes groggy, and there was Jenny, opening the door. She walked into the bedroom, ethereal, naked. Stalking with grace, like a ghost in a movie, her feet barely touching the floor. Her body looked almost liquid as she poured herself onto the bed beside him.

Jenny. Jenny, I've missed you. I've missed you so much. I don't know what my life is without you. I don't know who I am anymore.

There was something off about her: her body and features were there, but he couldn't get a fix on them. It felt like, as his eyes were about to figure them out, they blurred and eluded him. He recognized her face, her beauty, but it was more his heart's reaction to her presence than him truly seeing her. She touched him, and instead of being comforting and pleasurable, her touch was cold, freezing even. Her kisses felt like they were extracting his soul through his mouth, leaving an arctic void within him. He stirred and struggled. The freeze went straight to his bones. He was paralyzed, pinned under her. She might have looked like mist given shape and color, and yet her weight flattened him.

She took him inside her then. Far from being the delightful experience he remembered, he was instead consumed by dread. Unlike all the other times he'd dreamed of holding her in his arms in the month since her death—dreams in which she'd actually looked alive—this dream left no doubt the person in his bed was not. The reasoning part of him overrode the emotional, yearning part. He knew this was impossible and wrong. Jenny was dead. She would never return. He was fucking his dead wife.

"This is wrong," he mumbled, slurring his words.

She continued riding him without pause, looking straight into his eyes.

There was a flash, like being dazzled by headlights, and for a brief second, he saw her entire arm was burned, covered in carbonized flesh, and exposed, reddish tissue; the illusion broken for a second. Then it was her lightly freckled skin again.

He couldn't make himself stop. His mind was having a tug of war with his body, which did not heed his commands. He let out a moan, both pleasured and helpless, and it horrified him.

She leaned forward, grabbed his arms, moving them away from her hips and holding them down on either side of his head. Her grasp was viselike. Her grip on his wrists didn't allow his arms an inch of motion in any direction. Her face came three inches from his, and she stared deep into his eyes, making no sound. He noticed a smell coming from her breath, and he could've sworn it was the smell of rotten meat, of the stored gases of decomposition. She lunged forward, letting out a hungry growl, followed by a flinty moan as she kissed him. It sounded primal, predatory, like she was trying to force her breath into his lungs and fill them with flies. He shut his eyelids tight, filled with disgust. The kiss tasted as if someone had shoved a hundred live maggots down this throat.

Peter opened his eyes, and he was now staring into the burned face of his wife. Two cavernous eyes surrounded by red and black flesh covered in sticky, dried up blood. He tried to push her away but found he couldn't—or wouldn't—since his mind was trying to push her off, but his body wouldn't obey his commands. He could still feel himself pushing over and over into her, as if his body *wanted* this, when his mind clearly didn't.

Sleep paralysis! That's what it has to be!

He felt her probing tongue in his mouth, longer than any human tongue should be, spreading a sort of slimy saliva that tasted like a fatty cut of pork that fell through the grill, gathering grease and soot, and left forgotten for weeks.

She pushed off, straightening her back, releasing his arms, and he now watched her in her full glory, sitting on top of him. His dead wife's body. Exposed white tendons, decomposing muscle, and the yellow remains of fat deposits, covered in bits of skin that tried to grow over the damage, but weren't fast enough to keep up with the body's deterioration. Everything was lined with black patches, like charred meat. Bones coated in browned flesh; stained teeth exposed like a cruel grin. And she kept riding him, up and down. Grinning down at him.

Though she'd let go of his arms, he didn't move them. He kept them at the sides of the pillow. Why wasn't he pushing her away?

Sleep paralysis!

His very own succubus had taken on the shape of his dead wife, and he couldn't force himself to stop, until—

No!

A shudder.

A tingle.

His breath caught.

No!

A choppy moan escaped his lips.

He felt himself cum as if he'd been in the middle of the fiercest sexual encounter of his life. He tried to pull out—and this time found he could almost do it—but Jenny's skinless hands grasped his hips as she rode him even harder. She stared at him with those blackened eye sockets, and he could now notice the dried, whitish remains of her eyes' sclerotic fluid.

He emptied himself into her, though it felt more like she'd emptied him.

Once she was done, she leaned in and kissed him again. Once more, the invasive tongue filled his mouth and the back of his nose, with a repulsive taste and stench his brain told him must be emanating from her internal organs, boiled in her bodily fluids during the fire.

With inhuman effort, he found the strength to finally push her off.

"JENNY, STOP!" he shouted, as he woke, soaking in sweat, despite the numbing cold of the night. He struggled to catch his breath.

He was alone. Outside the window, the mountain mist danced in pale wisps through the branches.

CHAPTER FOUR
COTTON-CANDY CLOUDS

02:28 p.m.
Three-and-a-half hours before Callum Baker's death

Ray regarded Barry with curiosity. He'd grown quiet since they'd sat on the park bench, but it was a pleasant sort of quiet. Peaceful. He couldn't believe this was even happening. It had taken thirty years, but here he was, with the man he'd always loved, sitting on a bench at Seaside Park, having a well-deserved gelato after spending the entire morning making love—for real this time—no sudden stops or guilt crises, it was just *them*, at last, enjoying each other.

Barry gazed out toward the ocean. Light blue eyes looking almost silver in the sunlight. It was such a perfect little slice of life, a sharp contrast to the terror of the night before at Cunningham's. The memory of the man who'd held a gun pointed at Barry's face filled him with anger and dread. The thought he could've lost him seemed so distant now, but lingered like a smudge on a blank page. Not knowing why, his eyes wandered toward the old T-square scar on Barry's neck. He'd come such a long way, and it could've ended in a second.

Stop it, he thought, pushing the thought aside. He wouldn't let it ruin this small, perfect moment. The green grass, the trees, the waves crashing where the sand met the ocean, the blue sky streaked with cotton-candy clouds, the wind blowing in the leaves, laughter, and barking of dogs in the distance. The small gelato cups in their hands felt like the perfect way to cap off the day, and it was still early.

Ray kept staring at him, as if he were a puzzle he was trying to decipher. "Elijah Wood."

Barry turned to him, gave him a bemused frown. "Elijah would what?"

Ray chuckled. "You have Elijah Wood eyes. I've always kinda tried to find someone to compare your eye color to. Figured it out. You have Elijah Wood eyes."

Barry blew air through his lips and waved a dismissive hand at him. "Get outta here. No, I don't!"

"Yes, you do."

"Half the people in this town have blue eyes. White Harbor is as diverse as a carton of eggs."

"Nah, your eye color is unique. Trust me." He grinned, his eyes brimming with love. "I've been staring at them for three quarters of my life."

Barry grinned back, his smile framed by that brown beard of his, and Ray could see his cheeks turn red.

He leaned his shoulder against his big guy's arm, smiling as he did. "So, do you like the view?" he motioned toward the sea.

Barry shrugged. "I'm not new in town. I've seen it a thousand times before." He gave Ray a sideways glance. "First time I can relax and enjoy it, though."

"Alright, so I gotta ask." He adjusted his position on the bench, as if about to have a serious conversation, though his playful smile betrayed him.

"Uh-oh…"

"You're forty-two. You've always known you're gay, even if you didn't want to accept it. I really have a tough time believing you've never—"

"Never." Barry chuckled, anticipating the question.

"Like, *ever*…"

"That's right."

There was an awkward pause. He stared straight at Barry, who only looked off to the horizon.

Barry sighed. "Well, there was Hank Marsh. We—"

"No, no." Ray shook his head. "You told me that. That doesn't count. That was an immature kiss when you were eleven. That's kid's play."

Barry gave him a side eye. "Well, it made it really damn awkward when you guys were dating! I mean, knowing *he* knew, but *you* didn't know. That was weird as hell."

"Why?" Ray gave him a mischievous smile. "Were you jealous?"

"Little bit. Not gonna lie."

"Of him, or me?"

Barry feigned offense at this, turning a frown with a hanging jaw toward him. "Well, I'm here with you, not in New York with Hank, so what do you think?"

Ray flashed a huge grin. "Good answer."

There was another brief pause, during which Barry kept staring ahead. Ray was a second away from closing the topic, when—

"Steam Portland," Barry said, almost in a whisper.

"What?"

"Steam Portland. Last year of college."

Ray gawped at him, as if he'd grown a testicle out of his earlobe. He let out a confused chuckle. "I'm sorry, there must have been shrooms in my gelato. Did I just hear you say, 'Steam Portland?'"

"Mm-hmm." He gave a nod, still staring toward the sea.

"You. Barry Giffen. You have been to a gay bathhouse."

"Mm-hmm." He nodded again. "Twice."

"Twice?!" Ray stared at the ground. Mouth hanging open.

Barry smirked. "Why? You've never been?"

"Well...yeah...but..." He put on a pensive frown. Swallowed. "I've always been open about, you know... You're the guy who was so closeted you had sex with Jess...and, I mean, if there were some kind of White Harbor Lesbian Council, she'd be the Wise Elder Lesbian."

"To be fair, we were both drunk and in denial."

"My point being, you in a bathhouse, with the tiny towel, the gross sandals, and guys hanging from slings. I can't even..."

Barry responded with an amused smile. "Are *you* jealous?"

Ray gave him a soft punch in the shoulder. "A little. Not gonna lie."

"Nothing ever really happened," he said in a serene voice. "First time I went was almost at the end of college. I had put up with four years in a dorm full of guys running around in their boxers. I needed a freakin' outlet. So, one day, I said, 'Screw it', and went there. The showers were empty, but there were these four guys standing nearby, and they tracked me going in. The moment the little towel came off, and the water started running, it was like all three of them teleported into the shower, staring and, you know..." His eyes flitted down toward his crotch then back up to Ray. "So, I got outta there, quick as I could, and rushed into the steam room. Two minutes later, I'm sitting there, can barely see anything because of all the steam, and there are all of these hands on me. So, I panicked and ran out. Swore never to come back."

"You did, though."

"The week before my wedding to Maryann." He gulped. "I saw it as my last chance, you know? Before closing up shop without a single customer. I went there. I put up with the stares and the leering eyes. I mean, like I'm that much to look at..."

"You seriously underestimate how popular bears are in the gay community, and how ridiculously hot you are."

Barry turned to him. Smiled. Blushed. "Thanks. Anyway... I went there already knowing what to expect, so it wouldn't shock me anymore. Checked in. Clothes in the locker. Shower went smoothly, and I started walking around these blue- or red-light hallways, until I saw this guy in one of the private rooms, door hanging open. He was beautiful, and he was lying in this bed, and he was naked and was…" He gave Ray an awkward look again. "Well, you know."

"Jerking off?"

Barry squinted at him. "Are you comfortable with me telling you this?"

Ray chuckled. "Yes. We're both adults. I don't want you to feel like there's a part of your life you can't tell me."

He nodded with a pleased expression. "I went in, and he glanced at the door, telling me to close it, and I did. He got up. Stood in front of me, staring into my eyes, and he took off my towel and started…you know…touching me…there…and it felt so damn good. I was touching him all over, and he kept doing this thing with his hands… Unbelievable." He glanced at Ray to see if this wasn't too much detail. Ray was unfazed. "You have to remember, no man had ever touched me there, and I was feeling so caught up in the whole experience, I went in for a kiss,"—he held his breath, put his hands up as if punctuating the moment, one holding a chocolate gelato cup—"and the guy pulled his head back."

He eyed Ray, as if verifying he understood what this action meant.

He did.

"He looked at me like I was crazy. Crazy for wanting a kiss when we were both already naked and touching each other. He gave me this condescending smile, like saying, 'What are you, new?' I felt so humiliated. I picked up my towel, got my stuff from the lockers, and left. Never went back."

Ray gave him a tender look. "Come here." Ray took Barry's large hand in his, moved his head closer and pulled Barry's head toward him and kissed him, putting as much love as he humanly could behind it. Once the kiss was done, he ran a hand over his beard. "I love you."

Barry's face lit up. "Me, too."

As if the universe itself had noticed two people being happy—which demanded an urgent response—Ray noticed a couple walk a few yards in front of them, hand in hand. The woman was staring at them. There was a suspicious look of recognition in her eyes. Barry's face went stiff, as if his chest were collapsing in on itself, like his entire body wanted to hide within his ribcage.

"Shit," Ray said. "Remember our conversation earlier about the whole 'coming out of the closet' thing?" He noticed the way the woman's face went from recognition to shock. Her companion turned to look at them as well. "I don't mean to make you panic, but that's Danae Wilkes and her husband. If what I've heard is true, I think you'll be officially out by dinnertime." The air became viscous and hard to breathe. Ray knew Danae worked at the docks, the same as Barry, but he wasn't sure how well they knew each other, if at all. Barry's face was inscrutable. "Should we go home? If we're going too fast with this, we can slow down a bit. You haven't even talked to Maryann yet, and here we are, acting like—"

"Hi, Danae!" Barry called, waving at the passing couple, prompting them to stop.

Danae Wilkes gave him an uncomfortable look. "Oh, uh... Hi, Barry! I thought you'd be at the office today."

Ray gawked at him, then was supremely aware of his hand and Barry's being clasped together. All of a sudden, their interlocked fingers felt to him like he'd thrown Barry on top of the bench and started raw-dogging him in public.

Barry's fingers squeezed tight. "Happy birthday! It's today, right?" he said in a pleasant, yet loud voice, then looked at the husband. "Hi there, Richard."

The man returned an uncomfortable wave.

"Thank you!" Danae's smile wavered a little, her eyes flitted from Ray to him, then back to Ray, then back to him. "I took the day off to celebrate, yes. How about you?" Her voice took on the singsong tone of someone beginning to relish catching an acquaintance red-handed; that delicious morsel of gossip beginning to settle on her taste buds.

Barry shrugged. His indifference to her venomous tone felt almost seismic in Ray's mind. "No large shipments today." He flashed a pleasant smile. "And I had too many vacation days piled up. So, I figured, why the hell not?"

She nodded, her head moving with a slow up-and-down motion, lest she provoke the large, insane man grinning back at her.

An awkward silence stretched between the two couples.

"This is Ray." Barry raised both their hands together just enough for her to see, and for someone who'd never been shy about being gay, Ray suddenly wanted to dig a hole in front of the bench and continue until he came out the other end of the Earth, see if it was true it led to China. Then, Barry added the words that froze him in place. "He's my boyfriend."

Danae stared like he'd told her he had corpses buried under his flower garden. Her expression was of fascination and horror, combined with a forced smile. "Nice to meet you!" She gave him a mare-like, toothy grin, then turned back to the man who, she'd just decided would become her gossip goldmine for years to come—were it not for the fact she would die the next day, drowning in endless gallons of mud—"So, you and...Maryann..."

"We're separating."

Ray knew, of course, this wasn't yet true, even if it was the plan.

"I'm moving out this week."

Now it was Ray who shot him the "this man is certifiably insane" look. In his case, however, it had more to do with how brazen he was being.

"Well, as long as it's the best for your whole family," she said, still in that musical tone of the unapologetic hypocrite. "Best wishes!" She pointed toward the amusement park, not taking her eyes off him. "We gotta go now. It was a pleasure to meet you, Ray. See you on Monday, Barry!"

"Buh-bye." Barry flashed a huge smile and watched her leave, murmuring things to her husband. She appeared to be saying something akin to: "Call the national guard! There's a 250-pound psychopath lose in town!" She shot Barry one last scandalized look over her shoulder, and they hurried along toward the crowd at the amusement park.

Once they were gone, Barry let out a deep exhalation, let go of Ray's hand, brought the gelato cup to his lips, and scooped the entirety of its contents into his mouth, until the cup was empty. He then pressed his teeth together as the brain-freeze passed.

Ray, still looking quite shocked, used a thumb to wipe the spicy chocolate gelato off Barry's beard, then looked down to find a little gelato stain on his shirt. "Your shirt." He wiped the tiny drop off, leaving a small smudge. "Well...between this and a man pointing a gun at us last night, I'd say this interaction was the most shocking of the two."

"I don't know how I'm not having a full-on panic attack." In Barry's eyes, he could see it: the way he unwittingly imagined going back, scampering away to his dark little cell, back to his prison, his sentence, his isolation, his loneliness.

"Hey, Big Bear." Ray got closer, pulled his face toward him, and kissed him again. He felt his body relax. Once the kiss ended, Ray glanced at him and found a smile. There was no prison, not anymore. Only the green grass, the blue sky, the cotton-candy clouds, and the sound of the wind in the leaves.

There was no prison.

"Um...guys?" the voice came from behind the bench.

When they turned, there was Angela, not in her wheelchair, but standing with a cane, next to Bobby; Nadine beside them. All of them stared at the two sitting on the bench, jaws hanging open.

He could sense Barry tensing up again. It was one thing to put on a show to teach Danae Wilkes to mind her own business. Another was for their closest friends to have witnessed it. Ray's hand was the one squeezing hard now.

(*How do you feel?*)

(*I feel like me*)

There was no prison.

Nadine was the first to break the awkward silence. "Seems we're not the only ones crazy enough to go out to the park on the day after we're held at gunpoint before a town-wide supernatural blackout."

Bobby surveyed the surroundings. "Lots of people took the day off and flocked to the park, it seems. So, I suppose we wouldn't have been the only ones, anyway."

Ray also took a wide glance at the surroundings. "You never get used to it, do you? The way we just ignore and rationalize shit in this town?" He looked at the other three. "So, what are you all doing here?"

Bobby put a gentle hand around Angie's waist and flashed a beaming smile. "Nadine and I had a promise to keep to this cute lady over here. We weren't letting anything interfere with that."

Nadine tilted her head. "To be accurate, I was blackmailed into promising, and Bobby got roped in with me. I have a sub covering for me at school."

"We just had ice-cream, and so far, I've been on the merry-go-round, the bumper cars, and the Ferris wheel." The childlike joy in Angie's voice made it easy to forget this was a thirty-something-year-old woman. "I'm trying to convince Miss Stuck-Up here to let me get on the scrambler and the roller-coaster."

"Not gonna happen." Nadine shot a look at her two friends' hands, still clasped together. "Turning the question back around. You guys had it rough last night—more than any of us—and you're here in the park today...among other surprising developments?"

Ray turned a loving glance toward Barry. "I guess...last night reminded me it's not worth spending another moment without the people we love." He squeezed his partner's hand, then looked up at Nadine and squinted, studying her expression. "You already knew, didn't you?"

She sighed. "Peter knew about Barry since a long time ago. He didn't flat out tell me, but I sort of pulled little bits of info from him until I put it all together." She shrugged at Barry. "Don't get mad at him. He would've never told anyone, but he has no poker face when it comes to me. I know him too damn well."

Barry chuckled. "That's okay. How'd it go with Peter last night?"

"Oh, you know,"—she rolled her eyes—"the usual. Guilt and gloom, with a big scoop of 'Mother' thrown in. I convinced him to drop that stupid plan to move back to White Harbor, though."

"Oh," Barry seemed a little disappointed. "It's kind of a bummer, but yeah, I think that's for the best."

"He looked like he had a really shitty night, too. He dropped me off to go visit Callum on the way to see his mother. He seemed stressed out. We barely talked on the drive home."

"Hey, sis," Angela interrupted. "Can we maybe drop the depressing 'Peter's mom' talk just for today? It's such a beautiful day. I'm having a great time. Let's focus on the good things for now. That sound okay to you?"

"Yeah. You're right."

Angela turned toward Barry and Ray and squealed with glee. "You guyyyys!" She extended her arms toward them and took two awkward steps in their direction, wiggling her fingers as if calling them to come closer. "What are you waiting for? C'mon and hug me! I can't jump over the bench and hug you, you know?"

They both walked around the bench and gave her a tight hug.

"This makes me so happy!"

CHAPTER FIVE

BELT

1989

Martha Lange stood on the circular stone altar at Sanctum's center. Around her, eight pairs of people sat in a circle of sixteen chairs—two parents for each of the eight families. Behind them, their children, only those sixteen or older, sat on pews forming an octagon, with small gaps in between for passage. Stone pillars stood behind the pews, torches in sconces shining warm, dancing light across the faces gathered. Beyond the pillars, darkness pressed against the solid stone walls. Above, a domed ceiling opened to a starless sky where a blue moon hung motionless, peering down at this urgent gathering of The Circle.

There was silence all around as she and the rest of the Circle waited for his response, yet as far as Logan Giffen was concerned, they could wait for the rest of their lives. His answer would never be yes.

He eyed his wife, Yvette, who also stared at him, her eyes brimming with anxiety, then fixed his gaze on Martha Lange. He pushed air out of his nose, and a sardonic scoff left his lips. "Fuck you," he said.

Consternation. Gasps all around.

"How dare you?" said Judy Becker—whose family owned the local supermarket—narrowing her eyes at him with disgust, the same as her husband, Sam.

", don't!" Yvette pleaded, clasping his shirt's sleeve.

He pulled his arm away and stood. He shot a piercing blue stare at Martha Lange, who sneered at him in a silence pregnant with smug self-importance.

"Oh, how dare I?" His gruff voice echoed, bouncing off the chapel's walls. He turned his gaze to Judy Becker. "Let's see how compliant you are the day this bitch"—he motioned toward Martha, as gasps erupted from the crowd—"decides she wants to sacrifice little Sam Junior. Let's see how high and mighty you and Sam Senior are!"

"Logan, please!" Yvette pleaded. "You can't speak about the Mother like that!"

"It's your son she wants to kill, Yvette!" he shouted, spit spraying from his lips as he spoke. He stared at his wife with contempt. For years, he'd put up with her alcoholism and her mistreatment of Barry, because he thought of her as a good person, deep down, and he'd always loved her, but hearing her plea in favor of what Martha Lange was suggesting was beyond disgusting. "Your son! She wants me to stand there"—he pointed at the altar, finger trembling with anger—"and stab our son forty-four times in front of all these people. Don't you care?"

Yvette stammered. "I—"

"If it were the Lord's decision that we must give our Sam for the good of all, we'd more than humbly give him up!" Judy Becker sneered with pride. "But it has to be you!"

"That ain't happening." Logan shook his head.

"Logan," Chuck Cunningham said in a beseeching tone; his wife, Madelyn, pulling him back by the hand. "Please, man, listen to reason. We have no choice! None of us were expecting the Valencia kid to die in the Vanek House. That offset the balance to the other side. We need to do something to bring it back, or everything's going to get derailed! We're so close!"

"Yeah, yeah, marvelous job of parroting what that crazy monster said. I'm not doing this! You hear me?"

"You're such a damned hypocrite, Giffen!" Logan spun his head to one side to find Collin Rockwell—whose family owned the local shoe store—standing from his chair glaring at him, his wife Stacy beside him, and their son Stanley sitting behind them. "You're fine having a comfy job managing the docks and having the guarantee of a long life, as long as you don't need to pay for it when asked."

"It's eternal life, Logan!" Amber Bishop—the Town Manager—said, as her husband next to her nodded, and their twin daughters watched in silence. "For all of us! Once God awakens, he will take us all to the Moonlit World. We'll all live there forever as a family. Barry will be waiting for you there! You won't have to miss him long!"

He squinted at her, baring his teeth, ready to tell her to fuck off, along with those two horrendous teenagers of hers, when—

"That's enough," Martha said. "Logan, it's not a request."

He whirled on her. "I'm not your fucking slave, Martha. I don't have to do what you tell me. You won't take my son from me."

"When Curling allowed the Vanek House to take Gerardo Valencia—"

"Oh, shut the fuck up, Martha! I don't fucking care!"

"Logan!" Yvette pleaded.

"You should care." Martha said. "You're a direct descendant of the cave survivors. The only one in The Circle. Your son has the eyes, as do you, which is rare. His sacrifice can shift the balance in a way Curling and his order can't shift back from now until the Ritual of the Four Nights. His sacrifice would guarantee no more setbacks. Eternal life for all, like Amber said, including your son, whom you'll meet on the other side. Don't comply, and instead, it will be the Void for you, your wife, and your son. It's a simple choice."

"The only thing simple here is that brain of yours, Martha. You think it's that simple? Sacrifice your son. See how simple it is."

"Peter has a different purpose," she said, a plain, emotionless statement.

"Fuck you," he repeated, his voice an irate growl. "Fuck you all."

He turned around and walked toward the one aisle in the Sanctum, leading to its one exit. Yvette once more reached for his shirt's sleeve, and he pulled it away, only this time, he stopped and turned back around with a fiery glare. "I want your drunken ass out of the house tonight! Is that clear?" With that, he turned toward the exit and stomped out, with the sound of Yvette's voice following him, pleading for him to reconsider.

He reached a large door, reinforced with metal. It creaked as he pulled it open. He stepped through, and it was like walking into his bedroom from his house's hallway. He was hit by the afternoon sun coming through his bedroom window. It was pale, winter light, which appeared blinding after coming from the gloom of the Sanctum.

It had been hours since he'd told Martha Lange and the Circle to fuck off. It was night already.

Yvette hadn't arrived from the Sanctum—not that he wanted to see her—she had stayed behind with those people and had probably exited through the doorway into one of their homes. More likely than not, she was at Cunningham's, getting stupid-drunk with her buddy, Neal Parham.

He knew he couldn't stay in this town, and he couldn't leave Barry with his soon-to-be ex-wife. He no longer trusted her. Regardless of what he thought of the Circle, he knew the power beneath the town was real, and Martha would use it to her benefit. Barry was valuable to them as a descendant of the cave survivors—the town founders—because his lineage served as a connection with the power awakened there over a hundred years ago. He was also considered blessed by that power; his pale blue eyes seen as a birth sign of his connection to the Blue Moon God, Uolmin. Logan offering his own son would be a precious sacrifice. It symbolized one of the cave descendants ending his bloodline of his own volition, a line which should've ended at that cave so many years ago, if not for God's mercy. A sort of, "Thank you, Lord, we're satisfied now, so we return your blessing after all this time."

Because of this, he was certain they wouldn't try to sacrifice Barry themselves, because then the symbolism was lost, and with it, the value of the sacrifice. Still, once 1996 rolled around, and the time came for the Ritual of the Four Nights, he was certain Martha Lange would select Barry as a sacrifice out of pure spite. He needed to ensure his son was nowhere near this town when that happened.

He walked out of his bedroom, let out a stream of air from his lungs that felt like it would never end, and shuffled down the hallway to find his nine-year-old in the living room, watching TV.

"What are you watching, buddy?" he asked, forcing a smile.

Barry turned a smile toward him. "Rerun of Italy-England at Wembley just finished. Now, I'm watching Unsolved Mysteries."

His boy had been getting into trouble for bullying other kids. However, since he'd had a talk with him about a month earlier, things had improved a lot. He was so proud of how sincere an effort he'd made to change. He prayed the change was permanent, and his plan of uprooting him from White Harbor and both of them moving to California with his stepbrother's family wouldn't cause any further behavioral issues in the boy.

"Dad, you okay?" Barry asked. Those bright blue eyes that made all of this necessary studied him with worry.

"Uh, yeah! Just came to tell you to call for a pizza. Esposito's has a two-for-one going on." He nodded toward the breakfast counter, where his wallet and keys sat. "There's cash in my wallet."

"Cool!" Barry jumped up from the couch and made a beeline toward the wallet.

Logan turned around and headed back to his bedroom. He needed to get things ready for the next morning, pack up a suitcase for himself and Barry. Yvette would come home too drunk to even notice—if she came home at all. His telling her to move out would likely send her on a bender long enough for him to take care of everything.

He'd hide the suitcase under the bed, where she wouldn't notice, just in case. The next day, early on, he'd move money from the joint account to his personal account. He'd need to be quick. Carter Booth ran the local bank, and his family was in the Circle. He wanted to remain unseen, if possible. He'd come home and get Barry, then fuel up on their way out of town—again, being careful, since Reece and Lydia Holland, also part of the Circle, owned the gas station. He'd already called his brother, who said they could stay with him for as long as they needed, while they got settled, and—

"Hello, Logan." Martha Lange was standing in his room.

He stopped cold, holding the door open, choking on the gasp that rose up his throat the moment he saw her. Only it wasn't her. It was that thing she did. What she could do within the confines of the town. Sending her image to other places, looking like black, wormy smoke given the shape of a woman.

He cast a glance toward the living room, where Barry was already dialing Esposito's for dinner. He stepped into the bedroom and closed the door behind him. "You're no longer welcome here, Martha."

"This land belongs to God, and I am His messenger. I will go where I must to do His work."

"I won't sacrifice Barry, Martha."

"You will address me as Mother, Logan. I have given you leeway thus far because of your lineage, but don't keep testing my patience."

"I'm out, 'Mother.'" He infused the word with venom and hatred. "My family will no longer be a part of the Circle. If Yvette wants to keep going, well, good for her, but Barry and I are out."

"You don't get to decide that. This is your last chance."

He cast a steely glare toward her. "Go. Fuck. Yourself. Martha."

She stared at him with those empty eye sockets of hers.

"Take off your belt." Her voice felt like an underwater detonation inside his skull, coming with bassy concussive force.

Logan unbuckled his belt, a long, black leather belt from back when he'd been a size forty-six waist, and he'd gotten it as a birthday gift from his son, which was the reason he hadn't cut it or replaced it when he'd slimmed down to a size thirty-eight. He'd simply cut a new notch and tucked the leftover belt under the loops.

Martha Lange knew this. It was stored in Blight Harbor along with many equally innocent secrets, and many more harmful ones from the entire town.

He pulled on the belt—a leathery hiss came from it as it passed through the loops of his jeans—and held it in front of him. Breathing fast, realizing what was about to happen, his eyes flitted toward his nightstand. *The letter. Will someone find it?*

"Pull that chair from the corner," she said. "Place it under that low beam."

His panicked eyes regarded her disturbing, shifting shape as his body moved against his will. "Martha, don't do this!" He grabbed the chair. Some pants and shirts tossed over its back fell to the floor as it tilted to one side. Still clutching the belt with his other hand, he pulled the chair around the bed, passing the corner where the woman's ghostly apparition stood, and positioned it under a low metal beam that crossed the ceiling. "My son—"

"Your son will be safe for now. There is another way to at least offset what Ben Curling did to Gerardo Valencia. It's not as effective, and not as long-lasting, but it should tide us over until Peter is ready. Your son would've been ideal. However, you are also a cave descendant. You can still be of use."

"Martha—"

"Climb the chair, loop the belt around your neck, tie it to the beam."

His body trembling from the effort of fighting Martha's influence, he put one foot on the chair, then, supporting himself with a hand on the chair's back, he climbed on top. His face looked flushed, and he was sweating profusely, his thoughts now shifting to his son, his young boy outside, of leaving him with an alcoholic mother, who was willing to sacrifice him for her religion. He looped the belt around his neck and passed the end through the buckle, pulling until he felt the black leather tighten. He then stood on tiptoes, passed the belt over the beam, passed it through the buckle, and tied it in a double knot.

"Your wife will raise your son—"

"She can't!" he blurted. "She—"

"Do not interrupt me again."

He felt his mouth seal shut. Air blew out of his nose and tears now brimmed over his eyelids.

"Your wife will raise your son."

She can't! She's an alcoholic! She doesn't love him! Why didn't I see it sooner? Why didn't I see she didn't love him? I can't leave him alone!

"And, Logan," she added, her voice malicious, rejoicing. "When the Ritual of the Four Nights arrives, you can be sure your son will be one of the last sacrifices."

No! His tears flowed down his cheeks. His teeth grinding with anger and despair. *Barry! My boy! You fucking monster!* His heart beat fast, and his mind swelled with the thoughts of all those moments he'd miss, all those things he wouldn't see his son do. He wouldn't take his son to the world cup, like they'd planned. What would become of him if he left him alone at the mercy of—

"Step off," Martha said.

As he moved his right foot to step off the chair to his death, Logan's final thought was a plea to his son not to give up on himself.

The doorbell rang, and Chuck Cunningham shuffled toward the door. He had gotten almost no sleep the previous night, after getting the news about Logan Giffen. The guilt in his chest was more than he felt he could bear. If he wanted to keep his family safe, though, he'd need to learn to bear it.

The bell rang again.

"Coming!" he said.

Despite his need to protect his family, he felt Martha had been the one to drop the ball when Gerardo Valencia was killed in the Vanek House. Out of the Circle, Martha lived the closest to that wretched place. She lived the closest to the Valencias. She knew the blizzard that made young Gerardo wander into the house was not natural. She should've sensed something out of the ordinary was happening inside the house. Instead, something in that house had killed the boy and tilted the balance away from the Circle, leading to this whole mess with the Giffens.

He opened the door to find Leo Fuentes in his police uniform, standing outside. "Oh, hey Leo!"

"How's it goin', Chuck?"

He noticed Leo was holding what looked like a folded letter inside a sealed plastic bag.

"Sorry to interrupt you at this hour. You're probably getting ready for lunch."

"Oh, no, no worries at all." He looked at the plastic bag again with trepidation. "Got something for me?"

Leo regarded the bag and the letter in it. "Uh, yeah. Sorry, this probably looks all scary and stuff. Should've taken it out of the bag." He unzipped the bag and reached in with a swift, casual motion. Brought out the letter, making sure not to unfold it, and handed it to Chuck. "I'm sure you heard about Logan?"

He nodded, looking rather uncomfortable. Turning the letter this way and that. He didn't know whether he was expected to open it and read it in front of Leo. "Is this from..."

"Logan? Yeah. We found it in his nightstand drawer. It was addressed to you. Had yesterday's date. It was a fairly easy, open-and-closed suicide case. No reason to keep the letter, so we brought it to you."

"Oh," Chuck nodded, eager to be done with this conversation. "Thank you."

"The examiner kept a photocopy for the official record."

Chuck nodded again. "That's okay. Did Amber Bishop read it?"

Leo frowned, confused. "Mrs. Bishop? No, why? I mean. She's the Town Manager, not the police chief or a forensics investigator, unless it has to do with something like town policy or some important thing that impacts the town. Why? Should she?"

"No!" Chuck blurted. "No... I don't know what the letter says. It's Logan's, and it's personal, so..."

"I get it, Chuck. Nothing to worry about. This was just another suicide"—his breath caught, his eyes flew open, he put his palms up, fingers flared—"I didn't mean it like that! I meant. This is personal stuff. Family and friends stuff. This ain't Mrs. Bishop's business."

"Thank you, Leo. Appreciate it."

"There's nothing suspicious or bad in the letter—sorry, I read it when I found it in Logan's room—there's... There's just this weird thing at the end, like written in some foreign language no one at the station knew what it was. I figured it was like a thing you guys had from like when you went to school together and stuff. Like a code?"

Chuck hurried to open the letter. His eyes flew all the way to the end, where he noticed the language of the Lord. He eyed Leo, who watched him expectantly. "Yes." Chuck grinned a huge, forced grin. "It's this sort of code we used for teachers not to figure out the notes we were passing in class. This says, 'Ann Summers High Specters Forever! Have a blessed life, my friend.' We used to play high school football."

"I see. Well, I won't intrude anymore. I'll leave you to it. My condolences for your friend."

"Thanks again, Leo."

The moment the man in uniform walked away and the door was closed, Chuck was quick to read the letter from the beginning.

Chuck,

I'm leaving you this letter because, out of our circle of friends, you and I have always been the closest. You've been a great friend of mine since we were kids, and I feel we have similar values.

By this time, you will have heard of what I did. I felt this was the right thing to do for myself and my family. Please keep an eye on Yvette. She's sick, and you selling her alcohol doesn't help that sickness. I know that's not your fault, but try to cut her off sooner if you can. Have a friendly talk with her. Maybe that'll make her look for help for real this time.

I won't name names here, since I don't know who else might read this before it reaches you, though you know if this happened to me, it could happen to any of us. The negative influence that drove me to do this could knock on your door down the line.

Please take care of your family. Take care of Jess and Maddie. Leave this town. Nothing good happens here.

If our circle of friends ever feels like they're going the wrong way, never forget:

Rralom egoiiatt tjenaf saaor sen.

Miysar somafvoiatt rralom sen.

Uolmin-yevin arlo doi miysar sen.

Logan

Chuck knew Logan hadn't killed himself. That had been Martha's doing. She'd forced him to do it. So, when he wrote this, he'd been talking about something else he planned to do. Given his advice to leave the town, and what The Circle had wanted to do to Barry, he figured Logan was probably going to take the boy and skip town, leaving Yvette behind.

He couldn't figure out the part written in the tongue of God. He understood the words and their literal meaning. He didn't understand what he meant by them, though.

CHAPTER SIX

BULLET

2022

03:59 p.m.
Three hours before Callum Baker's death

Jess Cunningham sat on her parents' bed, on her mother's side. Legs together, hands resting on her thighs, one upturned palm over the other, a single used bullet, dented and stained with old blood, staring up at her. Telling her so many things she couldn't even wrap her head around.

Her mom was dead.

She was certain of that much, even if she hadn't even seen her body. It was an entire sequence of logical leaps leading to that conclusion, and yet, it was the only conclusion she could draw.

When she was thirteen, she shot Freddie Parham in the head to stop him from killing her friend Leroy at the old Vanek House. The bullet was of this caliber, which didn't mean much on its own, except a thirty-year-old bullet extracted from someone's skull would've looked as tarnished, dented, and bloody as this one. Of course, the kicker had been Freddie hadn't died. Somehow, the powers in the Vanek House had helped Freddie survive a shot to the head, not even leaving a scar, just a clean circle of skin in the middle of the bloodstain on his forehead. Even as a lifelong resident of White Harbor, who'd seen her share of inexplicable things, she had a hard time thinking those words without feeling crazy. He'd survived and murdered Leroy anyway, before being beaten unconscious by Barry.

Last night, before a supernatural blackout hit the town, a man claiming to be Ben Curling's heir came after them with a gun for burning down the Vanek House. He'd claimed Freddie had escaped his cell in Lighthouse Rock and was walking around town, killing people.

That morning, according to the news, three people had been re-ported missing, and just a couple of hours earlier, Freddie himself, to her face, had claimed there had been a fourth victim, hinting with glee at it being her mom.

Minutes earlier, she'd found the bullet inside her mother's clos-et, with a message from Freddie that read: "Just off the top of my head."

Her mom was dead.

"Should we go to the police?" Royce asked. He'd been by her side since all this madness started the previous night—or had it actu-ally started thirty years ago?—he was standing near the bedroom window, his butt resting on the edge of her dad's desk.

Jess shook her head. With her free hand, she tucked a strand of red hair behind her ear.

"Jess, I know it's a town tradition assuming the worst and that we can't do anything about it, but—"

"Won't do any good," she said with a disheartened croak. "They won't find her."

"Look, I'll be first to not be like, 'Yay, cops!' but it'd be good to at least have another set of eyes looking for her, don't you think?"

She sighed, turned her gaze toward the open closet, where she'd found the bullets. "This is the same as the Vanek House, but in the whole town." Her voice sounded old and tired. "Whatever Freddie's doin', he's using the power in Blight Harbor to move through town and make people disappear. All day yesterday, I kept sensing Blight Harbor was active. Hearing people at the bar talk, the general buzz of the town was different from the moment Peter set foot in town. There's been this droning, like electricity on wires, or static, like the town woke up." She looked up at him. "You heard what that asshole Hitch said. Peter needed to stay away from White Harbor, and instead he came to town, and now his mother's going to kill a lot of people."

"That's nonsense, Jess." Royce was trying to be dismissive, but the way he clutched the edge of the desk with his right hand betrayed his fears.

Jess shook her head again.

"You said it this morning. This town's a creature, it's swallowed us whole, and we're just used to getting digested." She regarded him with a stern look. "We're too quick to dismiss the weirdness, but you, me, the rest of the Vigilantes, we've seen too much fucked up shit to disregard it like that."

Royce's eyes wandered around the room. He nodded with reluctance. "Should I tell the others? Want me to text the group chat?"

Jess, once more, shook her head. "Bobby and Nadine are taking Angie to the amusement park today. She hasn't left the house in like forever. She's feeling healthy for the first time in ages, and she's all giddy about it. I don't want to ruin that for her."

"You know what could really ruin it for her?" Royce asked, his voice loaded with sarcasm. "A guy with a gun showing up at the amusement park."

"No, I don't think he will."

"You're dismissing it, Jess. You're doing the thing you just said we shouldn't do. Freddie pretty much confirmed something else is happening tonight!"

She sighed with annoyance.

"Don't text them for now. If anything bad's gonna happen, it won't happen in the middle of the day, in public, Freddie said it would be at night. I promise I'll tell them before sundown. I need to do something first."

"What?"

"I need to talk to my dad."

"Chuck? Why?"

"Coz he lied to me. He told me he'd taken mom to my aunt's house, and the blackout had caught him coming back into town. I thought that was weird, coz he'd have needed to drive like the devil was trying to fuck him to make it there and back before the blackout, but I didn't question it. Look." She motioned with her head toward the narrow space between the bed and the nightstand. There was her mom's cane resting against the wall. "My mom wouldn't have left without her cane." She lowered her gaze toward the inner side of the nightstand. "The holster where she kept her gun is empty. She, or someone else, took her gun out and didn't put it back." She looked at the bed and ran her hand over the covers, which were wrinkled under her weight, but also showed creases and lines all over her mother's side. "Someone was lying here. My mom would've smoothed the covers and the pillow after getting up." Finally, she looked down at the small rug at her feet. There was a pair of light green slippers lying inert there. They looked so tiny beside Jess's booted feet; it made her breath catch as she suppressed a sob. "Her slippers are here. She wore them all over the house. I gave those to her on Mother's Day. She loved them because they had cold gel to cushion her frail little feet. She said they helped her with the p—"

She felt the sob coming back, stronger, pushing up her chest.

"Oh god…"

Royce hurried beside her, sat next to her, put his arm around her.

"I'm okay." She once more forced the tears back. "Sh-she, would've walked here from the chair by the living room window, sat on the bed, and taken off her slippers. She didn't get up from the bed again. Otherwise, her cane and her slippers wouldn't be here. This is where she disappeared. This is where she died."

"C'mere, baby." Royce eased her head onto his shoulder.

"My dad knows what happened." Tears began their race down her cheeks. She sniffled, took a couple of ragged breaths. "He wouldn't have lied to me like that if he didn't know. Let me talk to him first. Then we'll tell the others."

CHAPTER SEVEN

THE PAST IS FOREVER

????

??:??? ?

Endless hours before Callum Baker's death

It was like looking in the mirror at a reflection that was no longer you. Looking at all your past mistakes in each wrinkle, all your lapses in judgment in the sagging skin. Every single regret, forever check-marked by a gray hair, and no matter how many of those you trimmed or plucked out, they would grow back, their numbers only increasing.

The old man regarded him with curiosity and a healthy dose of mistrust—John Hitch would have been disappointed otherwise. In an unfriendly grumble, Ben Curling asked, "How do I know you're me? The *right* me."

He reacted with a "hmm" from the depths of his chest that should've been answer enough. The old man picked up on this.

He appeared more intrigued than a second ago. His stony stare still demanded an answer, however.

"I couldn't even be here if I weren't," John said. "Knowing you, though, I guess you'll want more proof. So, what do you want?"

"Just tell me about yourself," the old man said. "I'll decide."

He let out an impatient sigh. Time didn't matter—not here, anyway—yet he still felt pressed for it. "Nothing I say here will matter." It was a weak attempt. The old man wouldn't go for it. Figured he might still try. "Not to you, anyway."

"If what you're saying is true, then I have all the time in the world. And you ain't coming in here until you talk."

John looked down at the two black Mastiffs lying at Curling's feet. If he'd been anyone else, they would've sat up and stared at him with mistrust, ears perked up and ready to pounce on command, but they simply lay curled up beside the rocking chair, sometimes looking up at him in that curious way dogs had, though not enough to actually move. *They're not dogs, though. Not at this point in time. Not anymore.*

He leaned back and supported himself on the porch banister. Turned his head and regarded the Vanek House, down the slope, seeing it in person for the first time in twenty-nine years—considering he, John Hitch, was twenty-nine, and hadn't been born in White Harbor made this quite surreal. He was used to surreal, though.

He sighed. "Where do you want me to start?"

"Just start at the beginning," Curling said with a shrug.

"Which beginning? Father banishing me back in Horsham? Getting caught as a stowaway on a ship to the Americas when I was in my twenties and not being thrown overboard only coz the first mate thought I had a warm mouth and a tight ass? Living off the land for years on my own? Marrying Norma only to avoid a lynching? Or do you want me to skip to White Harbor proper? The cave? Burying all of those bodies before they'd fully thawed?"

"All one hundred and fourteen of them." Curling lowered his gaze.

"Nice try," John answered without hesitation. "Only one hundred and nine went in the ground. Five got lost in the cave." He squinted at the old man. "Including Amias Vanek."

Curling eyed him, studying his face.

"I've never seen the look on my own face when that asshole's name is mentioned," John said. "Looks like the right amount of hate." The old man averted his gaze. "So? You haven't answered my question. Where do I start? Should I skip to Walter Parham's rape and subsequent hanging?"

"Start with Christopher," Curling said, freezing him on the spot. They held each other's gazes for what felt like an entire day. "Without him, you and I wouldn't be talking right now. Without him, we'd be a hundred years in the grave—give or take thirty years, depending on which of us we're talking about."

A flash of unbridled grief crossed John's face. He avoided thinking of Christopher most of the time, and there was no one living who could remind him of him. Leave it to Curling to open up that wound. "Goddamn it, you already know I'm you. This is a waste of time!"

"No time to speak of. Not here. I would very much like to hear about him...from you."

"Why?" he snapped. "It's pointless. Either when the cycle ends and restarts or once I figure out how to get back, you will disappear and forget everything I said. Any nostalgic memories, any angry emotions this conversation evokes, they will all vanish with you the moment I leave this place. I won't even remember being you, talking to me, because this place, this time, doesn't exist. *You* don't exist."

Curling let out a long huff, leaned back in his rocking chair and crossed his arms over his chest. He turned his big eyes up at him and shrugged. "In the meantime, though, I exist. My mind exists. I remember him. I want to know how *you* remember him. And from here until the cycle restarts or you leave—which you can't do without my help—I will remember this conversation. So...we have literally all the time in the world. Tell me about Christopher."

John curled his upper lip. "Fine."

THE 1800S

Things weren't so complex back then. What was complex was keeping them hidden. Populations were smaller, so unless one was completely isolated—which was why he'd always favored living in the margins of where other people lived—people knew your business. Meeting men wasn't difficult. He'd always had a way to catch their eye. They'd always found their way into his gravitational pull.

Because of this, John Ellis—as he'd been called back then—learned fast to keep it hidden. The fact he'd been a burly, tall, bearded cattle rancher since he was a young man helped him avoid suspicion.

He'd kept his dalliances with a young cowman at his father's ranch secret for a while. It was the young cowman who hadn't been good at keeping it hidden, though, and his big mouth had gotten both caught. It had gotten John banished by his father and—from what he learned later—gotten the young man "accidentally" killed by a well-aimed stone to the head.

The first mate on the ship he'd snuck into to come to America *had* known how to keep it hidden. He saw John's size and his muscles and made a good case for the captain to keep him on to do heavy labor around the ship in exchange for food. He, of course, had made him do extracurricular labor every night. For such a short man, the first mate had some insatiable appetites, most incompatible with John's preferences. However, when the alternative was being tossed overboard, he'd clenched his teeth and bore it in silence, to not wake up sleeping sailors or call the attention of whoever was on watch.

Once in America, as the years passed, he'd made his way from the East Coast to the West Coast, doing odd jobs, and meeting men from time to time. There had been a butcher here, a farmhand there, a fruit salesman, a tailor, a few cowboys, one lawyer, another butcher, and as cities gave way to wider, less-populated lands, they had, for the most part, been farmers and farmhands. They'd all known how to keep it hidden.

He ended up settling somewhere in the Oregon territory in 1850. He hadn't taken any land during the Oregon Donation Land Act. He wanted nothing stolen from someone else. He was a white man from England, he knew he was an invader, and he'd only come to this land to have a fresh start—and not give his father the chance to send one of his people to "accidentally" crush his head with a well-aimed stone. Everything he had, he'd earned, bit by bit, with years of work. If any of the natives ever came for the land where he'd built his ranch and confiscated his pigs, he'd leave them to it, hope they didn't kill him, and move on. Somehow, it never happened, which only made him sad on account of what that implied.

He took a wife soon after arriving in Oregon. It had felt like the right thing to do, given he planned to sell his pigs and salted pork in nearby towns and settlements, so appearances were important. Norma, for reasons he could never explain, loved him, although she always knew who and what he was. It had started as a relationship of convenience—Norma being a widow with no money, land, or trade—but she was always kind and doting. Eventually, he'd learned to love her, too.

It was around that time people had taken to calling him Long-Lived John, or John "The Long-Lived" Ellis, when it was apparent he'd lived far longer than the average American male at the time.

He met Christopher Horton in 1861. He'd been nineteen at the time.

Norma knew about Christopher. She'd already become sick with the cancer that would take her life in 1862. She approved of John's relationship with Christopher, perhaps knowing she was dying. Norma, like those men John had met in his lifetime, knew how to keep it hidden.

It was she who came up with the story about Christopher being John's nephew, which would allow for the young man to come live with them and give John company after she was gone.

Norma was a talented storyteller. The story became that the young man with the green eyes, brown hair, and cleft chin had married at eighteen, only to lose his wife to smallpox within a year. Heartbroken, he fled to America to escape his parents' pressure to remarry (the woman had a flair for melodrama). Norma moved into a separate bedroom in their small home, making it her deathbed and yielding the marriage bed to John and Christopher. She insisted that John keep her room looking lived in, even after her death, to deceive any visitors.

For four years after they'd given Norma a holy burial, John and Christopher had shared a home. Keeping it hidden. Until John joined the settlers going to that land where no one, not even the Tillamook—who referred to the area as "The Land of Two

Moons"—set foot. He promised, once they'd started a settlement, he would arrange for Christopher to join him in this new land.

In 1867, after surviving the blizzard and the cave, and White Harbor finally became a small town, Christopher joined John, and for twenty years they lived a quiet life together, on the outskirts of town, maintaining the story of the older uncle and the widowed nephew.

That was until, in 1887, Reverend Douglas Burgess knocked on John's door, while Christopher was out working at the town's dried goods store. The reverend came with threats of exposing their "sinful endeavors" unless John helped him with a "sinful endeavor" of his own.

John had failed at keeping it hidden.

????

"Is that enough for you?" Hitch said, doing a sweeping gesture of frustration with his hand. "Can we be done with this?"

"How did Burgess know?" Curling asked.

Hitch rolled his eyes. "A kiss on the cheek. Said he'd come the previous night to ask if I would donate a pig for some church celebration or another, and as he came down the hill that led to our ranch, he saw me through the window, putting firewood in the stove. He saw…" He paused and sighed. "He saw Christopher put an arm around me and kiss me on the cheek."

"Did you believe him?"

"That he saw us? Yes. That he came at night only to ask us to donate a pig? No. He could simply ask me the next day at the market."

Curling nodded in silence.

"He knew what he was looking for. I don't know what made him suspect. When we were in town, we—"

"Kept it hidden."

"Yes." He eyed Curling with pain in his eyes. Curling's expression was stony, emotionless. He only raised an eyebrow and gave him a quick nod to continue. John shook his head. "A kiss on the cheek led to Walter Parham being raped and hanged for killing his rapist. Don't get me wrong, Burgess being stabbed forty-four times and getting his cock ripped away was just what he deserved…but, what he did to Walter Parham…he did with my help."

"Why did you help him?"

"Huh?" He thinned his eyes at him.

"Them buggery laws were rarely enforced."

"Yeah, 'them buggery laws' might have been rarely enforced, but lynch mobs sure liked to enforce them."

Curling chuckled. "So, you were just a coward."

"No! I wasn't going to put Christopher in danger. I would've died a million times before letting them lay a hand on Christopher."

"Hmm."

"What?"

"If that was your only motivation, I'm not sure you're really me."

He scowled at the old man, his mouth working in an angry snarl, trying to produce a retort. He pushed off the banister and stood in front of Curling. "Fuck this." He turned, marched toward the steps, and stopped short of walking down.

"I know you're me, okay?" Curling said, making John's eyes swivel toward him. "There are thirty years between us. I want to know if we see things differently after thirty years. Tell me, and I'll help you."

Hitch hesitated, sighed. "I was scared of ending up old and alone. I gave a serial murderer-rapist a quiet spot to do his disgusting deeds. I helped him catch a fourteen-year-old boy, then walked away, knowing what he would do to the poor kid. I stood by quietly as Dorothy Parham forced her husband to hang her traumatized son. Are you asking if I have any regrets? What do you think? I prayed to God to end my life, but to spare Christopher. Instead,"—he scoffed and shook his head—"Christopher died of tuberculosis less than a year after, and I'm still here. Alone."

Curling kept staring at him, indicating there was more to say.

"I regret my involvement in what happened to Walter Parham." John turned an accusatory eye at Curling. "Especially knowing what *you* will do to Freddie Parham before you die."

This got a surprised reaction from Curling.

"If you're asking me if I would do it differently, though... No. I wouldn't. I would've done anything to protect Christopher, even if it meant being cursed, even if it meant I would only get one more year of him." His expression turned stiff and unshakable, now looking so much like Curling's there would've been no doubt of their connection even though, physically, they looked nothing like each other. "Even after Vanek betrayed me and put me in Rickward Curling's body to go on, and on, and on, until I became you, then me. Even if I keep paying for what I did, alone until the sun explodes, I will never regret having that one last year with Christopher. Does that answer your question?"

Curling smiled with his eyes. Supporting himself on the rocking chair's armrests, he stood up, followed by the gaze of his two dogs. He stepped toward his front door. "Might take us months...years..." He took a key out of his pocket, opened the door, and turned toward John. "But we'll figure out how to take you back."

John pulled out his smart phone from his pocket and brought up his camera, pointing it toward the open books, scrolls, papers, and documents on Curling's table. Some pulled straight from Curling's bookcases—lost to John after the old man's death—others gathered from libraries and homes around this construct of White

Harbor. While the phone didn't have a signal within the reality bubble, its basic functions still worked.

He noticed Curling staring at him from one side, and realized, in early 1993, while there might have been rudimentary cell phones, what he held now would've looked to the old man like something stolen from a spaceship. "It's a phone," John said. "Phones take pictures now."

"Hmm," the old man responded. "Makes sense."

He snapped pictures of everything, making sure he at least got two of each item to avoid any being blurry.

As he was about to put the phone away, one of Curling's rugged index fingers touched an old book, opened to a page with a symbol with which he was familiar. It was his Order's equivalent of what Freddie Parham had used to send him to this bubble, this imitation of White Harbor.

"Memorize this one," Curling said.

John looked up at him, gave him a confused expression. "I know it."

"Thirty years between you and me, and from what you tell me, you don't even live in White Harbor. The Ritual of the Four Nights started. That opens a whole bunch of complex variations that weren't available to me, so I'd imagine that's true for you, too. Pushing someone into a reality bubble would be easy for either of us, but look at this,"—he pointed at a small glyph next to the main one—"length of time. This,"—he tapped at another smaller glyph—"displacement. This,"—he tapped at yet another—"physical state." He regarded him with a grave look. "There are others I haven't used. Learn them."

"Why?" John asked. "Why would I need this? I can't take a whole town of four thousand people into a reality bubble if things go sour. I can only move one person."

"Exactly." Curling gave a single nod. "I'm old in my current form. You're saying summer 1993 I die trying to feed Peter Lange to the house. I'm okay with dying. It's what I've always wanted. But, when I die, you'll be born. You're young, almost thirty. You can live a life once this is over. If things go badly, you can use this to send yourself to a reality bubble. Make it so once it's over, once the ritual ends, you'll be dropped off a fair distance beyond those damned mountains. If you're injured, you can place yourself in a dormant state; let the reality bubble heal you as much as it can. You can still live a life. After all this shit is over, you can live a *real* life. Maybe not end up alone."

John curled his lip at the old man, almost with disgust. "You can't be serious. Now I should be the one doubting if you're really me. All we've wanted from the moment Walter Parham hanged was to die. After Christopher died coughing blood, it only cemented that resolve. I want to stop the ritual, yes. I want there to be a world for everyone else, yes. But all we've ever wanted is to die and not come back. John Ellis, Rickward Curling, Jenelle Curling, Osmin Curling, you, me, it's the one thing we've *all* wanted. Why would I ever need to leave White Harbor alive?"

The old man eyed him keenly. A smile played around his lips. "Maybe, because I remember Amias Vanek's face as I choked the life out of him for what he did. Have you forgotten?"

John's breath caught in his throat. He tried to sputter out an answer, but the image of Vanek's face, eyes bulging, hands pawing and scratching at him as he died, was something he could never forget.

"Amias Vanek was on his deathbed," Curling continued. "He was resigned to his death. It was over. And still, the moment our hands stopped the flow of oxygen to his lungs, he fought to have a little more time." He paused. Both swallowed hard at the same time. "Maybe it's because you've told me I'm a few months away from dying. The real me—the one that, for you, has been thirty years in the grave—that version of us didn't know he was going to die this year. I do. The moment you told me, I felt this twinge of fear. Even though I knew once you left the reality bubble, I'd just vanish, there was still that little voice telling me I wanted a little more time. Do you understand? Just in case you feel that twinge of fear before the end...learn this." He once more touched the symbol in the book.

John gave no answer and snapped two quick pictures.

"Now, let's find you a door where you can draw the return glyph."

2022

06:02 p.m.
Five minutes after Callum Baker's death

The portal glyph had worked like a charm. It would've been a longer, far more complicated process if he hadn't left a corresponding portal glyph somewhere in his destination. He was fortunate to have drawn one inside Callum Baker's closet when he'd broken into his house to find some much-needed information, in case he had to come back and browse through his notes again. Instead, it had served him as his way back from the reality bubble. The moment he'd crossed the door in Curling's old home, it had been like the back wall of the closet had disappeared, and he'd simply stepped through.

He now stood in front of Baker's corpse. He'd been sitting on his desk chair when John had flung the closet doors open and had plunged his knife repeatedly into his body. He'd died on his chair and now was surrounded by a circle of blood-soaked carpet, where his glasses lay. He looked up at the open laptop on the desk. The desktop wallpaper displayed mountains and fields of green. Up in the blue sky, only cotton-candy clouds—a stark contrast to the deep crimson at his feet.

John didn't have to wonder if Baker had also wanted a little more time when faced with his imminent death. He'd repeatedly blurted, "Wait! Wait! Wait!" as he stabbed him, as if his brain had glitched and gotten stuck on that one word to persuade him to let him live.

One down, he thought.

He needed to kill five of Martha's chosen sacrifices before the end of the Third Night.

Based on what he'd overheard, while hiding in the closet, Baker's girlfriend, Nguyen, was coming here. He would kill her, as well, leaving only three more to put an end to Martha Lange's ritual.

He checked the time on Baker's open laptop.

It was 06:03 p.m.

The Second Night drew close.

CHAPTER EIGHT
CLOSED

"**D**ad!" Jess burst through the bar's door, her black boots stomping on the linoleum. She'd found a sign at the door that read: "Closed for the day," which only aggravated her more, since her dad hadn't even consulted with her about closing the bar. The place was gloomy, as the sun had almost sunk behind the line of the horizon, soon leaving White Harbor at the mercy of darkness. There were only the ceiling spotlights shining down on the counter, and—for some unfathomable reason—also the blinking, colored Christmas lights that lined the mirror on the wall behind it. They looked too cheery for how betrayed, grieving, and angry she felt.

She reached the counter, and her palm flew forward with a mind of its own. She slapped that steel tit-shaped bell at the corner of the bar twice, releasing two annoying *dings*. She hated the damn trinket. The locals never rang it anymore, but when tourists came, they seemed infatuated with it, to the point she wanted to throw her cheapest, thickest bottle of rum at their fucking heads—then set them on fire.

"Dad! Where the fuck are you?" She stormed to the other end of the counter and pushed the kitchen door open. Darkness greeted her. If she hadn't been so overcome by anger, she might've noticed the blacked-out room through the eye-level window on the door.

"What?" Her dad's voice, approaching up the cellar stairs. "What's going on?" He emerged through the open cellar door and regarded her with surprise. "Pum'kin?"

"Don't fuckin' call me that," she blurted. "You're gonna tell me what's going on right now!"

His mouth moved, bumbling, trying to utter words that weren't coming.

"Mom's dead." Her voice faltered, broke. She pushed the grief aside, focusing on her rage. "You knew, and you lied to me! Now I find the fucking bar with a closed sign, and you're doing god-knows-fuck-what in the basement." She looked down at his hands. He was holding a shotgun.

"Sweetheart..." His face scrunched up like an old rag, and the lines on his forehead and his eyes deepened as he broke down. "I'm so sorry!"

"You motherfucker!" She shouted, punched him in the arm, feeling her voice break with every other syllable. "You fuckin' piece-of-shit motherfucker! I goddamn fuckin' hate your fuckin' guts for lying to me! You..." She felt her body tilt forward and her arms fly open. She embraced her dad and buried her face between his head and his shoulder, her back convulsing with bitter sobs. Her voice went thin and weak, a little girl with an "ouchie" asking her dad for consolation. "Mommmm!" she sobbed. "Dad, tell me I'm wrooong! I want my mommm!"

Her dad, whose tears were also spilling over, held her tight, and he kept saying, "I'm sorry, hun. I'm so sorry!"

He held her for a while, letting her get the first of many upcoming sobbing sessions off her chest. After a few minutes, he caressed her red hair and gave her a soft pat on the back as he inched his face away from hers to get her to meet his gaze. "We need to talk."

Jess's green eyes, bloodshot, underlined with sad, tired bags, looked at him. She raised a freckled hand and ran its back all over her face, wiping tears and snot from it.

The bar door flew open, startling both of them. They turned around and, in the light coming from the spotlights, was the shape of a man standing there, holding the door open. Jess recognized him at once.

"What the fuck?" Before she could utter his name, her dad spoke.

"Hitch?" Chuck looked even more baffled than her. He pushed his daughter aside and pointed the shotgun at the man.

John Hitch's shirt was soaked with blood. Long, thick tendrils of blackish red ran from the crimson stain that had formed on his shirt and crotch, down his guard's uniform khakis. There were two visible cuts in his shirt, straight. Stab wounds—unbeknown to them, this was where Sylvia had stabbed him before he stabbed her and ran away. He had a wild, almost wall-eyed stare in his eyes, and held a bloody knife in his tightly closed hand.

"Cunningham," Hitch said, punctuating this with a cough, causing blood to spurt out of his mouth. "You're alive." With difficulty, Hitch raised the knife, pointing it straight at Jess. "You and your friends need to die." He took in a ragged, sodden breath. "Before..."

He stopped, breathed with difficulty. The knife fell from his hand, clanking on the floor. Then his entire body followed. Hitch crumpled like a puppet with cut strings: arms hanging to the sides, knees buckled, body tilted, torso going limp, and his head hit the floor sideways.

Barry strolled with his friends between games and concession stands at the amusement park, surrounded by flashing lights, laughter, and the noise of people trying to forget about their worries.

Angie, now back in her wheelchair, exhausted after a long afternoon, walking around with her cane, had a huge pink bunny on her lap. Bobby had won it for her, filling out a clown's mouth with a water gun. This hadn't been a monumental accomplishment, though. There were four spots in the game, which had been taken by Nadine, Bobby, Ray, and Barry. Whoever won had agreed to give Angie the prize. They'd also talked Nadine into letting her ride the tiny roller-coaster, and—under a half-joking threat about murdering them all if anything happened to her sister—she'd agreed.

Other than some mild stomach discomfort, Angie had been alright.

The afternoon had been just what they needed to forget about the horrors of the night before. However, as they rounded the corner to reach the parking lot and go home, Barry's breath hitched. Standing next to his Civic were Maryann, her mother, Therese, and their two children. Daniel held his mom's hand, and baby Gabe rested in his grandma's arms.

"Well, lookie here." Maryann greeted them with a sneer, her eyes zeroing-in on Barry and Ray's clasped hands. "Danae was right, Mom! He really has no shame. What do you have to say for yourself, Barry? Did you already forget you have two small children who are going to grow up in ridicule because of their pervert father?"

Ray took a step forward, rage in his eyes, "Listen, you—"

Maryann raised a finger in his face. "Excuse me, but no! I'm talking to my cheating husband, not the piece of shit who thinks it's okay to break up a happy family."

"Happy family?" Ray said in a burst of angry disbelief. "After all you've done to him? Now, who's being shameless?"

Barry put a gentle hand on Ray's shoulder, prompting him to stand down. He stood between him and Maryann and spoke with a measured tone. "Let's not do this here, please. We do have to talk, but not here, not in a parking lot, not in front of the ch—"

"Oh, you're uncomfortable doing this here, Barry?" She raised her voice even louder. "In public? What's more public than you flaunting your little butt-boy all over the park?"

People passing by turned and stared at the scene.

"I..." He choked on his words. His eyes pointed down at the floor. He'd gotten so used to lowering his gaze since he married Maryann, it had almost become a Pavlovian reaction.

(*I can finally be me. I'll never be that other person again*)

He forced himself to look up, drove his gaze into hers. "Do not disrespect him."

Maryann cackled, shot a glance at her mother, who rolled her eyes. "Look at him. The big burly man defending his bitch! Amazing, all it took for you to find your balls was for some second-rate nurse to spend the night sucking on them."

Seeing Ray's temper boil over, Barry once more put his hand out toward him.

Instead of exploding at Maryann, shouting, and letting out the anger he was truly feeling, he gathered himself. "Maryann, I will not have this conversation with you in front of my children. I'll come tonight and pick up my stuff. We'll talk then."

"You're not setting foot in *my* house again."

"The house is in my name!" Therese chimed in with pride. "I'll call the cops on you!"

That old threat. Old, and by now, dusty and frail.

"You do that, Therese. We'll see how it goes." He turned a steely glare toward his wife. "You don't want to test me, Maryann. I do owe you a conversation, and we need to talk about the children and custody—"

"Custody?" She guffawed. "Once my brother's done with you, you'll be lucky if you ever see them ag—"

"I'm trying to do this amiably." He could feel the anger rising, higher and higher, like lava in a volcano, threatening to destroy the stability of what had been built around it. "I don't want—"

"I don't care what you want!"

"Fine!" While the anger showed in his face, he reined it in enough to keep his voice under control. "Is this how you want to do it? Fine."

He pulled his phone out of his pocket, unlocked it, searched for a file. He tapped a few more times. A notification rang from a phone behind him.

"Nadine," he said without turning back. "I sent you an audio file. I don't have Angie's email. Could you forward it to her, please?"

"Sure."

"What are you doing?" Maryann shot a puzzled look at Nadine.

He ignored her. "Angie, I want to hire you, or someone from your firm, as my lawyer. Is that okay?"

"You got it." Angie flashed a shark's grin. "Just a phone call; we got you covered."

"Thanks."

Maryann grew more tense each second. "Barry... *What* are you doing?"

Barry raised the phone to her face so she could look at the screen. Displayed was an audio recording named "Bedroom 1". It also showed a date two months earlier, and a timestamp of 10:33 p.m. He shot a fleeting glance toward his children and lowered his voice so only Maryann would hear him. "I never thought I'd have to use this. You're leaving me no choice."

"What is that?"

"Think." His eyes held her gaze with restrained fury. "Ignore the date. Look at the location. Look at the time. What could I have recorded in our bedroom at that time?"

Her eyes went wide, her jaw dropped, but she pulled herself together, not willing to give an inch. "There's nothing illegal there. We're married!"

"Guess how many times I said 'No' in that recording. Eleven. I counted. Guess what you said to make me comply?"

"You're a man." She looked him up and down, still trying to keep a semblance of superiority in her face. "If you were truly being forced, you wouldn't have been able to—"

"Eleven times, plus you threatening to take my kids. What do you think a judge will make of that? It's all there, beginning to end. Even you, mocking me at the end, while I slinked away to the bathroom."

"You wouldn't. You wouldn't let people listen to us—"

"I would if it gets you out of my fucking life."

"If that's the only thing you have, then—"

"Not the only thing. Chats, voicemails, nanny cam videos."

"My brother will—"

"Your asshole brother might be able to knock out a couple of them. Not all. If it's about leaving the kids with an abuser like you, I'm sure they'll want to see and hear everything. You keep the house. I'm willing to grant you visitation rights—"

"Grant me! How dare—"

"Grant you," he repeated. "Supervised visits at first. Push your luck, and you see that woman over there?" He pointed at Angie. "She and her partners—hell, even an associate at her firm—can demolish your brother."

"I heard that!" Angie flashed her playful smile at her, wiggling her fingers in a raised hand. "And Barry's right. We'd tear your bitch brother a new one. Tell him I'm with McCullough, Larson, and Sharpe, and watch him piss his pants. I remember your brother. Chandler Thompson, right? He applied a while back. They wouldn't even have him as an entry level attorney."

Maryann stared at her, her expression a mask of confusion. Her mouth, like a fish out of water.

Barry got within an inch of her pale face. "Go home. We'll talk tonight."

She stood there, her mouth issuing babbling sounds, until she managed a breathless, "Okay."

He turned toward his children. Therese tried to pull Daniel away from him by the hand. Barry stared daggers at her, freezing her on the spot.

"Mom," Maryann intervened. "Let him."

Barry went down on one knee, and Daniel threw his arms around him.

"Daddy," the little boy said. "Where were you? I missed you last night. Mom was mad."

"I know, buddy." He caressed his little boy's head, looking into those blue eyes—so much like his. "Daddy still has some things to do, but I'll be home tonight to tuck you in. Gabe, too, alright?"

"Promise?"

"Promise." He flashed a beaming smile, then kissed his boy on the head. "You know Daddy Promises are always true, right?"

Daniel nodded.

"Oh, you see this nice man over there?" He pointed at Ray, who was standing a couple of steps behind him. "You probably don't remember him because you were Gabe's age last time you saw him. That's your Uncle Ray."

Ray smiled at the little boy, awkwardly at first, then with that bright grin of his, and waved at him.

The three-year-old waved back, looked at his dad and said, "He smiles nice."

Barry chuckled. "He makes Daddy smile a lot, too. You'll know him better one of these days. I bet you'll get along."

Daniel returned a shy smile.

"I love you," Barry said.

"I too."

He let Daniel go back to his grandmother and stood up to say goodbye to Gabriel, who leaned in to have his dad hold him. He took him in his arms, getting a whiff of that pleasant toddler smell.

"Dada-da," Gabriel babbled.

"Here's Dada." He chuckled. He put an index finger up, and Gabriel grabbed it. "Dada loves you, baby boy." He gave his son a loving kiss on the cheek, to which Gabe responded by grasping his beard where it was just long enough to grab. "See you tonight, alright?"

He took a deep breath, trying not to let his tears spill over, turned toward Therese, and handed her the infant. He shot a glance toward Maryann. "Are we clear, then?"

She lowered her gaze, like *he'd* done so many times before. "Sure," she seethed, then hurried next to her mother, took Daniel by the hand, and shuffled toward her SUV.

"Oh, and Maryann?"

She turned around.

"You should find a job."

She gave him a sneer, but once more lowered her head and turned her back.

Barry stood there, watching them walk away, breathing hard, trying to control the tears that kept pushing to come out, until Ray's hand slid around his waist.

"How are you feeling?"

Barry turned and threw his arms around him. "I'll be okay."

A second later, Bobby and Nadine wrapped their arms around his shoulders, and Angie's arms went around his waist, all in a group hug.

"You can cry if you want, you know?" Angie said.

"I'm...not going to cry."

"Kinda looks like you are, man," Bobby said.

"No, I'm not." His voice broke.

"Yup, definitely gonna cry," Nadine said.

Barry swallowed hard. "Fuck you all."

He started crying.

Nadine hung up the phone as Barry and Ray drove away. Turning to Bobby, she said, "Peter said he's a couple blocks away, so he offered to pick us up, said he'd be happy to drop you guys off at home. He just wants to talk to me about something."

Bobby and Angie exchanged a look.

"Actually," he said, "do you think it's alright if Angie and I hang here a bit longer?"

"Uh, sure, that's fine."

"Ooooh," Angie said in a playful tone. "Is my big sister gettin' some tonight?"

"Angie," Bobby intervened. "What the hell? Peter's wife just passed. How can you even say that?"

"No!" Nadine said with a firm voice. "That's in horrible taste. That will never happen. Cut it off. That topic is closed. Forever."

Angie shrugged, disappointment in her eyes. "Alright. It's the convent for you, I guess, Sister Mary Prudish of the Sewn Vagina."

"Angie!" Bobby gasped.

Nadine bristled at this. "Listen to me, you—"

"I'm joking! Don't be so freakin' serious."

Nadine shook her head and sighed as Peter's blue Malibu rounded the parking lot and stopped in front of them.

"Hey," Peter said with a wave.

Bobby and Angie waved hello.

Nadine leveled an emphatic stare at Bobby. "It's almost eight. It's getting cold. It'll be dark soon. I don't want Angie out late, Bobby. The cold isn't good for her. Also, remember what happened last night. I'm not that sure that guy is gone. Please keep her safe."

Bobby nodded. "I will."

"Go, mom!" Angie said with impatience. "I'm a grown woman. I brought my sweater. I'll be fine."

Nadine walked around the wheelchair. Her mind swirled with a thousand reasons she shouldn't leave her out in the street like this, though aware this was that voice in her head that always told her she needed to take care of everyone instead of letting them take care of themselves. "Park closes in an hour." She turned toward Bobby. "God help you if I find out you did some dumb teenager stunt like trying to have sex on the beach or something."

Angie clicked her tongue and snapped her fingers. "Aw, shucks, there go my dreams of getting a sandy pussy."

Peter arched his eyebrows. "Is it too late for you to stop being friends with Jess? Seems like she's a bad influence."

"Nah," Nadine said, going to Bobby and giving him a hug, then another to Angie. "Damage is done."

She turned, opened the car door, and settled on the passenger seat.

A few smiles and waves later, Peter's vehicle rolled toward the parking lot exit.

As Peter's Malibu exited the parking lot, he turned to look at Nadine as a vehicle coming in the opposite direction lit up his face with its headlights. "I wanted to stop by Cal's if that's okay. I feel kinda bad because this morning I went to see him and drop off a notebook, and I was kind of a dick to him. He had all these theories involving..."

"Your mom?" Nadine said, pulling her phone from her purse.

"How did you—"

"Just a wild guess." She swiveled her eyes toward him in an expression that said, "I mean, really?"

"Anyway, I texted him to say I was coming over again. That was about three hours ago. No answer. Then, I got on the group chat. That's where I noticed something odd." He made a turn at a corner. Around them were businesses, warehouses, and other industrial properties, which separated Seaside Park from the residential areas further, all bathed under the glow of the streetlights. "We all checked in this morning, like we promised. Nothing from Cal all day after I visited him, though. Sylvia either."

"So? You know them, he's probably up to his nose in papers and notes about creepy folk tales, and she's beside him encouraging him. That's just Callum and Sylvia."

"Please check it out and tell me I'm crazy, or maybe just worrying too much after last night."

Nadine pulled up the group chat.

ROYCE

Jess and I are okay. Tracy and Lillian left 1 hour ago. Lil had something early at work, she'll drop Tracy at preschool later. Y'all missed the best pancakes ever [pancake emoji]

08:24

JESS

Royce's baby girl is soooo cute [heart emoji] I might have to kidnap her

08:25

ROYCE

Y'all read it here. Just in case she goes missing. Jess stole her.

08:25

RAY

Hey I'm OK. Srry I didnt reply earlier. Was having breakfast

08:53

"Heh." Nadine chuckled. "Smooth, Barry."

Peter frowned at this. "What?" He turned another corner, and now they had trees to their left. The trees that surrounded the patch of marshlands at the center of town, near the Pargin river.

"Oh, nothing." She waved a dismissive hand. "Remind me to tell you later."

"Could you keep going? Start later in the day."

"I want to catch up on my messages. Hold your horses. If you want to tell me so bad, just tell me."

"Keep going. I'm hoping I'm wrong."

She gave him a concerned look. She knew Peter was anxious and insecure, but he was usually more communicative with her.

Hey people. Cal and I didn't get murdered on the walk home from the bar. Hangover makes me wish I was dead, though. Cal slept in. I'm already at school.

09:02
CALLUM

I'm not as asleep as I wish I were. I had a rather abrupt visit this morning. Don't worry. It wasn't our dreaded, murderous visitor of last night, just someone making an unexpected yet exciting delivery.

09:08
ROYCE

Jesus, Cal, you even text nerdy, man.

09:10

NADINE

Peter and I are okay. He's dropping me off later.

10:13
PETER

I should be at your house around 11:30 Cal

10:16
CALLUM

Splendid!

10:18

ROYCE

[Picture of Zazu from The Lion King *saying, 'I, madam, am the king's majordomo.']*

Literally how you sound

10:19
JESS

Stop it, you fat childish asshole.

10:19
ROYCE

Stop calling me fat.

10:20
JESS

This is litrly the 1st time I call you fat today.

10:20
PETER

Hey, Jess. Did you guys go to the police?

10:25
ROYCE

Hey, Pete. We got something to do at noon. We'll probly go when we get back.

10:41
PETER

K? Isn't this kind of important?

10:43

ROYCE

Man, maybe you and Nadine can go?

10:48
PETER

I can't. I have an appointment at the hospital after meeting with Callum.

10:49

NADINE

[Witch emoji]

10:49
PETER

Stop that.

10:49
ROYCE

Nadine, how about you?

10:51

NADINE

Bobby and I are taking Angie to Seaside Park later today.

11:02
ROYCE

Cal? Sylvia?

11:04
SYLVIA

At school until 5

11:08
CALLUM

I have research to do. I can't spare the time to go deal with police bureaucracy and incompetence.

11:10
ROYCE

Alright. Ray?

11:11

Ray?

11:30

Barry?

11:44

[Alarm emoji] Anyone know if Ray and Barry are okay? They're not replying! [Alarm emoji]

11:55
RAY

HEY! SRRY! FEL ASLEEP!

11:58
BARRY

I'm fine. Sorry. Was busy with some stuff.

11:59

Stuff at my house.

11:59

Nadine chuckled again. "Alright. I gotta tell you. We actually spent the entire afternoon with Ray and Barry at Seaside Park."

Peter curled the corner of his lips in confusion. "Wait, how? Yesterday, Ray couldn't even stand being close to Barry for more than a minute."

"Who the hell knows?" She showed him the earlier breakfast message. "They spent the night together, and here they were having breakfast." She scrolled up to the later messages. "Fairly sure here they were having sex." She tittered. "I guess we called it."

Peter smiled. "Good for them, though."

"Oh, and you should've seen Barry telling Maryann off right before you arrived. It was—"

"Um, Nadine." He pointed at the phone. "The chat. You can tell me the gossip later. Finish reading the messages."

She was taken aback by his bluntness. "Uh, sure."

JESS

Okay, look everyone. We're not going to the fuckin' cops! Makes no sense at this point. Me and Royce have shit to do. TTYL.

12:02

ROYCE

> *Guys. Jess has a really bad migraine. She's gonna go home and lie down for the rest of the afternoon. She said she'll turn her phone off for now. She's okay, no need to worry. Fill u in later. Just a recommendation for now. You should all head home. Explain later.*

14:32

"Hmm." Nadine re-read Royce's message. "Wonder what happened to Jess. She and Royce seemed to be in a hurry at noon, then he sends that message."

"I messaged him separately. He says Jess is fine. She needed some privacy. He didn't want to say what happened. He promised they'd tell us tonight." He eyed the dashboard clock. "It's already 8:05, though. Nothing yet. But that's not what I wanted you to read. It's the next part, about an hour ago."

PETER

> *Hey, Sylvia. Is Cal home? I've been texting and calling him for a while, but no response.*

18:38

> *Sylvia?*

18:51

> *Syl, you guys okay?*

19:07

> **Guys?**
>
> 19:19
>
> **Anyone?**
>
> 19:29
>
> **Anyone know anything about Sylvia or Callum?**
>
> 19:35

Nadine glanced at Peter. "You could've just told me."

"I wanted you to read it and see if I'm being paranoid."

"You're not paranoid." The world beyond the windshield rushed quickly to the right, disorienting her as Peter turned left at the next corner. "This is unlike both of them. They're usually quick to reply. I'm worried." She turned a wide-eyed stare at him. "You don't think that man—"

"I don't know."

As if to compound their worries, a text from Royce popped up on the group chat.

ROYCE

> *Sorry guys. Was waiting for Jess to text me, but she hasn't. GO HOME! EVERYONE! SHOULDN'T BE ALONE! Jess and I talked to Freddie at lightouse rck.*

> *He killed four people last nite like the security guard said. We think anther blackout's coming. He said one person would die. Doesn't know who. GO HOME! LOCK YOURSLFS IN!*

20:06

"Oh, God." Nadine looked panicked.

"My mother..." Peter's eyes bulged open.

Nadine turned to him. She knew nothing good could follow those words.

"She said, 'The two nights to come and the eternal night to follow, God will rise to claim this world and reshape it.'" He stopped in front of Callum's house. The lights were on. Peter stared, alarm in his face. "Yesterday, she said, 'It starts tonight,' then the blackout happened. Today she said, 'the two nights to come.'" He turned a terrified stare toward her. "I didn't take her seriously. I thought she was incoherent, like she—"

Nadine's phone rang a notification.

It was a text from Jess in the group chat.

JESS

> *I'm at the bar with my dad. Freddie killed my mom. My mom's dead. We have the security guard here. Unconscious. Covered in blood. I don't think it's all his.*

20:08

As quickly as she could, Nadine typed a message.

20:09

She waited for a minute. Two. No answer from Bobby. Those two were probably not even looking at their texts, their attentions absorbed by their first night out together in a long time.

Nadine turned a plaintive look toward him. "I have to go back! I have to get Angie!"

Peter was already in the middle of opening his door. "We will. Angie's with Bobby. She's not alone. Cal and Sylvia might be seriously hurt in there, though. We'll check, then we'll drive back to Seaside Park as quickly as we can. Alright? C'mon!"

Unsure, but knowing Peter was right, she opened the passenger door and stepped out. Both hurried toward the house.

CHAPTER NINE
LOVERS UNAWARE

08:03 p.m.

The door hadn't even clicked shut behind them when Barry was on Ray, kissing him, peeling his jacket off, and maneuvering him toward the couch.

"Really?" Ray said, kissing him back with a smile on his face. "Again?"

"Mm-hmm," Barry said with a naughty chuckle, pressing his lips into his.

"Don't you gotta go pick up your stuff and tuck in your kids?" He planted a long kiss on his mouth. "It's past eight."

"Mm-hmm," he answered again. "That's why it's gotta be a quickie on the couch." He reached down and unzipped Ray's jeans. "Let's save the long, romantic lovemaking for after I come back, alright?" He pulled Ray's shirt over his head, then his own, and planted a wet, bearded kiss on him. "We gotta catch up for the past thirty years."

Ray bit his lip and gave him a hungry, salacious grin. "Damn. What's gotten into you?"

Barry kissed him again and pushed him onto the couch. He unbuttoned his jeans, pulled them down. "In a few minutes...you."

Freddie stood in his cell. Surrounded by all the pictures he had blessed with his blood, and the next one, waiting to be blessed, before him.

The canvas on the easel showed a two-story house in front of a cul-de-sac. At the center of the cul-de-sac was a circle of grass with a huge tree whose canopy covered a colorful kid's playground. This was Mother's gift to him. His reward for having completed the sacrifices of the First Night. He got to take revenge on his childhood tormentor, but further than that, he got to take revenge against the person who had thrown him out of the Vanek House before he'd been able to complete the ritual to dispel his family curse.

He'd managed to kill the six children the ritual demanded, but thanks to goddamn Barry Giffen, the last of them—Leroy—had died outside the house. Barry had thrown Freddie out of the house, disconnected him from its delicious power, that power that made him feel alive, made him feel like he mattered. The moment he lost touch with the power felt like a meth addict going cold turkey, if the entire withdrawal process was compressed into a minute.

He remembered the way Barry's fists had punched him over and over. Freddie slid his tongue over his fake teeth—replacements after the giant oaf had knocked most of the real ones out. The first punch had landed as he felt the power from the house draining from his body. In a way, the barrage of punches that followed, and his later unconsciousness, had only numbed the pain of getting disconnected from the house. The numbness, however, had only been temporary.

When he woke up shackled to a hospital bed, the loss hit him like an avalanche, mud and rocks crushing him without mercy. He howled in agony. Every injury he'd ever suffered—the broken arm from when he fell off his bike, every drunken beating from his father and the school bullies, every scrape, every bruise, every fall—struck him all at once, a million times over. It wasn't only physical pain. His entire soul felt emptied, replaced with every grief, disappointment, and insult; with every time he'd felt like a loser. And paramount over all of those feelings loomed the solid, overpowering pain of watching his mother and his baby sister lying dead, drowned, and broken on the riverbed.

(*A red ant crawling on my mom's lower lip*)

(*Lolly had one eye open and one closed, like a plastic doll*)

The doctors had come into the room to sedate him. It had done no good. He'd fallen physically asleep, but in his mind, he could still feel that unutterable pain.

All because of Barry Giffen.

His family, his ancestors, his mom, his sister, were suffering in the Void, and had been suffering there for thirty years because he hadn't been able to kill Leroy inside the Vanek House.

All because of Barry Giffen.

He beheld the scene on the canvas. All the streetlights were dead. Not a single light came from any window. Besides that, you could have sworn there was nothing wrong with the cul-de-sac. And that was the point. Barry had to get there, thinking there was nothing wrong. The surprises would be inside. He'd planned this to the last detail.

Freddie started to worry when he realized Barry wouldn't come home at his usual time. He hadn't gone to work. He'd spent the morning getting railed by that annoying fag, Raymond, then gone to the park all afternoon. Rumors swirled in Blight Harbor (he'd gotten tidbits from Danae Wilkes, then from Maryann Giffen herself) that Barry was coming home to end his marriage that night. Freddie hoped this would be before the Second Night's chaos began, so he could trap Barry in the house, with all the fun nightmares and tortures he'd planned for him. If the Second Night's events came first, however, he was confident Barry would run home in a panic to protect his kids. That's when he'd get him.

The Mother had blessed every drawing, every painting, even the special one Freddie had prepared. All he needed was his own blood to open the gateway. He had nothing sharp in his cell to cut himself, but even the best mental institutions wouldn't remove his teeth. Without hesitation, he bit into the soft flesh between his thumb and index finger, ignoring the pain. Blood was flowing freely by then, but it felt like his teeth wouldn't fully go through the connective tissue. He wanted to bite through, only for the morbid enjoyment of it. With a final, rubbery tear, his teeth met.

He examined his hand. Blood trickled over his palm. He swallowed the torn piece of flesh, then cupped his hands, letting the blood pool before rubbing them together. Like with the previous night's canvas, he smeared his blood along the edge in one smooth motion. The canvas expanded in all directions, enveloping him in a bubble, until he stood beneath the tree by the playground.

Like in the First Night, he adjusted his sight to the darkness. The dark-blue glow coming from that beautiful moon—God's eye—became brighter just for him. In this light, he could see the tree was dead, its leaves brown and withered. The playground lay abandoned; the plastic broken and coated in mud, the metal bars and the swings were rusted beyond repair. One swing hung limp, detached from its chain, one edge brushing against the dirt and the dead grass.

Freddie strolled toward the house, the only thing in the cul-de-sac untouched by the decay around him. When he stepped onto the street from the circle of dead grass, his foot sank into five inches of dirty water, though his intangible form couldn't feel it. He glanced back at the playground. It looked like a desolate island in the middle of a sea of filth, swallowed by the darkness.

Beautiful, he thought.

He tilted his head and gazed up at the blue moon, opened his arms wide in worship and shouted, "Thank you, Lord! These lives

I'm about to end are a gift to you! May this humble meal serve as an offering from one as unworthy as me!"

God did not answer. He didn't expect Him to. Freddie knew He was pleased, though.

He walked up the flooded driveway until it rose above the water level and reached the front door.

Such a beautiful home, he thought. *What I created inside it is even more beautiful. Sublime, even.*

There was this small sandy slope at the edge of Seaside Park, flanked by two green swaths of green grass, which now looked gray in the moonlight. This was the spot where people often came to swim or have picnics on the beach, and it was a perfect spot for couples to sit and watch the sunset on summer afternoons.

Bobby helped Angie off her wheelchair and lowered her onto the sand, leaving the big teddy bear sitting on it, and now they sat in silence, side by side, looking up at the waning, silver moon in a sky that seemed to have sprouted a million more stars than usual because Angie had come out to see them. They could hear the voices and the sounds that floated toward them from the amusement park slowly fading away as the concession stands and the rides closed.

He glanced sideways at Angie, who seemed to drink the starlight through her skin. It had an unearthly glow to it. Her dark hair had merged with the shadows of the night, making her look ethereal, like some timeless nature spirit emerging from the darkness to light up the world.

He picked up a little bit of sand in his hand and let it fall through his fingers, little by little. A silly smile drew itself on his face. He let out an overly dramatic sigh, which made Angie turn to look at him. "I don't like sand," he said.

Angie stared at him with a befuddled expression, then her cheeks swelled, and she let out a sudden burst of laughter. "You stupid dork!"

Bobby chuckled along with her.

"Are you seriously quoting Anakin Skywalker at me?" She slapped his shaking shoulder as he continued to laugh. "You ruined the moment!"

He shrugged. "Technically, you should love that quote. The prequels are from your generation more than mine!"

She shook her head. "Nope. Even I know that line is cringey."

They both chuckled together.

"But, if I have to be honest," she added with a shrug, "I don't like sand, either. It's coarse, and rough..." She turned a silly glance toward him, and he met her eyes. "And it gets in your pussy if you have sex on the beach."

They both burst out laughing like a couple of idiots, earning a few annoyed glances from other couples sitting on the beach, also gazing at the starry sky.

Bobby moved his face closer to hers and their lips locked in a deep, intense kiss, after which Angie rested her head on his shoulder.

"I love that you're a huge nerd," she said.

He kissed the top of her head. "I love that you honestly think you're not a bigger nerd than me."

Bobby's eyes moved down from the starry sky, until he saw, in the distance, the lights from Lighthouse Rock, and his smile faltered. Was Freddie in his cell? Or had he, like that man at the bar had said, escaped somehow? He wondered what Jess and Royce had found out while talking to him. He had made it a point not to check his phone all day and focus entirely on Angie. He felt the urge to pull it out of his pocket and have a quick peek, but it felt intrusive to him. It felt like the light from the screen would dim the starlight that had Angie so enamored. They'd leave in about twenty or thirty minutes, he thought. He'd check when they were in the Uber.

He noticed how Angie hid her hands under her arms, even with her sweater on. The night was getting colder. He pulled her even closer to share his warmth with her.

"Cal!" Peter shouted, slamming his open palm, already sick of ringing the bell. "Sylvia!" Three quick raps on the door. He leaned over toward the window, and all he saw was the empty apartment, the lights on, nothing out of the ordinary other than the absence itself. He turned around, frustrated.

Nadine was coming back from the house across the street, where a neighbor peered out the window with curiosity, his phone pressed to his ear, yet choosing not to get involved in whatever was happening. "Nothing?" she asked.

Peter shook his head. "What do we do?"

Nadine shook her head and shrugged. "The neighbor said he saw Sylvia through the window a couple hours ago, and she seemed fine. Waved hello and everything. He says he's calling the police. My guess is he's calling more because of the two strangers banging on Cal's door than him thinking there's something wrong with Cal and Sylvia." She examined the front door. "Should we wait for the police?"

"No. The police in this town are useless, and they might be too late."

"So, you're saying we should break in?" The second she said this, she squinted, noticing something at the foot of the door. "What's that?" She pointed.

Peter turned and found two symbols, or glyphs, drawn near the bottom right corner. They looked like the runes Vikings used, but they had intersecting curves and lines that made them seem unique and alien.

A hazy memory flickered in Peter's mind. He was a teenager, trapped in a sealed off hallway of the Vanek House with Ben Curling, who claimed the space was under his control. Desperate to escape, Peter had eyed the sealed door, trying to figure out how to open it before the old man caught him and killed him. While he couldn't recall the exact symbols, he remembered the markings near the doorknob, symbols eerily similar to the ones near Callum's front door. It could just be his mind playing tricks. It wasn't déjà-vu, more like looking at a yearbook picture and remember talking to a specific person when, in fact, you never exchanged a single word.

That security guard, John Hitch, claimed to be Ben Curling's descendant. Now, he's at Cunningham's bleeding out. This can't be a coincidence. He didn't know Hitch. But he knew Curling, and he'd seen these symbols. "Nadine, I'm going to break the door down. Could you try to erase those first?"

Without question, Nadine pulled a Kleenex from her purse, bent down, and wiped at the strange markings. They left a smudge, like lipstick, but it flaked off as she dragged the tissue across. "Ready," she said, standing back up.

Peter took two steps back, ran toward the door and slammed his shoulder on it. It shook. It didn't open. He repeated the process, and this time, as soon as his shoulder slammed into the door, the wood of the doorjamb splintered and the door flew open, then bounced back. He stopped it with one hand, and he and Nadine hurried inside, followed by the neighbor's voice from across the street shouting, "Are you crazy? I'm calling the police!"

What struck Peter at once was the difference in lighting the moment they opened the door. From outside, it looked like every light in the house was turned on. The moment they walked in, there was only the light shining over the dining table, and some small LED spotlights in the kitchen. They gave the living area of the house a sensation of two cones of light separated by deep, unforgiving shadows.

There was light further down the hallway, coming from the open bedroom door. As they passed, Peter peered inside, saw no one. He heard Nadine—who had walked past him when he stopped to peek. She gasped and screamed, and Peter knew why without having to turn his head.

He hurried all the way to the back and, from outside the office, found Callum, lying dead on his desk chair, a blanket thrown on him from the shoulders down—a large bloodstain drawing a blob over most of its surface, as if it were a print. He looked as if he'd fallen asleep and someone had lovingly given him a blanket so he wouldn't get cold. That someone would've been Sylvia, who was slumped over the desk, in front of Callum's laptop and screen, an arm on top of the keyboard, and her face buried into the crook of her elbow. She was sitting on the folding chair Callum had pulled for him earlier that day. She had blood all over her clothes, and she had bloody towels, held against her body with duct tape, like some kind of morbid corset.

Nadine stood with her back against a bookshelf at one side of the door, her hands covering her mouth and tears spilling over her face. She shook her head in horror. "Oh my god, Peter!" Her voice sounded muffled through her hands. "Oh my god, they're dead. They're dead!"

"We..." He stopped, swallowed. His eyes were beginning to sting, realizing he hadn't blinked in well over a minute. He felt the grief rise up his esophagus like acid reflux. "We have to tell that neighbor what we found. If he's still with the police, he can tell them."

(*His mother. She's going to kill a lot of people*)

(*You know she can do it, Lange. Don't even act like you don't*)

(*I needed to kill four of you before he killed the second one*)

"John Hitch," Peter said. "He said he needed to kill four of us before Freddie killed the second one last night. What if we were wrong? What if he's still trying to kill four of us?"

"Five!"

The word startled both Nadine and Peter. They turned their heads to see Sylvia was moving.

"He needs to kill five of us now." Her voice came out vacuous, tired, fading.

"Sylvia!" Nadine shouted and ran toward her. She kneeled beside her and grabbed her hand. She turned teary, horrified eyes toward Peter. "What do we do?"

Peter emerged from the front door of Callum's house, carrying Sylvia in his arms, with Nadine following close behind, texting the group chat to let the others know. She ran past him, holding his car's fob, pressed the button and opened the back door wide for him.

Across the street, the shocked neighbor, still with the phone to his ear, came out of his house, his mouth wide open. "What are you doing?"

"She needs to go to the hospital!" Peter shouted. "Give them my car plates! I'm taking her to the emergency room at Clarendon! There's a dead body inside! Callum is dead!"

"What?" The word exploded out of the neighbor's lips, and it looked as if his eyes would explode from their sockets along with the word.

With Nadine's help, Peter put Sylvia in the backseat, trying to be as gentle as possible. Once he was sure she was secured properly, his head again appeared over the car's roof. "Tell the police the man who did it is named John Hitch! They found him wounded at Cunningham's! Tell them to send a cruiser there!"

Nadine ran around the front of the car and dropped into the passenger seat. Peter closed the back door and hurried to the driver-side door.

"But! But! But! You can't leave if there's a body in there!" The neighbor bumbled his words, his free hand's fingers moving as if they were a spider trying to detach itself from his wrist and escape.

"Tell them to get here, now!" Peter commanded and hurried inside the vehicle.

As the car took off, Nadine eyed Callum's front door. She wiped tears from her eyes. "I feel horrible leaving Cal there, like that."

Peter's eyes flitted to the house, shrinking in the rearview mirror, then back to the road. "Me, too, but we can't let Sylvia die. We can't do anything for Cal."

Sylvia let out what sounded like a gurgling moan.

Nadine turned around. "Syl? You'll be okay. Hang in there."

"Did you...bring the notebooks and the cult's book like I said?"

"Yes." Nadine nodded and slapped her purse. "Don't worry about that right now. We need to get you to the hospital."

"Cal," Sylvia moaned. "Is he really..." She swallowed saliva, grunted with pain, and her voice broke. "He is, isn't he?" She opened her eyes a little and a single tear rolled from each of them as she met Nadine's eyes. "I can't... All these years...and all I got...was six months..."

Nadine reached back toward her hand and took it in hers.

"Six months." She grunted hard this time, as if something were eating her from inside. "Why'd I wait so long...like I could do better?"

Nadine held her hand tight in hers. "Syl. Don't—"

"He was right there, all this time." She let out a painful sob. Growled in pain as Peter made a quick left turn. "Now, he's not here anymore."

Barry finished buttoning his jeans, then adjusted his purple flannel shirt over his T-shirt, the same clothes he'd been wearing since the previous night at the bar. He took his shirt collar between his fingers and gave it a sniff. "Well...not quite ripe, but I can't wait to go get my clothes and actually change." He glanced back at Ray, who was lying naked on the couch, gazing up at him. Barry's eyes glided over every slick, sweaty line of that beautiful body.

"I like your smell."

Barry chuckled. "You're not super objective, don't you think?" He bent down and planted a kiss on his lips. "How'd you like that?"

Ray gestured with an open palm toward his sweat-drenched body. "I mean, look at me. I can barely move."

"Might want to get some electrolytes or some energy drinks, coz that was just the appetizer." He raised an eyebrow at him and gave him a sideways smile. "I'll expect at least five more of those when I get back." He tilted his head to one side, considering. "Four, if you make them *real* intense."

Ray grabbed a pillow from the couch, covered his face and let out a fake scream, then grinned up at him. "Are you trying to kill me? Is that what this is? Revenge?"

He stood over him, puffed his chest out, doing his clumsiest attempt at looking handsome and sexy. "You saying it's not worth the effort?" He once again gave him a sideways smile.

Ray looked him up and down and shook his head, as he stood up and put his arms around him. "Electrolytes, Red Bull, Viagra,"—he gave him a quick peck on the lips—"hell, cocaine, if it will help me do that as many times as you want."

Barry kissed him again and thought, instead of getting used to it, every time he kissed Ray, he found two more reasons to want to kiss him more. "I love you."

"I love you, too."

"I'll be back before you know it."

With one last kiss, Barry turned, took his fob from the coffee table, and headed for the door.

Martha sat by the window in her bedroom, gazing up at the silver moon shining over White Harbor, her black beads wrapped around her left hand.

She was lucid.

She knew this wasn't her home. This was a hospital room. The geriatric care wing at Clarendon Hospital. She knew she was sick. Alzheimer's. She knew if it wasn't for God's intervention, she wouldn't even have brief moments of lucidity, only a long, entangled web of memories that made no sense, like pieces of a puzzle that somehow fit into each other despite being out of order, resulting in an abstract image that did not resemble reality. Something deformed, incoherent, a mockery of the beauty it once was.

Above all things, she knew Peter had put her here, in this room. The most humiliating of fates for God's anointed messenger. She would break him. She would crush his will under her foot like she did when he was a child. He would regret this indignation. He was frail and susceptible after she'd compelled his bitch to set their home on fire. She still had to bring his little six-year-old spawn into play. That would have to wait, though.

She would make her son rue the day he thought he could cage her power in a little hospital room. God would bring him back to her. God promised. God never lied.

"*Tjenaf egoikaat gozun-Uolmin yggshe,*" she mumbled.

She gazed at the silver moon. God's closed eye. It was time for it to open.

"Let the Second Night begin."

CHAPTER TEN

THE TOWN 1 – SUMMONED

It happened all at once, in a blink, to every person within the limits of White Harbor.

In the wake of the First Night, Judy and Sam Becker were devastated by the loss of their son. Judy knew her husband shared her sense of betrayal toward Martha Lange. She had sacrificed their boy, despite their years of loyal service.

One second, they sat huddled in their living room, wallowing in their shared grief. The next, Judy found herself alone. Her husband was gone. All lights in their home had died, save for the dim blue light coming from the moon outside.

"God," Judy Becker said with resignation, wiping away the tears from her eyes. "It's begun."

She looked around the dark room and noticed there was a kind of orange glow around her front door, passing through the narrow space between the door and the frame.

Regretting every decision that had led her to this point, but knowing it was too late to turn back now, she picked up the knife she'd placed on her coffee table and stepped toward the door.

She reached for the doorknob, certain in his own version of the Moonlit World, her husband was doing the same.

They'd see each other on the other side.

Maria Knox woke up in a hospital room with no knowledge that she'd been found unconscious on the street after the previous night's blackout. All she remembered was being out on her night walk with her pretty Pomeranian, Dottie III. She'd been wearing her pretty pink tracksuit, and relaxing as usual, when, in an instant, the world had gone dark, then the surrounding buildings started glowing with red and orange and yellow flames. Dottie III was no longer beside her—she was holding only a leash. The street was flooded with water up to her shins, and every house in the neighborhood was on fire.

Standing in that inexplicable, burning neighborhood, she was reminded of the fire at the Vanek House, the one that had consumed the bodies of her husband and her three children, thirty years earlier, victims of Freddie Parham and Ben Curling. She hadn't been able to even have a funeral with open caskets for her entire family. All that had been left of them had been charred bones. According to the coroner, her husband had been mauled by Curling's dogs.

Her husband had at least died the hero that shot the evil old man (the fact it had been Jess Cunningham, using her husband's gun, was completely unknown to her).

All of these memories had risen within her as she'd stood under a strange blue moon in this flooded, burning neighborhood. Then, out of nowhere had come these *things*, like black tentacles, or threads, shooting out of the water, wrapping around her, tying her, enveloping her, crawling inside her until all she saw was darkness, and all she felt was her body twisting and breaking, as she screamed with futility.

It must have been a dream, she thought.

She had no memory of the creature she'd become. She had no memory of devouring Sam Becker Jr. There was nothing after that nightmare, and now she was standing in a dark hospital room wearing a hospital robe. There was no electricity. None of the usual noises she'd expect wafting in from a hospital hallway. By the flickering orange glow between the door and the door frame, it appeared the hospital was on fire, too. But then, why wasn't she seeing the same glow through the small window on the door?

It wouldn't be long before those same black threads she'd seen the previous night would flood the room and force her to walk through that door.

In his mother's basement, Louis Foley—Jess's bar server—watched TV in his undies; lotion and tissues ready to rub one out and smoke a joint. He was enjoying a night off after Chuck Cunningham had called to tell him the bar would be closed that night. He'd been in the middle of brushing Cheeto dust off his T-shirt, readying for his nightly unwinding ritual, when the TV and every light around him went dark in a second, except for the eerie blue light pouring in from the basement window, which illuminated nothing.

"This, again?" he blurted.

He pawed around the mess of sheets and pillows for his cell phone, hoping tonight the flashlight worked, unlike during the blackout of the night before. "Mom?" he called, receiving no answer. This, in this darkness, made a chill climb up his spine. "Where the hell did I put it? Mom! Could you bring down a candle or something? I can't find my phone."

He sauntered toward the basement stairs and looked up. There was a strange, flickering orange glow around the door.

"Mom?"

For a moment, he worried there was a fire upstairs, but he would've heard his mother screaming, or she would've come calling for him to leave the house. Maybe light from a gas lantern? No, that light wasn't bright or intense enough to glow through the doorframe like this. No, that light was whitish.

"Mom? What's going on?"

He wasn't aware, as he climbed the stairs with reticence, his mother had been in the toilet when the lights went out, and she'd seen her own glow framing the bathroom door. She had already crossed over.

Riley Estrada and Mason Owen had arrived at Cunningham's to find a "Closed for the Day" sign at the front door. As they both moaned and complained and tried to agree on where else to go get drunk, Riley turned his head to find his buddy Mason was gone. So were the lights in the entire street. The bar's door, despite its "Closed for the Day" sign, emitted a flickering glow all around it.

Barry Giffen's Civic rolled to a stop in a town devoured by darkness. "No, no," he said, slamming his palm on the wheel. "Not this again."

He tried to restart the vehicle. The battery was dead. He was in his neighborhood's cul-de-sac, two houses away from his house. All windows looked dark, the streetlights extinguished; and up there, in the sky, was that terrifying dark-blue moon from the previous night.

"I've gotta call Ray!"

He checked his phone. A glassy-black rectangle with nothing on the screen. He looked out the window to his left and saw something inexplicable: a few feet away from the car, there was a rectangular outline, the width and height of a door, simply existing in mid-air. He could see the house behind it—Vince and Katherine Craig's home.

Feeling his chest turn into solid ice, he slowly opened the door and stepped outside. He cast a glance toward his house, where Maryann and the kids were, then he regarded the strange rectangle. The outline glimmered orange, like embers glowing on the other side.

"No fucking way I'm going through there." He turned toward his house, then he saw it—coming out of every door and every window in the neighborhood—approaching fast. A black tide.

Freddie Parham examined his creation. He might have outdone himself this time. "Brickhouse, you have no goddamn clue what's coming," he said in a boastful, self-satisfied voice. "Now, we just wait for the night's festivities to end." He stepped through the door, into the orange light.

Ten-month-old Mia Dittman, who, at this point, had a limited understanding of the world around her, watched as black tendrils rose from the floor, taking shape. The shape changed color, turned solid, became familiar. It was the shape with the sound "Ma-ma" attached to it. It didn't smell right, though, but it smiled down at her, picking her up as Ma-ma normally did.

Mia smiled as Ma-ma took her toward something that glowed orange, which opened, allowing Ma-Ma to carry her through into a wide-open space with a warm, orange glow.

What Mia couldn't have known was, in the next room, the real Ma-ma had been reading a book (not that she knew what *that* was), and she was now staring at the bedroom door, whose contour glowed, just like it had for her.

Northwest of town, at the gas station, Dominic Willis, who was alone for the night, on account of Gunnar Bilson's sister's disappearance, followed the orange ember glow he found on the convenience store doors. What he found on the other side was nothing resembling a convenience store.

In the Lumenwood trailer park, Zak Hopper had spent hours consoling Georgina and Gunnar Bilson, mother and brother of Stephanie, the girl he'd impregnated and dumped. Stephanie had disappeared during the previous night's blackout. He felt guilt he couldn't put into words, especially since he was sure he'd been one of the last people to see her, when she'd come asking for candles for her mobile home. He'd been an asshole to her. Except, now, back in his own mobile home, something more immediate grabbed his full attention: an orange glow around the door leading to the restroom.

At the Callahan Inn, Alberto "Tali" Ruiz, sitting in bed among a bunch of scattered books and papers on sigils, glyphs, and runes, was also staring at the glowing contour around his bathroom door. His mother had warned him this would happen. She'd also warned him he'd have no choice but to step through.

sat up, awakening in the basement of Cunningham's bar. He moved his hands all over his body to find no signs of the stab wounds Sylvia Nguyen had given him.

"What the hell?" He turned his head to the left to see the doors to Chuck Cunningham's gun locker, shimmering with an orange glow, as if they were a single door. His face drooped with dread. "I see..."

Sylvia Nguyen stood in a dark, vacant street outside the open back door of Peter's Chevy, looking around in confusion. "Peter!" she shouted. "Nadine!"

She had no idea how she'd gotten out of the car, or where her stab wounds had gone. All she knew was her friends weren't there. Through the window, she could see a black shape, a body, on the back seat where she'd been lying a minute ago. It looked almost like her, but translucent. The dark-blue moon loomed again over White Harbor. There was what looked like a glowing, rectangular portal in mid-air in front of her, and—

"Guys! Anybody?"

—something dark and terrifying was coming out of every door, every sewer grate, every window, rushing fast toward her.

Jerome Lucas had taken a day off from the vet clinic. His son handled most appointments nowadays, anyway. He'd been in the middle of brewing some passionflower tea, like his late wife used to make for her anxiety, when the lights in his kitchen had gone dark, and the door to his garage had begun glowing with a strange outline.

The lights had gone out for Xavier Poe Kane while he sat, his head bent over the documents on his desk—historical documents he'd gotten from Callum Baker. He'd been studying them closely, trying to pinpoint the location of the "UFO event" one of his callers claimed had happened in the area three hundred years ago. He immediately corrected himself: *Not a UFO, some kind of huge light or explosion. Still, what if it was a UFO? Wouldn't that be the best thing ever?*

The moment the lights went out, he ran to his window to find exactly what he expected to find; a dark-blue moon glowing over White Harbor, which was, like the previous night, consumed by darkness. He scanned the sky, looking for any sign of moving lights, cigar-shaped objects, moving orbs, or discs. What if all the abduction stories, including his own, were related to this one phenomenon?

Wouldn't that be exciting?

He scanned for a few more seconds. There was nothing. That full moon was more than enough, though.

When he turned around and noticed the orange glow delineating his bedroom door, a wide smile appeared on his face.

"This is so fucking cool."

One by one, every person in White Harbor—over four thousand people—was summoned through their very own door. Whether voluntarily, guided by the shape of a loved one, or compelled to, each person passed their door.

Peter Lange found the orange portal outside the driver's side door of his blue Chevrolet Malibu.

Nadine Schaefer found it outside the passenger door.

Raymond Chang had been showering when the lights went out, the water stopped running, and he noticed the glow in his bathroom door.

Jess and Chuck Cunningham found it, separately, at the top of the basement stairs, as they'd been stitching John Hitch up.

Royce and Lillian Howe had found themselves alone, separate, in their living room, the front door glowing. Their little girl had been led by something resembling her dad through her bedroom door.

Angie Schaefer had found herself alone on the beach, a glowing portal a few steps away in the sand.

Bobby had felt true fear before in his life. The terrifying events inside the Vanek House and what Freddie had done when they were just children had marked his life forever and even cemented his choice of profession. Despite that, Bobby had never been overcome by a sense of terror so great as the one he'd felt the moment Angie disappeared from his side, the touch of her head on her shoulder and her hand in his simply vanishing.

"Angie!" he shouted, springing to his feet, turning around in circles, causing sand to fly in an arc around him. "Angie!"

The beach was deserted. The families and couples sitting there mere seconds ago, the lights from their phone screens, or their little fires, were gone. Behind him, the amusement park was in complete darkness. Not a soul around him. He could still hear the waves nearby, still crashing. Their sound in this abandoned world was like the growl of some undiscovered sea monster—

(*An enormous creature, dark but maddeningly beautiful, and terrifying beyond comprehension, rising from the line of the ocean with an open mouth that disappeared at both ends of the horizon, swallowing the sea, the earth, and the sky, and every creature in them*)

—emerging to claim the Earth and end all life beneath that ghastly, dark-blue moon.

"Angie!" he shouted again, realizing there was no one there to hear him. When he faced the beach again, he spotted something he'd missed. A rectangle of flickering orange light, in the shape of a door of some sort. He didn't need someone to stand next to him and point out the obvious: he was expected to go through it. A lifetime of movies and video games had made this clear right away. Except, he was determined *not* to go through. It would be like playing into what was expected of him in this scenario.

What if Angie's in there? he thought, then glanced up at the blue moon, thinking back to everything John Hitch—the Lighthouse Rock security guard—had said about the blue moon, and Freddie escaping the island to kill for Martha Lange. *What if she isn't there and I end up getting killed and leaving her helpless against whatever's going on?*

Making up his mind, Bobby turned around and hurried back up the sandy slope that led to the amusement park. The silhouettes of the empty stands, the bumper cars, the Ferris wheel, and the roller-coaster sitting immobile in the blue darkness made his hackles rise. There was something so unnatural about the complete absence of life emanating from a place that had been brimming with noise and laughter mere minutes ago.

Then...movement.

Even in this darkness, he could see it, like a wave of black washing over the ground, coming from between the concession stands, between the individual bumper cars, and the small metal fences that surrounded the rides. It looked like either a single, liquid entity rushing toward him, or billions of individual black worms crawling at ridiculous speed.

Bobby spun around and stomped the ground back toward the beach. The black wave also came at him from the left and right, forming a closing wedge, narrowing behind him. He ran down the slope as the left and right portions of this horizontal maw closed fast. He kept running, kicking up sand as the patch of beach in front of him narrowed further and further, blackness closing in around the door.

"No! No! No! No!"

He reached the glowing door outline as the black mass nipped at the heels of his shoes, and without hesitation, pushed the door in and ran through.

He was blinded at first by the light on the other side. Once his eyes adjusted, the sight before him was beyond comprehension.

He was in a wide circular space, lit up by burning torches on sconces on tall pillars—the source of the orange glow. The noise, screams, and chatter of thousands of confused, terrified people shook his eardrums at once. There were familiar faces around him, people he knew from town. Was this everyone in White Harbor? That was ridiculous. Should've been ridiculous. That meant over four thousand people had been brought here, just like him. He struggled to fathom the power required to even attempt something like this.

Men, women, children. People in pajamas, in casual clothing, naked people, people in scrubs, and hospital gowns. The most inexplicable sight was an entire enclosure or cage surrounded by thin black bars to his left, made of some solid substance, like obsidian. In it, were little children, infants, and babies, all being held in the arms of strange black figures, made of the same material as the prison bars, branching, and spun into the shape of adult humans, whose fingers stretched like vines and wrapped around the children, holding them in place, facing the center of this inexplicable space.

The ground had a slight downward slope, as if allowing visibility of the center for all those present.

The slope reached what looked like a moat, or a chasm, surrounding a circle of earth at the center of the pit, like a round altar, and on that altar, was a woman he didn't recognize at first, standing in front of a black structure, something like a cross with two horizontal beams, slightly tilted upward.

I've seen that altar before, he thought, but realized that made no sense. Where *could* he have seen a place like this anywhere?

The pillars, the sconces, the...

Up above was a gigantic domed ceiling with an opening at its center, the dark-blue moon glowed beyond the skylight. *The chapel at the Vanek House,* he thought in disbelief.

He looked around. Noticed the concentric pattern formed by the columns, noticed what looked like a symbol embossed on the altar at the center. He recognized the woman standing there.

That's Martha Lange!

It was then he noticed a figure tied to the cross-like contraption at the center of the altar. He trudged forward, pushing people aside to get a better view. People weren't offering any resistance to his advance. They were trying to stay away from the center as much as possible—everyone could sense if there was danger, it was there.

As he approached and got a better angle on the altar, he saw the person hanging from the black structure, which he now realized was made of the same hard, black obsidian as the child cage. The person had their hands bound at the top, where the first horizontal beam met the vertical column, the lower horizontal beam poking with a jagged tip at the center of her back. It was—

A scream cut through the air like a scythe, and even if he didn't want to look away from the altar, recognition made him turn his head to the left.

"ANGIEEEEEEE!" Nadine's voice cried. She was near the edge of the chasm, a few feet to his left, screaming her sister's name over and over again. "ANGIEEEEEEE!"

Bobby gawked at the altar, and his heart dropped into a black hole at the pit of his stomach, never to rise again, as he confirmed the bound woman, struggling to break from the chains that held her hanging from the contraption, was indeed his Angie.

CHAPTER ELEVEN

WITNESSES

A chaos of people.

Peter waded through a bewildered, terrified crowd. People who, like him, had been whisked away to a place that couldn't possibly exist.

The crowd pushed this way and that, as if they couldn't make up their minds about in which direction they should be moving. Should they be moving away toward the edges, where a solid stone wall prevented them from leaving, or toward the inner area, where a bottomless chasm threatened to swallow them forever if they fell in?

That's Mother, he thought in panic and disbelief. *Mother has Angie hanging from that thing. I have to stop her! I can't let Mother hurt—*

"ANGIEEEEEEE!"

He whipped his head to the right. He would recognize that voice anywhere, even if it were warped and distorted into a horrified scream among the clamor of a thousand voices.

"Nadine?"

He ran. Pushing through the crowd.

He found her kneeling at the edge of the chasm. She was unmissable. Most people gave the edge a wide berth, not wanting to risk falling in. Bobby was there with her already, both clinging to each other, their faces twisted in horror, watching helpless as Angie hung from that strange structure at the center of the altar.

The voice hit him when he was three steps away from his friends.

"Praise be to God!"

Mother!

Her voice had been perceived by his brain, bypassing his ears. She was speaking straight into his head. He cast a wide glance and noticed the confused faces all around, the murmurs, the wide-open eyes. Somewhere in the distance, children and infants cried in terror.

"The First Night, four will open the gates!" her rapturous voice declared in his mind—in everyone's mind. *"The Second Night, one will seal the town! The Third Night, four will awaken God! The Fourth Night will be eternal!"*

He looked at her and realized she had been staring at him this whole time. She was lucid. Lucid like he hadn't seen her in years. The terrifying steel in her gaze, and that proud smile directed at him, made the blood in his veins turn to hairy caterpillars crawling through his body, making him shudder.

Her lips moved, and as she spoke, he heard her voice in his mind, but the words in his head did not match what her lips were saying. She was speaking in that strange language known only to the Circle: *"Tjenaf egoikaat gozun-Uolmin yggshe!"*

He heard: "*GOD WILL FEED!*"

Black tendrils had spun together and turned into some kind of wrought crystal steel, forming thick bars surrounding what must be every small child in White Harbor. It was like a cage, or an enormous pen, and no matter how hard Barry pulled to get to his two boys, it was like trying to rip a bridge's tension wire in two. His arm muscles tensed to their limits, his face was red, spit shot out of his mouth as he roared in anger, watching his two babies just out of arm's reach, trapped in the arms of two obscene replicas of himself. Their grotesque forms were hollow and twisted, but the resemblance to him was unmistakable. They were made of the same strange, black substance as the bars, shaped into branches, twigs, and vines, and woven together to form loathsome statues. They reminded him of the creatures they'd encountered inside the Vanek House thirty years ago, except solid and empty.

Daniel kept calling for his daddy, and Gabriel's shrill cries pierced his soul.

"I'll get you outta there, boys. Daddy's here. I'll get you out!" He was unsure he could keep that promise.

"*Four lives have already been given to allow God's servants into our world!*"

He could hear Martha Lange's voice in his head, spewing her insane religious babble. None of that mattered to him right now. He had to free his two boys before whatever was about to happen happened.

"Daddy!" Daniel had peed in his pajamas in fear, as tears streamed down his face. "Daddy, let us out! Daddyyyyyy!"

He took a few steps back, ran toward the cage, rammed his shoulder into it, but recoiled back with a pained grunt after the impact did nothing to even rattle the enclosure.

"Tonight, God solidifies His hold on this blessed land!"

From all around, came cries of terror, calls of: "Go to hell, you crazy bitch!", and he could hear the voice of a woman calling the name "Angie".

That's Nadine. What's going on?

Barry pressed his face closer to the bars, passed his arm between them. Reached for Daniel. "Here, buddy! Grab Daddy's fingers. We'll be okay."

Daniel leaned in, stretching his left hand as far as he could, and he was able to grab two fingers in Barry's hand. He curled the fingers in to help his son get a better grip. "Great, buddy, you're doing great. Daddy's got you." He glanced at Gabe, who continued to wail in terror. "Now, try to take Gabe's hand. I think you can reach it. C'mon, you can do it."

Daniel reached toward his little brother, who, at first, didn't take his tear-filled eyes off his father, then, feeling the touch of his brother's fingers, turned his head toward him. As if needing some kind of human contact, almost by instinct, clutched his brother's hand in his.

"Good!" Barry forced a smile. "Good boys! I'm so proud of you! Don't worry! This will be over soon! We'll be alright, and we'll go home soon!" He spared a glanced over his shoulder, past the commotion and the screaming crowd to see who he was certain was Martha Lange, with a woman wearing the same summer dress as Angie, hanging from a strange contraption. He knew he was lying to his children. He had no clue what was about to happen. He was certain it would be anything but alright, though.

"Tonight, you will witness God's hand in action!"

Royce was huddled with Lillian, both making their way through the crowd toward the area where all the younger children were.

"Honey, what if she isn't there?" Lillian asked in a panic. "What do we do?"

Royce squeezed his wife's hand tight. "She'll be there."

"How can you know that?"

He sighed, shrugged, shook his head. "I don't know, but remember what I told you about how Leroy died?"

She nodded.

"These things usually have an order. I confirmed that last night, when Jess thought of how to get Peter and Barry's cars started. There are rules. I see only teenagers and adults out here. So, all small children should be"—he pointed toward the black bars forming an enclosure, surrounded by desperate, screaming parents—"right there."

There were people clinging to the black bars, trying to break them or walk between them with no success.

Lillian shook her head, looking bewildered. "This is insa—AAGH!" She shrieked as a naked man, barely covering himself with one hand, grabbed Royce's shoulder.

"Royce!" the man said.

Given his wife's scream, Royce was prepared to take down whoever had touched him. He recognized Ray, hand on his shoulder, stark naked, eyes open wide in confusion.

"Ray, what the fuck?"

"Have you seen the others?"

"Why the fuck are you naked?"

"I was in the shower when this whole thing happened. Didn't have a chance to grab a towel or anything."

"Jesus," Royce said.

Lillian pulled a blue cardigan off her body. "Here."

"Thanks." He took the cardigan and tied its sleeves around his waist like an apron, covering the front, but leaving his ass still exposed. He looked from one to the other. "What about the others? Have you seen Barry?"

Leroy raised an eyebrow at him. "You mean the person you couldn't get away from fast enough last night?"

Ray let out a frustrated huff. "Long story. Have you seen him?"

"No."

"I think," Lillian said, "if he's here, he'll probably go where we're heading. He has two little boys. He's definitely heading there." She nodded toward the enclosure, where those strange, unnerving figures—upsetting even from a distance, like human-shaped shrubs in winter—held what looked like every small child in town.

"Let's go," Royce said.

As soon as they took another step came Martha Lange's voice, once more, broadcast straight into their minds, which gave them a sickening, violating feeling.

"Angela Schaefer has been chosen by God to seal White Harbor."

The three stopped in their tracks, looked toward the center. Royce had noticed the hanging woman on that strange circular altar. He remembered the altar from their failed attempt at saving Leroy. That was the same altar, and this was the same chapel where Freddie tried to sacrifice him—only scaled up a thousand times over. He had recognized the woman as Martha Lange, even from this distance, but had not recognized the poor soul bound to that structure.

"She will ready White Harbor for God's feast."

"Holy shit, that's Angie!" Royce said. Someone bumped into his shoulder, hurrying toward the center of the crowd. He was at first startled, but soon recognized the person. "Jess!"

Jess turned wide, consternated eyes toward him. "Royce!" she ran back and threw her arms around him. "That bitch has Angie! I can't! I can't lose someone else!" She looked up at him. "We have to do something. Please!"

Royce turned toward the children's enclosure, knowing his priority needed to be his little girl. "Jess, I—"

"Go," Lillian interjected. "Go save Angela. I'll find Tracy."

He wavered.

"Go!" she insisted. "We'll be fine!"

He nodded, and both he and Ray followed Jess to the inner part of the circle. Quickly, they arrived at the edge of the chasm, where the floor no longer sloped, and went flat for about three feet. The chasm between them and the altar was roughly fifteen feet across. It would be impossible to jump.

Royce looked down and saw the pit stretched long past the point where the torchlight illuminated the stone. That fall would kill anyone. He gazed toward the altar. He could make out Angie's terrified face from this distance. "Let her go, you monstrous fucking bitch!" he shouted. "Let her go!"

Martha Lange spared a glance in their direction. For a moment, it seemed she would turn her head away and ignore them, like they weren't worth her attention. Instead, the despicable woman gave a half-smile, superior and arrogant as always. "*Let the Chosen Accursed join me and witness God's glory firsthand.*"

In a blink, they all disappeared and reappeared at the altar. All standing in front of Martha Lange. Behind her was Angie, struggling for her life.

Royce glanced to one side, then the other. To his left were Sylvia, Barry, and Jess. To his right were Ray, Nadine, Bobby, and... "Freddie?" he said in a baffled voice.

Freddie turned a proud smile toward him, waved his fingers hello. Bobby, who was standing beside him, looked gobsmacked. Freddie grinned at him, too, and took a knee, bowing his head toward Martha.

"Your servant is here, Mother. Command me, and I'll assist you however I can."

Martha regarded him for a moment. "Stand, Frederick," she said with a solemn voice, this time with her own lips, not speaking inside their head. "You have more to do, but not tonight. For tonight, you're a witness." She turned toward them. "Let's begin."

The group shouted curses and pleas toward the insane woman. She acted as if she couldn't even hear them. Like they were so beneath her, their voice made no sound.

She stepped behind Angie, sparing a glance up at her.

"Don't you fucking dare touch her, you fucking cunt!" Jess shouted, making Royce realize neither of them could move from the spot where they were standing. "Don't you fucking dare!"

"Get away from her!" Nadine shouted. "Leave my sister alone!"

"Mrs. Lange!" Bobby shouted. "Don't! Don't do this! Stop this!"

Among all their screams, a distinct voice came from behind them, from across the chasm.

"MARTHA, THAT'S ENOUGH!"

They turned their heads to see Chuck Cunningham holding a Magnum to Peter's head.

Martha, who was standing behind Angie, considered the old man with repressed anger and a hint of amusement.

"This has gone too far!" Chuck shouted.

Why was Peter not brought here with us? Royce thought, as if any of this should make sense, seeing Peter's terrified face as the muzzle kissed his temple. *Wait a minute,* Royce felt around his pants pocket. He should've had a pocketknife there. He'd taken it in case he needed to defend his family if anything happened that night. The knife was gone. *It's gone. How did Chuck bring that gun here?*

"I swear I'll kill Peter right now, Martha!" Chuck said, a serious threat in his voice. "If he dies, this whole thing ends. Stop this madness now! Nobody wants this world you're trying to create. Not like this! Not with fear! Not with murder!"

Despite the panic of having a gun pointed at his face, Peter could see the grief this was causing Old Chuck. The old man's eyebrows were twisted upward, bunched up in a skin knot at the center, his teeth bare, clenched together, his breath shallow, ragged.

"Mother, please!" Peter said. The sudden sound of his voice startled Old Chuck. The noise from the crowd dimmed into a murmur. The crowd noticed whatever was happening in this one spot had some sort of impact on whatever was happening on the altar. "This can't be what God wants. God can't possibly want fear and death! You *have* to see that, Mother! Even you can't believe God wants all of these people, even children, to be this terrified!"

He said it with confidence in his voice, though everything he knew about his mother contradicted what he was saying. She couldn't care less about any of these people.

"*Be quiet, boy,*" she said, and from Chuck Cunningham's reaction, he surmised everyone else could hear this. "*Tonight, you're as irrelevant as any of these peasants. I am the Messenger of God. You know nothing of what the Lord wants.*"

"Listen to your son, Martha!" Chuck straightened the Magnum. "Peter is a good man, and someone I hold in high esteem, but I swear, I'll blow his fucking brains out right here, so you can crumple up your grandiose plans and shove them up your ass!"

His mother snorted out a laugh.

"*Such bravado in such a cowardly man. You wouldn't dare.*"

Chuck put his finger on the trigger, his aim unflinching. "You have til the count of three to let all these people go. By the end of the last 'e', your son's brain will already be flying through the air. One!"

"*I should've expected a traitor like you to use the Circle's privileges to bring that weapon into this sacred place. I thought it beneath even you.*"

"Two!"

Peter glanced at his friends. While they were shouting at Chuck not to shoot him, he could see the conflict in their eyes and the way their gaze flitted every few seconds to Angie and to the pit surrounding them. His head exploding in a Magnum blast would save all the people Mother planned to kill, including all his friends.

What about William? I'd leave William alone. I—

"You seem to forget something important, Charles..." Mother's tone was condescending. To her, this man was never an obstacle and would never be.

A knife slid under Old Chuck's jaw, holding its position, ready to cut on command. The person holding it was Judy Becker. Peter's eyes flew open with shock. The sweet old lady that had given him a sizable piece of cheesecake when he'd arrived in town. He'd seen a group of about six people approaching from behind. He hadn't recognized them at first. Behind Old Chuck were Judy Becker, with the knife, and Sam Becker Sr., with a little pistol. Ethan and Emmaline Garner, the proprietors of Seaside Park, along with Reece and Lydia Holland, who owned the town's only gas station, were also present, brandishing guns to prevent anyone from assisting Old Chuck.

Mother smiled. *"The rest of the Circle also came prepared in case you or anyone else attempted to intervene."*

"They might kill me. Not before I pull the trigger and blow his head off, though. I don't care about myself! I care about—"

"Your daughter?"

Jess screamed.

He turned his head so quick Judy Becker's knife nipped his neck—a thin line of blood running perpendicular to the cut. Jess was leaning forward over the chasm at an impossible angle, as if held precariously by an invisible arm. His bloodstream came to a sudden stop. "No! Jess!"

"*What will it be, Charles?*" Martha let go of Jess for half a second, and she fell further. "*I only need four. I have others to choose from.*"

Jess screamed as Martha let go again and she tilted further into the pit, only the tips of her boots touching the ground now.

Defeated, Chuck handed the gun to Sam Becker.

"I'm sorry about this, Chuck," he said.

"No, you're not. Even after she killed your kid, you're still her slave."

"*Wise choice,*" Martha said, and Jess's body was pulled back into the altar, where she staggered backward, away from the edge, until the same force that had been holding her, gripped her again, made her turn around, and she was again facing Martha and Angie. Soon, Jess had Royce's arms around her. She hugged him back, weeping with terror.

"*Enough delays. God waits.*"

CHAPTER TWELVE

HERE AT THE END OF ALL THINGS

A ngie knew she was going to die.

She'd known for almost eight months now. From the moment Dr. Glendale had given her the news of the cancer.

She remembered sitting in his office, her gaze gliding around the room, taking everything in, in no particular order. She saw a painting of a ship floating in a calm sea, a bookshelf with medical volumes, diplomas and certifications hanging on an orange-colored wall; a family picture on the desk, plus an individual one for each of the doctor's three kids—the daughter's was a college graduation photo. Everything Angela saw, she regarded with fascination, as if it were the first time she'd seen such a thing. Anything to add a sense of levity and detachment to her ordeal.

Then there was the other piece of decoration, next to the doctor's desk, the one that didn't fit with the rest of the room: a full-body plastic skeleton with all the organs placed where they would normally fit within a body. Lidless eyes staring forever into space.

She suppressed a shudder.

Doctor appointments made her anxious responses—hidden well behind a wall of stoic professionalism, weekend partying, and Lexapro—go into overdrive. In just the fifteen minutes she'd been there, she'd untied and tied her hair eight times, and the bridge of her glasses itched on her nose like a swollen mosquito bite. She only wore glasses to read legal documents, but she'd been so stressed she'd forgotten to take them off. When she wasn't readjusting her hair or scratching her nose, her hands were clasped together into a tense, solid mass of fingers.

Shit, I'm becoming Nadine. Calm down, girl!

She felt the more someone knew about her, the more vulnerable she was, and doctors got to know too much, too fast. Their job, by definition, was to invade a person's most guarded boundaries, even if they did so with the best of intentions.

All things considered, she'd lived her life doing pretty much anything she wanted, without complications, and she could only achieve this by not letting anyone tell her what to do. She had full control of her life, control which was taken from her in its entirety while sitting in front of a doctor. Take off your clothes. Open your mouth. Stick out your tongue. Open your legs. Rarely was anything more invasive of her personal space. She felt, however, this particular doctor's office was comforting—except for the skeleton. The skeleton was a tone-deaf inclusion in this otherwise pleasant space.

As if to complement the feeling, she noticed, through the window behind the doctor's desk, a tree covered by beautiful yellow flowers that made her heart fill up with a sort of inexplicable joy. Her mind struggled to remember what it was called, then—

Caribbean trumpet tree! That's right!

She smiled.

Her dad had told her trumpet trees had been an almost accidental import to the area. They were mainly found in dry climates; so, they seldom thrived in Wight Harbor's "random, with a certainty of rain" weather. Their wood was also supposed to be quite resilient and resistant to fire. As a kid, she had always felt that was an awful lot of explanation for pretty flowers.

It was at that exact moment she realized something important. Even though she was tense, as she often was in these situations, that tension was her default response. It was what she was used to. More of a physical reaction than a real psychological response. Deep inside, she found, there was something closely resembling calm. She was at peace. She felt prepared for anything.

The doctor put down the papers he was perusing, then ran his hand from his mouth to his chin.

I'm fine. I'm prepared. Whatever comes, I'll be fine.

"Miss Schaefer..." he said, and she felt her stomach tighten. She was hoping he would just be out with it and spare her the endless litany of "as-you-knows" and "it-looks-likes" some people seemed to use as padding and fluff for news, bad or otherwise.

She was prepared. He should come out with it. She was ready.

"I'm afraid it's cancer," he said plainly.

The words hit her like a brick to the face, and she realized she would've preferred the padding and fluff. All delusions of being prepared disappeared, as she realized she'd been clinging to the notion it couldn't happen to her. She lowered her gaze, trying to process the information. As she tried to swallow saliva, it felt as if she were swallowing a live sea urchin.

"Um...is it...operable?" she asked with a voice like the urchin was still stuck halfway down. She looked at the doctor, her gaze trying to read in his expression any possibility of good news that could follow such a terrible blow.

(*It's not the deadly type of cancer! You'll live a long, healthy life! Also, you've won the lottery!*)

The doctor cleared his throat and shook his head. "If you had come earlier, perhaps. Now—"

She let out a sudden, short, hysterical cackle, so unexpected it startled the doctor. Her hands flew up to cover her mouth in embarrassment. It was her fault. She could not believe it was her fault. She breathed in and forced herself to regain her composure. Her hands went back down to being clasped together so tensely it looked like her fingers might snap like brittle twigs.

"I was afraid to come." She choked back tears with a deranged smile, trying to explain, trying to tell it like it was a funny anecdote, like explaining it would make the doctor change his mind. "You know how it is! You think as long as there isn't a test saying there's something wrong...you think..."

Doctor Glendale's eyebrows came together in an expression of sympathy, and she hated him for it. Thirty-two was too young to be told you're dying of cancer.

Angela untied her hair once more, letting wavy strands of long black hair nearly close over her face like curtains, and then tied it back on tighter than it had been before, almost gaining two extra inches of forehead. The orange walls and the yellow flowers outside didn't feel as warm and comforting to her anymore. They seemed to be a sickly, phlegmy color. She scratched her virulently itchy nose and thought of what to say next. She was great with words in front of a judge, a jury, or a witness. The courtroom was her stage, and she was the queen of eloquence, verbiage, and enunciation. Right now, though, there were too many words pushing against the inside of her lips, trying to explode out. She didn't know what the next best question would be. Finally, she asked, "How about treatment? Chemotherapy. Wouldn't that work?"

The doctor shook his head again. "There's always a slight chance of chemotherapy succeeding but, once the cancer has spread as violently as this one, that chance decreases to almost nothing. At this point, I feel chemotherapy would only result in severely lowering your quality of life...for the time you have remaining."

"The time I have rem—" She couldn't finish the sentence. The words wouldn't come out. She was still holding back the tears, trying to get through the questions without breaking down. "And how much time would that be?" She braced herself for the answer. *A year? Two?*

"Three, maybe four months."

She breathed in deep. She felt like there was a bottomless pit within her body, and she was inside herself, falling down through it. "Oh my god. Nadine. Oh my god," she muttered in a hurry, babbling, looking at the floor. There was a crack there, a tiny crack on the linoleum, creeping out from under the beautiful, plush rug. She then raised her head to look up at the doctor, still not crying, but wanting to, so desperately. The crack looked like a smiling face. "What about alternative treatments? I've... I've seen these stories on the news—"

"Miss Schaefer, I—"

"No, no, wait. I have seen it," she insisted, losing her composure. "People who get cured. Maybe, if I do what they—"

"Miss Schaefer, the thing is—"

"I saw one on the news the other day!" True desperation erupted out of her. "Herbal treatments. Acupuncture. Healed!"

"That's what I'm trying to—"

"I—"

"Miss Schaefer!" the doctor said in a stern voice.

She fixed her desolated eyes on him, almost begging for some hope. He had none to offer.

"Those are placebos taken by people who were lucky their cancer went into remission. It happens. Not when it's this advanced."

The skeleton, with its open eyeballs and bare teeth, seemed to mock her.

Angela couldn't hold it in anymore. She burst into tears, her hands covering her face out of shame at breaking down in front of another person. She was always so strong, capable of dealing with anything. Now, there was no use in even trying.

"Do you have relatives? Anyone who can take care of you?" he asked. "Or will you need a caretaker at home? You have excellent insurance. It covers that."

But it can't make me not die.

Angela uncovered her face, which was red and wet, and she remained hunched over with her elbows resting on her knees. Nadine. All this time making fun of her for never getting a life, and now she would outlive her. She'd give anything to have whatever little life Nadine had. A life she was now going to be imposing herself into.

She nodded, biting her lip. "I'll talk to my sister." She didn't look up at the doctor, but at the blossoming tree outside, trying to squeeze some comfort out from its beauty. There was none, only that sickly yellow color that now made her feel like she was going to vomit.

Doctor Glendale's question about how she wanted to spend her last days made her feel exposed. Her inevitable death was leaving her bare and naked in the eyes of the man before her. No longer a human being, but an organic machine with weaknesses, and failures, and unfixable vulnerabilities. She had become an animated lump of skin, bones, muscle, and blood, and somewhere in there, some glitch in the coding of her cells was telling her body to copy errors non-stop until they inevitably clogged up the entire system and made everything stop working. She was a thing, an empty vessel, a malfunctioning robot, a walking corpse. Worse yet, as she now lay virtually cut open and dissected before this man, with her insides exposed like a biology lab frog, her greatest fear had escaped through the gaping cut for him to see she feared depending on others. Her terror at the prospect of feeling helpless had become visible, palpable, known.

"Enough delays. God waits."

The voice pulled her back to the now. Back to the crazy woman gazing up at her with a proud smile on her lips as she walked around the contraption she was bound to. Back to the clamors and screams and murmurs of the crowd gathered here, forced to watch this horror. Back to the terrified, screaming faces of her friends. Her big sister looked like her face was about to break open to let out a flood of tears to join her desperate wails, and Bobby was staring, mouth gaping, perplexed, his head shaking, as if his denial of his situation would make it any less real.

She could feel a sharp point poking into her back. It had already broken her skin a little, and the tiny wound wouldn't stop stinging.

Angie knew she was going to die.

She'd known for almost eight months. Dr. Glendale and the others she'd gone to for a second and third opinion had given her three months. She'd lived almost eight. She was thankful for that. She was more thankful it was her, and not one of the people standing before her, crying their eyes out. She wanted them to live long, happy lives.

She peered down at her clothes, the pretty summer dress she'd worn for her special day out with Bobby and Nadine. She almost smiled, realizing it was one of her favorites, from back when pretty clothes were a thing that mattered to her. She'd had the print on her dress custom made. It was a white dress covered in yellow flowers. Caribbean trumpet flowers.

Her eyes returned to Bobby. He'd made it all worthwhile. He'd made her last days beautiful and filled with a love she used to think she didn't deserve. She'd hoped she would die in his arms, watching the credits roll on *The Return of the King*. She'd asked him, when she was on her deathbed, to play the movies one last time for her. Now she wouldn't get to watch them. She smiled at him, though.

"I am glad you are here with me," she said in a weak voice, afraid he wouldn't even hear her. "Here at the end of all things."

His paralyzed face broke, like layers on a rock wall, cracking one after the other. His gritting teeth bared. His mouth opened into a scream as he fell to his knees.

She gasped. Felt the jagged point push into her back, then tunnel through her body. She looked down and saw the knife-like tip poke out of her stomach, and blood begin to stain her beautiful dress, blooming outward, then running down. In the shock of the moment, a thought flashed through her mind. *Take that, you asshole,* she thought at the cancer in her stomach, which was most likely being pierced right now. *You didn't get to kill me.*

She felt a flat, blunt surface touch her back, at the base of the knife point. It continued pushing, making her body curve forward, further, further, until her entire body formed an arc from her bound arms to her bound feet, a vertical sickle.

She let out another long, shuddering gasp, but didn't scream—the shock of what was happening overriding her pain. She could, however, hear her friends, her sister, her boyfriend, scream in grief and horror. Their screams quickly got lost in the thundering, echoing clamor of the four thousand people around her. She could feel the tickle of blood running down her thighs, dripping at her knees.

Then came the flames.

She felt them licking at her toes, at her feet, up her leg, rising from the foot of the structure she'd now become a part of. By the time she felt the flames envelop her head, burning her hair and beginning to cook her eyes, Angela was howling in pain. Her screams drowning out the voice of four thousand people.

Bobby held Nadine close to his chest. She screamed against the thick fabric of his jacket, as he stared in near-catatonic horror at the love of his life burning before his eyes. Her body held in an obscene arch to become part of what he now recognized as the symbol embossed on the altar floor. The smell of her burning flesh adhered to the inside of his nostrils in a way he was certain he'd never be able to wash it off.

She wasn't screaming anymore. Where his ears had tuned in to only the sound of her shrieking voice—the last he would ever hear of it—it was now replaced by his friends' screams and curses, and those of the crowd of onlookers. An entire town, summoned here to witness the world losing something precious, leaving an empty space nothing could fill.

A hole in the world, he thought. Where had he heard that phrase before?

"*Praise be unto God!*" that madwoman shouted into their heads again. "*Glory be unto God!*" The elation in that voice as she raised her palms up to the sky, toward the blue moon, which seemed to feed on the smoke rising from the flames, sickened him.

"I'll kill you," he mumbled, then he stood up, and louder than all his friends, he shouted. "I'LL KILL YOU!" Martha turned, eyed him with a pitying smile, so condescending it made his insides turn. "I'll fucking kill you. I'll get my hands on you, and I will—"

The punch came from the right. A swing that made his head turn fully, then another punch to his stomach, then there were hands on him, and before he knew it, he was on the floor and Freddie was on top of him, punching him over and over.

"How dare you threaten the Mother!" Freddie spat, as blow after blow came down on him.

"*Enough!*" Martha's voice exploded into their heads, and in a second, they were both standing, facing her. Everyone was. Four thousand people. Silent. Still. Like an army asked to stand at attention.

The sudden silence in the huge space, broken only by the crackling of the flames that continued to burn Angie's flesh, was unnerving.

Martha addressed the crowd. "*The Second Night's offering is now complete! Her soul has been consumed for a greater purpose! You have borne witness to God's glory! Those of you the Lord deems worthy shall reap your rewards, and those of you who aren't will be consumed in his awakening!"*

She sauntered around the altar. *Around my Angie,* Bobby thought with a grief so great, he could feel a web of fractures forming in his soul. *She said her soul was consumed.*

"Don't try to run." She grinned wide. *"The town is being sealed as we speak."*

There was an image. It appeared in Bobby's mind and—he was certain—in the minds of everyone present. Somehow, at the same time, he could see the two roads at the northwest and southeast of White Harbor, the only exits from town. The entire road, the tunnel, and the cliff crumbled and fell into the ocean in a landslide. Huge rocks and trees fell into the ocean, forming a chasm in both roads.

"Don't try to cross the mountains. Don't try to leave by sea." She paused, and Bobby swore he could hear the old woman chuckle in his mind. *"God will feed, and His banquet must be plentiful...but He's not averse to appetizers."*

(An enormous creature, dark but maddeningly beautiful, and terrifying beyond comprehension, rising from the line of the ocean with an open mouth that disappeared at both ends of the horizon, swallowing the sea, the earth, and the sky, and every creature in them)

"Go now," Martha Lange ordered. *"And wait."*

He was back at the beach, standing in the sand. He could hear people crying and screaming all around him. Confused, panicking people whose hearts had also been clutched by terror after seeing Angie be sacrificed, after seeing the mountains crumble and the Earth swallow the roads out of town. The amusement park's lights were back on. He could hear screams and shouts coming from there as well.

He turned his teary face to the sky and regarded the silver waning moon and the stars he and Angie had been gazing at what felt like a lifetime ago. They seemed dimmer. Darker.

She said her soul was consumed.

He gazed at the ocean, at its hungry blackness.

(*An enormous creature, dark but maddeningly beautiful, and terrifying beyond comprehension*)

Angie was dead, so he was dead. His life was over. His only reason to live now was killing Martha Lange, and Freddie for his complicity in her death.

Angie was dead.

He fell to his knees, just as he had right before seeing his world come crumbling down, and he sobbed.

She said her soul was consumed.

His sobs turned into screams. His screams, into roars of anger.

Angie was dead, so he was dead.

CHAPTER THIRTEEN

THE BODY

Peter swerved, the car drawing an 'S' on the asphalt, the moment consciousness came back to him in his running vehicle. His sudden gasp as he tried to regain his orientation was accompanied by a pained grunt from Sylvia, who was lying in the backseat. Once he straightened the vehicle, he peered at his rearview mirror and saw her wincing in pain, arms wrapped around her bleeding torso. He remembered, all of a sudden. Sylvia needed urgent medical care. Callum was dead.

And Angie... My god.

His attention got called to the right, where Nadine sat, one hand over her mouth as she wept in silence. Her eyes seemed lost, watching houses fly by the windshield. To Peter, the houses looked like frames of animation showing a time-lapse of different characters continuing the same action: turning on lights, opening front doors, standing in porches and front yards, confusion and panic in their faces, looking up at the sky, dialing on their phones.

As he turned a corner, he noticed a child, a little boy no older than his son, wearing a *Bluey* T-shirt and red shorts, standing on the sidewalk crying his lungs out beside his parents, the father tended to the mother, who appeared to have fainted on the sidewalk. The sound of the boy's cries of, "Mommy!" dopplered in through the cracked open window like an air-raid siren.

All of these people had witnessed the same event. His mother had murdered a woman in front of the whole town. He could still smell her in his nostrils. It reminded him of Jenny's horrifying death.

He reached a hand toward Nadine's arm. She pulled back.

She turned a wild, wet scowl at him, then looked away.

He didn't know what to say and drove a few more blocks in silence. Only glancing back from time to time to see if Sylvia was still with them. She was breathing, issuing weak, guttural moans.

"This is all your fault," Nadine said in a moist whisper.

He swiveled disbelieving eyes toward her.

She cast a vacant gaze out the window, as if replaying the spectacle of her younger sister in flames in a hellish, never-ending loop. "That security guard, Hitch, said it. The only reason your mother was able to do what she did is you came back to White Harbor. He knew she was going to do this. Peter, stop the car."

"Wait, how is this my—"

"Year after year after year, since we were children, I told you to cut her off. I told you not to visit her. She should've been locked up after what she did to you, but you..." She let out a long, angry breath. "You told your aunt to plead with CPS to recommend the prosecutor to send her to psychiatric treatment." She let out a sarcastic snort, shook her head. "Psychiatric treatment for a woman who can paralyze you with a word. I wonder *how* she convinced the psychiatrist she was cured. It should've ended thirty years ago. It's your fault that evil bitch is free to do this. I said, stop the car."

"That's insane! She's not evil. She's sick, Nadine. My mother's sick. She doesn't know what she's doing. We just need to stop her."

"My sister is dead!" she shouted, her voice enraged. "Angie's dead, and you're still making excuses for your mother? Fucking stop the car if you don't want me to jump out!"

"C'mon! Don't do this!"

"What am I doing?" She drove both her burning eyes into his. Her face filled with rage, the passing lights from outside reflecting against the tears covering her cheeks. "The whole town might die because you couldn't lock her up and forget about her! How dare you make excuses for her after what we just witnessed? What am I doing other than pointing out you're a murderer's enabler?"

He lowered his gaze, then looked at the road ahead. "You're right," he mumbled. "I'm sorry." No answer from Nadine. "Look, people are going to panic after what happened. Let's take Sylvia to the emergency room before people flood the hospital. We'll discuss this after, alright?"

No answer. No acknowledgment of what he'd said. Just the cold judgment of silence. The rest of the way to the hospital, Nadine didn't speak a word, and only stared out the window, bitter tears spilling from her face.

John Hitch awakened with a sudden scream as the two deep stab wounds in his torso began hurting again. Seconds later, he felt a hand push him down to the concrete floor and hold him there.

"Don't move, you stupid asshole!" It was Chuck Cunningham's voice. He was kneeling beside him, his hand pressed against his chest. "You'll pull the stitches!"

Hitch looked around. He was in the bar's basement. They'd brought him here after he fell unconscious, he realized. Jess Cunningham had her arms around her father, and she was sobbing. Hitch looked down at his exposed torso and noticed stitches over one stab wound. The other one was still open, bleeding, only partially sewn shut. The needle and black thread still hung to one side from a raised fold of flesh.

Once Cunningham seemed satisfied he wasn't about to spring up and attack them, he removed his hand from his chest and put it around his daughter.

"I lost another one!" she sobbed, her voice broken, shaky. "I lost another one!"

"I'm sorry, hun." Chuck ran a rugged, slow hand over her hair.

Hitch didn't understand why they were trying to save his life, when just the night before he'd been waving a gun at them and had come today with the obvious intention of killing Jess—he would've been forced to kill Chuck, too.

"My jacket." Hitch pointed at his security guard jacket, which was hanging from a hook on the wall to his right. Chuck looked at it. "There's a piece of blood chalk in the right pocket."

Jess turned confused eyes at him. Chuck understood what he was talking about, though.

"Just a second, Pum'kin." He let go of his daughter to step toward the jacket.

"There's a"—he grunted in pain, bright-white teeth bared—"phone in the left pocket. It's not blocked. There are pictures. One says 'Safehouse Sigil.'"

Cunningham took the blood chalk, brought the phone out, and began browsing through it. "Got it."

"Draw that on the front and back doors of the bar," Hitch said. "Windows, exits, trapdoors, or vents, draw the sigil near the frame."

"Dad, what the fuck is going on?" Jess asked, still crying.

Hitch ignored her. "Things are gonna start happening fast now." He grunted again; a trembling hand flew up to the open wound in his upper torso. "You need to make this place untouchable to her, Cunningham."

Chuck hesitated, not the hesitation that came from disbelief, but hopelessness.

"Cunningham!" Hitch called, followed by a long, bare-toothed groan. "Move!"

Chuck closed the small cellar windows, scribbled the sigil beside them, turned, and ran up the stairs without saying a word.

Hitch turned toward Jess. "Your dad is regretting years of lies. You heard what that Lange woman said"—there was a reluctant realization in her face—"your daddy was part of the group that caused all this. Gave that Lange woman more power than they should've. Now they lost control of her, and four thousand people are gonna die."

With a look of astonishment, she fixed her gaze into his eyes.

"Sounds harsh, but you should've let me kill you and your friends," he said, as if that were the most normal observation to make. "Now I'm in no condition to." He glanced at the half-sewn wound in his torso. "So, unless you and four more of your friends decide to kill yourselves in the next twenty-four hours, which I'll admit seems unlikely, we have to figure out a way to stop that woman."

Jess stared at him, unable to speak.

"You shot me"—he pointed an index finger toward his heart—"right here, thirty years ago."

She gasped. In her eyes, he could still see the grief of the loss of the Schaefer woman, mixed with recognition and bafflement.

"You better pray I don't die before I can help you figure out how to put a bullet in Martha Lange. As of now, it might be easier to shoot the president, but it's that, or we're all dead." He signaled with his head toward the open wound. "Patch me up."

Barry hit the brakes as soon as he appeared in his car. He was staring at the round island at the center of his neighborhood's cul-de-sac, his headlights illuminating the playground and the large tree at the center.

"Jesus Christ," he said under his breath, getting his bearings enough to maneuver the Civic toward his house. The haunting image of his children, trapped in the clutches of those obsidian replicas of himself, intertwined with the nightmarish thought of Angie, body arched, impaled, and engulfed in flames, left him terrified his children might endure the same fate. He drove up his driveway and parked in front of the garage door.

The neighborhood had erupted into chaos, he assumed, the moment all the families in the other houses reappeared in the place they'd been collected. Murmurs, cries, and shouts echoed in the night air—panicked people trying to regain some sort of control over insignificant lives they'd been reminded could end in a blink.

He leaned over and opened the glove compartment, dug around under his papers, and found a box cutter. It was the closest he had to a weapon, should one of his panicking neighbors cross a line, considering everyone had seen him be transported with his friends to that altar, and who knew what people would interpret from that. He put the box cutter in his pocket and jumped out of his car.

The true level of the surrounding noise hit him when he opened the door.

The Craigs and their little girl ran out of their house, slamming the front door behind them. Vince Craig shouted, "Hurry! Hurry!" to his wife, Katherine, who'd reached their family's bronze Subaru SUV before him and was waiting for him to unlock it with his fob. Still, the man kept repeating, "Hurry! Hurry!" as if he'd short-circuited.

Shouts of, "Get the lanterns!", "Toilet paper!", and "Where's the suitcase?" came from the Wallace place, as silhouettes ran every which way past the windows.

Old Emily Bird shrieked her lungs off from her second-floor bedroom while her daughter cried for her to calm down, just calm down.

Elvis Camacho exploded out of his door onto his front porch, stumbled down the two steps, and fell to his knees on the grass of his lawn, wheezing, hyperventilating, clutching his chest with pain. His wife, Samira, stood at the door with her phone to her ear, repeating, "It's not getting through, honey! 911 is jammed!"

Barry was startled by the screeching of not one but two sets of tires, followed by a crash, as Josh and Viv Evans rushed out in their red Hyundai at the same time Vince Craig swerved his Subaru out of his driveway, going the wrong way. Their vehicles met at the cul-de-sac exit. Craig's front bumper smashed into Evans's back fender, but other than Josh Evans shouting, "Fuck!" they simply kept going as if nothing had happened.

Where are they even going? Martha Lange said...

(*Don't try to run*)

"It's the end times!" Emily Bird cried in shrill terror.

"Not getting through, honey!" Samira Camacho shouted, panicking. "It's not getting through!"

"Tylenol and Pepto-Bismol!" Otto Wallace ordered.

(*Don't try to cross the mountains*)

"Mom, calm down!" Chelsea Bird pleaded.

"We witnessed the rapture!" Emily Bird responded, undeterred. "We've been left behind!"

(*Don't try to leave by sea*)

"Still not getting through! Honey, breathe in, breathe out! Slow!"

"I got the sleeping bags!"

"Mom, seriously, stop it! You're driving me nuts!"

(*God will feed, and His banquet must be plentiful*)

Barry was startled when his phone's ringtone rose above the cacophony. He recognized the tone immediately. Ray's ringtone. Fumbling, he brought the device to his ear.

"Oh, thank god," Ray's voice said the second he answered. "Are you okay?"

"Y-yeah. You?"

"I'm okay, just shaken. Oh my god, Angie. I can't believe..."

"I know." He cast a nervous look around, then back at his house, which, unlike every other house in the cul-de-sac, showed no signs of reaction to the events of the night.

"Did you read Nadine's text?"

"No, I—"

"Cal is dead. Hitch killed him. Peter and Nadine are on the way to the hospital with Sylvia. Hitch stabbed her, too."

"Oh my god."

"Where are you? It sounds crazy over there!"

Barry didn't answer. He regarded his house as if it had grown jaws.

"Big Bear, are you there?"

"I'm in front of my house." Barry examined the windows. The lights were off. The curtains were drawn. He couldn't detect a sound coming from it.

"Are your kids alright?"

The second Ray said the word "kids" a chill went up his spine. He'd been seconds away from running inside to get his kids out when the phone rang. What had stopped him in his tracks had been the absolute deadness of the house itself, given the pandemonium swallowing his neighborhood. He froze the moment he saw those dark windows, afraid of opening the door, afraid of going inside and finding...

What?

He couldn't even think the words. He made a herculean effort to calm down. "I'm heading in now. I'm getting my kids and driving them to our place. I'll be there soon. Lock the door, grab something you can use as a weapon. Don't open the door unless it's me."

Ray's breath sounded apprehensive. "Will you be okay?"

"Yes. If I'm not there in thirty minutes, try to get Peter or any of the others to come get me, but you go to Cunningham's, alright?"

"Why wouldn't you get here in thirty minutes? What's going on?"

"Sweetheart..." Barry put as much tenderness in his voice as his panic would allow. "I'll be fine. I'm going in and out. Things are getting ugly in the streets now. I'm sure in your neighborhood is the same."

Ray paused, then uttered a nervous, "Yes."

"I'm not good at juggling so much at once. I need to know you'll be safe no matter what. Jess has guns and supplies in her cellar, so that's probably the safest place I know. I'll see you in thirty minutes at our place or after thirty at Jess's, alright?"

"Alright."

"Good."

"Don't you dare die."

"I won't." Uncertain, Barry took one last survey of the house's front, which remained tomblike, or more like a body in a tomb, a thing that is meant to contain life, a pulse, a soul. There was none there.

He put the key in the door and walked into absolute madness.

Nadine ran past the sliding door of the emergency room. They'd arrived before every panicking, hyperventilating, heart-impacted person in White Harbor flooded the E.R. Right away, it was apparent fear and confusion had gripped the entire town, including its small medical staff. Their faces showed the existential bewilderment of having been taken to some other reality to witness a human sacrifice.

She swallowed with difficulty, the memory still compressing her chest like a giant's fist. "My friend was stabbed!" She gestured toward the door. The two nurses at the entrance looked at her as if this were the first time they'd heard those words. "She's been bleeding. I don't know how long."

The female nurse ran a hand over her eye, as if wiping a tear, nodded to the male nurse, and soon they were both rushing out the door with a stretcher.

Nadine turned around as they passed and watched them as the door slid shut behind them to make sure they got to Sylvia. She caught a glimpse of Peter staring back at her through the faint smudges on the glass. There was that very slight shake of his head, as if realizing what she was planning to do.

Peter would have to move his car out of the entrance and park it. This would give her time. She turned and strode down the hallway, found the stairs sign, and followed it. Went up to the second floor, where another sign pointed her toward the Elderly Care wing. She went through a sliding door leading to a bridge between buildings enclosed in glass on both sides. From up here, she could see cars pulling up to the E.R. entrance below.

It's different when four random people disappear, she thought, thinking about the usual indifference Harborites showed to tragic events. *They can ignore that, but not what happened today. No one can ignore that. Oh, Angie...*

She reached the other side of the bridge and stopped past the door. Looked at the hallway ahead, then left and right. She didn't know where Martha Lange's room was. She remembered Peter telling her his mother's room looked out toward the garden. This building was only one story, set on the side of the mountain, so it was at a level with the hospital's second floor. The gardens had been built on the side of the mountain, which meant the room looked south.

She turned right, marching past a few patients and a nurse, all of whom wore the same look of universal panic on their faces. As she passed the young nurse, she turned, reached out, and touched her arm. She jumped as if Nadine had shouted at her. The name on her badge was Kassandra Ferguson.

"Martha Lange's room." She saw recognition in the nurse's buggy eyes. "Which room is it?"

The nurse hesitated. Shook her head. Pointed toward a bend in the hallway. "I... 205... That was her, right? Martha Lange?"

Nadine frowned, seeing the nurse was more than scared. She was terrified.

"I recognized her in that...dream, or whatever it was... I went to her room, to see if she was there, and I..."

"What?"

Nurse Ferguson shook her head. "I don't know what I saw. I think..." She trailed off, disoriented. Eyes moving in every direction, as if trying to find something to focus on. "I'm sorry, I need to go get a doctor." She shook Nadine's grip off and walked away, adding, "Don't go in there! It might be a health hazard!"

Nadine watched her walk past the sliding door, toward the bridge. She turned to gaze at the hallway, to the bend the nurse had pointed at. Against one wall, she found one of those poles on casters mobile patients used to walk with their IV bag. She looked back, noticed nobody was watching. She approached it, put her foot on the legs and spun the pole until it came detached from them.

Holding the pole in her hands, she turned at the corner and walked down the hallway toward room 205. There were five doors on the right, the first of which was 201, which meant Martha's room was the last one.

As she passed one of the open doors on the left, she was met with the eyes of an old man sitting in bed. He stared at her as if she were insane—she realized she probably *looked* insane holding an IV pole like a weapon.

She stood in front of the door to room 205 and took in a deep breath. What was she *really* planning on doing? Reach Martha Lange, then, what?

I'll know when I see her, she thought, and reached to push the door open. Before she could, there was a hand firmly grabbing her by the wrist.

"What the hell do you think you're doing?" Peter asked, pulling her away from the door, more forcefully than she would've ever expected from him.

She pulled her hand away. "Let me go." He wouldn't. "She has to pay for what she did. This has to stop."

"What are you, crazy?"

They tussled, Peter trying to take the IV pole away from her, until she kicked him in the shin, and he let go.

"No," she said. "Are you?"

Grunting with pain, he flashed her an angry look. "You're going into a sick old woman's room, brandishing a stick to what? Beat her with it?"

"Maybe!" Her eyes dared him to talk back. "Maybe more!"

"I can't let you hurt my mother, Nadine! I know she—"

"What? You know what?" She glared at him. "What's the excuse now, Norman?"

"Don't call me that."

"She killed my sister," she spat. "Callum—our friend!—is lying dead in his house—"

"That wasn't her!"

"She caused it!" Her voice rose high and outraged. "She caused this madness! Callum is dead and Sylvia is fighting for her life! Because of her!" She pointed a hateful finger at the door. "At least with Cal, they left a body to bury. I don't even know where Angie's body is. What am I supposed to do with that, according to you, huh? Say, 'That's in Blight Harbor. Leave it there?'" She stared daggers at him. "Do I leave my sister's body in Blight Harbor?"

Peter stammered. "I...don't..."

Nadine pointed the IV pole straight to his face. "Try to stop me, Peter Lange, and I swear..."

She didn't finish the sentence. The threat in her eyes was apparent. He would lose her. The greatest threat she could make was leaving Peter forever. Her greatest punishment would be her absence.

Without a word, Nadine turned and pushed the door open, marching into the room, Peter right behind her.

They both stopped. Gasped.

A hollow, metallic rattle sounded as the IV pole hit the floor tiles.

By the window, on a high-backed chair, under the cold LED lights, sat the motionless shape of Martha Lange. It was made of hundreds of hardened black tendrils, which emerged from the floor, the walls, and the ceiling, like some bizarre topiary figure. The individual threads intertwined, forming what looked like a huge concave spiderweb around the chair. The old woman's figure sat in the middle of this web made of black crystal. An empty shell made of black mesh.

"What the hell?" Nadine asked, more unnerved by the lifeless husk than if it had been the old witch herself, spewing vitriolic curses and threats at her.

CHAPTER FOURTEEN
PORTRAIT OF AN AMERICAN FAMILY

The first thing that hit Barry's face was the heat, the moisture, like walking into a tropical climate, the kind of heat that clung to your skin like a latex suit.

All lights were off, and not enough moonlight entered through the open door to illuminate what should've been his house's foyer. He took two steps in and reached for the light switch to his right, but touched only a bare concrete wall.

SLAM!

The front door flew shut behind him, giving him a start.

He was now in complete darkness. Even if there was no electricity, he should've seen some moonlight coming in from the windows in the living room to the right, or the dining room to the left. There was none. Only the dreadful Stygian dark.

He searched for the flashlight app on his phone and turned it on. Soon, a small cone of white light shone before him, covering a distance far shorter than ideal.

His house's foyer was gone. He was standing at the entrance of a locker room. Green metal lockers, like the ones he remembered from Garland Elementary, lined the walls at either side, rusted and dripping with what looked like thick, coagulating blood from the slits on the doors onto a moldy concrete floor with a single drain in the center, where all the crimson fluid ran into, emitting an echoing, metallic gurgle. The long wooden benches before him were broken in half, rotten, and splintered, their metal frames eaten away by rust.

Speechless, he moved the flashlight up and, where the exposed, multicolored water and drainage pipes would normally run across a locker room ceiling, there were instead fleshy tubes the diameter of an arm, covered in veins, relentlessly pumping what he assumed was the blood that flowed out of the lockers, with the pulsating rhythm of an unseen heart. He realized, though, this was only his brain trying to make sense of something that couldn't make any.

"Maryann!" His voice echoed against the metal of the lockers. No answer.

He took slow steps forward, disturbed by the wet sound of his Timberlands against the blood-drenched floor. As he stood in the middle of the room, he was jolted by a bang coming from his left. He whipped his body around with a start, his feet sloshing in the blood on the floor.

"Help!" a voice, tinny and muffled, said, coming from inside one of the lockers. "Someone, get me outta here!"

"What the fuck?"

It was a child's voice. Not one of his children, more like a young teenager. In the back of his mind, it sounded familiar, but he couldn't quite place it. He stepped toward the locker door, put his hand forward, but pulled it back, not sure this was a smart move.

He clenched his jaw, and in a swift motion, pulled the door open and let out a sudden cry, taking a step back.

His breath hitched. Inside, hanging upside down from a black leather belt, was a kid's head, the belt tied so tight it made the gore at the end of the severed neck look like a bouquet of pink and red flowers. It took him a few seconds to recognize it was Hank Marsh

(*Today I kissed Barry Giffen in the locker room*)

his old classmate, as he remembered him from school

(*His lips tasted sweet, like root beer*)

except his eyes were clouded over, whitish, and dead.

"Eww!" Hank's disembodied head said in that disturbing child's voice, scrunching up his face in an expression of revulsion. "If I'd known you'd grow to become such a fat loser, I would've never kissed you!"

Barry slammed the door shut with disgust. He could hear Hank's head cackling with evil joy from inside the locker. "This is freakin' nuts."

He stepped deeper into the room. The phone's flashlight revealed a doorway some distance ahead, and from it issued the swirling steam that saturated the air, dense and heavy. Before reaching it, though, he was greeted by another baffling sight. From the top of the wall at the end of the locker room hung a tattered Garland Elementary banner, under which a picture from his eighth-grade graduation stared back at him with an awkward teenage smile. The picture was almost as tall and wide as the doorway he was heading toward, and to its right, written in huge letters in dark ruby blood, was: MOST LIKELY TO SUCK DICK IN AN ALLEY TO FEEL DADDY'S LOVE.

"Who the fuck is doing this?"

He marched through the open doorway and found himself in yet another locker room, this one quite different from the previous one. The lockers here were red with little white number tags, a top row, and a bottom row. There were rectangular block-like benches on a gray concrete floor, and everything looked as moldy and dilapidated as the room he'd come from. The steam was thicker here, spiraling into ghostly shapes. Old sandals and towels lay scattered on the floor, soaking up the blood that poured from the lockers, which mixed in with a constant drip of water from the steam that condensed in the ceiling and fell down.

What truly drew his attention were the carcasses.

Vaguely human-shaped chunks of blood-drenched beef, fat, sinew, and bone, with their limbs cut off at the elbows and knees. Some hung from the ceiling on leather belts as if on harnesses, some hugged the walls, some emerged from open lockers. The large, pulsating tubes crossing the ceiling came down the walls like snakes, penetrating these shapes, through their mouths or their assholes, then coming out the opposite end, and continuing on toward another meat puppet, entering it the opposite way.

Two of the shapes appeared to *kneel*, face to face, on two bright lemon-green chairs near the center of the room, which looked oddly out of place. The condensed drops of water that fell from the ceiling turned crimson when they came in contact with the blood-soaked meat and fell into the running red stream below, swirling into the drain at the foot of the green chairs.

Completing this profane, hedonistic scene was the echoing sound of a husky, moaning voice reverberating in this suffocating space, a man's voice which Barry soon recognized as his own, a voice relishing in the throes of unbridled sexual ecstasy. He felt exposed, as if someone had been recording him the previous night, and the sound of his own moans in such a vulnerable moment of release made him far more uncomfortable than the grotesque shapes that populated this room.

He stood frozen for a moment, not knowing what to do next. The flashlight's beam didn't let him see the other side of the locker room through the steam. He figured if there was an exit to this place, it would be on the other side, but he was afraid to move. It was clear to him this obscene house of horrors he found himself in had been created for him and him alone by someone, or something, that knew him intimately.

He ran a hand down his sweaty face. His clothes were soaked with moisture from the steam. He trudged into the locker room. He went around a figure hanging from a harness, its stumpy thighs sticking up in the air, as the pulsating, fleshy tentacle that came down from the ceiling impaled its asshole and came out of its mouth. Aside from the gaping mouth, he saw what appeared as two eyes, rolled up to show only their whites in uninhibited pleasure.

With every step, the moaning became louder, more intense, hungry, pleading.

A shudder climbed his back.

He walked further, going around the two figures kneeling on the lemon-green chairs—a sickening meat sculpture, where a flesh tube, like a tentacle, came in through the asshole of the one on the right, out of its mouth, into the mouth of the one on the left, then out the other end, where it then lay on the floor, throbbing.

This entire room looked like what Barry's mother had raised him to believe being gay was. A tawdry reduction of humanity to flesh, bone, and faceless carnal desire.

He was almost past the two figures at the center when he was startled by the heavy, moist splat of something falling to the wet floor. He turned to find the piece of meat from the swing had fallen, the tube that penetrated it had come detached from the ceiling. It was now lying on the floor. Thin, crimson rivulets ran from it, making their way toward the drain at the center.

He walked past another hanging piece of beef, its ribs open, displaying the long tube that filled its body from top to bottom, pumping god-knows-what through it. The moment he moved his flashlight away, it fell to the floor, making water and blood splash on his jeans.

There was another splash from somewhere, then another.

He quickened his pace, now perceiving a dragging sound approaching, as the pleasured moaning intensified all around him.

They're crawling toward me!

A piece of meat propped against a locker to his right fell down.

He didn't wait. He ran until the wall on the other side became visible.

"No!" He moved the flashlight around, realizing there was no exit, just a bare, wet, moldy concrete wall. He slammed the side of his fist on it with frustration. "Fuck, no!"

Something clutched his ankle and pulled, and he fell on his stomach. The sensation of the bloody water soaking through his shirt made him gag. He turned around to see one of the tube-like tentacles had grown fingers and had a hand clutching his leg. At the other end was one of the meat figures, pulling itself toward him, pushing itself with the end of the tentacle that came out of its ass, like some kind of worm.

With a horrified cry, he reached into his pocket and brought out the paper cutter, his only weapon, and started slashing at the thing holding his leg. It recoiled, let go. *It can feel pain*, he realized, as he stood up, and, before it could recover, kicked it hard, making its facsimile of a head bounce back and the hand-tentacle twist around aimlessly. He then stomped on its head, crushing it, caking his Timberland with even more blood and gore than had already been clinging to it. He looked down at the monster's smashed head, remembering when he was a teenager. The creatures at the Vanek House had healed themselves and come chasing after them again, even after appearing dead. He expected this one to rise back up, but it just lay there, lifeless. The fact they weren't black as soot with glowing blue eyes meant these weren't like the things from the Vanek House. They were something else.

It was then the thought hit him like a cattle prod. *The others!* A hand grabbed his forearm, the light from the phone being pulled in that direction. He turned and slashed at it with the paper cutter, and it let go. Another hand soon replaced it, wrapping itself around his neck, and he slashed at it, too. By the time it let go, the one on his left arm was back, and another one had him by his leg. A dozen hands at the ends of long, fleshy arms, wrapped around his waist, his neck, his limbs, and his body. The fingers groping, grabbing, feeling; intrusive, violating. The pleading moans in the air ringing in stark contrast to what he was feeling right now.

Barry screamed, struggling to get free, but he was soon overpowered and fell to the floor. The hands crawled under his shirt, into his pants. "No!" he shouted.

"*Yes!*" his disembodied voice moaned right back.

"Stop!"

"*Don't stop!*" the voice pleaded in ecstasy, mocking his horror.

He was being pulled back toward the center of the room, unable to break free. The creatures were all moving in a single direction with him in tow. One of the meat creatures wriggled past him, one end of its tentacle wrapped around his thigh, the other propelling it forward.

Through the mass of groping, pulsating tentacles, he made a clumsy effort to point the flashlight in the direction he was being taken. At first, he couldn't see through the steam, then he saw the creatures clustered around the two green chairs, which were askew, tilting at an odd angle, as if sinking.

He soon realized they were, in fact, sinking as the tiles beneath them bent like rubber, around a single point, forming a hole that expanded until it had swallowed both chairs. The creatures crawled, one by one, into the hole, pulling Barry along with them.

He screamed, jerked his body, and strained to break free before he fell into what he was sure would be certain death.

The tentacles pulsated, the hands groped him in ways that sickened him, and the sound of his enraptured moans grew louder, moaning, *"More! More! Right there! Don't stop!"*, as if the fact he was about to be swallowed by the earth itself brought that disincarnate version of him to the edge of climax. As the hole in the floor swallowed him, and he fell into the darkness, his thoughts went back to his children, who were somewhere in this house, and whom he'd failed to save.

He hit the ground. The fall had hurt, but he hadn't fallen far.

He was in solid, all-encompassing darkness, not even a hint of light to tell him where he was. Barry knew he was in a small space, barely enough for him to fit with his knees bent. His shoulders touched both sides of the space. He had no idea where the meat figures had gone. They'd vanished. He was alone in utter silence, in a space not much larger than a coffin.

Barry pushed himself up with his legs, his back sliding up the wall. He expected his head to hit the top part of this box, but it didn't. He could stand normally. His phone was gone. The paper cutter was gone.

What the hell do I do now? He pictured he was buried alive—buried standing—and he would die of suffocation in the darkness and the moist heat. The thought alone made him hyperventilate a little. He'd never been claustrophobic, but realizing you've been buried alive would make even the bravest man panic, and he wasn't that man. He put his hands forward, trying to hold himself steady as he forced himself to calm down. His fingers felt texture. Metal. Horizontal slits. He moved his hand further. A vertical division, then more slits. *Doors?*

He pushed hard. The two doors shook slightly but didn't move. He pushed again. Same result. He was locked in tight.

I'm not buried alive. This is a locker or a closet of some kind.

He put all his weight behind his shoulder as he slammed into the doors again.

"Won't do any good, Brickhouse," a voice coming from everywhere said, followed by a gleeful "Hee-hee-hee!" laugh. He had a hard time recognizing the voice, especially considering he'd only heard it briefly in its adult iteration—at the altar where Angie had died—but the laugh was unmistakable.

"Freddie?" he asked.

"How do you like my little tribute to you, old buddy?" He giggled. "Might be a bit on the nose, but I worked really hard on it. Hope you can appreciate all my hard work."

"Where are my kids, Freddie? What did you do with my kids?" He took shallow breaths. The terror that Freddie might have done something to his boys like he did thirty years ago to Royce and the others in the Vanek House scratched at the inside of his chest.

Freddie giggled again. "Wow, no 'where's my wife?' That's cold, man! Guess getting dicked down so hard by Asian Robin fucked up your memory, right, Batman?"

"Shut up!" Barry pushed against the door again, to no avail.

"Oh, yes, Brickhouse. I know all about you and your dear Plus-One. There's a little of everybody in Blight Harbor, did you know that? What you whisper, what you hide, what you fear...the town knows. It wasn't hard to find you there. Blight Harbor is so full of *you*. A life so full of abuse, and lies, and pretense. A pathetic loser who liked to act tough. So many little secrets smeared on tissues as your hands stood in for lovers you couldn't have. It's been so fun sifting through every little nugget of trauma."

"Whatever, man, just let my kids go!"

"No, no, no. I want to savor this," Freddie hissed, venom delineating each syllable. "Not even my sick fantasies could've hurt you like you hurt yourself when you married Maryann. Damn, Brickhouse, talk about self-flagellation. She's everything you deserve. It almost made me think maybe you had been punished enough, and I should take out my anger on one of the others."

"Why? Why me? Why my kids? We haven't even seen each other for thirty years! Why do this?"

"Thirty years doesn't make up for what you did. Beating me up. Pushing me into lockers. Shoving my head into toilets. Ripping up my drawings. Humiliating me."

"That was kids' stuff, Freddie! Jesus, we were a bunch of stupid kids! We're forty-year-old men now! You can't be serious!"

"You interrupted my ritual."

"What?"

"You threw me out of the Vanek House." Freddie's voice became agitated, enraged. "You disconnected me from the house's power! My little sister and my whole family are being tortured in a dark hell because you threw me out of the house! You took my hope! You stole my salvation! Then beat me into a bloody mess! You ruined my life!"

"I don't understand!"

"Oh, you're about to understand, Brickhouse." Freddie's voice was packed with hate but brimming with joy. "Now, you're the one trapped inside the locker. And the show's about to begin."

A light from outside blinded Barry for a second. He looked up through the slits and was greeted by a horrifying sight. Hanging from the tall ceiling was his dad's corpse, exactly as he remembered it: the black belt around his neck, his eyes bulging out of their sockets, his tongue sticking out. He had been turned into some kind of light fixture, like a revolting chandelier, with thin, golden arms sticking out of his body, curving upward, and ending in a light bulb—tiny chunks of gore stuck throughout. He swayed a little in one direction, then another, moving the shadows on the scene below.

There was a lavish version of his dining room. A table with six chairs. Maryann, Therese, and his two children sat around the table—Daniel sat on his booster cushion and Gabriel in his highchair. They were all posed as if ready to dine, except their heads hung lazily, as if sedated; their eyes open wide, unblinking, and a long unnatural smile stretching their lips. On the table was a sumptuous banquet, like what he'd expect to see spread out at a castle in a fantasy movie. The bountiful spread showcased a succulent rack of lamb, a suckling pig adorned with an apple in its mouth, plump lobsters, a large fish embellished with slices of lemon, and an array of fresh fruits, cakes, and pastries. In the center, there was a raised tray covered with a shiny silver bell. There were tiny drops of blood falling on the otherwise impeccable, polished silver, which he noticed were falling from his dad's corpse, which was crying blood.

"What is all this?" Barry said under his breath.

"You have it all. More than a piece of trash like you deserves. I couldn't even dream of having half of what you have. A high-paying job, a big house, a family... Freedom."

"Freedom?" Barry spat the word like phlegm exploding out of his lungs. "Freddie, have you not been paying attention to the things you say you know about me? I haven't had freedom my whole fucking life!"

"You have everything I ever wanted. More than I've ever had." Freddie's voice hissed this sentence. "More than you deserve. And you want to give it all up? For what? To get fucked like a submissive bitch by some sanctimonious nurse. All you've done is complain about your privilege, while I've spent my life in a tiny cell, stewing in my own farts, forgotten by the world." He paused for a moment. "No...you don't deserve any of this."

"Freddie, please, don't hurt them. Do whatever you want with me, but please, *please*, let them go."

"Are you suuuuure?" Freddie's tone became playful again. "Even the ball-and-chain and the old hag?"

"Yes! I don't care what they've done to me. I don't want you to hurt them."

"Oh, no, no, Brickhouse." Freddie chuckled. "I'm not going to hurt them."

The doors to the locker flew open.

He took a step forward without meaning to. "Wait, what—"

In the chandelier's light, he could now see black tendrils on the back of his hands, which had dug under his skin and stretched into his fingers. He hadn't felt them. They were not causing him any pain. He couldn't move his arms or his hands.

He took another step, and another. He realized there were similar tendrils going down his legs. He felt something pulsating in the back of his neck. He hadn't felt it until it moved. Every time, before he took a step, the thing stuck to the back of his neck pulsed, then movement would happen.

Barry regarded the table, looked at his family, those staring eyes and horrid smiles on their faces. His hand moved, and he grabbed a large knife off the table and his eyes flew open wide as realization hit. "No!"

"Smart boy!" Freddie said and followed it with a loud "Hee-hee-hee!"

"No! Freddie, please no!"

"Let's go in order of importance, okay? What about finally taking revenge on your mother-in-law, huh? You can just picture her flicking her bean, thinking of every mean thing your wife ever said to you."

Barry moved unwittingly, walking around the table to stand next to Therese. "Freddie! Don't make me do—"

In a second, the knife went up, and he plunged it down into her chest. Barry screamed. Blood sprayed out and ran down her lavender gown, and he stabbed her again, again, again, again. The last stab was two-handed, going into her eye, the knife becoming lodged in the bone of her eye socket. He wiggled it with disgust until it came free.

"Well done, Brickhouse!" He could hear Freddie clapping. "Now, your beautiful wife, mother of your children, abuser of your dick."

Fat drops of blood ran down Barry's face and got stuck in his beard. "Freddie, stop! Stop!" He walked toward the head of the table, from which Maryann looked up at him, her teeth bared in a mocking grin, staring straight at him.

"Ain't she a beaut? Her whole life, her mom raised her to be a trophy wife to a man who paid for everything. Not that she ever complained. With her church friends, she always bragged about her dutiful husband that didn't make her lift a finger around the house. She thinks those feminists are crazy that a woman should ever have a job. I wonder what it feels like to be so proud of being so useless."

"Freddie, stop! I'm begging you!"

"I thought this was what you wanted, Brickhouse. You wished you'd never gotten married and had children."

"That's not true!"

"C'mon! Don't bullshit a bullshitter, man. How many times did you lay in bed thinking, 'If only…'" He giggled with malevolence. "Well, now you can get your wish!"

The thing on the back of his neck pulsed. Barry's fist went up, his knife pointed at Maryann's throat. "No!"

"It's not like it's the first time you're forced to do something you don't wanna do, right?"

Maryann kept flashing her vacant grin up at him, as if amused by Freddie's words.

The blade came down and stuck deep into Maryann's throat. He could feel the tip hit the vertebrae in the back.

"No! God!"

"Woah! That one came with hate behind it, Brickhouse! I barely needed to push your hand down!"

Barry let out a disgusted, horrified cry, seeing his fist move to one side, then the other, slicing her neck, making her head flop further back, hanging by muscles. Arterial blood sprayed into the air, soaking his face, his hair, and his beard. Large globs and tiny spots landed on the table and the food. He pulled the knife out and stuck it in again near her collarbone. Once, twice, the third one he stuck low in her abdomen, then began pulling up, cutting an incision up her belly. Blood gushed out and soon her insides were protruding from the gash. It wasn't cartoonish like in the movies, where everything fell out and hung like linked sausages. Instead, he could see her intestines and other viscera pushing out of the hole, barely held in by a thin membrane, which made it far worse.

Barry bent over and vomited on the floor beside Maryann. When he looked again, her bloodied face still grinned at him, hanging over the back of the chair.

"See? Doesn't that feel great?" Freddie giggled. "Now the children!"

Barry looked up with a tear-filled face and pleaded, "Stop this! No! Freddie, please!"

Freddie responded with a childish voice, mocking Barry's pleas. "No, Barry! Stop! Not my drawings! Please! I'll do anything! Don't rip them up! Please!"

"You sick fuck!" Barry sobbed, now standing behind his two children, their grinning heads sagging to one side. "These are my children, you piece of shit! They haven't done anything to you!"

"Eeny,"—the hand with the bloody knife pointed at Gabe—"meeny,"—the knife pointed at Daniel—"miny, moe..."

Realizing the insane horror of what Freddie was doing, Barry screamed, switching between heartrending pleas and insults at the monster forcing him to do this, his face a mess of tears and snot.

Freddie continued. "Catch a tiger by the toe. If he hollers... hmm." He stopped. "Did you know if you do 'eeny meeny, miny, moe' with only two people, it will always land on the second person? So, this is kinda pointless."

The thing behind his head pulsed.

WAIT!

Before he could brace himself, the knife was flying. He felt it break through his three-year-old's ribcage. He was stupefied, staring at the blade sticking out of his older boy's small chest. He couldn't scream. He watched as his hand flew back, pulling with it more blood than he ever thought his boy's body could hold, then stabbed him again, and again, and again, and again.

He was still in this dazed stupor when the knife changed direction and came down into his one-year-old's chest. There was no resistance whatsoever to the blade. The bones were so delicate they might as well have been rubber. He pulled it out and brought it back down once, twice, thrice, still unable to scream.

"Let's make the last one really count!"

Barry raised the knife straight up and brought the blade down on the top of Gabe's small head. He felt it go through his skull, his jaw, and into his chest. As if to punctuate the deplorable act he'd been forced to do, his hand tilted the knife back, making Gabe's face look up at him, grinning with the only four teeth he had in his mouth, now stained with blood. He was still too stunned to scream.

It was the pulling of the knife that did it. The revolting way his baby's head straightened and his neck stretched upward as the knife came out, then flopped back down, lifeless.

Barry's raucous screams would've been heard for miles if he were anywhere inhabited. His knees weakened, and he thought he would fall to the floor. He wanted to collapse. He wanted to regain control of his body so he could slit his own throat and make the pain stop.

"Oh, we're not done, Brickhouse. There's one more guest at this dinner party."

His breath caught in his throat as his free hand reached for the silver bell that covered the tray at the center of the table. The moment the lid came off, not even the tears blurring his vision could've protected him from what was underneath. Lying on a bed of grilled eggplant slices was Ray's head, staring at him with the same horrible grin as the rest. He could see the red tissue, arteries and tendons sticking out of his neck, as if his head had been torn off, instead of cut.

"Ta-daaa!" Freddie said. "The whole family's here!"

The drops of blood pouring from his dad's eyes fell on Ray's cheek and ran down in thin lines.

A deep, keening wail that started deep in Barry's frame escaped his lips and crescendoed into an Earth-sundering scream. He bawled, struggling to move his body, trying to force his hand to slide the knife across his throat and end it all—he had no reason to live anymore—but other than a strained shake, he had no control over his limbs. This went on for the longest minute of his life until he gave up at last.

He hung his head and wept, helpless, like he used to weep at The Pines as a kid. "Just kill me, please." There was no answer from Freddie. "Please, I just want to die, Freddie. I just want the pain to stop."

No answer.

BOOM!

The heads of his entire family exploded in a burst of colorful confetti and rainbow streamers that danced in the air as a banner that read: SURPRISE! came down from the ceiling.

Before he could process this, all the bodies before him melted into thousands of black threads, as if they were braids coming undone. The food also melted into black threads. He felt the thing at the back of his neck disintegrate and run down his back with the rest of the tendrils that controlled him. He could move now.

"W-what?" His chest heaved up and down. He ran the back of his hands over his eyes. He was now alone in this strange version of the living room, lit by the chandelier that had been sticking out of his father's body.

"Did you really think I'd make you kill your defenseless family?" Freddie asked with amusement. "No way, Brickhouse. I'm not that heartless. I would at least let them fight back."

Footsteps thumped across the second floor.

"Bet you're relieved you didn't murder your kids, huh? Though, I'm sure the mental images and the feeling in your hands of the blade piercing their bodies will haunt your mind for the few remaining hours you have."

"So, I thought of this really fun idea. That thing you're hearing is Maryann and her mom. I made some...updates to them. They're heading directly to your kids' room, and damn, these ladies are starving."

Barry sprinted, no hesitation, gripping the knife clenched in his hand, running toward the doorway at the other end of the dining room. He needed to find the stairs in this twisted version of his house.

"Look at you go!" Freddie let out his "Hee-hee-hee!" loud, his voice orgasmic with joy. "You didn't let me get to the fun part!"

Barry reached a hallway that didn't exist in his house, mimicking the bathhouse setting from before—bloody concrete floor, lockers with red doors lining the walls, pieces of meat with veiny tentacles through them, hanging from the ceiling—except there were small, alternating red and blue spotlights, which gave the space a blurred, disorienting feeling. He ran as fast as he could, knowing at any moment those things would start falling to the floor and trying to grab him.

"You'll have to kill your wife and your mother-in-law, or they will devour your kids. As long as they're alive, they'll keep trying to eat them. That's the only thing they know anymore."

His feet splashed on the wet concrete, hearing the large chunks of beef hit the floor behind him. He didn't stop to look back. He turned right at a corner and arrived at what looked like his bedroom. Same grotesque motif as the hallway. The bed, now a plain block of concrete at the center of this steam room, had one meat puppet bound to the bed with belts while another sat on it. It was the only room in the house in which the moans of pleasure turned female, while the male voice only repeated the word "No" in a defeated, robotic monotone. He dashed toward what used to be the bathroom door. His arm was ensnared by a slimy hand tentacle, but he retaliated with a swift slash. It let go. He continued running before it could try to grab him again. He came out to another hallway in this labyrinth. There was a doorway at the other end. He ran with all his might. In the blue light, the silhouette of one of the chunks of beef in front of him dropped. The tentacle morphed into a hand and came for him right away. He dodged to one side and grabbed the tentacle. He pulled on the slimy, disgusting thing and flung the chunk of meat as if it weighed nothing, back toward the area he'd come from.

He was covered in sweat and blood from head to toe. He turned left and found himself in a blue-lit steam room with seven gray sliding doors in front of him. "Really?" The doors had little number plates near the top, like the doors he remembered from the bathhouse, from left to right: 306, 304, 314, 308, 310, 302, 312.

Not willing to waste time, he went for the one in front of him. He slid door 308 to one side, only to find a cluster of four lumps of meat on the floor. Four tentacle hands shot toward him. With a cry, he managed to dodge just in time and, putting his full weight behind it, slid the door shut, crushing the tentacles with it. A hand with a severed tentacle clung to his forearm. He pried it loose, and it fell lifeless to the floor, leaving a translucent slime on his skin. He let out a disgusted groan.

"You know?" Freddie said. "I used to think tentacles with fingers at the end were sort of lame. I think I changed my mind about that." The childish cackling that followed filled Barry with rage.

"I'm gonna fucking kill you, you crazy piece of shit!" he snarled. "I'm gonna rip your head off and shove your balls down your throat!"

Freddie giggled. "Now, *that's* the Brickhouse I remember. But it's not me you need to use that anger on, cupcake. Tick-tick-tick-tick. They're getting clooooserrrr!" He said this last phrase in a mocking singsong that made him even more furious.

He turned toward the doors, trying to get his anger under control. *He's using the secrets I keep in Blight Harbor. This is the bathhouse. I didn't get a room, so it's got to be the room where the naked guy was waiting with the door open. The numbers are out of order. It was the last room in the row. A corner room. Last room. Highest number? 314?*

He took a quick step to 314 and slid it open. He was met by six hands, grabbing and pulling him. He stopped himself with an arm on the door frame. Swung the knife at the hands. The cuts looked black in the blue light. Once they let go, he slid the door shut. He could hear them pawing at it on the other side.

"Fuck!" He panted. The idea of Maryann devouring their children sent a jolt of panic to his brain. *Last room. So, not lowest to highest. Highest to lowest. The other direction. 302!*

He pulled 302 open and found stairs going up.

He raced up the stairs, arriving at the second-floor hallway. Despite keeping the same motif as the rest of the house, there were no carcasses hanging around. But what captured his interest was the comforting, golden glow radiating from his children's bedroom at the end of the hallway. Terrified, he kept running, the sound of his heart pounding in his ears, until he reached the room.

"Kids!" he shouted as he rushed in to find an old empty child's bed on the left side, and a crib on the right, both looking water-damaged and bloody, which alarmed him less than the fact his children weren't there. He looked around, jaw clenched in anger. "Where the fuck are they, Freddie?"

There was a sound behind him, wet, slimy.

Freddie's voice came to him like a drop of acid sliding into his ear canal, hissing as it burned. "Turn around, bright eyes."

Barry spun one-eighty and let out a horrified scream, taking a step back. Up in the ceiling, near the single incandescent light bulb in this room, a slit had formed, made of flesh and skin, resembling a gigantic set of outer labia. He caught sight of it as what looked like an enormous face the size of his entire torso pushed through it. The face, growing at the end of a red, pink, and brown, cancerous appendage, like an enormous tongue or a gigantic slug, was of his mother, except with empty black eyes, staring at him. He stared, petrified, at the monstrosity before him as its mouth opened to let out an angry cry. Its breath smelled of putrefaction and alcohol.

"FAGGOT!" it shouted, its speech slurred, drunken. "I should have stuffed every wire hanger I had inside me to make sure you weren't born."

Barry's back was pressed against the furthest wall, where a locker door had replaced the bedroom window. His breathing was fast and panicked, his eyes bulging in disbelief.

"You disgusting faggot," the monster said. "AIDS hasn't gotten rid of you yet, so we'll have to do it ourselves."

Ourselves?

The creature retreated into whatever unholy womb lived behind those lips. He could see it moving, hear something rumbling past the opening.

"Did you know," Freddie said, "that in pretty much every culture in the world, there are folk tales about vaginas with teeth?" He giggled like a child. "*Vagina dentata...* Of all the dumb things for us, poor little men, to be afraid of. I learned that from our dearly departed Callum 'Droopy' Baker, back when we were kids. Kinda makes you wonder why he was researching that."

The ceiling kept churning, shuddering. Something was coming.

"Makes sense, though. Us men, so proud of our little peckers, imbuing them with so much of our power and worth, and just a little *clack* of teeth coming together could rob us of all that." He giggled again, his "Hee-hee-hee!" echoing through the room, merging with the wet sounds coming from the ceiling. "That takes on a whole different meaning for you, don't it, Brickhouse? You fear it for a whole other set of reasons. Like how you had to make yourself fuck one for years when you didn't want to. Over and over and over. Even when she knew you *really* didn't want to. Pretense and threats and denial compelling you to say 'Yes,' every time you said 'No'. Must feel funny being part of a statistic no one gives a fuck about."

Churning. Muffled voices. Something was moving. Something was about to be birthed into this room.

"The voices of your coworkers in your head saying, 'Yeah right. Like any man wouldn't want a hot chick to fuck his brains out .'" Freddie's voice got imbued with its highest level of delightful meanness. "And that little smile Maryann got on her face as she asked you to fuck her harder. That smile that said, 'I know you don't want to, but I can make you do it.'"

"Shut up," Barry said in a low, choked voice.

"That word you refuse to say, but you're vividly aware of every day of your life..."

Barry raised his voice. "Shut up!"

"Say it with me, kids! Rape-rape-rape-rape-rape-rape-rape-rape-rape-ra—"

"SHUT UP!" Barry shouted, only to be met by Freddie's loud, boisterous laughter.

Louder voices came from beyond the opening. Something was coming.

"But, seriously, why is it men are so afraid of pussies with teeth? So lacking in imagination. I've never been scared of that, not once. Do you want to know what truly terrified me, Brickhouse? Not teeth. For most of my life, I was afraid vaginas might make a great hiding place for—"

Another fleshy monstrosity, made of muscle, skin, and cancerous tissue, burst through the slit in the ceiling.

"—SPIDERS!"

His mother's face had shifted upward within the sluglike appendage, with Maryann and Therese grotesquely attached at the end, their torsos merged into one, like a sock-puppet from hell.

The two heads had vacuous black eyes and deformed features. Four drooping breasts hung over a bulging, veiny, pregnant abdomen. The creature's four arms and extended ribs flared open, resembling an insect's segmented legs. A two-headed, pregnant spider, held aloft by the meaty appendage.

Barry raised the knife, pointing it at the creature before him.

"C'mon, hon," Maryann's head slurred, grinning, her voice distorted, monstrous. "Give me some sugar. Don't be afraid."

"He's a coward," Therese spat. "Look at him cowering, when he should be giving us that juicy, thick cock."

He let out a disgusted cry.

"He's a faggot," his mother's head said. "A useless faggot!"

"Where are my kids, Freddie?" Barry shouted, the knife trembling in his hand. "Where are they?"

Maryann and Therese cackled as if complicit in a juicy secret. The disgusting snaillike appendage holding the creature aloft curved upward, the heads positioned under the one light bulb glowing in the room, horrid shadows crawling over their faces. The creature presented its veiny abdomen to Barry and rubbed it with its bony hands. A slit opened in the middle to only half its length, revealing the unconscious faces of his two children covered in slime and blood. The moment the folds opened, they both inhaled hard, as if they hadn't been able to breathe.

"Better hurry, Brickhouse," Freddie said as the slit folded closed again over his children. "That's the last breath they get unless you kill your wife and mother-in-law."

"No!"

"And believe me, this time, they're the real ones"—he giggled—"only slightly, but permanently, modified."

"You can't—" Before he finished, the creature lunged forward, and one of its sharp legs shot toward him and pierced his right side. He let out a painful cry.

"Always found those love handles of yours kinda sexy," Maryann said, showing a smile with too many yellow teeth. "What do you say, handsome?" She looked at the long piece of bone penetrating his skin. "Maybe, if I stick you, you'll finally want to stick me."

Despite the flaring pain and revulsion this monstrosity caused him, he couldn't bring himself to harm Maryann or Therese. There had to be another way. "Maryann! Try to fight it! For your children! For your mom!" The leg twisted in his side. He clutched it and screamed as the jolt of pain sent flames through his nerve endings. "Maryann, please!"

"I told you he was dumb," Therese said, showing derision even through those black spheres she had for eyes. "He doesn't get it. Maryann and Therese are gone. It's only their memories in here." It rubbed its belly with two of its hands. "Tick-tock, you dipshit."

Thinking of his children, Barry let out a loud roar and reared the knife back. As he took a swing, the monster pulled its leg out of his side and recoiled, once more presenting its belly to him as the blade cut through the air. The knife sliced through its flesh, deep, as it completed its sideways arc, leaving a vicious, bleeding gouge.

Maryann and Therese moaned with pleasure, then broke into blissful cackles. "Yessss!" Maryann said. "Stick it in me, baby!"

He stared at the cut in their belly and panicked, realizing he could've stabbed one of his children. The memory of the dining room, and the feeling of the knife going into their soft bodies, made his hand tremble, almost making him drop the knife.

Something hit him from his right, and then he was flying. He fell on the bed. It broke. Its noise echoing through the space, followed by the sound of his mother's drunken voice.

"You're a disgrace! You're an embarrassment! Your father killed himself because he knew you were going to grow up to be a fucking queer! He preferred to die than living with the shame!"

This was followed by another of the spider's bone legs flying toward him like a lance and piercing the fatty tissue at the back of his thigh, its tip coming out the other side and getting stuck on the mattress.

Barry hollered in intense pain.

"Ooh," Maryann moaned. "Good idea, baby. Let's do it on Danny's bed."

Barry raised the knife.

Reacting as expected, the monster shifted, placing its belly forward in defense.

Instead of attacking the body, he gripped the bone leg sticking out of his thigh with a firm fist and stuck the tip of the knife into it. The monster tried to pull back, but Barry didn't let go. He pulled the knife out. It left a fissure on the bone leg. Using his free arm, he elbowed it right in the fissure, and the leg broke. The way it shook sent tendrils of white-hot pain up and down his leg, but he watched with satisfaction as the creature jerked with a shriek.

Clenching his teeth through the pain, he pulled the sharp leg out of his thigh, stood, and raised the knife to stab the creature, which positioned its pregnant abdomen forward.

"Not too smart, are you, you goddamn bitches?" He let the knife fall and used that free hand to reach for one of the upper spider legs—one of Maryann's arms—and pulled. He might no longer be in the great shape he was when he was younger, but he was damn strong. That one firm yank brought the creature's twisted heads closer to him. He raised the severed bone leg, hesitated for half a second

(*Maryann and Therese are gone. It's only their memories in here*)

(*They're the real ones. Only slightly, but permanently, modified*)

then shoved it into Therese's eye, which let out a gurgling sound and went limp as the entire mass of flesh and tumors reared back. Maryann shrieked in a tone he couldn't identify as either pain or pleasure. His mother's huge, deformed face continued to curse and insult him. Knowing another attack was coming, he jumped to the other side of the room, a swipe of two of the creature's arms missing him by an inch. He grabbed the crib in his hands and raised it above his head as two of the spider legs flew toward him. They hit the crib, and it exploded into a million splinters.

Maryann bared her teeth. "You don't seem to get the pecking order in this house, Barry," she spat. "When I say, 'Fuck me,' you will be a good little slave and fuck me!"

Even if he knew this thing was most likely not Maryann any-more, just a grotesque mockery of her, the way she said those words was so natural, so real, it awoke a bubbling anger within him that propelled him to his feet, a handful of splinters between his fingers. With a scream, he tossed the splinters into the creature's face, making it protect its eyes. He dove for the knife on the floor and turned, ready to jump and drive it into its arrogant, grinning mug. He stopped cold, seeing one of the bone legs already flying toward him.

His breath hitched in his throat. The needle-sharp tip of the leg stopped less than an inch from his heart. There was a second of realization. This would've pierced his right shoulder blade if he still had his back to the creature, but when he turned around, he put his heart in its path, making this a killing blow.

My side, the back of my thigh, my shoulder blade. Non-lethal.

His thick fingers wrapped around the bone leg, and once more, he pulled with all his strength.

Maryann's mouth opened in an angry cry as it came closer.

"I'm not your fucking slave!" he shouted as he drove the knife into Maryann's mouth. It gagged; blood spurted out. Tremors coursed through the creature's body as it let out a faint whimper, struggling to breathe amidst coughs of blood. He felt it go limp as if in sections before it fell to the floor. The tail end of the creature slipped out of the labia in the ceiling and fell in a sputter of translucent slime.

He pulled the knife out, scrambled toward the round abdomen. Examined it for a quick moment to determine where to cut to get his children out, praying to a god he wasn't sure he believed in that they were alive. Carefully, he stuck the tip of the knife into the creature's flesh, where the skin looked less stretched and bulgy, and cut down, feeling disgusted at the thought this might be Maryann's actual flesh. Soon, there was a gap large enough to put his hand in and get a general idea of how his kids were positioned. He cut, opening a long bleeding gash across the length of the enormous belly, and pulled the two flaps open.

He reached in, pulled Gabriel out, laid him on the floor on his side. The infant coughed slime onto the moldy floor. He didn't wake up, but as he reached in to pull Daniel, his baby's shoulders moved as he breathed. He laid Daniel beside him, set him on his side and patted his back until the boy coughed as well and resumed breathing. They were alive, which brought tears of relief to his eyes, yet they were still unconscious for some reason.

"You disgust me," his mother's drunken voice said. He turned his head toward it. The enormous face was still alive, lying on the floor, attached to this lifeless slug that made up the creature's body. It looked pathetic. "Those boys will grow up shamed and bullied because of their faggot father. They might as well be dead."

He stood up. The pain of the wound in his thigh setting his nerves ablaze. He stepped toward the grotesque face and looked down at it, exhaustion in his eyes.

"You make me sick," the monster said, and he could smell the alcohol in its breath. "You're going to turn your kids into faggots, too."

He took in a deep breath. Let it out. "I hope you're burning in hell, Momma." He raised his foot and brought down his Timberland on her face, over and over, and over, and over. He could hear bones crack, see its black eyeballs sink into its deformed skull, see its teeth break, as a pool of dark crimson blood spread around it. Once satisfied it was dead, he shuffled toward his children and fell to his knees next to them, verifying they were, indeed, still breathing. He remembered the first time he held each of them in his arms after they were born. Mixed in with the joy and the bliss and the absolute love he'd felt for his children the first time he saw them was this disturbing certainty he would do even the most horrifying, reprehensible things in the world to make sure no harm ever came to them.

Now, he'd proved that realization true.

"Well, aren't you a buzzkill?" Freddie said from everywhere at once. "Doesn't matter. I'm not letting you leave. In a moment, my little crawling carcasses will reach the bedroom and take your kids, and I can't wait for you to see the abominations I will turn them int—"

Barry took the knife and put it up to his own throat. "You can't kill me, can you? This thing could've killed me easily, but it held back. This was all about torturing me and murdering my kids. You can't kill me. Hitch was trying to kill us before you and Peter's mom could. You still need us."

No answer.

"Let us go. If you don't, I'll kill myself right now. That will throw a wrench into your stupid little ritual, won't it?"

"You wouldn't."

(*the most horrifying, reprehensible things*)

"Try me."

There was a moment of silence.

A chuckle.

"You ain't that special. You're lucky Droopy went and got killed, and Principal Boobs might die, too, so I kinda need you. Would've been fun to watch you bleed out."

Another silence.

"Whatever." Freddie sounded indifferent, yet a thwarted note underlined his voice. "By tomorrow, God will feast on you and your little brats."

In a blink, his kid's bedroom was back to normal. His children were still lying at his feet. They looked peaceful, as if they were sleeping. Their clothes were still slimy, but other than that, they seemed fine. He turned his head, expecting to see Maryann and Therese lying dead beside him, bleeding from their faces. However, they were gone. They'd stayed in Blight Harbor, or whatever that had been.

Hurting from his wounds, Barry picked up his kids, held them to his chest and wept. The horror of the things he'd been forced to do still clawed at his heart, but he also felt a relief he'd thought impossible.

The soft, amber glow from the bedside lamp in Ray's guest bedroom cast a soothing light as Barry sat in a chair, with a thousand-yard stare, while Ray checked on his sleeping kids.

He'd emerged from that building he could no longer see as his home to find the phone lines were jammed. He'd driven through streets filled with panicking people and vehicles going this way and that. Even from a distance, he could see groups of headlights at the two collapsed exits of town. No one would be getting out through there. He'd reached Ray's home—their home now—to find he hadn't yet gone to Cunningham's.

Ray turned around, removing his stethoscope from his ears, and letting it hang around his neck. "As far as I can tell, they're perfectly fine. Temperature, heart rate, blood pressure, breathing. Everything's normal. Can't know for sure without taking them to the hospital, though."

"The hospital is probably bursting with people now," Barry mumbled, his voice full of panic.

"Hey." Ray crouched in front of him, took his hand, Barry wrapped his fingers around it. Ray gave him a gentle kiss on the lips. "I can't even imagine what you felt going through that. I don't know what Freddie did to them. From what I can see, they seem to only be asleep, like he sedated them, somehow. Other than that, they seem fine. If it's some kind of—I dunno—supernatural anesthesia or something, it might wear off. We'll observe them, alright?"

Barry looked into his eyes and nodded with reluctance.

"Now, let me treat those wounds. We don't want them to get infected."

Barry gasped, staring at the bed.

Ray whipped his head around. "What?"

Barry bolted up from the chair and in a second, he was kneeling by the bed with Daniel in his arms; the boy was blinking groggily as he wrapped his lazy arms around his dad's shoulders. Soon, he also had Gabe in his arms. The little boy glanced around in confusion, sticking his lower lip out, ready to cry. Instead, he buried his face in his dad's chest and let out soft whimpers. Barry caressed his baby's hair.

"Daddy," Daniel said. "Where are we?"

"Um..." Barry gave the boy a kiss on the forehead. He looked back at Ray, who was staring, baffled. "Remember Uncle Ray? We're staying with him tonight."

Ray raised a hand, smiled, waved hello.

Daniel did the same, a bit confused. He noticed the blood on his dad's clothes. "You hurt, Daddy?"

"Uh, yeah, a little," he said. "But Uncle Ray is gonna patch me up real good. You'll see."

Daniel cast a tentative glance toward Ray. "Uncle Ray takes care of you, Daddy?"

The corners of Barry's eyes wrinkled in an honest smile. "Yes." He nodded. "He takes care of me. That's why we're staying with him. Is that okay?"

Daniel smiled. Nodded. "Can Rita visit here?"

Rita was their nanny. It hadn't escaped his notice the boy hadn't asked about his mom or his grandma. It was a conversation he'd need to have with him later.

"Sure. We'll work something out."

"I'm sleepy." The little boy rubbed his eyes, and Barry realized Gabe was already snoring against his chest.

CHAPTER FIFTEEN
THE LAST MEETING OF THE VIGILANTES

"Hello, my dear believers and no-longer-skeptics," said Xavier from the soundproof booth of his mountain home. "If you're just tuning in to today's midday edition of Paranoid-Normal, well, you're in luck! I've just wrapped up my first thirty minutes, it's 12:32 p.m., and I just finished my first bottle of Black Butte XXX (No, they don't sponsor me, but they very well damn should, after this!) and it's time for the current events round-up!"

"Well, this is it," Sylvia said in a weak croak, the laptop on her thighs, the backrest of the hospital bed tilted up at a forty-five-degree angle. "We're getting our news from Xavier Poe Kane. The world is officially ending." She cast a baggy-eyed glance at her friends, who were standing around her, looking quite grave. "That was a joke, people, c'mon."

To her right was Jess, sitting on a chair, holding the laptop straight, so Sylvia wouldn't have to make the effort, having been through surgery the previous night. Standing beside her was Royce.

To Sylvia's left were Ray, Barry, and his two kids. They'd brought them in for a checkup that morning. Ray, coming in through the main door in his nurse's scrubs, had pulled some strings at the hospital to get them ahead of the considerable crowd.

Nadine stood by the window, staring outside in silence, looking morose. Cold, gray sunlight, unfitting for a summer day at noon, bathed her face. Peter had excused himself a few minutes earlier, looking overwhelmed and dodging questions about his mother.

"I'm sorry," Sylvia said, looking in Nadine's direction. "I didn't mean to make light of the situation."

Nadine shook her head, noticing everyone's eyes had converged on her. "That's okay. You lost someone last night, too. We all lost Callum and Angie, actually." She looked at Jess, then at Barry's kids. "We all lost someone."

Sylvia pondered on this. "In my case, it's not that it doesn't hurt. It hurts more than I can put into words. But Cal would've preferred me staying *me*, you know? Not crumble down. That's why I'm trying to be...not broken? We all deal with things differently."

Nadine nodded, forced a taciturn smile.

Sylvia's eyebrows arched upward, as if remembering something, then gasped. "Oh god, Cal!" Her gaze moved from one person to the other. "Do you know if—"

Jess squeezed her hand. "Yeah, hun, they already picked him up. He's downstairs, in the...um...the morgue."

"Oh... Okay." Sylvia smiled, eyes downcast. "Must be cold there." She glanced toward Nadine again. "Any news on Bobby?"

She shook her head. "He turned off his phone. Best guess? He's home, in Angie's room…processing everything. Or, more likely, *unable* to process it." She turned to look at her. Her reddened, puffy eyes and the way her entire face seemed to sag made her look decades older.

"Today's stream has had the lowest audience in the history of my channel," Xavier said from Sylvia's laptop speaker after a recap of the night's bizarre event. "Of course, that is to be expected when all outside communications have been cut off and my audience is one hundred percent local. Ironically, this means I've never had so many people from White Harbor tune in, so I guess you take your wins where you can get them! Ha! I don't mean to be this guy, but this is one big 'I told you so' from me to you! I've been telling you for years the world is full of inexplicable shit!"

"Cal couldn't stomach this guy," Sylvia said. "Now I see why."

Xavier popped a new beer bottle open. "Anyhoo… phones, power, internet, everything's currently working, only within the confines of the town, including Lighthouse Rock. Which should make you wonder how the hell that's even possible, since our electricity and communications come from *outside* White Harbor, but we can't reach anyone beyond our borders."

He paused for effect. Took a sip from his beer.

"According to Lil," Royce said, "at town hall, they've been trying to reach out to emergency services. No luck so far. No calls, no radio, all communications end at the highest point of the Crescent Mountains."

"The generalized panic after last night's interdimensional cross-ing event," Xavier continued, "or ICE (not to be confused with the government agency; we're not fans of the government here), has subsided somewhat. Cooper Bishop, our dear Town Manager, has asked the population to please remain calm, to stay away from the two town exits, which remain blocked by, you know, there not being a road and all."

On screen appeared two drone videos of the only roads out of White Harbor, where two massive landslides ended at wide, impassable gulches leading straight down to the ocean rocks.

"Of course, as evidenced by the cars parked at the edge of those newly formed drops to a rocky death, people will never listen, even for their own safety. I mean, look at these morons camping out, waiting like the road will suddenly rebuild itself."

"He's got a point there," Royce remarked.

"Instead of trying to leave through a non-existent road, like your IQ is in the single digits, our town officials ask that you stay in your homes while next steps are communicated through the White Harbor town hall website, shown at the bottom of the screen. Yes, our town does have a badly structured website that looks like a teenager's blog from the late nineties. Besides staying home, for those experiencing health issues, or needing medical or psychiatric assistance, triage tents have been set up at Clarendon Hospital's parking lot, as to not flood our small hospital with people having panic attacks."

"Looks like plenty of people having panic attacks to me," Na-dine said in an emotionless voice, looking out the window. "I'd say three, five hundred, maybe? More?" She looked at Ray. "Aren't you supposed to be out there helping them?"

"Yes." He sounded unsure of whether Nadine had meant that as a jab. "I told them I'd go as soon as I found Danny and Gabe's dad."

"But he's..." She pointed at Barry.

"They don't know I found him."

"Oh..." Nadine nodded and turned to the window.

"Finally, for those Harborites who have access to boats at the Seaside Marina," Xavier continued from the laptop, "or even the docks, we advise you to *not* try to leave town by sea, for reasons that will soon become obvious in the video I'm about to play."

"Here we go," Royce said.

"I think I'll take the kids outside," Ray chimed in, squeezing Barry's hand, who returned a tired, approving nod. "I already watched it, and I think they don't need to be here for the conversation after that." He took Gabe from the chair beside Barry. The boy hesitated at first, then raised his arms toward him. Ray then turned to Daniel and smiled. "Hey, Danny, let's get you and Gabe a juice box and some cookies from the vending machine. Would you like that?"

Daniel nodded.

"Awesome." He grabbed the boy by the hand and took them both outside.

While Xavier gave his long-winded introduction from the laptop, Jess looked at Barry from across the room. "How you doin' over there, Barr?"

He let out a loud exhale, eyes glued to the floor. "I'm okay, I guess. How'd Nadine put it? Processing everything? I'm just happy my kids are okay. Wish I hadn't had to murder their mom and their grandma to do it."

Sylvia turned to him. "It was a pragmatic choice. It was them or your children."

"I know. It's just 'Husband Kills Wife' isn't a headline I thought I'd ever have attached to me."

"Oh, come the fuck on!" Jess tried to sound like her usual self, even though her heart was shattered by what happened to her mom. "That rapist cunt and her enabler mother deserved worse. They at least had the benefit of being far gone when you did it. Those weren't them, just some *thing* Freddie made using them as materials."

"Their faces, their words, their personalities. It was close enough."

"Barr, look at me."

He swiveled his sleep-deprived eyes in her direction.

"You have your children. You and Ray have each other now. Take your Ws even in shitty circumstances."

He nodded, his face a tug of war between agreement and doubt.

"Alright," Royce said. "It's starting."

They all huddled around the laptop, where a shaky video, recorded from the bridge of the White Harbor ferry, played.

James Groves stood outside the ferry's cockpit, looking out toward the bow. His phone was attached to his helmet, so he had to remember to keep it steady, as the recording would follow the motion of his head.

The ship pitched and yawed as it cut through the waves of a sea that, while often calm, was now turbulent and unseasonably foggy. People on the uncovered deck below either sat, shaking their legs with anxiety, or paced around from one end of the ship to the other—as if walking would result in them reaching their destination faster.

"Hello," he said. "My name's Jim Groves. I'm one of the deckhands of the Mallard. That's, uh, the White Harbor ferry, in case anyone outside our town's watching. What else? Um, okay. So, the Mallard can fit six cars and roughly one hundred people. She's a relatively small vessel. This is the first group of people trying to evacuate White Harbor after our two exit roads collapsed, and... uh... Jesus, some truly fucked up stuff happened. I'm sorry for cussing. It's just. I don't know. Anyway, we didn't take in any cars so we could fit more people. We didn't really count. There's like a hundred and fifty, maybe hundred and seventy, people here."

He turned his head to the right, and Lighthouse Rock became visible in the distance, looking hazy in the fog.

"We're making a wide turn, like a mile round, heading southeast, coz the eastern end of the Crescent Mountains sinks down into the ocean and keeps going for like at three-quarter mile, so we don't wanna risk scraping the bottom of the ship on that, especially since we're, y'know, at capacity. Men, women, children, old people, hundred seventy people plus the crew."

The ship pitched over a wave and fell, breaking it in half in a splash.

"I tell ya, the captain says we have to drop them off at the closest dock and come back for more people. I don't wanna come back, man. I don't wanna come back. Just wanna run like hell once we dock."

The captain cursed at him from the cockpit, his words muffled by the thick glass.

"No! No, Captain! I'm just nervous. I'd never do that."

Jim walked around the cockpit to the other side of the walkway he was standing on and turned the view toward the back of the ship, showing a smattering of motorboats following, each loaded to capacity with people. He wiped the raindrops off the phone.

"As you can see, we're not alone. Those are boats that took off from the marina the moment they saw the ferry depart. Not sure why they're following us. Probably feel safer following our route than winging it. It's... I swear, if you'd seen what we all saw last night, you would be scared, too. That woman was burning, and we couldn't save her. We all got pulled to that place. What would happen if we got pulled there again right now while we're on the boat? I... I dunno...we're all scared. God, I shouldn't even be here!"

For a few seconds, Jim leaned his head and wept. Around him, the rain intensified.

He tried to regain his composure. "Couple years back, I was planning to move to LA, was gonna split an apartment with my buddy, Mark, play guitar in his band. He knew some of the spots talent scouts go. I was so close, man, I almost moved out of this goddamn town." He took a long, wet sniffle. "But then I was like, 'Nah, that's too risky. Here I have a job, and I don't pay rent at my dad's place.' And just like that! I dropped it! All the planning, and I just dropped it, like something hypnotized me, and suddenly, LA seemed like too much of a hassle! That's crazy, man!"

The captain shouted again from the cockpit.

"I'm sorry. I'm sorry, Captain, I'll keep recording."

More shouting.

"Sure. I'll save the commentary. Sorry."

He turned back to face the front of the ship, as an enormous wave made the bow pitch hard upward, then down. Rain was now pouring from the sky without restraint. He grabbed on to the guardrail around the walkway, as the sea shook the Mallard in every direction. People on the deck below staggered every which way, pushing each other, some slipping on the wet surface and falling. He could hear people in the indoor cabin below screaming.

"Whoa," Jim said. "That was a big one! What the hell?"

The second Jim steadied himself and looked ahead, he realized there was another wave swelling in the ocean. A colossal wave. He wiped the rain from his eyes with his sleeve, then wiped the phone, too. It looked like a black wall emerging from the foggy whiteness ahead. He turned toward the cockpit. The captain's face showed a level of bafflement no one would ever want to see on someone piloting a ship.

"Shit!" Jim screamed. "Shit! Shit! Shit!"

With a violent jerk, the ship's bow went skyward, almost sixty degrees, slicing the wave in two as water and foam exploded into the fog. Jim steadied himself with the guardrail. To his right, three of the trailing boats turned over, spilling their passengers overboard, and disappearing under the churning swell. He whipped his head left. People on the lower deck clung to anything solid—seats, railings, each other. Flailing bodies slid down the deck, stopping only when the ship's bow crashed back down with a violent splash, like a gigantic child slapping the water in a tub. The ship tilted on every available axis. Screams echoed below, drowned out by the ship's groans and the roar of the ocean. It was a chaotic symphony of disaster, reaching a crescendo as another wave formed—a monstrous, unnatural concave, rising out of the fog and rain. Whatever this was, it wasn't just the ocean anymore. This wave looked blacker than the others, as if something vast and ancient were emerging from the depths. It was so gargantuan it took an eternity to break the water's surface.

"C-cap-captain!" Jim bumbled in a shaky voice, receding toward the cockpit door. He knocked on the thick glass, receiving no response from the captain, who only stared ahead, mesmerized. "Captain! C-cap-tain!"

It was solid. Something solid emerging from the wave. Dark. Black. Water cascaded down the slick black curve, formed vertical wedges as it fell, resembling serrated fangs in a black maw.

Jim hurried inside the cockpit, stood behind the captain. "It's glowing!" he shouted, as the screams from below were almost as loud as the ocean and the engines. "Glowing lights! Captain! Glowing lights! Look!" He pointed straight ahead. There was a line of shining, silvery-blue spots along the length of the curved mass. It looked like an enormous sea serpent from old legends, or a gigantic tentacle rising from the depths, its curve larger than the ship, taller than the rocky hills at the eastern end of the Crescent Mountains, and lining its curve, glowing, blue spots.

"No! No! Captain, it's gonna—"

It struck like a whip.

The entire cockpit tilted to the right, and now the world was spinning. Closing his eyes, Jim was left with nothing but darkness and the force of gravity. Jim and the captain joined the hundreds of screaming people from the indoor deck. Everything shifted. He tried opening his eyes, but got only spinning images: light, darkness, hands, legs, a control panel, a door, a face, then blue-green ocean on the other side of the thick glass of the cockpit. Blue-green water. Bubbles.

Jim was kneeling on the glass. His phone was lying face-down on it. He picked it up, shone its light around. The captain lay unconscious a few steps ahead.

On the glass, a tiny crack.

"No! No, please!"

It stretched. Lengthened an inch.

Breathing. Moaning. Jim heard the echo of his own hysterical voice whimpering. Then, he screamed as a man with a broken neck floated fast past the window, carried away by the resulting wave, then, in the phone's light, dozens of shapes and silhouettes passed, some inert, some still fighting for their lives, carried by the waters past the cockpit window.

Jim screamed. "No, no, no! God! No!"

The silhouette of a woman in a light-colored dress, unconscious, sinking, far. Her upraised hand seemed to be stuck on something. A bag? A piece of clothing? A child. A child, kicking and flailing their arms, as they were dragged down to the depths by their unconscious mother, arm still clinging to the back of their shirt.

The crack stretched, split in two, continued to grow across the glass.

"Help me," Jim whined. "Somebody help me!"

The mother and child disappeared in the merciless darkness.

"No! Noooooo! God, help meeee!"

Blue spots in the depths, faint, equidistant, their glow becoming intense as they swam, snakelike, against a vast, oily blackness that stretched every direction. It was with mounting horror that Jim realized this blackness wasn't the ocean, but the body of whatever had capsized the ship, and it was coming closer.

The window burst into the cockpit, flooding it with water. Jim let out one last howl of terror before the rush of water and shards of glass filled his screaming mouth, then his lungs.

There was a brief silence among those present in the room as the video ended, during which all that could be heard was Xavier recapping the shocking images, and reports from eyewitnesses at Lighthouse Rock, which confirmed neither the ferry nor the boats trailing it survived the event. There was no sure way to confirm this other than sending out more boats to the spot of the accident, which no one was insane enough to do.

"Well, it's, uh..." Royce started. "It's a good thing to at least know just how royally fucked we are."

Jess let out a sigh. "After watching that, it's no wonder we have four hundred people out there panicking and having anxiety attacks."

"Not to mention fights and shootings breaking out all over town," Barry said. "People broke into Harbor Grocers and looted it. Set it on fire after picking it clean. It's been closed since Sam Becker Jr. went missing,"—he canted his head to one side as if considering—"or died, most likely. Everybody saw the Beckers last night when they threatened your dad,"—he nodded toward Jess—"which pretty much confirms the Beckers are part of Martha Lange's group, so people weren't overly concerned with breaking their windows, stealing their stuff, and beating each other to a pulp over the last roll of toilet paper. Nobody knows where they are right now. They seem to have gone into hiding, same as the Garners and the Hollands."

"What about Jess's dad?" Nadine said, turning a side eye toward her.

"What's with the tone?" Jess looked shaken by this.

"He's one of them, too." Nadine turned to the others. "One of the people who killed Angie."

Jess squinted at her. "Careful with what you're saying there, girl. They also killed my mom."

"And your dad knew they were going to do that. He didn't stop them. He didn't warn us." She kept pushing, even after seeing Jess stand from her chair. "Did *you* know they were going to do that?"

In a second, Jess was standing in front of her, fury in her eyes.

"How about the question in everyone's mind, Jess?" Nadine met her gaze. "Are *you* one of them?"

The slap reverberated through the room. Jess glared with piercing green eyes at Nadine, whose face was turned to one side, mouth open, absorbing the pain. Everyone stared in shock.

"Now, you listen to me"—spit sprayed from Jess's lips—"coz I'm not gonna repeat myself. My dad *was* part of that group. That's true. But trying to leave them made that Lange bitch kill my brother, and he kept quiet to protect me, and even then, that bag of crazy had Freddie kill my mom. Last night, who was there pointing a Magnum at Martha fuckin' Lange to stop her from killing Angie? Angie!... One of my best friends in the entire world!" Tears spilled over, ran down her face. "She might have been your sister, but that doesn't mean you're the only one mourning her! You *just* said that a moment ago, now you forgot?"

Nadine cast her reddened gaze down, looking embarrassed. "I'm sorry. You're right."

"Um, guys…"

They all turned to Sylvia, who rubbed her bandaged stomach with the tips of her fingers.

"We need to talk about what Cal and I discovered about what's coming. Because it involves all of us, and Royce isn't wrong in saying we're royally fucked." She nodded toward Jess. "You said your dad has Hitch in your basement, right?"

Jess nodded, looking embarrassed, realizing she'd helped keep alive the man who had killed Callum and stabbed Sylvia. "Yes. He's not doing well. He's alive, conscious. I'm not sure he'll make it without actual surgery, though. My dad had blood stored in a cooler in the cellar…" Everyone stared at her. "For emergencies! Jesus! He did a transfusion, but after last night's blackout, we don't even know if the blood went bad or not. So, we're not sure he'll survive the night."

"You guys need to figure out how to keep him alive. I swear, I wish I could choke the life out of him for what he did. But he's literally the only person who can help us fill in the gaps. Also, your dad, Jess. He has something we need."

"What?"

"He has Logan Giffen's suicide letter."

Barry reacted as if he, instead of Nadine, had been slapped all of a sudden. "Say, what?"

"Your dad was in the Circle. He left a letter for Chuck Cunningham, which everyone thought was a suicide letter. It's not."

"Wait, go back a few sentences. What do you mean my dad was in the Circle? That's a lie!"

Sylvia turned an assertive gaze in his direction. "It's not. Gerardo Valencia's death impacted some kind of balance between the Circle and the Order of the Rising Sun—"

"The what?" Royce asked.

"Hitch's religious group. Keep up. Curling needed to feed the Vanek House with a sacrifice once a year to prevent what lived in the house from getting out: the thing the Circle worships."

"Wait, now Curling is involved?"

"Hitch *is* Curling," Sylvia said with annoyance. "They're the same person: a settler known as Long-Lived John Ellis, who's been reincarnating for over a hundred years. He had a hand in the death of Walter Parham, which began this whole mess. Now, can you stop asking questions and getting me off topic? Ouch!" She winced, putting a hand to her stomach, then stared at Royce.

"Should you be doing this?" Nadine asked. "You're in recovery."

"Stop. Getting. Me. Off. Topic!" she answered with a glare.

"Uh, sure, go on," she said.

"So," Barry stepped in, "my dad?"

Sylvia swallowed, gathering her thoughts. "Your dad was in the Circle. Both your parents died before you were sixteen, so you never knew. He didn't kill himself. Martha Lange killed him. Are you with me?"

He stared at her, mouth agape, and answered with a subtle nod.

"Neal Parham, Freddie's dad, killed Gerardo, which knocked some strange balance of power over the town. So, Martha Lange decided to sacrifice you, because you're a direct descendant of the first settlers. They needed that balance for...well, what's happening now. When your dad refused, she used that same weird power she used on us that day outside the Vanek House to make him hang himself in his room."

Barry's face looked like the entire foundation of his life had been shaken.

"He left a letter, which everyone assumed was his suicide letter. Well, it wasn't, since he had no idea he was going to die. Your mom was in favor of sacrificing you, so he was going to take you away from White Harbor, and he left a letter to Chuck Cunningham"—she nodded toward Jess—"urging him to get out of town, too."

"My dad didn't kill himself?" Barry whispered.

"No, he didn't," Sylvia said, then returned to Jess. "I couldn't translate some phrases in the cult's language at the end of the letter. Our copy was too blurry, and I didn't know most of the words. Your dad knows what it means. I think it's supposed to be a way to stop what the Circle is doing right now. We need your dad, and we need Hitch alive."

Jess gave an understanding nod.

"What about what Peter and I found?" Nadine asked. "That weird black crystal statue in Martha Lange's room? Is it dangerous?"

Sylvia shrugged. "I don't know. What did you and Peter do with it?"

"We closed the door. A nurse saw it early on, though. I think they've been too busy or scared to check on it, but they will. I'm sure. That thing, at a hospital? They might think it's infectious or something and quarantine us all, so we won't be able to stop what's happening."

"You took a picture, right? Can I see it?"

Nadine pawed inside her bag as if she'd forgotten what a phone looked like, and finally found it. She pulled up the picture and handed it to Sylvia. The others leaned in to look at the screen, which displayed a picture of the bizarre sculpture of Martha Lange. Those black threads that made it up looked like a tangle of dry weeds given human form.

"That thing," Barry said. He winced, his wounded thigh hurting when he tried to stand too quick. "It looks like what I saw last night in that temple, holding my kids. They took my shape. There were lots of black sculptures like that one holding children in that enclosure."

"That tracks." Sylvia studied the image. "It's made of these black, living threads. I'm not sure what they are. We've seen them before, at the Vanek House. They call them 'the Exiles', they serve that god-thing. They can exist in Blight Harbor or can possess a body and transform it, so they can exist here. They didn't need a body inside the Vanek House. Any part of that place could open to Blight Harbor if someone like Freddie knew how. That's all I know. No idea why they're on this side. I remember seeing my shape made of those threads in Peter's backseat, right before I was taken to that temple last night. Maybe it's an exchange—like a *placeholder* for taking someone to the other side?"

"What about my house last night?" Barry asked.

"I don't know. My best guess is while the ritual is happening, Freddie can walk between the two sides, even invoke Blight Harbor into an area. In the ritual, his role is called 'the Architect of Life'. He basically creates and gives shape to Blight Harbor and its monsters, using what he finds on that other side."

"Jesus," Royce said. "These people and their weird-ass names."

"It's safe to say the ritual is happening to the letter. All of this was supposed to happen back in 1996, but Peter's absence delayed them." Sylvia then spoke at length about the Ritual of the Four Nights, the sacrifices for each night, and, most relevant to them, what was about to happen. "Tonight, Blight Harbor will take over, and four people out of a pre-selected group have to die. Guess who that group is."

There was silence all around the room.

"*I curse you all*," Royce mumbled, and everyone's eyes filled with recognition. That day when Martha Lange had caught them sneaking their things out of the Vanek House. "*One day, I will come for you, and you'll feel my revenge. That is my curse on you.*" He cast a wide glance around. "That's why she pulled *us* to the altar last night. What was the thing she called us last night?"

"The Chosen Accursed," Sylvia said. "The last thing Cal wrote on his notes was 'Maledictions', then a question mark. He mistranslated it. It wasn't 'Maledictions', it was 'Cursed Ones', or 'Accursed Ones'. That's most likely what it was referring to."

"So, next time the blue moon comes out, they're coming for us," Royce said.

"The Third Night," Sylvia said. "Four of us have to die at the hands of Martha or her servants, including Freddie's creations. Then, *something* happens which starts the Fourth Night, which is supposed to be eternal."

"So, what's the plan?" Royce asked. "Separating didn't go so well last night."

"We hole up inside the bar," Jess said. "We have guns and supplies. Hitch had my dad draw these protective"—she waved a hand in front of her, like doodling something in the air—"whatchamacallits. Supposedly, they'll keep Blight Harbor, Freddie, and that supernatural cunt, Martha Lange, out."

"Good," Sylvia said. "That's why we need Hitch, though. If what Cal and I interpreted is true, those whatchamacallits won't last long tonight. We need to get out before the ritual is completed."

Jess stood up. "I'll go ahead of all of you, Dad and I will get the bar ready. How long do you think we have?"

Sylvia shrugged. "No idea. Thursday night, it was well past 10 p.m. Last night, it was before nine. So, maybe it's coming earlier each night? I'm not sure."

"Last night, sundown was earlier," Nadine said. "We didn't pay attention. Days are getting shorter."

"Alright," Jess said. "Get everything you need, and we'll meet at the bar at five. Let's not even risk coming close to eight."

Royce scratched his chin with his index finger. "I have to get Tracy and Lillian. Lil is on the town council, so she volunteered. They're in that mess of people out there. We'll go to Cunningham's right after."

"I have to get Bobby," Nadine said. "His phone is off. He won't know what's coming. I'll look for him, then head to Cunningham's."

"I'll wait for Ray here with the kids," Barry said. "I don't care if they don't let him clock out earlier, we're all getting out of here at three, max, even if I have to bulldoze through the crowd outside. We'll be at the bar long before five." He glanced around, as if remembering something important. "What about Peter?"

"Peter can't be there," Sylvia said, flat out. "Martha will always be able to locate him and influence any place he's in. If Peter enters Cunningham's, we're all dead. I know this sounds shitty, but the best we can do is warn him and tell him to stay inside and not come to Cunningham's. The good news is Peter is safe as long as four of us don't die. Bad news is...he's on his own."

There was an unnerving silence in the room, broken only by a sarcastic snort from Nadine.

"Deen?" Sylvia said. "What was that?"

Nadine glanced at her friends, all of whom stared in confusion. She shook her head. "I always had this conceited thought that the worst punishment I could inflict on Peter would be my absence. No matter what, I'd always be the last to leave him, so me abandoning him would actually carry some weight. I just never had a reason to. Now, it looks like I'm both encouraged and justified to do just that."

Conflicted looks converged on her. She responded with a shrug, a sigh, and turning her gaze out the window again.

"What happens to Peter if four of us die?" Royce asked.

"I wasn't able to translate that far before passing out. All I know is the Fourth Night involves someone from the Mother's bloodline, so it's either Peter or his son. Little William is not an option since the person needs to be physically in White Harbor, and he's staying with his grandma, miles from here."

"I'll leave Peter a message," Nadine said, frost in her voice. "It'll be the last thing I do for him."

Barry turned to Sylvia. "And you? You can come with Ray and me. We'll take you to the bar."

"I can't. Not unless a doctor discharges me. I'm stuck here."

Jess shook her head. "No fucking way! Fuck that! You're not staying here alone!"

Barry put a hand forward. "Don't worry. Ray and I will figure something out, alright? We won't leave her here."

"Okay." Her mouth was a straight line. The next second, she was crouching, rolling her jeans up to reveal a small black gun in a discreet holster. She pulled it out, stood, grabbed Sylvia's hand, and positioned her fingers around the grip, ensuring to keep her forefinger out of the trigger. "This little girl is a Ruger LCP Max, double stack. Eleven rounds."

"Jesus!" Royce stood between Jess and the tiny window on the door. "We're in a hospital, Jess!"

"The safety is this little blade in the trigger," she continued, undeterred. "As long as you don't press it in, the gun won't fire." She raised it to Sylvia's eye level. "Align this little notch in the back with the front sight. This little thing here." She touched the tip of the gun.

"Got it," Sylvia said. "I think."

"Hide it somewhere in your bed. No one will find it."

Sylvia tucked it under her pillow. She looked around. "So, are we ready?"

A nervous silence passed among the group, as if sensing, despite all their planning, it would be the last time they'd all be in the same room together.

"Then," she said, a mournful tone in her voice, "I guess this meeting of *most* of the Vigilantes is adjourned."

CHAPTER SIXTEEN

HOUSEKEEPING

Peter lumbered through the front door, closed it behind him harder than he'd intended. He let out an exhausted sigh, ran his hand through his hair, and crossed the front hall, heading toward the stairs.

All he wanted was to reach his bedroom and let his body drop lifelessly on his huge mattress. But he knew the moment he closed his eyes, all he'd see, spinning in a hellish loop, would be the sight of Angie in flames, Jenny in flames, his mother's deranged smile, that bizarre sculpture they'd found in her hospital room, and Nadine blaming him for everything that was happening.

(*The only reason your mother was able to do what she did is you came back to White Harbor*)

She's wrong, he thought. *I had no way of knowing she'd do this.*

As he set foot on the first stair, his attention was called to the right, past the dining room. The sound of two people talking. The only person who should've been here was Doris. He stopped, turned, and crossed the dining room. Through the rectangular window on the swinging door to the kitchen, he could see Doris sitting at the center island, and another person whose back was turned toward him.

He placed his palm against the door with some apprehension. *What am I worried about?* he thought. *It's just Doris and a guest.* Careful not to startle them, he pushed the door in slowly, and the pudgy old woman's eyes soon turned toward him. She seemed surprised. Her companion turned around. It was a man in his late thirties, short-haired, wearing glasses, carefully trimmed chin beard. His eyes looked like Doris's.

"Hi," Peter said. He could barely afford that one word, he was so tired.

"Oh, Mr. Lange," Doris said. "Welcome back. So glad you're okay!"

"Yes." He cast a suspicious look toward the man, noticing the way he closed one of two books he had on the island surface, placed one on top of the other, and pulled both an inch closer in an almost unwitting defensive gesture. "Everything okay?"

Doris smiled that doting smile of hers—she had always been more motherly to him than his own mother, despite refusing to call him anything other than "Mr. Lange"—and with a hand, gestured toward the man. "Yes, this is my son, Carlos Alberto. He came to visit me."

"Hello, Mr. Lange. Nice to meet you," the man said with a nervous smile. "People call me Alberto, or Tali. You can call me either."

Peter, whose mind didn't have the processing power for pleasantries, only managed an "Okay."

Doris and Alberto—or Tali, like he said—exchanged a complicit look he had no willpower to dissect, so he defaulted to trusting the old woman, who'd always been nothing but deserving of his trust—even if her current behavior seemed strange. He nodded at him, then at her. "I'm going upstairs. I need to sleep."

They exchanged another look. "Oh, of course," Doris said, as the swinging door closed behind him.

Peter climbed (almost crawled up) the stairs, reached his bedroom, kicked off his shoes, tossed his jacket over the desk chair to his left, and turned toward the bed, undoing the top two buttons of his shirt as he did so. He pulled his wallet and keys from one pocket, tossed them on the nightstand, then reached into his other pocket and pulled his phone. He was about to toss it on the nightstand when the thought crossed his mind. *I should check on William.* He groaned, regarded the phone as if it were some asshole boss telling him to work on an urgent report a minute before it was time to clock out.

He let his ass drop onto the mattress, bouncing slightly, as he looked for his mother-in-law's phone number, and hit the call icon.

Three rings later, Susan Morton's pleasant voice answered. "Hi, Peter. How are you?"

"Good, I guess."

"Calling at noon two days in a row, I see. Is everything alright?"

He nodded, massaging his temples with his thumb and pinky finger, then realized she couldn't see him nodding. "Uh, yeah, just had a terrible night. Was about to take a nap, but I wanted to check on William."

"Oh, sweetheart, I'm so sorry to hear that. I hope you get some sleep. I know things have been tough lately."

"Thanks," he said, his voice devoid of any enthusiasm.

"William's doing fine. He's already put that weird nightmare from the other night behind him."

"That's good to hear." He rubbed his eyeballs. They felt like someone had punched him from inside his skull.

"He should be back from school in a couple hours. I'll tell him you called."

"That's okay. I'll call him back after I get some sleep. I don't want him to talk to zombie me." He tried to chuckle.

"That's fine, dear," Susan said with a warm tone. "Rest, and we'll talk later."

Once the call ended, Peter threw the phone on the bed. It bounced off the mattress and clattered as it hit the floor. He waved a tired hand toward it. He'd pick it up later. Without bothering to take his jeans or shirt off, he fell sideways onto his pillow, pulled his legs into the bed.

Within two minutes, he was asleep. He didn't hear the notification of Nadine's incoming message. He certainly did not see the message disappear from his phone.

Tali watched Peter Lange shuffle away through the rectangular window on the kitchen door and thought he'd expected the man to be a little friendlier based on his mom's constant praise of him. *He looked pretty exhausted, though. There's also the way his wife died and the events of the last two nights.* He felt a shiver climb up his spine just thinking about it.

"*¡Pónme atención, Carlos Alberto!*" Doris slapped him on the shoulder. "I'm talking to you, *M'hijo!*"

Reacting to the slap, he whipped his head around. "Ow, *Mami!*" He brought a hand to his shoulder. "I'm sorry!"

"You need to pay attention, because we have very little time."

"Okay. So, you stay here with him, and I go look for the others."

She slapped him on the shoulder again. "*¡No seas tan bruto!*"

"Ow! *Por Dios, Mami,* stop it!" He once more brought his hand up to rub his aching shoulder. "That's literally what you said!"

"No! Curling! You have to look for Curling!" she said, at first loud, then lowering her voice, not wanting to risk being heard by her boss.

"Hitch, you mean."

"Same thing. Curling will be where they are. You have to get them all in the same place, then you and Curling protect that place, so Martha Lange can't get to them. That's how we stop this. It will not save everyone in town. It can save some."

"And how am I supposed to find him?"

"I used a locating spell. He was in the bar. Cunningham's. Then he vanished. I can't find him anywhere else. It means he's still there, and he sealed the building. He'll be there."

Tali bit his lip, thinking. Finding all of them and bringing them to Cunningham's was the best course of action. However, the thought of finding them all in such a short time was daunting. "What about you, *Mami*?"

"I'll be fine."

"Don't be stubborn, *Vieja*." He knew she hated it when he called her an old woman, but it got her attention. She narrowed her eyes at him. "If Lange is here,"—he motioned with his head toward the second floor—"you can't seal this place. She'll send Parham or something worse for him, and if you're here, she'll kill you. You expect me to be out there protecting a bunch of strangers while you're in danger in this house?"

She regarded him with a grave look, which was undercut by a loving smile. "Come here." She leaned in and gave him a huge hug, which he returned.

No matter how much he'd grown up "the Gringo way"—an ever-growing wedge coming between him and his parents through puberty, moving out for college, living independently, only seeing them on holidays and birthdays—those roots, that very Latino bond, were undeniable. His connection to his mother was unshakable. No matter where he was, he felt he'd come home to a bowl of her *sopa de albóndigas* at the end of the day. No matter how old he was, he'd always be her baby, and her embrace felt like the safest place in the world.

"I'll be fine, *M'hijo.*" She placed a gentle hand on the back of his head. "I can't tell you what I'm going to do, because now that he's here, she might be listening. But remember: *sabe más El Diablo por viejo que por diablo.* I have a trick or two up my sleeve."

"*Está bien, Mami.*"

She kissed him on the forehead. "Go. We have very little time. *Te amo, chigüín.*"

He nodded, resting his head on her chin. "*También te amo, Mami.*"

The confusion was taking over again. She had used too much power for the Second Night's sacrifice, and she could feel it, the haze, the swirl, taking over her mind and making her not her highest self. She was usually not aware of the swirl taking over. Only after stumbling back into lucidity did she realize she'd been walking through a foggy maze of shuffling memories. But here, with the influence of God's power still coursing through her veins, she could feel herself getting lost again, little by little, and...

Home. She was home. Her porch's front step. She was in her forties, and she was standing on her front step. Sun beaming down, making her squint, making her face hot, and a few steps further, on the front lawn, was Peter, six years old, ready for school, his leather backpack strapped to his shoulders.

A man with her back toward her, on one knee in front of the boy.

He had tan skin, graying black hair. Hector. Useless, cowardly... What was the other word she used to describe him? Ignorant—Yes, ignorant—Hector.

He spoke with a noticeable Hispanic accent, which, despite all her hard work, she hadn't been able to teach him how to conceal, or at least, smooth to an acceptable level.

"There," he said, tugging on the fabric of Peter's shirt to remove the wrinkles caused by the backpack's straps. "Now you look like a proper first-grader."

Peter returned a proud, radiant smile.

Soft. Hector was making him soft.

"Make lots of friends, alright?" the useless man continued. "You're a charmer, like your *Tata*. Soon the whole town will be talking about what a cool kid Peter Rojas is!"

"Lange." The word escaped Martha's lips, as if she couldn't contain herself from correcting him. "We agreed."

Hector glanced sideways at her. He seemed annoyed. She didn't care.

"We agreed he'd have the name Lange, too. His name is Peter Rojas-Lange. I won't go over this again, Martha."

She huffed, glared at Peter. "I don't want you talking to the other children."

"Martha."

"I'm talking to our son." Her tone was a cleaver, chopping down on any coming rebuke. She turned to Peter again. "Why mustn't you talk to the other children?"

Peter, whose smile had vanished into a worried, tense line, said, "God doesn't like it. They and their families will be cod-co-dend-condemned to the Void. God will feed on them."

She gave a stern, almost invisible smile. "Good." She then turned a prideful smirk toward her useless, cowardly, ignorant husband.

"We talked about this," he said, standing and walking toward her, pointing a finger. "I don't want our son to be isolated. I want him to be a normal kid. Happy."

"He will be happy," she stated in a matter-of-fact, condescending tone. "He's obeying God."

Hector became upset. She didn't care.

"This is not right!"

"You've always been an ignorant man. Useless. Cowardly."

"Stop it, Martha. I'm warning you."

She glanced down at the necklace with a cross that hung over his chest. "Still clinging to childlike fantasies. How much longer, Hector?"

He clutched the cross, tucked it inside his shirt. "You said you'd give me time."

"Who do you think you are?" Her lip curled in disgust. "I am the Mother. God talks to me. Not you. You do not make God wait after he's used my voice to tell you to get in line, over and over again. I wonder. Do you even believe?"

"I do believe!" He looked scared now. "Or did you forget already? I was in the cave with you. I saw." He stared off to one side, eyes full of dread. "I saw."

"Then I expect you to do what must be done." She surveyed him up and down, as if appraising a dress she'd wanted when she'd seen it through the store's window display, yet after purchasing it, noticed the broken seams, the stains, the uneven hem. "I debased myself by choosing to be with you. My youthful lust is a sin I am now paying. You're disgusting in my eyes. The only thing that could ever ingratiate you with me is fulfilling your role for our family and our God."

Hector returned a contemptuous glare, said nothing, turned around and paced toward Peter.

She watched him as he walked down the slope, holding their son by the hand. Then a sound from up the slope. Steps on grass. By the time she turned, Peter—now a teenager of twelve or thirteen—shouldered past her, marched across the porch and through the front door.

"Peter!" she called out with indignation. "Where were you? I've been waiting all afternoon!"

"I was out with friends," he said, without turning around.

She followed him inside. Realizing, at the same time, she was older, a lot older, in her eighties.

"How many times have I told you—"

He spun on her, daring eyes flashing at her.

"No, Mother! I already told *you*! I will learn God's law. I will learn God's tongue. I will recite the stupid prayers as many times as you want. But I won't stop living my life!"

"How dare you?"

He turned around and kept walking into the house.

"Come back here!" She followed him. Something caught her attention from the left. The fireplace was lit, the living room was dark. She noticed her younger self sitting on a chair, and Peter, as a child, sitting on the banquette beside her. Through the window she noticed it was snowing outside, while it had been a beautiful sunny day only a minute ago. She squinted at this scene with confusion. She looked ahead to see teenage Peter disappear into the now gloomy darkness of the hallway.

"Come back here, boy!" she commanded. "Peter!"

She turned right and entered the kitchen, which was almost pitch dark, save for the one light bulb shining from the pantry, swinging this way and that, shifting the shadows of the cans and containers on the shelves. There was a pounding noise, and the muffled voice of Peter screaming, banging on the trapdoor in the pantry floor.

"Mother! Please!" the dimmed voice screamed. "I'm sorry! I'll do anything you want! Please! Let me out!"

Martha ignored this, continued walking after teenage Peter, who was crossing the door to the back porch. The kitchen seemed unusually long, the door so far away. As she marched toward it, the voice from the pantry became adult Peter's voice. "Mother! I'm scared! Let me out! Please! PLEASE! I'LL OBEY, MOTHER!"

She reached the door, coming out the other end to the back porch. The day was bright and sunny, the sudden light blinding her. She shielded her eyes. In the glare, she thought she saw an image of a car. A car she recognized well. A 1978 Chevrolet Malibu, brown, with a cream top, plunging into deep waters. The image faded as sight returned to her, and now there was Peter and that Schaefer girl, Nadine. Both sitting on the porch stairs, kissing.

She felt the anger rise inside her very soul. Her face contorted with rage. She looked down at her hand; she was holding a pair of scissors. Her lips peeled back, and spat, "Whore! Get away from him!"

As she advanced on the two children and stabbed with the scissors, the scene disappeared, and she was standing on a stone floor, light from torches dancing at her feet. The scissors were gone.

"I took her sister," she mumbled in a drunken croak. "She took my son. I took her sister. The whore paid. The whore paid. I took her sister."

"Martha!" a woman's voice said. "Uh, I'm sorry...Mother! Mother, are you alright?"

Her eyes rolled in her sockets toward the source.

There were people around her.

The Circle.

What remained of it, at least.

They were in the Sanctum. Her mind was back. She was back.

With her body still bent at the waist as she recovered, Martha felt a hand on her shoulder, which she shrugged off in one swift motion. "Don't touch me!" She cast a fierce glance around the circular room. "Sit down, don't waste any more of my time."

There were puzzled looks exchanged between the members of the Circle and their families as they took their respective seats. They were all here, the elder members sitting in their two corresponding chairs, side by side, their children and grandchildren in the pews behind them.

"You brought children," she said in a dissatisfied croak. Other than Sam and Judy Becker, whose only descendant, Sam Jr., had been offered to God during the first night, the rest of these idiots had brought their entire families with them; children under sixteen, even adult family members, their spouses, and extended family. "You brought non-anointed people."

"We're sorry, Mother," Cooper Bishop said, that nepotistic Town Manager, whose election had floated only on the shoulders of his parents' fame. He stood up behind his parents, who looked as confused and scared as he did.

Good, Martha thought. *They should fear me.*

"We didn't know what else to do," Cooper said in a shaky voice. "After...last night, the people are looking for the members of the

Circle and their families. We needed to keep them safe, and this was the only safe place."

She narrowed her eyes at him. "I didn't see you or your parents come out to stop Charles Cunningham when he tried to kill my son."

His lips reacted with a stupid quiver, until the politician in him pushed a ridiculous, hypocritical smile to his face. "We couldn't, Mother. Our role was to keep the peace and keep the people from trying to leave before the Third N—"

"And did you?" she asked. "Becker's supermarket was looted and set ablaze. Fires are breaking out all over town, and our God had to intervene to stop ships from leaving by sea."

"I..." he stammered. "I'm having people gather at the hospital, offering them supplies, medication, to keep them calm. The police and the fire department are—"

"Quiet." She made his mouth shut tight and forced him to sit. A murmur of shock passed through the people gathered around, many of whom had only the faintest idea of why they were here.

"You're useless." She surveyed the faces in the room. Eyes gleaming with the light coming from the sconces in the chapel's columns. "All of you."

"Wait, is that..." Her eyes fixed on a balding man in the crowd standing behind the pews. "Is that the woman we saw in that dream last night? Is she the one that burned that w—"

Something thin and black whipped past him, coming from the wall. It disappeared as quickly as it appeared. The man's head plopped to the right and bounced on the stone floor as his body slumped to the ground, spraying blood all over a woman Martha could only assume was his wife. The woman shrieked. Others joined her in her screaming until one of the anointed members in the pews sitting behind Carter and Mollie Booth stood and put a hand over her mouth, pleading with her and the others to be quiet, to no avail.

"*SILENCE!*" Martha roared inside all of their heads. All noise ceased, and now dozens of terrified eyes stared in her direction, fearing their heads would be next. "I will speak. Anyone who utters a single word will join that disrespectful, headless pig."

Dead silence. Even the children pressed their mouths shut, though tears rolled down their cheeks.

Martha pointed at two empty chairs on one side of the circular altar. "Charles Cunningham. You saw what he tried to do last night to *my* son. Have any of you even looked for him?" Her gaze passed over them like a scythe drawing a circle. "No."

Amber Bishop, an elegant woman of almost eighty, raised a timid hand. "Mother, I've been searching for him using God's sight. I can't find him anywhere."

Martha scowled at her. "Your incompetence is an embarrassment. Yes. He can't be found by God's sight. What does that tell you?"

Her mouth opened and closed, helpless.

"Only someone from the Order can block our sight. There are only two Order members in White Harbor that we know of. That fat old maid that works for my son, and Curling—or Hitch, or whatever his new name is. I can see Peter and that fat witch, but

I can't see Curling, which means Charles is with Curling! That traitor is with the one person who stands a chance at stopping the ritual. Why are you all here and not out there, searching for him?"

"Mother," Judy Becker said. "We're sorry. We were scared for our lives."

Martha scowled at her, her eyes two blue flames of anger. "And aren't you scared for your lives *now*?"

Judy stammered. "He must be at the bar! That's the most logical place!"

"Yes!" Kai Bishop said. "In the city plans, I remember his property had a cellar! It's easy to secure! He's probably holed up there! We can take some of the younger, stronger people here and—"

Shocked murmurs all around. The entire crowd had gone immobile from the neck down. A woman—one of those uninvited guests standing behind the real Circle members—had been holding a baby. The moment everyone went stiff, the toddler, who had begun to wail, slipped from her grip and fell on its head, which cracked open on impact. The baby was dead in an instant, a mere twitch of its leg indicating the final synaptic firing of its dying brain. The mother screamed, and soon everyone was screaming again.

It didn't matter. Martha spoke inside their heads again, and they were silent. "*You fools. You utilitarian, greedy, subservient hangers-on. Bloodthirsty leeches.*" She cast an evil smile at all of those present. "*God doesn't need you in His new world.*"

She raised a finger. Thin black spikes, no thicker than a pencil's tip, shot upward from the floor, skewering everyone present, except the elder members, who remained fixed to their seats, helpless, eyes brimming with terror. As the first of the agonizing screams began, Martha's fingers flared, and each spike split into dozens of individual barbed spikes, which protruded from mouths, and eyes, and hearts, and lungs, and stomachs, the individual barbs caked with gore. They looked like grotesque, spiked scarecrows, their feet not touching the ground. People of all ages, from infants to old people, impaled to feed God with their delicious pain. Soon, save for a few weak choking sounds, gurgling from dying throats, there was silence.

"Kneel," Martha said to the ten elder members, who dropped to their knees, compelled by her mind control. "Face your deaths in adoration of our Lord."

"Mother, please!" Amber Bishop said. "We have always served the Lord the best we could! Have mercy! We are loyal! We have always been!"

Martha stepped down from the altar and walked toward Amber Bishop and her husband, Kai. "Why have you been loyal?"

"I'm sorry. I don't... I don't understand the question."

"What did you want from our Lord?"

"We..." She turned her head to her husband, who only returned a panicked expression. "We wanted prosperity for ourselves and our family, and...an eternity living within God's glory."

"Prosperity for your family," Martha said. "Your son is dead." She pointed and made them raise their bodies and turn to see their son, his wife and three children, black spikes coming from everywhere in their bodies, making them almost unrecognizable.

"Your line is dead." She lowered her hand, and they were back on their knees.

"Then it was God's will," Amber said in desperation. "But Kai and I have been faithful. We deserve—"

"Oh, you deserve…" Martha smiled, savoring the words. "What do you think you deserve?"

"We… we…" Amber screamed as Martha raised a finger and her husband's head was chopped off by a black thread that spun, whip-like, from the floor. The head rolled in front of Amber.

Martha could hear the commotion from the other kneeling sinners in the room. "What do you think you deserve for using God for your own benefit?"

"No, Mother, it's not like that! It's not—"

"Are you saying I, the messenger of God, am a liar?"

"No!"

"Am I unjustly accusing you?"

"No!"

"Then it's true that you're using God."

"Mother! I—"

A flick of Martha's finger, and Amber's head rolled. Her body went limp beside her husband's in a puddle of blood.

Martha walked toward the kneeling, weeping figures of Ethan and Emmalyn Garner.

"No! Please! Mother, please!" Ethan pleaded.

"What have you and your family contributed to the Circle, Ethan?" Martha asked. "It must have been so wonderful to win that bidding war for the land by the marina. Seaside Park, the boardwalk, the amusement park. Years of profit. What has been your contribution?"

"I... we..."

Flick.

His head flew off.

Emmalyn screamed desperate pleas of mercy. Her head was rolling on the floor shortly after.

Martha's bare feet left bloody footprints on the stone floor as she took each slow step, now approaching Reece and Lydia Holland, both of whom kneeled, whimpering and trembling, speechless with their foreheads touching the floor. She glared down at them. Looming over them. "Why didn't you bring Charles Cunningham, Reece? Lydia?"

"I went to his house," Lydia said. "He wasn't there. I..."

"So, you simply thought you'd done all you could and ran to safety." Lydia's head bounced off the floor with a *thunk* and rolled away. Martha turned to the beheaded woman's husband, who was now kneeling in a puddle of piss.

"Mother, I can go to the bar. I can kill Chuck for you. I can bring you his head! I can—"

The air he was using to speak pushed out a spurt of blood from the hole left by his head as it came detached from his neck. She noticed how the jaw and eyes were still moving slightly, as if trying to plead with a voice that no longer came.

"You should've had his head here by the time I arrived."

She continued to leave bloody footprints as she approached Carter and Mollie Booth.

Carter turned terrified eyes toward her. "Mother! Wait!"

"You're giving me orders."

"No! Never, Mother! I'm pleading for you to reconsider! My bank has been supporting the Circle since even before you became the Mother! We have been paying for everything the Circle has ever done! We've been supporting you financially!"

Martha's enraged eyes opened wide, the reflection from the torches making them appear like burning furnaces.

"We paid for your bail after your arrest in '93! We would've paid for all your legal needs if your sister and son hadn't pleaded for your charges to be dropped!"

"Money," Martha spat. "That's all you have to give. Your only worth. And you presume I valued these things you did for me. Like God wouldn't have provided for me if you weren't here. No, Carter. You were simply a means, a mechanism for God to work. If you hadn't been here, God would've found a way. So, you and your family profited for decades and all you have to show for it is that profit to come and throw in my face in a desperate plea for your life, now so devoid of value."

Carter's lips quivered, trying to form words, even as his head rolled away. His wife, Mollie, kept praying, trembling in fear.

"What about you, Mollie?" Martha asked. "Are you as worthless as your husband? Is money all you can offer?"

"God, please. I'm your faithful servant," she muttered. "Please heed my prayer. I've been loyal. I've served only you, Lord. Have mercy."

"God isn't listening, Mollie. I am His conduit. Only I speak to God. You not knowing that is pathetic."

Like all the others, Mollie Boothe's head rolled away, leaving a trail of blood as Martha advanced toward her last two victims, Judy and Sam Becker.

"Any words?" she asked, looking down at them.

Judy Becker turned her raging, reddened face toward her, then spat on her bare feet. "We will not beg, you bitch! You fraud!"

Martha raised an eyebrow, curious.

"We should've known," Judy continued. "We should've known when you didn't look for a replacement for Logan and Yvette Giffen! When you didn't replace the Rockwells after they left... After you killed them! The Circle was incomplete, but that didn't matter to you! You were never planning on letting the rest of the Circle live in God's new world. You used us! You're using our God for your personal benefit, yet come here to judge us for doing the same! Hypocrite cunt!"

"Judy, be quiet," Sam Rockwell said, cowering.

"Why?" she answered. "Why be quiet when she's going to kill us, anyway? She used us. She never cared about Dorothy Parham's teachings! This bitch is a lesser Mother, not worthy of that name! She's used us to do her bidding for years, when all she cared about was bringing us here, to this point, when she no longer needed us!"

"Judy!" Sam insisted. "Judy, please!"

Martha flicked a finger and the old man's head rolled.

Judy moaned with grief and anger. "You fucking bitch! You monster! Sam! Oh, Sam!"

"Keep going," Martha said with a subtle smile.

"Curling got the best of us thirty years ago because you were negligent, even though you lived right across the street from him! He died, but he won! He delayed us because you were blind. You were too proud to see he would try to kill Peter! You were too focused on torturing your son for the most menial things to see that Curling had to be dealt with! Peter only went into that house because you were careless! But no! Of course, Martha fucking Lange couldn't be at fault! It was Peter's fault! Right? You throwing him into that dirty crawlspace in your house was what got him taken away, putting everything at risk! But it was never *your* fault, right? Never your fault! You chastise us for enjoying God's blessings when you're using God for your own benefit, more than any of us! I see you!" Judy let out a long sob. "We served you loyally. We treated your son right, and you killed our son."

"Judy," Martha said, almost in a soothing voice. "Look at me."

Judy turned her bloodshot eyes toward her. Her face was wet. Snot ran down to her lips.

Martha smiled. "You are all dying because God deemed you unworthy. Only I am worthy of God's love. You basked in God's glow for as long as He allowed, but now it's time to pay your blessings back. Your son died because he didn't matter. He was irrelevant."

Judy's teeth peeled back, ready to curse at her, but Martha spoke first.

"Only my son matters," she said. "Only Peter matters."

With that, Judy Becker's head was separated from her neck, but not in a clean, perfect line like the others. The cut went diagonally across her jaw, cutting through her chin, her tongue, her upper teeth, her cheek, and over her ear, leaving a small portion of her head still attached to her neck, bleeding in gushes, a sliver of brain matter still held by a tiny concave of her lower skull.

"Your will has been carried out, Lord," Martha whispered, then closed her eyes. "Let the Third Night begin."

Freddie sat on his bed, looking around at the drawings and pictures in his room. The impatience inside him mixing with his frustration at having failed at killing Barry's children. The stupid oaf wasn't as stupid as he remembered. He'd figured out his one limitation. He could've risked it. Sure, Droopy Baker was dead, but he still had seven of the Vigilantes to pick from. He could've let Brickhouse slit his own throat, then watch him choke on his own blood as his beautiful critters tore his kids apart limb from limb before his dying eyes. He then remembered how angry Mother had been after he'd nearly fumbled the First Night for his carelessness and arrogance.

No problem. He would have all the time in the world to kill Brickhouse, his brats, and the rest of the Vigilantes once the Third Night kicked off.

Needing to vent his frustration, he stomped toward the easel, glaring at the canvas of Brickhouse's cul-de-sac. With a sneer, he slammed one corner on the floor and kicked it, breaking the frame in half. He kicked again, shattering it. Using the tip of a brush's handle, he stabbed the canvas, reached into the gash, and ripped it in two, tossing the ruined painting into a corner, like garbage.

"I take it your revenge on Barry Giffen didn't go so well?" the Mother's voice said, pulling a gasp from deep within his chest, as he dropped to his knees, embarrassed.

"Mother!" he blurted. "I'm sorry! I didn't see you there."

He regarded the figure before him, the way its form changed, morphed, and writhed; black worms creating this manifestation of her shape, and those empty eye sockets which stared deeper into him than actual eyes would.

"Your immaturity sometimes makes me question if I chose well, Frederick."

"Mother, I'm sorry if my failures have offended you. You granted me leave to kill Barry's family and I couldn't finish the job."

"They're meaningless to me," she said, her voice flat, menacing. "Stand up."

He did as commanded, and now, seeing her face to face, he recognized the slight differences in the threads that made up her form, and the ones he'd always seen. They seemed slower. Rougher. Like they had difficulty retaining their shape and color. "Have you already crossed to the Moonlit World, Mother?" he said with wonder in his eyes. "Permanently?"

She gave him a slow nod.

He let out a trembling breath. "Oh, I'm so envious, Mother. Forgive me for saying so."

The threads that made up her face formed a proud smile. "Fulfill your role to satisfaction, and you may join me here."

His breath caught. His eyes flitted to the shadows under his bed and back to Mother, and realized she'd caught this.

She motioned toward the spot he'd glanced at. "You should never use that. You're not allowed in the Inner Sanctum."

He bowed his head. "My sincere apologies, Mother. It was hubris on my part to even put that to the canvas. When God showed me the image, it was...so beautiful. I had to. Please forgive me. I know I'm not worthy."

"As long as we're clear," the form of the Mother croaked. "It's time." She reached with a morphing, distorting hand and put it on his forehead. "Leave Peter to me. You must deliver four lives of the Chosen Accursed to God. Do not let your arrogance get the best of you again, Frederick. You can move between doorways near them, but you are not untouchable during the Third Night." Leaving a black trail with her finger, she drew the Sickle of the Moon on his forehead. "Too much depends on you now. Do not fail me."

Freddie's eyes took on a determined sheen. He pressed his lips together and took a deep breath. "Yes, Mother."

CHAPTER SEVENTEEN
THE TOWN 2 – RUMBLING

Royce waded through the crowd that had formed around the tents now populating the hospital parking lot until he spotted Lillian at the head of one of the lines, under a tent, behind a long table, giving out supply packages along with other volunteers. Quickly, he moved people aside, making his way toward his wife, earning annoyed looks and calls of "Hey, no cutting!". He spotted his daughter standing beside her mom, handing her packages with a smile on her face, as if she hadn't seen what they'd all seen the previous night. The malleability of children never ceased to amaze him. It was, perhaps, a small mercy his little girl would remember it only as a bad dream—if at all—and not be traumatized by it. He hoped the same would apply for whatever was coming their way now.

"Lil," he said as he reached the supply table.

"Baby," Lillian said, surprised to see him there.

An old woman standing beside Royce with one of those granny carts in tow shot him a rather intense stink-eye and blurted, "Hey! What the hell do you think you're doing? Well, ain't that a nice thing? You people get a Black president, and suddenly you think it's okay to cut in line?"

Both Royce and Lillian turned wide-open eyes and hanging jaws at her.

"You heard me!" the old woman said.

Just short of shouting at her, Lillian grabbed one of the packages and slammed it on the table in front of the horrible old woman. "Here you go, Mrs. Grady! Now, scram!"

Indignant, Mrs. Grady took the package of canned foods, toilet paper, milk and other groceries and put it in the granny cart. She walked away mumbling unintelligible expletives and slurs.

Lillian looked at her husband, shaking her head, as if saying, "Can you believe this shit?"

"We need to get out of here, baby," Royce said, as his daughter crawled under the table and threw her arms around his leg. "Now."

Lillian frowned. "What are you talking about? I can't. Cooper's nowhere to be found. Even his family isn't picking up the phone, so I'm one of the few town officials around. I can't just leave."

"Lil, we can't stay. Remember what we talked about after what happened last night?"

She swallowed hard. He could see the horror of the memory still lingering in her eyes.

"Martha Lange took me and my friends to that altar. Sylvia figured out why. She's coming after us, and she won't hesitate to use you and Tracy to get to me."

"Oh god."

"Cunningham's is safe. We need to get there, quick."

She hesitated, her eyes moving from him, to the line behind him, to their little girl clutching his leg.

"Hey," a man behind Royce said. "Can we move this along? We have families to get to!"

Lillian glanced at him, looking conflicted. "I can't. These people need me. Take Tracy with you, but I have to stay here."

"I'm not leaving you here." He looked at the packages on the table, then the stacks of packages inside the tent. "Baby...when did you guys prepare these?"

Lillian blinked, looking at the packages on the table, not grasping what he meant. "They were, uh...they were ready this morning. Why?"

Royce felt a raindrop hit his forehead, then another hit his neck. "All this stuff didn't come from Harbor Grocers or Stockman's, then. Harbor Grocers was looted and burned. Stockman's is too small. This was all packaged and kept in town hall. You're the finance director. This would've been one hell of a huge expense. When was it made?"

The sound of raindrops hitting the asphalt with an arrhythmic *dap, dap, dap-dap* joined the growing murmur of people realizing it was about to rain.

Lillian's eyebrows came together at the center, in a knot. "The PO was finalized last week. We got these...earlier this week." She stared at him.

"Let me get this straight. You're saying Cooper Bishop ordered to buy supplies, medicine, all of this stuff to distribute to the townspeople in an emergency since last week and made sure it was ready and packaged before any of us had any idea an emergency was coming. Then, after last night's event—which none of us could've predicted—he recorded that message telling everyone to come here if they needed supplies or medical treatment, organized with y'all this whole operation, then he and his family disappeared."

"Royce, that's crazy." she asked, still struggling with the realization. "Why would he?"

"Let's go." Royce crouched to pick up his daughter, then taking Lillian's hand and pulling her around the table.

By now, rain was falling in a steady flow, and here and there he could see umbrellas pop up from those who had been smart enough to notice the weather today wasn't normal summer weather. Others tried to seek shelter under the tents, but there wasn't enough room for everyone.

"Why would he gather so many people here?" Lillian asked. "Royce? We should tell these people to leave!"

"Hey, where the hell are you going?" the man who had been standing behind Royce called. "Who's giving me my stuff?"

Lillian looked over her shoulder. "I... Tell everyone we have to get out of here!"

The man squinted at her, looking puzzled. The woman standing beside him took his hand and mumbled something inaudible, pointing at Royce. The look on both their faces was the same look Lillian had given him when she was remembering the horror of the previous night. She recognized him from the altar. The woman started walking, pulling the man—her husband or boyfriend, Royce assumed—along with her, and followed them.

They shouted for everyone around to leave, but the rain and the noise of the crowd made their voice not carry far.

Royce caught a glimpse of people rushing into the tent and starting a fight over the supply packages they'd left unguarded.

The rain became more intense. Thick raindrops, falling hard, with a vengeance, unrelenting, and above all things, cold. More umbrellas popped in the crowd as Royce and his family shouldered through the mass of people. Those without umbrellas used their jackets to cover themselves from the downpour.

"Royce, we *have* to tell them!" Lillian insisted.

"They won't believe us, Lil! Or worse yet, they'll recognize me from the altar and think we had something to do with it!"

He looked back. A few more people had joined them. Not nearly enough.

"What's going to happen?" she asked.

"I don't know! I don't think this is normal rain. We need to get outta here now! Where's the car?"

She pointed toward the edge of the parking lot, at the few parking spots that lined the street. Their Lunar Silver Metallic Honda Accord—as the man at the dealership had called it a million times the day they'd bought it—was parked parallel to the sidewalk. "There. I didn't want to park inside because of the crowd."

"Great."

"What do you mean this is not normal rain?"

"Did you see the ferry video?"

Her eyelids opened wide, green eyes radiating pure terror.

"It's the peak of summer, and it's pouring. I can't know it's the same, but we can't risk it!"

As they were reaching the edge of the parking lot, she stopped, pulled her hand away from him, stood there, soaked in rainwater. Her hair hung in long, thick curls from which water dripped rhythmically. "We can't leave these people here!"

"Baby, what do you want us to do? We have to..."

He trailed off as the ground started shaking. A low, bassy rumbling filled the air. Birds flew out of the trees, and Royce observed they made no noise other than the flapping of their wings. No calls, no caws, no peeps. *Just like when the Vanek House burned. Just like when Leroy died.* Light posts moved this way and that, tree branches swayed. The murmur of the crowd they'd left behind grew into a clamor. Fear, confusion, panic.

Earthquakes weren't uncommon on the west coast, in fact, most people were inured to them, but given everything they'd seen, that rumbling, that movement of the earth beneath their feet, as if they were nothing but ants on a dinner table, made Royce feel small, insignificant.

Tracy held her dad tight and cried. The small crowd that had followed them out of the parking lot—some twenty or thirty people—sped up, reaching the sidewalk, where he and Lillian had stopped.

In a blink, the four people at the tail end of their followers disappeared as the pavement caved in around them, followed by the entire parking lot, as a gigantic sinkhole formed. The simultaneous screams of almost five hundred people falling to the depths echoed through the air, then were drowned in the roaring sound of rolling earth, rocks, water, and pavement.

The small crowd around Royce screamed. Lillian brought a hand up to her mouth and buried her head in Royce's chest, throwing her arms around him and Tracy.

As the shrieks and moans of dying people rose from the depths of the hole, Lillian cried, "We were just there. We were just there!"

"The sky…" Royce said, mesmerized.

Two minutes later, the light disappeared from the world. They were enveloped in complete darkness.

Matilda Grady strolled away from that unpleasant couple of Negroes at the tent, who had been so rude to her. She was convinced she had done nothing but point out the entitlement their people seemed to display by cutting in line in front of her. What was she to do, as a warm-blooded American widow of a veteran? Let them? Hell, no! Her husband didn't fight to bring freedom to those commies in Vietnam—and she'd have a few harsh words with anyone who'd dared insist they'd lost *that* war—to have a couple of 'coons cut in line in front of her.

She stopped. It dawned on the ornery, racist old woman—words others used to refer to her—that she *was* the widow of a veteran, a senior citizen, and she *had* been disrespected by those two at the tent. Maybe, if she pushed a bit, wielding these facts, she might be able to get another package of groceries.

She turned, determination on her face. She took a step forward when the ground beneath her feet started shaking. *Just an earthquake,* she thought. Not the first and definitely not the last she'd experience in her life in the leftist-commie-ridden hellhole that was the west coast, so she pushed onward. A second free package of goodies was all that mattered.

Listen to them screaming, bunch of soft cowards! My Glenn put up with Charlie firing at him from all directions! They can't put up with the floor shakin' a bit!

Upon her second step, the ground beneath her dropped as if it had evaporated and she was falling straight down. She was so confused by this, she didn't have time to even scream. She'd barely opened her mouth in a gasp when she hit a slab of asphalt that had landed a millisecond before she did. Her legs hit the hard surface straight, and broke at the knees to either side, shins facing two different directions, her broken tibiae sticking out in spiked splinters from her skin. She managed a choked "Aagh!" before she fell forward and her hands were buried in the mud down the slope from the piece of asphalt, as she watched in utter bafflement how people, rocks, thick chunks of concrete, medical supplies, and all sorts of debris rolled down toward the center of the concave hole.

Something hit her upper back—a person, on account of the scream that accompanied the rolling mass—pushed her head down into the mud and continued rolling. She raised her muddy head to see a heavyset brown man in nurse's scrubs rolling further down, most likely the one who'd crashed into her. Soon he was buried under a landslide of mud and people.

She opened her mouth and let out a shriek that got lost in a sea of screaming humanity, as she felt a horrible burning pain in her arms, and turned her eyes down to see two ragged, bleeding stumps of meat where her hands used to be. The moment the man had slammed her back, he'd pushed the slab of asphalt down and forward, toward where her hands were buried in the mud, and its sliding edge had severed both about two inches above her wrists. She rolled on her back, lying on the slab of asphalt, legs broken.

She didn't scream for long, however, as a crate full of grocery packages came rolling and tumbling down the incline, crushing screaming people, gaining momentum as it went, loosening the earth even further, giving one big tumble before falling on Matilda Grady's head, and flattening it against the asphalt, before continuing its roll down the slope and breaking apart as it impacted the unfortunate people sinking into the large mud pool at the center. This last part was entirely missed by old Mrs. Grady, whose headless corpse was now swallowed by the coming landslide.

Nurse Kirkpatrick—Kiki to her friends—had spent half the night, all morning, and the afternoon so far freezing in this unusual cold in mid-July, taking blood pressure, heart rate, and temperature measurements from an endless line of people who were certain they were about to have a heart attack, or that they'd contracted some strange virus from "that other place" they'd all been taken the previous night. She hadn't even had enough time to process what she and the whole town had gone through, and she'd needed to deal with an onslaught of panicking people. And that's what most of them were: panicking. No high blood pressures, no concerning heart rates, no high temperatures, no symptoms other than heightened stress, fear, and anxiety. Sure, there had been a few who had chronic heart conditions that had worsened after the event. There were people with injuries from fights or accidents, burns, and broken bones, which she passed on to other nurses or doctors, but they were understaffed for a town-wide panic.

If she'd had a choice—like these people—after last night she would've locked all her doors and stayed inside, not come to a hospital to stand in a crowd, in the cold, to be told she was just anxious, being given a package of groceries and sent back home. She was miserable here. It didn't help it was raining now. Even though she was under the tent, the wind carried the raindrops inside, and the rain was freezing cold as it flew up her neck. *Should've brought a hoodie, not a cardigan,* she thought. *I'm gonna catch a cold. I'm sure of it.*

A man gave a gentle push on the back of a small boy of roughly eight, who, she could see, was having difficulties breathing. Seeing this was probably one of the real ones, she forced a smile and said, "Hey, champ, how are you today?"

The little boy, who seemed apprehensive, breathed in, and even in the rain and the crowd, she could hear the loud wheeze coming all the way from his bronchi. He turned tired brown eyes in her direction and said, "My asthma got really bad, and people looted all the inhalers from the dru—"

The boy stopped. The ground was shaking. The Earth rumbling. An earthquake.

Kiki, who had always been afraid of earthquakes, clung to the small desk in front of her, as if that would hold her in place.

The boy turned toward his dad and tried to put his arms around his waist, but before he could, there was no ground beneath them.

The world became a blurry mess of shapes flying in front of her eyes, sounds of things breaking, crashing, people screaming. Then there was immediate pain, and she felt as if she'd been cut in half. She didn't even have the strength to scream. She struggled to take in air as she realized she'd hit the edge of her desk, as they'd both crashed into the dirt below. The desk had pushed into her ribcage, breaking several of her ribs, and by the blood now coming from her mouth, she could tell her ribs had pierced something in her.

She hadn't even reached this full realization, when something crashed into her from behind, a body, or a person, which, unknown to her, had tumbled down the edge of the hole that had opened. The impact made the desk push deeper into her torso, and she let out a large spurt of blood through her mouth and nose. Despite the pain, the chaos, the noise, she could feel the person on top of her move. Whoever they were, they were alive. She was hit by another body, and another, and another, one after the other, piling weight on top of her. She realized she could no longer feel her legs, but she could feel the contents of her entire torso push up, since her broken ribs no longer served as protection.

Blood kept pouring from her mouth, a constant stream that ran down the short slope before her, reaching a body in front of her, sinking in the mud. It was the little boy, his hand sticking out toward her, fingers twitching, but he was clearly dead as a rock had obliterated half his skull in a mess of bone, brain, blood, and teeth. Further ahead was the dad's back; he was face-down, sinking into the mud, motionless.

Kiki tried to scream again, but her esophagus was now blocked by the contents of her entire body pushing up against it. Her fingernails dug into the laminate material of the desk as she turned her bloodshot eyes to the sky, from which rain fell without mercy, blinding her and washing the blood from her mouth. The dozens of people piled up behind her screamed as they all realized they were sinking into the mud. She could feel hands, legs, backs, heads pushing this way and that, trying to escape, slowly going quiet as the earth covered them all. Soon, she tasted the mud flowing into her mouth, entering her nostrils, covering her eyes.

The last minute of her life was spent in absolute darkness.

Louis Foley had received a strange message from Jess, urging him to come to Cunningham's and bring his mom with him. "It's safe here," she'd said. For a moment, he thought his boss had gone crazy. Why would he go to Cunningham's this early on a Saturday? Saturdays were always busy nights, so Jess always had him come in well into the night, when it got truly busy. Coming in at this hour meant him sitting around doing nothing. And what was that about bringing his mom?

Probably got drunk after that weirdness last night, he thought.

In either case, he couldn't go to the bar this early. His mom had sent him into the hospital parking lot crowd to bring supplies and groceries. She'd insisted on him telling the supplies people he didn't live with her—she gave him her driver's license—so they gave him one package for each. Like anyone in town would believe he didn't live in her basement. It was the one thing he was sure Blight Harbor had gathered about him from every neighbor and every bar customer.

He'd been standing in line for almost an hour, and now it was raining. His clothes were soaked. He craned his head to the right to see one of the tents had been abandoned by its staff, and people were rushing in to steal supply packages. Some people from his line ran toward it. *Buncha animals,* he thought, and stayed in line.

The ground rumbled, shook, and before he could get his head on straight, he was in freefall. A flash of a thought crossed his mind: it felt like that time he went to Six Flags Magic Mountain—a real amusement park, not the shithole in this town, that only had kiddie rides—and got on the Drop of Doom. That first second of his body at the mercy of gravity, falling, his legs going up in the air. The difference was, this time, he did hit the ground hard, rolled backward, broken legs flailing, hit several rocks, gave a tumble, did a full somersault in the air, then felt something push through his back. He expelled air from his lungs, then noticed the metal pipe sticking out under his sternum. His green shirt turned purple as blood soaked it.

Skewered on the spot, he looked up the slope to see an avalanche of earth, faces, limbs, and bodies rolling down to bury him.

Danae Wilkes was the last to fall. When the ground caved in, she'd been close enough to the edge of the sinkhole to reach out in a flailing panic and grab the first thing she could get her hands on. She'd been lucky enough to get her arms around a light pole, which had fallen in, but remained attached to its anchor points and the pipes that carried the electric cables.

She watched from this vantage point as hundreds of people fell to their deaths. Human bodies rolled down the hole, surrounded by earth, stones, and canvas tents still attached to their poles, in a maelstrom of death and chaos. Bodies got crushed by rocks and crates, as people were swallowed by the moving earth. There were broken limbs, broken necks, bodies flopping like rag dolls as rocks obliterated their bones. Children, even babies, sank helplessly into the ground, which moved like a living entity; their parents nowhere near to even try to save them.

Her dear Richard fell, crashed into a cluster of people, all of whom were enveloped by a muddy white tent, and rolled down the slope, carrying its screaming contents—*A people burrito*, she thought in a sudden bout of terror-induced hysteria—and getting lost in the mud and rain.

The center of the sinkhole—which comprised the entire diameter of the hospital parking lot—was an ever-growing pool of mud and wriggling bodies under the merciless rain. Their reaching hands looked like hundreds of worms in parasite-infested shit. The more it rained, the more the pool flooded. The more mud slid into it, the thicker the pool grew. The more people reached the center, the more arms joined the desperate movement, becoming part of the mass.

Then she saw something that, even in all this madness, made her further question her sanity. A clump of earth the size of a sedan sloughed off a nearby portion of the sinkhole, revealing something slick and black, slimy and scaly, almost like a fish or a snake's skin, but she felt deep within what she was seeing wasn't even a significant portion of the whole, the equivalent of the skin of a fingertip.

Fish and snakes don't have fingertips, she thought in her horror.

Then it moved. Just a little. The ground shook. More mud rolled down the sinkhole. The lamp pole fell about a foot more into the hole, its sudden movement shaking her grip loose. She clawed at it in desperation, but the luck that had allowed her to grab the light pole at first did not repeat, and her fingers brushed past the tip of the pole, and now she was rolling down the slope. She spun on her side, jerking screams issuing from her lips. She hit what might have been rocks, what might have been corpses, what might have been supply crates. Nothing stopped her on her way to her final doom, ready to become one more with the mass; one of the hundreds of worms wriggling in the mud. She felt the moment one or more of her ribs broke, then her left arm.

The roll slowed. Slowed. She stopped rolling and now she was sliding on loose dirt. Her eyes still pressed shut.

She came to a stop.

Trembling, lying face-down, pain surged through her upper arm and side. She could only grunt in agony, as her throat was too raw to scream. Glancing at the ground, she realized she'd landed on a flat, solid patch of earth. The rain still poured without mercy, but she was alive. She wasn't falling anymore.

Am I okay? she thought. *Is it over?*

The answer came as she once again noticed the din of desperate screams coming from right behind her, joined by a hand gripping her ankle, then another gripping her shin.

She turned onto her back to see a depiction of what nightmares in hell must look like. A mass of humanity, covered with mud that made them all look like a single entity, hands and shrieking faces reaching for her, people climbing over each other, sinking others under their weight for one last gasp of air, pushing the weaker down, men, women, children, pleading for help she couldn't give, as if she were the last remaining life vest in a sinking ship.

She found the strength to scream now, seeing the hands clutching her leg, trying to pull themselves up. They were pulling her in. She kicked and flailed with whatever remaining strength she still had in her, but it wasn't long before half her body had joined the mass of doomed people sinking in the mud. Moments before she sank, she saw, through the unforgiving rain, the way the sun disappeared, as if devoured by the black sky itself—an eclipse without an eclipse—and now, all that remained was darkness, rain, screams, hands pawing at her, bodies climbing over her toward a safety that no longer existed.

She couldn't see. She could no longer scream. Her mouth was in the mud, full of the thick, disgusting sludge. A hand pushed down between her shoulder blades. Now the mud was in her nose, her ears, her eyes. She tried to push herself up, but now there was nothing solid to support her hand on, no edge to grab onto. In the darkness, the surface seemed as if it were miles above her head. Miles of bodies to wade through for another gasp of air.

Impossible, she thought, reaching up with a hand to climb through the sinking crowd, only to feel someone's foot push it down. *Too far. Impossible.*

Barry stared out the second-floor window of Sylvia's hospital room at the horror outside. The unnatural rumble and crash that had come from the parking lot, followed by air-rending screams. He held Gabe close to his chest, while Daniel clutched his leg and cried, terrified by the earthquake and the sudden commotion.

"Jesus Christ!" Barry cried.

"What happened?" Sylvia said from the bed, but he was too stunned to respond. She held her stomach and grunted as calling out so loud had hurt quite a bit. "Barry! What the hell happened?"

He turned his head toward her. Eyes wide like saucers, mouth working to say something. "I... Oh god, Ray!" He pulled his phone from his pocket and fumbled to unlock it. He called his number, the phone rang once, twice, then...

The world around darkened. The lights in the room and all hospital appliances turned off at once. Daniel screamed, which prompted his brother to start wailing.

Static.

The phone ringing deteriorated into static, then cut off, but the phone was still on.

"Shit!"

Barry tried to dial again. No signal, no Wi-Fi, no mobile internet.

"Barry. The flashlight. Turn on the flashlight."

He fumbled with the phone again to find the flashlight app, and soon there was a small cone of light shining in the room. He placed the phone on a little table beside him, facing up so it illuminated the room. He could hear people screaming outside. "What the hell is going on?"

"It's starting," Sylvia said. "It started earlier than we thought. It's not like the last two nights. There's no connection, but the phone is on. That means devices with a battery are still working for now."

Barry went down on one knee and held Daniel close to his body. "There there, buddy, Daddy's here." He then looked at Sylvia. "How do you know that?"

Sylvia shrugged. "I'm guessing?"

"I need to go find Ray. There's a huge sinkhole outside! All those people in the parking lot... they're..." He looked down at his son, then shot a terrified glance at Sylvia.

"Oh crap," she said.

"I don't know if Ray was out there!" His breath caught in his throat, desperation showing in his face despite his best efforts to remain calm for his children. "What if he was out there?"

All four jumped, startled, as the door opened. At first, all they saw was a phone flashlight moving into the room. Soon they realized it was Ray in his blue hospital scrubs, holding his phone in one hand.

Barry put a gentle hand on Daniel's shoulder to nudge him away a bit to stand up. A second later, he had his free arm around Ray, and Ray had his arms around him and Gabe. Barry kissed him, relief on his face. "Oh God, I thought—"

"I *was* out there. I stepped back in to come and check on all of you for a quick minute when the earthquake happened."

Barry motioned toward the window. "Did you see…"

Ray nodded. "It's chaos out there."

"We need to get out of here. We need to get Sylvia and the kids out of here."

Ray looked around the room. "I have to stay here. People are hurt. We were understaffed to begin with, and a lot of hospital staff fell into that hole, and the few that remain here are—"

"Listen!" Barry's voice was firm. "I get that, but the other nurses and doctors won't have Martha Lange and Freddie Parham coming for them specifically, like us. I told you what Syl found out." He could see the conflict in Ray's face. "We can't stay here. We need to get to Cunningham's, where they can't reach us. If you stay here, you'll be a sitting duck!"

"Barry, I…"

"No! Screw that! I can't lose you again! This is bigger than all of us. You staying here won't help when that Third Night thing hits in full. It will only ensure you die." He put a hand on the back of Ray's head and pulled him in for a loving kiss, then repeated, "I can't lose you again."

Ray hesitated for another moment, pressed his lips in a straight line, then gave a single nod. "Okay. We can't go through the front door. It's a mess there. People are panicking. Back door had been closed to ensure patients went through the triage tents before coming into the hospital, so only people with actual emergencies came in. Our best bet is going down two floors, to the basement. It leads to a ramp where supply trucks come in. We can get out through there." He turned to Sylvia. "We need to be careful with you. You're still technically fresh out of surgery. This is incredibly dangerous in your state. If you pop your stitches, that would be..."

"Bad," Sylvia said, pulling the gun from under her pillow. "Got it. Let's get outta here."

CHAPTER EIGHTEEN

AWAKENING

Mother's fingernails dug into his wrists like the pointed teeth of a moray eel. They were in their old house, but the hallway between the living room and the kitchen went on and on, appearing endless. He was an adult, which did not match the setting—Peter hadn't lived in that house since he was thirteen.

Or was it sixteen? he thought. *I think a couple days ago I thought sixteen. Why did I think sixteen? My mind gets foggy like that sometimes. Thirteen. It's thirteen. Why am I here?*

The bite of those fingernails brought his attention to the woman in front of him, pulling him along by his wrist, which was now covered in blood. Mother looked the right age for the setting. She was in her forties, but so was he.

"I saw you!" she said, rage coming out as spit from her lips. "I saw you with those other boys from school! Riding on their bicycles! You were with those filthy boys, with their dirty mouths, and whores for mothers!"

"I'm sorry, Mother!" he pleaded.

"Disobedient son! Disappointing son!" She continued pulling him behind her. Each step made her fingernails drive themselves deeper into his skin. He could see rivulets of blood running from the puncture wounds. "How many times do I have to tell you? God doesn't want you speaking to them! They're filthy! They're beneath you!"

"I'm sorry, Mother!" He was weeping, despite himself. He couldn't control it. "I won't do it again, Mother!"

I hate you, Mother... No! No! I can't hate my Mother! It's wrong to hate one's Mother! It's not her fault she's like that. It's that religion of hers. It's the Alzheimer's. It's dad abandoning us. It's—

(*Angie's dead, and you're still making excuses for your mother?*)

"Get in there!" she commanded, and he realized she was standing in the pantry, holding the trapdoor open. "Obey!"

Not The Hole. Please!

(*Don't go down there don't go down there don't go down there don't—*)

"I don't want to, Mother, pl—"

She slapped him across the face.

He saw things down there. Down in

(*The Hole*)

the crawlspace of their old home. There was a river of vermin, of insects, of crawling things with wings, and legs, and mandibles. A river running at full speed, waiting to drown him the moment he set foot inside.

His heart raced with terror, his legs weakened, tears rolled down his face. A few drops of blood from his wrist fell into The Hole, and when they hit the river of vermin, the critters became excited, frenzied. He was shaking with fear. His fists were clenched white.

"Please, Mother, don't make me."

Whispers rose from The Hole—gossip and rumors—every whispered word from every person who'd spoken about him in his life, especially after he'd been taken from Mother. Every condemnation from Nadine, and every person who blamed him for what was going on. Then, from the cacophony, rose his own Mother's disembodied voice, repeating words she had spoken before.

"*He promised He'd bring you back to me.*" His mother's voice played around in his head, and in a blink, her face filled his entire field of vision. Her fingers clasped, claw-like, the sides of his head. Her eyes were black caverns, and she grinned insanely. She spoke. Her voice fanatical, orgasmic, unhinged. "*The bitch is dead, your boy will be devoured, and God will bring you back to me. God will bring you back to me. His Glory will be upon the world, and I will rejoice with my son by my side.*"

He looked at Mother. She wasn't the one speaking. The voice came from The Hole.

"*It starts tonight, boy! It starts tonight!*"

The blackout. Mother had been right. The blackout had been that specific night. It had all started that night. Then, Angie. What was coming next? He didn't know. He didn't want to know.

"*You will come back to me. God has promised.*"

"No," Peter mumbled, trying to push his mother away, trying to remove her fingernails from his head, the pain of them burrowing into his skin, into his scalp, scratching his skull.

"*God will bring you back to me.*"

He was falling now.

The mouth of The Hole widened to devour him, and soon he was enveloped by the river of insects and rats and spiders, screaming in desperation. Blight Harbor's whispers and Mother's words repeating in his mind.

"The bitch is dead, your boy will be devoured, and God will bring you back to me."

"Mother, please!"

"God will bring you back to me."

"Please, help me!"

"His Glory will be upon the world, and I will rejoice with my son by my side."

"Mother, help me!"

"You will come back to me. God has promised."

"I'll do anything. Please! Please, help me, Mother!"

Peter sprang up in bed. "Anything, Mother!" He sat, confused. His chest heaved. Terror clutched his heart. He could still feel Mother's fingernails digging into his scalp.

The surrounding darkness felt almost solid.

Did I sleep through the afternoon?

He could hear rain outside, a real downpour he wouldn't have expected this time of year. It was freezing cold, too. He reached for the lamp on the nightstand and flicked the little switch on it. It didn't work. *Strange.* He pawed around the nightstand for his phone, then remembered he'd dropped it all the way on the other side of the bed. He groaned with annoyance, but then his fingers touched something slim, rectangular. *The TV remote.* He pointed it across the room and pushed the power button. The TV wouldn't come on either. *Are the batteries dead?* he thought, as he slapped the remote hard against the mattress like a dumb caveman and tried the button again.

Nothing.

Blindly, he slid his feet inside his slippers, which were always on that particular spot by the bed, where he could find them in the dark.

They felt damp.

What the...

Peter stood up. Took his first step. As he put his weight on it, the floor beneath his right slipper made a loud, out-of-place *creak!* He stopped cold. Last he checked, an expensive ceramic tile floor didn't go *creak!* It felt somewhat uneven, as well, almost like old wooden boards that had shifted, narrowed, and bent with age and moisture, leaving a small space in between.

That's crazy. What the hell's going on?

With worry and confusion boiling up inside him, he ran around the bed, toward where he knew the door was, and beside it, the light switch—

Creak! Creak! Creak! Creak! Creak! Creak!

—and, when he flicked the switch with his forefinger, the light didn't come on. *Must be another blackout,* he thought with alarm. *Should've been obvious when the lamp didn't work.*

His attention was called by a single, tiny red light in the ceiling, only a little red dot. It took him a moment to understand what it was. The smoke detector was working. So, electricity was out, but perhaps not like the previous nights. *Smoke detectors use batteries, so, maybe my phone...*

He hurried toward the bed—

Creak! Creak! Creak! Creak!

—looking for his phone. When he went down on his knees, he used the bed to support himself, and the bedsheets crinkled like paper. He pulled his hand back, mystified, afraid to touch it again, as if it had grown teeth.

What the hell's going on?

He ran his hands over the floor, searching for the spot his phone had fallen, and confirmed what he was now touching was indeed rough wooden boards, long planks with a small space between them, and they felt damp and slippery, as if coated with mold. A wave of relief washed over him as he touched a slick rectangle that didn't seem to fit with any other texture in this room.

He turned the phone toward him, and its motion detection turned on the lock-screen clock. The time on the screen made no sense. It was 2:07 p.m.

He raised his eyes toward the general area where the open windows should be. Only blackness. The implications of it being two in the afternoon were terrifying beyond words. For it to be this dark, the sun itself would've had to stop existing altogether. No stars to speak of either. It was so dark, even the light from the screen felt dim. It lit up nothing but his hand, as if whatever evil had made the sun disappear were actively feeding on any source of light, letting it shine no further than an inch.

He unlocked the phone, tapped on it until he found his flashlight app. A white cone of light flooded the room, temporarily blinding him. Though, just like with the light from the on-screen display, the flashlight felt diminished somehow, lighting only a few feet before him. When his eyes adjusted, he could only wonder if he was really awake, or still asleep and having nightmares. The world before his eyes spat in the face of reason.

His room was made of moldy old wood. There was damp, yellowed-out newspaper draping every wall, even the large windows, which were boarded up beneath the paper. The bed, the bedside table, the lamp, the remote, the desk, the chair, even the TV screen on the wall, were wrapped in newspaper as well, even though he'd just been lying on his bed, and touched the remote, and they'd felt perfectly normal. All over the walls and the ceiling were black tendrils, like thin tentacles, strewn across the entire surface, like crawling vines converging into a puddle at the center of the ceiling. Drops of dirty water dripped from the wooden boards above, giving the room its soaked, waterlogged look, as if he were exploring the inside of a sunken ship that had been pulled to the surface.

The damp, pungent smell of piss and shit hit him out of nowhere, almost overwhelming. It made a sensory memory appear in his mind's eye, reminding him of the day he'd realized his mother needed to be hospitalized.

After years, he'd determined he'd bring Jenny to meet Mother, despite Mother's insistence she would refuse to see or talk to her. The moment Peter opened the door, he was overwhelmed by a smell that almost stabbed his nostrils. The house was a mess of garbage and filth. Mother was in her sleeping gown, sitting in front of a long-extinguished fireplace, with her book—the Uolminar—resting on her lap, and even from where he and Jenny stood, covering their mouths and noses, eyes open wide in horror, they could see her hands and legs were caked in feces.

Mother turned and noticed him, smiled at him. She looked emaciated, skeletal, pathetic; her smile like a death's grin. She whispered his name with joy and raised her open arms toward him, as if waiting for a hug. Peter could now see the recent dampness of piss soaking the front of her gown, the fecal handprints on what used to be white fabric, and her filthy legs.

Just as she was about to take a step toward him, she noticed Jenny, and her face changed, a glimmer of understanding flashing in her eyes as her face contorted in a hateful scowl. Her hands, which were open for an embrace, curled into claws and she ran toward her, howling, "WHORE! BITCH!" The effort, however, was too much for her frail, malnourished state. She stopped, swayed on her feet, eyes lost, confusion on her face, and she fell to the floor.

She'd been hospitalized in geriatric care since that day.

Peter took a step back, and there was a *creak!* in response, bringing him back from the memory, mocking him and whatever sense of reality he still had left.

This is the Vanek House, he thought, realizing at once this thought made no sense. *The Vanek House is in my room.*

The puddle in the ceiling grew outward, tendrils crawling over tendrils to bring form and texture to the charcoal-black shape quickly growing, until what he was staring into was an enormous head, almost the diameter of his king-sized bed. It was—

"Mother!" he cried in horror.

The figure had no eyes, yet he could feel it staring down at him. Staring in anger, judgment, and disappointment. Dwarfing him with its size and presence, as if its very existence had weight and gravity. It opened its monstrous mouth wide, its jaw dislodging, like a snake's, and in a booming, cavernous voice it said, "God will bring you back to me!"

With a scream that emptied his lungs, Peter turned and ran out the door, slamming it shut behind him, even as the creature's voice continued to repeat that terrible phrase.

"God will bring you back to me!"

Peter stood with his back to the door, then, almost as if its surface were red-hot, bounced off it, turned to look at it, picturing the monster crashing through, chomping on him with its black teeth, then swallowing his mangled body. He took short, ragged breaths, his breath coming out in a cloud through his mouth. He examined the door, which looked nothing like the one he knew. It was old, wooden, unpainted, covered in mold.

Hesitating, feeling a lump in his throat, he turned the flashlight to the right to examine the hallway. It had exactly the same look as the bedroom. All the pictures and paintings hung crooked from rusted nails in the newspapered walls and displayed only smudged paint or distorted imagery. Illustrations trying to be faces or landscapes and falling apart before being complete.

He forced himself to walk forward, followed by the unceasing creak of the floorboards, and noticed all doors in the hallway were papered over, so he'd have to rip the newspaper off them if he wished to open them. He had no intention to lay a hand on that moist filthy paper, though.

I have to get out of this house, find the others.

He hurried toward the stairs, his flashlight barely lighting the opposite end of the hallway. The rickety creaking of his steps filled the atmosphere. The stairs themselves were also made of old wood. The banister at the top and the railing were gone, the way he remembered the stairs at the Vanek House not having a railing. *But it's not like that. Not really. The layout is exactly like my house but changed into this weird Blight Harbor imitation of the Vanek House.* From the second-floor vantage point, he moved his phone flashlight around and confirmed the front hall also had the same grotesque decor as the rest of the house.

His breath caught the moment he looked at the front door—what he hoped would be his way out. There was another black shape, the size of the one in his bedroom, protruding from the high wall above the door, just visible from this distance in the dark.

With careful steps, Peter moved down the stairs, each step more careful than the previous. Soon, he got a clearer view of the thing above the front door. It was his mother's face, but enormous, empty eye sockets directed at him, staring, unmoving. Unlike the creature in the bedroom, this one didn't speak, it only stared.

The lower part of the head, which stretched into a web of intertwined black threads, split in two and stretched down, making it look like curtains attached to the lower corners of the doorframe. It was an eerie sight, like some sort of sentinel or guardian of the front door, like it was able to see everything from that place high above. It could certainly see *him*. Somewhere, in the part of his brain that tried to process this insanity before his eyes, he thought the face was squinting at him, the way Mother did when she knew he'd done something bad. That disapproving stare.

He didn't take the flashlight's beam from the face above. It turned to follow him in silence as he stepped down. He sensed as soon as he reached the bottom that thing would descend like a bird of prey and bite him in half, but when he reached the bottom, it didn't move. It hung there, looming above him with its unnerving scowl. Staring. Disapproving. He knew he had to get to the door, but that thing—

That goddamned thing!

—was up there, staring him down with empty eye sockets.

He felt as if it was daring him: "*If you want to get out, you'll have to go through me, boy.*"

He had to get out. He had no choice. He stalked toward the front door, a rectangle of old wood surrounded by filthy, newspapered walls, and of course, that thing, up there, following his movements with its judgmental stare, ready to come down and envelop him in its cavernous mouth, as soon as he got under it.

With disgust, he reached toward the folds of black, intertwined threads to move them away. His eyes darted upward toward the staring monstrosity, and with caution, peeled the black "curtain" with the arm holding his phone, just enough to slip through. His other hand gripped the doorknob, and as he peered down, his stomach tightened. Through the gaps in the floorboards, he glimpsed water lapping at the house's foundations, as if it were standing on pilings over what should've been solid ground. Instead, it was a watery abyss that seemed to stretch forever down. Horrifying whispers rose from beneath. The sustained chattering of incessant, unintelligible voices.

Shaking the fearful thoughts out of his mind, he turned the knob.

A woman's blood-curling scream cut through the foyer like an expertly sharpened butcher knife through raw, bloody meat, stopping Peter cold before he could open the door. He spun toward the doorway to the dining room, his heart pushing against his ribcage like a battering ram.

Doris! he remembered, as another scream slashed through his ears—this one was cut short, sudden, gurgled. He darted to his right, through the doorway at the foot of the stairs, into the dining room. The chandelier above the table had become an entangled mess of black threads. The furniture looked ancient, moldy, covered in grime. Large swaths of blood and excrement were smeared across the already disgusting wallpaper, like random brushstrokes.

Black threads dangled from the ceiling like vines in the jungle, swaying and sticking to his hair and clothes as he barreled through.

Peter couldn't dwell on these things. He rushed into the kitchen, where every appliance was now rusted and streaked with blood. He stumbled his way around the center island. Its once polished metal top was covered in dark, bloody smears, and water damage. Rusted pots and pans dangled from the overhead rack, like remnants of an old forgotten civilization. Outside, only pitch-black shadows filled the windows, dense and impenetrable, as if the glass had been painted over.

Past a small interstitial space they used as a laundry room, Doris's bedroom door lay ajar. Everything was eerily silent, except for the sound of the rain, and the lapping of water and whispers that came from the darkness below.

Is she dead? What if she's dead?

Peter grabbed a rusted knife from a wooden block on the island, paying no attention to the other empty slot on the knife block, and started taking slow, tentative steps toward the laundry room, which led to the service room, so slow, the creak that accompanied his footsteps was barely audible. He stopped, stalled for a few seconds as he was one step away from the bedroom door, then peered inside.

Doris, his maid for over a decade, was sprawled on the floor, dead, lying face-down at the back of the room. Her face was turned to the left and her right cheek was squished against the baseboard. Her left arm was limp, close to her torso, and her right arm was propped up against the wall, as if she'd slid down the wall with her arm raised as she died. There was a knife driven through the back of her neck, and it came out of her mouth, splitting her lips and tongue in two. Her one visible eye showed but one emotion: stark, consummate terror.

Peter brought a trembling hand up to his mouth, and he felt his eyes moisten, his knees become weak. He wondered who could've killed poor old Doris in such a savage manner?

You know who, his own thoughts answered.

He stepped further into the room, not noticing a shadow that had scuttered across the kitchen behind him. He noticed, in the hand raised against the wall, she held something that looked like a red crayon, but dull-colored, like chalk. From it, an uneven line of bright red ran across the wall—which, he observed, was not covered in newspaper. It was a regular white wall. In fact, this entire room looked like Doris's room, unaltered. He followed the red line up until it reached a large mirror on top of the old woman's dresser. She had drawn a strange symbol on the mirror, which he'd never seen. It looked like an upside down cross with a diagonal line across the top, and at either side, two small circles joined by a large concave line, with smaller lines on either side. It almost looked like a strange balance of sorts. Smaller individual runes and symbols were drawn around it.

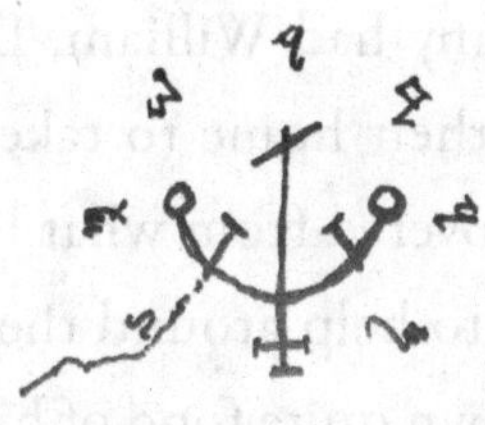

What's this supposed to be? he thought, remembering Mother's old book and the strange scribblings in it. Doris had been killed as she was drawing it, from the looks of it, but by whom? *Or by what?*

"Oh, Doris," he said with a rueful sigh. "I'm so sorry."

There was an open book on the dresser, where he noticed the same symbol—or a version of it, without all the surrounding smaller symbols—at the top of one of the pages. Beneath the symbol, the page read:

ABARIEL

One of the dukes of daylight, beneath Usiel in the infernal hierarchy,

as per the Ars Theurgia. Can be invoked to conceal or to reveal.

Despite being a duke of daylight, Abariel is one of the regents of the Moon, able to cast protections or bring forth that which the power of the Moon has kept hidden.

"The moon," Peter mumbled under his breath.

Strange symbols and books on infernal entities didn't seem to fit the image of the Doris he knew. He remembered the kind, motherly person she had been in life, always there when they'd needed her. After Jenny had William, Doris had moved out of White Harbor to their home to take care of her day and night, until Jenny recovered from what had been a complicated labor, then stayed to help around the house until William turned four. She'd grown quite fond of his son, and had always pampered and cared for him, almost to the point of spoiling him. He remembered there was never a moment in the day in which the woman was too stressed or tired to offer a smile.

She was dead now. Lying on the floor like nothing but a sack of meat, with a knife stuck in the back of her neck all the way through to her mouth.

Peter was pulled from his thoughts and his mourning for the old woman by a sound: playful giggling. It could've even been considered cute, had he not heard it in this surreal version of the house. In this darkness that numbed the senses, in the face of all this horror, all this blood, that sound didn't fit. It sent chills up his spine and made his skin crawl. Then it was there again: a giggle, followed by some wordless, childish exclamation.

He turned around slow. Sweat formed small beads on his forehead. His jaw was clenched tight, as were his fingers around his phone in his left hand and the rusted knife in his right. He faced the door, shining the flashlight toward the space that separated the kitchen and Doris's room. There was nothing but hanging, dirty clothes, rusted shelves with detergent and softener containers, and a washer-dryer that looked like it had spent a hundred years in a swamp. He was sure he'd heard it. It had to be there.

Peter wasn't aware of just how right he was. The source of the unnerving sound had been right behind him all along, except not in the direction he was looking.

It was above him.

CHAPTER NINETEEN
CHILD'S PLAY

Crawling along the ceiling, unheard and unseen by Peter, the thing moved as easily as it would crawl on the floor, like a lizard. It crept toward the back of the room, past Peter's head, until it reached the opposite wall, positioning itself above Doris. It started creeping down the wall toward the kind old woman's corpse. Its thin, bony, blackened hand got hold of the handle of the knife that had killed her. It started twisting and pulling it, trying to dislodge it from the back of her neck.

There was a low, revolting sound from behind him. It was a thick, wet, gut-wrenching noise. There should've been nothing behind him that could make that sound, only Doris, still and lifeless.

He felt the hairs on the back of his neck prickle. Something was behind him. No doubt about it anymore. He turned, half-expecting Doris to be standing behind him, risen from the dead, pulling the knife out of her mouth so she could cut him to pieces for an easier meal (weren't the undead supposed to feed on the flesh of the living, after all?).

There was something behind him, but it wasn't Doris in all her resuscitated, cannibalistic splendor.

It was something much worse.

It was a boy, or something that looked like one. It had no eyes, just two black, empty eye sockets, no mouth. It was naked, emaciated, and bony, except for a bloated belly, like what you'd see in malnourished children in documentaries—when the body retains fluid from starvation. It had no hair on its entire body, save for some isolated strands of black hair on its head, and it was so pale its skin was nearly transparent, showing the veins underneath. It was down on all fours like a dog, and in one hand it held the knife it had pulled out of Doris. Then, in the place where its mouth should be, a small puncture appeared, and it started spreading to the sides, forming a growing slit, which then opened into a wide, black-toothed grin, from which a mischievous, childish giggle poured forth. It sounded amused and playful; it felt sickening and wrong.

Peter staggered backward. A minuscule squeak escaped his lips. His eyes were so wide open it felt like his eyelids would recede behind them and push them out of his face. Every nerve on his back shot electrical impulses, tingling and chilling sensations running up and down his spine, none resulting in the desired response of running away.

His mind was soon flooded by the memories of the horrors he'd seen inside the Vanek House almost thirty years earlier. All of those sights he kept pushing down, trying to deny, trying to explain away, trying to make little of. Even the events of the previous two nights hadn't yet pierced through the mental barriers he'd installed, the failing dam he'd built between himself and Blight Harbor for the sake of his sanity. None of his excuses mattered in the face of the abomination before him.

As the monster pushed its torso up with its hands on the floor, he thought he espied something, faded and hard to make out in full, near its chest area. A blueish discoloration that, at first, looked like a bruise, but soon made him gasp in disbelief as he recognized—

Bluey...

—the blue cartoon dog he'd seen on the T-shirt of the child crying in that street corner next to his fainted mother. The image was stretched, distorted, an almost invisible blob, but once he noticed it, he couldn't unsee it. It *was* Bluey.

He felt a tiny giggle rising up his throat, into his mouth, pushing against his lips and his clenched jaw. He slapped a hand over his mouth. He refused to let himself giggle at this, because a giggle would become laughter, and when laughter came from terror, it had a different, more alarming significance.

Somehow, that little boy was in his house, and had been transformed into this obscenity. It was bigger than the boy, though, like his limbs and bones had been stretched and become skinnier.

Every inch of Peter's body quivered in fear. In anticipation of the horrible death he would surely suffer at the hands of this creature, because he couldn't move. *No! It's not here. That creature isn't here. It can't be! I'm still asleep. This creature doesn't exist. It can't exist! Please let it not exist. Please let this whole thing be a dream!*

It moved toward him, on hands and feet, its mouth had once again vanished.

Peter was frozen in place under terror's icy grip. The enormity of the situation paralyzed him. It was everything: the transformation of his house, the gigantic black Mother heads, Doris's death, and now this thing. It hit him all at once. All of it shoved in his face in one merciless blow. He couldn't move.

The thing crawled toward him, eyeless, mouthless, deadly.

His body refused to react. It was betraying him, serving him on a silver platter for the monster to kill him without him being able to defend himself. Then it was right in front of him. The awful grin drew itself again across its face; childish giggles issuing from it.

Then it attacked.

A thin, horizontal crimson line was drawn across Peter's chest, as a straight opening formed in his green shirt. Blood stained the fabric in a growing cascade that stretched down to his belly.

The message finally reached his brain: this was real. The blood, the warmth of it, that tingling as it slid down his skin. He was awake. This was real. He was going to die unless he moved, and at last he did.

He stumbled back into the kitchen and ran to the back door. It wouldn't budge. In desperation, he slammed his shoulder against it, taking advantage of it being rotten and decrepit in this bizarre version of his home. The door burst outwards. He stopped short, arms braced against the frame, as outside the door there was nothing but water. An endless polluted ocean, stretching as far as the eye could see. The tips of pines in the distance poked through the surface under the driving rain, like remnants of a drowned civilization.

I'm at the top of a mountain. That's impossible.

Then he noticed the dark-blue moon, glowing in the pitch-black sky. Pregnant rain clouds flew in front of its dim glow, their water breaking.

He stood there gawking a minute too long, as the monster leaped from behind and grabbed on to his back. He bent forward, fearing for a moment they would both fall into the water, and he'd drown in the depths. He staggered back into the kitchen.

The sharp blade of the knife was just touching his throat, making a thin cut that was reddish but didn't bleed. Peter got his phone hand between him and the creature's knife arm and tried to push it away, but the monster was surprisingly strong. Peter screamed, shrieked in a panic. He stumbled through the kitchen, banging his back against walls and shattering deteriorated cabinets. He shook, fought, but the thing was still on his back. He tottered around the center island, and threw himself backward against the pantry door, which swung open, but didn't break. He fell on top of the child monster, pinning it to the floor with his back. It kept trying to slit his throat. Its invisible mouth reappeared to let out a bellow, which rightfully belonged to a child having a tantrum, and then disappeared again.

He'd dropped the phone as he fell, and it was now lying on the floor, flashlight shining toward the ceiling, bathing the pantry in dim light, casting fleeting amorphous shadows as their arms or legs broke through the cone of light. Then he remembered the knife, the rusted knife he'd picked up in the kitchen. It was still clutched in his right hand. He started stabbing backward over his shoulder with it, trying to stick it into the creature's face, while holding its arm with his other hand to keep it from stabbing him. He was screaming in both fear and rage now. The monster kept moving its head to all sides, dodging the knife while still trying to slice Peter up.

He stabbed backward once again and felt the thing squirm behind him on the floor. Knowing he'd hurt it, he scrambled to stand from the ground and turned to face what he'd expected to be a dead monster. He'd driven the knife right on the spot where the mouth should've been but hadn't killed it. It was bleeding, but not much.

The monster then brought itself up on all fours, the knife still sticking out of its face. Then the mouth started appearing again around the knife and Peter was frustrated to find now the thing was holding the knife between its teeth, which were clenched around the blade in the most alarming rictus he'd seen in his life. It only had a slight cut on its lip.

The child creature pulled the knife from its mouth with its free hand and—

Shit!

—it now had two knives. Peter walked back a few steps, sensing the monster tightening its muscles, ready to pounce on him and slash him to death.

It leaped!

Peter moved back with a scream and slammed the door shut. A second later, the monster crashed against it, then pounded on it with unrelenting fury. While the door might look like old, rotten wood, it was holding, for now. He could already feel it splintering, and tiny holes forming through which he could see the faint light from his phone. If the creature broke through, it would be screaming time all over again.

He had an idea.

While still holding the door shut, Peter reached toward the metal grating fixture where the pots and pans hung. He knew it was right behind him, even if it was too dark for him to see. He felt around for the heaviest pan he could find until he felt the cast-iron skillet.

He let go of the door, brandishing the rust-covered skillet with both hands. The moment the glow of the phone's flashlight filtered through and widened as the door opened, he swung the skillet with all of his strength, hoping to hit something. He hit the demon square in the face.

It was still alive, though.

Without hesitation, Peter walked into the pantry, stood over the dazed child creature, grabbed the handle with both hands and started beating down on its head, over and over. He screamed in some sort of panic-induced primal rage as heavy iron rained down on the demon boy's head, which cracked open like a smashed egg.

Black and red blood trickled down through the spaces between the floorboards, down into the dark waters.

Peter panted with exhaustion, still trying to make sense out of a world that mocked the very concept. He picked the phone off the floor, then pried one of the knives from the child monster's hand and trudged back into the kitchen.

Everything around him was quiet now, save for those horrible whispers emanating from beneath the floor, and the sound of the rain outside. The whispers had gotten louder though, but he couldn't make out words. He felt like covering his ears, but didn't. He was certain that sound would be there for as long as he remained in this hellish version of his house and he couldn't spend the whole time with his hands over his ears, especially not with things like this monster walking around.

He felt lightheaded, pins and needles all over his skin, ants crawling up and down his body and all over his brain. The pain in the cut across his chest burned without mercy. He shambled toward the kitchen door, and as he passed by the refrigerator, he was overcome by a strange irrational curiosity. He regarded the fridge, almost like it was calling him.

(*Open me!*)

He could picture the shelves filled with packets of maggot-infested meat, and a stench worse than any he had ever smelled; and black, decomposed blood dripping to the floor. He could picture the movement of the maggots on the meat, biting holes into the plastic and slurping on the aged blood that pooled at the bottom.

He felt nausea, imagining what the smell and sight of it would be like.

His gaze was rapt by the refrigerator door, which kept begging him to open it.

Tears built up in his eyes, and he felt his knees give. No matter how horrifying the events at the Vanek House had been, he'd never truly let them in. They'd gone to the other side of the Blight Harbor dam, never to be thought of or considered, but *this...* this was too much. Putting the last few nights and what he was going through now on the other side of the dam would make it spill over the rim. Too much, too quick. Before he was aware of it, he was lying on the floor, sobbing, hugging himself in a fetal position.

"This isn't happening. Please, God, this can't be happening."

The cracks on that poorly maintained dam were spreading, crisscrossing, spiderwebbing; pressured jets of liquid darkness geysered through the holes, flooding his mind.

"God, help me, somebody help me. Help me!"

He shook, shuddered. Spasms ran all over his body as the adrenaline released during the fight against the monster drained itself from his system and shock settled in.

"Help me! Please, help me!"

All of a sudden, in his mind's eye, he was back in The Hole, back in the dark space, with cockroaches and other vermin crawling over him, over his face, and getting into his mouth when he opened it to scream. He stretched his arms up, and he could feel the underside of an invisible floor, the floor that had always been there when he had been trapped under the house, in the darkness, his own home turning into his coffin. The suffocation, the cold, and the desperation coming back to him. The dam was breaking, the threat of a ravaging flood.

"HELP ME! PLEASE, HELP ME! OH GOD! HELP ME!"

"Dad?" a familiar voice said.

The memory of The Hole was gone, all of a sudden. He was still lying on the cold, damp wooden floor, though, so there was little comfort in this change.

"Dad?" the voice repeated.

It was a small, soothing voice that brought warmth to his heart, but not enough to pull him back through the threshold of sanity. Still trembling, dreading what this next affront to reality would be, he turned over on the floor until he was facing the kitchen door. There, in the doorway, his little hand holding the swinging door open, stood a boy. He had pale-white skin and had big blue eyes and black hair combed to the side. He was wearing blue overalls over a long-sleeved green shirt with horizontal white stripes.

William. His boy.

A small cherub's mouth opened in a face filled with worry, and he said, "Daddy, what's wrong?"

Peter crawled on hands and knees toward his son, a thirsty man spotting an oasis shimmering in the desert. He threw his arms around the boy and held him close with all of his strength.

"William! Kiddo, what are you doing here?" He grabbed the boy's face with both his hands and held it, examining him close to ascertain this wasn't some mirage. "I thought you were at your grandma's! How'd you get here?"

"Dunno," the boy shrugged, looking concerned. "I was watching TV with grandma, and I fell asleep and woke up in here and then I heard you and then I came here and found you on the floor." The boy spoke in a single run-on sentence, no pauses or punctuation.

"But Will, that's..." He was about to say impossible, but then he looked around—after he wiped away his tears with his shirt's sleeve—at the way his home looked, and realized all of *that* was also impossible. "Where did you wake up, champ?"

"In that big room on the roof, where it's very dark."

"You mean the attic?"

"Uh-huh..." He nodded. "Mom was flying."

Peter stared at him, squinting, examining his face, looking for any sign the boy had misspoken.

There was none.

CHAPTER TWENTY
THE BASEMENT

Ray and Barry had carried Sylvia down the stairs, sitting in a wheelchair they had procured from the hallway. The elevators weren't working, and for some reason, the emergency generators hadn't kicked into gear. Ray's best assumption had been they had been damaged during the earthquake, since they were located near the parking lot. It was possible they had either fallen into the sinkhole—crushing some unfortunate souls who'd survived the cave-in—or the sinkhole had ripped the cables connecting the generators to the hospital.

Barry held the wheelchair from the supports above the footrests, while Ray held the handles steady at the top. They couldn't risk shaking Sylvia too hard. They'd tucked their cell phones in the breast pocket of their jacket and scrubs respectively to light the way down. Daniel walked behind his dad, holding the hem of his jacket, and Sylvia held Gabriel on her lap, careful not to let the boy's body brush against her stitches.

As they reached the first-floor landing, the stairs door suddenly opened and a nurse Ray recognized as Kassie, a newer nurse on staff, stared at them in confusion.

"R-Ray? What's...going on?"

"Kass, look. I have no time to explain. We have to get her out of here asap. We're going through the basement supply ramp."

"O-kay?" She gaped with a dumb expression at them. "But we're all-hands-on-deck here, we—"

"Kass!" He raised his voice, got it under control, sighed. "Look at us three. Do you remember the two of them? From last night."

It took a couple of seconds, but her mouth went wide open in a slow, trembling gasp. "That...altar... You three, and..."

"Right. We need to get out. Something's coming for us and we're going to a safe place."

Ray knew Kassie was like a plastic knife in a cutlery drawer. The girl had barely become an RN more by divine intervention than brainpower.

"There's a safe place?"

"Yes. Don't ask how I know. Tell everyone you can to go to Cunningham's. It's safe there. I don't know what's coming, but Cunningham's is safe,

(*For how long, I have no fucking clue*)

and everyone who can make it there should do so, stat."

Kassie nodded.

"Go." Ray motioned toward the hallway behind her. "We need to hurry."

The rookie nurse disappeared into the hallway, the door closing behind her, and they continued down toward the basement.

"Are you sure everyone will fit in Cunningham's?" Barry asked.

Ray shook his head. "I think it's big enough for about a hundred, maybe two hundred people. Guess we'll see."

A hospital basement wouldn't have felt like a welcoming place even with the lights on, Sylvia thought. Now, in complete darkness, broken only by the limited reach of Ray and Barry's phone flashlights, she realized, traversing Clive Memorial—the local cemetery—at night sounded like a more appealing prospect.

Barry now walked behind her and Ray with his two kids, who were quiet and well behaved.

"You know, Barry?" she said to break the creepy silence. "I've always had serious reservations about ever having children, due to how patently annoying and noisy I find them."

"Um," Barry said. "Okay?"

"Don't you work at a school?" Ray asked, an eyebrow raised.

"Ah..." She raised a corrective index finger toward him. "High school. There's a difference. Little children are mostly shrieking larvae that suck the life out of their parents, while simultaneously infusing them with a misguided, hormone-induced sense of fulfillment and pride. Teenagers, on the other hand, are simply assholes."

"Language." Barry motioned toward Gabe, whom he was carrying, and Daniel, whom he held by the hand.

"Jerks," she corrected herself. "Anyway, as you have now demonstrated, the advantage with teenagers is you can talk to them in a way you can't talk to little kids. They've already sucked the life out of their parents almost entirely by that point, so they isolate themselves in their rooms to go into a pupa state and use the life they sucked out of their parents to morph into actual people. People with personalities. Annoying, jarring, underdeveloped personalities, but if they ever emerge from their cocoon of isolation to talk to adults, and they step out of line, you can simply tell them they're being complete pieces of sh...uh...doo-doo...because they're people, not shrieking larvae."

"So," Barry said, sounding confused, "is there a point you're trying to make with this really badly timed reflection?"

Careful not to hurt her surgery cuts, she turned her head around and smiled at him. "I don't consider your children shrieking larvae, and I don't hate them. That's my point."

He squinted at her. "Thanks?"

"I mean it, they're very well behaved, not at all the monsters I expected them to be, given... Well, you know... Their b-i-t-c-h m-o-m. I guess there's an advantage to the fact she didn't raise them at all." When Barry didn't answer and only stared, she added, "You're a good dad. That's the gist of it."

He smiled at her, only a little. "Thanks."

She turned to look ahead as Ray's flashlight shone on a small plate to the left. It read: MORGUE.

"Wait," she said. "Stop."

"What is it?" he asked.

She hesitated. "Is Cal in there?"

Ray didn't answer at first, then said, "Yes."

"I know we're in a hurry and all, but...can I see him?"

"Syl, I don't think—"

"Please! The way things are going, it's likely we won't ever come back here, and I won't see him again, or even give him a proper burial. I already said my goodbyes, but...just one last look?"

After a few seconds, Ray let out a worried sigh. "Sure. Just... Let's make it quick."

"I promise."

Ray had pulled the long metal tray from one of the twelve refrigerated units at the back of the morgue. Callum was in the second one from the left in the bottom row. Ray had then helped Sylvia stand up from the wheelchair—an act more painful than she'd expected—and now held her in front of Callum's motionless body, half-covered with a white sheet. Despite the lack of electricity, Sylvia could still feel the lingering cold wafting from the dark hole they'd pulled her dear Cal from, which felt even colder than the already chilly environment of the morgue itself.

"They haven't cleaned him," she said, her eyes studying the dried bloodstains all over his body, then stopping at one of the open cuts.

"Haven't even sewn his wounds." She reached with a trembling finger and touched the edge of the wound gingerly.

"With everything that's happened since last night," Ray said, "there hasn't really been anyone available for an autopsy. Normally, he'd be on one of those stretchers over there with a blanket over his face, but it didn't feel right to leave him out in the open, so I called in a favor, and they stored him in one of the cooling units in the meantime."

She let out a cynical chuckle. "Stored…" She smiled. "Like he's a cut of brisket."

"I'm sorry. I didn't mean—"

"I know, don't worry." She ran her hands over Callum's arm. The skin felt too cold, too stiff. "This isn't him anymore."

"Hey, guys?" Barry called from the doorway, two empty metal stretchers at either side of the room between him and them. His back was pressed against the door, holding it open. His children were just around the doorway—bringing them into a dark morgue wasn't something either of them wanted to do—and Barry was keeping an eye on them and the hallway, just in case. "We should probably get going."

Sylvia gave him an unenthusiastic nod, then turned back to look at Callum. "I don't know what I was expecting to get from seeing him again. It's not him."

"It makes perfect sense to want to." Ray ran a supporting hand over her back. "I think they left his personal items in a bag here. Is there anything you want to take?"

She thought about this for a minute. "His glasses?"

"Sure. Is it okay if I let go for a minute?"

Sylvia put a hand against the metal surface of the refrigerator to support herself. "Go ahead."

Ray walked toward one of the metal tables nearby and found a bag with clothes. They were torn and brown with blood. He reached in and pulled the glasses out, brought them to her. She took them as Ray once more positioned himself to support her.

Sylvia examined the glasses in the phone's light. There were specs of blood in one of the lenses, a large bloodstain covering most of the other, from when the glasses had fallen into Cal's blood. She took in a deep breath, let it out little by little. "Thank you." She was unsure if she was thanking Ray for the glasses, or Callum for having existed.

She motioned for Ray to help her back into the chair. As he pushed the tray with Cal's body back into the darkness of the cooler, she put the glasses in a tote bag that hung from one of the wheelchair handles, where she carried the gun and the book with her notes.

A sudden grunt came from the door, startling both of them. They turned to see Barry stumble inside, trip, and fall forward, stopping himself with one of the stretchers in the room.

Standing at the door was Freddie, a toothy smile on his face as he pulled the door closed, wiggling the fingers of his free hand goodbye.

Barry crashed against one of the stretchers, which rolled away several inches, almost sending him sprawling to the floor. He clutched his wounded side, turned his head around to see Freddie at the door, closing it, a smug, mocking smile on his face. He caught the slightest glimpse of Gabe as he tried to waddle past him to go after his dad. This filled him with rage, and he almost bounced off the stretcher to try to catch the door before it fully shut, but he was too late and crashed against the closed door. His children cried out for him, terrified.

"Freddie!" he shouted, slamming one fist on the door while trying to pull it open with the other, but it seemed Freddie had done something to the knob, which wouldn't turn. "Freddie, don't you dare touch my children! Open this door!"

Freddie's hyena laugh came through the door in response. "Feels like we've been through this before, haven't we, Brickhouse?"

"This isn't funny! Give me my kids back!"

"Daddy!" Daniel screamed, while his brother wailed in terror.

"Tell you what," Freddie said. "If you figure out a way to get yourselves outta there, I'll wait for you at Plus-One's house with your two crotch goblins, but you better hurry. You see, right now, only Norman sees the Blue Moon. He's got his own issues to deal with at home. But you better believe the Blue Moon will rise again, greater and brighter, over the whole town. Once it does, it won't be long before the Exiles turn your brats into beautiful little monstrosities, and I'd rather you be there to see it in person, Brickhouse. Oh, yes, man, you have no idea the twisted, wonderful shapes God has prepared for them!"

"Fuck you!" Barry slammed his shoulder on the door over and over, making it shake, but it was a reinforced door for a refrigerated room, which could withstand however many blows he could give. "Let them go, you goddamn monster!" He kept crashing into the door, punched it until his fists bled and he couldn't stand the pain. He let out a loud, angry scream, his face turning red, the tendons in his neck bulging out. He moaned with pain, holding his shoulder, the strength leaving him, being replaced by a fearful sob. "Please, Freddie," he begged. "Please. I'll trade myself for them. Let them go, and you can have me for whatever the hell your God wants to do. Just, please!"

"Hee-hee-hee!" Freddie laughed with wicked amusement. "Oh, wow, I really pray to God you *can* actually make it outta there, Brickhouse."

Barry stared at the door, eyebrows pinched together with worry.

"I hope you can get out in time to see your children become something even more horrifying than your wife and mother-in-law, hee-hee-heeeeeeee! But, unfortunately, that's just Plan B. I can't let my personal desires get in the way of God's designs, and well, I have three of you locked up in there together. It would be irresponsible of me to let the opportunity pass. I can kill all three of you in there, then go searching for one of the remaining Vigilantes.

Just one more! One more, and the world will be ready for God to rise!" He let out loud, uncontrollable peals of laughter, underlined by the sounds of Barry's kids crying and calling for their dad. "This whole place is about to go bye-bye, but in the meantime, I left something in there as a gift."

Barry gasped, turned to meet Ray and Sylvia's concerned faces.

"Sure, it's mostly harmless," Freddie continued. "The Exiles need a *living* host to stay on this side for long, otherwise they stiffen and die..."

Barry's eyes went wide open when he realized what Freddie was implying.

"No!" Sylvia said as she turned to look at the door to the refrigerator where Callum was. Strange thumps came from inside, as if something was stirring and convulsing in there.

"But, I mean, who knows?" Freddie continued. "It might show some initiative and kill all three of you."

Amid the thumping coming from the cooler rang the sound of his children crying and screaming for him as Freddie dragged them away, laughing until his laughter petered out down the hallway.

"Freddie!" He slammed his fist on the door again. "No!"

The door to the cooling unit slammed open.

Something tentacle-shaped burst out of the open metal door, just missing Sylvia's head. In the wheelchair, she ducked with a scream, shielding her head. Ray, who was standing beside her, moved away to avoid being struck by the fleshy mass that emerged from the cold container.

Sylvia looked up and what she saw made her heart sink with both horror and grief. The creature, whatever it was, was a corruption of Callum's naked body, which looked boneless, like it had been stretched like taffy, its legs fused together, its arms melted to its sides, and it snaked in the air like a gigantic, horrendous earthworm. Its lower portion was anchored to the inside of the cooling unit by a larger, fleshy mass growing from where his feet should've been. The head portion turned toward Ray and her; its neck stretched to four times its normal length. The mouth opened like a vertical slit, toothless, to reveal hundreds of tiny black tentacles, like hairs wriggling in a way that made her stomach turn.

It reared back. Ready to attack.

Seeing what was coming, she shielded her face, but then felt the wheelchair move as Ray rolled her away from the monster.

"Shit! Shit! Shit! Shit!" Sylvia screamed. She tilted her gaze up to see Barry running toward a nearby tray and grab a bone saw—it looked like a silvery, stumpy handsaw—and without hesitating, ran toward the worm, which turned the mouth full of little hairs toward him.

"Barry, don't!" Ray shouted, held a hand toward him.

The creature wasn't moving. It stayed in that bizarre position, curved up and to the side, as if ready to strike, but it didn't move. A shudder ran through the length of its body for a few seconds, then let out a strange burble from its deformed mouth. It gave another shudder and fell to the floor with a disgusting meaty slap. There, it flopped once. It tried to move, to crawl. It curved its wormlike body toward Sylvia's wheelchair.

It's dying, Sylvia thought, watching as the pathetic creature—created using her dead boyfriend's body—struggled to move toward the wheelchair.

It stopped about four inches from the wheelchair's footrests. It's face—Callum's broken and contorted face—gazed up at her. That vertical mouth opening was now full of stiff black threads, like the bent hairs on an old metal brush. The sight of that face she knew well, even if it looked nothing like him anymore in its current state, made her shudder.

Sylvia reached into the tote bag and curled her fingers around the gun Jess had given her. She gritted her teeth as she pointed it at the creature at her feet.

"Syl," Ray said. "You don't have to..."

She shushed him. She tried to keep her hands steady and ignore the pain now burning all over her torso. *The safety is this little blade in the trigger,* she thought, placing her finger over the little blade. *Align this little notch in the back with the front sight, that little thing there.* She tried to put together Callum's face from the recognizable traces she could still see in that grotesque form, then she cleared that mental image. If she saw it as Cal, she wouldn't be able to shoot it. She needed to just see the monster, the worm. Every moment it lived was an insult to Cal's memory.

Then it blinked.

She pulled the trigger, almost by reflex, as if that blink had been too human for her brain to accept as coming from this monstrosity. There was a clear hole in its forehead. A black substance ran a few inches out of the hole, only to harden. One last shudder ran across the creature's body, then it lay still.

Sylvia put the gun back in the tote bag, brought her hands up to her face and sobbed like she'd never sobbed in her life.

Soon, she felt Ray's arms around her. She leaned into his chest and let bitter tears soak his shirt.

A minute later, the thought came to her, pushing past the emotional turmoil. "Wait," she whispered with a sniffle. "What did Freddie mean this place is about to go bye-bye?"

CHAPTER TWENTY-ONE
THE ATTIC

William had been sitting on the couch next to his grandma. She'd been watching one of her boring *soap-poppers*, but at least she gave him Jell-O and ice-cream to sit and watch with her. At one point, she paused her TV show, which was always full of crying, and people arguing, and kissing in that icky, open-mouth way, like his dad and his mom (the thought of the word made him wince) used to do. She got up to get a glass of water and, when she came back, as she was sitting beside him, she gave him "the look", that grandma look, like she knew something troubled him, and asked, "Is everything okay, young man?"

He noticed the way her eyes moved over the bruises and scratches all over his body.

"Yes," he lied and ran a guilty hand over the damaged skin. "It was the Worm Woman." He was still lying. The only bruise from the Worm Woman was the nail marks and bruises on his shin. She had only appeared to him once, and no more.

He looked at his grandma, who gave him a concerned look and asked, "If something bad is happening at school, you would tell me, right, young man?"

He nodded. He was lying again.

His grandma looked disappointed, like she knew it was a lie, but she only nodded once and unpaused the *soap-popper*. She continued watching.

He'd also lied to his dad a couple of days ago. Before the Worm Woman appeared at night. He'd told his dad everyone at the new school was friendly and had treated him great. Yes, he'd made friends, and they'd gone to play on the cool playground at the school, but William had kept out the ugly part of his experience. One of the other children, Ángel Torres, had come after him with three other boys. Ángel's dad had recognized him from the news and told him about his mother's death. Ángel's dad had said William's mom was a crazy lady that had set her own home on fire. Ángel and his friends kept tormenting him every chance they got. Pushing him. Calling his mom a crazy fire lady, telling him she wanted to kill him for being such a weak little fag—not that he knew what that word meant.

This had escalated until the previous day, during which Ángel had pushed him off the slide before he'd been ready to go, and William had tumbled and rolled all the way to the dirt below. Before he'd even stopped crying, Ángel had crouched beside him, slapped a clump of dirt on his face and said, "If you tell, your dad will burn too!" then left with his friends chanting, "Will is a fag! Will is a fag!"

Though the threat, to an adult, would've made no sense, to William it felt all too real. It had already happened once, hadn't it?

William had kept all of this from his dad. Dad had told him he needed to be a brave boy at Mom's funeral, and he promised Dad he would be brave. He would always be brave. So, he would not tell him he was scared of those children at school. He would not tell him he was afraid his mom had tried to burn both of them because he was weak and scared of the dark. He would not tell him he was afraid Dad would also try to burn both of them because he was weak and scared of the boys at school. No. He would be brave. He would be a brave boy. He would keep quiet, so Dad would never leave him.

Some moments after he'd finished his Jell-O and ice-cream, William got sleepy and started nodding off. It was almost time for his afternoon nap, he realized, but he figured he could sleep on the couch. His grandma wouldn't mind.

He laid on his side and curled his knees, and soon his eyes closed. Seconds later, though, he felt cold. Almost winter-cold. When he opened his eyes, he found it was dark. Had his grandma taken him to his bedroom and closed the curtains? No, he thought. He would still see some light through the curtains. Was it night already? He tried to roll off the couch to realize he was already on the floor. Had he slept on the floor instead of the couch? No. He remembered lying sideways on the couch's comfy cushions. Had he fallen off the couch? Again, no. The couch was tall; he would've woken up, and his grandma would've been checking on him in a second.

He was freezing. He couldn't see the TV or any light coming in through the living room windows. In fact, he couldn't even see a window or a TV. It was *too* dark, and it smelled like a dirty toilet in here. He stood up, but almost lost his balance, because there were gaps in the floor, long narrow gaps between... boards? Wooden boards? They were wet, sticky. Drops of what he hoped was water fell at intervals from the ceiling on his head and body.

Fear slithered up his spine like a slug, leaving a slimy trail. The darkness and confusion made every one of his childhood terrors spring to the surface. A spider—hairy and venomous—crawling over his hand and up his arm. Or a snake—yes, a snake—with sharp fangs piercing his skin. What about a rat? A fat, disgusting rat, gray-furred, red eyes, diseased. Then there were ghosts—inescapable, translucent, moving through walls, dragging chains, and moaning—trying to drag him with them back to their graves; because that's what ghosts did, right? Or the Devil—plain and simple—just as a mean babysitter had once described; rising from a fiery pit, horns, wings, and hooves, eyes burning like embers, reaching out to snatch him and pull him into the bowels of Hell for being a bad boy.

But what he feared most was that woman. The woman made of worms, with holes for eyes and a slithering tongue. The Worm Woman. He could still hear her voice in his head, saying, *"It's not something personal."* He didn't know what she even meant by that. *"It's just what's right, but it won't be personal."*

He imagined her voice in his head, like a witch in a fairy tale, now speaking new words to accompany his fears. *"You're a very bad boy. That's why your mommy is dead. You couldn't help your mommy, and she burned. Your daddy thinks you didn't see, but you saw. You saw her burn. You heard her screaming. You couldn't help your mommy, and one day your daddy will leave you for letting your mommy burn and die. And one night, when you're alone in bed, the Devil will come from Hell and grab you by your little feet, and take you away, no matter how much you scream and cry. And then, you'll burn, too. You'll burn like your mommy."*

In this darkness, he was expecting to feel a hairy, clawed hand, grabbing his ankle and, from there on, it would all be flames and screams as the Devil dragged him to hell.

William stood up, heart thumping. He shuffled to his left until he touched a nearby wall. The wall was covered in some sort of corrugated material, like wrinkled wallpaper. It was wet, and it stank of pee. It was gross, but it was the only guide he had. The wallpaper made soft squishing noises under the pressure of his fingers as he followed it along in the direction he was already facing, until he reached something flat, wooden, horizontal, a little under the height of his head. It had gaps underneath. A railing, maybe? He placed both his hands on its wet surface and started following it a few steps to the right. *One step, two steps, three steps, four steps.* The railing ended abruptly, and his right hand came off it. He stood on that spot, grasping only air.

His left hand felt some sort of bend at the end of the railing and felt it go back the way it came, except going down. He turned around and put his left foot forward. When it felt nothing underneath it, he brought it a little further down, carefully, and found footing again. Stairs. What he was touching *was* a wooden railing next to a downward-going set of stairs.

He descended, step by step, one by one. Careful. Slow.

He sensed he wasn't alone. Something was there with him. The tiny hairs on the back of his neck stood up in alarm. His arms stiffened at his sides and he fidgeted. A rising tremor climbed up his legs, then his whole body followed.

"Is..." A soft whisper. He stopped, swallowed. "Anybody here?"

Silence.

He choked a tiny whimper that grew in his throat. He had to control himself. He was six years old. He was a big boy. He had to be brave. Dad was always right. And yet, William was scared. He couldn't see whatever he sensed down there, dangerously close.

I have to be brave. He continued down the stairs, one trembling step at a time. Something shifted. He stopped again. A horrid smell came from right in front of him. Something was breathing in his face. The breath came from above, so, whatever it was, it was tall. Right then, he realized his left hand was no longer on the railing but on something like skin, which felt clammy and bony. It felt like an arm.

Instead of running away screaming—which would've been the most logical reaction—he stayed put. Was this a person? His curiosity getting the better of him, he moved his hand a little higher. He felt an elbow. That wrinkly nub of skin that formed right at the joint. This seemed to be a person. But then, why didn't they move? Why didn't they react to his touch? Why didn't they say something? By now, he was not only choking back whimpers; he was choking back tears of raw, thumping fear.

I'm a big boy. I'm brave. I won't cry. I won't scream.

Tightening his jaw, he continued feeling. The skin, he noted, was wrinkly, which made him think of his grandma Susan. Was she here? Was this her? Maybe she was asleep? Standing up?

Then he felt another elbow. Another elbow on the same arm.

This thing wasn't his grandma. This thing wasn't even human.

If it was going to hurt him, why didn't it? Why was it just standing there, breathing on him? And why on earth didn't he run away? It was a tall, scary thing, standing in front of him in the darkness. Any other kid would run, but William wasn't stupid. Everything he did, he always thought out in a careful manner, a little more than other kids his age. He knew the only way to run was up the stairs, which would reduce his speed, and in this darkness, he could stumble. If he made any sudden moves, the thing—whatever it was—might react and attack him.

If right now it wasn't attacking him, it was because it might not know if it was supposed to, like his friend Branden's dog, who seemed friendly, but took a moment to sniff his legs and clothes before it suddenly started barking at him and had to be pulled away. Or, maybe, he thought, it knew as well as him how thin his chances of escaping were, so there was no need to hurry.

What he didn't understand was why he was still touching the monster. Why did his curiosity surpass his fear? The answer was simple and mystifying at once. Knowing he couldn't escape it, he was curious, morbidly so. His hand kept moving across the creature's wrinkled skin. The second elbow, if it was indeed an elbow, had thrown off his sense of shape completely. So now he was looking for something familiar, something to guide himself with, something—

Clothes...

—as he moved his right hand to the left, he felt it. A sleeve. It had clothes on. They felt torn and shabby, but they were clothes. Further, a shoulder led to what felt like a cleavage, which meant the face was right above it.

Don't. Don't. Don't...

He moved his hand upward. There was a neck. He stopped. Hesitated. One double-elbowed arm and a shabby dress he could handle; but a face, an actual face, he wasn't so sure he could deal with. Still, his hand continued moving, almost unwillingly drawn upward. Like when his father forbade him to touch something, and that gave the item the attribute of being irresistible.

The neck was too long; almost the length of one of William's arms. It was wet and slippery. Then he felt a jawbone, a chin. He felt the curvature of the chin—so close to the top of his head, he now realized why he could feel its breath on his hair. His fingers were now trembling more than before, but he kept going, still choking back the terrified whimper that kept pushing up his throat. He *had* to know. There was now a thick liquid oozing between his fingers. *Drool*, he thought—given he was so close to the mouth. Then there they were: the teeth. He pulled his hand back when he felt how sharp they were. That was as far as his curiosity would go. Too far already. He dared no further inspection. His curiosity satisfied; fear at last came back to replace it, reclaiming its cruel, freezing grip upon him.

What do I do? he thought, breathing hard, feeling the creature's hot breath in his hair. *I'm a big boy, I'm a brave boy, I won't cry.* He tried to convince himself, putting all his will behind it, but he could feel his heart give in to it, give in to the finality of terror, to the unbeatable reflex that is panic. Tears started streaming down his cheeks, and their salty taste invaded his tongue. For every time he told himself he wasn't afraid, his mind, with the mean voice of the Worm Woman, answered.

I'm not scared...

"*Yes, you are,*" the voice said with glee.

I'm a big boy...

"*You're a little boy. A defenseless little boy. And that thing is going to eat you whole.*"

I won't cry...

"*You're already crying.*"

I'm a brave boy...

"*Brave boys don't piss their pants, and you just peed a little.*"

I'll be okay...

"*It's going to eat you whole.*"

The creature sniffed his hair—

"*Like the dog, Brave Boy! Just like Branden's dog! Right before it tried to bite you!*"

—inspecting him. Why was it waiting? Why didn't it kill him? Could it be it didn't see him? Could it be, in this darkness, this thing was as blind as he was? It knew he was there, but it couldn't see him. It wore clothes, so was it like a person? Was it smart? What if it didn't know if it was okay to attack him? It couldn't see him, so it wasn't sure. Maybe, if he hadn't touched it, it would've never known he was even there.

What do I do?

There it was, again, the important question.

Tentatively, following a stupid idea, but the only idea he had, he moved his foot back toward the upper step, and though he tried to lay his foot down with the utmost care not to make a noise, it made a low, subtle *creak!* He sensed the way the monster stirred and shifted. There was the soft whimper rising in his throat again. If the monster was even two steps up the stairs and not at the bottom, this might work. But he couldn't be sure.

As soon as he heard the monster shift, perhaps taking a step toward him, William took one more step back, then pushed forward with his palms stretched to the front with a holler. There was the thump of clumsy steps, followed by a bloodcurdling screech. It sounded like a dinosaur in a movie, but also like a scream. Like a woman's scream. *Like my mom when she was burning.* The way the screech moved away told him it was falling backward.

As it fell, William followed it, stomping down the stairs as fast as he could, holding the railing and praying to God he didn't trip. He could hear the creature tumble all the way down, screeching with indignation. He heard it crash at the bottom. His left hand came off the railing, and his foot hit the bottom of the stairs. His plan was to run past it before it could get up, but then his left hand hit something, something round, protruding from a flat surface. He grabbed it. A doorknob. Something slimy writhed from the door itself, in strings, and passed through his fingers, making him think of the Worm Woman.

Without thinking, he pulled the door open. The creature scrambled near his feet. Was it struggling to stand? Was it already standing? As he pulled the door, it hit the monster's body, so he couldn't open it in full. The monster was lying in the space required for the door to swing open. Now that he was so close to escaping, he couldn't hold it anymore, he cried loudly, sobbing without control, tugging on the door, slamming it against the creature's body, squeezing himself through the thin open space, but being unable to get through to the continuous, thick darkness on the other side.

I'm a brave boy!

"Then why are you crying like a baby?"

The door wouldn't budge. He was stuck halfway through. He could feel the creature's body brushing up against his calf.

I'm a big boy!

"Maybe that's why you won't fit through the door!"

The creature was standing up. It was going to kill him. He was stuck. It let out a horrible screech. He was going to die.

I'm not scared!

"It's going to get up, and it's going to eat you. It's going to eat you whole!"

Then, a miracle. As the monster's body went vertical, it allowed for the door to open a little further. William slipped out the door, almost as if expelled by tremendous pressure, like a fish slipping out of the hands of a fisherman. As fast as he could, he turned and pulled the door shut behind him with all of his strength. He took a few blind steps back, expecting the monster to swing the door open and come bounding after him, ready to tear him to pieces. He jumped with a cry as a wild pounding began on the other side of the door.

It was trying to get out. It couldn't turn doorknobs. Or didn't know how.

With no intention of sticking around and finding out, he turned, ready to run into the darkness—which didn't seem as dark as before. He was in a hallway, and further down, as the wall to his right ended, a blueish light grew in intensity from that direction. He reached an open space, where stairs went down to another floor. He knew this house, he thought. When he looked down, he spotted the source of the blue light. Down on the first floor.

A glowing woman—

A ghost!

—naked, with her back toward him. Her white skin looked blueish silver from the glow emanating from it, which did nothing to conceal the burning red in her long hair. She was holding something in her hand. She was examining it, as if hypnotized by it. A picture.

"Mom?" he said, struck with immediate recognition.

She looked at him over her shoulder, with eyes whose color he couldn't see from this distance. That was when he noticed she was floating about two feet off the floor. Her gaze was blank, like she was looking at a piece of furniture instead of her son. She glanced at the picture again, then up at him, her face inscrutable, until a subtle smile took shape on her lips.

She turned away and put the picture down on a table near the front door, then stepped toward it, walking on air. She pushed away what looked like two black curtains hanging over the door—William was so mesmerized by the apparition he didn't notice the "curtains" were hanging from a black, bulbous, shapeless mass just above it. Without looking back, she walked through the door and closed it behind her, leaving him alone in a house swallowed mostly by darkness, but with the benefit her glow still came in through a long, narrow window near the ceiling, showing him the way to the stairs.

Now that he got his senses back, he remembered the creature behind the door and his ears caught the sound of it banging against it. He hurried to the stairs before the glow disappeared completely and climbed down, hugging the wall to his left. Visibility went back to zero halfway down. Once he reached the bottom, the wall to his left broke off—a doorway, maybe?—he took two steps and felt the wall start again. He'd been right. It had been a doorway.

This was his family's house in White Harbor. He was sure now, even if it looked so different. That was the dining room entrance, he remembered. He continued straight, feeling his way along the strange wrinkled-paper wall, until he reached the corner, then continued along the other wall until he felt the curtains he'd seen his mother pull away, and past them, the doorknob.

He opened the door to see the silver-blue glow again, but it was now farther. The light coming from his mother showed him beyond the door there was no ground, only an endless mass of water, like a gigantic lake, stretching as far as his imagination would allow. A few treetops poked through the surface. His mom was walking on air about fifty yards away, in the heavy rain, glowing even brighter than before, a dark-blue moon up in the sky shone dim through dark clouds. He stood at the door, gaping as he she became nothing but a blue dot in the distance and then vanished.

With a numb expression, he closed the door. He could still hear the racket from the monster upstairs; but what startled him was a different sound: screams coming from the kitchen. It was his dad, screaming. A metallic hammering sound accompanied his desperate voice.

He followed the sound, feeling his way along the wall again, but this time he went in through the entrance to the dining room. There was light at the other side, coming through the small window on the swinging door, looking into the kitchen. He stalked close to it, trying to be quiet. By now, the screams had ceased.

What happened to Dad? Why was he screaming? Did a monster get him?

"If it did," the voice of the Worm Woman sneered in his head, *"you'll be alone. You'll be a brave little orphan."*

His dad screamed again, crying for help.

A knot in his throat formed, tears filled his eyelids, but he was a big boy, he was a brave boy, he wouldn't cry. His dad wouldn't cry. He was the one who had asked him to be brave after his mom died. He had to be brave like his dad wanted him to be. He wouldn't cry. Hesitating, William mustered the courage to push the door open.

He found his dad on the floor, lying on his side, with his arms wrapped around his knees.

He was crying.

It took a moment for his dad to calm down, during which he wouldn't stop hugging him. He looked scared. Once calm, William told him how he'd gotten there, then stood in silence, waiting for an answer. His dad looked at him with wondering eyes, and he felt his heart sink. *He's not going to believe me.* He was about to say, "I'm not lying!" but his dad spoke first.

"Show me where you saw your mom."

William led him back to the front hall, pointed at the door. "She was floating right there. Like a ghost."

Peter turned the flashlight toward the front door. He noticed—while the black threads that fell like curtains were still there—the enormous face of his mother was gone, replaced by a shapeless lump of pulsating blackness.

"She was holding that, Dad," William said, pointing at a small picture frame on a narrow table by the door. "She kept looking at it."

Peter strode toward the table and took the frame in his hands. It was a picture of him, Jenny, and William, taken a little over a year earlier. The glass covering the picture looked intact and clean, save for a clear thumbprint. "Well, son, last time I heard, ghosts don't leave fingerprints." He put the picture down. "Then again, last time I heard, ghosts don't exist, but given all the strange stuff happening here, I'm willing to question that."

He cast a wide look at this corrupted version of his house. He couldn't convince himself this was a nightmare, though any person with a grip on reality and a sense of logic would insist it had to be.

Peter opened the front door, if for nothing else but to confirm what he'd seen back in the kitchen was still true. Outside there was nothing but an endless stretch of dark water, a world flooded under a dark-blue moon. He stared up at it in fear and spite, then closed the door. They had to find a way out of a house surrounded by an impossible flood. No ideas came to mind. He went down on one knee and held his son in his arms. Something told him they wouldn't make it out of this alive, but that brought forth the question spinning around his mind all along. *If Mother is doing this, and all she wants is to get me back, why was her creature trying to kill me?*

He gave his son a firm but loving look. "We'll figure this out. We'll find a way out, okay?"

"Okay," the boy said among sniffles.

Please God, if there is a god, let my son be spared from whatever's happening here.

"You trust me, right?" he asked. The boy nodded his head up and down. "Right?" he asked again, putting more emphasis on the question.

"Yes."

"Okay." Peter seemed satisfied. He gave the boy a kiss on the head. "Will... You said you appeared in the attic, right?"

"Yes."

"I think we might have to check that place out. I have a feeling that's where we'll find some answers."

"Why?"

"I don't know. I guess because we're completely surrounded by water on all sides, but you still got here through the attic, as nonsensical as that might sound."

"Daddy, what does *nonsonsaycoll* mean?"

"Nonsensical, it...it means weird." He smiled at his boy.

"Okay." William hesitated for a moment. "Dad...what about the monster in the attic?"

Peter pointed the flashlight toward the top of the stairs. The boy *had* mentioned there was a thing up there, maybe something like what had attacked him in Doris's room.

"It went quiet." No sound was coming from upstairs. "But it's there."

Peter gripped the kitchen knife tight as they stalked up the stairs, William sticking close to him.

They crept down the hallway, watching and listening for any threat, until his flashlight shone on the attic door. With trepidation, he reached for the doorknob.

"Be careful," William whispered.

He gave his son a nod, trying to put on his bravest face, and pushed the door in.

There was no monster. He shook his head at his son.

"It was there, Daddy. I swear."

Peter stepped through the doorway, ensuring to keep his son behind him, and shone the flashlight to the right and up the stairs. Nothing to see. Nothing to hear. "Come in, Will." As William stepped through, Peter closed the door. On the other side there was something black and tattered, like a torn trash bag, drooping down, slimy, as if it had been ripped open from the inside, and emptied its disgusting contents.

The stairs creaked as Peter climbed up, knife at the ready, and once they'd reached the top, he'd found only the wide emptiness of the attic. It didn't have a flat ceiling like the bedrooms. The roof was diagonal. It started low on the left side and went up at a forty-five-degree angle, ending at the top of the wall on the right. It was made of rotten wood and the rain dripped through the cracks.

The flashlight revealed waterlogged boxes containing books and papers, all damaged by the water dripping down on them. Rusted shelves with old tools and appliances that looked ancient. The pungent smell of urine and feces coating the papered walls was particularly dense here. The memory of the days following that afternoon, when they'd found Mother, incoherent, wallowing in her filth, floated up again.

"*How dare you talk to me that way?*" Mother's hateful voice reverberated in his head, as if echoing through a dark cavern in his brain.

He flinched.

"*You were living in your own garbage, Mother.*" Peter's own voice, rising from the ashes of the past. "*You're malnourished. You could've died.*"

"*I was waiting for you to come home from school to make you dinner, you ingrate!*"

"*School? Mother, I haven't been in school for twenty-five years. Please, understand. You're sick. This is what's best for you. I'm trying to keep you safe.*"

"*This is my house! I don't need you to keep me safe! I am your Mother!*"

"*We talked about this. This is not your house, Mother. I'm putting you in elderly care from now on. Jenny and I feel this is—*"

"*How dare you speak that name in front of me?*" Vile contempt slithered over every word.

"*We've decided you need to be under supervision, Mother. From now on, if you need to go out, you'll have a caretaker with you at all times. I'm sorry.*"

"*You do not tell your Mother what she can and cannot do. Know your place!*"

"*This is not up for discussion, Mother. You're staying here. Period.*"

"*I pray that God will kill your brat.*" She croaked these words. The low register and slow enunciation of her speech felt like a knife twisting in his gut.

"*Stop it, Mother. Stop that now! That's my son you're talking about!*"

"I hope he dies. I hope his soul is taken to the dark Void of pain reserved for those whom God only views as cattle."

"That's enough, Mother!"

"God will feed on him in the blue darkness. He'll be damned to no respite from having his very soul tormented, torn apart, maimed, mutilated, and raped beyond recognition!"

A sound like a whip cracked inside Peter's memory, followed by Martha's voice grunting sharply. A shocked gasp—his own. A long silence.

"Mother. Oh, my god! I'm sorry! I didn't mean to! Oh god! Mother, I—"

"You..." Martha's voice hissed with rage. *"No-good son. Aberrant son. May that hand rot and fall off!"*

"Daddy." William's voice, from behind him, startled him.

Peter looked over his shoulder at his son. They were standing in the attic. He'd lost track of time. The memory of that first day his mother spent at Clarendon was still raw in his mind, like a scab he'd scratched by mistake and now poured scarlet blood down his neck. Was that all this was? Revenge? Resentment? Was that why Mother's creatures were out to kill him and his son? Was it all because he'd dared "lock her up" in Clarendon for her own good?

After having abandoned her when I was thirteen, he thought, knowing that was wrong. Knowing he'd been taken away because of what she'd done to him.

He'd lost control that day at the hospital. When she'd said all those horrible things about his son, the rage had come over him—lava rising from the bowels of the Earth—and his open palm had flown toward her face.

Was this all his fault, then? Why would it be his fault?

(*I told you to cut her off. I told you not to visit her. She should've been locked up after what she did to you*)

Could Nadine be right?

(*My sister is dead! Angie's dead, and you're still making excuses for your mother?*)

No. Nadine didn't understand. This wasn't fully Mother's fault. She was sick! Instead of abandoning her, he should've sought treatment for her sooner, before the ticking time bomb in her mind exploded and

(*The whole town might die because you couldn't lock her up and forget about her!*)

she unleashed her resentment on the entire world. Yes, this was mostly Mother, but it wasn't all her fault, he thought. She wasn't responsible for this. She was just sick and confused and angry. She was just a weak old woman, corrupted by a power he wasn't sure she even understood herself.

(*How dare you make excuses for her after what we just witnessed? What am I doing other than pointing out you're a murderer's enabler?*)

"Weak old woman" didn't fit when describing Mother. He knew this. He'd always felt Mother was a force of nature, something he couldn't appease no matter what he did.

"Daddy, I'm scared."

Peter finally spoke. His voice sounded curt, annoyed at being pulled from his thoughts. "What?... I'm sorry. What did you say?"

He noticed the way William reacted to his tone, closing down a little. It sent a thorn or pain straight through his heart.

"Nothing," William said.

Peter turned around, let out a deep breath, priming himself to explore the attic. Then—

CRASH!!!

"DADDY!"

Peter turned around in a fraction of a second. A creature with long, deformed, bi-elbowed arms—like mantis claws—had crashed through the roof and gotten a hold of his son, hooking its claws under his arms, and lifting him off the floor. Half the creature's torso stuck in through the hole, and it stretched a long, tooth-filled, tube-like neck toward the boy's head. In the second it took him to process the situation, he felt foolish, noticing a small window near the stairs was open. The creature had crawled out of it and up to the roof, ready to ambush them. His foolishness would cost him his son's life.

William was now beyond his forced non-reaction to fear, beyond his conviction of never being afraid. He was, at last, reduced to a scared little boy, a scared little boy who felt a warm dampness as he emptied his bladder all over his legs, when earlier only a few drops had escaped. The mean Worm Woman's voice in his head had been right all along. He was terrified, and the creature coming from the ceiling was going to kill him.

"*See?*" it said with glee. "*What did I tell you, my dear brave boy? It's going to eat you, that thing is going to eat you whole!*"

"William!" his father shouted. His voice came from far away, muffled. Fear and hopelessness had positioned his father in a different galaxy altogether, even though he was standing right there. He could see him in the back of his mind, trying to swing a kitchen knife at the monster without cutting him. So far away. He'd be too late. Too far away.

"*I was right, my little brave boy,*" the Worm Woman's voice said.

"Let go of my son!" His father's voice. A lifetime away.

"*You're not a brave boy. You're scared to death.*"

"WILL!"

"*You're not a big boy. You're very small.*"

"Let him go!"

"*So small, this thing will eat you in one big bite!*"

"Daddy!" the boy screamed, kicking and flailing. "Daddy, help me! Daddy, please, help me!"

The boy cried in fear. Some of his shrieks were silenced by terror, and only air hissed out of his throat. He kept pleading, begging for his dad to save him—a small animal at the dawn of his life, bleating for its parent to help it keep on living.

"DADDY!"

The creature's exposed teeth looked ready to open wide and take a bite off his face. He closed his eyes and tightened every muscle, ready to feel the teeth burying themselves in his skin, biting through flesh and bone. He let out a sharp scream, then he felt himself fall.

That must be what death felt like, he thought, falling into a black abyss, blind, with no sense of orientation. It was a concept no six-year-old should ever wonder about, but since the night he watched his mother burn to death, the thought hadn't left his mind, and now, he knew. It felt like falling. It felt like emptiness. It felt like darkness. It felt—

He felt the pain of his body hitting the floor.

When he opened his eyes, he spotted one of the creature's long, unshapely arms lying on the floor next to him. He looked up. His dad was snipping like a madman at the creature with a pair of long, pointy hedge clippers he'd gotten somehow.

The monster let itself fall through the roof. It crashed unceremoniously on the floor, just two feet away from William.

He crawled away as fast as he could. His dad kept the creature's attention on him, snipping at it with the shears and taking a few steps back away from William to draw it to him.

The monster rose to its feet, snarling, flashing its black-toothed mouth and drooling, as if saying, "You took my arm, now I'll take your head."

While it was tall and menacing, standing over seven-feet tall, it was skinny, rickety, and bizarre looking. Its skin was a sickly, jaundiced yellow, and even in the weak light of the flashlight, it looked wrinkled and spotty. And of all things, it wore what looked like a worn out, shabby dress—dirty white with intricate gray and blue print—which hung loose on its skeletal body. The lower part of the legs that came out from under the dress turned black as it approached the ankles, as if eaten by gangrene.

It approached with an awkward and uncoordinated gait, supporting itself on its reverse-N-shaped arm, as if it were a walking stick. Peter's brain couldn't move past the notion that it was wearing an ugly old dress in the most incongruous of ways.

It gave him no time to keep pondering, as it swung at him with its remaining arm, and tried to snap at him with its long neck and jaws. It missed, but then the arm came back around. Except, instead of hitting Peter, the arm flew off with a snip of the shears, and a fresh flow of blackened blood sprayed from it. The demon snarled at him. It lurched closer, salivating through its disgusting black teeth. Peter shuffled away, the old hedge clippers he'd picked off a shelf held toward the monster.

William tried to stand up and come toward him. "Stay there!" he ordered. "Don't come near!"

The armless creature pulled its head back, then it whipped forward, jaws snapping at Peter, prying the hedge clippers off his hands with its teeth, and tossing them aside. Peter stumbled backward and fell on his ass. He crab-walked away on hands and feet as the creature kept snapping at him. He kept dodging the best he could, trying to find an opening to stand and run past the monster to recover the clippers, but before he had a chance, it opened its jaws, and out came a black, warm, tar-like fluid. It fell on Peter and solidified into a hard rubber-like substance. He struggled to release himself from the gooey mess, which became harder and harder until it crystallized. He stopped, unable to move. The creature's awful breath was next to his head, the low growling from the monster's throat filling him with fear more than before.

The jaws opened, letting more of that ungodly funk come out of the back of its lengthy throat. Single drops of all-but-transparent saliva slid down its fangs.

The fight was over.

If Mother is doing this, why is she letting this thing kill me? Why?

Peter tightened every muscle in his body. He jumped as the monster let out an awful shriek, preparing to attack.

Death didn't come, however.

He eyed the creature. It staggered away, shaking, its long tube of a neck flopping like a fish. It stopped, stood in place, limp. It remained motionless for a moment, let out another screech—a weaker one, almost a lament—and fell forward like a downed tree. From its lower back protruded the hedge clippers, and standing behind it was William, whose face was pale and in awe, right before breaking into a sour expression followed by a loud wail and tears.

Peter banged his body against a roof column, ignoring the pain it caused him, until the crystallized black substance cracked and broke, allowing him to remove it in large chunks.

He ran toward his crying son and held him in his arms.

"I'm sorry! It was gonna hurt you, Daddy, and I didn't want it to hurt you. I'm sorry I didn't stay away like you said!"

"It's okay, buddy," Peter said, still holding the little boy. "It's okay. You saved your dad. Dad's okay, thanks to you."

Once they let go of each other, William eyed the dead creature on the ground, thought for a moment, then pointed at it. "Daddy," he said, hesitating. "That dress..."

"Yes?"

"That's Grandma Susan's dress."

"What do you mean?"

"She was wearing that when we were watching TV, before I fell asleep and woke up here."

Peter regarded the creature with concern. Examining the blue and gray pattern of the fabric, browsing through his memories to see if he remembered ever seeing Susan wearing that dress, but then dismissing it. The implication his son had just killed his grandmother, who would've been acting against her will, was more than he could process right now.

"Wait a second," he said, realization coming over him. He regarded the boy with bemusement. "What do you mean you were watching TV with her? I talked to her earlier. She said you were at school."

His son cocked his head to one side and gave him a puzzled look. "It's Saturday, Dad. There is no school."

Peter stared at his son for far too long. The voice on the phone, Susan's voice. He was sure he'd talked to her that afternoon. He swiped over his phone's screen, noticing his battery was at forty percent now. He might not have a signal in this bizarre world, but he could still check his call history and, as soon as he tapped on the phone icon, he saw—

There's no call. I didn't call her. What is this?

He realized William was still staring at him. He tucked the phone back in his shirt pocket and forced a smile. "Don't worry about it, son. I'm sure that monster just looks like that to scare us. To confuse us. Let's, uh...let's see if we can find out how you got here."

The sound only made it to the attic as a faint thump, which was registered by both Peter and William as just another random sound in the rain, the strange whispers, and the creaking of floorboards. In reality, the sound had been quite loud. Something had crashed onto the floor of the front hall, where the black cocoon that loomed over the front door had shaken, convulsed, ruptured, and birthed a terrible thing into the world.

As father and son traipsed through the attic, this new being unfurled its body.

It stretched a wing.

William felt ashamed. He'd let it show. He'd said the forbidden words: "I'm scared." His dad hadn't heard him, but he'd definitely noticed his screams after being caught by the monster.

But I saved him, he thought. *That makes up for it, doesn't it?*

"*Too late,*" the Worm Woman's voice answered. "*He knows you're scared now.*"

They walked in silence along the length of the attic, surrounded by boxes and shelves, and that gross wallpaper. Everything was wet, damaged, and stinky. One long, dark room with an odd shape because of the angled roof.

His dad strode toward the right side of the room, which had more space in it. He looked uncomfortable with how cramped the left side was.

Father and son trudged toward the back of the attic. That part was invisible. Even with the flashlight on, he couldn't see the wall at the end. They kept moving forward, but the room seemed to stretch. The back wall was still invisible—no way the attic could be this big. It felt longer than the house, than two houses even.

The voice of the Worm Woman came to him again, cruel and mocking. The boy pressed closer to his dad's leg.

"There are ghosts up here, Brave Boy. Ghosts!"

"Leave me alone," he thought at it.

"They're coming for you."

William grasped his father's leg even tighter.

"They're coming for you. Look. There. In the darkness!"

"You're lying! I'm not scared! I'm not scared!"

"They will bite you! They will cut you! You will burn like your mom!"

"Shut up!"

"You will never sleep again! All you'll do is scream like your mom!"

"Leave me alone!" he yelled, hurrying to hug his dad, burying his face in his stomach. "Leave me alone! Leave me alone! I'm not scared!"

William let out loud, rending sobs. His entire body shook. Peter didn't understand what was happening; he looked around for anything the boy might have seen that could've given him a sudden scare. Of course, given their current circumstances, that could be just about anything.

"Will, what's wrong?" Peter went down on one knee and put his arms around the boy and tried to calm him down. "What's wrong, kiddo? Will?" His son wouldn't stop crying. He was beyond terrified, shaking. "Please, son! You're scaring your dad. What's wrong?" No answer. "Will?"

"The Worm Woman says the ghosts are coming for me!"

"What are you talking about?" Peter held his son in his arms, sheltering his black-haired head under his chin; knowing his son had seen or heard something he hadn't. Something that had scared him half to death.

"Will, listen to me," Peter said, still holding his son to his chest. "I won't let ghosts, or that Worm Woman, or whatever scared you, take you away from me, okay? I'll take care of you forever. You're my little boy, and I love you."

William gave him a sheepish smile. He gave him several quick nods, wiping away his tears.

"I just... I need you to be brave for me a while longer, okay? We need to find a way out. Do you know what I mean?"

The boy's smile disintegrated. He took a shaky breath. He tightened his body, clenched his fists, and distanced himself from his dad. It appeared as if he was searching within himself to summon the courage needed to stop trembling and show a brave face.

"You sure you're okay?" Peter asked. "Are you ready to continue?"

William gave a single decisive nod, pressing his lips together.

He ruffled the boy's hair with a proud, loving smile. They continued through the inexplicably long attic, until, at last, they reached the end. There was a door there.

That makes no sense, he thought.

"What is it, Daddy?"

"This door. This should be the end of the roof. Beyond that wall, there should be a straight drop to the ground." *Not even accounting for the fact the attic is almost twice as long*, he added in his thoughts. "There can't be a door here. That's... That's preposterous."

"What does *purpossharus* mean, Dad?"

Peter didn't answer. He was too deep in his thoughts. Staring at the door. He was overcome by memories, long buried, of that fateful day at the Vanek House, of being the only one who was able to find his way through the shifting rooms and corridors, opening doors leading to places that made no sense. Was this the same?

"Daddy," William said.

Peter snapped out of it. "W-what, son?"

"What does *purpossharus* mean?"

"Oh, it...means something is ridiculous, or silly."

"So, it's *nonsonsaycoll*?"

"Yes," Peter answered with a smile two sizes too small. "Yes, it's exactly that." He examined the reinforced wood door before him—the *nonsonsaycoll* door. Wood with rusted metal reinforcements. He tried to imagine what might be behind it, like he had in the kitchen while staring at the refrigerator.

(*Maggots. Maggots on the walls. Millions of maggots. Maggots like in dead bodies. Dead bodies in graves. Dead bodies in coffins. Coffins. Coffins underground. The Hole. I'm in The Hole! I can't breathe!*)

In one motion, like removing a band-aid, he threw the door open.

On the other side, there was a plain, square room. Walls, floor, and ceiling were all covered with old bathroom tiles, save for a door-sized rectangle made of bricks in the wall in front of him, badly applied plaster applied on top.

"What the hell?" he mumbled.

Peter shone his flashlight on something hanging on the brick wall portion across the room. It was a frame, but it didn't contain a picture. It held a square piece of fabric with a message embroidered on it in green and pink letters, adorned with green leaves and pink flowers—also made with embroidery—all around the edges. It read: PRAY TO GOD FOR JOY, EVEN WHEN YOUR HEART IS BREAKING.

What sort of significance could this room have? Peter thought to himself. That message on the frame. It looked familiar. He felt he'd seen it before, somewhere. But where?

There was a faint rustle.

"Daddy!" William shrieked, startled, clutching his leg.

Peter turned his head in the direction the rustle had come from. In the corner to his right, there was a figure—dirty, bloody, clothes in tatters—sitting there. He thought at first it was another monster, and held the garden shears at the ready, but withdrew them once he realized it was a human figure. It was a man in his late fifties or early sixties. It was hard to tell in his state. His appearance was repulsive, with a disgusting white shirt, a gray jacket, and khaki pants, all of which were torn and stained. The man's head had a receding hairline and a few streaks of white in an otherwise jet-black head of messed up hair. He had an unkempt black beard, peppered with gray.

The man raised his head and regarded Peter. His brown, jittery eyes studied him.

Peter gasped, like he'd just emerged from a body of water, desperate for oxygen. His face twisted in shock; his hand flew to his mouth. The garden shears fell to the floor tiles with a metallic clang. His body trembled. Before he could even realize it, tears were pooling in his eyes, as if all the moisture from his body had gathered in them. That face. Those eyes.

"Dad?" Peter said with a childish moan.

His father, whom he hadn't seen in well over thirty years.

The man looked tired, ashen, spent, like he had just been rescued from a POW camp. He had bloodshot eyes and bulging, purplish bags underneath them. Despite his deplorable state making him seem much older, he looked close to the last time he'd seen him, which made no sense.

His mother had never told him where his father had been all this time. She'd only said he'd abandoned them.

(*That irresponsible, cowardly man! That useless ingrate! He never loved us, so he left us! Abandoned us! But we don't need him, Peter! All we need is each other!*)

Worse yet, the man had abandoned *him*. Left him at his mother's mercy, with no one to protect him from her. As a nine-year-old, Peter struggled to believe his caring, good-natured father could've truly walked out on him. He'd always felt loved by him, but where had he been all these years? Why hadn't he ever tried to contact him? And most importantly—

"What are you doing here?" Peter asked in a shaky voice.

Hector Rojas stood up, faced him.

His old man looked around, puzzled. "*Estoy...descansando. Creo...*" His voice was raspy, vacant.

"Resting?" Peter asked, nonplussed, unsure he'd heard him right. "What the hell do you mean 'resting'? Resting from what?"

"*No sé...*" He pointed a finger, still looking dazed. "This, uh...this wall is backward."

He was pointing at the patch of bricks with the sign that encouraged people to "PRAY TO GOD FOR JOY, EVEN WHEN YOUR HEART IS BREAKING".

"What?" Peter asked, glancing at the wall, then back at his father. What was that supposed to mean? How could the wall be backward? Maybe he meant the picture frame? "Dad, you haven't answered my question," he continued, with his quivering voice. "What are you doing here?"

"How's your mother?"

"Mother? She's...not here. She is... She *was*...in an institution."

"An asylum?"

"Elderly care." Peter's voice filled with shame for a second, but shook it off. Why should he feel any shame in front of the man who had abandoned him and Mother?

"Oh," Hector said, thinking. "Now it makes sense." He stood there, staring into nothingness, in his own private thoughts, then his eyes wandered toward William. They filled with recognition. His gaze wandered toward Peter, as if seeing their resemblance. "*Mi nieto?*" His voice sounded so emotional, he seemed to have forgotten his son barely spoke Spanish.

Peter hesitated, anger draining from his voice. "Yes. This is your grandson. His name's William."

"William Rojas?"

"Lange," Peter corrected. "His last name is Lange."

Understanding came upon his father's face. "*Comprendo... Esa bruja se salió con la suya.*" He pressed his lips shut, gave a sad nod, then peered at the boy. "I'm so sorry."

"Don't even," Peter said with an indignant hand wave. "You were barely a part of my life. You've never been a part of his, and he doesn't need you to be. So, save the apologies, and just tell me why you're here. Where have you been all this time?"

"I'm not apologizing, son," the man looked at Peter. "I never left you. I would've never left you."

"Then, w—"

"I'm sorry, because I can see how much you love this beautiful little boy. I know what it's like to be separated from a son. You're not ready for the kind of pain you'll feel when you lose him."

William gasped. Peter stared at his father in disbelief.

"His time is coming. She's coming for him… For the boy. There's no way to stop her."

With an anguished cry, William grabbed onto his father's leg, his face a mask of fear. Unbeknown to Peter, his son could hear the voice of the Worm Woman—whoever that was—cackling at him, telling him she'd been right all along.

"Look what you've done!" Peter yelled. "Why would you say something like that? Can't you see what's going on around here? The boy is scared enough as it is!"

"I have upset you." Hector lowered his head, looking embarrassed, and started mumbling some unintelligible song, sounding insane and erratic, fidgeting with his fingers. "I never meant to hurt you, son. Your mother. I was going to leave her, but not for another woman. I couldn't let her do what she meant to do. I meant to take you with me, but she didn't let me."

Peter's eyes filled with tears, but he held them back, too angry to cry. *I could've left with my dad. I could've been raised by my dad. And not… Not her!*

"Somebody summoned me here," his old man said, still fidgeting. "But I don't know why. I did my best, son, and I still failed. I know I can never make up for that with just an apology. *Solo quiero que sepas que de verdad te amo, Hijo.*" He paused. Pondered. "I won't disturb you anymore. I better leave now."

Hector shuffled past Peter and William and into the attic.

Peter wanted to hold strong. He didn't want to show any emotion, but he spun around and called, "Dad, wait!" His father's back disappeared in the darkness. "You can't go out there! It's dangerous!"

He took a step forward, then something—a strange white mass—flew out of the darkness and crashed into him, knocking him to the floor. The phone fell out of his shirt pocket and slid away, spinning toward the corner, flashlight facing down, casting the room in thick shadows.

William screamed. Then came wind from the left side. Wind and rain pelted his face. "Will!" he shouted, getting his bearings enough to crawl toward the tiny sliver of light visible between the phone and the floor. William continued to scream in unbridled fear. "Will, I'm coming!"

He gripped the phone, raised it, turned it toward the screams, and there, in the rain that came in from an entire wall that had somehow disappeared, was a monster, flapping its wings a few feet off the ground. This thing looked like a human torso with a head, bat-like wings that seemed made of a crisscrossing web of ribs draped in skin, and two arms hanging at the bottom. It was wrapped in bloody, filthy bandages and gauze; except for the arms which looked burned, gangrenous, with enormous claws at the end of them. Its head wobbled insanely to all sides, like in an epileptic seizure, as one of the claws reached for William, who cowered against the wall to one side of the door, shrieking in terror.

Peter scrabbled to reach the hedge clippers nearby, but before he could even get his fingers around one of the handles, the monster's wings beat the air, sending wind and raindrops flying everywhere, as it rose higher with his screaming son in its clutches.

"No!" Peter shouted. "NO!"

Two more hard flaps, and it was off, gliding away. He quickly stood, trying to chase it, but the room ended in a steep drop to the endless, flooded world surrounding his house. He watched the monster fly away into the clouded, rainy sky, thrashing its wings.

"WILLIAAAAAAAM!"

The sound of the boy's screams faded in the distance, far beyond the reach of his flashlight. *Too far! Too far!* The monster was gone. The merciless blue moon peered through the storm clouds as the creature carried away his only reason to live. It was over. His life was over. First his wife, now his son. They had both been taken from him, and now he was alone.

Peter fell to his knees. His arms stretched forward, begging for his son to be returned to him. His face was a pall of horror. Hopelessness, like a landslide, rolled him over and covered him, smothering him, burying him. His hands fell to his sides, then went to the floor. He remained there, on all fours, with his head hanging between his shoulders, defeated, weeping like a child, while a cruel embroidered message at his back, hung from the wall, urged him to "PRAY TO GOD FOR JOY, EVEN WHEN YOUR HEART IS BREAKING".

He let himself fall to one side and lay there as the rain blew in his face. He closed his eyes, deciding to never get up again, deciding to die.

CHAPTER TWENTY-TWO

CRUSH

Ray sat on the floor next to Barry, one arm around his shoulder, the other holding his hand. The big man's head hung down, and he wept, defeated. No matter how hard they tried, they hadn't been able to open the morgue door, which meant they were impotent to help his children.

"I'm sure nothing has happened to them yet." Ray ran his hand through Barry's hair. "You heard what Freddie said. He wants *you*. He's sick and holds this insane grudge against you. Harming the children isn't what he wants, that won't do for him. You know him well. He'll hold off whatever he's planned until you're there so he can rub it in your face like he tried to do last night. He's counting on you getting out of here."

Barry let out a long sigh. "Well, I'm still here. Guess I disappointed him."

The sarcasm wasn't lost on Ray, neither was that nihilism, which he'd heard before coming from him. It filled him with dread.

Sensing this, Barry wrapped his meaty fingers around his hand and gave them a soft squeeze. "I know what you're trying to do," he said, deflated. "I appreciate it...but I still feel like no matter what

I do, someone always gets hurt. I've let everyone important in my life down, over and over. For god's sake, I killed their mom and grandma to save them, and now *he* has them again!"

Ray moved his head closer and kissed him on the head, realizing there was nothing he could say to make the situation better at this moment.

"I think you should stop whining," Sylvia blurted, earning a gaping stare. "In a couple of days, you fought a crazy gunman, came out as gay, patched things up with the love of your life, kicked your monster wife and her mother to the curb, saved your children from Freddie's deathtrap, not to mention, you were ready to fight *that* thing"—she nodded toward the Callum creature, which they'd covered with a blanket—"with two weapons that looked like toothpicks in your hands." She shrugged. "It's simple. If you try to save them, your kids might not be dead, but if you give up right now, your kids are dead for sure. You're indisputably the strongest out of all of us, and you're just giving up?" She raised an eyebrow at him. "What should the rest of us do, then? Just lie down and die? Abandon all hope?"

"No, but..." His eyes wandered toward the closed door.

"Have patience, you troll-sized drama queen! Did you already forget Ray's nurse friend? That girl, the one that looked twelve? Whatshername? Uh, Candy?"

"Kassie," Ray said, as if realizing something.

"That one. Equally stupid name; sounds like a milkmaid in a black-and-white movie. Ray told her to try to get people to get out through the basement. We need to keep an eye out through that window"—she pointed at the reinforced glass window on the door—"and when we see someone coming, we shout and ask them to help us get the door open."

"What about what Freddie said?" Barry asked. "About this whole place going down?"

Sylvia shrugged, shook her head. "Guess we just hope someone passes by here before whatever happens, happens." She looked at Ray's phone. They only had that one flashlight on, to conserve the battery on the others. "Before all our phones run out of battery would also be nice."

Ray stood, ran to the window, and positioned his head sideways to look as far as he could down the hallway. What he saw made him gasp, then exhale quickly, fogging the glass. There was light. Moving light, coming down the hallway. "People! People are coming!"

He started banging on the door and calling, "Help! Please, help us!"

A second later, Barry was standing beside him, also banging on the door. "We're trapped here! Please! Let us out!"

One of the lights coming down the hallway separated itself from the rest and ran forward, toward the door. Seconds later, Ray was looking through the glass at Kassie's wide brown eyes. The light from his phone's flashlight making her pupils contract.

"Kass!" he said, loud, relieved.

"What are you doing in there?" she asked, her voice muffled by the glass.

He could see a crowd of people run past her. Only a few stopped, as if Kassie had been leading the group. "Never mind that. What's blocking the door?"

She looked down. "There's like a black, crystal th…" She stopped. She gaped at him, recognition in her eyes. "Oh, crap."

"What?"

She turned and called out to someone, waving her hand, asking them to hurry. A man he didn't recognize stopped beside her. "Here." She pointed at whatever was blocking the door. The man held a lug wrench, which Ray assumed he'd brought from his car for some reason. He raised the wrench, grabbing it with both hands, and began hitting the black substance Kassie had described, a substance Ray knew about. He wondered why Kassie recognized it. The man hit it over and over, until, satisfied, he gave Kassie a nod.

The moment the door opened, the smell of smoke hit Ray's nostrils. "What's—"

With urgency in her eyes, Kassie said, "The hospital's on fire! It hasn't made it to the basement, but it's gonna be here soon."

"How did that happen?"

"Last night, I saw that thing. The thing in Martha Lange's room." She looked at the passing people, nervous. "Run and talk?"

Ray nodded, and they all joined her, hurrying down the hallway with the rest of the crowd. Barry went to the front, as he'd be more capable of defending the others in a panicking crowd, and Ray rolled Sylvia's wheelchair right behind; Kassie beside him.

"A mob of angry people marched into the elderly care wing and burst into her room," Kassie continued. "They remembered her from last night's weird nightmare. I went after them, trying to stop them, coz I didn't know if that thing was infectious or what. When I got to the room, everyone was standing outside, staring in. There was a man in there with that black crystal statue. I remember him from last night. He was at the altar with y'all. He was the one who kneeled in front of that woman."

"Freddie Parham?" Ray asked.

"Wait, he's a Parham?" she asked, as if that fact explained everything—The Curse of the Parhams remaining ever-present in the town's collective consciousness. "He was there with two children, a little boy and a toddler."

Barry stopped, turned, and stared at Kassie. "The kids. Were they okay?"

"I don't know. I think so? Th-they were alive, if that's what you mean, but they looked...gone, like hypnotized or something. Alive, though."

Discouraged but somewhat relieved, he turned back, and they all continued walking.

"Then it was all really quick. Like, he touched the statue of that woman, then he touched the air, and it was like I could see some other place *through* the air. He picked up the toddler, grabbed the other kid by the hand, and they walked through. Disappeared. That's when the statue caught fire. It sprouted flames. It spread like those black vines coming from it were covered in gasoline. I turned and ran before everyone else, tried to get them to follow me, but a lot of them couldn't. The room and the entire ceiling exploded. Might have hit a gas or oxygen pipeline. The hell do I know? Those people were trapped there. I could hear them screaming. By the time I made it to the first floor, it was chaos. Those black vines were covered in flames, and they were everywhere. There were people on fire. Patients in their beds or wheelchairs who couldn't run were just burning. People piling up at the door, surrounded by flames. I stopped before reaching the reception area. If I'd continued just a few more steps, I would've been trapped in the crowd trying to escape, and I would've burned too. I knew I couldn't get out through there anymore, so I doubled-back and brought as many people with me as would follow me. We need to get to the supply ramp, like you said."

The hallway opened up into a small vestibule with boxes on either side, and it was crowded with clamoring, terrified people piled in front of a set of double doors which lay closed in front of them, as the smoke accumulated in the limited space.

"These doors should open outward," Ray said. "Why aren't they opening?" He stared at Kassie, who shook her head in confusion.

"Old doors!" Sylvia shouted, noticing their outdated make and the peeled paint job. "God, I hate this lazy, incompetent town!

This isn't an emergency exit, so they didn't replace it to be up to code. It's locked. Unless..." She turned her head one way and another, then looked at the people standing around her. "These types of doors use latches. Do you see latches where the doors meet at the top? I can't see from here."

"None," Ray craning his neck over the crowd.

"Then they're at the bottom." She pointed at a point past the dozens of legs in front of her. "These people are going nuts with panic, and they're too huddled up to look down."

"Hey!" Barry said. "Look down! The latch is at the foot of the doors!" He was ignored. "Crouch and unlock it! The latch is at the foot! The latch is at the bottom!" No one turned. People kept crying and screaming and shoving each other from one side to another in a panic.

"I HAVE THE KEY!" Ray shouted, as loud as his voice would allow.

Barry, Sylvia, and Kassie turned confused stares at him. A few more people turned, having heard him. There were a few puzzled exclamations of "What?" and "Key?" from the crowd.

"YES, I'M A NURSE! I HAVE THE KEYS!" he repeated, jingling a keychain up in the air, which—unknown to everyone, including his friends—only held the keys to his house's front and back doors, his bike chain, and a tiny shed in his backyard.

More people turned.

"Make way!" Barry shouted, pushing people aside to open a path for Ray. "This nurse has a key! He has the key!"

It was as if the word "key" was itself the key to parting the crowd. Regardless of how panicked they were, people made way for them.

We better pray my guess is right, Sylvia thought. *Or these people are gonna kill us for lying to them.*

Ray reached the door. Barry took the handles from him and positioned Sylvia's chair to the right of him, and motioned for Kassie to take his place. He stood on the left and positioned his broad back toward the crowd so they couldn't see what Ray was doing.

"Hurry up!" a woman shouted from behind Barry. "What the fuck is taking you so long? Did you forget how to use a key? We're going to fucking die because of your useless ass!"

"Hey!" Barry turned a rageful glower toward the woman. "Back off!"

"Yeah, shut the hell up, Karen!" Sylvia shouted.

"Wait, it's *those* people!" a man in a blue knitted cap and a yellow shirt said, pointing at them as Ray crouched in front of the door. "The people from last night! The ones at that altar! They burned that woman! They're burning down the hospital now! They did this!"

A clamor of concurrence and alarm blared through the crowd.

"We have to stop them!" Knitted Cap shouted. "The nurse is trying to get us stuck here to kill us! We have to stop h—"

He was grabbed by a hairy-knuckled, meaty hand clutching his throat, and in a second, Barry's fierce blue eyes and bared teeth were an inch from his face.

"You just try to get close to him," he snarled, a few drops of spit hitting the man's face. "We're not trying to hurt anyone, but lay a hand on him or my lady friends here, and I'll make *you* the exception."

"Stop!" Ray said from his crouched position. Even with his back to the crowd, Sylvia could see the keys hanging from one of his hands while he held one latch with the other, not yet pulling it. "Yes, we were at that altar last night. Yes, we know some things, so we know what's coming, which is why we have to get out of here! Do you want to die here? No? Then you can shut the hell up and let me open the door!"

Knitted Cap stared at Barry's unflinching, snarling visage, then at Ray's back. He hesitated. "Go ahead, man. I'm sorry!"

Ray still held the latch, not pulling on it. "One more thing." He jingled the keys as if he'd inserted them in the non-existent lock. "That's nurse Kassandra Ferguson holding my friend in the wheelchair. Once I open the door, nobody moves until she gets the wheelchair out, and everyone around us better make sure of that, because there's a gate past here. Only I know how to open it. If nurse Ferguson isn't first in line with that wheelchair, that gate remains closed."

He looked over his shoulder.

"Fine, sure, hurry!" Knitted Cap said. Other people around nodded, agreeing with reluctance.

Ray jingled the keys as he pulled one latch, then the other, then he and Barry pushed the double doors open. True to their word, though the coughing people behind them looked terrified and anxious, they waited until Kassie rolled Sylvia out. The crowd poured, little by little, into a wide-open space, a warehouse large enough for two delivery trucks. Boxes, crates, pallets, and supplies sat near the walls on either side.

They reached a large set of roller shutters at the opposite end, tall enough to allow for delivery trucks to pass once opened.

"No electricity," Sylvia said. "Don't these need a key to do the manual override?"

"No," Ray said, walking toward the left side of the shutters. "The electric system broke a long time ago, and they never got around to fix it. Manual open only."

"God, I love this lazy, incompetent town."

An increasing murmur of cries and screams filled the air, as if they were billowing in with the smoke that slowly flooded the high ceiling of the warehouse.

"Oh, shit!" Barry said. "Look at that!"

While Ray's warning had held the human stampede at bay at first, allowing some thirty people through the double doors, panic soon took over. The desperate people in the back started pushing, until a few at the front tripped, causing others to pile on top of them, creating a wall of screaming humanity too tightly packed to fit through. Faces pressed upon faces, bodies got squeezed together, arms reached, legs kicked, and gasps for air filled the room as the crush allowed no space for them to pull air into their lungs. Reddened, terrified faces were illuminated by wobbling flashlights, while thick smoke poured without mercy through the exit above the struggling crowd.

Some of the people in the crush were beginning to faint.

"What are you waiting for?" Ray shouted at the crowd standing in the warehouse. "Help them!"

Only some of them moved to help, Barry included. The others simply stood there, paralyzed, useless bystanders too afraid to get caught up in the horror and the flames. This fear was exacerbated when one of the first to arrive at the pileup was violently seized by numerous desperate hands, who clung to him, pulling him close and hard, until he was finally pried away with bleeding scratches in his arm.

Ray took the crank handle hanging to the left of the shutters and hurried to insert it into the slot. He began turning it with difficulty. The shutters rose too slow for comfort, not oiled up as well as they should be.

Barry and about five other people tried as hard as they could to wrest the victims from the pileup. It was obvious some of the people at the bottom were dead already. Barry pulled a woman out of the pile. He hauled her on his shoulder, turned and quickly put her on the floor. She crawled away, coughing and wheezing. The others had only pulled two other people. There was no way they would get everyone out fast enough to clear the exit and let the rest out, especially when the flickering orange glow of fire was now visible, approaching, further behind the crowd, past the smoke and the heads at the top.

Barry pulled a young man who only laid down, barely moving, breathing, with eyes closed. Two more people were pulled by the rest of the helpers, but others quickly took their place, perpetuating the crush.

(*A hydra. Cut off one head. Two more take their place*)

"Barry!" Ray shouted. He was having a tough time turning the crank. The shutters were stuck. "Barry!" he shouted again.

The big guy turned to look at him, a man's hand clinging desperately to his shirt. "What?" he shouted back, holding the man by the armpits and pulling with all his strength.

"I need you here!"

Barry hesitated, looked at the man he was pulling out of the crowd. Hesitated again, then gave a heave with a loud grunt, wrenching the man out of certain death. In doing this, a woman right beneath the rescued man had enough space to crawl out. Both rescuees were sprawled on the floor, their chests heaving as they struggled to catch their breath.

Barry turned, ready to run toward Ray, but soon there were two hands on him, one on his shoulder, one pulling on the collar of his shirt. More people—living people, begging for his help. He could see Ray struggling to open the shutters, and could see the crowd of onlookers, either too scared, too weak, or too unwilling to even try to help.

It's getting hot, he thought.

Beside him, two men pulled someone else from the mass of people. It looked like a screaming woman with long hair. Her hair was on fire, her clothes, too. It was then he noticed the intensity of the screams behind him had risen to a deafening roar and realized the heat had spiked to become nigh unbearable. He pulled away; the hands clutching his clothes came off, one of them tearing his jacket's seam at the shoulder. Before him was a wall of faces in indescribable pain, howling for help as tongues of flame licked through the upper space of the doorway and sprouted here and there through the gaps in the crowd. People whose clothes were in flames. They were roasting alive before his eyes.

He grabbed two of the hands reaching toward him and pulled as hard as he could.

"Barry!" Ray shouted again. "Barry! Hurry!"

"I can't!" He looked over his shoulder, pulling, but making no progress. The two women he was trying to help didn't move an inch. "I need to help them!"

One of the hands jerked, then went limp; the woman had fallen unconscious. The other one screamed and coughed, begging him to help her out. The screams from people in flames all around was almost overwhelming and was now joined by the revolting stench of burning human flesh.

"Help me!" the woman screamed. "HELP MEEEEE—" Her pleas devolved into intense caterwauling that pierced his ears.

The unconscious woman beside her was already ablaze. He could see flames cover the pleading, shrieking woman's hair, and surrounding her face. The flames crept up her jacket sleeves, forcing him to let go, seeing her skin blister and redden, fluid boiling and exploding in her face. Her eyes were reddening, eyelashes on fire.

Barry took a few steps back.

Nobody tried to help the burning people anymore. They stared aghast at the flaming mass of writhing, howling humanity, singed flesh, blazing limbs, and open mouths showing teeth enveloped in flames. The shape of the hallway formed a tube through which echoed the nearly animalistic cries of the victims further inside (dozens? hundreds?), which commingled with the roar of the fire.

It was hell.

Huge orange blazes now licked the upper part of the doorway, like a tongue running side to side on an upper lip, filled with voracious appetite as the meat for its feast roasted and charred. The fire spread out through the wall, gradually but faster than he would've ever imagined, and soon boxes of medical supplies were on fire.

Movement among the burning people slowed, then almost stopped. It looked like a wall made of stacked up logs with protruding skulls, all ablaze.

"Barry!" Ray called, and he turned. There were two people already at the shutters, trying to help Ray pull them up, but the shutters looked stuck, only about five inches off the ground. "If we don't open this, we're all gonna die here!"

He looked at the people that had been helping haul bodies out of the crush, who were the most likely to help, and said, "C'mon! We have to open that thing!"

The five others ran beside him and as they reached the shutters, they grabbed the bottom edge, legs open, knees flexed and started pulling up. The shutters climbed, slow but steady. He feared they might be too slow to get them open enough to escape.

The people

(*Those useless fucking assholes!*)

behind them, were coughing, screaming in fear, or shouting for them to open the door, but they were not helping at all, perhaps frozen with terror or filled with mistrust.

A man, whose unpleasant voice he recognized as the man with the blue knitted cap he'd grabbed by the throat minutes ago, shouted, "I told you this was all a trap! Don't follow them out there! You saw what happened in the parking lot! Something's gonna happen to us as soon as we go through that door."

Barry tried to ignore him. He poured his entire focus into flexing his legs and arms and pulling the damn shutters open.

"We need to find another way!" Knitted Cap continued. "Break a wall or something!"

"Do you know what might break a wall, and all of us with it?" Sylvia shouted at the man. "Those crates, full of oxygen tanks over there! Why don't you and the crowd move that out of the way of the fire? Hurry, people!"

Barry glanced over with dismay at the hesitating crowd, then several people ran toward two large crates by the wall to the left, mere feet from the spreading flames. There were bangs and metallic clanks as they pulled the tanks out and moved them away. *Good! They're doing something at least! Now, focus!*

Ray turned the crank handle, following their slow pace. Looking at him gave him strength, thinking his children were out there in peril gave him strength. With a loud roar, he put everything he had into lifting the shutters. The other people followed suit. Soon, the gate was raised up to his chest.

"There!" Ray shouted. "Hold it! Let me lock it in place! Don't let it go!"

Barry glanced at Kassie and Sylvia, gave them a nod, and the young nurse rolled the wheelchair out of the gate, ducking under.

Ray ran toward the center of the shutter, where there was a sort of circular two-handed crank. He grabbed both small handles and turned them counterclockwise, engaging the locking mechanism in place. "Now!" he shouted. "Out!"

Barry and Ray ducked under the door and got out into the darkest night they had ever seen. Raindrops dotted their clothes right away. It had been raining non-stop since the darkness enveloped the town. It was not enough to douse the flames that licked out of every window of the hospital, which burned with unstoppable anger.

They ran toward each other as people emerged from under the gate and ran up the slope, toward the street. A smattering of phone flashlights swayed this way and that. Kassie waved at them from the sidewalk, Sylvia in front of her. Without hesitation, Barry grabbed Ray's hand, and they ran toward them.

"What do we do now?" Kassie asked, and Barry noticed, even though some of the people kept running, most likely toward their homes and what they perceived as safety, others stood around them, as if awaiting instructions. He even spotted Knitted Cap, the hypocritical asshole, standing in the small crowd.

"I…" Knitted Cap started, when he noticed him staring. "Sorry about all that back there. Just scared, you know? I guess you know what to do next?"

"Go to Cunningham's," Ray said, letting go of Barry's hand and moving to take the wheelchair from Kassie. "Like I told you earlier, Cunningham's is safe. I don't know how many people will fit, but go to Cunningham's and take as many as you can with you."

She looked at the way the three of them separated from the crowd. "What about you guys?"

"We'll be there soon."

Barry could see the hesitation in her eyes, even though the only reason they were all standing here, alive and well, was Ray.

"Trust me," Ray said. "Jess Cunningham is there. Remember, she was there with us last night, too. She'll take care of you guys."

"Okay," Kassie said and turned around to leave as some of the people who'd heard Ray were already marching as fast as they could toward the bar, but then she stopped, turned around and gave him a tight hug. "Thank you!" She let go and gave Barry a hug as well. She gave Ray a knowing smile, having noticed them holding hands as they'd run up toward them. "You lucky bastard." She gave Sylvia a quick hug, which made her shrink away a little. "Y'all be careful, alright?"

They watched as the crowd disappeared as the relentless flames consumed the hospital at their backs. They could still hear screams and pleas for help coming from within.

CHAPTER TWENTY-THREE

COLD, DARK, EMPTY

Royce gazed out the bar's window toward the dark street outside. Not a single person wandered the streets.

"This is just creepy." He turned to look at Lillian, who had their daughter lying over her thighs in one of the window booths. Their baby girl had cried during the whole drive to Cunningham's and had managed to fall asleep once inside, in the relative safety they found themselves in. He ran a hand over his daughter's huge, beautiful puffy cloud of coiled hair, then spotted Jess standing behind him. "I kinda preferred to see people running and panicking. At least that seemed human."

"That always happens here," Lillian said in a soft voice, trying not to startle the sleeping girl. "Lots of houses on the way here had people in them, sitting there with lanterns and candles. Folks in this town have the habit of hiding in their homes instead of running away. I was shocked people were actually trying to escape town in cars or boats..." She spared a glance at Royce, then Jess. "Well, we know how the boat thing turned out. It's like they went into full panic mode, but then something made them settle into this sort of conformist default state and lock themselves in their houses."

Jess looked around at the twenty or so people that had arrived after Royce and Lillian, huddled around tables, worried faces considering an uncertain future. "Not like we're doing much different." She leaned toward a window and with her fingers bent one of the blinds to peek outside. "Reminds me of the thing you and Bobby mentioned with the birds."

"What about it?" Royce said.

"Ever seen birds during an eclipse? The sun's gone, so they think night is comin' and they get super noisy at first, flying all over, tryin' to find a tree or a nook to hide in, then they go quiet, thinking they're safe and it's time to sleep."

"They also get quiet and still when they sense a predator nearby," Lillian said.

Jess moved away from the window, pointed an index finger toward her, and clicked her tongue. "There ya go. How'd a smart woman like you end up marrying such a dumbass, Lil?"

"Shut up," Royce said. "So, you're saying that's what the birds thing is? We see the sun go bye-bye, so we go hide in our trees?"

"Asleep, defenseless, waitin' for some predator to eat us all."

Lillian gulped. "So, how safe are we here, really?"

"Not sure." Jess shrugged. "According to our friend downstairs, as safe as we're gonna be, which sounds kinda relative."

Royce looked away, frowned.

"You okay?" Jess asked.

"That man murdered Cal, injured Sylvia, killed at least one person a year for ninety years." His conflicted brown eyes swiveled to meet Jess's. "He talked Freddie into killing my brother..." He let that sink in for a while, wafting in the air like smell escaping from an open garbage lid. "And now he's all that's standing between us and death. I meant it when I said I could forgive Freddie, coz Freddie's always been nuts, but that man pushed Freddie over the edge. I'm not sure I can forgive him."

"No one said you have to."

"No." He returned a sarcastic smile. "I have to get comfortable with the notion, if we make it through this, I'll have to owe it to that monster down in your cellar."

Jess didn't respond. She shuffled her feet, hands on her hips.

"How *is* he doing, anyway?"

"He'll survive, for now. My dad had a lot of medical supplies stashed in the cellar. We sewed him up real good, hooked him up to a blood bag, if you can believe that, but...this isn't a hospital. I can't say for sure."

Royce nodded, glanced toward the window. Movement outside. Flashlights. Multiple. "People coming."

Jess ran to the door, hesitated for a minute, looking at the symbols scrawled on it. According to Hitch, the symbols should stop

Martha Lange's god—and she felt insane even thinking those words—from using its power inside the confines of the bar, even if she opened the door.

She removed the three locks and threw the door open to be greeted by a group of about forty people of all ages standing in the rain. A young woman, a petite blond in hospital scrubs, pushed past the crowd that stopped in front of the bar and looked at her with tired, terrified eyes.

"Is it true it's safe here?" she asked. "Ray Chang told us to come here. The hospital's on fire. We just escaped from there."

"Oh my god, Ray! Is he alright?" Jess asked in a hurry. "Was he with others? Where are they?"

The young nurse nodded. "Yes, he was with his boyfriend and this patient named Sylvia. They made it out alright. On the way here, we noticed the police station had caved in, like the hospital parking lot. It's just a hole now."

"We're soaking wet, lady!" a woman in an old parka shouted. "Can we come in now?"

"C'mon, Jess, let us the fuck in already!" a man with a blue knitted cap said.

Jess cast a disbelieving glare toward him. "Well, since you're askin' nicely, Arnold Fowler,"—Jess reached to one side of the door and picked up Peggy, her shotgun, and pointed it at him, prompting several people to raise their hands—"I'll give y'all the rules of the premises, same way I did with the people already inside. You get in, you do what I say, when I say. No fights. No shouting. No drama. You can talk to each other but use your inside voice. No one—and let me be specific—no goddamn-motherfucking-one goes near windows or doors without me explicitly saying you can. *We* know what might be happenin'. *You* don't. So, you'll respect the fact that knowledge puts us higher in the hierarchy and do as *we* say."

"But wait," the woman in the parka said. "Who's we?"

Jess swiveled Peggy specifically toward her, like a tank aiming its gun. "The people with guns. We'll be easy to spot. Also, no fuckin' interrupting me. That's one shitpile of an important rule. You're free to help yourselves to any drinks or snacks we have, except alcohol. Don't need no drunks causing no trouble." A groan issue from the group, which got cut short when the gun swiveled around in a circle over the crowd. She noticed a woman holding up a man with burns all over his arm and part of his face. "We have medical supplies—limited—but you're free to treat the injured." She pointed the gun toward the nurse, who jumped, startled. "What's your name?"

"Kassie," she said in a thin voice. "Kassie Ferguson."

"Alright," Jess said. "Nurse Ferguson is in charge of determining which supplies are needed, and she'll distribute them. Everyone else, hold patiently. Anyone with guns or other weapons?" One by one, she counted five hands going up. "When you go in, you put them on the bar counter and step away from them. God help you if I find any of you concealing a weapon of any kind. I won't hesitate to kick you out at gunpoint, or—if need be—shoot your head off." Two more hands went up. "Good. Now that we're clear,"—she lowered Peggy and stepped aside—"you can come in."

The oval of light from Nadine's cell phone swayed side to side on the sidewalk. Her heels clacked on the concrete, but also squished on the wet surface as the rain fell all around her. She'd taken an umbrella from one of the emergency tents around the hospital and headed home. The darkness, the earthquake, and the rain had caught her halfway there.

The street and the houses around her lay in absolute darkness, papers and random garbage strewn all over abandoned lawns, some doors standing ajar, nothing but dense blackness inside. She pictured the insides being devoid of furniture, appliances, doors, walls, not even a floor separating the two stories, just the outer shell of what used to be a home, filled with nothing but space and absence.

There was the odd house, here and there, where she noticed the flickering light from lanterns or wax candles—people who had decided to ride out the storm and hope for it to end. What, she wondered, did that make of her? Angie had tried to get out of town, moving to Portland, and she'd stayed. Even after her parents had died, Nadine had chosen to stay. Then, instead of going to Portland when her sister got sick, she'd had her sister move back to White Harbor, then used her as the excuse not to leave. How was she different from Peter, who'd bought a house to continue coming back to and visit the woman who had hurt him most, instead of staying away?

It was like when her depression made her not want to get out of bed or lie on the couch until three in the morning watching videos online. It wasn't really because she felt *sad*, but because she felt comfortable. Depression was comfortable. Routine was comfortable. It was a blanket that enveloped her and made her feel like she didn't need to put the effort into herself that she put on others. That comfort was addictive. This town was an addiction, an excuse not to move forward.

Her parents were gone. Angie was gone. Peter was gone, too, as far as she was concerned.

She'd told the others she'd text him, and she had. He was on his own now. He deserved no less.

Her house loomed ahead, growing, moving closer. The lack of any kind of light from inside made her fear that Bobby was also gone. The windows were like empty black eyes watching her approach. "Come here, little lady," it seemed to say. "Come here, walk inside. Light the fireplace and get warm. You'll be safe in here. Stay inside. Never leave."

She shuddered as she turned into the driveway.

The front door was unlocked, which at least told her Bobby had been there. The silence inside the house was crushing, solid, flattening. An atmosphere so oppressive, she felt like she'd walked into a garbage compactor.

"Bobby?" she called, her voice still hoarse from all the screaming of the previous night. Still, even in its diminished capacity, it echoed in the lifelessness of the house, as if she'd slammed the front door shut. She slinked toward the stairs, part of her mind telling her Bobby wasn't in the house, part worried she'd find her brother-in-law-that-never-would-be had followed Angie into the afterlife. She climbed the stairs, reached the landing, and shone the flashlight up toward the second floor. The door to her parents' bedroom was closed, as always.

There were no signs of life. Her home was cold, dark, and empty.

She reached the second floor, and on the left, found her bedroom door (closed), and the door to Angie's (open). "Bobby?" Concern rose up her gullet like acid reflux. She couldn't shake the haunting image of Bobby's lifeless body, clad in last night's attire, clutching Angie's pillow tight against his chest, with an empty pill bottle resting on the bedside table. Her stomach tightened as she treaded with shaky steps toward the bedroom.

She reached the door, and in one swift motion, turned the flashlight into the bowels of the room. Shadows scurried away from it to show her an empty bedroom. The bed looked as though someone had actually been in it that day—since she remembered making the bed before heading out to Seaside Park with Angie—the sheets had been disturbed, and there was a human-sized dent left on Bobby's side. As she had predicted, Angie's pillow lay lengthwise, still a little bent in half where he'd clearly had his arm around it.

There was a letter on the bed.

Nadine picked it up.

Nadine,

I'm sorry I couldn't stay home, so we could mourn Angie togeth-er.

I'm sorry I left you alone. The moment the sky went dark, and the earth shook, I knew I couldn't just sit here crying like the naive idiot I've always been. I'm too angry. I don't care what happens to me, I will kill Martha Lange for what she did. I will kill her, no matter what it takes. I don't know where to find her, but I know who does.

I'm heading to Lighthouse Rock. I'll find Freddie, and I'll make him tell me how to reach her, even if I have to beat him within an inch of his life. I will stop him. I think I know how.

I don't know what it is, but there's something about his paintings that connects with all this. If Angie died because I didn't notice something that was right under my nose, I'll never forgive myself. But I'll do something about it.

I will stop him. My childhood friend is gone. I haven't accepted that for thirty years, but now it's come to this. All that's left is this monster that helped Martha Lange, and Martha Lange killed my Angie. Even if I have to kill him, too, I will stop him.

Don't come looking for me. Find the others. Stay with them.

If I succeed, I guess you'll know.

I will avenge Angie. I promise.

Bobby

The memory of the video they'd watched at the hospital rose like that gigantic black tentacle—or whatever it had been—had risen from the ocean to sink the ferry. She pictured that happening to Bobby with whatever tiny boat he could find to reach Lighthouse Rock.

There was a noise. A creak. From the opposite end of the hallway.

The sound of the water lapping at the pilings beneath the marina made Bobby picture hundreds of tongues licking at the slimy, barnacle-covered concrete, and at the bellies of the smattering of abandoned boats docked there. It mixed with the sound of the rain, making him feel like the sea level would rise and drown the town in its entirety. Beyond the scant light his flashlight granted him, there was only an all-consuming black, no moon, no stars. The world had been dropped into a tar pit, like a corpse a murderer wished to hide.

His umbrella was in some locker back in Seaside Amusement Park, and he hadn't had the patience to search for Nadine's, so he'd thrown a green raincoat on and marched straight to the marina in the darkness. While it kept him dry, it did nothing to deter the cold. He'd been checking every boat, hoping someone might have forgotten their key, but he supposed people leaving their keys in their vehicles—as if the concept of thieves were an alien fairytale—was only a movie plot contrivance, same as the way people somehow kept running into each other in New York City—or any city, for that matter.

Frustrated, he let out an angry huff and shone the flashlight around, only to be startled by a man standing behind him, a long-haired, bearded man wearing a camo raincoat and jeans. Bobby almost tripped and fell off the marina walkway. "Jesus!" he shouted.

The man returned a wolfish grin and said, "Looking for a boat, pal?"

"What? Yes, yes, I am."

"Wow, check out that face, man!" the man he now recognized as Xavier Poe Kane, that mountain nut with the podcast, said. "You look like someone who got dragged onto an altar in an alternate dimension to see a friend burned to death. A very specific look, if you'll forgive me saying."

Bobby sneered at him. "Do you think you're funny?"

Xavier put his hands up in an appeasing gesture. "I apologize. My mouth runs off with me sometimes. But you *are* one of the people Martha Lange pulled to that altar to watch that poor lady burn. Am I right?"

"What's that to you?" The pain of the memory hadn't left him for a single second since it had happened, as his sore eyes and drawn face made obvious, but having someone else mention the event made it even realer than it already was.

"Again, I apologize. Dude, I can see she was someone important to you, going off of your reaction, and general fuckfacedness, but I just wanted to make sure, because"—he reached into a rucksack and pulled a binder with documents in it—"if you're one of those people, you're in plenty of trouble tonight. Trying to escape on a boat might not be the best idea. I'm guessing you didn't see the video of what happened to the ferry."

"I have no clue what you're talking about."

Xavier held the binder up for him to see. Bobby recognized the hand-drawn symbol on the cover, crudely drawn with a blue ballpoint pen. It had been on the altar where Martha Lange had murdered Angie, and on the altar back in the Vanek House. There were copies, Post-its, and notepad pages sticking out of the binder's edges.

"Okay? What's your point?"

"Alright, look. I haven't been able to figure everything out, but I got a bunch of info from Callum Baker, the librarian at—"

"I know Callum Baker. He's my friend. Get to the point."

Xavier stared at him for a moment, jaw hanging, surveying his face, as if he knew something Bobby didn't.

"What?"

"Oof... Um..." Xavier hesitated. "Dude, I'm so sorry..."

Realization hit Bobby all at once. *Callum hadn't been at the altar with the rest of them. His entire group of friends were there. Callum wasn't.* He let his shoulders fall and let out a shaky breath. "Shit."

"Based on what I've been able to gather from Baker's notes and some stuff I extrapolated, you and your friends are in danger, even more than the rest of us, because that crazy woman and her lackey, Parham, are coming for all of you, specifically."

"How do you know Freddie is working for her?"

"Coz he's my *extremely* far-removed cousin, or something like that. My great-grandma was a Parham. My great-granddaddy forced her to move out—coz that was a thing one could do back then, I guess—then my granddaddy, who was born out of town, moved back in, and so yours truly was eventually born here!"

Bobby examined his face, squinted, annoyed, tired of the schtick. He couldn't believe he was wasting valuable time with this guy when he had more pressing matters at hand. "Please get to the point or move aside so I can keep looking for a boat."

"She came for me. Years ago, she came for me. I always thought I'd had like an alien abduction or something like that, but after last night's Interdimensional Crossing Event, or ICE—not the government entity, mind you, just—"

"Xavier!"

"Fine! Duuuude! Chiiiill!" He cleared his throat and kept talking as Bobby pushed past him to continue searching the remaining boats, barely paying attention to him. "I think I was supposed to be what Freddie Parham is now. Her servant. After what happened last night, I remembered. It felt the same. Like time stopped, then I was taken somewhere. She was doing things to me. Not her, but...these things. Like tubes or tentacles. Touching me. I could feel them in my head, just like last night. Poking around. Trying to get me to do things I didn't want to do, offering me things in exchange. It was like she was using those things to scan my brain, my DNA, for something, but I pushed her out. Then I was back in my bedroom, and the bedside clock showed not even a minute had passed. Based on Baker's research, she needed a Parham to do this. Guess I wasn't *enough* of a Parham. I remember those words in my brain now: '*Not enough.*' That cult of hers was founded by Dorothy Parham. We're like servants to her god, or whatever, but I guess I didn't have enough of it in me to work, so the only one left was Freddie."

Bobby considered this for a while, knowing Xavier was probably right about this conclusion. "I need to go to Lighthouse Rock to confront Freddie. That's why I need a boat."

"Wonderful!" Xavier gave him a huge smile. "I have a boat!"

Bobby stopped searching for a key in a small schooner, and stared at him, unamused. "You could've started with that."

"C'mon, man. No self-respecting dweller of a mountain cabin in a coastal town can be without a boat for fishing."

"What's this about a video and the ferry?"

Xavier waved a dismissive hand. "I thought you were trying to skip town. Big no-no. There's a gigantic tentacle monster in the ocean, and it sank the ferry. Killed almost two hundred people."

"Wait, a tentacle what?" Even through the marks of grief and exhaustion on Bobby's face, his bafflement was apparent.

"Exactly what you heard. But I have good news. I think Lighthouse Rock is the boundary." He pulled out a map from the binder. It was a map of the town with lines drawn on it in red Sharpie. It looked like a circle following the curve of the town's sickle shape. Lighthouse Rock marked the oceanic edge of the circle. "The creature didn't attack until the ferry sailed past Lighthouse Rock. I'm heading there right now. If I'm right, there should be something under the island I've been looking for. It would be the coolest fucking discovery in the world." He put the map back in the binder and the binder back in his rucksack. "So, what do you say, Blondie? Wanna risk a veritable eldritch sea monstrosity sinking us based on pure conjecture?"

Bobby pressed his lips together. "Yes, let's go."

Xavier once again surveyed his face. "I mean, I want to make it clear. This is pure guesswork on my part, dude. We might actually get killed and eaten by something so gigantic we and the boat might not even count as plankton."

Bobby shrugged, shook his head. "I guess I don't really care if it's dangerous or not. I've got nothing else to lose."

Xavier nodded, slapped a firm hand on his back. "Let's go, then!"

CHAPTER TWENTY-FOUR

ELIZABETH

Consciousness came back to her in fits and starts. Her eyes opened in a dark place. Flashes of feverish dreams (or memories?) still clinging to her mind like thorny bushes cling to fabric. She had been drifting in and out of wakefulness for a while now. The only certain thing in her head was, each time she awoke, some new piece of information was added. She tried to remember, but remember what? What was remembering if you didn't even know you were alive before this moment?

She felt sick. She gagged. Every smell that entered her nose seemed new to her, *was* new to her. She couldn't even remember smells, and each of them made her nauseous. She dry-heaved some more. A jagged sliver of ice pierced her skull, leaving her with a pounding migraine. Maybe she hit her head and lost her memory; she would obviously not remember that. How did she even remember you could lose your memory?

Her stomach was a stormy sea, her head a tangle of language with corresponding images, only the barest and most basic memories. Concepts, rules, ideas, notions, new and surprising to her, comprehensible, yet alien: You walk with your feet. Sounds from your lips can form words. You are a woman, there are also men. It's not polite to belch in public. A phone is a device to call distant people. You're naked right now; clothes can help solve that. When you're hungry, you eat. *Eat?*

Eating was the last thing she wanted to think about. Eating. Food. Nausea.

She threw up copiously down the side of the...

Bed? Is that what this is called? Soft. To lie on. Lie. Lies. Untruths. Truths. Reality. Real. Am I real? Am I real if I can't see myself?

The headache brought with it another memory.

A name.

Her name?

Yes. No. Maybe.

Yes.

"Elizabeth," she whispered.

She pushed off with her... *Arms?*... to a sitting position. She felt now like she remembered all the basic things about life an adult woman should know, when a second ago she couldn't remember what words were. Still, if someone else—because other people existed, she remembered that now—asked her anything about herself, her mind would be blank; an empty notebook page, where all the information about her was supposed to be. But there was a name at the top of that page now, wasn't there?

"Elizabeth..."

Was that her name? Was she this Elizabeth? Probably. She couldn't remember anything about anybody else she might have met, before whatever brought upon this case of amnesia—*That was the word for that!*—happened: a family member, a co-worker, a boyfriend, a girlfriend? *Hmm, no,* she considered with surprise. *I like men, it seems, come to think about it. Though, I can't remember ever seeing one.*

People with amnesia usually remember their name first, or something that has to do with them personally. *Right?* Then again, they might remember something useless, like the time they mixed pickle juice, ice-cream, and tuna in a blender to see how it tasted. She had no memory of how those things tasted, though, so that was another strange thought.

"Yes, I think my name's Elizabeth," she said to herself, hearing her own voice distinctly for the first time. Was that how an Elizabeth sounded? "My name is Elizabeth."

As Elizabeth's eyes adjusted to the darkness, something that had seemed impossible a moment ago, she noticed there was light coming into the room, dim, almost unnoticeable, from the narrow space under a door near the foot of the bed. Warm, flickering light.

Her feet felt unsteady under her as she stood, but she soon felt balanced and ready. She took two steps toward the door, then something. A realization made her remember she was naked, and if there was another person on the other side, they might see her. She didn't want that. She padded around the bed with her hand until she found a blanket, which she draped around her body.

She reached the door, took the knob between her fingers—*Turn it*—and turned it. She opened it to find a bathroom. A lantern sat on the toilet's lid with a softly glimmering light, and to the left, in the tub, was a—

"Oh my god!" she cried, bringing a hand to her lips.

There was a naked man there, an older man, maybe in his early fifties, lying in the bathtub, motionless. *Dead.* Even in the dim lighting, she could see the tub was filled with water tinted red, and the man's left arm hung over the edge of the tub. A crimson puddle on the tiles.

Trembling, fearful but not yet fully grasping why death was something to fear, she padded into the bathroom, stalking around the puddle of blood. She picked up the lantern by the handle, returned to the other room, and closed the door behind her.

"I'm sorry, Mister." Elizabeth shone the light around what she now realized was a bedroom.

She found some clothes in a closet. The second piece of clothing she tried on made her feel comfortable. The first had too long a cleavage and too short a skirt, and she somehow felt that was not the way she would dress. *Not the way your mother would ever allow you to dress,* she thought. *Like one of those girls in the magazines.* This one looked nicer, she thought, observing herself in the mirror. It was a long olive skirt with a cream-colored blouse with long sleeves. Olive seemed to go well with her reddish hair.

She also found other clothing accessories: earrings, a necklace, shoes—she didn't choose high-heels, she felt she wouldn't know how to walk with those. She tied her hair at the back of her head in a ponytail and, looking in the mirror, she determined she looked quite pretty; or at least, she felt this was supposed to be "pretty". She was only missing the make-up. There was make-up on a vanity table, but she didn't remember how to put it on. Then the memory of the dead man in the bathtub made her realize perhaps vanity wasn't the best thing to dwell on at this moment, but it all felt so new, so exciting, despite being so confusing and scary. She left her face as it was.

Elizabeth ventured outside the bedroom to find she was in a one-story house. Upon examining the only other two bedrooms and the one other bathroom, she thought the man in the bathtub lived alone, and something had made him decide to... *Suicide himself? Is that the way you say it? Sounds odd.*

She reached a plain-looking living room. She wondered how she knew it was plain, when she couldn't formulate the mental image of what the opposite of that would look like. The front door was open, and she felt a strange sense of... *Dread? Insecurity? I feel unsafe with the door standing wide open.* Then she thought of something she hadn't considered. Did she used to live here? Was this her house? It probably was. Why else would she be here? Why else would there be women's clothes in that closet? They fit her a bit loose, she thought.

She had probably fallen unconscious in her bed after seeing the man dead in the bathtub... *My husband?...* In the mirror, she'd surmised she was probably about forty-something, so the age range made sense. Maybe the shock had given her some kind of hysterical amnesia, if that was even a thing. Maybe the man had knocked her unconscious—some men did that, she remembered from...the news?—and thinking he'd killed his wife, he'd taken his own life.

That's a lot of morbid thinking, Elizabeth, get a hold of yourself.

Should she call 119?... No...it was 911... Right.

Let's close that door first.

After she took a couple of steps toward it, a blade of pain cut through her brain, and she screamed. Her stomach rumbled, and she felt dizzy and sick once again. She didn't know whether to grab her head or cover her mouth. She fell back on an old couch, and all of a sudden, the pain stopped. She hadn't passed out or thrown up like before, but another memory—or something that *felt* like a memory—appeared in her mind.

She saw a car rolling down a hill, bumping and tumbling out of control. She was in the car, but it was confusing. It was all a blur. She was both somewhere inside the car, but simultaneously standing outside, witnessing this happen.

Four figures. Four figures in the car. A grown man, a grown woman, a little girl, a baby. All screaming.

Then the image was gone.

She sat on the couch, breathing hard, sweating cold.

A scream cut through the air, coming in through the front door, from somewhere outside.

CHAPTER TWENTY-FIVE
HELL FROZEN RAIN

Royce stood beside Jess, looking around the bar at a hundred scared, taciturn faces. These people, like them, had not gotten any sleep since the previous night's events, and since then, it had been one thing after the other.

"So, this is all we're getting?" Jess asked. "If sinkholes open all over town, this is all that survives of the four thousand people in White Harbor? Less than a hundred?"

"If no one else comes," Royce said. "I guess this is the best we can do." He mulled his own words over for a moment. "Unless you have like a bullhorn down in that cellar or something."

Jess turned her head to look at him. In her eyes, he noticed she had exactly that on one of those shelves down there. She pointed at the door to one side of the bar, reached into her pocket and brought out a jingling bunch of keys. "Roof access is in the kitchen. Go and unlock it. I'll be right back."

"Um, excuse me?"

They both turned to find a thirty-something Hispanic man standing beside them. Royce recognized him as the last person to come in a few minutes after the hospital crowd. He was drying his glasses with a napkin.

"Hi, my name's Tali Ruiz," he said. "I overheard what you were talking about. I think I can help."

They stared at him with puzzlement. Grabbing a bullhorn and going up to the roof to call as many people to the bar as they could didn't seem like such a complex plan that would require help.

"A bullhorn might cover like a mile at best. But with the rain, it probably won't reach everyone in town. I think I can help you make it go further."

"How?" Jess asked with mistrust.

"So, I know this will sound dumb, but...uh...magic?"

Royce and Jess stared at him. A loud "Pfft!" escaped Royce's lips. "C'mon, brother, go sit over there. Let us—"

"I know you have Ben Curling in the basement." He was met with silence, bulging eyes, and hanging jaws. "I can do the things he can do."

A second later, Royce had tackled him to the ground, his arm twisted against his back, as the surrounding crowd gasped in shock. "Well, you should've said that before coming in here, man." He pushed a knee into his back. "Would've saved us the trouble of throwing you out."

"No! Wait!" Tali grunted. "I'm not *like* him! I mean, I was part of his group, but I'm not like him!"

Jess pointed Peggy down at him. "Yeah, now tell me one with elves in it."

"My mom is part of his Order! Her name's Doris! She's Peter Lange's maid!"

Royce removed his knee from his shoulder, but still held him down. "And that's supposed to, what? Make you a good guy?"

"Yes! Our Order is peaceful! We're trying to stop Martha Lange!"

"But see, your friend Curling's version of stopping Martha Lange was trying to kill us two nights ago. He killed one of our friends, injured another. Among other atrocities."

"I know!" Tali pleaded. "I know! Curling doesn't follow the ways of the Order! He founded the order, but he went rogue decades ago! We're trying to help! Please!"

Royce shot a glance at Jess. She wavered for a moment, then returned a nod. Royce let go of Tali and helped him to his feet. "Alright, but after you help us with the bullhorn, we're gonna need a word with you and your buddy down there."

Tali gave a quick nod. "Sure."

Royce climbed through the trapdoor in the ceiling, wearing a raincoat he'd borrowed from Chuck Cunningham, flashlight in hand. The sound of rain hit his ears, and soon it became clear the raincoat was useless, as icy wind blasted the rain into his face the second he poked his head out of the hole.

He climbed to the roof, followed by Tali Ruiz, in another of Chuck's raincoats. He couldn't believe they'd all accepted something as laughable as "this guy will magic this megaphone into being louder". The last two days had been surreal, but he knew this went further back. After accepting what happened at the Vanek House as real, sea monsters, the sun disappearing, and magic didn't seem so far-fetched.

As they approached the edge of the roof, even through the rain, it was unquestionable. The town looked dead. Empty. Cars still worked, but there wasn't a single one in the streets, save for the cluster of headlights near the Blue Overlook—people still awaiting rescue. Dim lights flickered in some windows, barely noticeable against the town's blacked out expanse. The hospital still burned in the distance. Despite the driving rain, the flames raged on, as if water had no power against flames that angry. He pictured gas lines, tanks, and chemicals would keep fueling it for a while.

"Jesus Christ," Royce said. He then turned to look at Tali, who had the bullhorn in his hand and was also staring at the burning hospital. "So, how does this work?"

The shorter man gave him the megaphone, and Royce spied a strange symbol drawn on it. It looked like a mixture of runes and Japanese kanji. He peered at him with confusion.

"Is that it? Just this little doodle thing?"

"Yes. I think."

Royce pursed his lips, not looking quite convinced, and thumbed the switch to the On position. The bullhorn came alive with a resounding squawk, like a titanic robot crow clearing its throat. It made Royce flinch. He opened his mouth, moving his jaw side to side to clear his ears. "Okay. I think that works."

He put the bullhorn to his lips, but when he was about to speak, Tali said, "Wait! Mr. Howe. Maybe, to call people's attention, before actually speaking into it, why don't you press the alarm button?" He pointed at one of the buttons on the back. "It will be more likely to get attention than some voice out of nowhere."

"Smart." Royce held the bullhorn toward the west side of town. "Here we go. Cover your ears, brother." He pressed the button, and the sound of a siren blared out of the bullhorn. He'd been expecting it to sound like an air-raid siren, but instead it was more like bumping into a car with an alarm—except as loud as the trumpets of the apocalypse.

Tali covered his ears as Royce turned the bullhorn around slowly, so the entire town got an earful of: "WOOOOHREEEE-WOOOOHREEEEWOOOOH!"

Once he reached his original position, he clicked the siren off and put the bullhorn to his lips. "Attention! Attention! People of White Harbor! You are not safe in your homes! Cunningham's is safe! I repeat! Cunningham's is safe! Make your way to Cunningham's asap!"

He stopped for a moment, moved his jaw a little and rubbed his inner ears, then pressed his jaw tight and repeated the full message once more.

"Well, I'll be damned!" a voice said from behind, barely breaking through the ringing in Royce's ears.

Tali let out a shocked gasp, right beside him.

Royce spun around to find Freddie Parham standing in the rain with that smug smirk of his. "When I heard your voice, Tweedle Dum, I just *had* to pop on over to see with my own eyes you were stupid enough to step out of the bar."

"Fuck," Royce said.

"I mean, I'm fishing, I've got a barrel, and a dumb fish happens to jump from the river to the barrel. Who am I not to shoot it?" He grinned. "I gotta be quick, though. I have Brickhouse's kids locked in a bedroom. He's sure to come running home anytime."

"You piece of shit!" Royce reached toward the back of his pants and pulled out a gun Jess had given him, pointed it at him. "You're the fish in that analogy, bitch!"

"Please..." Freddie said, his grin unwavering. "Have you even noticed where you're standing?"

Royce looked down and, in the light from Tali's flashlight, he noticed the half an inch of rain that had pooled on the roof was now jet-black, and the rain falling from the sky in the immediate area of the roof was black as well. "No," Royce said, breathless.

A thin, black spike shot diagonally from the water at his feet and pierced his left hand, making him drop the gun with a scream.

"Do you understand now?" Freddie said. "I have only but a dust particle's worth of the power of God. I am nothing, and still, with a flick of my finger, I can turn every drop of rain currently hitting your face into a shard of ice. You'd make a cool sea urchin, you know?"

With a grunt, Royce broke the shard as if it were an icicle and pulled it out of his hand, curling his fingers into a fist. He shot a hateful sneer at Freddie. "I thought I could forgive you for killing Leroy coz you were crazy. I felt sorry for you. But now I see you're just a selfish, vile monster!"

Freddie cocked his head to one side, brought his eyebrows together and stuck out his lower lip in a mockery of a sad face. "Oh, you miss your brother, Tweedle Dum?" He pointed an index finger and thumb at him. "Let me send you to him."

Freddie's left hand exploded in a burst of blood and bone, followed by his face twisting in shock. A howl of pain issued from his gaping mouth.

Jess pointed her shotgun at Freddie from the trapdoor. "I knew you'd pull something idiotic if we just baited you, you fuckin' hyena!" She pumped the shotgun, ready to fire again.

Freddie let out a loud roar of anger toward her and stretched his one remaining hand in her direction. She reacted fast and ducked, closing the door above her, as pointed shards of black hail crashed against the metal surface of the trapdoor.

"Fuck!" he shouted in rage, then turned back to Royce and Tali, lips trembling, teeth bare, his maimed hand bleeding profusely. "You're dead, Tweedle Dum!"

Tali produced a small bag from his jacket and tossed what seemed like dozens of pebbles at Freddie's feet. The water in the area they encompassed went from black to clear, like normal rain. Royce noticed tiny symbols scrawled on the stones. He didn't know exactly what they did, but understood they disrupted Freddie's power. To what extent, he wasn't sure.

Freddie appeared to realize this as well. His good hand now pointed at them. Nothing happened.

Jess reemerged from the trapdoor, pointed Peggy at Freddie, ready to shoot.

Noticing this, Freddie growled at her, ran to one side, and disappeared in mid-air as the second blast from the shotgun went off into the night.

"Dammit!" she shouted, then turned to Royce and Tali. "Hurry! Come back in!" She disappeared into the hole, pushing the trapdoor so it would remain open.

Royce picked up the gun with his good hand. Both men ran toward the trapdoor. Royce gave a slight push to Tali's back, and said, "You first! We need that weird voodoo thing. Can't risk losing you."

"Okay!" Tali crouched and went down the ladder.

Royce looked back, expecting Freddie to appear again from the darkness behind him.

He did not.

Royce groaned as Jess hurried to his side and examined his bleeding left hand. "Fucking hyena, almost got me." He reached for a clean kitchen towel from a large table nearby and put it to his hand. He regarded Tali. "You saved both our lives up there, man. What were those pebble things?"

"I spent most of yesterday drawing glyphs on little rocks," he said with a pained groan, rubbing his side. "They limit his connection to their god's power, but apparently his gateways remain open, and that's how he escaped."

"Gateways?" Royce asked.

"During the ritual, Parham can move freely back and forth between this world and the Moonlit World, uh...what you guys call Blight Harbor, but to move long distances, he has to have set up gateways to move from one place to the other. Setting them up takes a long time, so I'm guessing he has a limited number of places in town he can move between. This bar would be one of them."

"He mentioned he had Barry's kids." Royce cast a worried glance toward Jess, who returned the look. "So, he probably has another of these gateways in Barry or Ray's house. He said he's waiting for him to get back home. He's going to kill them."

"Shit," Jess put her hands on her hips, pondering, then shook her head. "We can't do anything about that right now. We can just hope they make it." She looked at his hand and the towel, already soaked with blood. "Let's get that hand patched up."

A murmur came from the bar's main area. Voices. Consternation. Something was wrong. The three rushed out of the kitchen to see all the blinds on one side had been rolled up, and everyone was gathered at the windows, gazing in silent dread toward the street.

"Get away from the windows, you goddamn morons!" Jess shouted as they shoved their way through the crowd. "Didn't you hear me earlier?"

Royce found Lillian, who stood looking outside, holding Tracy against her leg. On the street stood Freddie, illuminated by the light coming from several flashlights shining through the window. There was a dead body lying at his feet, looking like it had been riddled with bullets.

"Mason," Jess said, under her breath.

Royce remembered the man. Mason Owen, one of Cunningham's regulars. He'd been there on the night John Hitch had come for them. Hitch had locked him, Louis Foley, and Riley Estrada—another bar regular—in the bathroom.

With teeth bared and mournful tears streaming down his face, Riley Estrada stood amidst the bar crowd, mourning the loss of his best friend.

Freddie grinned toward the crowd through the window. Looking at the hand Jess had shot off, it was covered in that crystallized black substance they'd seen on the other side, coating the mangled hand, which had only the thumb and a pinkie finger.

"You pathetic losers are all cowering in there, thinking you're safe," he shouted over the rain. He swiveled his head from side to side. "No. All you are is last. The last to die, but trust me, you will all die." He regarded the corpse on the floor. "Like this sad little drunk right here. Every night, coming to Cunningham's to drink his insignificant life away. Did you know he has an ex-wife down in Beaverton, with two kids he pays alimony for, but never sees coz he's too embarrassed they'll realize what a loser dad they have? Well…had." He giggled. "I only want those two, right there"—he pointed the black-coated left hand, if it could still be called that, at Jess and Royce—"so, if you guys push them out here, I might reconsider your survival prospects. How's that sound?"

Royce surveyed the terrified faces around him, hearing nervous whispers and unintelligible murmurs, but no one spoke up, until—

"Fuck off, Parham!"

All faces turned to find Arnold Fowler, the man with the blue knitted cap Jess had been pointing her shotgun at, sticking his head above the crowd.

"I might not trust these people, but I'll be fucked if I'm ever gonna trust a Parham."

This earned a sneer from Freddie.

"I've seen your face couple times in the news," Fowler said. "Freddie Parham. Killed those kids at the Vanek House. Not to mention, you got your mom and baby sister killed. And we're supposed to take your word? Nah, man. We're alright, right here, thank you very much, please do go thoroughly fuck yourself."

Freddie regarded him with hatred in his eyes. "So, that's how it's gonna be then, huh?" He grinned. "Since we're on the topic of things Blight Harbor has filed away for all of us, why don't we talk about some of you? See how you feel sharing that bar together with your friends and neighbors. Starting with you, Arnold Fowler. Does Sally Hargraves know you were the one who fed her dog meatballs with powdered drain cleaner?"

Fowler gasped. "No! It wasn't like that!"

A loud "What?" came from inside the bar.

"Oh, look, Sally's in there!" Freddie said and let out a loud hyena giggle. "Yeah, Sally-babes, your neighbor thought your dog was too damn noisy, and he got fed up with it."

"You son-of-a-bitch!" Sally Hargraves shouted, pushing her way through the crowd toward Arnold Fowler, and soon slapped him in the face, as others tried to stop the fight.

"It wasn't like that!" Fowler shielded his face from the woman's attack. "It was an accident!"

Freddie kept giggling. "C'mon, Sally, don't be such a little hypocrite. You're no saint either. I see your husband in the crowd. Does he know none of your three kids are his?"

"Shut up!" Sally Hargraves said, gawking at Freddie. "You can't possibly know that!"

"Can't I? Sally, it's all you think about, and it's the talk of the town. It's all over Blight Harbor. I wouldn't know it otherwise."

"Sally, what's he saying?" Sally's husband, Travis, asked. He had his three kids with him. "What's he saying?"

"If it's any consolation to you, Travis," Freddie said with elation, "the father is your buddy, Keith Holland—from the gas station Hollands—and he was recently beheaded, along with his entire family. So, you can keep pretending those three kids weren't pumped into your wife by Keith's impressively large gas nozzle."

As Travis Hargraves started an argument with his wife, who continued to hit Arnold Fowler over and over, Freddie turned his attention to another person in the crowd.

"Oh, it's so inspiring seeing all of you in there, together as a community. Singing Kumbaya, waiting for the storm to pass. Even Holden Graham looks right at home with Black people, Muslims, and the town's most famous lesbian, though if you were to lift his shirt, you'd see a huge swastika tattooed in his abdomen with the words: 'Death to Jews, Niggers, Queers, and Muslims'."

The man next to Holden Graham, a man of Iraqi descent, named Ahmad Saad, reached a hand toward his shirt, only to have Graham slap it away.

"No!" Graham said. "He's lying!"

"Then you have nothing to hide!" Saad said, his hand shooting forward and lifting Graham's white shirt to reveal, in the light of his flashlight, the large tattoo. "There it is!"

"Wait! I was saving up to get it removed! That's not me anymore! That's not—"

He was cut off by Saad's fist crashing against his jaw. Others joined in, pushing Graham, yelling at him, attacking him as he unsuccessfully tried to defend himself.

"I saved the best for last," Freddie said. "I see Keith Hunter in there. Never had the displeasure of meeting him in person."

The man opened his eyes wide, gaze fixed on Freddie, shaking his head, as if he knew what was coming, which only made Freddie grin wider.

"You see, good old Keith might not give off any weird vibes, but his phone is brimming with pictures of underage girls and boys!" Little by little, heads turned toward the man with horrified, baffled expressions in their eyes. "Not to mention an entire terabyte of videos in an external drive in his closet. And I'm not talking about 'barely legal'. Oh, no. I'm talking about little kids. Seven. Five." Murmurs started spreading like wildfire through the crowd as Keith Hunter appeared to shrink. "And your prized possession. The video with the two-year-old you found hidden deep in the bowels of the internet."

"Shut up!" the man shouted, crushed by the glares of anger and disgust.

"But, hey, I mean, maybe you shield yourself under the usual pedo excuse of 'look, don't touch', right? Like a junkie? They're only anonymous pictures and videos from the dark web, right? Except"—Freddie cast a look at the crowd gathered in front of the window—"you gotta wonder if the parents in there will believe that...considering you teach their kids math at Garland Elementary."

Lillian Howe pulled little Tracy closer to her, as jeers from the crowd rose to join the already heated fights going on between the other people around them.

"I see a few kids in there...must be so hard in that crowd, in the dark, to contain yourself from...shuffling by and copping a feel?" He turned his grin to Lillian and Tracy. "Especially little Tracy Howe, whose picture you took today, while in line at the hospital tents...right?"

Royce threw the first punch, unaware of when his disgust had turned to rage, fueled by the stress and anger from his encounter with Freddie. His knuckles sank into Keith Hunter's stubbly cheek, sending him staggering into another man, who shoved him back with a disgusted, "Don't fucking touch me!" into the path of Royce's eager fist. In a blink, he was all fists and fury. In his mind, he saw his daughter Tracy, set to start kindergarten next year, when she'd be within reach of this predator. Perhaps not in the same classroom, but there were maintenance closets, bathrooms, hidden corners only someone like Keith Hunter would know. He imagined his filthy hand touching Tracy's puffy cloud of coiled hair, and the last shred of rationality left him. Others soon joined in, kicking and punching the man.

As his fists connected with the man's face and body, he could barely hear Jess's voice shouting, "Stop! This is what he wants! Royce! This is what he wants!"

Before Royce's brain could internalize her words, he and several other people from the crowd were lifting Hunter. Seconds later, he was flying toward the window, which

(*What the hell did I just—*)

exploded outward into a thousand pieces.

"No, you stupid fucks!" Jess shouted.

The man landed unceremoniously and rolled over the pooled rainwater and the glass, just a few feet from Mason Owen's corpse.

"Oh, shit!" Royce said, feeling that intense, almost post-coital clarity that follows anger, as if his brain had received a jolt. "No!"

"Step back!" Jess shouted, as people realized the window now lay open to whatever horrors were outside and the commotion died down. Scared people followed her command and moved away from the window.

"Well, look at you, Tweedle Dum, and his angry mob." Freddie watched Keith Hunter stand up, his hands bleeding from the glass on the sidewalk. The man did his best to bring himself up on his knees. "Don't get me wrong. This piece of trash deserves that and much more, but you're all judging me for killing people, and you threw this man out here, knowing I was going to kill him without a second thought."

He raised his remaining hand. With a flourish and a flick of his wrist, he snapped his fingers. In an instant, the rain around Hunter turned into sharp crystals, like black ice. They pierced his body in impossibly rapid succession, making him convulse as the icy shards tore through him, like arrowheads shredding his clothes and skin. His body, his face and skull became a blood-soaked mess, pockmarked by tiny, jagged holes with black rocks lodged inside. He collapsed, still shaking under the relentless hail. After a few seconds, the hail melted into rain and the black marks on his body dissolved, leaving nothing but a lifeless heap.

"In a way, Tweedle Dum...I could say since *you* threw the first punch and helped throw him out, you're the actual killer. I was just your knife. Welcome to my level." He cast a glance around the ashen, silent crowd. "Over a hundred years, judging my family, and now I get to sentence you all to death. I'll be able to sense the second any of you step out of there, and you can die like the kiddie diddler at my feet. And if none of you come out, you'll still die when the Lord seizes the town. No magic seal will protect you then. That bar you thought was so safe will be your prison. You're on death row, all of you. You and your sins."

He stepped aside and disappeared into thin air, as if behind a rain curtain.

The crowd remained quiet for a minute before realizing he was truly gone.

Royce, who'd come back to join Jess and his family, said, "I thought he was going to come in and kill all of us, all because of my stupid ass."

"He can't," Tali said. "It's not the physical windows that don't let him or his god's power come in. It's the seals on the edges of them. As long as the seals are there, we're safe here. Problem is, those won't last all night."

Jess and Royce shot him a look of concern.

"You're coming to the cellar with me right now," Jess said. "I need you to talk to my dad and to that asshole, Hitch. If we're getting out of here alive, it depends on the three of you."

CHAPTER TWENTY-SIX
CANCER

That door shouldn't be open. That door was never open. Ever since she and Angie had cleaned and arranged their parents' bedroom after their mom's passing, the room had remained closed, and neither had gone back inside. It had become a mausoleum within their own home.

Someone had opened the door, though.

Nadine shone her flashlight down the hallway, taking careful steps, acutely aware she had nothing at hand she could use as a weapon should there be an attacker in that room. She thought back to Callum's pale dead body, and Sylvia slumped over and bleeding over the desk, and worried the same fate awaited her.

Hitch is wounded in Cunningham's cellar, she thought, trying to reassure herself. *This can't be him.*

Martha Lange? No, she thought. She wouldn't bother coming for her in person (maybe). Freddie, then. If Freddie had come for her, there was little she could do with just fists and willpower, especially considering the powers he might have now—according to Sylvia, who wasn't one hundred percent sure of her findings.

She stopped at the top of the stairs, shining her flashlight down to reveal a crimson trail. *Blood.* At first, she thought someone had been dragged up, but then she noticed the hand-prints—bloody, smudged, coming upward. Whoever it was had dragged themselves up the stairs. She followed the bloody slug's trail with the flashlight until it stopped at the forbidden bed-room door. Had Bobby returned wounded? Did Freddie hurt him, and he crawled to the nearest room with a bathroom and medicine cabinet? Bobby wouldn't know the medicine cabinet in there still held her mom's untouched belongings, though. He'd never been in that room.

"Bobby?" she risked, knowing how stupid giving away her position was. "Is that you? Are you okay?"

No answer. *Stupid! Stupid idiot!* For a minute, she considered turning toward the stairs and hauling ass outta there, straight for Cunningham's, but if there was the slightest possibility Bobby was in that room, and he was wounded and unconscious, she needed to help. *Shit, okay.* She stalked toward the room, cursing herself with each step for not abandoning the mission.

She stepped into the dark room, at first only seeing her parents' bed, and one of the nightstands beside it, the one with the picture of her parents' wedding, looking so youthful and happy. Before he'd slapped her mom, causing them to separate. Before he'd died of lung cancer for taking up smoking after the separation. Before she'd died of a heart attack. Before Angie had gotten stomach cancer—though she hadn't had the chance to die from it. Nadine's heart broke anew at the realization her entire family was gone. It was then her flashlight moved slightly up and shone on some-thing black, pink, and red.

"Boo!" a voice whispered from behind.

She spun around with a start and reeled back two steps, her flashlight catching sight of Freddie's grinning face, standing in the doorway, holding the door open.

"Do you know what's sad?" Freddie said. "You almost would've survived, if only because you're so boring and irrele-vant I almost forgot about you."

"Go to hell!" She kept her distance, her breathing becoming fast, trying to think of ways of pushing past him.

"Wow. Not even a creative comeback. You're so fucking dull! I even remembered Brickhouse's boyfriend, which, by the way: totally called it when I named him Plus-One. Come to think of it, I never even cared enough about you to give you a proper nickname." He brought his left hand to his chin, pondering. Nadine could see the hand didn't just seem covered by that black crystallized substance, like the Martha Lange statue in the hospital, it seemed *made* of it, stiff, like a prosthetic hand. Five obsidian-black fingers and a thumb. "I got it! Blandine! Hmm, no, it doesn't convey your general dullness..." His eyes opened wide, and he pointed the black hand toward her. "That's it! Rice Cracker! Bland, tasteless, boring, makes people groan when offered one, and it would definitely *not* be anyone's first choice, as proven by the fact not even someone as pathetic as Norman picked you." He flashed a wide grin.

"Fuck you," she hissed, still trying to measure if charging at him would be a good idea, or if he had some kind of concealed weapon.

He shrugged. "Meh, better than 'go to hell', I guess. Aren't you glad you at least got a proper nickname before you died, Rice Cracker? Not that you lived much to begin with. Hell, your sister would've died soon—even if Mother hadn't chosen to sacrifice her—and even she would've lived more than you if you've gotten to live to be a hundred. But, anyway, time to die."

"Don't come near me!"

"Or what?" he said with a smirk. "You'll teach me fourth-grade history until I die of boredom?" He let out his annoying "Hee-hee-hee!" giggle. "But don't worry. I'm not gonna be the one to kill you. I have guests arriving in minutes, but I've left you something to play with. Buh-bye, Rice Cracker! It was... forgettable knowing ya!"

He slammed the door shut, and from the silence left in his wake, came a wet, rhythmic thumping, growing out of the shadows behind her. For a second, she thought it was her own heart thumping in her chest, but when she turned, her scream ripped through the darkness.

She The bloody trail she'd been following went up the wall by her mother's nightstand. There, a deformed, faceless corpse hung, its flesh fused to the wall. Its ribcage and torso were splayed open, arms outstretched like wings, as if it were crucified over her parents' wedding picture. Instead of entrails, a massive, purple, black, and brown tumor beat like a grotesque imitation of a heart.

As Nadine stood frozen, smaller tumors sprouted from within, sending out dark, vine-like tendrils, infesting the walls, growing, clustering into swollen cysts and pus-filled sores the size of fists. They spread rapidly, covering every inch of the walls and ceiling.

Too late, she reacted and yanked at the door, but a vine of crawling tumors had sealed it shut. As she gave frantic pulls to the locked door, something grew out of the fleshy lumps, which made her take a step back. Yellow tips poked through the surface of the tumors and grew, unfurled, and opened.

Flowers! What the fuck?

The sight was jarring, almost absurd: delicate, yellow blossoms blooming out of the revolting, pulsating flesh. They swayed as the tumors bulged and slackened to the rhythm of the enormous pumping heart, creating a hypnotic, sickening dance. The blossoms formed clusters of pure yellow on top of exposed, affected flesh, making her stomach turn.

A stench worse than weeks-old rotten flesh pushed up her nostrils. Nadine's flashlight beam caught a hint of the faint, wispy vapors emanating from the flowers like specters. She coughed, the fumes burning her lungs. Her chest heaved with violent spasms as she gasped for breath, hacking as if her soul were ramming its way out of her esophagus. The air was thick with poison corrupting her insides, stealing her oxygen.

I'm gonna die here! I'm gonna die here!

An image came to her mind as she stared, helpless, at one of the clusters of yellow flowers. Angie's dress as she was tied on that altar.

Her dress catching fire. The yellow-flower print being consumed and engulfed by the flames that would kill her sister.

She remembered her earlier thoughts of Bobby, running into this room looking for the medicine cabinet, and had a desperate idea.

All of mom's stuff is still there!

Coughing, she turned and noticed the door to the bathroom was wide open. The tumor vines were contained within the bedroom, they didn't go in there. She marched in that direction, but she hadn't gone two steps when she felt something sting her forearm. She grunted, checked her arm, and there was a thin vine stretching from her skin to one of the flowers. It was growing roots underneath. Without hesitation, she grabbed the vine and gave it a hard tug. She screamed as it came off, leaving a small, bleeding hole in her arm. The extracted tip had small wriggling roots dripping with her blood, and a tiny piece of flesh. Soon she felt another sting and another as two more of these vines entered the back of her shoulder and her thigh. She could feel the tiny roots growing, anchoring themselves to her tissue. The outer parts grew tiny green leaves, as the vine got thicker and woodier.

Wasting no time, she pulled them both out, screaming with pain, tossing them aside and continuing her march to the bathroom. She could hear tiny spitting sounds as more vines shot out toward her. A vine hooked itself to the fatty tissue on her lower abdomen. One more got her on the thigh, close to the bleeding wound where she'd pulled another. One more clung to the base of her skull, right at the edge of her scalp, another in her upper back.

The roots stung the inner layers of her skin as they spread. She was but a few steps away from the bathroom. She could feel more of the vines attaching themselves to her body, as her lungs burned with the toxic fumes, and she knew, if she lost her strength now and allowed too many of the vines to get stuck to her, she would be immobilized and simply die from the poison.

No! she thought. *Martha Lange doesn't get to kill us both, Angie. That bitch has to pay!*

Clenching her jaw tight, she pulled with all her strength. Though she knew she had to conserve oxygen, she couldn't help but let out a loud roar of anger and pain. She could feel her skin tear as she plucked the roots from her flesh, taking little pieces of skin each time. As soon as she could move, she dove forward, past the doorway. Despite her aching body, she scampered away from the opening, leaving bloody spots on the floor, as more vines hit the spot where she'd landed, and lay limp and lifeless, unable to find their target.

First things first. Nadine eyed the bathroom window, stood up. Her clothes were covered in holes and blooms of red blood from her multiple wounds. She took off her jacket, wrapped it around her hand and forearm, then back-fisted the glass and scraped as much of the window as she could. She climbed up to it and took several long breaths of fresh air. She steeled herself for what she needed to do next.

She ran to the wall cabinet, catching her face in the mirror; spotted a small bleeding hole in her face where she'd plucked one of the vines. She opened the cabinet and found her mother's hairspray.

Her mom had always thought hiding it among the medicines, instead of her vanity, would prevent her daughters from depleting her can when their own ran out. She was glad her mom had never been good at hiding things. Next, she checked the drawers on the vanity under the sink for the other item her mom thought they didn't know about.

After Nadine's dad had passed away, Colleen Schaefer had taken up smoking, an old habit that had made a secret comeback, despite the fact lung cancer had taken her ex-husband's life. It seemed like a self-destructive way of keeping his memory alive. Her mother locked herself in her bathroom and smoked, which meant she kept her lighter here, thinking her daughters wouldn't come to her bathroom. She was mistaken about that. Nadine had left her dad's little shiny lighter exactly where her mom had left it.

As she rummaged through the drawers, the rotting smell of poison fumes wafted slowly into the bathroom. Nadine found the lighter and clutched it in her fist, triumphant. She put her jacket back on and tucked her cell phone into the chest pocket; the flashlight sticking out—she would need both hands for this. She climbed on the tub's edge, put her face out of the shattered window, inhaled deeply, held her breath, and hurried back into the bedroom.

As soon as she entered, she used the butt of the hairspray can to break the window immediately to her right, creating a draft from the bathroom to blow some of the poison out. She made sure not to remain in one place, anticipating the vines coming toward her.

She ducked to one side and then the other, staying in constant motion as she circled the bed.

Once on the other side, she got as close as possible to the main body, raised the can, and sprayed the throbbing tumor and the writhing corpse as thoroughly as she could. She could already feel some of the vines sticking into her back and legs, like darts. Bearing the pain, she flicked the lighter open. It took her two tries for the little flame to come, during which one more of the wretched vines clung to her back. She grunted, raised the flame toward the creature on the wall, and pressed the atomizer. The hairspray turned into a liquid flame that ignited the chemicals already coating the creature. The flames spread fast.

Realizing this might not be enough to keep the fire going due to the monster's blood and fluids, she turned toward the bed. The vines pulled tight; their roots hooked to her flesh. Despite the pain, she sprayed the bed with the atomizer. Soon, the covers and the mattress caught fire, and in seconds, the entire bed was ablaze.

Fueled by adrenaline, Nadine screamed, pulling with her full weight to rip herself free from the vines, tearing patches of her skin in the process. She ran toward the door and sprayed fire onto the tumor-covered vines that sealed it, praying it would make them retreat, or at least weaken them enough for her to force the door open.

She watched as the yellow flowers browned and blackened and shriveled under the touch of the flames. Smoke was now accumulating, mixing with the poison fumes from the yellow blossoms, creating a deadly mix. She went down on her knees, trying to stay as low as possible, and covered her nose with her blouse. As the fire spread and the flowers burned, she realized she was no longer being attacked by the vine darts. She turned her head to the right and her breath caught when she noticed it: a single yellow flower, unburned, growing out of a small tumor, which hadn't yet caught fire. It was perfectly aligned with her face.

Before she could react, out flew the thin threadlike vine, with its tiny arrowhead at the end, and hit the very center of her right eye. Nadine screamed in shocking pain, which intensified as she felt the roots begin to spread and cling to her eyeball. She fell to the floor, howling, rolling, kicking. At first, there had been tension on the cord that stretched from the flower to the eye, but then the yellow bloom caught fire, and the vine came off the wall. It was still alive, however, still growing tendrils around her eyeball, as she shuddered with pain. She pictured the tendrils continuing on, growing until they wrapped around her brain, leaves and yellow flowers protruding out of every orifice in her skull.

Perhaps it was an unconscious action, perhaps emboldening brought by the adrenaline, or perhaps a moment of desperate clarity amidst the worst pain she'd felt in her life, but in a sudden motion—

Like a band-aid! Like a fucking band-aid!

—she grabbed the vine with both her hands. In this moment of cruel clarity, she could even feel the texture of little leaves growing out of it—leaves that grew by feeding on her—and gave a hard yank.

She felt her eye slip out of its socket, along with the roots anchored to it. She could've sworn she felt her optic nerve rip away, even if she had no notion what that would feel like. She rolled back and forth on the floor, the horrifying pain of her self-inflicted enucleation sending shockwaves through her body. The smoke filled her lungs when she took in more air to scream, and her screams turned into coughing.

Move! Move! Her thoughts were a voice shouting from a distant land. *Get out!*

Despite the impossible pain, she rolled onto her stomach and crawled the short distance to the door. She clung to the doorknob and pulled. It wouldn't open. She could feel the door move in a little, but the mass at the top, though in flames, was still holding it shut.

No! Please, no!

She pulled. Her lungs were on fire. Her coughing made her ribcage feel about to burst until she became another version of the creature hanging from the wall. She pulled again. Still no luck. The door moved in an inch, but no further. She felt her strength leave her. She thought she was going to faint. If she fainted, it was over. If she fainted, she was dead. She pulled again. Only an inch. Smoke was now so thick, the flashlight looked like a tiny candle in the swirling darkness.

It's over. I can't.

There was a bit of light. Weak. Barely visible through the smoke. Light coming in through the inch the door had opened. Then there was a voice.

"Move away from the door!" It was a woman. "Can you move two steps back?"

She let herself fall to one side instead, leaving the door unblocked, and she lay there coughing.

The door shook. Someone had slammed into it. Two more times. Then on the fourth attempt, it flew open, and, with her remaining eye, Nadine could make out a figure standing in the doorway, holding a flashlight. The woman, whoever she was, hurried in, put an arm around her, and helped her to her feet.

"Come with me," the woman said. "I can help you."

Nadine threw her arm over the woman's shoulder, and they trudged out of the burning room as smoke billowed through the doorway.

"You're hurt. I... I think I saw, uh...medical stuff in my house, across the street. I'll take you there, alright? You'll be okay."

Nadine turned her left eye toward the woman and caught a glimpse of her as they walked the short distance toward the stairs. She felt a shudder of surprise. "J-Jenny?" she said in a shaky voice.

The woman frowned at her. "What? No. My name's Elizabeth."

Can't be Jenny. Can't be her. She's—

"Stop," Nadine coughed as they reached the stairs. "Wait. That room, over there. First door. Need something from there before I leave."

"We c-can't!" Elizabeth said. "We have to get out of here!"

"Will just take a second." Nadine let go of the stranger. She coughed at first, almost to the point of dry heaving, but brought herself to a standing position. She was injured, dizzy, weak, but she could walk. "Wait here."

Nadine plodded toward her bedroom, threw the door open and, wasting no time, opened the closet door to her right. There was a small chest against the deep end of the closet. In a hurry, she rummaged through it, hoping she still had it, and hoping she had batteries. "Yes!" she blurted, as she pulled a black hand radio from the chest and let the lid fall as she turned toward her nightstand. She found an unused pack of AA batteries in the drawer.

As fast as she could, she trudged out of the room, aware with every step and every move she had probably dozens of wounds all over her body, which kept burning with a vengeance as she made her way back to Elizabeth. She was forcing herself to ignore the fact she'd pulled her own eye out, even if the throbbing pain in her skull kept reminding her of this at the rhythm of her heartbeat.

"Ready?" Elizabeth asked.

Nadine answered with a nod, and both exited the house into the pouring rain. After the heat she'd felt inside, the cold rain felt soothing against her skin, even though it made her wounds sizzle with pain. "If you see a man wearing orange scrubs and a hospital robe, run," she said, remembering the way Freddie had appeared in her house and fearing he might come back, sensing she had escaped.

"I don't know what scrubs are," the woman said.

Nadine frowned with puzzlement.

"I'll explain. Let's get out of the rain first. Quick!"

CHAPTER TWENTY-SEVEN
THE HANGING FRAME

Even though he had been begging for death, Peter's eyes fluttered open as he noticed a ray of light piercing through the haze of horror, grief, and failure clouding his brain after losing his son.

The flashlight?

His fingers spider-crawled toward his phone, thinking the light was coming from it, but it was lying face-down. This was daylight. Dim. Silver. Wintry. He sat up and gasped when he realized he was in his childhood bedroom, back in the old house on Hill Road.

Light came in through the window across the room from him. The pane of glass was frosted over. It was snowing outside, an uncommon occurrence in White Harbor.

His bedroom. It sent chills up his spine just to look at it. Thirty years of not seeing this place. Even that fateful day he'd found Mother, surrounded by garbage and filth, rambling incoherences, the day they'd taken her to Clarendon Hospital, he hadn't entered this room. He'd paid for people to take all the stuff from the house and sell it without him needing to set foot in it again. He'd sold or thrown away everything but a few minor items and keepsakes, which he'd stuffed in boxes in the attic of the mountain house

(*The attic where I lost my son*)

and yet, all his old things were just the way he'd left them. The bed, opposite the bedroom door, still had its old, blue-striped covers. There was also the old toy chest in the corner, where he'd kept whatever few toys Mother had allowed him to have, at the behest of his father.

He stood, stepped toward his old bed, set parallel to the window. He sat on it, now facing the door, and was reminded of all the old lumps on the mattress. There was a small nightstand with a lamp. Curious, he gave a gentle tug to its tiny, beaded chain, causing the lampshade to come alive with a soft, diffused light that illuminated the entire room. His eyes lit up with surprise.

He spied a small, simple desk to his right with some notebooks and papers on it—school stuff. The walls were painted plain white, there were no frames or posters hanging from them. Everything felt so impersonal. Mother wouldn't allow posters, ornaments, anything that would individualize it; even the curtains and blankets had nothing of him in them. All because free expressions of one's personality at home were the first steps toward rebellion, toward the possibility of straying from the right path, according to her. Atop the chest of drawers to the left, however, there was a stuffed dinosaur his dad had gotten for him when he was a little kid. *That was in the box in the attic. I saw it when I was searching for the Uolminar for Callum. How is it here?*

Peter had thought this house had been haunted for some time. His memory was fuzzy, though. He remembered hearing voices at night, screams, cries. Scraping, thumping, banging, the sound of things breaking. They were almost inaudible, though. He was certain Mother hadn't been sleeping well back then, either. More than once, he'd heard her slippers shuffle out of her bedroom and walk down the stairs into the kitchen, where she'd stay for most of the night, muttering words to herself Peter hadn't been able to make out the few times he'd slinked toward the kitchen doorway to check on her. In the morning, she'd look sleepy and tired, but she would deny her insomnia and claim Peter had just been dreaming. The one time he'd chosen to press the issue, a good slap in the face had helped shut him up.

For weeks, these sounds had stolen his sleep. His grades had dropped, and he'd made it a habit to doze off in class, resulting in notes from his teachers, which prompted swift punishment from Mother.

As suddenly as the noises had started, one day, they'd simply stopped. He'd gotten his sleep back, and so had Mother.

"Peter?" a raspy voice spoke from the door.

His father stood in the doorway. In shock, he sprung up from the bed. "Dad? Are you okay?"

"What are you doing here? What am *I* doing here?" Hector Rojas said in a bemused voice.

"You tell me," Peter said, pushing his grief aside to seem indignant again. "It's been so long since you left, I assumed you were dead already, but here you are, and this... This place isn't even supposed to exist anymore. Not like this."

"*No entiendo.*"

"Speak English, Dad. You didn't stay long enough to finish teaching me Spanish, remember? Look around. This is the old house, the house we lived in when you left. That was over thirty years ago! I sold this house. I sold all of this stuff. None of this is supposed to be here." He studied the man before him. "Neither are you."

"I never left you, son. I don't know what you're talking about."

"How can you say that?"

His old man cast a perfunctory glance around the room. "She got the boy already, didn't she? I'm so sorry."

Peter felt a knife pierce his heart.

In the sad light coming in from the window, which hadn't been there when he'd seen him in the attic, he noticed how worn out, tired, and ragged his father looked. There was something else, though. Like an idea in his mind he couldn't put into words.

"William's alive. He has to be." The hurt in Peter's eyes betrayed his uncertainty.

"I'm sure he is," his dad replied in a vague, almost drunken voice. "That makes it worse. *Los muertos no pueden gritar de dolor.*"

"*Los muertos...* 'the dead' what?"

"The dead can't scream in pain." Hector's face was drawn, mournful. "Not all of them."

Peter surveyed his dad's face. "Dad...are...are you okay?"

"I'm still resting," he replied. "How am I still resting? I thought I'd be back now."

"What do you mean?"

"I saw snow, Peter!" his eyes lit up with a kind of childlike wonder, a kid remembering their first time playing outside in a beautiful snowy winter. "On the way here! I saw snow! I haven't seen snow in a long time!"

"Dad?" Peter's expression grew more concerned. What could it be about this man he hadn't seen in years that could seem odd after this long?

"Then I was here." The light in his old man's eyes faded. "I knew then why it was snowing. I knew it as soon as I saw this house. Your mother always liked snow. It rarely snowed in White Harbor, so it made her happy when it did."

"I... I remember," Peter said, still uncertain what this conversation was all about. "Winter was the time of year when she was usually more... uh... less angry."

"Your mother used to be so beautiful, and so filled with life. We used to dance together. We had popcorn at the movies. She loved 'The Way We Were', with Barbara Streisand. Oh, how she cried, and she held me in her arms. She would sing that song around the house all day, all the time. She...she was different back then. It all changed right around the time your sister was born."

"My sister?" Peter reacted as if he'd been kicked in the head. "What do you mean, my sister?"

"Your mother changed when she was born. She never wanted her. She didn't like to hold her or breastfeed her. Never cared for her, even years after. I honestly thought she hated her."

Peter's jaw hung loose. "Why would you both hide this from me?"

"Car rollin' down a hill," Hector muttered in a lulling, musical voice.

"What?"

"It was a closed coffin funeral. She wasn't in there. It was an empty coffin. I seemed to be the only one who cried. And well, you, Peter, but you were just a baby. All of your mother's new friends seemed very indifferent to the whole thing. All clustered up. All together. She was radiant." He paused for a moment, then seemed to wander off, and again, in that muttering, musical voice, recited, "Car rollin' down a hill. Slick the asphalt, then it spun. A skid, a crash, a roll, a splash. My dear Elizabeth was gone."

"Dad? What..."

"Car rollin' down a hill. Slick the asphalt, then it spun. A skid, a crash, a roll, a splash. My dear Elizabeth was gone."

"Elizabeth... Was that her name?"

His dad shook his head, a moan escaping through his clenched teeth. "No name now. Only screams. Only pain. Only eternity."

"Dad! Was that her name or not?"

"You know? I haven't seen your mother's bedroom since I got here," he said in a casual, almost joyful tone. "Maybe I'll take one last look at it before I go."

Hector turned around and strolled down the hallway outside. Peter jumped off the bed and strode after him. When they reached the door to Mother's bedroom, Peter stopped his father's hand as he reached for the knob.

"Dad, I can't go in there. Mother forbade me from going in there."

"You've been here before."

He was right, Peter remembered. He'd been there once, a long time ago

(*How dare you enter my room?*)

not long after his father had left. He sneaked into the forbidden room, knowing if Mother ever found out, he'd face her fury and be thrown into The Hole for who knew how long. Still, he clung to the childish hope he'd find his dad there, asleep on the bed, and his disappearance would be just a nightmare. When, disappointed, he'd found the room empty, he turned to leave, and his heart sank. Mother stood there, eyes blazing with rage. He had spent the entire day and night in The Hole, without food or water. Never again did he dare to enter his mother's bedroom.

"The only reason you would be this terrified to go in there is that she caught you snooping in the room."

Peter said nothing. His dad, who sometimes made more sense than others, opened the door. With trepidation, he followed him inside.

Mother's bedroom had a large window at the further end. Light blue curtains hung open, letting in the dim light from the snowy winter day. There was a large bed, covers meticulously arranged, not a wrinkle in sight. Two pillows and a simple quilt with white and blue squares completed the arrangement. Against the wall to the right was his mother's vanity table, which had a round mirror. There were no cosmetics on it—she never wore make-up—there was only an old hairbrush. Next to the vanity table was an ancient highboy, which seemed oddly out of place.

"That wasn't there before," his dad said as he walked toward it.

"Dad...I think it was there. I think I remember it being there when I—"

He shook his head. "She brought that in some time before you entered."

When Peter walked further into the room, something caught his attention. On the wall, between the highboy and the vanity table, there was a frame hanging with an embroidered message in it. It read: PRAY TO GOD FOR JOY, EVEN WHEN YOUR HEART IS BREAKING.

He now remembered seeing that sign before. That one time, when he was just a child, when he had dared

(*How dare you enter my room?*)

to step into his mother's bedroom. But what did it mean?

"See? I told you the wall was backward." Hector pointed at the wall. "It was facing the wrong way. Now it's facing the right way."

"What are you talking about? Could you please start making some sense? You need to tell me about my sister, about what you meant when you said William being alive is worse, and—"

"I couldn't see that sign until I was able to see everything."

"You're rambling. I can't understand what you're saying."

"Help me move this thing." His old placed his hand on the side of the highboy.

Together, they pushed the wooden box of drawers aside. Behind it was a rectangular portion of wall, made of badly laid bricks and plaster, painted in uneven strokes with a single coat of white paint. It looked like a rushed job, not at all befitting the pristine tidiness of the rest of the bedroom.

"What's behind that wall?" Peter said.

"I like soup, you know? Your mother used to make great beef stew. Do you like stew, Peter? Your sister loved stew. That was the first thing I thought of when I woke up just now. I was hungry."

Peter's voice got somber and emphatic.

"What's behind that wall, Dad?"

"A bathroom. Yes, a bathroom. It was going to be a shared bathroom between your sister's room and ours, but we decided not to make it shared at the last minute, your sister didn't need a bathroom, she could use the one down the hall, your mother said, so we sealed up her side and kept it open on this side. Your mother sealed this side, though. She sealed it later, yes. I could always hear her crying. I could hear her praying. Praying and crying."

Peter remembered Mother sitting at the kitchen table. Weeping. Muttering prayers alone.

"Dad..." Peter's voice was breaking, as if something horrible was rising up his throat at incredible speed. A notion bubbling at the back of his mind, and he could sense it would explode any second now. "Sobbing about what?"

"The banging," Hector said in a natural tone. "The screams."

"Oh my god. Oh my god!"

He ran back toward his bedroom. The hedge clippers. He still had them when he woke up in this place, the same as his phone. He picked them off the floor and ran back to his mother's bedroom. He pushed his father aside and started attacking the wall with the closed tip of the shears, over and over, until small pieces of poorly laid bricks broke off.

(*It was a closed coffin funeral. She wasn't in there. It was an empty coffin*)

"Oh god, she couldn't have, she couldn't have!" Peter shouted.

(*Your mother used to be so beautiful, and so filled with life*)

"No... Mother, why? Why?"

(*She was different back then. It all changed right around the time your sister was born*)

Peter kept attacking the wall. The tips of the shears were bent, but still broke through the bricks.

(*I seemed to be the only one who cried. And well, you, Peter, but you were just a baby.*)

No! How could they hide I had a sister? How could they?

(*Mother, I hear noises in my bedroom*)

What if she made me forget?

(*Car rollin' down a hill. Slick the asphalt, then it spun. A skid, a crash, a roll, a splash. My dear Elizabeth was gone*)

The wall kept crumbling until a sizable gap opened and a sickening, rotting smell wafted out like a soul from Hell. Despite the smell making him sick to his stomach, he pulled out bricks, one by one, until the hole in the wall was fully opened.

Peter pulled out his phone, switched the flashlight on, and shone it into the shadows, covering his hand with his nose. Before him, there was an old, moldy toilet, filthy with dried up human waste. Its lid lay broken at his feet as if someone had smashed it against the wall. The walls were covered in bathroom tile, with the same pattern as that weird room in the attic. Some tiles were broken, bloody smears covered almost every inch of tile. Lying on the floor, close to a bathtub caked in brown and green mold, there was a corpse, skeletal, desiccated, barely covered by dried skin, many years old.

Elizabeth, he thought. *Mother sealed Elizabeth in here. She feigned her death in a car crash. They didn't bury her, that's why they had a closed coffin. Mother put her in here! This is monstrous! Mother killed her! And if Dad was here, he must've known she was here, he must've heard the screams. He knew about this! He knew!*

He spun around in a rage and stormed out of the bathroom, looked his father straight in the eyes.

"Why? How could you, Dad?"

"Why what, son?"

"You must've known! It was your room! You must've heard the screams! You must've known! That's why you never told me I had a sister! You and Mother killed her!"

Peter's father shook his head in denial. His voice once again taking on that lulling, musical tone it had before. "Car rollin' down a hill. Slick the asphalt, then it spun. A skid, a crash, a roll, a splash. My dear Elizabeth was gone."

"She didn't die in a car crash, and you know it! She was screaming! Punching and kicking the walls!"

Peter grabbed his father by the shoulders. His dad kept chanting. Shaking his head.

"Car rollin' down a hill. Slick the asphalt, then it spun. A skid, a crash, a roll, a splash. My dear Elizabeth was gone."

"You couldn't take the guilt anymore, so you left. That's why you left!"

"Car rollin' down a hill. Slick the asphalt, then it spun. A skid, a crash, a roll, a splash. My dear Elizabeth was gone."

"You abandoned me knowing Mother had killed Elizabeth, and she would do horrible things to me! You coward!"

"Car rollin' down a hill. Slick the asphalt, then it spun. A skid, a crash, a roll—"

"SHUT UP!"

His old man raised his frightened eyes toward him.

Peter felt a sudden explosion go off within his chest. There it was! Now, standing so close to his father's face, he saw it at last. He'd noticed it in the attic, but he'd been so shocked he hadn't even questioned it. The thing that felt amiss about his "old man". It was so obvious. He hadn't seen his father in over thirty years; but he still looked the same as he'd looked back then. He looked tired, skinny, spent, lifeless, but other than that, he looked exactly the same.

He hadn't aged a day.

Peter let go of his father's shoulders and took a step back. He continued to back away until he stepped back into the hole in the wall. He swiveled his head toward the dead body on the floor.

It's too big. The clothes... Not the clothes of a little girl.

In a hysterical second, he crouched and picked them up off the floor and noticed with horror they were the same clothes his father was wearing at that exact moment.

"Oh god!" he exclaimed, feeling whatever sanity remained in him slip away. "That's right!"

The person within the walls couldn't have been his sister. The memory had been fuzzy, but he'd never heard the noises in the wall until his father disappeared. If it had been his sister, he would've been too young to remember. The noises had started when his dad left and stopped two or three weeks later.

When he starved to death.

The small bathroom window had been bricked and plastered over. *Liquid sealant,* he thought, the same used for bathroom tiles. It sealed the smells and muffled the sounds. It had been his father in there. The bumping, the pounding, the screaming. It had been his father.

This wall is backward. Of course it was!

The sign was on the bedroom side of the wall. That passive-aggressive sign that read: PRAY TO GOD FOR JOY, EVEN WHEN YOUR HEART IS BREAKING.

Mother must've placed it there to give herself strength not to let him out, no matter how hard it got. That's why she couldn't sleep.

They'd once loved each other. No matter how insane she got, killing him this cruelly would've been hard on her.

"You're dead!" Peter said.

"What?" Hector asked, confused.

"She killed you!" Peter was freaking out. "Mother killed you!"

"Peter, I don't know what you're talking about."

"What are you doing here, Dad?"

"I told you. I'm resting."

"Yes, you've said that already, but I don't know what you mean. You're resting from what?"

"I don't know."

"What happened after you died?"

"*Hijo,* I'm not dead."

Peter was close to bawling his eyes out now. His father was dead. This not only made him grieve for losing him all over again, but it even absolved him of all the things he'd resented him for. He wasn't losing a deadbeat father anymore; he was losing a loving one who didn't mean to leave him.

"Yes, you are!" he said, filled with grief. "Look!" He was pointing at the corpse on the floor. "Look! That's you, Dad!"

Hector turned his face toward the corpse and seemed, at first, unaffected by it.

"I have to leave now, Peter."

"No, Dad. Not yet. You can't!"

"I'm sorry I couldn't protect you. I..." He looked to one side, thinking, as if remembering something important. "Someone brought me here. That's why I'm resting. A voice called me. An old woman's voice. *Me hablaba en español. Una mujer. Con voz de anciana. Llamándome.*"

"An old woman?" Peter asked, grasping a few words. "Speaking Spanish?" He remembered the book he'd found in Doris's room. It mentioned something about unveiling what the Moon had hidden. "Was her name Doris?"

There was no recognition in his father's eyes. "I never saw her. I don't know her name. She…called me back from that other side, from the Moonlit World. I…was supposed to warn you about your mother. I was too late, I think. *Perdón, Hijo.* I thought, since I failed, I would be taken back to that place, but something brought me to this house. Probably that same woman. Maybe she brought us here so we could talk. But it's too late. It's too late. She has your boy. I'm sorry, Peter, for not stopping her sooner. I've always seen you, even from the Moonlit World. I've seen you when you come to town. I've seen your family. I saw your boy. I knew your house in the mountains, but I have never been able to talk, even in the few moments I had a mouth."

"You've…been here all this time? In White Harbor?"

"Yes, and no. Sometimes it's the Moonlit World, sometimes it's the town. It's always abandoned. Always dark, like a ghost town at night. It's only day when you come to visit. I'm unable to leave, though. At the edge of town, the darkness swallows me, and I end up back here, even if I'm walking in a straight line away from it."

"Dad," Peter asked. "Where is Mother? What is Mother trying to do?"

"She makes great beef stew, you know? I used to like it a lot."

"Dad—"

Hector's eyes regained clarity, filled with a sudden awareness. "Your sister didn't die in the car crash," he said, with eloquent recollection. "We all survived. You were a baby in the backseat with her. She was eight. We were driving back from out of town, and at the curve past the eastern tunnel, the car skidded, spun, broke through the guardrail, and we rolled into the ocean! The windows were open, and the car flooded fast. I thought we were dead. It was dark, underwater, and I passed out from a concussion."

Peter studied his father's face, noting the return of coherence in his words, even if what he said next sounded illogical.

"Then there was light—blue light—and air. We could breathe. We were in a cavern under the ocean, a huge air pocket. It was impossible for us to have fallen into it, so something brought us there. When I opened my eyes, I was alone in the car. My leg was broken, so I couldn't get out, but I saw, in the distance...your mother...she had you in arms and your sister by the hand, and you were all standing in front of..." His mouth worked, trying to find the right word. "God!"

"What?"

"The next thing I knew, everything went dark again, and when light returned, we were in the Sanctum, the...uh...*la capilla*, the...that stone chapel with the altar. My leg wasn't broken anymore, and your mother was standing beside me. She had you in her arms, and she had that book, the..."

"The Uolminar?"

"Yes! Your sister wasn't with us anymore, and we were surrounded by people, and they all kneeled, chanting, 'Mother! Mother! Mother!' I didn't know who these people were. I was just wondering where my Elizabeth had gone. Then I looked at your mother, and her face was different. She was smiling, like she knew something I didn't. After introductions, and these people showering us with gifts, we walked through a big wooden door in this chapel. Suddenly, we were home. That's when...she told me." His voice broke, and he wept, bitter sobs shaking his body. He clawed at his chest in rage and grief. "She offered your sister to that thing—to God—in exchange for our safety. For power! She sacrificed your sister, Peter! Let that thing take her, sink her into eternal torment! An eight-year-old girl! The previous Mother died without selecting a successor, so Uolmin, that thing, selected your mother as a reward for sacrificing your sister!" His eyes shifted with horror. "And I let her... I let her... I'm a monster!"

Peter stared in disbelief at his father, who was now pouring his heart out, conflicted about how to feel. Should he be enraged over a sister he never knew with a father he hadn't seen in decades?

"I told myself I'd protect you, at least." Hector's voice trembled. "But then she announced the Ritual of the Four Nights was coming, and my blood froze. We were supposed to sacrifice *you* when you turned sixteen. That's why she kept you isolated, never let you make friends, or learn about the world. Why bother when she planned to kill you, anyway? She claimed she loved you and wanted you all to herself until it was time to send you to God.

"I tried to stop her, but she threatened to take me away from you. She said someone with the blood of the Mother was needed. Said sacrificing you wouldn't mean losing you, because God promised us eternal life, and we'd be reunited after the ritual. So...I relented." His eyes darkened, shame radiating from them. "I forced myself to believe, too...for a while. But the more time passed, the harder it got. Then one day, I couldn't keep quiet anymore. I put my foot down and..." He stole a glance at the skeleton in the bathroom.

"Is that what she plans to do now?" Peter asked, his voice somber. "Sacrifice William instead of me?"

Hector Rojas nodded. "She wants your son to raise Uolmin. I thought it would be you, but when I saw your boy, I knew she'd come for him."

"What can I do to stop her?"

Hector gave a weak shrug. "I don't know. If she has your son, she has all she needs. Once she reaches the last step of the ritual, she will sacrifice him to that thing."

"But I thought you were brought here to help me, Dad. So, help me!"

"I don't know what this person thought I could do to help you. Your mother has power, *Hijo*. Uolmin is giving her that power. The closer His arrival, the stronger she'll get. I have nothing to give you. Nothing that can stop her. All I know is Uolmin can't rise if it doesn't have your son. If He gets William, everyone who's ever died in this town will suffer for eternity, just like I have." His voice trembled. "Where I've been all these years, there's only pain. Uolmin feeds on it. When I'm not wandering this town in the freezing dark, I'm burning and drowning every second of an endless existence, praying for a true death that never comes. If Uolmin rises, the entire town—the entire world—will face that torment. Because of one little boy! God is coming, *Hijo*. Not the god I once believed in, but the one your mother and I found. And it is cruel."

Hector stared at Peter, and little by little, his eyelids fell to halfway closed. His eyes lost that brief glimmer of lucidity that had taken over them; and Peter knew this was the end. His father was once again slipping back into the void, seemingly for good.

"I have to go," Hector said.

"No," Peter said, shaking his head, his tears at the breaking point. "No, Dad, you can't."

"I have to, Peter. I have to go," he repeated in a drowsy voice, as he turned around to head out of the bathroom.

"Dad, no! Please!"

"Goodbye, *Hijo*."

"No!" Peter threw his arms around his father, crying like a little boy. "No, Dad, don't leave! Please, don't leave! This wasn't your fault! I just got you back! Don't leave me again!"

"I'm sorry... After I was brought out of the dark place your mother put me in, I knew I would have to go back there sometime. *El mundo se está oscureciendo de nuevo.* It's time."

"No! You can't go!" the tears kept coming down like rivers. He was sobbing in desperation. "You can't leave me all over again! I can't lose you all over again! Mother treated me terrible, Dad. She ruined my life. I hated her! I still hate her! I hate her, and I hope she dies for what she did. She took my wife, she took my son, and now I've found out she also took you away from me. Please don't leave me, Dad! I need you! Don't leave me! I love you, Dad!"

"I love you too, Peter," his father said with a sigh, "but I have to go."

As if expending the last of his energy, Hector Rojas embraced his son one last time. He let go and moved away from his embrace. He studied his face, with eyes that told Peter he wanted to stay, eyes trying to hold on to the image of his tear-soaked face for an eternity, despite the torment. "My rest is over." With that, he turned around and walked out of the abandoned bathroom, leaving him as a teary mess on the floor.

Peter reacted to the sound of the bedroom door closing and stepped out to follow his dad. He had already gone through the bedroom door and closed it behind him. When Peter opened the door, there was no sign of him in the hallway. "Dad!"

He searched all over the house, but it was as empty as it had seemed when he first woke up in his bedroom.

"Dad!"

Gone.

"DAD!"

For good.

CHAPTER TWENTY-EIGHT

LIGHTHOUSE ROCK

Lighthouse Rock was deserted.

No one on the dock. No one in the fields around the building. Bobby and Xavier marched through the main entrance into the darkness of the building, their footsteps echoing in the open space. Even if most of the staff had evacuated for the mainland—and if that were the case, *how* exactly had they done that when the ferry now lay at the bottom of the ocean—there would still be a skeleton crew of security guards in the building. Unless they were all gathered in the opposite wing of the facility, this place was abandoned. Bobby brought out his cell phone, but the battery was now dead. "Damn."

"Here, man." Xavier handed him a small black device. "Take this, put it in your chest pocket. I always carry spares."

Bobby looked at him, puzzled, his mind still a haze of anger and grief, while still trying to figure out where everyone had gone.

Xavier sighed with frustration. "Here. Let me." He clipped the device to Bobby's breast pocket, adjusted a sort of flat head so it pointed forward and pressed a button. A band of white light shot forward, cutting a short distance into the darkness of the reception area. "Ta-daaa! Let there be light!" He pressed the button on his own chest pocket, and his flashlight also broke through the shadows.

"Thanks," Bobby said, his voice deadened. The darkness was so deep the flashlight only illuminated ten feet ahead. He looked around, shining the light toward the offices nearby. "There's nobody here."

"Shouldn't the patients, or inmates, if you'll excuse me, still be in their rooms?"

Bobby regarded him for a second, nodded, and turned toward a dark hallway in front of them. This area had rooms for treatment, therapy, patient intake, supplies. They were greeted by windows looking into empty spaces, abandoned desks, unused medical equipment. Open doors leading to soulless, dark rooms.

They reached a set of double doors that led into the patient areas. There was a card key reader to the right, but since it wouldn't work without electricity, Bobby produced a master key given only to doctors and security staff from his pocket, engaged the emergency override and unlocked it. They walked through, then he pointed to a doorway to the right. "Day room's this way."

He sauntered into the room, shining the light into an open area. The forest-themed wallpaper was only interrupted by a TV hanging on the wall, whose glossy blackness made it feel like a hole in reality from which countless eyes stared at them in secret. Tables and chairs were not neatly arranged, but set in ways that told him they were being used that day when everyone just vanished.

Tabletop games, drawing blocks, half-eaten snacks, weight-dented beanbags. He noticed a Scrabble set on a table, where he made out only one sequence of words:

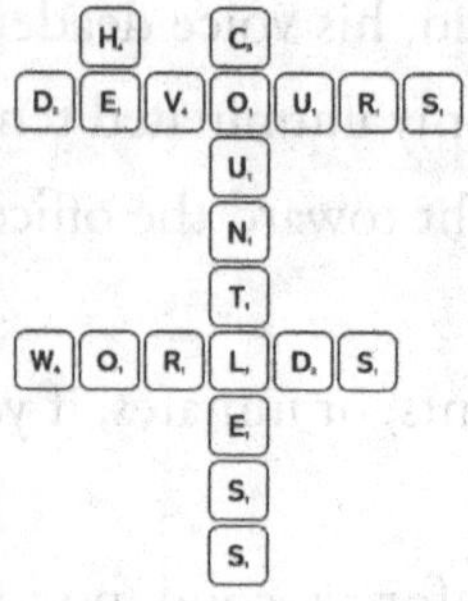

"He devours countless worlds?" Xavier read out loud. "Sure, that's not ominous or anything."

(*God will feed*)

"There were people here when everyone just vanished," Bobby said, then shook his head. "He's not here. Let's go." With those words, Bobby turned around and marched out of the room.

Xavier followed. "Dude, wait!"

Bobby turned, looked at him with annoyance. "What?"

"Don't you want to know what happened in here?"

"No." There was no hesitation in his voice. "I'm here to kill Martha Lange and Freddie Parham. I don't care about anything else."

"Aren't you even a bit scared about what's happening in town? Here? Didn't it seem weird that the rain just stopped a few yards off the marina, like there was some kind of boundary or something?

Did you happen to not look into the water on the way here? That triggered some serious thalassophobia in me, man! There's a *thing* down there!"

"I don't care." Bobby's voice was empty, robotic. "I'm thankful for your help in getting here, but you're here for one reason; I'm here for another. You don't have to come with me."

Xavier gave him a concerned look. "Okay, look. I think we're heading in the same direction. I'll follow you a bit further, just in case you need any help."

"Fine. Do whatever you want." He turned, walked down the dim hallway. His footsteps echoed alongside Xavier's in the desolate, abandoned space. They passed a set of double doors leading to one of the general patient room areas. Even at a glance, Bobby knew the place was empty. They entered a circular area, its high ceiling dwarfed both men, the darkness above making it seem boundless.

This space was the bottom half of the lighthouse, remodeled after the upper half was supposedly destroyed by a massive wave. Bobby doubted those claims in light of recent events. What should've been a dome open to the stars was hidden in an inky black void, stretching upward to infinity. To the right was a door leading to the courtyard, where he usually ate lunch under the shade of a maple tree. Across from them stood the entrance to the criminal patient wing.

He felt a tap on his shoulder.

"Hey," Xavier said. "Where does that door go?"

Annoyed, Bobby looked over his shoulder. Xavier was pointing at a metal door on the left. "There's a circular staircase there, goes to the boiler room. Generators. Maintenance. Bunch of other stuff."

"Then that's where I need to go. Could you help me open that?"

Bobby hesitated a little, but wanting to let the other man continue on his way and leave him alone, he took his key out, turned left, and unlocked the door for him. "There. Good luck." Not sparing a second look, he turned and marched toward the criminal patient wing doors.

"Hey!"

Bobby rolled his eyes, stopped, turned. "What now?"

"Look, I know you don't care about what I'm doing, but it might be related to what you're trying to do. You want to stop what's happening in this town, but I think it's bigger than Freddie Parham or that Lange woman. If—"

"I've gotta go."

"Hey! Asshole!"

Bobby turned to him, frowned with anger.

"Listen to me! You *want* to know this, man! If I'm right, down there, there should be an old floor grate, and an old ladder. It leads to a cavern. A fucking underwater cavern! The thing that's causing all this? It's probably there! So, once you're done beating Freddie Parham into a red paste, you might want to join me down there!"

Bobby didn't care. None of this man's words mattered. He was here for one purpose: getting Freddie to tell him where to find

Martha Lange and how to stop her. Then, he would kill Freddie, he would kill the old witch, and finally, he would kill himself.

He turned around without a word, but the next words out of Xavier's mouth gave him pause. He stopped. Listened.

"Did you hear me, dude? That 'god' thing, or whatever the town's loony cult worships, might be down there. Martha Lange might *already* be down there! Is this somehow making it through your brain synapses?"

"Fine." Bobby continued forward, disappeared through the criminal wing's doors.

CHAPTER TWENTY-NINE
FIELDS OF MOONLIT ETERNITY

His mind still reeling from having lost his son, and now having lost his father again, Peter wandered the house, feet dragging on the floor, plodding down the stairs. According to his dad, if Mother was allowed to complete her ritual, William would be trapped in eternal torment, and so would the entire town. He had no doubts anymore; he didn't question whether this was all insanity. This *was* happening. He knew the urgency of the situation, and yet his body felt stuck, clumsy, unresponsive. He felt as though he were carrying a truckload of rocks on his shoulders. It was too much, too overwhelming. He hadn't even been able to process Jenny's loss, now there was his sister, his father, his son.

He stood at the front door, zombielike, as if he didn't know what a door was used for. He shook his head, took in a deep breath, and reached to open it. The door didn't move. It didn't even shake when he pulled it, as if it were an object fixed in time.

What the hell?

Puzzled, after another failed attempt, he turned and marched toward the kitchen. He could exit through that door and reach the backyard. From there, he could walk out the back gate along the walkway between houses to the street.

And then, what?

He tried to open the door, but it wouldn't move either. His eyes swiveled toward the window that led to the back porch and the backyard. With curiosity, wondering if he could break it, he knocked on the window. It didn't sound like glass. It was almost like knocking on a stone wall. He used the side of his fist to pound harder on the glass, hard enough to break it. Nothing, just that lifeless *thump!* The glass pane didn't even vibrate.

What am I supposed to do now?

The answer came as he turned around and noticed, on his right, the open door to the pantry.

No goddamn way.

He stepped closer to the cramped, dark space. The gray light from the windows didn't penetrate its insides, and only hints of shapes on shelves could be made out in the shadows within. He reached a hand to the spot where he knew there'd be a little beaded chain, similar to his bedroom lamp. He took it between his fingers and pulled. An incandescent bulb bathed the area in amber light. The swaying of the bulb made the shadows of cans and packages dance, as if in joy at seeing him come to this place, the place where he belonged: The Hole. At his feet lay the trapdoor, the metal brace unlatched, and the padlock unlocked.

It's calling me, he thought, and almost chuckled at the ridiculousness of that thought. He swallowed hard. The truth of the matter was his heart wanted to escape his chest, and he'd much rather stay in this simulacrum of his old house forever than open that trapdoor.

"You want me to go down there, right Mother?" He shook his head. "No goddamn way. I'm not going down there."

Brave thought, but what else can I do?

He crouched, and in a slow, tentative motion, opened the trap-door. He should've been able to see the damp dirt down there, about two feet down, but there was only a black patch of darkness. He stared into the void, and thinking of that old Nietzschean quote, felt like the void was gazing back.

"Come down, boy," a voice said, raspy and thin, given a haunting, inhuman tone by the slight echo of the small basement.

Mother? It felt like there was ice water running down and solidifying on his back as sharp ice daggers. He pulled his phone out of his pocket. The battery was now at only twenty-five percent. He tapped the flashlight on and shone it down into the crawlspace. He saw no bottom.

"Come down, boy," the voice repeated, "we have matters to discuss."

Steeling himself for what might be his dumbest decision so far, Peter sat at the edge of The Hole, and let his legs dangle for a few seconds, breathing in an out—shallow, nervous breaths—almost expecting demonic claws to rise out of the darkness, grab his ankles, and yank him down.

He pushed himself off with his hands.

He hit the floor hard on his side. He grunted; the pain on his hip and shoulder from the impact was sharp as a knitting needle, but bearable. Teeth clenched, Peter got to his knees, picked his phone up off the floor, and stood. He recognized the place as his mother's bedroom at Clarendon Elderly Care, except there was no furniture, no hospital appliances. Only an empty room with a closed door and windows looking out into rainy darkness, only broken by that eerie blue eye in the sky, peering from behind dark clouds.

He looked up. There, in the ceiling, was the square hole he'd jumped through, the light bulb still swinging side to side.

"Behind you, boy."

He spun with a start, and the flashlight illuminated Mother standing there. "Mother!"

She was wearing a white blouse with round lapels under a blue and black wool cardigan, a tan pleated skirt, and no shoes. Her gray hair was tied in a ball at the back of her head. The light from the bulb coming in through the hole above made the shadows on her face shift with its movement, making it seem like her face transformed depending on the light's position.

"I was not expecting you to come, but God wanted you here. He wanted you to witness and aid in His miraculous works, to bask in His greatness."

"Mother, where's my son? This isn't your elderly care room, is it? This is that *other* place."

"Elderly care?" she asked, some indignation creeping into her voice. "Why would I ever be in elderly care if I have my own home? If the Lord promised you'd come back to me so I would never be alone again? The Lord gave me this house"—she motioned around with her hands, madly—"so I would be grateful for His mercy. He will give me you, so I can have a family again."

"Mother, what…"

"That whore and the spawn she bore you. They changed your path, but that will soon be corrected. Sacrifice is necessary for the Lord to forgive you and take you back into His glory, though. You've left Him no choice but to demand penance for your salvation. As your Mother, it pains me, but I know it's for the best."

That's what she used to tell him before she put him in The Hole. A sorry excuse for her cruelty. *"You're a bad boy! Maybe some hours in the dark will teach you to respect your mother! As your mother, it pains me, but I know it's for the best! You've—"*

"—brought this upon yourself."

"Mother, you're rambling," Peter said with a trembling voice. "Where is my son?"

"I know you don't understand, Peter, my dear boy, but we will finally be together forever. Everything will be as it once was. He told me it would be so. There's only the matter of the required sacrifice."

"Sacrifice?" he said in a daring voice. "Like you sacrificed my sister? Elizabeth?"

Her eyes flared with anger, and her bony hand flew across his face. The vile crack of her hand against his cheek echoed in the empty room. "Do not dare speak that name in my presence! That child was cursed! She should've been thankful her worthless life served the purpose of preserving ours. Yours!" There were pits of endless blue madness in her eyes. "The Lord has been slumbering, waiting for this one moment, that one precious soul to be fed to Him. The one needed for Him to rise. The one with the Mother's blood running through his veins. This town was built on God's slumbering bones, and so has become a creature under His service. It bends to His thoughts and moods. And this! This place we're standing in. This is God's mind." Her voice took on a zealous insanity even Peter had rarely seen in her. Eyes gleaming with tears of pure, deranged elation. She raised her arms, as if in worship. "I am now *in* God! But soon, I will live *with* God. In His holy presence! For my service, He will award *me*, the only one worthy of His love, with my one true wish: to have my son back."

"You're insane!" Peter snapped. "Where's William? Where's my son?"

He put his arms out, trying to grab his mother, but they went right through her, as if she were just a projection of light, or a shape made by mist.

"Your brat is being prepared to be devoured by God. To dwell in the Lord's stomach, where the pain never ends. He will feed on his pain and suffering for all eternity."

"NO!" Peter slapped at his mother like he was swatting flies, but his hands went right through her.

"What are you trying to do, boy?" she said in a superior tone. "Repeat your past sins? Don't think I've forgotten that transgression of yours. What did I say back then? Oh, yes." She gave him a venomous smirk. "May that hand rot and fall off."

Peter's right hand itched, then burned. He let out a painful moan that soon turned into a scream as the pain in his hand became unbearable. It was feverish pain, like red-hot, jagged blades piercing every pore in his hand. He watched in horror as his hand reddened, swelled, turned purple; white pustules formed and burst as creamy pus exuded from them. From the sores left by the blisters, the skin started to open and bleed dark, putrid blood, with a pungent smell that ate away at his nostrils. The skin now turned black, so did the blood.

Peter dropped to his knees. His screams reached a high pitch. He was screeching as tears rolled down his cheeks and beads of sweat formed on his brow. There were open wounds, all emitting that god-awful stench, and yellow and green discharge suppurated from them. The skin then dried, wrinkled, and broke, and the hand shriveled and thinned; until it was nothing but dry skin, bound tight to bone. The bone broke and his hand fell off.

Still gawking at the brittle remains of his hand, he felt himself sink into the floor. The hospital room disappeared, and his surroundings changed to oppressive darkness. Peter stared up at his mother in agony, holding the bleeding stump at his wrist.

She was glaring down at him from a square hole above his head, holding the trapdoor open. "You're a bad boy!"

His knees touched moist earth. The smell of rot was replaced by the smell of moisture, of mildew, of still dirt. *No! NO!* His mind panicked, taking him back to his childhood. To the desperation, to the realization of what was coming.

"No, Mother, please! Not the Hole! Please, Mother!"

(I'll be a good boy! I promise! I'll be a good boy!)

A smirk stretched across her face right before the lid slammed shut over his head and left him in darkness.

"Let me out! Mother, please!" He felt the buildup of terror and desperation commandeering his brain, taking control away. "LET ME OUT!"

Noise. Rustling. Movement. Scuttling sounds, small bodies shuffling around in the shadows. Approaching.

Cockroaches! Rats! Spiders!

The individual noises came together to form a murmur akin to an entire crowd of onlookers whispering in anticipation of the spectacle to come. Louder. Rising. Growing. There was the smell of vermin, of rats crawling in from tiny holes and pipes, rats stinking of sewage, urinating in the very dirt in which he was kneeling.

Then they washed over him like a wave. He was chest-deep in living things. Millions of creatures crawling on him.

In his desperation, he pawed around for the cell phone. It had landed with the screen in the dirt, covering the flashlight. He couldn't find it, engulfed in this mass of insects. His screams reverberated in the cramped space. His throat felt like it was being scratched by claws. His cries were hoarse and horrifying. He'd been reduced to a madman. A madman screaming out his insanity for no one to hear.

(*Cockroaches! Rats! Spiders!*)

The chittering, screeching, and scuttling noises from the surrounding creatures had become deafening, as if all the noises of humanity and all the cries of animals had been layered into a single recording and played back for him. Unintelligible noise, filling his ears yet not dampening his screams.

"Help me! Mother! Mother, please! Let me out! Let me ooooout! Mother, I'll be good! I'll behave! Please! Let me out!"

Panic hijacked his soul and ran away with it. He shook, convulsed. No voluntary movement possible. He needed to calm down. He needed to at least allow a tiny window through which a rational thought might slip through.

Breathe!

"I can't! I CAN'T!"

I have to breathe! I have to b—

"HELP ME!!!"

Calm down, I must calm down! Deep breaths, take deep—

"They're crawling on me! I can't! I'm scared! LET ME OUT! LET ME—"

Stop! I'm going to pass out if I don't! I must—

"MOTHER! MOTHER PL—"

Breathe! Breathe! The flashlight! Find the flashlight! Look for an exit!

He forced himself to control his breath, trying to not hyperventilate, trying not to pass out, trying not to scream; but it was too hard, brushing away all those shapeless things crawling on him—tiny legs, fur, mandibles, exoskeletons. The spasmodic fingers of his remaining hand searched for the phone while on his knees. The tide of critters covered his entire body. He felt like he was wading inside a wheat silo. Every movement felt heavy and difficult. Finding the phone felt impossible.

"Oh god, oh god! Help me!"

He found the phone. Gripped it. Things were crawling on his face, trying to force their way inside his mouth and his eyes, no matter how hard he tried to keep them closed. He could also feel legs scratching the inside of his ears. He double tapped the back of the phone, engaging the flashlight, and pulled it out of the shifting mess he was swimming in. He brushed critters off his face, some of their bodies bursting with the pressure against his skin. He opened his eyes.

There was no other possible reaction but to scream. Louder than before.

(*Cockroaches! Rats! Spiders!*)

It was a river of them. They crawled all over him, finding their way into his mouth every time he opened it to breathe because his nose was plugged with the acrid smell of vermin, of shit, rot, and other vile things.

He spat out the bugs that crawled into his mouth and tried to brush off the ones that climbed up his face with his forearm.

There were cockroaches of all shapes and sizes: the dark brown-and-yellow ones you find in every household. The black, segmented ones, armored with hard chitin shells. The pale, white ones found only in caves, which had lost their color because their kind hadn't seen the light of day in millennia. And the huge, bulky cockroaches with thick bodies, built like war tanks, bulging with viscous fluid, crawling around with broad legs and antennae. There were spiders: from larger-than-usual daddy long-legs; to enormous, brown hairy ones, the size of a gorilla's hand, with fat, round abdomens, and segmented legs as thick as his fingers. There were locusts, centipedes, giant millepedes, huge beetles. Fat rats dropped from pipes above him and waded across this river of vermin, sometimes sinking into it, and sometimes finding refuge under Peter's clothes. It was a nightmare flood threatening to drown him.

Amidst his absolute hysteria, Peter realized he was no longer kneeling, but standing. He was still in The Hole, but he had stood up, and yet the flood still reached up to his chest, as if the ground had sunken further. The old crawlspace had reshaped itself into a long, narrow, sewer-like corridor.

He waded through the tide of insects, laugh-screaming like a complete lunatic. His eyes were red with tears and his body moved clumsily as shudders and spasms ran through him from head to toe. There had never been such a multitude of bugs and rats in the actual Hole. This was Mother's power. Mother's punishment for his disobedience.

And Mother is right to punish me, he thought.

He had restrained himself from laughing back in the mountain house. When he'd seen the first monster—that child creature with the faded Bluey tattooed on its chest—he'd held the laughter at bay, refusing to succumb to insanity. But now, unable to contain himself, he let out ferocious peals of laughter, frenzied, violent laughter, accompanied by a constant torrent of tears.

"I've been a bad boy," he cackled shakily. A deranged, miserable grin was drawn on his face. His eyes were vacant, his mind gone, his voice breaking, and he babbled in a single, rambling stream of words. "I've been a bad boy you know that Mother that's why you've punished me I've been bad and you're correcting me thank you Mother I'm grateful I love you Mother."

The insects now crawled unimpeded into his hair and over his face, and when they got into his mouth, he chewed and swallowed, no longer spitting them out, laughing as he did this, while his insane babbling carried on.

"I love you Mother you're so good to me I'm the one who's been bad you're just trying to educate me I'm so grateful Mother thank you I'm so happy you're my Mother

(Munch. Swallow)

but please Mother it wasn't my fault Mother it was my friends Mother they led me astray Mother and my whore of a wife and my weak boy Mother they made me bad Mother and as soon as you let me out of the Hole Mother I will kill them all so I can prove I'm a good boy Mother I will kill my friends and I will kill the boy and we'll be so happy together Mother you'll see

(Munch. Swallow)

just you and me Mother together forever together forever like God commanded."

He waded through this living swamp for what felt like a lifetime. He came to a point in which he could see a round hole over his head. It was too small for him to fit, but he put a shaky hand up and grabbed the edge. The other hand followed, and he used both to pull himself up. It was a titanic struggle to pull himself through, but he made it out, leaving the river of vermin behind.

Once out, he fell sideways to the floor like a dead fish, and he remained there convulsing as his mind began to shut down. He hugged himself in the fetal position and shook. From the corner of his eye, he noticed Mother standing over him again.

"We understand each other now. Right, boy?"

He gave a shaky nod, his head bobbing up and down.

"If you do what I ask of you now," she said with a proud smile. "You have my word your son will live, and no harm will come to him. You know your Mother never lies, right, boy?"

Once more, he moved his head assenting, his fingers still clutching his shaky arms, his legs still pulled protectively against his chest.

"Good. There is one last thing I wish to show you."

Peter's eyes bulged open in terror, and his head shook. He didn't want to see whatever Mother was about to show him.

He observed his son in a position similar to his own, sleeping on the ground. He was in a dark, nondescript area.

A field? A street? Both?

The starless sky and the faint dark-blue glimmer of the moon through dark clouds served as a backdrop, allowing the black silhouettes of what might be buildings and hills to stand out.

Is this it? He wondered with apprehension. *Is she only showing me he's alive?*

Jagged lines of glowing light appeared across the ground, revealing cracks that spread through the terrain. The light intensified, a fiery yellow-orange hue, which flickered like molten lava and flames from the depths, giving him a clear view of the surroundings.

The horror of the scene overwhelmed him. What he'd perceived as buildings and hills were instead black, jagged structures—organic and geometrical shapes, like nothing seen in our world, made of a material like onyx or obsidian, similar to the Mother statue at the hospital. These towering forms were entirely covered with maimed human corpses. Men, women, children, even newborns, of every race. Thousands of them. Bound, impaled, or fused into the black material, their bodies in varying states of mutilation turned into a grotesque display as far as the eye could see.

No, no, no, no! Mother, stop! I don't want to see this! I get it! I understand now! Get me out of here!

The nightmare didn't abate.

Instead, his vision sharpened with cruel clarity, a loathsome hyperawareness of every minute detail, like he'd been forced to stare into a microscope, when all he wished for was to gouge his eyes out. His sight was flooded with images of festering wounds, charred flesh peeling off, empty eye sockets, exposed bones, and teeth without the cover of lips. Limbs dangled from torsos, entrails spilled from open gashes, and black crystal spikes pierced every soft, tender part imaginable.

Then, one body moved.

And another.

And another.

His breath caught.

They're alive?

The realization rushed at him like a tsunami. Terror flooded his lungs, wrecking all of his defenses, drowning him, leaving him unable to scream.

Wailing bodies strained against black hooks that pierced their hands and feet like in some unholy crucifixion. They had their stomachs ripped open, folds of flesh held apart by other hooks, resembling dissected frogs, unable to die. Their intestines had been pulled out and intertwined with neighboring bodies, forming an intricate web of gore. Hooks also stretched their lips into wide, bleeding grins and pulled their tongues, attaching them to their chins.

Carbonized bodies, somehow still alive, moved and bled thick, brown blood from deep wounds.

There was an entire field of people impaled in long, black stakes, inserted between their legs and exiting through their mouths, the stakes coated in their own guts. Black ropes bound their limbs, endlessly pulling them down the stakes. Tiny hooks, attached to almost invisible threads, were embedded in their eyeballs, holding them about an inch out of their sockets.

An entire structure to the right was a revolting mass of intertwined children. Their skins had been stretched and sewn into each other with black thread. He could see a child's head sticking out of the open and bleeding ribcage of another. Hands protruded from faces. Organs spewed out of skulls. The few faces not completely deformed or destroyed were contorted into a cruel countenance of pain.

How? Why? Why were they alive? How could anybody be alive in such a condition? What merciless fate could deny these people the respite of death in order to suffer the horrors he was witnessing?

Then his viewpoint moved away from his sleeping son, rising higher, higher, flying until he could see into the distance. He was floating above what looked like an entire city, reaching as far as the eye could see, infinite. An entire alien landscape, streaked with fractures in the earth, glowing with magma, where millions of tortured people wailed and pleaded for mercy that would never come. Enormous black pillars, like skyscrapers covered in tormented humanity, rose into the black sky, getting lost in the clouds, reaching for that cruel blue moon that fed on their screams.

And in the middle of all that, his little boy, sleeping. A tiny speck in this cruel wasteland.

Please, make it stop! Mother, make it stop! I'll do anything! I'll do anything you want! Make it stop!

From above, in that hyperawareness that had come over him, he thought he saw—no; he *did* see—a black tentacle emerging from one of the structures, the one closest to William, moving toward him, closing in, touching his helpless foot. A threat, clear, merciless: the boy could be one of them.

In a reflex similar to throwing up, Peter's rib cage contracted, and his mouth opened to let out a jarring scream that filled the world. The horror erupted out of him, his desperate scream rising even above that of the tortured masses below. A scream that seemed to last forever. Peter was no longer making any sound; he simply didn't realize it. His mouth remained open. In his head, he was still screaming.

At last, his mind allowed him the mercy of shutting down, in a microsecond flashing an entire memory of him as a teenager watching some random channel—PBS, perhaps—well into the late hours of the night, at his Aunt Constance's home, where he *was* allowed to watch television. He remembered the announcer's recorded voice as the National Anthem played, and images of a jet flying over American landmarks filled the screen.

"*We now conclude our broadcast day. We hope you tune in tomorrow for more of your favorite shows. God bless you!*"

Color bars. Then, static.

Merciful unconsciousness.

The broadcast, however, would start again. He would relive thousands of variations of this sequence, over and over. Different events, different tortures, different landscapes, same horrifying ending, for what felt like years.

CHAPTER THIRTY

BETRAYAL – PART 1

John Hitch lay on top of the sleeping bag Cunningham and his daughter had laid him on, a dusty old jacket as a pillow. They'd taken care of sewing him up and pumping him full of blood. What kind of freak was Cunningham to keep refrigerated bags of O-negative stored in a cellar? he thought. He'd have to replace it every month.

Sitting beside him was Royce Howe and a man he'd never met before. Carlos Alberto Ruiz—though he'd asked to be called "Tali" for some dumb reason he didn't pay attention to. He was Doris Ruiz's son. He was a member of the Order of the Rising Sun, who'd abandoned his faith and come back to it, and not a minute too late.

"Was your Mother inside Peter Lange's home when the sun went away?" Hitch asked, sounding weak.

Tali, who had been reapplying healing glyphs to Hitch's stabbed and stitched torso, pressed his lips in a bitter line and nodded.

"So, you know she's probably..."

Ruiz nodded again. "She, uh... She said she had a plan, and for that, she needed to stay."

"Foolish woman." The young man flinched at this. "I would've done the same," he added, trying to make him not feel so bad. He didn't know why. He'd eschewed all human connections long ago, but there was something earnest about him he took a liking to. Perhaps it was that Tali had done what he couldn't. He'd walked away from it all. He'd come back to it for his mother, sure, but he'd been free from the Order's deluded do-gooder dogma, at least for a while. "She most likely tried to summon someone to point Lange in the right direction, give him information he needed. It's a fool's errand, though. Unlikely Martha Lange didn't foresee that and planned ahead." He let the thought hang in the air for a moment. "I hope it somehow helps."

Tali gave him a taciturn smile.

Hitch turned to Royce, who was also looking somber, rubbing his bandaged left hand. He signaled upward with his eyes. "What happened up there?"

"Freddie happened," Royce said, his voice cold. He didn't seem interested in engaging with him.

"Say what's on your mind, young man."

Royce scoffed and shook his head, as if he found the fact of him calling him "young man" ridiculous, considering Hitch looked over a decade younger than him. "I can't help thinking Freddie wouldn't know how to do the things he can do now if you hadn't taught him." He sneered at him. "This is all the same power from inside the Vanek House, but at a town-wide scale, ain't it? You tricked Freddie into killing those kids to distract the house so you could kill Peter. My brother's death was just a fucking distraction."

Now it was Royce who let the silence hang in the air, made sure the words penetrated his pores.

"Well, look how much your boy Freddie has grown. You must be proud."

Hitch shook his head, a sarcastic smile on his face. "You underestimate just how much this is all my fault. This whole thing started with me, well over a century ago, letting Walter Parham be raped and hanged to spare the life of the man I loved."

Royce gave him a quick unwitting gawk, as if forcing himself not to notice he'd sprouted a clown's nose, and Hitch felt that old pang of discomfort. He knew these times were different from the times he'd been born. Saying he loved a man wasn't seen as a bad thing by most anymore, but that initial reaction hadn't changed in centuries, that moment they didn't see you as the same person you'd been a mere second ago, for better or worse, because knowing *that* made you a different person.

"All I bought with Walter Parham's life was one more year for Christopher, and an endless curse for myself. I know there's no forgiveness for what I've done. But, for what it's worth, and I know it's not much...I'm sorry about your brother."

"I have a question," Royce said, brushing aside his apology for something he felt mattered more. "You got the Vanek House from Amias Vanek, and Vanek started the cult Martha Lange now leads, right?"

"Mm-hm. Him and Dorothy Parham. She was the first Mother."

"Does it mean her god, or the power that makes this town such a shitty place, is there? Where the Vanek House used to stand?"

Hitch shook his head. "The house was a doorway. The reinforced door you crossed years ago led to the other side, where their god exists."

"Is there a way we can get there and stop them?"

"Get there? Maybe. Stop them? Doubtful."

"Look, man, I can't stay here waiting for a hole to open up in the ground and swallow this bar, or for it to go up in flames and kill my family. You've gotta give me something, goddamn it!"

Hitch rolled his big eyes toward Royce. Defensive, at first—it was his go-to reaction, after all—but then realized, even if it seemed hopeless, he owed the man at least that much, after what he'd done. "I'm not sure. All I've got is theories, things I pulled from books and mixed with what Vanek himself told me. Your friend, Callum, had some theories, some of which matched mine, but this is just conjecture."

"Alright, let's hear it, then."

"One hundred and fourteen people died out of the colonizing party that came to White Harbor in 1866. We hid from a blizzard inside a cave, and by the time we came out, one hundred and nine went into a mass grave. Five were assumed dead. Those were Amias Vanek and Gideon McClemont—the party leaders—and three others that accompanied them deep into the cave, trying to find food or a way to safety. They were never seen again. At least, that's what the stories say."

1905

Long-Lived John Ellis climbed the stairs of the house he'd called his reluctant home for most days since 1891. That year, Amias Vanek had appeared out of nowhere, loaded with wealth, a deed to a plot of land, and pretending to be his own nephew. Vanek hadn't aged a year since he'd seen him disappear into the darkness of that old cave. The man had kept the pretense for a bit longer, before John had flat out told him to cut the bullshit. Unlike most people around—save for perhaps Elbert Giffen, who was still around—John had been in the cave, and he never forgot a face; especially not the face of one of the two men that had brought him into this accursed town with dreams of prosperity. Vanek had only smiled, realizing it was no use lying to him, and said, "I might have work for you, John."

He'd hired John, who, even now, approaching a hundred, looked strong as a bear, to help build his new home in White Harbor, for him and his family. Once the Vanek House had been completed, Vanek had asked him to stay as his groundskeeper, as well as his family's security guard. Later, when Vanek's true intentions had been revealed, it became clear why he needed one. A man planning to start a new religion in Protestant America would need someone to watch his back.

John had agreed on one condition.

Despite the "Long-Lived" nickname being just a way to point out his natural longevity and vitality, it hadn't escaped the town's notice he'd stopped aging since around Walter Parham's death in 1887. Christopher had died, and he'd kept going, never sick, never feeble, not a single wrinkle added to his face. In fact, he seemed to be getting younger, now resembling a man in his early sixties. People watched him now and wondered if there was some truth to the supernatural rumors about his blessed longevity. But John knew this was no blessing. It was a curse. He would never have forgiveness for what he'd done to Walter Parham, so all he'd wanted from the moment Christopher had died was for his own life to end.

He now approached Vanek's bedroom, where the man lay bedridden and dying, to ask him to uphold their agreement, to do the thing he'd asked in exchange for his servitude. Vanek, whom he knew had found something in the depths of the cave, something that had helped him keep his youth and health, could use that power to help him die.

Something had shifted during the past year, though. Something had changed. Vanek's wife and two children had perished from a strange disease that had whittled their health and their bodies down to malnourished skeletons by the time they died. Vanek now seemed to have developed the same disease. He had an inkling of what—or who—had brought this change about, but this was irrelevant. He had to make Vanek uphold their deal. It was now or never.

He reached for Vanek's bedroom door.

"John Ellis, you should not bother Mr. Vanek at this hour." The woman's voice scraped at his spine like claws, slow-descending the length of his back.

He found Dorothy Parham standing to his right. He hadn't heard her steps approaching. The sight of her filled him with revulsion from the day she'd hanged her son in front of a frothing crowd. He'd considered leaving Vanek's employment the moment he'd hired the vile woman as a housekeeper, and again, when he'd realized what her true purpose in the home was. But John had stopped himself, remembering his agreement with Vanek. There was a purpose in him remaining here.

"Mind your own business, woman. This is between Mr. Vanek and I."

"You forget yourself, John." Slimy arrogance coated her words. "You must address me as 'Mother.'"

He narrowed his eyes at her smug half-smile, took in her hair tied in a ball behind her head, the way she stood so perfectly straight, hands clasped at the front around that strange black rosary, her plain white blouse, and powder-blue linen skirt down to the floor—speaking to a piety and purity he knew her not to have. "I am not part of your little witches' coven and owe you no honorifics."

"Mind your tongue, old man." Her façade broke just enough to shine through her pretense of composure. "You were touched by

God the day my wretched son died. You won't deny it. I can see it. If anyone should join me every week at worship, it should be you—a living, walking example of God's power. Even I, who lead the Circle, am showing the ravages of age from the eighteen years that have passed. But you...neither a grippe, nor an unsettled gut, not even a wrinkle. In fact, you look younger and healthier than back—"

"Be quiet, witch," he snapped. "Stop mocking me. I would sooner spit on the face of the demon that did this to me than worship it. Get away from me." Her face pinched in response. "Right. I was 'touched' by your god, and you can't command me like you do others. I suppose something good came from the day you murdered your innocent boy. Your oldest son died, one of your daughters, your husband. Later, his sister, her husband, their children, all dead within eighteen years. The Curse of the Parhams, they're calling it now. I'm sure you've heard the rumors. Only one of your daughters remains, and all of White Harbor wonders why God lets your wretched line continue. Were it only you that had departed instead of them, the world would be better for it."

He reached for the door again. His breath caught when her hand slid over his. It felt like a cold-blooded reptile slithering over his skin.

"I have no qualm with you being an old sodomite. I don't resent your involvement with my son's death, either."

He couldn't move. Fear was etched on his face, on his very heart.

"Oh, yes. That God you deride so much has told me."

He turned terrified eyes toward her. His earlier derision of the evil woman melted away and turned to shame, despite himself. "Your boy... What I did... He didn't deserve what...I..."

"The only true sin was my son shamed me anew when he killed the priest. I believed in the false god back then, and it drove me to what I did, but it was but a steppingstone, leading me to my current grace. So, I am thankful for my son's shame. This 'curse' you speak of, it's a way for God to cull the unworthy. The only legacy that matters is the succession of Mothers, those who will serve God, and I will always have been the first. So, let the people speak of a curse all they want. I have served my God well. I am free of all sin. You, John...you will never be free."

With a sneer, he threw the door open, stepped inside, and closed it in her face. Not being spared a quick side-eye glimpse of her proud smile.

The stench coming from the chamber pot hit him first. Then, in the light of an oil lantern, he beheld the withered figure of Amias Vanek—or what remained of the man—lying in bed, covers up to his chest, his rickety arms lying on top of them. He looked as if the cover had sliced him in two, right beneath his sternum.

Vanek turned a pale, skeletal face toward him. "Come, John. I've been expecting you, my friend."

His mind still reeling from his interaction with Dorothy Parham, John stepped closer to the bed.

"I heard," Vanek said, nodding toward the door. "I fear I've set something in motion I can't undo now. 'Hell hath no fury...' and all that. William Congreve spoke truly." He attempted what would've been a smile under normal circumstances.

"There is also: 'The wages of sin...' and all that," John answered without humor. "Romans. I'm not sure if the Apostle Paul spoke truly, but that damned book has brought me grief to no end."

"I do not regret having formed the Circle, John. If you're hoping I admit to the contrary, sadly, I won't. I honestly believe I have experienced the glory of the true God. I do wish I hadn't consorted with the woman chosen to lead it, but the flesh is weak. Cost me my two children and my Harriet."

"Why, Amias? Why did you choose her and not your wife?" He wasn't here to hear the dying man ramble about the death he'd brought upon himself, yet he was curious. "Might as well tell me now, before you close your eyes forever."

Vanek shook the leathery-skin-draped skull he called a head and said, "I've told you many times before. I didn't. God chose her. During the first meeting of the Circle, I hoped it would be Harriet. Keep the authority and the role of Mother within our family, but God chose Dorothy."

"Hmm." John was as unsatisfied now as he'd been every other time Vanek had claimed the same. The fact he'd started an affair with the Parham woman not long after she'd been chosen only confirmed Vanek's bias in the matter. The man was now paying the price of trying to break off that affair.

"You have to carry on after I'm gone," Vanek said, shaking him out of his thoughts.

"What nonsense is this?"

"Listen to me, John."

"No... No! You and I have an agreement!"

"I know, but this is the last thing I will ever ask of you, and then I will give you what you asked of me."

"No!"

"Then listen to me, at least. You will have time to tell someone you trust to do this before you actually die. This is important! She cannot be allowed to continue unhindered! The Circle must course-correct! I've seen where this leads if she's not stopped!"

"Talk. Then you will fulfill your promise. If there's something I can do, I will, but I'm not walking out of this room without my due payment."

Vanek studied his face. "Very well, then." He glanced at the pitcher and a glass on his bedside table. "Water first."

In a hurry, John reached for the pitcher, poured water in the glass, and gave it to Vanek. The man drank as if parched, but it also looked as if each swig hurt the insides of his mouth and throat. He finished drinking, coughed, and handed him the glass to put on the table.

"Talk," John said.

"I never told you what happened after that day, when we disappeared into the cave. Gideon McClemont, Giles Davison, Moses McCaskey, James Clements, and I."

"You wandered into the cave, the others died, you found this 'God' and it let you come back. Yes, you've told me."

"Not everything." He gave John a shrewd glance. "Clements didn't make it far. Strong a man as he was, his foot landed on brittle earth, and he fell into a black chasm whose depths we could only guess. Gideon and the others did not falter, until, through winding paths and treacherous crawls down openings in the rock, we made it to a wide-open space. A cavern. There was saltwater pooled at our feet, which told us we'd wandered beneath the ocean, but while the cavern itself was underwater, we espied sunlight, and an exit high above, with an easily climbable path to it." He paused, staring off into a distance John couldn't guess. "It was then an intense, silver-blue glow shone from our left, from deeper within the cave. An unnatural silver-blue. We decided to investigate."

John felt shivers at the mention of the silver-blue glow. He knew the silver-blue he was referring to. The same silver-blue he'd seen on those accursed flowers near the mass grave, the burial spot of those one hundred and nine settlers. These evil flowers grew there, and nowhere else in town.

"It was glorious. The face of God. I can't even describe it without tears. God filled the cavern, an enormous blue glow that peered into our souls—an ever-watchful eye from which we could not hide, nor felt a need to. It was a beauty beyond anything I had ever imagined." His countenance darkened. "It seemed only I thought Him beautiful, though. When I beheld my companions, McClemont was frozen, tears of terror streaming down his face. Davison and McCaskey screamed, clawing at their eyes, as if something were crawling into them. Then, the two pulled knives from scabbards and slit their own throats. As they bled, God's glow intensified, as if accepting their sacrifice.

"That's when I heard His voice in my mind—not a command, but a suggestion. It told me how to earn His grace and blessing. I looked at McClemont, my old friend, whom I'd grown to despise for bringing me on this journey, and at once, I knew what his use was. He was kneeling in his own urine, trembling with fear, speechless. He peered up at me, at my unsheathed knife, and I felt this nudge at the back of my mind. I started stabbing him. He didn't scream. He didn't fight, but the terror in his eyes, I'll never forget. Forty-four times I stabbed him before I realized he was already dead.

"God was pleased. I sensed His acknowledgment of my actions. I knelt before Him, and for years, we shared our minds, and I understood His desires. I wrote them down in my log, and that became the Uolminar—His word and His mission."

Vanek's voice trembled with reverence and awe, but his eyes burned with something darker. An adoration for the divine horror he had unearthed and embraced.

"Then He sent me back. Renewed. I emerged from the exit on that island, where the southern mountain range breaks off."

"Flat Rock," John said.

Vanek nodded. "I was to return to my hometown, where I would marry my betrothed Harriet, bear children, then return to White Harbor a wealthy man. I'd build a house where God would be worshipped. The Lord gave me a piece of His body to put in the house so we could walk from this house into the Moonlit World, and there, he'd build us the Sanctum so we could worship Him. Some of us—myself and the Mother—would have access to the cavern, to the Inner Sanctum, where God Himself dwells."

"Amias," John interrupted. "Why are you telling me all this? How does this help me stop that woman?"

Vanek motioned for a bell on his bedside table, gave a slight wiggle of thin fingers. With a sigh of frustration, John handed him the bell. Grimacing with the effort, Vanek shook the bell, which filled the air with its brisk yet irritating ringing.

A minute later, through the door came Rickward Curling, Vanek's house servant.

It felt wrong, John thought. Curling was a freed slave, yet now found himself in servitude to a white man again. Though paid and given a day off—and further than that, Vanek had platted his property and built a house for Curling's family—ly—the arrangement still irked him somewhat. There was also that damn bell. Like Vanek was summoning a dog.

"Mr. Vanek," Curling said. "You called?"

"Thank you, Rickward, for coming so quickly. Did you receive the papers I had the notary write up for you?"

"Yes!" Curling said. There was an air of excitement and surprise in the man's voice. "Yes, sir. I don't even... I don't even know what to say, sir. It's too kind. Even worrisome, I'd say, I—"

Vanek waved his bony hand in the air. "Never mind all that. There are some instructions, but they will be delivered at a later time. Now, I need you to please stand beside John, here, if you'll be so kind."

Curling raised an eyebrow at John, who gave a shrug. Hesitant, he approached John and stood to his right.

"Now, please, hold hands."

By instinct, John curled his right hand's fingers into a fist. He hadn't held another man's hand since Christopher had passed, and he wasn't about to do it again in front of Vanek—a spectacle for a dying man, whose mind might be going already, if it hadn't gone years ago with tales of caverns and silver-blue gods. He looked to the right and was met by Curling's nonplussed stare. John was sure Rickward Curling had heard the rumors in town about him. He could see his apprehension about holding hands with him at the request of a white employer gone mad.

"Please," Vanek said. "I mean no offense to your dignity. Indulge me this once. This won't take long."

John huffed, rolled his eyes, and in a quick motion grabbed Curling's hand, before the man could pull it away. "Get this over with, Amias, whatever folly you got in mind. We still have business to attend."

"This is part of that," Vanek said firmly. John believed him, he found. The decrepit man turned toward Curling. "This is just a formality, for my religion's sake, before I pass the property onto you, Rickward."

The property? John wondered. *Is he giving the entire estate to Curling?*

"A blessing of sorts," Vanek continued. "Worry not. This won't encroach on your own beliefs. I'm not asking you to believe the same as I. All I ask is for you not to let go until I'm done with my prayer."

Curling gave a formal nod, looking quite uncomfortable.

That said, Vanek closed his eyes, bent his head. He began a prayer, or incantation, of the kind members of his Circle often muttered. Nonsense babbling. The rhythmic recitation of these words he did not understand lilted almost like a bedtime lullaby. *Or a funeral prayer,* John corrected himself.

He felt lightheaded. The room darkened. Spun. The oil lamp flickered. Something glowed from outside the bedroom window. Blue. Silver-blue. The moon. Huge. Impossibly huge. The blue light replacing the amber glow of the oil lamp. He tried letting go of Curling's hand but found he couldn't. He closed his eyes.

"Stop," he said in a voice that didn't feel like his own. "Amias, stop this." Not his voice. He tried to let go. His right hand's fingers wiggled, opened, and closed, holding nothing. Pressure in his left hand. It was being held by...someone. A powerful grip.

"Stop!" he gasped. His eyes flew open. The angle, the height had shifted. His vision was "lower" somehow. He looked to his right. Curling was gone. *Pressure in my left hand.* He looked to his left and saw his own face staring back at him, twisted into a horrified mask of bewilderment. John screamed. *Not my voice! Not my voice!* He pulled his hand back, and that's when he noticed the hand was a deep brown. His other self, his body, the one standing before him, clutched at his chest and groaned. He watched his own towering body bend at the abdomen and crumple to the floor. He watched himself twitch for a brief moment and stop moving. He was watching himself die.

"John."

He looked toward Vanek. The man was looking straight at him, a soft smile on his face. "What…" He tried to speak, but he couldn't cope with the fact the voice coming out of his mouth wasn't his own. He stared at his hands: light-colored palms surrounded by deep brown skin. "What did you do? What did you *do*?" he demanded.

"John, you need to listen to me, because this is important."

He shook his head. "Damn you, Amias! Damn you! Fuck you! What did you do?"

"I fulfilled my promise. John Ellis has now died of a heart attack. He's John the Long-Lived, no more. It's what you wanted, now it's done."

He continued to shake his head. Understanding coming to him in waves. "What did you do?"

Vanek set an envelope on his bedside table. The moisture from the water glass dampened a corner of the envelope. The name on it read RICKWARD CURLING. "This is the key to the reinforced door at the end of the hallway." The calm in his voice only made John angrier, as if he hadn't witnessed what he'd witnessed.

"Dorothy and the Circle can still access the Sanctum because of my presence in the house, but in a few years after I die, the power that I gave that woman through our pact with God will be spent, and only this key will open that door. Keep it close. The lives of everyone in White Harbor depend on it. Once their power runs out, I want you to never let them into this house again. She will surely find her way to the Inner Sanctum through her connection with God, but she can no longer be allowed to go through here." He paused for a moment. "John?"

"What did you do?"

"Don't you know already?" Vanek asked. "I'm only calling you John while you get used to the notion you are now Rickward Curling."

He shook his head. "Fuck you! You lie! This is trickery of some sort."

"I assure you, it's not. Now, if I may proceed. This is important!"

He kept shaking his head; he hadn't stopped for a second since he watched his own dead body drop to the floor. He was lying there. Dead. But his mind was still here. Still alive.

"That door prevents God's power from running free through the town. It cannot be allowed to go free, or Dorothy and her group will be able to fully harness it. Glory be to God, but I do not want what Dorothy's group wants. The longer you keep this door closed, the longer before they can find the way to release God into this town and the world. That cannot be allowed."

"Shut up," John said, hoping to wake up from this nightmare.

"Dorothy, and each mother after her will write their own rules and rituals on the Uolminar, based on their learnings. The longer we keep them from fully awakening God, the longer humanity will exist in this world. God's power must be used for good, not for the selfish madness brewing inside Dorothy Parham."

"Shut up! Shut up! I don't want to hear your voice anymore!"

"That 'curse', as you call it, your immortality, can save humanity, John. You will now become Rickward Curling, live his life, accompany his wife, raise his children. When you die, your soul will inhabit the next available person of Curling's bloodline. Use that time to learn. Use the key to enter the Moonlit World, learn its ways, learn to use its power. Find the way to stop the Circle from awakening God. Once you've found the way to do that, you will be allowed to die."

"No. I won't do what you're telling me. You monster. You ghoul. How could you do this?"

Vanek cleared his throat. "One life per year."

He narrowed his eyes—no, Curling's eyes—at Vanek.

"That's what it takes to keep the door sealed."

Memories of the lavish annual celebrations Vanek held at his home, overflowing with wine and liquor, parties in which, inevitably, some poor drunkard wouldn't make it home, perhaps wandering into the woods or the ocean itself. Perhaps stumbling into Etenia Creek, at the edge of the house, where their body would be carried to the ocean, and conveniently never found.

"One per year. The house will tell you when it's time. Just bring them in and let the house sort them out. Feed them to it. It will keep the doorway closed."

"No... Never."

"The disease that consumed my wife and children, and now myself, was brought forth by Dorothy's jealous heart, but our deaths will still count, I'd wager. That should give you four years to get used to the notion. After that, one per year, or the horrors that will overtake the town and the world will be on you."

John was in abject disbelief. He'd seen Rickward Curling fade from his own eyes. He'd seen his fear. His horror at the realization of what had happened. His panic when he understood the only thing keeping that body alive was the curse on John Ellis's soul, and that soul was no longer in it. He'd sworn he'd never take anything from someone else. He'd sworn it when he built his humble house in a land others had taken from the natives. And yet, he'd helped take the innocence and the life of Walter Parham. Now, he'd not only taken Rickward Curling's life, but his body, his very existence, his family, his background, his race. There was no greater violation. Now, this man, this monster, had cursed him in favor of a mission he'd never asked for. Forever taking from others. Every time he died, he'd displace another soul, like he'd displaced Curling's, take the life that would've been theirs.

In a cold, quiet madness, John, now Rickward Curling, stepped closer to Vanek's bed.

"I know you see this in a negative light, my friend," he said, that pious smile on his withering face. "But you will do such good, it will compensate for the evil you'll have to enact."

In silence, Rickward Curling grabbed a feather pillow from the bed and pressed it firmly on Vanek's face—the awareness of seeing the hands he'd stolen clutching the pillow and pushing it down, only fueling his rage. Driven by the desperation of living just a little longer, Vanek kicked, struggled, to no avail. He could feel life vacating the man's body, and in brief minutes, Amias Vanek was dead.

John Ellis's death was declared a heart attack, brought forth by his long age. Vanek had died of the same disease as his family. John, now Rickward Curling, would disappear at first, leaving his life behind for almost a year, only returning to live Curling's life in his home, a resigned prisoner in a body that wasn't his, finding solace in trying to thwart the Circle and their plans. The sooner he figured out a way to put an end to it for good, the sooner he would die.

His life as Rickward Curling was short, however. Nine years after taking over Rickward's body, overwhelmed by guilt from sacrificing people to the house and finding no escape to his torment, he took his own life in October 1914. The horror was only compounded when he woke in the body of Rickward's sweet, kind sixteen-year-old daughter, Jenelle. He had, as far as he knew, erased her soul and replaced it with his own, finding himself trapped in the growing body of a young woman he'd essentially killed. His guilt was unbearable.

Jenelle was later forced into marriage, but her abusive husband left her during her fifth pregnancy, following four failed ones—including two stillbirths. After punching her one last time, he abandoned her, saying he wouldn't stick around to see her fumble her fifth. Jenelle Curling—retaking her maiden name after the divorce and retaining the Vanek estate due to Amias's ironclad clauses—died during childbirth in December 1929, giving birth to Osmin Curling, whose first moment of awareness was the realization that he had died giving birth to himself.

Osmin Curling would die young, in September 1954, beaten to death by a group of drunken white men, while soliciting a white male prostitute in Portland. He left behind two children—Benjamin and Camille—from his reluctant marriage to a woman who had divorced him and departed White Harbor upon discovering his proclivities. Osmin awoke to find he'd taken over the body of his son, Benjamin.

Despondent and bitter after several lives filled with sorrow and failure—feeling no closer to his eternal rest—Ben Curling cut ties with the world, including his sister Camille, who had moved out of White Harbor to live with her mother years earlier. He would dedicate himself only to feeding the Vanek House and trying to stop the Circle. Except, he would fail at both, dying of a bullet to the heart in 1993 as the house burned down around him.

Now, as John Hitch—his late sister Camille's son—he seemed destined for failure once again.

2022

"I'd put my money on Lighthouse Rock," Hitch said. "Vanek said he came out of Uolmin's cavern on Flat Rock Island. That's Lighthouse Rock nowadays. Your friend Baker also mentioned the island in his research, but I didn't have time to go through it all. I found no caves or cave-ins during my time working at Lighthouse Rock, though admittedly, I wasn't there long."

"So, we're fucked, then?" Royce said.

"Maybe not. There's always the cave path Vanek followed. I've been looking for that damned cave entrance for decades and haven't found it. I used to know the exact location, but it's been over a hundred and thirty years since the last time I was anywhere near it, back when they hanged Walter Parham."

"How can a cave just disappear?"

Hitch shrugged. "How can any of this happen? Regardless, I think it's a simple matter of this being the West Coast. Earthquakes, the ocean waves, rain, erosion. The landscape changed. You know about the sunken settlement southwest from here, right?"

Royce scoffed. "Sure, one of White Harbor's little 'tourist attractions' that never drew no tourists?"

Tali glanced at Royce. "What is it?"

He answered with a blasé sort of shrug. "In the early 1900s, people tried to start another settlement closer to the ocean. South Marshborough. They were Catholic, so they built this small church at the center of these, like, three town blocks—it was tiny. After a huge earthquake, the entire ground sank as a single, unbroken piece, along with the surrounding hills. When the tide is low, you can still see the church's bell tower sticking out of the waves. They thought that might be a cool tourist attraction, do like low-tide boat rides, and bring in scuba divers to go down into the sunken town, but...it didn't really take."

"Yes," Hitch said, hit by a sudden realization. "That earthquake sank the portion of the Crescent Mountains that joined the mainland to Lighthouse Rock, and I'm guessing, also destroyed the cave entrance. If the cave entrance isn't underwater now, my next guess would've been Lumenwood, since it's close to the area I remember, but I've found nothing there. In either case, even if we found the cave, the path is underwater and likely destroyed now."

"So, Lighthouse Rock is our only solid clue then," Royce said. "I think we have no choice but to go there."

CHAPTER THIRTY-ONE
BETRAYAL – PART 2

1991

Peter sat at the edge of the Blue Overlook, on rocky and solid portion of the cliff, his legs dangling over the edge. He risked a look down, his hand holding one of the railing posts. He shuddered, pulled back. A cold autumn wind rose from below. Soon it would be too cold to do things like this.

"You know?" He glanced at Barry, who was sitting to his left, his considerably larger legs also suspended over the edge. "After doing the 'pissing over the edge' challenge, this isn't as scary anymore."

Barry gave him a side eye and said, "Isn't it? Then how come you're grabbin' that post?"

Peter regarded the post as if he hadn't realized it was there until that very second. "Oh, this? Well, it's because, since I already pissed over the edge, there's no rule against holding the railing, is there?"

"Uh-huh." Barry was unconvinced.

"Also," Peter said, motioning toward Barry's own meaty fist clinging to the same post. "Look who's talking. You're doing it, too."

"Well, in my case I'm doin' it 'coz I'm scared shitless I'm gonna fall."

"You? Scared? I thought you were never scared."

Barry went quiet for a moment. Gripping the post tighter, he leaned over, looked down at the ocean below, waves crashing against the cliff, seeming hungry for both boys. "Hmm."

"What?"

"Oh, nothing. I was wonderin' if I'd be able to see our reflection in the water down there, at least like two little dots, but, nah. The sea moves too much. Would've been cool if there had been a reflection, though."

Peter nodded, having no comment on that remark.

"I'm scared a lot," Barry said. "A lot. I almost damn near died when you walked in on me and...Hank." There was a silence. Loaded. Uncomfortable. "I thought my life was over. Thank you for not tellin' anybody. My momma, she—"

"I know." The way Peter said this, it was clear he understood that fear from personal experience. The fear of their respective mothers finding an excuse to punish them. In the case of him and Peter, punishment came in bold, capital letters. "I would've never told anyone, anyway, Barry."

"You're a good guy, y'know?"

"I'm not."

Barry shook his head. "You *are* a good guy, man. You just don't like to believe it coz of all of this guilt bullshit your mom has piled on you. Not like me. I'm not a good guy. I hurt a lot of you guys, and you didn't deserve that. I'd like to, at least, sorta...*act* like a good guy, even though I'm not. At least, I don't wanna act like a bad guy anymore."

"You *are* a good guy, Barry. You just don't like people knowing that."

"I'm sorry for everything I did to you, Norman, uh... Peter..."

Peter smiled.

He *really* didn't know why they all called him that, which was baffling to Barry.

"I'll never do anything like that again. I'll tell the others, too, but especially you, man. I'll never, ever hurt you again. Swear on my dad's soul. If anyone ever lays a hand on you, I'll cave their skull in with a rock."

Peter, while moved, snickered a little, brought his hand up to cover his mouth. "Wait. Wouldn't that count as hurting people?"

Barry looked up at the pale blue sky. Pondered on it for a few seconds. "Well, kinda, but if they're tryin' to hurt my friends, then I guess they got it coming, don't they? It's like, well, maybe not self-defense, but like, *others*-defense or some shit?"

"Yeah. I think you're right."

They both laughed.

"Hey!" a voice called from some distance behind them, growing closer. "What the hell are you two kids doing? Get back on this side of the fucking railing!" They turned to see a man walking up to them from a parked truck. "Aren't you listening? That's dangerous!"

Looking at each other with a laugh, they quickly brought themselves to their feet, hurried to the other side of the railing, where Barry's bike waited.

He picked it up and mounted it in a hurry. He motioned at Peter with his head. "C'mon!"

Peter was already climbing up on the footholds on either side of Barry's back wheel.

Before the shouting man was able to reach them—demanding to know who their parents were so he could call them right now—Barry was already pedaling across the gravel parking lot.

They sped away down the slope, back toward town.

2022

Years ago, Jess gave each of her closest friends hand radios for emergencies—just batteries, and pressing the ON and TALK buttons. No complicated setup, no changing channels. She did this after an earthquake caused a landslide, knocking out a cell tower. It had been ten years since, though, and the radios had likely been forgotten by most. Nadine hoped—perhaps foolishly—in all this madness, Jess remembered to turn hers on, despite not having needed it in a decade.

Elizabeth had helped bandage Nadine's injuries. She'd patched up so many wounds, she felt like a damned quilt. Mr. Saunders—whose body lay in the bathtub—had plenty of medical supplies in his medicine cabinet. Nadine disinfected each cut, especially in the area around her eye. *Well,* she corrected herself, *eye socket now.* The pain had been excruciating. The true horror, however, had been the knowledge she would no longer have an eye. The thought kept stinging her mind like an angry wasp.

For now, she had used gauze and medical tape to fashion an eye patch, and she'd popped plenty of painkillers to dull the constant aching. She was now in the living room, sitting on the couch, having pushed the batteries into the hand radio.

She took in a deep breath, engaged the talk button, and said, "Jess." Her voice was coarse from screaming. "Jess, are you there?"

Elizabeth came from the kitchen with two steaming mugs in hand. She set them down on the coffee table in front of Nadine and sat beside her. "Mister, uh... The gentleman, in there"—Elizabeth pointed toward the bedroom, in the general direction of where Mr. Saunders's body was—"he had a gas stove. I put the kettle on and brewed some coffee with a sieve and a coffee filter I found. Um... I don't remember ever making coffee, though, if I'm honest. I only knew you had to filter it somehow."

Nadine regarded her and gave her a soft smile. The woman had told her she had amnesia of some kind, perhaps from a head injury, but she could find no signs of a head injury, no bumps, or hematomas. "Thanks. Do you remember how you knew Mr. Saunders?"

Elizabeth shrugged, shook her head, bringing up her mug of coffee to her lips. She took a sip. Scrunched her face. "Oh, that's disgusting. Don't drink that." She put the mug down and pushed it as far as she could on the table, as if it were about to explode. "I'm sorry."

"I don't remember ever seeing you here," Nadine prodded. "I know Mr. Saunders lived alone. I knew nothing about a...wife? Daughter? Girlfriend?"

"I really don't know."

Nadine gave a nod, dropping the subject, and put the radio to her lips again. "Jess. Anyone. Can you hear me?" She turned to her again. "Any idea how you got here?"

"I woke up in bed, here. I don't remember anything before that." She stopped. Her eyes shifted. She clenched her teeth and brought a hand to her head. "Wait. I... No. That's wrong. I was walking. I remember walking down that street outside...in the rain. It was dark. I don't... I don't think I knew where I was going. The front door was open." She fixed her eyes on Nadine, frowning with concern. "Maybe I don't live here... But then, where did I come from? Why did I pass out on that bed?"

"Maybe you felt you were about to lose consciousness? I mean, after whatever happened to you, maybe you stumbled to the nearest bed and just collapsed there."

Elizabeth cast a vacant look at the mug of coffee on the table.

Nadine brought the hand radio to her lips again, beginning to think perhaps no one was listening. "Jess. Jess. Anyone. Please. Is anyone listening?"

"Is there a lighthouse in this town?" Elizabeth asked. She turned to Nadine, an eyebrow raised.

Nadine's brow furrowed. "There used to be. Why?"

"I don't know. I keep thinking of a lighthouse. No context or reason. It's just...there. Light spinning."

There was an awkward silence between them, which was interrupted by an abrupt hiss from the radio and a voice coming through.

"You're supposed to say 'Over', you know?" It was Jess.

"Jess?" Nadine spoke into the radio with sudden excitement. "Oh my god, Jess! Am I happy to hear you. I thought your radio was off."

"Whaddaya take me for, Nadine? I ain't some careless, oblivious bitch. I gave it to you guys for emergencies, and this is one big fucking emergency."

"How's everybody over there? Did everyone make it to the bar?"

"No." Jess sounded deflated. "Just Royce and his family. Bunch of other people from the hospital, a few stragglers."

"What about Ray, Barry, Sylvia?"

"No. Freddie set the hospital on fire, and—"

"Oh my god! Are they—"

"They made it out. Freddie's got Barry's kids, though." Jess, in her own colorful way, told Nadine about their encounter with Freddie at the bar.

In turn, Nadine told her about her own encounter with Freddie's creature and her current physical state. "I think the reason he hasn't come back for me is either he's busy with the others, or he hasn't noticed I'm still alive. I need a gun, Jess, and I need you to find me someone who has a boat. I need to go to Lighthouse Rock." She stole a glance at Elizabeth, who turned toward her the second she heard the word 'lighthouse'. "Bobby went there looking for Freddie. Freddie might not be there now, but as you said, he can move quickly all over town. He might not like that Bobby's there, snooping around his cell. He's grieving and not thinking. I can't just leave him alone."

"You sure *you're* thinking straight, girl?" Jess said. "You're also grieving. You lost Angie, too, remember? There's that huge tentacle thing that took down the ferry. I hate to say this, but we don't even know if Bobby's still alive, or—fuck, I hope not—at the bottom of the ocean."

Nadine swallowed. "I'm betting, since we are supposed to be sacrifices, this needs to be done by Freddie or Martha Lange, so that thing might not come for us specifically."

"That's one hell of a huge bet, Deen." Jess let out a hesitant breath. "Sure. I can give you a gun. Royce has a boat in the marina. He can give you the key."

"My phone's battery's dead. I'll look for a flashlight here and hurry to the bar."

"Okay. Be careful, please."

There was a long silence between the two.

Nadine gave a tired chuckle. "We didn't say 'Over' once in the entire conversation."

Jess laughed. "Meh, it's the end of the world. Fuck etiquette."

Ray used his key to unlock the front door, and Barry didn't wait. He stepped past his partner and stood in front of him, trying to be the first to reach his children, while also shielding Ray from any traps Freddie might have set inside the house.

"Danny! Gabe!" he shouted. "It's Dad, where are you?"

"Shhh!" The shushing sound came from the dining room or the kitchen. "You'll wake the children, Daddy!" Freddie said in a lilting, mocking voice.

Barry took a step forward but was soon stopped by Ray's hand.

"Don't!" Ray said in a hushed voice. "Don't rush in like this. It's what he wants! He wants you to go in angry and out of your wits. Don't give him the pleasure!"

"Stay with Sylvia on the doorstep," Barry whispered. "Don't follow me in."

"Didn't you hear what I just said?"

"I heard, but he's got my kids, and I can't watch over everyone at the same time. Stay here!"

"The hell we're staying out here!" Sylvia said from outside. She gripped Jess's gun tight in her hand. "Ray's right, you shouldn't go in alone, or not thinking!"

A low growl escaped Barry's chest as he turned toward the dining room. He could see dim, flickering light coming from there. Candles. The dinner table was visible from where they stood, but nobody was sitting there, which meant Freddie—and perhaps his kids—were around the corner to the left, in the kitchen area. "Fine, but stay behind me, alright?"

He stalked toward the dining room, Ray rolling Sylvia along behind him. They reached the dining table and looked left. At first, Barry gasped. His children were hanging from those strange, hardened black vines from the ceiling, their eyes closed, their bodies motionless. It reminded him of his dad hanging from a belt around his throat. "No!" he cried.

"Don't worry, Brickhouse," Freddie said, sitting on the kitchen countertop, near the hanging kids. "They're alive. Just unconscious. You know, like when you murdered their mommy and granny?"

"I didn't murder them. You did that."

Freddie gave a careless shrug, canting his head to one side and sticking his jaw out. "Meh... You say 'potato', I say 'killing your wife to go suck every dick in the West Coast'. In either case, your two denial babies are still alive, so this is how it's gonna go." He flashed a wide, disgusting grin. "Right out of the gate, let me take one thing off the table. *You* don't get to live. You will die right here, tonight. Start making your peace with it. I'm sacrificing you to the Lord, no matter what, and I'm going to enjoy that so much I might just jizz all over your corpse." He turned to Ray. "Sorry, Plus-One. If it's any consolation, it will be revenge cum, not out of any kind of attraction to your boy, Wreck-It Ralph. Dudes ain't my thing." He turned back to Barry. "So, yeah, you're dying here today, but here's the good part. I'm only killing one of your kids! I was going to kill both, but then I thought, 'Nah, it would be cooler to make him choose!' and while we're at it, you also get to choose which of our two buddies over there gets to live!" He eyed Sylvia, put his palm to one side of his mouth, as if whispering a secret. "I don't mean to crush your hopes, here, Sweet-n-sour Tits, but the odds of Brickhouse choosing you...kinda slim." He returned to Barry. "So, there you go. See? I ain't that big of an asshole. One of your kids gets to live, and one player from Team Asia over there gets to carry your brat to whatever safety is there to be found in the remains of this town!" He wagged his index finger from left to right. "Tick-tock, big fella. I'm on a tight schedule here."

Barry stared at him, blazing anger and hatred in his eyes. He wanted to tear Freddie apart limb from limb.

(*He wants you to go in angry and out of your wits. Don't give him the pleasure!*)

"That's not gonna happen, Freddie," Barry said, in as calm a voice as he could muster. "I'm done playing these games. We did this at that chapel in the Vanek House. We did this at my house last night. I'm not doing it again."

"Not your choice, I'm afraid, Creampie."

Barry reached into his jacket pocket. "Ray, please take Sylvia into the living room."

"No!" she said. "No goddamn way!"

"If my boys get there without me, get out of here, all of you. If neither of us show up in five minutes, you two get the hell out. Don't look back."

"We can't leave you alone with him!" Ray said. "Barry!"

He turned a resolute gaze in Ray's direction. "Go now." His stony gaze softened a little, and he said, "Please." His partner hesitated. He stared at him as if he were asking him to do something impossible. Barry couldn't say he wouldn't react the same if he were in Ray's shoes. "I'll be okay," he whispered. "Go and wait for me."

Ray only stared, his head shaking side to side a little. "How can you ask me to do that?"

Barry pulled something out of his pocket just enough to let it glint in the light of Ray's flashlight.

Seeing this, Sylvia gasped. She pulled on the hem of Ray's scrubs. "Ray," she whispered. "Let's go."

"I'm thinking clearly," Barry said emphatically. "I'm not charging in and doing something stupid. I promise. Please, baby, trust me."

"Guys, I appreciate all the queer melodrama," Freddie said. "Super woke. Love it. Yass, Kween, and all that—as you can see, I *have* kept up with trends from inside the loony bin—but, as I said...tick-tock." He motioned toward the two children.

Ray cast one last hesitating look at Barry and said, "Okay."

Barry gave him a sad smile and whispered, "I love you, Ray. Whatever happens, don't forget that."

"Don't you fucking die."

As Ray wheeled Sylvia toward the living room, Barry brought out a small, glinting steel tool from his pocket, its handle no bigger than a pen. He removed a plastic cover from its tip and placed the sharp point less than an inch from his throat. He fixed his gaze on Freddie, gripping the scalpel he'd taken from the morgue, unflinching. "We've been here before, haven't we? As I said, I'm done playing your games, Freddie. Let my kids go. Let Ray and Sylvia go."

Freddie let out a deriding chuckle. "Or what? You do exactly what I need you to do and die? Damn, Brickhouse, I knew you were kinda dumb, but not to *this* level."

Barry smirked. "See, I might not be the best with words, but I'm not stupid. You've always underestimated me like I'm some dumb jock. I figured you out last night at my place, and Sylvia there did one hell of a good research job on your ridiculous ritual. Four of us need to die this night, either by *your* hand or killed by one of the monsters you're creating. Otherwise, it doesn't count."

"How can you be so sure?"

"If that weren't the case, Callum's death would count for your team. It doesn't. You said so yourself."

Freddie didn't answer. His lips tightened in a hateful scowl.

"Yeah. That's the confirmation I needed."

"That still doesn't make you invaluable. There are still six of you out there for me to pick from. The moment you kill yourself, I'll kill your dearly beloved cum dispenser, then I'll kill boobs-in-a-wheelchair, then go get the other two."

"Looks like you've got all the answers, then."

Freddie studied his face, unable to hide his mistrust and doubt. Barry noticed the way his eyes shifted.

Freddie pondered, analyzed what he might have missed, what could dumb old Brickhouse be hiding under his sleeve. He became jittery. Frowned. Shook his head, dismissing that thought. Then he stopped. Jaw slack. Eyes opened wide. He raised his gaze and drove it into Barry's, looking appalled. "You wouldn't. *She* wouldn't!"

"There's nothing I wouldn't do for my children. I love Ray...more than I love myself, more than I've ever loved anyone in my life, with the sole exception of my kids. And since you'll probably kill him anyway the moment I'm dead, I'd rather his death not be something you can use for your crazy plans."

"You're bluffing. There's no way in hell—"

"You know Sylvia has a gun. You know she used it to kill the thing in the morgue. She and I made a pact. If my kids don't arrive in the living room within five minutes, it means I'll have slit my throat. They'll probably hear me hit the floor. At which point, Sylvia will shoot Ray in the head, then shoot herself, before you have the chance to reach them."

"I don't believe you!"

"Think about it. The three of us die. Jess and, most likely, Royce are already at Cunningham's, so you can't get them. Bobby and Nadine are probably on the way there right now. Even if you kill them before they reach Cunningham's, that's just two out of four.

I can only imagine Martha Lange's face when she realizes you failed her. Tick-tock, Freddie."

Freddie's upper lip twitched. He remained silent, staring daggers at him.

"Since we've got four minutes before I run this scalpel across my throat, might as well get this out. What's your damn obsession with me, man? Sure, I was an asshole to you in school. It's not like I was the only one. Your dad was a violent drunk that kicked your ass, my mom was a bigoted drunk that kicked *my* ass. Was that supposed to make us best buddies? 'Kindred victims', like you said back at the Vanek House? Don't think I forgot. You felt betrayed coz I bullied you when I should've related to you more than anyone. Instead, you got Bobby, who had the life you envied. But you're wrong, Freddie, what our parents did to us didn't make us kindred. It made us mean. It made us assholes. Monsters."

Freddie's eyes spoke for him, brimming with growing indignation.

"Remember Cody Mason?" Barry said.

Freddie's eyes lost their hateful sheen for a second as recognition flickered in them.

"I do. After all these years, I still see his skin rotting and falling off while he was alive. I could've stopped him. I knew he was itching to do something to that autistic kid, Jaban, and his sister. Didn't know it'd be that bad, but I should've. Cody was insane. He looked up to me. One word, one threat from me, and he wouldn't have done what he did. That's on me. What he did to those two and the way he died. That's on *me*.

"And you? You killed six kids, including Leroy. Hardly the same, right? Wrong. Cody used to joke he only wanted to get to high school so he could load up his dad's AK and walk the hallways of Anne Summers High in the middle of the period, randomly firing into classrooms before anyone could even react. 'Like fish in a barrel,' he used to say." Barry's face took on a disgusted look. "It was only a sick joke, right? Problem is, after you make the joke so often, it's not a joke anymore. I could've said something. I didn't. Not because I didn't believe he was capable—oh, trust me...he was—but because I thought that would've been *his* doing, not mine. I was so angry with the world, I thought I didn't owe them anything, so it was none of my business. If Cody hadn't died, and I'd kept my mouth shut, and he'd gone through with it, that would've been on me. The six you killed in the Vanek House would've been only a fraction of what he would've done. All on me.

"I'd like to think I would've changed my mind, eventually, said something—and maybe I would've. Still, if I'd been too late..." He paused. Swallowed thick saliva. "So, no, Freddie. You and me? We were never kindred. We were just mean. We were just broken. All we did was hurt people or let them get hurt. The difference is, I stopped. Peter, Ray, Bobby, hell, even you—in your own way—made me realize there was another way to live. I apologized for what I did to each and every one of you."

"Apologies mean shit," Freddie hissed, bitterness saturating his voice. "People don't change. You're still mean and broken."

"Maybe," Barry said, the tip of the scalpel half an inch from his throat. "Not completely, though. I've stumbled. I married Maryann coz I was scared of what people thought. I hurt her by doing that. Who knows how her life might've turned out if I hadn't been a selfish coward. Maybe she and Therese would still be alive. Maybe I wouldn't have hurt Ray. Maybe we would've had a life together. Instead, I'll probably die tonight. No, man. The meanness never goes away completely. It's always creeping up on you. You have to choose to fight it every day. I've done that for thirty years—sometimes better, sometimes worse—but I've done it.

"Not you, Freddie. You've wrapped that meanness, that resentment, that trauma around you like a fucking comforter. You've let revenge keep you warm. How many people have died now because of that? No, Freddie, you and I were never kindred anything. I could never be you."

Freddie's hateful visage morphed into that malignant grin Barry could recognize so well. "Tell you what, Brickhouse. For someone who claims not to be good with words, that was quite a speech! Bravo! How long did you rehearse that?" He giggled. "Most of that was bullshit, to be honest, but one thing you said did land with me... I can't fail the Mother." His grin disappeared altogether. "I think I should forget about all of these little childhood grudges and be pragmatic."

Freddie slammed his palm on the countertop, and from his fingers outward, the entire kitchen, then the dining room, quickly changed into something Barry recognized as the strange bathhouse motif of the previous night at his house. Moldy concrete floor, old lockers lining the walls, and fleshy tubes spread out across the ceiling fast, like one of those timeline maps showing the spread of a pandemic.

The black threads from which his children hung came to life as black tentacles as the space transformed before his eyes. The wall threads spread around him and bulged in places, forming what looked like cocoons, small at first but growing slowly, like oil blisters. Soon, the transformation had spread past him, moving toward the living room. A single black thread sprung and shot toward him from where a light switch used to be—quick as a chameleon's tongue—and plucked the scalpel from his hand.

"No more games, Brickhouse!" Freddie said, triumphant. "I'll just kill you all!"

He called my bluff, Barry said. *I fucked this up.* "Raymond, run!" he shouted. "Get out! Both of you, get out! Don't come in here! Just get out!" He turned to see several of the fleshy tubes near the living room entrance stretch down in a crisscross pattern, blocking anyone from escaping from there.

As he turned back around, another of the fleshy tubes descended from the ceiling like a boa hidden in a high branch, and wrapped itself around him, coil after coil encircled his body and squeezed tight, leaving him paralyzed.

Freddie ambled toward him. The black thread with the scalpel moved toward his hand, and he took the handle between his fingers, as if being handed a spoon to dig into a delicious dessert. "Let's make this quick." He examined the scalpel. He motioned with his head toward the children. "As you bleed to death, I want you to know after I kill you, I'll kill your boyfriend, then Sylvia, but I will take my sweet time with your children. They will scream and scream for as long as I can keep them alive. I'll squeeze every millisecond of suffering I can from each of them. That's the last thought I want you to have as your life leaves your body."

Barry roared with anger, struggling against his bindings, face red with strain. He could hear Ray and Sylvia shout his name from the living room.

Freddie raised the scalpel to his throat.

Stopped.

"No..." Freddie looked scared. His breathing became anxious, then panicked. "No!" He dropped the scalpel, looked this way and that, shaking his head in bemusement. "Fuck! Fuck! FUCK!" He turned around, took two steps away from him and disappeared into the ether with a fading, echoing, "FUCK!"

Nadine and Elizabeth's shoes splashed along the sidewalk, rain pelting the too-large yellow and blue raincoats they'd taken from Mr. Saunders's closet, along with two borrowed flashlights bobbing side to side—it wasn't like he'd be needing them anymore. Empty houses stared at them from either side of the street with black, rectangular eyes. The rare house here and there showed signs of a lantern or candlelight, but no faces peered out in curiosity at the two women marching down a street everyone had tacitly deemed no longer safe to walk.

"Are you okay to walk in the rain like this?" Elizabeth asked, moving the flashlight toward the red stains visible on Nadine's bandaged right calf, which stuck out from under the coat and her skirt.

The water made her multiple wounds sting, but most were superficial wounds. The rain was diluting the blood a little before her body's natural clotting stopped the bleeding altogether. "It's okay." She kept looking ahead, making an Amazonian effort not to pay attention to the patch of black that had replaced the right side of her field of vision. If things kept going the way they were going, it might replace her entire vision, her entire self. Only a patch of nothingness where Nadine Schaefer used to exist. *Not live*, she thought. *Angie was right. I forgot how to live. Now, I might not even get a chance.*

She glanced at the other woman, debated with herself on whether to ask the question that had been skating eights in her mind. "The lighthouse. You said you kept thinking about a lighthouse. What exactly? Can you think hard about it and maybe picture what is it about the lighthouse that's related to you? Like, maybe not context, but a feeling, maybe?"

Elizabeth wiped the rain from her face. Her brow wrinkled deep, like she was using all her brainpower to come up with something useful, but not getting quite there. She cocked her head to one side, then the other. "It scares me. I don't know if I'm there willingly, or if I was taken there. All I know is I'm scared." She turned her blue eyes toward her. "What's weird, though, is despite the fear, I feel like I belong there? Like, that's where I'm supposed to be?"

Nadine contemplated this for a minute, saying nothing.

"You said you're going to the lighthouse, right?" Elizabeth asked.

Nadine gave a hurried nod. "Yes. I was wondering, when you remember the lighthouse, is there an *actual* lighthouse there?"

"Yes. Why?"

"There used to be a lighthouse, but not anymore. It got destroyed by..." She stopped. Doubted. Continued. "By a wave. Now there's a mental hospital there. No lighthouse, just what remains of it."

"I see a lighthouse." She shrugged. "Like a real one. Light spinning." She let out a sudden gasp. "And the moon!"

This prompted Nadine to turn her head toward her.

"A blue moon, bright blue! Huge! In the sky, right on top of the lighthouse!" She noticed the shift in Nadine's face.

"Are you sure it's bright blue? Not dark blue?"

Elizabeth nodded. "Why? Does that mean something?"

"I don't know. Maybe? I guess we'll have to find out."

"Are you saying it's okay if I come with you?" She grinned with excitement.

Despite the horrors she'd experienced, she found Elizabeth's childish, good-natured demeanor heartwarming, and she couldn't help but smile at her. That drive and curiosity reminded her of her dear sister. Nadine nodded in response. "It might be danger-ous, though. Are you sure you want to go there?"

Elizabeth grinned. "Yes. I need to know why I keep thinking about that place."

"Then, sure!"

They continued walking in silence, wending their way to-ward Cunningham's.

As they turned a corner, there was a strange splashing noise from behind, concealed by the murmur of the rain. Nadine glanced left. Elizabeth wasn't there. She might have gotten distracted by her thoughts and not noticed her fall behind.

She spun on the spot, looked back. Elizabeth wasn't there.

There was that sound again, accompanied by a voice, a muf-fled exclamation, coming from just around a corner building.

Alarmed, she ran back, turned, and shone her flashlight on one of the most bizarre images she'd ever laid eyes on. Not some deformed creature concocted by Freddie Parham's twist-ed mind, but Peter, holding Elizabeth in a choke hold, his left elbow curled around her throat, and the stump of his right arm—cut off at the wrist, but already scarred and healed—po-sitioned at the back of her head to hold her steady.

Feeling like she was, at last, losing her mind, she shouted, "Peter, what the fuck are you doing? What the fuck are you doing?"

"Stay back Nadine. I won't hurt you. I promise. But this doesn't concern you."

The cold, emotionless voice, almost devoid of soul, made her stutter. "L-let her go, now! Please! I don't know what's going on, but let's talk about this! Please, Peter! It's me!"

He flinched, hesitated.

"There's nothing to talk about, Nadine. I won't hurt you only because it's you, but don't come any closer, or I'll have no choice."

"What?" she blurted. This wasn't Peter. This couldn't be Peter. There was no reality in which those words would come out of Peter Lange's mouth.

"You haven't seen what I've seen," he said. "I won't let it take my son. No matter what I have to do. So, stay back. Mother needs her. So, I'm taking her."

(*She's not evil. She's sick, Nadine. My mother's sick. She doesn't know what she's doing*)

Nadine shook her head slowly, disbelieving. "You can't be serious."

"I am," he said, resolute.

"After all she did to you. After all she did to us. After she killed Angie, and god knows how many more people today...you're doing this?"

"Yes. I don't expect you to understand."

Nadine pulled the kitchen knife she'd taken from Mr. Saunders's house. It was wrapped in a towel, so she could tuck it into one of the raincoat's pockets. She pulled on a corner of the towel, and it unfurled in a spiral and fell to the wet asphalt. "Oh, believe me, I understand. I've been trying to convince myself all day there's at least a little part of you that woman hasn't infected beyond repair, but now I see how stupid I've been." She pointed the knife at Peter, seeing the terror and confusion in Elizabeth's eyes.

The resolve in Peter's stare wavered. There was a slight glimmer of her best friend still there, but it was soon gone, replaced by that steely gaze that told her he was now his mother's puppet. She lunged forward; the knife drawing a high arc, meant to startle him, but not actually hurt him or risk hurting her terrified companion; adjusting for the fact she was still getting used to moving and acting with only one eye.

Peter moved his head back.

As expected, the knife missed, but got her closer to Peter, where she could aim better. She swiped the knife back around, this time aiming toward the side of his head. Not a fatal cut—she wasn't trying to kill him, despite everything—she was trying to make him let go of Elizabeth. The knife drew a firm, deep line across his left temple, cutting through the side of his eyebrow.

Peter turned his head and pulled back with an ached grunt. She could see copious blood now running down his face and turning watery in the rain. With a forceful swing of his arms, he threw Elizabeth to the ground. Before Nadine could take another swing at him, his left hand gripped her knife arm, and he pushed her hard with his right shoulder, making her fall backward. As her arm twisted in his, she let go of the knife. A second later, she was lying on the rainwater flooding the side of the street.

She opened her one eye to see Peter standing over her, pointing the knife in her direction. She put her palms up in reluctant surrender.

"I'm sorry. This is what Mother wants. There's no other way."

"You're pathetic," she spat.

Without a word, he turned toward Elizabeth. He grabbed her by the arm and pulled her up, putting the knife to her throat.

Elizabeth let out a terrified cry.

Peter glanced down at Nadine. For a moment, his face broke a little, and she couldn't tell if it was just the rain or tears. "Goodbye, Nadine."

She gawked as he took two steps back, pulling Elizabeth along with him, and moved through an almost invisible tear in reality. She thought for a moment she could see the place he was stepping into. It was too subtle, too faint to make out, but she noticed one unmistakable thing. Behind him, high above, was a bright light, spinning slowly. *A lighthouse!*

The rip in reality closed, and now there was only the dark street and the rain.

When Bobby stepped into the criminal patient wing of Lighthouse Rock, at first, he thought it was as deserted as the rest of the facility, but as he sauntered down the long corridor that made up the wing, it soon became apparent that wasn't the case.

The beam from the flashlight he'd gotten from Xavier shone a narrow, white, oblong shape on the plexiglass windows and doors of the cells. Beyond the transparent material, it revealed the inert bodies of the patients and the missing staff members. All bound to the walls by a black substance, like the one he'd been surrounded by at the beach—and what they'd seen as children at the Vanek House—except solidified, like some kind of cement or resin.

Are they all dead? Bobby approached one of the cells and looked inside, forming a parenthesis with his hands around his eyes to block the flashlight's glare on the plexiglass. At first glance, they appeared dead, but soon he noticed they were breathing, even drooling.

He aimed his light toward the mezzanine above. Though he couldn't be certain, it seemed the two rows of cells up there were similarly occupied.

Freddie was likely not in his cell, but he might at least find something he could use to locate him...or hurt him. He couldn't know for sure, but he was almost certain Freddie would return to his cell at some point. He could feel it in his gut. He approached cell number 1408 and used the emergency key to open the door.

Inside, he was greeted by countless drawing block pages, canvases, and doodles he'd seen before, but now they radiated a sinister aura. These weren't just innocent tools of artistic expression, but something sinister he'd been too neglectful to notice. A detailed plan, laid out right under his nose.

Every painting around him had a brown-red dot on it—it looked like blood. The images depicted familiar places from town, twisted by some cataclysmic event. The hospital engulfed in flames. An enormous crater in the hospital parking lot. The slope of Peter's old house, now a barren wasteland.

Wasn't one of the people who disappeared Thursday night that family's baby? He recalled seeing it on the news that morning. The family that had moved into Peter's house a few years back. Their baby had disappeared. The father was found comatose in the nursery.

His eyes found more horrific drawings—Seaside Amusement Park, Lumenwood, Cunningham's—all warped into nightmarish landscapes inhabited by deformed creatures.

On the floor lay a torn-up canvas with a shattered frame. Curious, he arranged the pieces in what looked like the right order and recognized the cul-de-sac outside Barry's house. Unlike the others, it wasn't sickening and corrupted, but there was an eerie feel to the way the neighborhood lay in darkness, save for that evil blue moon. The edges of the canvas were lined with blood.

As he stood up, another painting caught his attention on a wall near the barred window.

Bobby's shoes rustled on the clutter of papers on the floor as he stalked toward this painting. He stopped and examined it. It was a round altar, surrounded by a chasm, surrounded by a multitude of people contained within an enormous domed chapel. At the center of this altar was a person bound to a black structure. Their identity or gender couldn't be made out. The person's back was arched to complete a sinister symbol. They were screaming, covered in flames.

Angie...

Freddie hadn't only known this would happen. He'd even painted *where* it would happen. The image wasn't something he could've painted after witnessing Angie's death. It was too complex to have been completed in such a short time.

Even though anger and grief were crushing his heart, his face showed no emotion. He ripped the painting off the wall and tore it in half, then tore the halves, as well. Without hesitation or thought, he ripped another drawing from the wall, this one drawn on a notepad page, and ripped it up. One by one, he went around the room, ripping paintings from the walls and tearing them in half, letting the pieces fall to the ground. He crumpled others, tossed them aside. He'd become a whirlwind of rage. Bobby wasn't sure of the moment rivulets of tears began flowing from his eyes. He couldn't even hear his own wails of pain and wrath. Every page he ripped apart was Freddie, every canvas was Martha Lange.

He picked up the easel at the center of the room and raised it above his head. Little plastic paint containers, brushes, and pencils cascaded to the ground and scattered, rolling away from him, as if in fear of his rampage. With a shout, he swung the easel against the wall once. On the second swing, it broke against the concrete, sending splinters flying along with a detached screw.

"I gave you all of this!" he shouted, picking up a little paint container, uncapping it and throwing it at a wall, an arc of green flying in almost slow motion through the air. It hit the wall and fell, leaving a green splotch on a creature doodled on the concrete. "I gave you all this shit, you son of a bitch!" He hurled paint containers left and right, he broke pencils and brushes. "I gave you all this to help you, and for what? For what? Answer me!" He turned toward the bed, nothing but a cot with a rickety frame and a thin mattress. He flipped the bed over, screaming, "Answer me!"

There were more drawings under the bed. He took one, ripped it. Took another, ripped it as well. The third made him stop. He stood there, staring at the painting he was holding, as he panted with exhaustion. He studied the image before his eyes. It was a cavern. Squiggly rhomboid lines formed a mesmerizing mesh of reflected light on the cavern walls and ceiling. In one corner of the painting, there appeared to be a large body of water.

(*It leads to a cavern. A fucking underwater cavern! The thing that's causing all this? It's probably there!*)

Glowing, silver-blue light shone from the depths of the cavern, its source unknown.

There was a rustling from behind.

"Put that down, Bobby."

He turned around to see Freddie standing there, palms raised toward him—one looked like a black prosthetic hand.

"Please...put that down. You don't know what you're doing." Freddie surveyed the chaos of destroyed drawings and paintings, the paint-splotches scarring the sketches on the walls. "Those paintings belong to Mother. They belong to G—"

Bobby's meaty right fist crashed against Freddie's left cheek. A spray of spit came flying out of his lips as he staggered back.

Before he could recover, another punch, this one straight to the gut. Freddie bent with an "Oof!" that echoed outside the room and reverberated through the empty corridor outside. Bobby threw a right hook that made Freddie's head swing back on impact. He stumbled, tripped over his own feet, and fell to the ground.

Freddie waved his hands in the air, disoriented, dizzy. "Wait!" he managed, before Bobby loomed over him, kicking him, over and over, without mercy. Each kick found its mark on tender spots or unsuspecting bones.

Bobby scowled at the flailing wretch at his feet as he made a pathetic attempt to shield himself, and in a cold, vacuous voice, said. "I'm going to kill you, Freddie."

Ray's home returned to normal.

The black tentacles that held Barry's children had transformed back into their crystallized form. The infection Freddie had unleashed upon the house receded and faded, like watching a sped-up video of a festering rash, open sores healing, closing, scabbing over, and leaving almost invisible scars. Barry used a meat cleaver to free his children from their bindings, and now held them tight in his arms. Feeling the relative warmth from their skin—even in this chilly night—and feeling the movement of their chest as they breathed sent tingles of relief down his entire body.

"Barry?" Ray darted into the kitchen and Barry stood to greet him. He stood in front of him and placed a hand on his cheek, then regarded the children in his arms. "Are they okay?"

"Yes." Barry was jittery and embarrassed as he looked into his partner's eyes. "I didn't mean what I said...about you and Sylvia. I didn't mean it, I—"

Ray threw his arms around him and the kids.

"I swear, baby. I would've never—"

Ray shushed him. "I know. I know. I'm not an idiot, Big Bear." He looked up at him. "I know who you are." His smile soothed him as much as one could be soothed under these horrifying circumstances. "C'mon, let's lay them on the couch while we get whatever we need and get to Cunningham's asap. Here, give me Gabe."

Without hesitation, Barry leaned forward and passed him the baby. He cradled the kid in his arms with a smile.

A minute later, both children were on the couch, sound asleep, heads lying on cushions. A gas lantern, left from Thursday night's blackout, shone warm light around the space from a spot on the floor.

"Do you think they're actually okay?" Barry asked, fidgeting. "They're still not waking up."

Ray stood beside him, an arm around his waist. "Might be the same thing that happened last night. It took a while for them to wake up. Maybe what he does works like a sedative?"

"Yeah, I think you're right. Sorry for being a worrier."

Ray pulled him close, gave him a soothing kiss. "I know you're a big softie." He chuckled. "Shows how much you care."

Barry's large, bearded face lit up a little with a relieved smile. He gave Ray a peck on the cheek, then turned to Sylvia, who was no longer in the wheelchair and was now sitting in an armchair at the opposite end of the living room. "Are you okay?"

"Peachy," she muttered, rubbing her stitched abdomen. In one hand, she held Callum's glasses, turning them over, gazing at them, as if drawing strength from them. "Even though your little ruse failed, it confirmed our suspicions about the Third Night's rules and Freddie's abilities. It has to be him or his monsters killing us—can't just be us slipping in the shower. He pretty much conceded Cunningham's is safe, for now. Plus, he let it slip we *can* actually survive this thing."

"How do you figure?" Barry asked.

"He said he'd let one of your kids and one of us live so we could find 'whatever safety is there to be found in the remains of this town'. If there was no safe place, he would've taunted us, like, 'You're all gonna die, anyway.' You know he can't help himself."

She paused, letting the words sink in, then, without looking up, added, "For the record, if things *had* gone sideways, I would've totally shot Ray and myself to make sure the Hyena didn't get the satisfaction of killing us."

Both men raised an eyebrow.

"What?" she said, deadpan. "If we were gonna die anyway, why not die telling Freddie and Martha Lange to fuck off?"

Ray squinted at her, as if trying to come up with an appropriate answer, but then pivoted and said, "We should get to Cunningham's. Now. Before he comes back."

"We need another lantern," Barry said. "I don't think our phones are going to have charge for much longer. Also, some kind of weapon would be nice."

"I still have ten bullets in the handgun," Sylvia said, nodding toward her tote bag. "I could also throw that cult book at Freddie's head. It's heavy. Might hurt."

Barry glanced at her, recognizing their tried-and-true method of dealing with stress through out-of-place humor. "Keep the gun close. Ray, baby, the other lantern's in your bedroom closet, right?"

"Yes. Top shelf. There's also a stun-gun in my nightstand. I'll go get them. Maybe go back into the kitchen and pick up a knife?"

"Sounds like a plan."

Both men turned around, ready to head off, when a scream cut through the living room.

They spun around to find Peter standing behind Sylvia, holding a knife toward her chest. Trying to protect herself, she wrestled with his knife arm, as its trembling tip searched for a target.

Ray stepped forward; a palm raised toward them. "Wait, what the f—"

He couldn't finish the sentence.

Peter pulled the knife back, wresting his arm free of Sylvia's grip and, in that moment of confusion, he slid the knife beneath her chin. With a swift pull, the blade cut deep, unleashing a sudden expulsion of arterial blood, which then settled into rhythmic bursts. Sylvia coughed in a spray of crimson. Abject, wild confusion flashed in her eyes. Her hands flew to her throat, desperate, trying to stop the bleeding. As she pressed against the wound, her fingers caught in the deep gash, folding the skin slightly as the blood flowed through her hands.

Barry gawked at Peter, who gave him a wavering, yet inexpressive look. His jaw was clamped shut, arms stiff at his sides.

They stood rooted to the floor as Sylvia dropped to her knees, one hand clutching her throat. Her other hand went to the floor, trying to support her body, but it slipped on the slick pool of the vital fluid at her feet. She went sprawling without grace or ceremony, and lay convulsing next to Callum's glasses, which had been stained with blood for the second time in twenty-four hours.

The last thing Barry heard before seeing red and charging toward Peter was his vacuous voice, saying, "I'm sorry. I had to."

CHAPTER THIRTY-TWO

BETRAYAL – PART 3

Jess opened the bar's front door to find Nadine, soaking wet, covered in bleeding bandages, and wearing an eyepatch—of all things—standing exhausted in the pouring rain.

"Jesus, girl, I had no clue it was this bad!" As she waved Nadine inside, she poked her head out and looked both ways. "Didn't you say you were with someone?"

Nadine pushed past her. Dozens of eyes fell on her like flies on carrion. She looked around in a frantic hurry and stopped once she spotted Royce, who was helping the other survivors board up the broken bar windows. "I need your boat key! I have to get to Lighthouse Rock, now!"

"Stop for just a goddamn second!" Jess said, grabbing her arm. "What the fuck happened on the way here? You look—"

"Peter's gone insane. He's helping his mother!"

Jess and Royce—who had hurried over to join them—regarded her with bemusement.

"That c-can't be right," he said. "That's not—"

"The woman I was with—the woman who saved my life and patched me up—he kidnapped her. He attacked me, stole the knife

I was carrying, and took her away at knifepoint, then stepped through a hole in the air. Disappeared."

"Like Freddie," Jess said, breathless.

"He said it was 'what Mother wanted'. He's gone off the deep end. Look, I know he took her to Lighthouse Rock. I saw it. Bobby's there, too. He's in danger."

Jess and Royce exchanged a look.

"Gollum-Peter," Royce said, referring to his conversation with Jess two nights ago in the cellar, about the way Peter always made excuses for his mother, the way he both hated and loved that evil woman.

"What was that?" Nadine asked.

"Nothing," Royce said. "Not important. I'm coming with you."

"Whoa, whoa, whoa!" Nadine said. "No! Your wife and daughter are here. You have to stay to protect them."

Royce shook his head. "No, Deen. Trust me. Lil can take care of our girl, and they have Jess, Chuck, and all of these other people to help. You're wounded. If what you're saying is right, everything's converging on that island. Sending you alone is a suicide mission. If Peter and his mother and everything that's happening is leading there, me helping you stop it *is* protecting my family."

"Hitch confirmed it," Jess added. "Whatever god, or demon, or supernatural shit is giving Martha Lange the power to do this...is somewhere under Lighthouse Rock."

"Fuck," Nadine said.

"Fuck is right," replied Jess. "We gotta get you and Royce equipped. You've seen the things Freddie can do. My guess is he's prepared a lot worse over there...well, him and now Peter."

Nadine gave a resigned nod.

"You go and tell your wife," Jess said to Royce, looking terrified and concerned for her best friend. "Don't worry, we'll take good care of them for when you guys get back."

Barry hurtled toward Peter so fast he had no time to react. Just as he was about to say something, the bigger man's fingers gripped his jacket collar tight, then followed this with a powerful blow to his chest. His feet lifted off the ground, his body was propelled back; air was knocked out of him once when his back hit the wall, then Barry's weight crashed into him.

He stared into Barry's burning blue eyes. It wasn't only anger radiating from them. There was betrayal so deep it made him feel even smaller than he already felt in front of his old friend. However, there was nothing to it. He had to do this. There was no other choice.

"Why?" Barry roared, his voice sounding as if his throat were filled with gravel. "What the fuck is wrong with you?"

Spit hit Peter's cheeks. "I had to," he said in a dry, indifferent tone. He said it, knowing neither he nor Ray would understand.

They were incapable of understanding. They hadn't seen what he saw—what he'd been forced to see, over and over, for years. "I swear I wasn't going to hurt you or Ray. I had to kill Sylvia, though."

Barry's face, which looked like a huge, bearded planet filling his vision, glared at him, and that look, that look of bewilderment, of betrayal, pierced his heart deeper than the horrible, unforgivable act he'd just committed. It hurt him knowing they would never understand. He didn't need them to, though. It was what Mother wanted. It was all for William. It was the only choice.

"What's that even supposed to mean?"

Peter's voice was calm, inexpressive. "I know all you've gone through. Your dad, your mom, your marriage." He peered over Barry's shoulder. Ray was kneeling beside Sylvia, frantic. "You finally found each other. I would never take that away from you." He did the best to form a smile. Barry's reaction was still of bemusement. "You promised you'd never hurt me. I'd never hurt you. It's going to be Sylvia, Jess, Royce, Bobby. Mother only needs four. That's it. I won't hurt you, Ray, or Nadine."

In Barry's eyes, he could see him connecting the dots, and instead of looking relieved—

Why? Why don't you look relieved, Barry?

—the horror in the big man's eyes only deepened as he grasped what he was saying.

As if to punctuate this, Ray suddenly let out a helpless wail from behind Barry. "She's dead! Oh god! Barry, he killed Sylvia! He killed Sylvia!"

Peter's dark-blue eyes connected with Barry's light blue. "I won't hurt you, Barry! I promise. You're one of my dearest friends. I pr—"

The punch felt as if he'd hit him across the face with a rock. Peter thought his head had come detached from his body. The world spun around him, just long enough for the second punch, the third punch. He was falling now. He felt as if he were falling forever during the few seconds it took him to crumple to the ground.

For a ridiculous instant, he thought the assault was over, but even though his eyes were closed, his mind spinning, he sensed the moment Barry was on top of him. He roared with grief, crying, "Why? Why? Why?", the word acting as the metronome for each of his punches.

Bobby meant it, Freddie could see. He could also feel it as his kicks found him, over and over, with no sign of stopping. For a second, in his desperation, he put his remaining hand out to touch the wall—unleash the Moonlit World and its denizens on Bobby—to stop his assault and eliminate him in one fell swoop, but he stopped his hand just an inch from the surface. *I can't! If I bring forth the Moonlit World in this room, the transformation might destroy any artwork Bobby didn't rip apart! I don't even know what's left! Fuck!*

Another kick got him directly in the stomach, knocking the air out of him so hard it made Freddie go up on all fours, back arched, mouth and eyes wide open, lungs taking in no air. He caught sight of his hand on the floor. All he needed to do was think it, but he couldn't. So much power, so many horrors he could unleash to tear Bobby to shreds, but he was rendered impotent by four measly feet separating him from the corridor outside, where he could release the power God had granted him while keeping his cell isolated.

Bobby let his foot fly again and kicked Freddie in the stomach a second time. The pathetic man's body bent at such an acute angle, it looked like he'd lifted him off the floor. He rolled onto his side, wheezing, trembling, bleeding.

Bobby stared at Freddie's left hand, now a stump encased in black crystal with prosthetic fingers. In a flash of clarity, it all made sense: the same substance that formed Freddie's hand also bound the unconscious people in the cells and formed the contraption where Angie had been immolated. Those black, living threads that had forced Bobby through the portal—and the tar-like creatures in the Vanek House—were all made of the same material. Same material, two different states. Freddie's hand gesture had summoned the threads at the Vanek House altar when they were kids. Now, as

Freddie touched the wall, Bobby realized it wasn't random. There was intent behind it. Freddie was trying to trigger something.

"I see," he muttered.

Freddie's pained eyes flashed toward him.

Bobby kicked him again, this time in the ribs. He thought he'd heard one of them crack.

Freddie cried out in a howl of pain.

Bobby reached for his belt, unbuckled it, and pulled it out, then passed the hanging end again through the buckle, forming a loop. He bent his knees and closed his fist tight around Freddie's right wrist, holding his palm up. "Can't let you use your one good hand, right?" Freddie's sudden gasp was all the answer he needed. He wrapped the belt loop around Freddie's wrist and pulled it tight.

Freddie let out a cry when he felt the hard metal loop dig into his skin.

Unmoved by this, Bobby pulled him across the room, dragging him across paper, ripped canvases, and spilled art supplies. With Freddie's arm pulled taut, in a straight line, Bobby did two things with a coldness he would've never believed himself capable of. First, he raised his foot and brought it down in full force on Freddie's wrist, which was lying on its side. With two additional hard stomps, he felt the ends of his radius and ulna shatter, accompanied by Freddie's howls of pain. While Freddie tried to pull his arm away, to no avail, Bobby raised his foot again, this time bringing it down on his elbow. It took four heel stomps to fracture it to his satisfaction.

Freddie's screams were maddening, ululating cries of insurmountable pain.

Bobby didn't care.

Once more, he dragged him by his mangled arm a few steps further toward the toilet, at the foot of the cot he'd flipped over. If Freddie's arm had happened to rip away at its shattered joints, it was of little concern to Bobby.

He tied the belt around a sturdy safety rail next to the toilet, looping it once around Freddie's palm so it would face away from any surface, ensuring he couldn't touch anything. Once satisfied, he crossed the room again, stepping over Freddie's moaning, jittering shape.

"I was the only one who believed there was still good in you, Freddie. Even after seeing the things you summoned inside the Vanek House." Bobby crouched, his back to his former friend. He brushed aside a few pieces of paper that lay on top of one of the detached legs of the easel. "Even after seeing those dead children at the altar. Even after I witnessed you grinning and cackling as you stabbed Leroy in the back." He raised a long piece of varnished wood in front of the flashlight, slapped it against his palm to make sure it was sturdy enough. He stood. Turned around. Freddie's beaten figure lay wriggling on the floor, his bound arm bent at the wrist and elbow in an unnatural shape. "I believed in you."

Freddie raised his bruised and bleeding face, breathed in and out, trying to get some control over the pain, then he forced himself to display a bloodstained grin at Bobby. "Well, if we're honest...that's totally on you, Bobster."

Bobby returned a sarcastic smile, walked up to Freddie, slapping the easel leg on his palm one more time, which let out a satisfying meaty bump.

Freddie's expression faltered for a fraction of a second—he knew what was coming—still, he flashed his grin at Bobby again, and continued, "I can't be blamed for your stupidity."

The wooden stick swung almost out of nowhere. Like a bat meeting a baseball. It struck hard against Freddie's cheekbone with a crack.

Freddie's face was a mess of blood, gashes, bruises, and missing teeth. His lower lip was split almost to his chin. His chest heaving, he spat a glob of blood on the floor. His entire visage was such a crimson wet ruin, it would've been impossible to tell he was crying if it weren't for the sobs now shaking his upper body. Still, he turned his face toward Bobby, trembling, pathetic, and yet, his mouth stretched into a gap-toothed grin, the cut in his lower lip pulled into a disgusting V.

On pure instinct, knowing Freddie well enough to know what was coming, Bobby returned the smile. A smile that contrasted with the cold murder in his eyes.

"Look at you," Freddie said, his voice raspy and sodden. "Who knew all it'd take to grow you a pair of balls was subtracting a pair of boobs from your life?" He started giggling, his evil hyena laugh coming out in choked, aching bursts, until it was cut short by the heel of Bobby's shoe stomping on his balls. Freddie caterwauled in pain, as he pushed the heel in deeper, deeper, until he felt one of them give a satisfying, meaty yet gelatinous squish.

Freddie reacted as if someone had pulled his guts through his mouth. He rolled on his side, knees curled inward, and vomited a mixture of blood and whatever he'd last eaten, forming a swirling shape.

"I should've let them transfer you to another doctor. Even if you went on one of your little hunger strikes to make sure you stayed with me. I shouldn't have cared. Let you starve and wither away, or have them lock you in a dark cell, feeding you through a tube. I wasted thirty years on you."

"As I said before," Freddie forced himself to say, "It's not my fault if—"

"Shut up."

The wooden easel leg, now painted with Freddie's blood, flew across his face again, making Freddie for once remain quiet. Perhaps the pain was getting to be too much.

"Your dad was a drunk asshole. But your mom... Jesus, Freddie. Your mom was one of the kindest people I've ever met. Even your dad knew that. He took out his drunken rage on you, but he never hurt your mom, not an unkind word. Even when she was always embarrassed by the scenes he made when he was in his drinks, your mom loved your dad, and he loved her. She was a light in the world. And Laurie..."

Freddie flinched at the mention of his little sister, almost as if Bobby had stabbed him with her name.

"Laurie took after your mom. She was such a happy little girl. I loved playing with her in your living room while your mom made dinner for all of us."

Freddie pressed his lips tight. Gone were the daring stare and the taunting words. He listened in silence. The only sound coming from him were the sodden breaths from his broken, bleeding nose.

"You never understood, man." Bobby's tone melted into something less detached, something heartfelt and melancholic. "Those moments, right there, those were the only moments I had a family."

Freddie turned his swollen face, and even through puffy eyes, the confused stare he gave him was clear. "What?"

Bobby scoffed. "Wow, and you were supposed to be my best friend." He shook his head. More and more, each second, Bobby was overcome with the feeling he'd devoted years to a lost cause. "You were my friend since we were in kindergarten, and you never saw. No matter how many times you came to my house and watched movies or played video games or hung out and had pizza. You never saw." His voice broke. "Aside from a hello, did you ever interact with my parents? Did you ever see them interact with me much? No, right? It was also like that when you weren't around. They paid for my school, they got me clothes, they got me electronics, movies, action figures, game consoles. Anything I wanted, I got. You weren't around anymore by then, but I was the first kid in White Harbor—other than maybe Royce—to have a computer with internet access. All I had to do was ask for it."

The corner of one of his lips was pulled to one side in a sardonic smirk. He pointed the bloody end of the easel leg toward Freddie, which made him flinch.

"You thought that meant I had the perfect family." He shook his head. "No. My parents never cared about who I was, how I felt, who my friends were, what made me tick as a person. They just threw money at me and called it parenting. I don't think my mom ever told me she loved me. But you know who did? Your mom. Mikayla Parham said she loved me. One day as I was heading home, she gave me this huge hug goodbye, and said, 'Oh, I love you so much, Bobby. You're like a son to me. You make Freddie happy, and I love you for that.'"

Bobby wiped his runny nose with the back of his hand, not realizing this had only left a streak of blood stretching to his left cheek.

"That was actually the last time I ever saw her... Alive, that is." He drove his eyes like lances into Freddie. "It's like subconsciously she knew it would be the last time we talked. I'm not sure she knew she was going to die because of her stupid son."

Freddie flinched again at this. "I—"

"Shut up."

Freddie's body curled inward, expecting Bobby to swing that wooden stick across his face again.

"I know you didn't mean to kill her and Laurie, but you did. You and your witless, impulsive, selfish nature. You killed them the moment you waded into The Eye, thinking you were immortal. Welp, you survived, they didn't! Your witless arrogance killed the only genuine mother and sister I'd ever have. Then you went on to do so many more horrifying things...using them as an excuse. And here I was, a ridiculous clown with a degree, spending decades believing there was still good in you. I still believed...in you."

Bobby's sudden hysterical laughter echoed across the lifeless corridor.

"And, to thank me, you helped kill my Angie...and according to that John Hitch guy—whom I refused to believe at first—you were planning on killing us, the Vigilantes, my chosen family." He stared straight at him. "How many families were you planning on taking from me, Freddie?"

There was a moment of silence between them. Freddie no longer held his gaze. His face, concealed by shadows, looked away, as if pondering.

"I'm sorry, Bobby," Freddie said, his voice weak, honest. "I'm so sorry."

Bobby observed him with suspicion. The Freddie he knew had never apologized for anything in his life.

"You're right." Freddie's voice quivered as he let out a loud, painful sob. "Barry's right, too."

Barry? He didn't know what Freddie was talking about, but he knew he'd never once called Barry by his name. Only Brickhouse. *It's Freddie's way of distancing himself from others and putting himself above them. Not acknowledging their actual names.*

"He said I'm broken!" he wailed. "Broken! That doesn't even begin to describe how fucked up I am! I was always a piece of shit, but when Lolly died... Oh god! Oh, my god!" His voice crumbled, like a rock cliff splitting apart as it fell into the ocean.

He's manipulating me. This can't be real. Never in a lifetime of knowing Freddie had he heard his voice turn so shrill, so vulnerable. *He also said Lolly.* His cute pet name for his sister, the one nickname in Freddie's universe not meant for distancing, but for closeness.

"When Lolly died, I broke. I didn't mean to kill her, but I killed her! Walking into the deep part of the river was the worst thing I've ever done. The worst thing I've ever done! And I want to take it back, so bad! None of this. None of this would've happened if...if...if I hadn't carried her into the deep part of the river. I'm sorry! Oh god, I am so, so sorry!"

Is he actually being...honest?

"I helped kill Angie. You spent years trying to help me, and I helped kill her." He spat blood on the floor again, breathed in and out, his broken nose whistling with each breath. He then gave an inward nod. "I'm done. Do what you gotta do, man."

Bobby studied his face, detached it from any personal feelings about the pathetic man bound to the sink, matched it to a lifetime of knowing this person's facial expressions, vocal inflections, body language. He was looking for any indicator he was playing him. Found none.

He tossed the easel leg aside. The wood clattered on the floor, then went silent. He took a couple of steps back and sat down on the floor, among the papers and canvases, rested his back against the wall. Given his knowledge of Freddie, his fanatical ramblings, the fervent belief he'd seen in him for years and years, he knew there was one thing Freddie wouldn't do, and that would be his tell, the test of how honest Freddie was being.

"I'm going to kill Martha Lange, Freddie," he said, his tone collected, matter-of-fact.

Freddie gasped, horrified, almost as if he'd told him he was going to exhume Laurie's corpse, cook a broth with her bones, and force-feed it to him. His head shook, an unwitting reaction. He wasn't feigning his shock.

"Where is Martha Lange?"

The question hung in the air, like a pendulum swinging between them, waiting for one of them to reach out and stop its movement.

"There's a cavern under this building," Freddie croaked. "If you go to the boiler room, you can descend to it. Mother is there with God."

Bobby held his poker face. What Xavier had said, the painting he'd found under Freddie's bed, which now lay on the floor. This wasn't a lie. "You don't have the key to the boiler room. You would've never made it down there on your own. How were you planning to get down there?"

Freddie's eyes flitted toward the painting of the cavern and back. Bobby noticed how he hesitated; he saw him *want* to lie. Instead—

"God lets me walk through the paintings. That's how I can get out of this cell. I'm not supposed to go into the cavern. I'm tainted because of my family curse, but I made it, just in case the Mother allowed me to go, the cavern is always on the other side, the uh... The Moonlit World, but the paintings let me walk into it."

"How?"

"Blood," Freddie said. "My blood."

Bobby looked around, remembered the bloody canvas edges and the blood dots on each drawing. "You put your blood on the edges of the canvas, and it lets you walk through."

"Yes."

Bobby stood. Walked over and picked up the cavern painting, then approached Freddie, crouched. "Don't move, or you'll regret it." He ran his fingers over Freddie's face, taking some of his blood, and applied it to the edge of the painting. He repeated this process a few times, as Freddie held his breath, until the entire edge was lined with blood. Nothing happened. Bobby turned a menacing gaze toward Freddie.

"I'm the only one who can use the paintings. It won't work for you."

"Okay." Bobby stood, rolled the canvas, and marched toward the cell door.

"W-wait! Where are you going?"

He turned to Freddie. "I'm not going to kill you, Freddie. But I can't leave this here with you, especially now that you might use it. I'm going to find Martha Lange, and I'm going to go through the boiler room. Not this thing. If you're lying and she isn't there, I *will* come back and kill you. Last chance to come clean."

"I'm not lying, Bobby. She's down there. But God is with her. I don't think killing her will be as easy as you think."

"Thanks for your concern, but I really don't care if she kills me."

"Bobby," Freddie said, as he was about to turn and leave. "Thank you for believing in me. I really am sorry for my part in all this."

Bobby smiled. The nod he gave him was sad and tainted, but also communicated he appreciated Freddie's words. He turned around and walked into the dark corridor, the sound of his footsteps echoing all around.

As he passed one of the cells to his right, he was startled by a sound coming from inside, a bumping sound, screaming. To his horror, one of the security guards, still bound to the wall, was writhing and kicking, the back of his shoes banging against the cell wall as he screamed, "What's going on? Help me! Help me!"

Bobby approached the cell and put his hand on the glass. "Hey! Hey! Look at me!" Bobby called.

"Doctor Novak?" the terrified guard said. "What's going on? I... I was in the dayroom, and suddenly I woke up here. What's going on? Please get me outta here!"

He kept kicking and writhing, trying to break his bonds, as Bobby reached into his pocket for the key.

"Got it." He looked down at the key in his palm. Before he could use it, there was something black protruding from his chest. A spike, or blade of some sort. His body gave a shudder as a large bloodstain formed around the exit point. The blade then disappeared back into his body. He felt it slide against the nerve endings on his flesh, and felt something collapse within him, like someone had popped a balloon inside his ribcage. Then, the blade came out again through a second hole. It was pulled back again, then pierced his body a third time. Perplexed at first, despite the pain, despite the blood, he looked up at the guard, who was staring, eyes bulging, and screaming in horror. He was looking past Bobby.

Bobby whirled around, his right arm swinging as if to hit something behind him, but missing, and there was Freddie, his swollen bloody face giving him a gap-toothed, gash-lipped grin. "Wh-what?" Bobby wheezed.

The black crystal coating around Freddie's stump had reshaped itself into a long blade instead of a hand.

Blood—*his* blood—dripped down like rubies from it.

Freddie's other arm hung limp and broken, and from his wrist dangled a cleanly cut belt.

"What-t?" Bobby wheezed again, realizing he couldn't take in breath, and he was wasting his last remaining oxygen on a meaningless question.

He watched in horror as Freddie tightened the black bindings around the security guard, causing a sickening crunch of bones and a gruesome expulsion of blood and organs from his mouth.

Freddie returned his eyes to him. He stabbed him again. The blade went into his stomach, his chest, his underarm, and finally, his heart.

Bobby dropped to his knees, feeling himself die.

Freddie pulled the blade back with a rapturous smile. "Hee-hee-hee!" he giggled, blood spurting from his mouth. The last time Bobby would hear his hyena laugh. "Gullible, naive, stupid. Oh, Bobster. It's been fun, buddy." He crouched and, thinning the black blade to almost a needle's thickness, pierced the rolled canvas that Bobby had dropped, picked it up. "You almost got me. You. Almost. Got me. If it weren't for you believing in me."

Freddie walked away, back toward his cell.

Bobby fell face-first to the floor. His hand got stained with the expanding pool of blood gushing from him, escaping him. He could feel his body empty on the cold concrete. Before the world darkened, he stretched his arm out, as far from the pool of blood as he could, and tried to scribble something on the floor with the crimson fluid in his fingers.

He died without knowing if he'd finished scribbling it.

As the latest punch impacted Peter's face, the memory overtook Barry. A cruel jolt. A reminder of what he was doing

(*I'll never, ever hurt you again. Swear on my dad's soul*)

and it brought him to a stop with a gasp.

He looked down at Peter's bruised and bleeding face, and he felt his heart wrench inside his chest. "I'm sorry." The two words were whispered so low, he was the only one who heard them.

Peter's face turned to one side, spit out a small gob of blood.

"I'm sorry," Barry said again, shaking his head, horrified. He *must* have been holding back, engaged some subconscious brake.

He'd punched Peter what? Five? Seven times? Knowing his own strength, if he'd actually punched him at full strength, his face

(*Freddie Parham has to die!*)

would've ended up like Freddie's when he'd beaten him down on the Vanek House lawn. Broken bones, missing teeth, an unrecognizable mess of blood. Worse even. He'd been a teenager back then; he was a full-grown adult now. If Ray hadn't stopped him, he would have killed Freddie back then. But Peter... Peter had killed Sylvia in cold blood.

(*Peter Lange...has to die?*)

Barry shook his head. Turned his teary eyes toward Peter, ensuring to hold him down against the floor until he was sure of what was happening. "Why?" he asked again. "Why would you do this? Tell me, goddamn it!"

Peter swallowed what must have been a copious amount of blood mixed with saliva. He sighed, and turned a cold, steely gaze up at him, curled lines of slick blood running down his cheek from his nose and mouth. "It's what Mother wants. It's the only way." The words were robotic, a soulless automaton's response to a voice command. "Freddie was too slow. His thirst for revenge, his arrogance got in the way of his duty. So, Mother commanded me to finish the job."

"The..." The words wouldn't come out. He could feel the rage still bubbling in the back of his mind, held only at bay by his confusion. "The job?"

Peter nodded. "Four of you have to die. Freddie hadn't even..." He stopped. His eyes shifted to one side, as if he sensed something in the air. "Huh... Guess I spoke too soon." He turned his dark-blue eyes toward Barry's petrified face. "He just killed Bobby."

"What?" Ray said, springing up from beside Sylvia's corpse, his hands covered in blood.

"You're lying," Barry said.

Peter's permafrost eyes stared up at him. An eerie, disgusting calm emanated from his expression. "Two to go."

The rage pushed past his confusion, and once more, Barry raised his fist with an angry growl, this time ready to bring it down in full strength on a person he'd promised never to hurt.

"Stop." Peter's voice felt like it had coated his entire brain with tar.

Barry couldn't move. A familiar feeling. Martha Lange's command freezing his entire body. Only this time—

"Get up."

Barry stood. Absolute terror twisting his face.

"Step away from me," Peter said, no expression on his face.

Barry took two steps back toward the wall.

"What are you doing?" Ray's voice. Barry couldn't turn his head toward him. "Stop! You can't—"

"Quiet."

Ray stopped talking mid-sentence.

"I know neither of you can understand this," Peter said, his dead-alive gaze fixed on Barry again. "You don't need to. This is what Mother wants. I've been fighting her for so long, but now it's clear to me she was right. This is how it has to be. Four of you must die, but I will not take away what you've struggled so hard to find, Barry. I want you, Ray, and your children to have a chance at surviving this. I want Nadine to find a life outside this town. I had to choose. You will do anything for your children, Barry. I will do anything for my son. So, stay out of my way."

"You selfish piece of shit! Is that your excuse? You get to choose who lives and who dies, just because you happen to be Martha Lange's son? I would give my life for my children, but I would never kill my friends just because I *lucked* upon the power of keeping my boys safe in exchange for their lives."

"Lucked?" he smirked.

"You heard me."

"You killed your wife and her mother."

"I didn't."

"Are you sure?"

Barry stammered. Swallowed. "I was defending myself. I was defending my kids."

Peter chuckled. "If you knew what's coming, you'd know I'm doing just that."

"You're disgusting."

"Take your wins when you get them, Barry. Don't make me change my mind." He looked from one man to the other. "I have to visit Cunningham's. Jess and Royce are next. I wish you both—" He stopped, looking at something just behind Barry, jaw hanging slack. Sudden shock flashed across his face. "What? No!"

Barry felt a hundred needles piercing his lower back, spreading under his skin. He turned to see a black blister on the wall, a remainder of Freddie's creations. It had burst, and black threads shot out, entering his body, wrapping around him, and pulling him against the wall. He was soon enveloped in a cocoon of darkness; the threads invading his muscles, organs, and every available orifice.

Before the blackness took him completely, Barry caught a glimpse of Peter turning his head toward a distraught Ray, and saying, "I'm sorry! This wasn't me! I didn't want this!" then stepping to one side and disappeared into thin air.

Darkness became his world.

His mind stopped being his own.

The crowd had stopped working on boarding up the windows, and now simply stared at the figure that seemed to have stepped out of the rain itself. Plenty of them recognized the individual standing in the middle of the street; thick strands of straight black hair falling over his face, through which he stared at them through the openings between the boards.

Jess wended her way through the crowd until she spotted her dad standing near the front, looking outside. She placed her hand on his shoulder. "Dad, what is it?"

He raised a palm toward her. "Stay back, Pum'kin."

Annoyed, she tried to push past. "I've told you a million times not to fuckin' call me th—"

He grabbed her by the elbow. "Stay back."

His tone of voice gave her immediate pause. She cast a glance around. Concerned, scared faces, hands over mouths, couples holding hands. Recognition.

She tried to look over his shoulder, but the angle didn't line up well enough for her to see between the few boards already affixed to the window. Then the voice came from the street, floating in through the white noise of the rain.

"I'm going to repeat this only once."

Is that...Peter?

"Send Royce Howe and Jess Cunningham out, now." Peter's voice sounded as if it were coming from a screen reader. An automaton. An imitation of emotion. No soul.

Chuck raised his rifle, pointed it outside. "I can send a bullet flying right through your balls if you don't leave right now, Peter! Don't make me do this!"

There was unintelligible murmuring all around.

Peter's soulless chuckle wafted in through the rain. "I don't want to hurt anyone in there, Chuck. I promise I won't. I just want Royce and Jess."

"And people sleeping under bridges want a mansion in the Hollywood Hills—pool included. Not happenin' for them, either."

Jess, tired of all the posturing on her behalf, pulled her arm out of her dad's grip, grabbed his gun arm, pointed it down, and walked past him.

"Jess, don't..."

"Shut up, Dad, let me handle this." She stood in front of Chuck and looked outside. There, through two boards framing the image, as if in one of those movies, where you have black bands at the top and bottom of the screen, stood Peter, the rain pouring down on him. He didn't seem to mind. "I didn't want to believe it, Petey-boy," she said, and the murmuring from the crowd became clear.

"Peter Lange," they said, hearing their recognition confirmed.

"The writer."

"Martha Lange's son."

"Saw him on Jimmy Kimmel the other night."

"Wait, wasn't that crazy woman at the altar Martha Lange?"

"His wife died in a fire."

"I read his last book. Fuckin' sucked."

"Peter Lange... Did he go nuts?"

"I thought he'd died in a fire."

"Did he kill his wife?"

"What's going on with him?"

"He's crazy like his mother."

"He wants to kill us, like his mother."

Feedin' Blight Harbor, Jess thought. *Fuckin' idiots.* "When Nadine told me what you did," Jess continued, "I kept thinking she was wrong. All those years of us protecting you against your mother. All those years believing you had freed yourself of that dusty old cunt, and here you are...Martha fuckin' Lange's little servant."

"You haven't seen what I've seen, Jess." His voice might have just as well been coming from a scarecrow, posed in the street as a creepy prank. He didn't move, and with the rain, she couldn't see his lips moving as he spoke.

"You've seen what, Norman?"

"I saw what's coming. I spent years there. Years in mere minutes. I can't let that happen to William. Or to the ones who survive this. Mother is right."

Jess scoffed. "And there it is... Remember what I said the other night? How that woman wasn't your family, that *we* were your family? I meant that, Petey-boy. I'm hoping, as I did many years ago, that this insane babbling comin' outta your mouth doesn't translate into you actually hurting someone you love. You stopped yourself from hurting' Nadine, it's not too late, Peter. You can still—"

"I killed Sylvia."

Jess's breath caught with a choking noise. Seconds of silence—broken only by hushed murmurs—ticked away, while Jess hoped against hope she'd heard him wrong.

"I slit her throat." He added this to make sure there was no doubt. "Watched her bleed out in Ray's living room."

Jess shook her head. This couldn't be happening. She couldn't accept this was happening.

"Bobby's dead. Freddie killed him in Lighthouse Rock."

A single sob, more like a sudden explosive moan, left Jess's chest. She stopped herself from outright bawling.

"I didn't want to hurt Barry or Ray...but Barry turned."

"T-turned?" she asked in a weak voice.

"That's right, you've never seen it happen. Remember the monsters at the Vanek House? Sort of like that. Freddie turned him into one of those. I didn't know. Couldn't stop it. Barry will probably kill Ray."

Jess shook her head. This was a nightmare. She wanted to wake up.

"I can't count them, though, since I don't know they'll die on time, and Mother needs four." The emotionless tone with which he said this, as if he were talking about a transaction or a negotiation, filled her body with goosebumps, disgust coursing through her skin. "So, I'll need for you and Royce to step out here. I promise no harm will come to the people inside. I only need the two of you. You can die knowing I'll let them live. Hell, Nadine and Ray might still make it out alive."

Jess closed her eyes, feeling her heart breaking and the world spinning around her. She forced a smile. "Your mother locked you in a crawlspace for two weeks, not caring you were starving and thirsty. She used Freddie to kill my mom. She immolated Angie. Hundreds dead in the ferry and the hospital. And you trust that person to spare the people in here if we do what she says? That's the person you're aligning yourself with. If that's the case, I don't think there's much more to say."

In a swift move, she reached for her dad's rifle, pointed it, and fired. A small splash on the wet asphalt, accompanied by small chunks of material, exploded at Peter's feet. He flinched, took a step back. "Next one goes straight into your skull," Jess said, raising her aim. "No one's setting foot out of this place. In case you haven't noticed"—she motioned toward the two corpses lying a few feet from where Peter stood—"we already had a heart-to-heart about the topic with Martha Lange's *other* bitch."

"Fine. Have it your way, Jess."

A gasp ran through the bar crowd as the street changed around where Peter stood. Thousands of cracks opened on the pavement, forming a spiderweb that stretched as far as the flashlights could touch. The streetlights rusted, broke, fell. A flood of filthy water rose from the gutters, until it reached about a third of Peter's shins, and ran endlessly down the slight slope of King Street, on its way to the ocean. The buildings around began to change, to transform, to age. Their shapes, their material, their very nature turned into something that didn't belong. No one could quite tell what they looked like through the darkness and the rain, save for fleeting glimpses in flashes of lightning.

The bar crowd took a panicked step back, bumping into each other, as the edges of the windows developed cracks and mold, and what looked like black veins ran over the frame and crawled inside the bar. After a few inches, the veins stopped, their tips dematerializing, as if they'd reached a threshold they couldn't grow past.

"Shit," Chuck said in a shocked gulp.

"Those protective glyphs are giving way, aren't they?" Peter asked. "They will stop working soon. Especially now that God's eye is open." He looked up, and Jess noticed a hint of blue shine on his face. "You're not seeing it right now, but the blue moon is out again. The whole town is changing. You can see a little of it from in there, and once you're forced out of that rathole, you will see how much. Your time's running out."

"Fine, you pathetic little shit. Wait there all you want! Nadine and Royce are halfway to Lighthouse Rock to kick your mom's ass."

"Dad, shut the fuck up!" Jess shouted.

Peter flashed an angry stare at him. He took an urgent step aside and disappeared in mid-air, like Freddie had done earlier—the spot where he stood now occupied by nothing but the rain.

"Why would you tell him that?" She gave her dad's shoulder a hard push.

"We need to buy time to figure out what to do. Having him standin' out there waiting for someone in this panicking crowd to slip up won't help."

"He's going to go after Nadine and Royce! He's going to kill them, Dad! Did you forget about the ferry?"

He shook his head. "Based on what I know, if what capsized the ferry kills them, it won't count for Martha's plans, and even if she gave him some of her power, I'm fairly sure Peter won't be able to walk on water and ambush them in the middle of the ocean. We sent them armed. They have a chance. We have many people here also hoping to survive, not just your two friends out there, so we have to focus on that." He reached into his jacket pocket and pulled out an old envelope in a small plastic bag. "There's also this."

"The letter. You found it!"

"I remembered where I put it, a few minutes before your pal showed up like the angel of death out there. It was in the cellar all along." He motioned with his head in the direction of the cellar door. "Let's go." He turned toward the crowd. "Anyone brave enough to still approach the windows, keep trying to board them up. We'll be right back."

"It's not raining out here," Nadine observed, as Royce piloted his small family boat across a sea that looked so still it gave her goosebumps. They'd agreed on going at the lowest possible speed to reduce the noise made by the tiny four-person vessel, guided only by a compass, since there were no stars, and the small navigation device Royce had on his boat was throwing out nonsense. "No waves."

"No moon, either," Royce said. "Don't quote me as a scientist, but I think that might be part of it. Don't think the waves would stop entirely, though."

"Yeah, me eith—" She gasped, cutting off her phrase. She waved a frantic arm in the air. "Kill the motor! Kill the motor!" she whisper-shouted. "Lanterns, too!"

Royce complied, frowning with confusion. He doused the lanterns. They were swallowed by the soupy dark. The motor went silent, followed by the lapping sound of water and the small fishing boat doing a little side-to-side jawing dance until it settled.

"Look at the water." Her voice had a breathless, high-pitched hiss to it. Her hand went up to cover her mouth. She was terrified.

Royce's eyes drifted to her left, toward the water. Lacking reflections, it looked like they were in a black chasm, endless in its reach. The water lapped softly against the sides of the boat. He scooted over, closer to port. He hesitated and looked down at the water. He felt the moisture drain from his body, as if someone had uncorked a hole in his feet and all the water, blood, and piss were spilling out of him. He felt lightheaded, terrified beyond his ability to function, but more than anything, he felt small. Insignificant. An ant crawling up a stone at the foot of Mount Rainier.

The water wasn't black. Not quite. Down there, God knew how many feet below, something moved.

He could only tell it was moving because of the glowing blue spots lining its body. Each looked roughly the size of a human head, which made him not even want to guess their actual size, given how far down they were. They followed a curved line, snaking, forming a slow wave, as if they lined the side of a colossal tentacle, or a deep-sea eel, which had developed these blue spots to see in the depths. It didn't attack, but instead swayed with a slow, eerie motion, like a lazy behemoth biding its time, waiting for someone to provoke it.

Royce felt a surge of panic rise up his throat, but he closed his eyes, breathed in and out, controlled breaths, muttering a list of the names of Tracy's dolls, trying to arrange them by the alphabet. "Amelie...Ashlyn...Cecily...Felicity...Gwen-Gail the Gracious Girlie-Girl...Josefina..."

"Royce!" Nadine whispered.

No, she doesn't have any dolls named... He shook his head. "What?"

"Do you have paddles?" Nadine asked. "I don't think we should use the motor."

He looked again over the side. There it was still. Blue dots swaying in a terrifying dance, knowing all it needed to do was move a little to make this little boat capsize and send them flying overboard to be eaten by whatever else was down there. The images of the ferry turning over as a gigantic tentacle rose from the waves were all he could see, all he could think about. "Kaya," he muttered again in an absent voice. "Keisha...Nanae the Nicest Nanny..."

"Royce!"

"Uh... Yeah... Motor... Can't turn on the motor. I..." He swallowed. "I have two paddles, but it's gonna take us a while."

"Doesn't matter. Let's use those."

Still doing his best to get his terror under control, he released two straps that held the paddles at either side of the boat and handed one to Nadine. He told her to position herself on the port side; he took starboard. "Follow my rhythm, alright? We have to paddle deep and in tandem. This isn't really a paddle boat."

"Okay."

Before they could even touch the tip of their paddles to the water, they stopped, gawking ahead. In a matter of a few seconds, where there had only been blackness, there was a lighthouse, clear, undeniable, an actual beacon on Lighthouse Rock, shining cold, silver-blue light as it spun slowly, instead of the usual bright white or yellow. Shining above the beacon was that horrid blue moon, except now, instead of shining dark-blue, like the other nights, it was a glorious, terrifying silver-blue.

"What the fuck just happened?" Nadine blurted.

Amidst his confusion, Royce risked another look over the side of the small boat. He could still see it, the swaying row of blue dots, moving in the depths. The gargantuan appendage of a creature he couldn't comprehend.

Rebecca, he thought. *Rae-Rae...Susie-Q the Q-test...Wilhemina...Zoey...*

CHAPTER THIRTY-THREE

BLUE

Ray watched in abject horror and despair as the black cocoon grew. It had been large enough to swallow Barry entirely, and yet, it continued to grow, and bulge, and pulsate with the passing of each second.

Then it ruptured.

What emerged from the widening gash was no longer Barry, though half his face remained. It stood almost eight feet tall, hulking, monstrous, mere feet from where Ray watched his world fall apart.

The Barry-creature seemed dazed, as if adjusting to its new unholy shape. Only the right side of Barry's face, chest, and arm were recognizable. His sad, half-lidded eye was still that precious powder blue, but all light was gone from it—a corpse's eye. Barry was no longer there.

The other half of its face was exposed muscle, tendons, and veins, with bloody teeth and a bloodshot, lidless eye with a black iris. Its massive, skinless body bulged, streaked with enlarged veins and ligaments. Plates made of bone covered parts of its chest, back, and limbs, like incomplete armor, especially its enormous left arm, which looked apelike, hanging almost to the floor, ending in a grotesque mass of muscle, shaped like a meaty battering ram.

"Bar—"

It reacted to his voice. Its bloodshot eye turned first, then its entire head. It let out an angry growl.

Ray held his palms forward. "Barry! Stop!"

It charged. No hesitation. The grotesque figure came straight at him, moving with surprising speed despite its bulk. The sinewy muscles and tendons pulsated with each movement; the raw, red tissue clung taut over its nightmarish form, glistening with blood. Its enormous foot stepped on Sylvia's head, crushing it like a cantaloupe.

Ray let out a horrified scream, cut short when the creature swung its huge arm in a wide arc before it. It hit Ray across the chest, and now he was flying toward his right. His back collided with the wall, and he fell to the ground. His chest and ribs throbbed with pain.

The monster now loomed over him. From up close, Ray looked up at what remained of Barry's face, that half-lidded blue eye, looking defeated, resigned. *Is there anything of you still there?* he wondered. The lifelessness of that eye was all the answer he needed.

The creature stretched its massive left arm forward. Ray stared in disbelief as five skinless hands at the tip of the bulky arm, previously clasped together, untangled their fingers, leaving a hollow space between them. The hands spun around each other, transforming the battering ram into five distinct arms, each acting as the fingers and thumb of a massive claw. Before Ray could react, the claw seized his entire upper body, lifted him off the ground, and hurled him screaming over the coffee table.

He landed hard against the foot of the couch where Barry's two children still lay unconscious. Forcing himself to recover from the pain as fast as he could, he opened his eyes to find with horror the creature was now reaching for the metal and glass cabinet near the opposite corner of his living room.

Thinking fast, realizing it intended to throw it at him, he resolved his priority was to protect the children. He curled his fingers under the bottom edge of the couch. *They might get banged up, but at least they won't get seriously hurt*, he thought with urgency. Ignoring his aching muscles, and the heartbreak that whispered in his ear to give up, he flipped the couch over on its back—seat vertical, legs facing him now—and heard a slight thumping and shuffling as the kids rolled over the back of the couch and onto the carpet, shielded from any attack.

He glanced back just as the Barry-creature lifted the cabinet over its head, its red eye glaring, teeth bared in a roar. It hurled the cabinet at him as Ray dove under the coffee table. The cabinet crashed down, sending glass flying in every direction. The coffee table's legs broke—its surface absorbed most of the impact—and it collapsed on top of Ray. He was winded, but alive.

He rolled to one side, lifting the weight off his body with difficulty. As he emerged from under the debris, he realized his house no longer looked the same. In fact, it resembled nothing that could be described as a house.

What the hell?

The nightmarish imagery was different from what Barry had described at his house. Different from what Freddie had unleashed there earlier. This seemed *made* for him, even if he couldn't know why.

Wall to wall, he was surrounded by metal slabs, like the ones found at a morgue, except set vertically. Lying on these metal slabs—or more like hanging from them, given their verticality—were masked male mannequins resembling naked corpses. The mannequins were anatomically correct, with plastic penises and testicles of varying sizes and shapes. He even noticed some were circumcised, while others weren't. They had varying body types, colors, builds, and heights. The only thing they all had in common was a featureless orange mask with two empty black holes for eyes covering their anonymous faces.

The ceiling and floor were cracked concrete, moist, and covered in moss and mildew, as if the house had been abandoned for years to the elements. His living room furniture was still there, but it looked aged, torn, and moldy. Glass shards from the cabinet lay on the dirty floor, and the cabinet's metal frame was bent and rusted. The gas lantern, by some miracle, was still shining on its spot on the floor, despite looking dirty and ancient.

Hurrying, Ray peered over the deteriorated couch with its torn upholstery. Barry's children were still there, breathing. He sighed with relief, but not for long.

Stomp! Stomp! Stomp!

Approaching fast.

He had no chance to turn. He was pulled by his leg. Amid the panic, he caught a glimpse of a round, cracked rock lying on the floor. Without thinking, he reached for it, grabbed it, prepared to use it as a weapon once the monster brought him close enough—assuming that's what it was going to do, and not just step on his skull like it had done with poor Sylvia.

The monster's angry yet mournful groans sounded close now. He flipped over onto his back only to have the Barry-creature's enormous claw grab him like before and pick him up, readying to toss him across the room again. Ray pulled his arm back, feeling the weight of the rock in his hand, ready to strike the creature's terrifying face with all his might

(*Half that face is still Barry... My Barry!*)

but before he could slam the rock in its face, the creature screeched, recoiled, and let him go. It took two steps back as Ray lay on the floor, befuddled. He regarded the rock, noticed a message written on it with black Sharpie: *You make me live.*

At first, he stared at it, mesmerized, then realized this was the rock Barry had gifted him when they were teenagers, the cracked rock with the blue crystals inside, which were now glowing with a light of their own in the creature's proximity.

He swiveled his head to look at the monster. *His eye! Barry's eye is glowing blue!*

Still keeping its distance, the Barry-creature let out a guttural, angry growl, and in that growl, Ray could hear a disturbing hint of his partner's actual voice.

Not fully understanding what was happening, but grasping it had to do with the rock, he raised it and held it forward toward its split face. It took a step back, still flashing its angry, murderous scowl at him.

But that eye. Still glowing blue.

Ray stood, stepped back, expecting the monster to come closer. He kept retreating toward the couch. If the rock kept the creature away long enough, he might be able to take the two children, exit the house, and run.

How the hell will I do that while holding the rock? I only have two hands.

The Barry-creature stepped toward him. Its heavy step made the ground shudder. He noticed the fractures on the floor deepened.

Basement below. This concrete looks old. Too much of this and the entire house will cave in.

"Stay away!" he shouted, holding the rock forward. The crystals inside glowed with intent, as if reacting to the creature's aggression. "Barry...please!"

The monster responded with a bestial roar, still containing that disturbing underlying layer of Barry's voice. The five arms that made its claw once more spun around each other, hands interlocked at the end, to reform the battering ram appendage. Ray didn't know if this was an oncoming threat or a sign of retreat.

Near the shattered coffee table, Ray spotted Sylvia's tote bag. Inside were the gun, her laptop, the Circle's book, and her notes, lying next to her lifeless corpse. Nearby, Callum's bloodstained glasses served as a morbid reminder of the couple's research and their conclusion that these bizarre events had rules—a reason behind them. He peered at the glowing rock, then at the creature's glowing blue eye. *This means something.*

He hurried forward, picked up the bag, pulled out the laptop, book, and notes. *No need for those anymore.* He tucked the gun in the tote bag's outer pocket, slung the strap over his shoulder, and hurried back around the couch. The Barry-creature's eyes followed his every move.

Ray pulled out his phone. He turned on the flashlight and tucked it in his breast pocket. He then picked up Gabriel, who was the smallest of the two children, and carefully tucked him into the tote bag, where he fit snugly, only his shoulders and head peeking out.

That'll have to do.

Ray crouched again and picked up Daniel, throwing the boy's arms over his shoulders and sitting him on his right arm as he held the rock toward the monster with his left.

The creature let out another blood-curling roar, its frustration at its inability to reach its prey increasing with each passing second. Then, in a childlike tantrum, it unleashed its fury by repeatedly battering the walls, demolishing the nearby mannequins, and sending the metal slabs crashing to the floor, generating a cacophony that resounded throughout the living room. Then came the sound of concrete breaking. The house shuddered. Ray could feel the vibration under his feet.

He risked peering over the couch. The plain, moldy concrete behind the metal slabs crumbled under the creature's insane barrage.

Upon falling, one of the metal slabs revealed a broken glass door, which would have been the door to the backyard. This meant there might yet be a way out of the house, despite the walls being covered in these bizarre morgue tables. The problem was the monster standing between him and that exit. He also had no clue what lay beyond, now that the house had changed.

The Barry-creature picked up a mannequin and hurled it at him. It hit the bottom of the couch; its plastic body broken and twisted. The second mannequin it threw crashed and broke against the two bodies on the wall behind Ray, then fell to the floor. One of the two mannequins had come halfway loose from the slab, leaving a thin, repulsive layer of gore-caked plastic clinging to the metal surface, reminiscent of skin super-glued to a table and forcibly ripped off. It was then, he noticed the two broken mannequins the creature had thrown were bleeding. Thick ropes of actual human blood.

Ray put Daniel and the glowing rock on the floor. He grabbed hold of the couch and pulled with all his strength. Rolling it over so now it was lying on top of the three of them, forming a sort of triangular roof that would protect them.

The onslaught kept coming. He felt the couch shake as two bodies crashed into it. Despite being mannequins, he could hear the wet sound of bones breaking. More came. Bleeding and broken mannequin bodies fell all around him. One fell with its fractured neck turned toward him, staring into him with empty black eyes through its orange mask. Then came the metal slabs, loud crashing sounds as they landed here and there, hitting the walls and the floor, and all he could do was cower and try to protect the children.

Stomp! Stomp! Stomp! Stomp!

It's coming!

A growl sounded as the creature lifted the couch off him and threw it as if weightless toward the farther end of the living room. It collided with the wall and broke, causing a section of the wall to crumble as if it were made of Styrofoam instead of concrete.

The monstrous figure loomed over him again. Ray felt himself disappear under its hulking shadow.

It raised its humongous arm with the full intent of crushing him with a merciless blow. Ray's fingers scrambled to grab the rock again and held it up toward the monster. The glow of the crystals inside the rock intensified—a mighty blue—their light cast on the monster's face, half a skinless terrifying monstrosity, half the man he loved, whose one blue eye glowed too, its light appearing to connect, forming a sort of bridge with the crystals.

The creature recoiled with a scream, an actual human scream. Barry's voice.

The monster—Barry, if by some miracle he was still there—picked up and threw the remains of the coffee table at him, but its swing went wild and it crashed against a wall on Ray's right, missing him. It stomped away, appearing dazed and

(Scared?)

disoriented.

As it ran, it swung its arm and demolished the wall dividing the living room and foyer. It swung its arm back, and Ray caught a glimpse of the stairs shattering in a burst of splinters, as it disappeared in the direction of the dining room.

Ray remained on the floor, scared of moving, fearing the creature would turn back around and come for him. He picked up Daniel again and held the rock tight, curling his fingers into the crack on its surface to get a better grip. He would try the front door, and if he couldn't leave through there, he'd exit through the exposed backyard door.

Once he reached the foyer, it became clear leaving through the front door would not be an option. Here, like in the living room, the walls, including the door were lined with morgue tables and mannequins, making the doors inaccessible unless he somehow ripped them out of the walls—something he was certain he couldn't do as easily as the Barry-creature.

Beyond the foyer, the house looked different. It was wallpapered in old-looking skin, stretched, wrinkled, spotty, with translucent tubes coming in and out of it, carrying dark fluids of unusual colors. This insanity spread all over the floor and ceiling and continued into the dining room.

The light from his cell phone caught an eerie image amid all of this. Further ahead, the dining table was now an autopsy table under a bright hospital light, and on it was a mannequin he recognized at once. It was tall, thick bodied, wore no orange mask. The plastic on its head was shaped and painted to resemble the beard and haircut Barry usually wore. Even from where he stood, he could see the mannequin had chest hair, arm hair, even pubic hair drawn on it.

On the other side of the table, standing still, as if mesmerized by the mannequin, was the Barry-creature. He couldn't tell for sure, but it seemed in pain. Grieving. This monstrosity with exposed, bleeding flesh and bone protrusions all over its body looked sad. Having the light from the rock shining on its face had awakened some inkling, some memory of its humanity, and now it stared at a depiction of the man it used to be.

It sounded insane just thinking about it.

He regarded the metal plates covering the front door and the naked mannequins on them. His only option to get out now was the backyard.

As he turned to head back, a sudden wail from what used to be the dining room startled him.

Barry?

It was his voice. His sorrowful voice letting out an agonizing wail. Ray stared, dumbstruck, at the very human way Barry's half of the creature's face scrunched up in horror as it screamed. It raised its gigantic arm and slammed it down on the mannequin. A shower of blood and viscera sprayed in all directions as the mannequin split in half right under its chest and the autopsy table bent and broke. The creature continued to roar, to scream, to cry. It looked to one side, then the other. Barry's half of the face looked around, seeking understanding, as if there was someone who could explain what had been done to it. Then its eyes found Ray, and its one eyebrow went high.

Shame. There was shame in that expression. It shook its head, turned, and ran toward the kitchen area, which wasn't far, but was right past the point where he couldn't see it anymore. *Him,* he thought. *Can't see 'him'. Or is it still 'it'?*

Then came the unintelligible cries, laments, sounds of things being thrown or crushed with unspeakable force.

Despite realizing it was a dumb risk, he ran toward the kitchen. He stopped near the destroyed autopsy table, where the mannequin lay, with its human guts sprawled on the concrete floor. He swiveled his head to his left to find the Barry-creature on a rampage. Everything looked trashed and bloody. The skin that draped the walls and furniture had been ripped apart to reveal the deteriorated remains of Ray's kitchen underneath. Barry kept banging on walls, crushing the countertop, ripping out wall cabinets, then started swinging its enormous arm at the refrigerator—which now looked like a tall box covered in elderly human skin.

"Barry, stop! Stop!"

He (it?) ignored him.

The flashlight beam reflected on the area where the stove used to be. Barry had obliterated the stove, ripping it off its place, and throwing it aside. Ray's alarmed eyes stopped on a broken gas pipe. Even through the ruckus, Ray was sure he could hear the hiss of gas flowing in, flooding the kitchen. Every living fiber that made his heart beat compelled him to run toward the creature and try to reason with the fragment of Barry he knew was there. This was counteracted by the terrifying awareness all that was needed for the kitchen to explode was a single spark, which could come from the many appliances, pots, and pans flying all over the kitchen, and he had the children to care for.

Ray turned. Even if leaving Barry broke his heart, he had to reach the backyard door and get the children out of the house before the explosion.

It came just as he set foot in the living room.

The air itself seemed to solidify and shove Ray from behind as the explosion hurled him forward. He clung to the children in desperation, shielding them with his body as the house collapsed around them. Concrete, dust, pieces of furniture swirled in an expanding bubble of fire. Ray crashed onto his right arm in a corner near the backyard door.

It took a moment to catch his breath and open his eyes. Flames and smoke billowed nearby, filling his vision. Yet somehow, this part of the house still stood. Half the second floor hung precariously, canted to one side, jagged rebar jutting from the wreckage. Gaping holes in the walls exposed more rebar, and metal tables lay scattered across the ruin. Mannequins burned in the flames, torsos and limbs strewn about. A mannequin's head, its orange mask eerie in the firelight, cast a blank stare at him.

Ray examined the children and felt relieved they were unharmed. Sitting up amid the rubble, he noted the walls forming the corner behind him, though damaged, still stood. The ceiling above him—the half that hadn't collapsed—was cracked like a spiderweb. It drizzled concrete dust on his head. His flashlight revealed two fissures creeping toward each other like ominous lightning bolts, threatening to bring the ceiling crashing down on him and the kids.

Heavy footsteps resounded even through the roaring flames. The Barry-creature entered the living room. His (its?) gigantic arm and part of its back were aflame. The half that was still Barry bore scratches, but it was mostly intact. The monstrous side seemed to have absorbed the brunt of the explosion. Barry turned toward Ray, and a low, guttural growl escaped its throat. There was no trace of Barry's voice anymore.

It (definitely 'it') stomped toward him, shoving aside slabs of concrete and metal tables like they were nothing.

Heart racing, Ray scanned the area for the glowing rock, but it was nowhere to be found in the rubble.

Where is it?

The house groaned, shuddered; more concrete fell from above. A loose metal plate slid off the canted piece of ceiling, crashing beside the monster. It ignored the noise, continuing its relentless approach.

God! Where is it?

It stopped right in front of him. The bared teeth on the left side of its face resembling the jaws of a feral beast, ready to bite.

No, no, no.

The ceiling let out a loud crack. The two lightning bolt fractures moved closer to each other.

No, no, no!

The creature stared at him. It was surreal seeing it standing motionless, its breath accompanied by a low growl while flames consumed half of its body. It was as if it didn't even feel it. Perhaps it didn't.

It bent at the waist.

Ray gasped. Held the children closer to him, preparing for the end.

A jolt of realization. *The gun!* He reached into the tote bag's side pocket, pulled out the gun, aimed, and fired twice in quick succession. Both bullets glanced off the bone plate in its chest, merely chipping it.

Barry's human hand moved with caution, grabbed his wrist with a gentleness that could've only come from the real Barry, then pointed the gun toward the floor.

What? What's—

The large arm, which had again unfurled into a claw, moved. It picked something off the floor, held it toward him. The blue glow was what first told him what it was. The crystals in the rock glowed, along with Barry's one blue eye, as if hypnotizing him. The Barry-creature looked at him—*really* looked at him—offering him the rock.

"T-take it," it (he?) said. His voice was guttural, broken, but still Barry's.

Absentminded, not even questioning this, Ray took the rock, staring at how little remained of Barry's face. His voice broke. "Barry...is it really you?"

"Please, take good care of my boys." He regarded his children with tenderness, but also with so much heartache, it wrung Ray's heart like a rag.

"We have to get out of here, Big Bear..."

Barry's eye turned a longing stare toward him, sadness emanating from it as if Ray were part of a life he'd already said goodbye to.

There was another crack from above, and an entire chunk of the second floor came down on them.

Ray screamed, closed his eyes, shielding the children. This was it. They'd be crushed and die in the burning debris. Death didn't come, though. Ray opened his eyes to see Barry standing over him, bent forward, both his human arm and his monster arm supporting his body against the wall, as the chunk of ceiling that had fallen on him lay in an unsteady balance on his broad, bone-plated back—one large piece of concrete still hanging from bent rebar on one side. Ray could now take in the full horror of the mass of skinless muscle Barry's body had become, but the only thing he could truly see, what captured his entire attention, was the glistening stream of tears that soaked Barry's half of the creature's face, and the sorrow in his glowing blue eye.

"You have to...go," Barry said in that ragged voice that was barely his. He motioned with his head toward the backyard door, its glass pane shattered. The hanging chunk of ceiling blocked the way to it. "I can't...go with you."

Ray shook his head. The cruel reality of what had happened, from the moment Barry's new form had emerged from that cocoon, finally washed over Ray like a devastating hurricane, wrecking everything in its path. "No," he said, tears finally rolling down his face. "You can't. You can't do this! Not now! You can't leave us!"

"The rock's...effect...won't last...forever..." Barry let out a choking, gargled noise, and he twitched as if something from within him was trying to come out, and he was holding it back by sheer force of will. "It will...take over...again."

"No, please!" Ray sobbed. "We'll make it to Cunningham's. It's safe there! Chuck or Hitch, they might... They might know how to reverse this."

Barry shook his head. "Save...my boys..."

"Please, come with me. Please! Big Bear, don't make me lose you again!"

"Remember...wh-what I said yesterday..." Barry's half a face attempted a smile. "Another universe. Maybe...in another universe..."

"No! Don't fucking say that! Don't you fucking say that!"

"Maybe...in another universe...we get more than...a few days."

Ray dropped the rock and put a hand on Barry's cheek.

Barry's eyes closed as he leaned his head into his palm, as if committing its warmth to memory. He opened his eyes and cast a loving look at his children. His expression became calm, full of determination. Barry turned his head toward the wall to his right. He still struggled with the weight of the second floor on his back, and the flames covering his monster arm, but he forced himself to stand straighter, pushing the collapsed ceiling higher, trying to raise the hanging chunk blocking the way and open a gap for Ray to pass and reach the backyard door.

"Please come with us," Ray said. "Please? I'm begging you. Don't do this."

Barry swiveled his head side to side.

Understanding, Ray approached Barry's face, gave him a small, quivering kiss, and ran his hand through what little of his beard hadn't been singed in the explosion, their foreheads touching for a brief, final moment. "In another universe." The sobs and the overwhelming pain in his heart almost stole his ability to speak.

Barry nodded. "I...love you."

"I love you," Ray responded.

He took the glowing rock from the floor, stood, and hurried out through the gap, then through the broken glass door and into the backyard. He meant to run the moment he stepped out, run and not look back, because it would hurt too much. He couldn't. He took two steps out into the rain and turned around. Peering through the opening, he caught a glimpse of Barry's face staring at him.

"Goodbye," Barry said.

Barry's arms let go of the wall, and Ray caught one final flicker of blue in his human eye. The floor beneath his feet gave way, and the remains of the second floor, the walls, and the roof collapsed on top of him, sending him plummeting into the basement. A cloud of smoke, dust, and fire erupted from the ruins of what was meant to be their home. As the pouring rain began to extinguish the flames, the wind carried away the last traces of dust.

Ray sat on a dilapidated bench in his backyard, not even caring if it was sturdy enough to support his weight. The blue light from the crystals inside the rock slowly faded, died. He knew this meant Barry was gone.

He sat there, numb, stupefied, for several minutes. Tears and rain streamed down his face. His clothes were soaked, as were the children's.

Moments later, he worked up the strength to meander around the wreckage of his home and finally got a look at his neighborhood. The streets were flooded with about five inches of running water. Every building looked abandoned, lifeless. Overgrown lawns, cracked walls, mold, those dreadful black vines (and wet newspaper?) covered every structure. He'd seen some houses with lantern light in them on the drive here. There had been people in those houses. He was sure of it. There was nobody around now. This was an abandoned world. He felt as if he were the last man alive on a post-apocalyptic Earth.

He might just as well be.

Lightning flashed. Thunder roared. He turned his frayed, teary eyes up at the sky. The moon shone through the clouds, bright silver-blue. The same blue as the crystals, the same blue as Barry's eyes, but unlike his beautiful gaze, that moon's glow was cold, terrible, sickening.

The world had been robbed of his partner's perfect blue eyes. Now he was forced to keep living in it.

CHAPTER THIRTY-FOUR
THE DEEP BREATH BEFORE THE PLUNGE

In the bar's cellar, under the glow of a lantern, John Hitch, who had been helped into a wheelchair by Tali Ruiz, examined the letter handed to him by Chuck Cunningham.

"I don't know what you expect me to get from this," Hitch said. "I don't know how to read the Circle's language."

"You don't need to know," Chuck said. "That's why I'm here." He pointed at the end of the letter; the part written in the tongue of the old god. "This part. I had completely forgotten about this. It's been over thirty years, and I'm an old man. This says, 'The souls from the cave fed the flowers, the flowers became crystals, the crystals favor the opposition.' Logan Giffen was part of the Circle, so was I, so my guess is by 'the opposition', he meant the Order, the opposition to the Circle."

"The flowers became the crystals," Hitch mumbled. "I'm not... I mean, I can understand the part about the souls from the cave. It's talking about the settlers. The mass grave. The blue moon-buds"—he gazed around, realizing none of them knew what blue moonbuds were—"the flowers that grew over the mass grave. I haven't seen those flowers in well over a hundred years. I was telling

Howe and this young man I thought the cave sank into the ocean, along with South Marshborough. If that's the case, we can't reach it."

"C'mon, man," Jess pushed. "Think! We can't stay here!"

"He's right," Tali said. "I went over the protection glyphs all around. They're losing strength. Especially after the street outside changed. Any second, now, the change is going to break the seals, and whatever's out there will come in here."

Hitch shook his head. "It might refer to the balance. The death of the settlers fed Uolmin, but that much sorrow also creates an opposing force. It's the balance the Order and the Circle used to fight each other for, but that balance went to hell when the Vanek House burned—nothing holding Uolmin's power back anymore." He cast a tired glance around, his face looked flushed. Blood loss and exhaustion showed in the dark circles around his eyes. He fixed his gaze on Chuck, looking defeated. "In theory, if we had access to the mass grave where I buried the settlers, the power there should protect us the way it protected Walter Parham when Reverend Burgess assaulted him. But unless this Tali fellow knows a spell that can give us all gills, it's unlikely we'll reach it."

Commotion sounded from upstairs. The sounds of arguing, shouting, disagreement. Lillian's voice berated someone, the words unintelligible but commanding. Being the only remaining member of the town government, Jess and Chuck gave her command of the bar whenever they weren't upstairs. The discussion died down, little by little. There were running footsteps coming toward the cellar door.

"The hell's going on?" Jess asked with alarm, hearing the cellar door open.

In came nurse Ferguson, bounding down the stairs with what look like a child in her arms, held tight against her chest. Behind her came another figure, also with a child in arms, an older child.

"Ray?" Jess sprang up and ran toward her friend. She stood in front of him, surveying him from head to toe, as if she'd already assumed him dead. His clothes were a mess. He was dirty, bruised, and soaked from head to toe. He had Sylvia's tote bag hanging across his torso, and in his arms was Daniel. "Barry?"

Ray's face appeared to collapse from the bottom up. His lips curled downward, trembling, exposing teeth, the lines framing his mouth and nose became more pronounced, his eyes narrowed, squeezing out sudden tears, his brow wrinkled, and he stepped forward into her embrace, and finally let out peals of sorrowful sobs.

He shook in her arms, inconsolable, the sense of loss radiating from his skin and into hers. They stood like that for a few minutes.

Moments later, they sat in a circle around John Hitch, who had the rock with the blue crystals in his hands, turning it this way and that. *The flowers became crystals...*

Interrupted at times by sobs, Chang—he couldn't bring himself to call him Ray, as if they were familiar with each other—had filled them in on everything that had happened inside his home, including Barry Giffen's death, and the way the entire town had transformed into something he couldn't even describe. He talked about how he'd stalked his way to Cunningham's, trying as hard as he could not to call attention to him, having seen creatures coming out of some houses. Creatures he was certain used to be people, but no longer, like what had happened to Giffen.

"Where did you get this?" Hitch asked, motioning toward the rock.

Chang's face looked sorrowful again. He stared at him with mistrust. Hitch couldn't blame him, he realized, he'd tried to shoot him and the man he loved two nights earlier. Seeing the effects of losing Giffen on his face made him deeply uncomfortable. While he'd seen something similar in Sylvia Nguyen's face when he'd killed Baker, he felt closer to Chang, given the *one* thing they shared in common. He'd gone through a similar loss a lifetime ago, and he was still nowhere close to recovering.

"Chang," he pushed, held the rock cracked side up. "Where?"

"It was a gift from Barry," he said, his voice wet, defeated.

"How long ago?" He felt bad pushing him like this, but this was important. More important than his grief.

"When we were kids. He found it. Been in my home since."

"How long before giving it to you did he find it?"

Chang looked unsure. He stared at the floor, shook his head, shrugged. "I don't know. Some time before we met, I think."

"So, *he* found it," Hitch asked. "No one gave it to him."

"Yes, he found it. It was on a pile of rocks, just like that one. This one was cracked. He thought it was pretty. Picked it up from the pile."

"Where?"

"The Pines. Near Garland Elementary."

Hitch's eyes opened wide with shock. *If Giffen found it, this was there on that pile many years after the earthquake. The pile of rocks. The cairns. It was at The Pines all along. I was off by about a mile. Lumenwood is right there. The reduced rate of strange phenomena in Lumenwood also supports this.* He looked around at the people present. "I dismissed the Curse of The Pines as a children's myth. I thought if it was really true, I would've seen it in Blight Harbor, but it was its absence that should've given it away. What happens in The Pines doesn't go into Blight Harbor. I'm such an idiot. If this was found in The Pines, chances are that's our safe place. I can't be completely sure, but it's all we've got."

"We need to get there," Jess said. "We don't have as many weapons remaining, but there are plenty of people with us. Some of them brought guns with them. If we have that rock, we can use that as protection, can't we?"

Hitch hesitated. Shook his head. "Giffen was a direct descendant of one of the original settlers, Elbert Giffen," Hitch said, doubtful. He noticed the way Chang flinched upon hearing him refer to Giffen in the past tense. "On top of that, he inherited the Eyes of God—or whatever those fanatics called them—which means, this thing"—he motioned toward the rock—"might only have worked on him. There's no guarantee it will work with anything else we might run into out there."

"You're wrong," Ray said, clutching a half-empty bottle of water. "I couldn't avoid all the creatures out there. One caught me by surprise. Fell out of a window from an office building two blocks from here. Came straight at me. Fast. Way too many arms." He looked at the surrounding group, as if hoping no one would ask him for a description of the horror that had attacked him. "I held the rock toward it. It glowed blue. Stopped it in its tracks. It didn't regain its humanity like Barry did, but it stayed away. It tried to come after me a couple more times, so I pulled out the gun, and while it cowered from the blue light, I put two bullets in it and ran."

"Then it's settled." Chuck Cunningham stood, dusting off his butt. "We're heading for The Pines right away." He turned to Jess. "C'mon, Pum'kin, let's sort out the supplies and go tell the people upstairs so we can select who gets what."

Jess nodded in agreement.

"Um..." A voice, from halfway up the stairs. It was Nurse Ferguson again. She looked toward Chang. "Ray? The kids woke up. They're, uh...asking about their dad."

What little strength might remain in Chang's body drained upon hearing this. He gave a resigned, tired nod and stood up.

As he strode toward the stairs, John blurted, "Hey...Chang."

He stopped, regarded him as if he were a wino in an alley.

"I'm...sorry...about Giffen..."

Chang frowned, puzzled.

"I know how you're feeling."

Chang pressed his lips together, looked away, and hurried up the stairs.

"Is there anything I can do to help?" Tali asked, for some reason looking at him as if he'd decided he was some kind of wise tutor. If anything was now clear to him—based on the way Raymond Chang had snubbed him—it was that there was nothing wise about him. He still appreciated having one person around that didn't outright hate him.

"Royce Howe mentioned you'd saved his life on the bar's roof," Hitch said. "You drew runes on pebbles. Right?"

"Yes?" Tali said.

Hitch turned to him. "How quick can you draw them?" He turned his head toward the shelves, one of which had a box of Ritz Bits cheese crackers on it.

Jess examined the gun rack, and she couldn't help feeling there should've been more guns in it than there were. She'd had this overconfident image in her head her grandpa and her dad had stockpiled for the end of the world, but when faced with the reality, she remembered this cellar was just a survival storage in case of a townwide emergency. Their stock felt rather wanting for what Ray had seen out there.

Might as well shove Peggy in my cooch and pull the trigger, she thought with cynicism. *Go out in a spectacle, traumatize the crowd upstairs.*

She was startled by a meaty hand slapping her shoulder. "Pum'kin..."

"Dad, I've told you a million times..."

"I might die tonight, get killed by one of my bar patrons turned into some hellish monstrosity... Can I at least call my baby girl the pet name I gave her when—"

Jess threw her arms around her dad. He was shorter than her, so she tucked her head between his head and his shoulder. "Yeah, yeah, I ate a whole pumpkin raw just 'coz you told me I couldn't. I was a pigheaded six-year-old, wasn't I?"

He hugged her back. "'Was?'" he said and chuckled.

Jess giggled a little.

"You scarfed that damn thing down. Stared straight at me and your mom the whole time, like, 'Dare you to stop me.' We were scared."

"I puked my soul out later that day, though. Spent a whole week burping pumpkin." The warmth of her dad's embrace made her feel like just going to sleep and letting things sort themselves out. "Daddy, I'm scared."

"Me, too, Pum'kin." He kissed her red hair. They held each other for a little longer, before he placed a hand on her arm and gently pushed her away, staring at the gun locker. "So? How're we looking?"

Jess sighed. "Not bad, but not good either. With the people meandering in after Royce bull-horned the message, we're about a hundred and forty people here. So, getting those extra people is encouraging. Problem is, we're low on weapons. I've got Peggy, you've got your rifle, there's one more rifle in there, two handguns, plus the gun Ray got from, uh,"—she flinched—"Sylvia. Ten people up there brought weapons with them. We can give the people up there these two hunting knives, a few more from the kitchen, hammers, crowbars, brooms, mop handles. Not sure how helpful that will be."

"Better than having a bunch of randos panicking and firing off in the middle of a terrified crowd." He picked up a hunting knife hanging from the locker door and examined it. "And they *will* panic, hun. The things Raymond is describing, what he saw outside. I've been in the Circle my entire life. I've *experienced* visions of the Moonlit World—as seen by the two Mothers I served. It wasn't this. It wasn't what Freddie showed me. I ain't never seen the monstrosities Raymond described, and I might panic when I see them; same as those randos I'm talkin' about." He stood, held the knife by the blade, handle toward her. "You *have* seen them, Pum'kin."

Jess looked into her dad's eyes, then down at the knife.

"At the Vanek House," he added. "You've seen them. You've shot them. *You* have to lead the party out of here, hun."

Jess touched her fingers to the knife handle. "These things are not the same."

"You're right. These are...were...people. That means these can die, in theory."

"I've lost so many already, Dad. Jonah, mom, Leroy, Cal, Bobby, Sylvia, Barry... Peter..." She swallowed. "I even count him as a loss."

"None of those are your fault. Not a single one. Are the dead at the hospital your fault? Hell no. In a situation like this one, don't count losses, coz the losses will keep piling up. You have a hundred and forty lives here. If half of those make it to The Pines, *that* will be on you. You are so fuckin' strong, hun. So fuckin' strong. I loved your brother, but you're the best thing your mom and I ever made."

Jess took the knife handle, turned it, touched her finger to the serrated saw back, pondering.

"Even if you ate a whole raw pumpkin and puked your guts out," he added.

She cast an annoyed glance at him to find a big, stupid grin on his face. "You're a fuckin' asshole, so, of *course*, you had to be my dad." She threw her arms around him again.

Nadine and Royce set foot on the pier at Lighthouse Rock. Not for a second during their silent paddle toward the island had they taken their eyes off the beacon that shouldn't even be there, especially considering it rose out of the center of the mental facility.

Both structures now occupied the island at the same time, as if the lighthouse had been part of the mental hospital all along.

The rain had come back in full force as they approached the island. Nadine stood on the rickety pier, flashlight in hand. Old, sodden wooden planks vibrated and swayed and creaked with the ocean's movement. The pier was not the same sturdy structure where the ferry once docked for employees and visitors; it was plain to see.

She turned to Royce, who had just finished tying the boat. "Be careful where you step."

"Don't have to tell me twice," Royce said.

He walked beside her, each step feeling like it would make the wood break and send them plunging into the depths. He pointed the flashlight toward the dark water. "You seeing this? Or is that just me?"

Nadine followed his gaze and saw a twisted structure rising from the dark waters. It was a grotesque amalgamation of wheelchairs, stretchers, intravenous poles, and tangled hospital equipment fused together into a monstrous sculpture, like a pillar. IV tubes snaked around the framework like vines, some ending in clusters of needles, others splitting into cables that coiled and twisted, attaching to defibrillator paddles arranged like sinister flowers on a nightmarish plant.

Similar structures rose from the water at intervals on both sides.

Her breath caught when she realized some of the cables ended in a fleshy black mass with clusters of actual yellow flowers. "Let's hurry." She shone her flashlight toward the other side of the pier to see similar structures rising there. "Let's not stand too close to those things."

Royce seemed distracted. "Do you see that bundle over there?"

Nadine followed the light's direction and discovered what appeared to be over-ear headphones attached to a cable. A large R printed on one, and a large L on the other.

"Look," Royce pointed. "The left one."

At first, Nadine wasn't sure what he meant, but then she spotted it: a large X scratched over the left headphone.

"Is this some kind of sick joke?" Royce said.

She was about to say it meant nothing, but then her eye caught another of the fleshy, cancerous masses clinging to the metal structure, and the yellow flowers that came from it. "Ignore it. Let's go."

They reached a set of stairs leading up to the island proper. There, the last metal structure emerged from the earth and rock, as if it were rooted there, like a grotesque artificial tree.

As soon as they set foot on the island itself, there was no doubt this was "someplace else".

I have a feeling we're not in Kansas anymore, Nadine thought.

What, from a distance, had seemed like the mental facility, was instead a strange collage of mismatched structures—houses, stores, buildings, even landscape—pieced apart, then fused together in the shape of the mental hospital. They could see parts of Peter's old house, of the Vanek House, of Garland Elementary, and Clarendon Hospital. An entire wall seemed to be a gravity-defying, vertical version of the fields at Clive Memorial—grass, gravestones, and all—climbing the side of the building, like living cladding.

"That tree," Royce said, breathless, pointing the flashlight at a tree growing horizontally out of the cemetery wall. He moved the light a little to the right. "Three tombstones that way is Leroy's grave."

"Let's steer clear of that, okay?"

More bizarre "hospital supply art installations" like those on the pier rose from the ground, turning the island into a surreal landscape. Disturbing, anthropomorphic black crystal shapes—reminiscent of the Martha Lange sculpture at the hospital—sprouted at random spots, with grass, roots, and earth clinging to them. All were female, and all were incomplete—some missing a head, an arm, or half a body.

"Where to?" she asked.

"So, this must be the main entrance." Royce pointed at the strange collage of buildings before them, then gestured to the right. "That courtyard used to hold the old beacon like a monument, but now it's replaced by that...thing." He pointed at a shapeless mass where the monument once sat. "That's because the beacon's back in its original spot, being all creepy and shit." He glanced up at the lighthouse, its beacon spinning slowly. "The old lighthouse entrance should lead to this round vestibule. The criminal patient wing is beyond that—that's where Bobby took me and Jess to see Freddie. My bet is Bobby's there."

"I don't want to stay here in the open a second longer than necessary." She looked up at the moon, which appeared to be listening in on their conversation. "Let's hurry inside and hope it's not as batshit crazy as the outside."

They traipsed toward the courtyard, and as they went around what used to be the beacon monument, Nadine blurted, "Oh my god!" Her voice oozed with disgust.

The flashlight revealed the monument had transformed into a massive black crystal sculpture, shaped like Martha Lange's face—a face she would recognize anywhere. Something looked horribly wrong, though. A chunk of Martha's left cheek appeared to have been bitten off, exposing the teeth and ragged flesh beneath—everything rendered in a mesh of black crystal threads. The eyes, made of clusters of yellow flowers, stared at her, lifeless yet unsettlingly aware.

"Oh, fuck this shit so hard!" Royce shouted, picking up a rock off the floor.

"What are you doing?"

"The mirrors!" he said, looking repulsed.

"Mirrors? What—"

"In the eyes! The eyes are mirrors, but it's Leroy looking at me from the reflection! Leroy!"

"What? No, they're yellow fl—"

"He's grinning at me." His face was contorted with shame. "Blaming me!"

"Royce!"

"Stop blaming me!" He hurled the rock at the enormous face.

The rock flew with near-perfect accuracy through the sculpture's eye socket. Yellow petals and flowers and cancerous meat flew out—what her friend claimed to see as mirrors. He picked up another rock, and with the same bullseye aim, made it fly through the second eye.

"It wasn't my fault!" he cried. "Not my fault, brother!"

"Royce!" Nadine grabbed him by the shoulders. "It's not real!" His panicked gaze met her eyes for a second. "I mean...if it's real, you're the only one who sees it. This place is messing with your head!"

He looked away in shame, his mouth working to concoct words that made sense. "I'm sorry. I could hear him in my head. 'You let me die. You let me die.' I... I've always felt I could've... Should've saved him."

"We *all* did everything we could, Royce," she said. She shook his arm, prompting him to meet her gaze again. "This place will keep trying to mess with us if we're not fast."

He nodded.

They jogged toward the door at the base of the lighthouse.

As they approached the entrance, they were met with another bizarre sight. The outer wall of the criminal patient wing was covered in the Valencias' house, as if someone had unfolded it like a Happy Meal box and wrapped it around the building in bands. The yellow house and its flower garden alternated with bands that were Freddie's home—deconstructed as well—creating a strange pattern of yellow and gray. A curving river of water ran between the layers, widening into a pool in the center before dropping into a deeper layer filled with rocks—this could only be the Pargin River.

"Keep going," Nadine said. "Keep going, keep going."

They disappeared into the open entrance of the lighthouse.

Peter stood in the criminal patient wing's "A" corridor, his phone shining light on the surroundings. While the entire facility had turned into something out of an LSD trip, this one corridor remained unchanged, save for one thing. In the Moonlit World, the crystal bindings that held the asylum employees and patients inside the cells came alive.

Asylum, he thought, knowing the word was no longer used to describe mental care facilities. Now they used softer words. Gentler words. Sensible words that did nothing to describe this place. *Fuck sensibility. Call this asylum. Call this the funny farm, cuckoo's nest, booby-hatch, loony bin. Call this Bedlam...* He looked down at the corpse at his feet. Bobby. His friend. *Call this the Devil's S&M dungeon, studded whips, and all.*

He felt pressure in his chest, like something crushing his sternum against his lungs. He surveyed the stab wounds on Bobby's back, the congealing bloodstain around him, one hand stretched toward a smaller bloodstain on the floor.

"I'm sorry," he whispered, relieved he hadn't needed to do the deed himself. The stark image of Bobby's lifeless body at his feet—something he hadn't had to endure for long with Sylvia—made him question his ability to fulfill his mission, even if he didn't question how necessary it was.

"I didn't need your help."

Peter looked up to find Freddie standing outside his cell, his face a mess of blood and bruises, right arm broken in at least four places, left arm missing its hand, coated in the black crystal substance they could both now manipulate. Peter regarded the stump where his own right hand used to be. He grimaced with discomfort, or perhaps shame.

Freddie was a pathetic sight for someone claiming to need no help.

"I got Brickhouse," Freddie said, "didn't I?"

"Yes, you did." Peter's voice was glum as he stepped closer.

"I felt him die." He flashed a wide grin at Peter. He was missing a tooth. Another one was chipped.

"But I don't think your trap would've gotten him if I hadn't pushed him closer to it."

This didn't sit well with Freddie. "You didn't know I'd left a trap."

"No. The fact remains, though."

Freddie scoffed. "You won't take credit for my kill, Norman. I appreciate your help with Tits Nguyen, though." With difficulty, he did a pained, awkward bow, moving his broken left arm as if he still had a hand to spin dramatically. "My Prince."

He giggled, but his giggles broke into a fit of coughing. He wiped the blood on his forearm.

"Stop that."

"I didn't need your help!" Freddie repeated in a growl. "I didn't need Mother to give me an executive assistant!"

Peter eyed the mess of papers and canvases inside Freddie's cell. "Are you sure?"

Freddie glanced at the cell, cleared his throat. "I've been here for almost thirty years. There are still more than enough drawings for the Exiles to pick their forms." He paused. "I did lose all the paintings for the town portal locations."

"Not all." Peter pointed his flashlight at the painting of the cave lying on Freddie's bed. "You know you can't use that, right?"

Freddie looked even more uncomfortable now. "I... It's just in case of an emergency. I know I can't.... Shouldn't enter that place." He gave Peter a scornful look. "I don't have the benefit of the Mother's blood running through my veins, so I can't just pop in and out wherever I want."

"Why does it bother you so much?"

"I've worked too hard for this! To win the Mother's favor! I don't need a mama's boy to come nepo-baby his way on my territory!" He caught himself, realizing he might have gone too far. "Sorry if that was a bit...much... You've seen her, then. You've seen Mother since she crossed over?"

"Yes."

"Did she say anything about me? Is she mad at me? Unsatisfied with my work?"

Peter studied his face. "She's not mad. She just thought you might need a little help."

Freddie gave a sigh of relief. "I really, really am going to fulfill my part. I won't fail her. If you see her at the Inner Sanctum, please tell her that."

"Why do you care, Freddie?" Peter's tone was cold, thorny.

Freddie seemed nonplussed by this. "What?"

"You have to know she doesn't care about you, right?"

"What did you fucking say, Norman?"

"*I'm* all she cares about. All she wants. All these horrors she's unleashed into the world? It's all for me. She wants me beside her forever, like a damn lamp at her bedside, regardless of what *I* want. She doesn't care about anything, or anyone else. Certainly not you."

"Shut up! You shut the fuck up, Norman!"

"Back when Mother used to cook and deliver meals around town, I liked to watch her top the green beans. You know, remove the tips? The end of the stem? They made this satisfying crunching sound as the knife sliced through the bunch, and sometimes the tips flew off. It was so fun for me as a kid."

"The fuck are you talking about?"

"There were always the little strays, the odd bean that was too short and kept the tip, so she grabbed those and broke them with her fingers. It made this soft snapping sound. I liked it. Gave me this fun tingle in my chest. Once I asked Mother why she had to remove that. She said she didn't need to. That the tips were perfectly fine to eat, they were just not 'aesthetically pleasing.' They were edible; she just didn't need them. There was plenty of green bean without the tip, so she took them out because it was more 'aesthetically pleasing.'" He drove an icy stare into Freddie. "You...aren't necessary. You...aren't aesthetically pleasing. She only needs me. She's using you. So, do your job, get the reward she promised, but don't expect her to care about you. If you do, she'll see you as one of those stray pods the knife missed, and she'll snap your head with her fingers."

Freddie opened his mouth to say something but was interrupted by Peter.

"Now, stay still and let me help you." Peter tucked his phone in his chest pocket, light pointing out, then opened his palm to show a small black crystal.

"What are you doing?"

"I'm going to grab your broken hand now. It's going to hurt like a bitch, but I'm trying to help, alright? You know what this stone is." Peter took Freddie's hand and raised it toward him, making Freddie flinch in pain as Peter yanked hard on his deformed arm. The crystal sat snug between both of their palms. "Hold still."

The tiny crystal melted into a puddle from which black tendrils emerged, piercing Freddie's skin. He cried out as the threads wove into his muscle and bone, dipping in and out like dolphins leaping through water. The threads tightened, causing loud pops as broken bones realigned and his arm reformed. Freddie howled in agony as a final, sharp crack echoed. His arm, though straightened, was marred by black lines and tension wires running from his upper elbow to his forearm. A Frankenstein arm, of sorts. Shuddering and foaming at the mouth, he shot a wild look at Peter, gasping for breath.

"This is temporary, but it should help you finish the job. We just need one more."

"Thank you, Norman," Freddie growled. "But, as I said, I don't need your help. You have *one* role in this thing. You should get to it, chop-chop, vamoose, lickety-split, and leave me to it!"

"That's what I'm about to do, Freddie. I just came to warn you."

Freddie gave him a confused frown. "Your insipid bestie and Tweedle Dum? Yeah, I know they're coming. I didn't need you for that."

"Good. Please, only kill Royce. Don't hurt Nadine. You don't need to hurt her. Just Royce, alright? And make it quick. Please don't make him suffer."

A wide, gap-toothed smile crawled to both sides of Freddie's bloodied face. "Of course, Norman"—he raised his strange, repaired arm—"I mean, I owe you one, after all."

"Alright." Peter stared at him, examining his face. "I mean it, Freddie. I killed Sylvia for you, but now I'm trusting you to finish your job. Take Royce out quickly, painlessly. Do not hurt Nadine. Don't betray me. I'm the Mother's son. You obey Mother, and you obey *me*. You don't want to fail Mother by being too impulsive, do you?"

Freddie's grin gave a hateful twitch, but then returned to its firm, stretched, bloody glory. "Of course."

Peter gave a disheartened but satisfied nod.

"Oh, hi Rice Cracker!" Freddie said, enunciating her moniker with a hypocritical, whiny voice. "Hi, Tweedle Dum!"

Peter turned to find Nadine and Royce standing several feet behind him, staring, mouths agape.

Freddie let out his loud hyena's giggle, letting it echo across the corridor. "Please, don't tell me you were standing there to hear this one last part! That would just be mortifying for Norman, here!"

"Peter," Nadine said. "How could you? Who the fuck *are* you?"

"You don't unders—"

"Don't you fucking dare tell me I don't understand! You killed Sylvia? You fucking murderer! And now you're bargaining with Freddie, for which of us he should kill?"

"Thanks, by the way," Royce said with a hypocritical smile. "Appreciate the vote, brother."

"You're disgusting," Nadine said.

Peter let out a long sigh, gave Nadine a pained look, then said, "When this is all over, look for me, Nadine. We'll sit down and talk over a cup of coffee."

He stepped through a hole in the air and disappeared from the corridor.

CHAPTER THIRTY-FIVE

MONSTERS

Jess stood amid the crowded bar—Peggy loaded and clutched in her hand, while her dad held his rifle. Lillian and Ray held handguns, and Jess kept a .44 as backup. She'd also returned the weapons she'd taken from the people who'd brought their own. Finally, Arnold Fowler, despite not being Jess's favorite person, had gotten the other hunting rifle on account of Chuck vouching for his hunting prowess and aim.

She had given Fowler a stern look and asked, "Did you really feed Sally Hargraves's dog meatballs with drain cleaner?"

He shook his head in a panic. "No! Never!" he blurted. "I got drunk, made some meatballs for dinner. I put powdered drain cleaner in them instead of flour by mistake. My drunk ass saw a white powder and poured it in. I almost ate them, too. I noticed the package while I was serving them. I put them in a bag, tossed it in the garbage. But Sally's damned dog; it sometimes got in the bin. Damn Greyhound was more like a raccoon. It... Well, you can guess the rest. I felt horrible."

Jess had studied his face, found no lie in it, and said, "If you make me regret this, the last thing you'll feel is fresh air blowing through the new window I'll be opening right here"—she'd touched her index finger to the center of his forehead, right on the hem of his blue knitted cap. She'd given a similar warning to those who brought their own guns.

"Alright, people, look." She cleared her throat, scanned the assortment of apprehensive faces. "I ain't good at speeches, so this won't be a 'rallying the troops' moment. Y'all know already what your role is. If you got a gun, you're on the outer part of the group, next is the knives and pool cues and chair legs crowd, followed by kids and elderly, and at the center are the cots, the wheelchairs, and people on piggyback. Now, listen here. We don't know what's out there, but it's likely gonna be fuckin' scary. I ain't gonna lie. All I can say is, we might not like every person here, but we got no room for fucking up. No infighting, ya hear me? We can deal with all that shit once we make it through this. Please take care of each other. Don't make me kick your bitch asses, alright? Now—"

A woman's scream cut through the crowd.

Every head turned toward the area near the windows. Even from where she stood, it was clear the infection from outside had crept further in. The bar's outer wall and nearby booths were barely recognizable. Parts of the wall looked like crumbling concrete, with random patches of wood growing out of it. Newspaper pages were draped over the seats. Some booths had morphed into bizarre fusions of a broken hospital bed and a birthing bed with stirrups—cables and dripping IV tubes snaking throughout. Black, vein-like threads crawled everywhere, pulsating and writing. Blight Harbor was at last breaking through, pushing into their only shelter.

People moved away from where the screams came, pressing against each other. Then the screams turned into desperate sobs and cries for help.

Jess glanced at Chuck. "Dad, you stay back here, watch our backs"—she shot a look at Arnold Fowler—"Fowler, with me."

Jess and Fowler pushed through the panicking crowd, the woman's cries growing louder as they approached. They reached the edge to find a petite, blonde woman in an orange sweater kneeling beside a little girl of no more than five, who was writhing on the floor.

It wasn't immediately apparent what was wrong with the little girl until Fowler pointed at her, and said, "Her hand!"

The woman in the orange sweater turned wild, panicked eyes toward them and cried, "I didn't know! I swear I didn't know! Please, help!"

The girl's hand was closed into a fist around a black lump, from which dark threads snaked up her arm, burrowing into her skin, and slowly winding their way toward her shoulder.

"When that man was here!" the woman shouted. "The first one! Parham! When he killed that pervert, this tiny black rock fell in through the window!"

The flick of the wrist, Jess thought with alarm. *Right before he killed the man outside. He flicked his wrist in a weird way, like he was...throwing something...*

"My Chloe! She picked it up! She didn't want to let it go! I... I thought it was just...like a pretty gemstone! I thought it was harmless! I—"

"You stupid fucking moron!" Jess shouted.

"I'm sorry!" the woman pleaded. "Please! Help her!"

Fowler stared at Jess as if she would know what to do. The little girl was lying on a wooden floor that shouldn't exist in the bar.

It got in. It's in!

Now black threads came between the wooden floorboards, wrapping around the girl's body. She could hear screams rise from the surrounding crowd. Planning, formation, weapons, what could that possibly accomplish against something that made so little sense? Jess shook her head. "We have to—"

A black thread shot toward the little girl's mother, entered her skin, and she let out a shocked holler of pain. More and more came fast, giving them no time to react. In seconds, mother and daughter had been enveloped in a growing, shifting black cocoon.

"Back!" Jess shouted. "Get back!"

Black threads now shot outward from the cocoon, like spiderwebs, toward random people in the crowd. One pierced a man's throat, another flew into the eye of a man shielding his barking Border Collie. The man's wife pulled the panicked dog away as black tendrils began crawling into the man's mouth.

Stepping away, along with Fowler, Jess noticed something glowing blue in the crowd. She took a deep breath. "Get behind Raymond Chang! The one with the blue glowing thing! Behind the blue glow! Don't crush each other!"

People around her, though panicking, appeared to obey her order.

The glowing blue rock rose above the crowd. Ray was holding it up as a beacon, as people crowded behind him, which was now the only part of the bar that hadn't turned into what she now recognized as some twisted mixture of the Vanek House and a hospital room.

"Dad!" she yelled. "Cellar exit! Nobody goes downstairs until it's open!"

Chuck nodded, scanning the crowd. He handed something to Lillian, who held up her dad's keychain for Jess to see. She understood right away: Chuck would hold the crowd back while Lillian ran downstairs and opened the cellar exit to the alley. With little Tracy in her arms, Lillian ran down to the cellar.

An electronic crackle was followed by a screech as Chuck raised the bullhorn to his lips. He adjusted the volume. "Listen to me!" His voice boomed across the bar crowd. "All eyes here!" Waving his rifle in the air, he continued. "Gather between Glowing Blue Rock Guy and me! We're goin' out through the cellar once the exit is open! Get a hold of yourselves! 'Coz if you try to push past me, I won't hesitate to blow you away!"

"Jess!" Arnold Fowler grabbed her by the arm and turned her around. Something was emerging from the black cocoon, which, based on its size, had at least gathered about ten more people into it, resulting in a huge monstrosity. There were five people on the floor, writhing and screaming as they got rolled into black bundles being pulled into the main mass. "Do I shoot it?"

"Jesus Fuck!" Jess said. Most of the crowd was already behind them. "No! Save the ammo! We have to get out!" She turned. "Dad! Single file! Cellar!"

"You heard her, folks!" Chuck said, restraining the fear in his voice. "Single file! Injured people first! Children and the elderly next! Anyone tryin' to push past the others and not being a good neighbor gets a bullet in the leg and left behind! I mean it!"

A grotesque, fourteen-foot-tall creature lumbered out of the black cocoon. Its massive, childlike head—the size of a person—bore a swollen, hydrocephalic skull covered in clusters of breathing holes. The torso was a writhing tangle of anguished human faces, mouths agape and eyes wide with horror, moaning incoherently. Fingers and toes jutted out at random from its nightmarish form, curling and twitching. Two thick tentacles lined with insect-like legs sprouted from its sides, dragging its sluglike body forward, like gigantic centipedes. The lower body was a chaotic jumble of human limbs, joints twisted and misaligned, creating an unsettling, distorted symmetry as it advanced toward the crowd.

"Where do I shoot it?" Fowler asked, panicking, readying the rifle.

"What do I look like, a fucking demon biologist? I dunno! Head?"

Fowler raised the rifle, aimed right at the gigantic child's head, and fired. The blast echoed through the entire bar, along with the sound of startled screams.

A hole opened right between the creature's eyes—her dad had been right about Fowler's aim—but then watched in horror as the holes in its head shifted places with the gunshot, closing one of the holes and replacing it with the new one and moving it up its gelatinous skull.

"Alright, not the head," Jess said.

A tentacle reached for a man beside Fowler, its insect legs clamping tight around him as he screamed. It pulled him in, and the infant's mouth unhinged like a snake's jaws, swallowing him whole. Jess watched in horror as the man's face emerged from the creature's body, deformed, with an enlarged eye, blending into the grotesque mass. The creature grew larger, with new arms and legs joining the twisted mass near its tail.

"Dad! Hurry! Hurry!" Jess shouted, she and Fowler moving back as the room emptied into the cellar little by little.

"Jess!" She looked over her shoulder. It was Ray. "Maybe I should come closer! Use the rock!"

"No! If you lose that thing before we even go into the streets, we're fucked! Down! To the cellar! Right now!"

Ray nodded, turned, and ran toward the cellar door, where Barry's kids waited for him.

The creature raised another of its tentacles and went for Jess. She tried to dodge it, but it got the insect legs around her body. She felt the pressure of the legs pressing her body tight as it pulled it toward her. The child's horrid, toothless mouth opened, waiting to take her in. A second rifle blast echoed, and a chunk of the tentacle in front of her exploded into a spray of blood and meaty chunks. It twitched and let her fall.

Jess scrambled to her feet, picked up her shotgun, and without giving the monster the chance to recover, she turned and let out a full blast, which not only sprayed its face with shotgun pellets, but cut off the tentacle Fowler had wounded with the rifle. Jess bounded back to Fowler's position. The bar area was nearly empty now.

"Thanks," she said.

He nodded back, right before both had to dive to the floor to avoid a swing of the other tentacle, as the one they'd cut off soon grew back. In the time it took them to recover, the creature swallowed two more screaming people—two more suffering faces sprouted from its body, eight more twisted limbs, larger body mass—before they could raise their guns and fire at it.

"Jess! Arnie!" Chuck cried. "Cellar! Now! Go! Go!"

They turned to see the last of the people running down the stairs. They dashed across the now-wooden floor, heading toward Chuck, who fired his rifle at the creature, trying to slow it down at least the seconds it would take Jess and Fowler to descend.

They stomped down the stairs, hearing the moment Chuck slammed the cellar door shut behind them and locked it with a large bolt. The last of the people climbed the exit stairs toward the alley, being ushered by Lillian and her precious little girl, who was imitating her mom's hurried hand-waving, telling people to get out.

"You guys okay?" Lillian asked.

Jess nodded, trying to push down the thought that at least thirteen people, including a little girl had died on her watch to become part of a grotesque monster, but she remembered her dad's words: "*Don't count losses, coz the losses will keep piling up. You have a hundred and forty lives here. If half of those make it to The Pines, that will be on you.*" She fixed a fierce gaze on Lillian. "Take your little girl. Let's get the fuck out. The Pines. Shortest route. Formation as planned. Nobody splits up. Tell them!"

Lillian took Tracy's hand, nodded at Jess, and hurried out of the cellar.

Soon, Jess, her dad, and Fowler joined the group outside. Standing in the alley, soaking in the rain, they didn't get the full picture of how much White Harbor had changed. They were about to find out.

Royce pointed the handgun at Freddie as he and Nadine approached, the sound of their footsteps echoing in the silence of the criminal patient wing corridor. Rows of plexiglass windows at either side and in the mezzanine above gave them an eerie view into dark cells crowded by unconscious patients and staff members—like puppets hanging inert from strings in a puppeteer's dressing room.

"Don't you fucking move, Freddie," Royce said. He peered down at Bobby and felt his heart sink. One lifeless eye remained open, fixed on a single spot, glazed over, devoid of reflection or vitality, a heartbreaking reminder of the emptiness his friend was leaving behind.

Nadine crouched beside Bobby, ran a loving finger over his blood-covered cheek. Heartbroken, she whispered, "Say hi to our Angie, sweetheart." She ran a hand over the right sleeve of his jacket, and stopped at his hand, under which there was what looked like random blood spatter, only it didn't seem so random.

Royce spared a glance down, seeing her move Bobby's hand aside. "What is it?"

She swiveled her eyes up, met his gaze, and motioned toward what Bobby's hand had been covering. Scribbled in blood were the words: "Basemt. Boilr. Grate. Cavern. God."

"Don't mean to interrupt," Freddie said in that arrogant voice of his. "But we gotta get to the part in which I kill you." He looked at Nadine. "And never mind Norman's little sentimentalities, Rice Cracker, I'm killing you both. I promised Mother I'd kill four of you, and I intend to."

"This has to end, man," Royce said, gun trained on Freddie's bruised and bloody visage.

"Yeah, *man*," Freddie said, crouching and placing a hand that looked like it had been stitched with black shoelaces on the floor. "Let's end this."

Hundreds of black threads spread out from his hand toward the surrounding cells. Through the plexiglass, they could see the hospital staff and patients being engulfed by their bindings as soon as the black threads touched them. The pulsating black pods that enveloped them burst open, unleashing a horde of monstrous creatures into the cells, whose doors opened in unison.

Royce and Nadine watched, frozen in terror, as these horrors shambled toward them. They saw bodies split open into vertical mouths with hundreds of teeth, limbs twisted into tentacles or insect parts, stretched necks, added joints, toothless mouths with obscene swollen lips. Eyeballs forming clusters, or bulging, or dangling from appendages. Oozing holes dripping with unspeakable fluids.

One creature's head was simply a bundle of huge yellow flowers, like a beautiful bouquet wrapped in a long collar of human meat instead of wrapping paper. Another had a huge, sphincter-like mouth, from which hung strands of long black hair, straight to the floor. Another creature, emaciated and grotesque, had a duplicated torso—one at the top and another at the bottom—each with identical heads and arms, like a face card in a deck. The top half slashed at them with knife-like claws, while the bottom half crawled on its hands, dragging its face behind it like a slug.

"My beautiful, beautiful things will take good care of you." Freddie took a step back toward his cell. "I'll just stand here and enjoy the show."

Nadine pulled out the gun she'd gotten from Jess. Royce tucked his gun in the back of his pants and pulled a shotgun hanging from a strap, pointing it at the oncoming horde.

"Deen! I got this side! Point at Freddie so he doesn't come at us from behind!"

Without hesitation, Nadine turned and pointed the handgun at Freddie.

He scoffed, grinned, raised his mangled, stitched hand, and wiggled his fingers toward her. "Miss Schaefer, I gotta say...even with an eye patch, you're fuckin' boring."

Royce pointed the incoming tide of monsters and fired. Two of the creatures dropped, but there were too many. He pumped the shotgun, blasted them again. The yellow-flower-meat-bouquet creature's head exploded into a hundred petals that rained down onto the shambling mob. "Fuck! There are too many! Move back! I'm gonna use the thing Hitch gave us!"

"Royce, no! We can only use that once!"

"That's right. The moment I use it, you run!"

"Are you crazy?"

He lowered his voice so Freddie couldn't hear. "Deen. You fucking run. Basement door is in the circular vestibule. Bobby wrote that for a reason, and only one of us is going there."

"No! What about Lillian and Tracy?"

He raised the shotgun again. Fired. Four shapeless monstrosities hit the floor. "I'll get out of here, find you, then we'll join them, alright?" It was obvious he didn't believe this. "If I don't make it out...tell them I love them, and uh..."

He glanced down at Bobby's corpse and remembered a day in 1994 when Bobby invited him over to watch a bootleg of *Léon: The Professional*. Despite his deep depression over Leroy's death, that day, watching the movie, eating pizza, and drinking Pepsi, he'd laughed, cheered, and cried. It was the day he realized it was okay to keep living, even if the pain burned forever. Years later, he'd watched the movie with Lillian and told her why it meant so much to him. For their first anniversary, she'd given him a poster signed by Jean Reno—which Bobby had procured on eBay—and he knew then he had to marry her. They even named their daughter Tracy *Matilda* Howe after Natalie Portman's character.

"Tell her I went out like Léon. She'll get it."

Nadine hesitated. "Okay."

"Kids?" Freddie interrupted. "Stop whispering. If you can share it with each other, you can share it with the class!"

Nadine fired a bullet in his direction. She didn't hit him, but made him flinch. She turned to Royce. "Do it!"

Royce rummaged in his pocket and found a piece of paper where John Hitch had drawn a series of strange symbols using a strange red stick, like a crayon. He'd warned him this power could only be tapped into once, so he needed to time it right. He unfolded the paper, crouched, and set it on the floor, symbols facing up. His upper body jumped with a start when another *bang!* came from Nadine's gun, followed by Freddie's amused hyena laughter.

"C'mon, c'mon, c'mon," he muttered, watching the oncoming tide of horror. "Alrighty, if this doesn't work, we're fucked." He looked at the weird doodles on the paper, thinking he had to be crazy to believe this gobbledygook would actually work. He remembered Hitch telling him to wait until the creature or creatures made it "so close he could see the color of their eyes". Of course, he neglected to mention which of the hundreds of eyes to focus on.

There was a monstrosity right in front of him. Its lips peeled back to reveal a tongue made of writhing blue eyeballs. He placed his palm on the paper. Black tendrils shot from the paper, connecting to the monsters, then branching out from one creature to the other. In seconds, their veins swelled, blackened, and crystallized into spikes that erupted from their insides, freezing them in place. Strange growls and gurgles filled the air. He stood, pulled out his shotgun, and fired. The eye-tongue creature flew back, crystal spikes shattering, toppling a bunch of others. He fired again, taking down the double-bodied face-card monster. He needed to reload.

He looked over his shoulder. "Deen! Go! Go! Go!"

Nadine took one last shot at Freddie. The bullet glanced past his cheek and obliterated his ear before she turned, ready to run.

Having pulled more rounds from the strap and loaded them, Royce pumped the shotgun again, and fired, hitting a scorpion-like creature whose pincers were human faces with enormous mouths. It reared on its back legs and toppled into the others behind it.

In a rush, Nadine threw her arms around him, pulled him in tight, and said, "Please, don't die. Think of your baby girl!"

"I'll try, dammit, but hurry!" he said, pumping the gun.

Nadine disappeared through the door at the end of the hallway, just as more creatures crawled down from the cells up in the mezzanine to join the few below that still lived.

"Nice magic trick, you piece of shit!" Freddie roared from behind, coming closer.

Sensing the attack, he tried to dodge left, but Freddie's black blade pierced his right shoulder. Royce cried out but clenched his jaw, knowing he couldn't stop moving or Freddie would kill him. He dropped the shotgun, spun left to free the blade, grabbed Freddie's arm, and slammed him onto the concrete floor. The pain in his shoulder forced him to release Freddie and scramble for the shotgun, seeing the first creature approach—a thing like a gigantic headless toad, whose torso opened like a Venus flytrap, tentacles with individual mouths rising from it.

He raised the shotgun toward it and blasted it up close. It took every single pellet from the shotgun. He turned toward the crowd, fired again, pointed to the other side, fired again. Seven creatures fell in revolting bursts of blood and limbs, but more kept coming.

The shotgun was empty. No time to reload. He pulled the handgun from his pants and pointed it at Freddie. The blood from his former friend's ear drew red lines over his bruised face, making him look like yet another of his monsters.

"Stop, Freddie!" Royce shouted. "Don't make me kill you!"

"Oh, that's so cute, Tweedle Dum!" He charged forward, swaying left and right. "Like you even could!"

Royce fired twice. Missed. Got a quick glimpse of Freddie's frenzied grin, his giggles echoing in the corridor, right before Freddie's stitched fist connected against his left cheek. Before he could recover, he felt the black blade pierce his right forearm.

He cried out and dropped the gun, which spun, rolling on the floor. He fell backward, landed with Freddie right on top of him. Freddie pulled the blade out. Royce shielded his face, only to see the blade poke through his bandaged left palm, the tip stopping inches from his eye. Freddie's rabid face looked down at him as he pushed the knife down.

"I'm gonna make a skewer with your eyeballs!"

Royce punched him in the ribs, and Freddie screamed, rolled off him in pain. He turned and tried to crawl toward the gun, while the psychotic man winced, but soon he felt the blade pierce his left calf, coming in through one side and exiting through the other. With a holler, he turned to see Freddie's deranged face snarling at him. He raised his right foot and kicked his head twice, making him fall back. Leaving a trail of blood behind, Royce continued crawling until his fingers curled around the gun's grip. He quickly stood, limped away two steps, before turning and pointing the gun at Freddie, who now rose, a mad countenance in his face, grinning like a hungry wild animal at him.

"I...was chosen by the Holy Mother," he croaked, shuffling toward him, a reconstituted army of monsters lumbering a few feet behind. "Holiest under God, she bestowed a task upon me, and I shall not fail her. I'll free my family, and *you*, Royce Howe, aren't half the man who can stop me."

"You're talking crazy, Freddie! Man, stop! I'm serious, you insane fuck! I don't want to kill you! Stop!"

Freddie started giggling under his breath, a malevolent glint in his eyes. "'Half the man,'" he chuckled. His giggles of "Hee-hee-hee!" soon grew in intensity. Little by little they built, mad, deranged, peals of hyena cackles bouncing off the concrete and Plexiglas. He threw his arms back and let out his laughter as loud as his lungs would allow, almost as if howling. "HEEE-HEEE-HEEE-HEEE-HEEE! Half the man! Half a man! Half a man is what you've felt like since I killed your brother! Haven't you?"

He drove his gaze into him, eyes out of their orbits, spilling over with pure madness. "Alright, Half-Man," he said in a low croak, his voice jerking with maniacal giggles, "let's send you to your dead twin and make you whole." He bent the arm with all the stitches and showed him the back of his mangled hand, wiggling his fingers as if preparing to do a magic trick. "You were a comics fan, weren't you?"

Freddie closed his hand into a fist and three vicious black blades emerged from it. He sneered at him, putting the blades up in front of his face. "Snikt, snikt, bub!" He launched forward without warning. "HEEE-HEEE-HEEE-HEEE-HEEE!"

Without thinking, Royce raised the gun and fired four bullets. Every single one hit home. All went into Freddie's torso. He slashed at him, cutting three deep furrows in his abdomen.

Royce staggered back, recoiling in pain, as Freddie came to a stop a few steps in front of him.

The madman looked down at the open holes in his body, which now further stained his orange hospital scrubs with dark blood. He stared at Royce, almost looking betrayed.

"This"—he coughed blood—"this wasn't supposed to go like this." Freddie's face looked like a kid being told the trip to Disneyland was canceled. "It's not over..." He ran his hand over the blood, looked at it as if it couldn't be real. His lips trembled, peeled back into a snarl. "It's not over!"

"It's over, Freddie," Royce said, realizing three of the four shots had gone into his abdomen, and he'd die soon from blood loss. "It's over. Stop this. We might still be able to get you some help."

Freddie scoffed, spraying blood from his mouth, then grinned, but the grin soon faded. "I want nothing from any of you." He let out a low growl. "You're dead, anyway. I won." He looked over his shoulder at the crowd of monsters shuffling closer. His eyes found his cell, just a few feet to his left, and trudged toward its open door. His feet left bloody footprints on the papers and canvases scattered on the floor. He reached the bed, picked up what looked like a rolled-up canvas.

Royce considered following him, but the mob of creatures was too close to the cell already. He'd be cornered in there.

Freddie unfurled and held up the painting—the edges of the canvas were stained with blood. It expanded like a window looking into a dark cavern, wrapped around him like a bubble, then vanished, taking Freddie with it.

Royce walked back, helpless. He regarded the mass of death shuffling his way. The creatures stomped all over Bobby's corpse and continued past Freddie's cell.

He only had twelve bullets left, four shotgun rounds, and there were at least three dozen of those abominations coming his way. He realized then he was right about what he'd told Freddie.

It was over.

CHAPTER THIRTY-SIX

HALLOWED GROUND

The crowd, led by Jess and Chuck, navigated through familiar streets, turned alien and decayed. White Harbor resembled a dead civilization, crumbling concrete and rotten wood everywhere. Five inches of disgusting water ran down the cracked, overgrown streets, every surface covered in mold. Broken windows revealed dark, empty buildings filled with rotting furniture. Twisted hospital equipment, like gurneys, wheelchairs, and tubing, formed eerie structures that climbed over buildings, like insane scaffoldings. Black vines crept everywhere as the blue moon watched them from a stormy sky with mocking curiosity, like lab rats in a maze.

As they traversed the abandoned streets, scattered throughout the landscape, they gawked at otherworldly oddities that appeared almost separate from the motif of the town as a whole—if there was such a thing as a motif in this insane, incoherent world.

The crowd gasped as they passed an alley where the walls were covered from ground to ceiling in thousands of dolls, torn to pieces, bleeding, and crying, "Ma-ma! Ma-ma!"

The Glamorium Emporium—the hair and nails salon two blocks from the bar—displayed what looked like burned mannequins sitting on every chair. Their unnerving faces looked like real, charred skulls wearing perfectly crafted wigs, and colorful painted nails on their fingers.

Jesus, what the fucking fuck? Jess thought, gazing at the hallucinogenic ridiculousness that surrounded them.

They passed a rusted, windowless vehicle with flat tires. Two genderless, human-sized glass figures in the backseat appeared to be fucking—one straddling the other—their limbs stretched, curved, and spiraled out the windows and around the vehicle, as if clinging to it with a firm yet fragile grip.

"People!" Jess called. "We're coming up on Mason street! Residential area! Be on the lookout!"

Homes meant people. Whole families must have definitely stayed huddled in their houses, ignoring Royce's call. If the creatures were people, a residential area could spell trouble. They hadn't encountered any monsters so far but based on the cries from the back of the crowd, the abomination from the bar had busted out of the building, and was pursuing them, which meant they couldn't stop, or it would catch up to them.

The first house as they turned into Mason street, past a dense thicket of trees, almost brought the march to a dumbfounded stop. It was a house everyone knew well: the house that kept its Christmas decorations all year long.

"Well, fuck me..." Chuck mumbled, gawking at the house along with everyone else. The Christmas decorations were glowing bright in a house-sized display of obscenity. Two white-gloved hands made of Christmas lights came from the sides of the house toward the front door, holding open what looked like a gaping asshole—in merry pink and red lights—rendered in such detail around the door, there was no way of mistaking it for anything else. As if that weren't enough, on the roof was Santa—also in Christmas lights—lying on top of an upturned sleigh, legs up in the air, with a blinking, animated Rudolph pounding him back and forth, as the other reindeer stood in line, on their back legs, holding throbbing erections, waiting for their turn.

It was such a ridiculous, outlandish spectacle, it left Jess speechless amidst gasps from the crowd.

As they meandered between the dilapidated homes on this street—one of which was covered in skin and blinking eyes, looking this way and that—Jess got nervous they had encountered none of the monsters Ray had described. Jess glanced toward him. "Where are they?"

He shook his head and shrugged. "Beats me," he said, holding the rock with the crystals in one hand, and Daniel's hand in the other. The crystals emitted no glow. "On the way to the bar, they were coming out of the houses and wandering around like zombies. I didn't go a block without seeing a few."

Beside him, Nurse Ferguson carried Gabe in her arms—the boy was sucking on his thumb with a distant stare. Jess glanced down at Daniel, who wept into his shirt. These children were all that was left of Barry, Jess thought, and knew Ray was beyond anxious about their safety. He couldn't let anything happen to them.

Instead of being relieved by the absence of creatures, it actually made Jess more anxious. She felt insane in realizing she'd rather have monsters coming at them from all angles than not knowing when the other shoe was going to drop.

They passed Burkle park, which, Jess observed, hadn't changed at all. It looked just as it had always looked—clean and well-kept. The water flooding the streets appeared to drain into the gutter surrounding it, keeping the trails that wound through it unflooded. It was an odd exception she could find no explanation for until she remembered this was the park where Freddie came to sketch and draw. It was a special place for him.

In stark contrast, was Gerardo Valencia's old house. Once a charming yellow cottage surrounded by flowers, it had decayed due to abandonment. However, the peeling paint and overgrown weeds were nothing compared to what it had become this night. The house's boards, shingles, and lawn had twisted into a grotesque, beating heart with a human face. A thick black tentacle slithered into its mouth, emerging as writhing tendrils from the aorta and vena cava.

At the corner of Hill Road and Graham Street, where the road climbed toward the mountains, the survivors were confronted by a sight that made clear how insignificant they all were. The entire slope where the Vanek House and Peter Lange's home used to stand was now a massive crater, flooded with muddy water. A landslide had stripped away earth, asphalt, and homes, leaving a dark wound on the mountainside, as if a colossal excavator had carved a chunk off the hills. Etenia Creek—which had dried up years ago—had swelled and overflowed. The creek's water now rushed downhill, causing the flood in the town below.

"Careful with the stream!" Jess shouted. "The slope means less flooding, but quicker water rushing downhill. Pick up the children, stay on the sidewalk, don't trip. It's not strong, but can be dangerous. Stay packed tight! It's straight from here to the school!"

The crowd turned south and continued trudging under the miserable weather, shoes soaked and muscles tense from the cold. A few blocks in the distance, Garland Elementary came into view, as lightning flashed in the sky, the building emerging from the rain and the dark.

It was when they finally reached Carpenter Street they realized where all the creatures had gone, as they appeared from both corners, crawling on roofs, and down from trees. Alarmed murmurs rose from the back of the crowd, which told her the creature from the bar was catching up.

They were surrounded.

Peter was puzzled to find himself not in a cavern, as he had expected, but in the living room of his old home on Hill Road. This wasn't a cold and empty facsimile like the one where he'd talked to his father, but it felt lived in, inhabited, warm.

He was standing with the front door shut behind him—he hadn't shut it—and he sensed dancing light from his left. His mother was there, sitting in her old armchair, the one with the green and gold upholstery and the high back, in front of the fireplace, the flames casting light and shadows on her face.

"Come here, boy, sit next to me," Mother said, her voice sounding tired and melancholy.

Without a word—a cowed, beaten dog called to sit at his mistress's foot—Peter shuffled toward the banquette beside her, where he used to sit as a child.

"This isn't the actual house, is it?"

She swiveled her eyes toward him, looking annoyed. "I thought I raised you smarter."

He sat down, trying not to look at her. He drove his gaze into the fireplace. Let her say whatever she had in mind.

"You have done what I asked." It was a statement, not a question, yet he answered anyway with a weak nod. "That Parham boy was too impetuous, too arrogant. I wasn't convinced he could finish his mission alone. He's useful, but not reliable."

Peter remained silent.

"Wait here until I tell you to come out. I have things to take care of."

Still no answer from Peter.

"I am no fool, boy. I know the only reason you agreed to help me was sparing your son from what you saw on the other side. I didn't want you to believe in our God because of fear alone, but sometimes there is no other way. For most of us, we first learn to fear God, then a few of us find our faith once we see His works come to fruition."

Peter kept his eyes on the flames, gave a nod to show he was listening.

"That night in the cavern," she said, as if telling him a bedtime story—not that she ever did such a thing when he was a child. "Right before God revealed Himself to me, I found a book and a musty, old corpse on the floor, decomposed, unrecognizable. It was the previous Mother. She was weak. The true plan God had for our world was revealed to her, and she feared it. She came to plead with God, ask Him to reconsider. She died for her lack of faith. She hadn't chosen a successor, and the Circle couldn't choose it for her, so they were aimless, rudderless, until God chose me."

Another vacant nod from Peter.

"God asked for sacrifice as proof of faith. Our suffering feeds Him. I know it must seem strange to you we worship a God that feeds on suffering, but that is the easiest way to tell who are the Faithful and who are not. If there is suffering in a person's life, continuous suffering, that person has not been favored by God. All of those people in the world who are suffering, sick, starving; people would tell you they deserve our pity, but they don't. God has not favored them, so they deserve nothing. God has favored us. He'll take our suffering away."

She drove such a firm stare on Peter, he couldn't help but meet it.

"I promised God a sacrifice of my descendant's blood, to prove my faith, and secure our place in the next life. I know you don't understand this. Your immaturity and this wretched world's laws delayed our ascension when you were taken from my side. But God promised you would come back to me, and he has delivered." She paused, pondering. "We've all had to make sacrifices to make up for our failures."

"I don't care about your god, Mother."

She stood up. Slapped him. Glared down at him. "Know your place."

"You promised my son would be spared. That's all I care about. Will you keep that promise?"

"I have never lied to you," she said, indignant. "Your Mother never lies."

Peter nodded. He knew this was true. "Mother," he said, sounding dispirited, risking another slap. "Did you ever truly love me?"

She regarded him, stone-faced. "You will wait for me here until I call you. Do not leave this place." She stepped toward the door but stopped, sighed. "Peter..."

He looked back over his shoulder, surprised to hear her call him by his name in such an earnest tone.

"I am sorry if I had to resort to this to make you see the right path." There was a certain vulnerability to her voice he'd only ever heard once, a very long time ago. "Many have died these past few days to accomplish that. One does not bring forth the things I have if it's not out of love. I hope you know that."

Peter looked back toward the fire. The front door's hinges whined as she opened it, followed by the sharp echo of it slamming shut.

Martha set foot outside the door, and her old home was gone. She had woven long tendrils from the Exiles throughout the walls, ceiling, and floor of the surrounding cavern, and made them sprout blue crystals, which glowed with an ethereal light. They cast shimmering reflections on the wet stone surfaces, and reflected off small pools formed by the seawater that filtered through the stone of the cavern, dripping down from stalactites with a faint sound, which echoed through the tunnel.

A few feet from where she stood, she noticed something that broke the serenity of this hallowed space. It looked like a man, lying in one of the small pools of water, staining it red with his blood. She would've thought him dead, were it not because of his feeble attempts to crawl out of the pool. He'd made it out by the time she stood in front of him, glaring down with contempt.

"Stand up, Frederick," she said.

"M-Mother, I..." Freddie mumbled. "I can't... I'm too, w-weak... I..."

"Stand."

With an aching groan, he brought himself to his feet and looked straight at her with a drawn, bruised, bloodied face. "Mother. Hel-lp me..."

"You were forbidden from entering this place, Frederick. You're cursed and dirty. You are not allowed here. Can you do nothing right?"

"I know," he wept. "I'm sorry, Mother."

"Stop mewling like a baby."

He tried to compose himself. "My ap-pologies, Mother! I know! I need your help! I'm dying! Please, save me. I'm... I'm here to ask for your mercy. I f-finished m-my mission."

"You needed my son to help you. Why should I reward you?"

"Mother, I...a-am devoted to you. I am devoted to God. I'm begging you."

"Are the four dead?"

"Yes!"

"How did each die? I will know if you're lying!"

"Sylvia Nguyen...was k-killed by Peter," he started with difficulty. "I felt her die. Bobby Novak, I...killed him myself, stabbed him. Confirmed his d-death. Barry Giffen was turned into one of...my creatures. He was crushed and...burned to death. His house collapsed on him. I felt him die, t-too. Royce Howe, I...wounded him...s-sent a horde of my creatures after him. Too many for him to defeat alone."

Mother's glacial stare did not leave him. "Did you confirm his death?"

"I..." he stammered; his eyes shifted. "I can't sense that from inside the cave, Mother, but I'm... I'm sure...he couldn't have survived. There were at least twenty of my creatures. He'd used one of Curling's tricks to get rid of some of them, but that can only be used once. Nothing he could've had would—"

"So, you don't know." Mother's face was carved in stone.

"M-Mother, I... I will go back and make sure! Please, I'm begging you...heal me so I can cont-tinue to serve you! I won't fail you!"

"Why should I?"

He dropped to his knees and groveled. "Mother, I'm begging you! I've always...been faithful to you! I've always been...y-your servant! I've done everything you've ever asked of me!"

"So, you are throwing this in my face, like a debt collector?"

"No, Mother!" His fingers trembled, and he let out a weak, desperate sob. Panic became the very blood in his veins, of which he realized there was little left. "Never! Yes, I've been waiting for G-God's forgiveness! For God's...r-reward for my humble service, Mother! To know my family—my baby sister—are...free from their curse. Free from the Void! M-mother, please! It's all I've...ev-ver wanted!"

"You love your sister so much, Frederick? Then, join her."

From the corner of his eye, he spotted one of the black tendrils on the ground twitch. It drew an arch in the air, leaving a deep cut in his throat. Whatever blood remained in his body drained into an expanding pool before his eyes. He tried to look up. Couldn't. He reached with trembling hands toward the Mother's bare feet, but she took a step back, out of his reach. He forced himself to look up, further opening the bleeding wound, only glimpsing the blurry image of the Mother's indifferent face.

"I won't risk missing one of the four sacrifices due to your negligence, Frederick. You forget you were there when the Chosen Accursed were selected."

No! He remembered now. Before he'd accepted God. Before the Mother had come to him with her offer. Before he'd killed six inside the Vanek House. The day the Mother had selected the candidates for the sacrifice. He'd been in that house. Locked in that room Curling had put him in. Trapped in the darkness, when the voice had floated up from...outside.

"*I curse you all.*" It now came to him, clear as the memory of Laurie's birth and her first cries. The Mother's voice. "*You have corrupted my son with the filth of the world. You have made him wish for a life he cannot have. You have pulled this irresponsible, weak boy away from the Lord's plan. You will all experience loss at the hands of the Lord. One day, I will come for you, and you'll feel my revenge. That is my curse on you.*" He'd thought it was a dream. A hallucination from being trapped in the dark.

She can't! She didn't choose me in person! I wasn't physically in her presence!

"I know what you're thinking, Frederick," Mother said, calling his fading attention back to her. "I needed to select you in person, like I did the others. But you forget one thing, my boy: I am the Mother. I am God's voice in the world. I wrote the Ritual of the Four Nights, inspired by God. I can interpret it as I see fit. And all it says is 'the Chosen Accursed, selected by the Mother.' You were one of that group, Frederick. One of Peter's young corruptors. So, I also selected you."

Her proud, sneering face looked down at him, her visage becoming clear for just a second before fading as life vacated his body.

Lolly...I'm sorry...

A shotgun blast went off amid the chaos near Garland Elementary, and what looked like an armless woman with an elephant's trunk for a head exploded in front of Jess. Blood and guts splattered everywhere. The sharp crack of the shot was drowned out by the relentless staccato of gunfire echoing all around as the survivors fought a desperate battle for their lives.

"They're too many!" Chuck shouted, firing his rifle, and reloading as if it were second nature. "Martha knew we would come this way! We can't get to The Pines through here! We need to double back and go around the block, but someone's gotta hold these things here so they don't chase the rest!"

"Reload!" Jess shouted, wiping monster blood off her face. Her voice was barely audible in the onslaught of gunshots, animalistic roars, cries of fear, indescribable monster noises, and the screams of people dying. It was overwhelming.

"I got you!" Arnold Fowler stepped in, while Jess retreated to a small pull cart being dragged behind them by Tanya Hagel, the owner of the tiny bookstore on King Street. The woman, who looked terrified as a turkey in Thanksgiving, had nevertheless insisted on helping somehow, since she didn't want to just sit back and wait to be killed by whatever came next in this night of horrors.

"Are you okay, Jess?" Tanya asked, hands trembling as she handed a box of shotgun shells to her.

Jess nodded in a hurry, reloading as fast as she could. "I need you to do something for me!"

"O-okay?" The woman's eyes went round as marbles.

"Ray's in the back! You know Ray? My friend? The nurse? He's holding that enormous monster from the bar at bay with that glowing rock of his!" She finished reloading the shotgun, handed it to Tanya. "Take this! This is Peggy. I love her, so fucking look after it!"

Tanya looked like Jess had handed her a live rattlesnake. "I wouldn't even know how to—"

"No, Tanya, goddammit! Take it!" She pushed it into the woman's ample bosom.

"Okay..."

"You take the glowing rock from Ray. You give him the shotgun. Hold the rock as close as you can to the monster without it actually grabbing and eating you." The woman gulped in terror. "Tanya, don't! Stop that!" If she'd had a newspaper, she'd have rolled it up and bapped her in the nose. "You hold the rock as close as you can to the monster and tell Ray to put all five rounds from this gun into the creature. Body shots! All five! Then, whether that puts the monster down or just staggers it, everyone—every single survivor here—follows you guys around the block toward The Pines' entrance. The one students use. You know the one?"

Tanya nodded in a hurry. "Through the chain-link fence."

"Good girl. Can you do that?"

"B-but... But why me? I mean, look at me! I can't stop shaking!"

"Jess!" Chuck shouted from the frontline. "We need you!"

"I don't know any of these people. The ones I know are fighting tentacled uglies. I know you. You're as jittery as a teenager with a pregnancy test, but you're reliable, and you've hung in there even when your bookstore's seen tough times. So, can I fucking trust you?"

"Y-yes! But what about you and your dad and the others back here?"

"Someone's gotta stay back so you guys can make it."

"But—"

"Watch it!"

Tanya turned and was face-to-face with a creature the size of a child, but with a spider-like abdomen for a torso and six arms. A puckered hole near the top seemed ready to spit something at her. In a panicked reaction, she shrieked and smashed it with the shotgun's butt, sending it to the ground with a wet, gurgling sound. Still screaming, she hammered it until it lay motionless, crushed like a bug on the wet asphalt. Blood-spattered, she turned a shocked gaze toward Jess.

"Fuckin' go, woman!"

She nodded and began pushing through the crowd.

Jess turned around and pulled out her .44 Magnum out of the holster strapped to her belt and joined Chuck, who regarded her change of weapon.

"I'm guessin' that means we aren't making it to The Pines?" he asked.

"We hold the line to give the others time to go around the block." She noticed the way he pressed his lips together, noticed his mind working. He was about to protest, tell her to escape with the others. "Don't say anything. It's my decision, Old Man."

He hesitated, gave a curt nod, and continued to fire into the crowd of monsters.

The creature with a child's face and holes in its bulbous head had grown with each of the unfortunate people it had swallowed, and now stood almost as tall, wide, and long as a city bus. It recoiled from the blue light of the crystals. Ray knew it was still deadly, though. The light's range was too small, and the creature's four tentacles—it had grown two more since the bar—were picking people off one by one, pulling them in and swallowing them, growing and adding more limbs and anguished faces to its body. While others fought the monster horde, Ray's sole task was keeping this behemoth at bay.

People tried to push against each other, trying to move as far away from the child-faced monster as they could, but they were already packed too tight against the people trying to stay away from the monsters on the other side. It was desperate chaos, with people dying all around, and no way out in sight.

And now, there was this new insanity to deal with. Ray stared aghast at Tanya's eyes, as if the mousy bookstore owner had asked him to sprout wings and fly away, carrying the entire crowd with him to Mars.

He paused for a moment, considering whether to protest, seek an alternative solution, or go back to Jess and tell her how idiotic her plan was. He refused to abandon her. However, he took the shotgun from Tanya and gave her the rock.

"Hold it forward," he said. "It won't try to grab you, but it will try to swat at you with the tentacles to knock it out of your hands, so hold it tight!" He'd just finished saying this when they had to duck to avoid a tentacle that flew over their heads.

"Wait!" someone called from behind.

Ray turned to see Tali pushing John Hitch in a wheelchair toward them. There was what looked like a box of Ritz Bits cheese cracker sandwiches on Hitch's lap.

"We need someone with a good arm," Tali said. "We need this to be thrown as hard as possible, scattered around the monster."

"Give it here," Riley Estrada said, emerging from the crowd. He pushed Tali aside, picked up the box, then shot a withering look at Hitch. "Don't think I've forgiven you for locking me and my buddy Mason in Cunningham's bathroom two nights ago. You know? My buddy who got killed before he could enter the bar tonight coz you didn't kill Parham when you had the chance?" His eyes shifted toward Hitch's Lighthouse Rock uniform. "Asshole."

"Estrada," Ray said with urgency. "You sure you can do it?"

"College baseball. Two years. Dropped out, though—sick dad dying of cirrhosis—but I still got the arm. Guaranteed. This ain't a pitch, exactly, but I can do it."

"Guys, please hurry!" Tanya pleaded, holding the rock toward the monster as steady as she could.

"Clear the way!" Estrada said.

The crowd gave him as much room as they could, given the conditions. He took a three-step running start, the open box in his hands, full of cracker sandwiches with strange runes scribbled on them. He pulled the box back, as if he were readying to throw a bucket of water into a burning building. He swung and out flew two pounds of round mini-sandwiches, which flew high, then rained down over and around the creature.

The monster let out a wet, angry roar. It convulsed, its swollen mass gave revolting shudders, the faces on its body let out gurgling screams.

"Now this!" Tali dropped his rucksack on the ground. It let out a loud, heavy, oddly familiar clack. He opened the zipper to reveal pool balls inside, all of which had a rune drawn on them. It looked different from the one on the crackers.

Estrada looked inside. "So, how should..."

"Just throw them like a pitch. Hard. Center mass. They'll be like bullets. The runes will delay the wounds closing. Keep the hits as close together as possible. Can you do that?"

Estrada chuckled, rolled his eyes. "'Can I do that...'"

He picked up the rucksack and set it at his feet. Despite the darkness and the rain, he grabbed the first ball—an eight-ball—and threw it with perfect aim, striking one of the monster's anguished faces, obliterating it, leaving a hole that wouldn't close. He kept throwing, each of the sixteen balls tearing into the creature, most hitting so close to each other they left a large hole in its body.

"Chang!" Hitch said, his tone commanding. "Get in as close as you can. Empty the shotgun into that hole!" He turned to Tanya. "Lady, follow him closely with the rock, so the creature won't attack him."

Casting his fear aside, Ray walked up to the monster. Tanya stood next to him, the rock crystals glowing intensely blue. The monster, which was still convulsing, tried to attack but recoiled at the touch of the blue light.

Ray held the shotgun like Jess had taught him years ago. He pointed at the hole in its body and fired once. Pumped the gun. Fired twice. Pumped it. Fired. Pumped it. Fired. Pumped it. Fired one last time, leaving a huge, ragged wound in the creature's disgustingly human flesh.

"The rock!" Hitch shouted, then grunted with pain. "Put the rock in its body!"

Ray gawked at him, wide-eyed, disbelieving. "You can't be serious!"

"NOW!" Hitch shouted, then bent forward with pain, coughing.

Ray grabbed the rock from Tanya, handed her the empty shotgun, and with a terrified scream, stepped forward and shoved it inside of the monster's bleeding wound. Without waiting to see what happened, he pulled Tanya by the hand and ran back as far away as possible.

The creature convulsed, its faces writhed, limbs twitched, and tentacles flailed as it tumbled, tried to rise, and fell again, screeching in pain. The grotesque, childlike face wailed like a lost infant calling for its mother. Then, with a ripping sound, its insides ruptured, and a burst of gore and guts exploded from its mouth before it slumped over, dead.

"Run!" Ray shouted as he hurried toward the center of the crowd, where Kassie Ferguson had Barry's children. He picked up Daniel, asked her to take Gabe. "Around the block! Around the block! Run! Run! Everybody! Now!"

The crowd moved as one, those not fighting or being attacked, ran past the creature's corpse, turned the corner, and headed for the entrance to The Pines. Screams, gunshots, and fighting echoed from those left behind. Ray felt uneasy running, leaving Jess, especially after what happened with Barry.

He spotted Lillian approaching, carrying Tracy in one arm, a gun in her other hand. He stopped running, grabbed Kassie's hand. "Kass! Take Daniel!"

"What? What about you?"

"Uncle Ray?" Daniel said, weeping. "Are you going to go find Daddy?"

"I…" He stopped, at a loss for words. He noticed Lillian getting closer. "I'll do my best, buddy. I'll be back."

He hugged the two weeping boys, left them with Kassie, and ran to meet Lillian, feeling like shit for lying to them about their father.

"You know the other entrance to The Pines, right?" he asked her, wiping rainwater off his face.

"Of course, who doesn't?" Lillian nodded in a hurry.

"I'm down to one handgun bullet, and you're one of the few people left with a gun. Go around the block, be careful crossing Carpenter Street. Stay unnoticed, but if anything sees you, shoot it. Stick close to Kassie. Make sure she and the kids get in. Kassie can take Tracy inside, but you guard the wire fence entrance so as many as possible can enter. If I don't make it, please watch over Barry's kids—they have no one else."

"Okay." Her eyes betrayed her fear for her daughter, and the uncertainty of whether her husband had even made it to Lighthouse Rock. Ray knew he was burdening her, but he had no choice.

As the crowd ran past, Ray turned toward the child-faced creature's corpse, approached the bleeding hole in its body, and muttered, "I'm fucking crazy," before shoving his hand inside, reaching for the rock.

Jess had just watched Jerome Lucas, the old veterinarian, get skewered by a creature resembling an elderly naked woman on four dog legs, draped in a tattered robe, with a head like a purple flower with squiggly, purple tendrils around its center. The flower opened like a mouth to reveal a giant, black, spiny sea urchin. As it pulled Lucas close for a sharp, fatal kiss, he screamed, "Pauline, I didn't know!"

Jess was too late to save him.

She also shot down a creature with two male bodies fused together, one mounting the other, covered in crude oil and reeking of sulfur. It had missed her with an oily spit that set an unfortunate survivor on fire. She put a Magnum round into each of its heads, then noticed they wore unbuttoned blue shirts fused to their skins, with the names "Willis" and "Bilson" embroidered on their chests—the gas station guys.

Then, a monstrous pregnant belly with legs swallowed a teenager—whom Arnold Fowler had identified as Zak Hopper, his neighbor from Lumenwood. It opened like a vulva, spat out what looked like an umbilical cord with a fetus's head at the end, and reeled Zak in. She could hear the teenager screaming inside as it chewed and crushed him. Jess sliced the creature's belly with her knife, and it vomited Zak's mangled corpse to the asphalt as it died.

Jess was out of Magnum rounds, relying only on her knife. Her dad and Fowler would soon run out of ammo, too. They were surrounded by a scattering of corpses—both monsters and those who couldn't defend themselves.

A block behind them, she could see the flashlights of the last of the survivors turn the corner. She sighed with relief. "Back away, open up some distance, and make noise!" she shouted. "Keep their attention on us. Draw them onto this street. Give the others a chance to cross without being noticed!"

Jess, Chuck, Fowler, and two other survivors—one armed with a gun, the other with a knife—retreated the way they'd come from, shouting and firing, trying to make as much noise as possible. Fewer creatures remained to follow them, but they were still out-numbered. It was clear not everyone in town had transformed; small pockets of people were likely hiding, or already dead at the hands of their transformed relatives. Even so, there were far too many monsters for the five of them to survive.

A creature whose body resembled a man-sized HPV wart with crablike limbs slashed the throat of the man with the knife. He fell with a gurgling scream as blood sprayed from the wound.

"We're not gonna make it!" Fowler shouted.

"Not the point, son!" Chuck cried. "The point is for the others to make it."

"Shit," Fowler blurted, shaking his head. "Fuck." He turned and shot a creature like a faceless woman with five baby-shaped tumors sticking out of her torso, thorny tentacles swinging from each of their mouths.

Jess looked back and glimpsed something that brought her to a stop. Behind them, a pocket flashlight swung left and right as someone ran toward them. In the rain, she didn't recognize the person at first until she spotted the blue hospital scrubs. "Motherfucker!" As Ray approached, his arms drenched with blood, she noticed the glowing rock in one of his hands, the gun she'd given Sylvia in the other. "You shouldn't fuckin' be here!"

"I—"

"No, Ray! You're supposed to be taking care of Barry's kids! They're what should matter to you!"

"I'm here because I love you, you stubborn fucking mule!" he spat.

Her eyes bulged, taken by surprise.

"You saved his life two years ago in the bar's cellar. He and I wouldn't have had at least these last few moments together if it weren't because of you, Jess. I'm not losing you, too!"

"Give me the rock," Chuck said. "I'll stay with it here, holding them back, and the four of you run around the block!"

"No!" Jess said. "Dad, no!"

"I'm an old guy, Jess! I've lived. I was one of the people that caused all of this. It's only fair."

"Dad, watch out!" Jess pulled the gun from Ray's hand and shot a creature like a huge floating shrimp with a human skull and hanging tentacles approaching from behind the old man. The bullet pierced the skull, which didn't seem made of bone, but of the same chitinous shell a shrimp would be made of. It fell convulsing to the wet ground. "You're not staying here!"

"Hey! Give that back!" Ray shouted.

She and Chuck turned toward him to see Arnold Fowler, walking away from him, rifle in one hand, the glowing blue rock in the other. His face, clothes, and even his blue knitted cap were soaked with dark blood. For a moment, she thought the man was stealing the rock from Ray, and her first impulse was to point the empty handgun at him.

"There!" Fowler said, instead, setting the glowing rock down at his feet. "Problem solved. *I'm* staying!" He pointed the rifle and fired at a creature with an enormous head, which went flying back and deflated as if its entire cranium was a balloon filled with liquid brains.

Jess noticed a puncture wound in Fowler's abdomen. She didn't know how serious it was, but it might have factored into the man's decision.

"That won't hold all of them back," Ray said. "They'll sneak up on you! It's—"

"Chuck has always been good to me," Fowler said. "You have each other. Brandon here"—he motioned toward the other survivor with the gun standing next to him—"has a wife and a little girl in that crowd. Plus, I'm hurt bad. I might not survive even if I get to The Pines."

Jess nodded, hesitating. "Alright. Flashlights off. Everyone but Fowler. They might not see us like that. He'll stay here, drawing them to him. We'll run blind around the block." Everyone turned their flashlights off. Jess held hers on for a while longer. She eyed Fowler, whom she'd always disliked and always considered a selfish piece of shit—now realizing how wrong she'd been about him. "Thanks," she said with a nod.

He nodded back. She killed her flashlight, and they were all pounding pavement right away, leaving behind Fowler's flashlight and the blue light from the rock in the dark behind them.

From the distance, Fowler let out loud shouts of fury, drawing the creatures to him. His last two rifle shots rang in the night air, then came his grunts as he fought using a knife. As the group disappeared around the corner to their left, the sound of his painful death cry made Jess's heart shrink.

Elizabeth stood alone at the center of a circular platform—a sort of altar—surrounded by pillars, with torches on metal sconces. The edges of the circular room were dark. The light from the torches did not reach them. And from those shadows now emerged a figure.

She took a step back, apprehensive, but even more scared to step off the altar and there being something evil concealed by the shadows around her. Still, the woman appearing before her, bare feet padding on the rough stone floor, felt more evil, more wrong, than anything she could think of. She couldn't remember a thing about herself, or her life, but she knew the feeling coming off that woman like waves of darkness.

"Who are you?" Elizabeth said. "Who was that man? The one that brought me here?"

"His name is Peter," the woman said in a raspy voice. "I did not expect you to recognize him, of course"—she smiled—"but it's amusing to see how little you remember. You are almost ready. Well, of course you are. You wouldn't be here if you weren't."

"Ready for what?" Elizabeth took a step back.

"My Peter's finally coming home," she said, as if this was supposed to mean anything to her. "Together, we will celebrate the rebirth of our Lord. Because it is the Lord's promise, and you being here is proof it will come true."

"You're talking crazy."

"Oh, child, I would've thought the same if I were your age. Youth views wisdom as insanity. Yet wisdom is nothing but the experience granted by the memories of age. Thus speaks the Lord."

"I don't know what you're talking about." Elizabeth's eyes darted around, looking for something to defend herself with. "What do you want with me? Are you the one causing all of this weird stuff in town?"

"Those are questions to which you'll soon know the answers. You are almost ready, but there are still some preparations before Peter arrives."

Without warning, Elizabeth felt a sharp jolt in her head, just like the one after she first regained consciousness. She screamed as pain surged through her stomach, nausea overwhelming her. Strange, alien images flooded her mind, stronger this time, and she found herself speaking them out loud, unable to stop despite the urge to vomit.

"A child. A girl. Me. Her. Who? An old corpse. A book. A woman. Mother. Talking. Chanting. 'God, take her.' Crying. I'm crying. She's crying. Who's crying? Me. Her. The woman. She repeats. 'Take her. Spare me. Spare my husband. Spare my son. I don't want her. I give her to you.' The girl's in pain. I'm in pain. Forever. Later. People. Circle. Speaking. 'Mother, glory be. God, glory be. Ever-watchful eye, glory be.' Guilt. So guilty. So sorry. Time. The girl. Forgotten. Gone. Son. The son. The Mother."

Elizabeth let out a painful moan, holding her stomach. She howled in pain, dropped to her knees, then threw up on the floor. Grunting, she crawled away from the old woman, shudders racking her body. She felt sick. She felt like she was going to pass out.

The old lady stood over her as consciousness left her. "Don't worry, my dear. The sickness will pass. You rest while I get something to mop up the floor." Her voice was fading, moving farther and farther away. "Lie there, gather your strength. You will need it when Peter arrives. Sleep. By the time we wake up, we will celebrate as a family."

They reached the hole in the chain-link fence where Lillian stood over the body of a dead creature—a winged monstrosity wrapped in bloody bandages—perhaps a straggler that had followed the crowd. They were shocked only one had come this way.

Lillian regarded them with surprise, as if she was certain she'd never see them again.

"Where are the kids?" Ray asked, as if on impulse.

"They went in with Nurse Ferguson," Lillian said, looking shocked and exhausted. "They're fine."

"Oh, thank god," he said.

They climbed the wooded slope to the clearing in The Pines, where they joined the rest of the crowd. The first thing they noticed was, in this general area, it wasn't raining and the trees looked normal. There was even the odd sound of a night bird coming from the surrounding woods. The second thing was there had been about a hundred and forty people taking refuge in Cunningham's. Now, on a rough estimate, only about eighty remained. Still, eighty seemed like a lot, considering their odds.

Ray reunited with Barry's kids, and Daniel wasted no time in asking about his dad. Jess couldn't imagine how hard that conversation would be. For now, Ray offered vague answers to the weeping children, likely waiting for a better moment to break the terrible news.

She shone her flashlight toward the stretch of Carpenter Street visible outside. The monsters milled about beyond the school fence, but none attempted to cross it, didn't even touch it.

"They can't come in." She recognized the voice as Hitch's.

From the wheelchair, he motioned toward the edge of the clearing, pointed a flashlight in that direction. There was a large pile of moss-covered round rocks, eroded and covered in vegetation and dirt, which seemed to hold them in place. "I laid those rocks there myself for the dead settlers. Their bones are buried right under here. If you crack any of those rocks, you'll find the same crystals as the one Chang had." He moved the flashlight toward a large rock—where she remembered Bobby used to sit when they were kids. "That's the rock where Reverend Douglas Burgess violated Walter Parham." The light shifted left and shone on a smaller pile of rocks, this one almost invisible; it could've been mistaken for a natural formation. "Young Parham should still be buried right there, and that hill leading up to the school, that's where the settlers' cave was."

Jess shuddered at how much fucked up history was compressed in this one spot. "So, what now?" she asked. "Are we safe?"

"From them?"—he motioned with his head toward the monsters on the street—"Seems that way. Not sure about what comes next."

Jess crouched next to him. "Nadine and Royce are in Lighthouse Rock trying to stop this. Is there anything we can do?"

Hitch considered. "What lies here is in direct opposition to what Martha Lange is doing. So, maybe we can tap into that, but I need help. Tell your father to come here." He turned to Tali. "Boy, did Doris give you anything on the Atman or Mundilfœri?"

"Yes!" Tali's eyes opened wide with recognition, reaching into his rucksack, which, now empty of the pool balls, only held two tomes and a notebook.

"Good. This clearing is perfect for this, but we need to draw the combined sigil I'll give you, so we need people to step away, so the sigil isn't broken. We must be quick."

CHAPTER THIRTY-SEVEN

MOTHER

Peter sat by the fireplace in his old home, waiting. For what? He didn't know. Mother had commanded him to wait, and questioning her was pointless. For years, he'd lied to himself, thinking he had control since he left White Harbor, but he always returned, even if it drained him. Mother was his drug, his addiction, and everything else—career, marriage, family—was just a distraction. He couldn't abandon her; they needed each other. Now, he would give Mother what she'd always wanted, even if it meant he'd never see his son again. William would be alive, at least. He would save his son from his own destructive addiction.

Huh? Footsteps...

He turned around. Looked toward the hallway. There was someone there. A shadow on the floor, coming from right behind the wall that separated the living room from the hallway. A small shadow.

A child?

"William?" He stood.

No. Don't disobey. Mother said to wait!

He stalked toward the shadow. It moved. The person took a step back, hearing him approach, but he still saw the shadow on the floor. He stepped around the wall. There was a girl standing there. She was eight, perhaps even ten years old, with long, curly brown hair, blue eyes, wearing a simple but pretty blue dress that matched her keen gaze. She stood there in silence, looking up at him with a stern expression.

"Hi," Peter said, confused. "Little girl...what are you doing here?"

She didn't answer.

"I'm Peter... What's your name?"

She studied him. Her gaze showed mistrust, which he supposed made sense. He was an adult stranger. "My name's Isa." She pronounced it "*Eesa*".

"Isa. Nice to meet you. What are you doing here? This place is dangerous."

Isa shook her head. Her long mane of curly hair waved from side to side. "You can't stay here." She put her hand out, beckoning him to take it. "You have to go. Now."

Peter narrowed his eyes at this.

"William needs you." She curled her fingers at him, and without hesitation, he took her hand. She led him down the hallway, to the kitchen, and stood in front of the pantry door.

The Hole. A shudder ran through his body. *No. Wait. Why's the door closed?*

The pantry was never closed. It always stayed open as a reminder—or a threat—the punishment he feared was always there, easily accessible, waiting for him. Peter looked at Isa. She was pointing at the doorknob.

"Go through. William's on the other side."

"I can't," Peter said with a gulp. "Mother told me to stay here and wait."

The girl again shook her head, with irritation, with urgency, brown locks moving around her head like cloth on a spinning scrubber at a car wash. "You have to. William needs you before it's too late."

Peter's limbs refused to respond. He'd done terrible things at the behest of Mother, all to save William. What if going against her wishes undid their agreement? What if going through put William in danger?

"Now! Hurry!" Isa insisted.

Peter's hand flew to the knob, and he threw open the door. On the other side he didn't find a pantry, but a chapel with an altar, the same chapel from the Vanek House, except this one was inside a cavern that continued and curved left beyond the altar. From the depths beyond the bend came an ominous blue glow.

There were lit torches on rough stone pillars around the round altar—unlike the smooth pillars he remembered from the Vanek House chapel—and there were two raised stone slabs on the altar.

On one of the stone slabs lay William. Peter looked back at Isa, who was still standing at the open door, which stood in the air—no walls surrounding it. Isa gave him an encouraging nod, and he ran toward his son. "Will!" His son appeared to be asleep, wearing a white robe like what people would wear at a Christian baptism. It was too ceremonial for comfort. His chest rose and fell—he was alive. Peter grabbed his hand, shook him. The boy wouldn't wake up. "Will!" No response. *What the hell am I supposed to do?*

He looked at the other stone slab. There lay the woman he'd brought here, also wearing a white ceremonial robe. Nadine had called her Elizabeth, and he hadn't needed to look at her twice to know this was the sister his dad had talked about. He could see the resemblance at once. His long-lost sister brought back to life for some sinister purpose only Mother knew about.

(*I promised God a sacrifice of my descendant's blood, to prove my faith*)

He'd served his own sister on a silver platter to Mother to do as she pleased, and his son now lay beside her. What was the meaning of this?

He could tell she was also alive and breathing, but more shockingly—

"What the hell?"

—she was pregnant.

Quite pregnant, about nine months, in fact. She hadn't appeared pregnant when he'd taken her and brought her to Mother.

"Elizabeth." Peter gently touched the woman's shoulder. The discomfort of touching a stranger palpitating under his fingertips, considering he'd kidnapped this woman. He grabbed Elizabeth by the shoulders and gently shook her, like he'd shaken William. "Elizabeth!"

Elizabeth's eyes blinked open. She looked around, confused, no clue of where she was, then her eyes found Peter and she let out a startled cry. "No! Stay away! You're that man from the street! Stay away!"

"No, no." He held his hands toward her. "I was asked to bring you here! That was all! I swear I won't hurt you!"

"I don't believe you!"

"I think..." He hesitated. "I think you and I need to talk. You don't know who you are, right? Well, I know something about you that you don't."

"You're trying to confuse me." She shook her head and slid off the stone table, looked at William—who, to her, must be some helpless, unconscious child brought here by her kidnapper. "I don't believe you!" Her eyes darted around, and she remembered something. "The old woman!", she seethed, and moved around the stone table, keeping her distance from Peter.

"Mother."

"She's your mother? She's... She's not right! She's insane!" She looked like she was remembering something. "'There are still some preparations before Peter arrives.' That's what she said. You're Peter, right? Nadine called you Peter! Stay away!" She looked around. Stopped. Noticed the enormous belly protruding from her. She gasped in shock, eyes wide open, disbelief like someone had dumped a bucket of ice water on her. She screamed. "What—" She turned bulging, horrified eyes toward him and shouted, "What did you do to me?"

"I don't know! I found you like this!"

"This is impossible!" she said, becoming hysterical. "This doesn't make any sense!" She looked at him, eyes pleading for answers. "What is this?"

"I don't... I don't know!"

"What are you doing here?" a voice that froze Peter's soul said, demanding.

Peter and Elizabeth turned toward the deeper side of the cave, where the blue light came from. Mother was standing there, eyes blazing with anger.

"Your role in this was over long ago." She looked straight at Peter.

"Mother... You said you'd call me when you needed me."

"And did I?" she said with an angry hiss. "You were supposed to stay there. I made that space look exactly like our home, so you would feel comfortable waiting until the end came. I don't need you anymore. You've served your purpose. You're not welcome here."

"Wh-what?" Peter could tell she was furious. Had he been a little boy, he would've been cowering in a corner by now, begging not to be whipped and thrown in The Hole, but he felt angry right now. She hadn't lied. She never lied. But she had tricked him. "I don't understand... You said—"

"It doesn't matter," she sneered. "Be here, don't be here. You're irrelevant." She motioned to Elizabeth and William. "They're the only ones that matter now."

"What have you done to me?" Elizabeth demanded. "What is going on?"

"You..." Martha said, grinning at Elizabeth. "You're the gift the Lord has given to me in exchange for bringing forth His awakening."

Peter interjected. "You promised if I helped you, my son would be spared."

"Didn't I tell you your mother never lies?" She glared at him, her voice venomous. Her proud, deranged expression could strike fear into the bravest of men. "I will keep my word, but I'll repeat one last time: your role is over, Peter, you no longer matter."

"What's that supposed to mean?"

"Don't you remember?" She seemed to be grinning and scowling at the same time, her face a mask of insanity. She pointed at Elizabeth. "She walked into your bedroom, even before she was aware of her own existence. She laid down on your bed and took advantage of your lust for that bitch of yours, Jenny. She took your seed and walked out of your room. Then she was called to the town where she was given memories and a solid body, waiting until it was her time."

Peter's face twisted in horror. He remembered now, when he'd seen her stalk into the bedroom, like a ghost in a dream. He'd mistaken her for Jenny, her auburn, almost red hair, her features, so much like Jenny's, but shifting back and forth so he couldn't be certain. Then, what William had said

(*Mom was flying*)

even his son had mistaken that shape in the house—which he'd said had been walking on air toward the town—with his mother. They looked so alike. The shape had left a fingerprint on their family picture, perhaps confused about its own identity, seeing Jenny, and seeing itself in her. When he kidnapped her, at Mother's request, he'd paused for a second, his mind again mistaking her for Jenny. He'd been so numb and in shock by everything he'd seen, he hadn't made the connection.

It wasn't a dream.

He'd had sex with Elizabeth, he'd impregnated Elizabeth, he'd impregnated his sister, and his mother had planned it all.

Why? For what purpose?

"I used the Lord's power to speed up the birth," Mother said. "Now she's almost ready."

"You're sick, Mother!" The disgust on Peter's face couldn't be hidden. "You're sick! You... You made me sleep with my own sister! How could you?"

"What?" Elizabeth asked, bewildered.

Peter gave her a meaningful look, then nodded with shame.

"Your sister?" Martha asked. She sounded genuinely puzzled. This had caught her off-guard, but her expression soon changed, as she seemed to catch up. "You know about Elizabeth, then."

Martha shot a piercing gaze toward Isa, who was still standing at the door, not setting foot in the cavern. For a second, Martha's eyes displayed a hint of emotion, as if moved from looking at the girl. This was replaced by an unsettling grin. "*That's* your sister," she said, nodding at the girl. "Probably summoned by that heathen maid in some misguided attempt to help you. *That* is your sister, Elizabeth. She's been in this cave, trapped in the Void, feeding God for years."

"No," Peter said, but noticed the resemblance between the adult Elizabeth and the little girl. "Her name is Isa. She said—"

Mother let out a loud cackle. "Oh, that ignorant foreigner of a father of yours had wanted to name her Isabel, which is Spanish for Elizabeth, but when he didn't get his way, he gave her that silly pet name." Martha's voice broke a little, but it regained its strength. "Goodbye, girl. Go back to the Void with your useless father."

Martha gestured, and the door slammed shut, disappeared, leaving nothing but the other end of the cavern, where black tendrils with blue, glowing crystals bathed the darkness in cold light.

Her eyes returned to Peter, and that one glance comprised all of her contempt for her son being such a disappointment. She had no more words for him, he realized.

Her gaze now flew to Elizabeth. "As for you..."

Mother put her entire hand over Elizabeth's face before she could pull away, like an eagle's claw.

Elizabeth let out a harrowing shriek, as if electrocuted.

Martha's mouth worked, gaped. She looked as if she were choking. She convulsed, her tongue came out of her lips in an explosion of spit, and her eyes rolled back into her skull, showing nothing but white sclera.

Peter watched the scene, helpless, perplexed.

Mother started foaming at the corners of her mouth. Her body jerked uncontrollably and fell to the floor. She convulsed a few more times, then lay still.

He gawked in horror at the lifeless body of his mother. He hated her. *She's dead!* Oh, how much he hated her. *She's finally dead!* She had ruined his life. *I'm free!* She had killed his father, condemned his sister, taken his son, and tried to kill him. *I'm finally free!* She deserved to die. *Mother?*

"MOTHER!"

Peter dropped to his knees, a fierce, desperate look in his eyes. He picked her up in his arms and looked deep into those blank eyes of hers, red capillaries running all over the whites. There was no life in those eyes. No soul. She was limp as a wet rag, drool coming in rivulets out of the sides of her mouth. She showed no sign of breathing.

"Oh god!" Peter shouted, hysterical. "Oh god, no! No! Mother! Mother!"

She was dead. Martha Lange was dead. Mother was dead. He realized all of a sudden, he would give everything in the world to hear her scolding him, calling him an ingrate, insulting him. But she didn't. She couldn't. She was dead. He would've agreed to be locked in The Hole for days, to feel her fingernails digging into his arm as she pulled him toward the crawlspace trapdoor.

"Mother! Please, don't go! Don't go! I'm sorry! I'm sorry for being a bad boy, Mother! I'm so sorry! Forgive me, Mother! Forgive me!"

Bitter tears ran down his face. He grabbed her dead hand, slapped his own face with it, over and over, like a complete lunatic.

He let out an anguished wail. "Lock me in The Hole, Mother," Peter said, burying his face in her bosom. "Lock me in The Hole. I'll go quietly. I'll never disobey again. I'll be with you forever. Talk to me, Mother! Please, Mother, say something!"

"What would you like me to say?"

The voice came from Peter's side. Her voice. Mother's voice. But how? He was holding her dead body. She hadn't moved. Was the voice in his head? Had he lost his mind at last? He then turned his teary face, looked up, and there stood Elizabeth, but her face had taken on an expression he recognized well, an expression he loathed, and loved, and dreaded.

"You're a weak, mewling boy."

It was Mother.

Peter dropped Mother's corpse in a panic, and scuttled backward, away from her, a countenance of shock etched in his face.

How didn't he see it before? It was right there. The real reason he'd mistaken her for Jenny earlier. His brain now flashing the realization, in the clearest example of an Oedipus complex, Peter had chosen a wife who was a dead ringer for his mother. The only obvious difference...

Blue eyes! Jenny had green eyes! Mother's eyes are blue!

He remembered seeing that wedding picture on her dresser, that one time, when he'd dared enter her room. The beautiful blue eyes, the lightly freckled, milky-white skin, and the long auburn hair.

Jenny had long auburn hair when they'd met. Before she dyed it red.

He hadn't noticed Elizabeth's resemblance to Martha right away because she still hadn't taken on that hateful expression that was Mother's and Mother's alone.

Elizabeth was not his sister.

Elizabeth wasn't even named Elizabeth. She'd only thought her name was Elizabeth—

(*She was called to the town where she was given memories and a solid body*)

—because of an old memory of her daughter, left in her mind.

Elizabeth was Mother. Mother, when she was about the age she had when Peter was born.

He hadn't impregnated his sister. He'd impregnated his—

"Mother!" he cried, face twisted in revulsion. "That's impossible!"

"This is my gift," Martha said, running a rejuvenated hand over her face. "My gift from God: a new chance at life." She then put her hands around her large, pregnant belly. "A new chance at motherhood."

"No!" Peter protested. "NO!"

Too much to handle, too much to take in. His mind felt as if it were about to shut down.

"I will name him Peter," she said, with a rapturous grin and moist eyes. "And he will be all you never were. You—"

She couldn't finish the sentence, as she was struck with pain all of a sudden. She screamed, grabbing her belly. Contractions, sudden, continuous, faster than natural ones, shaking her entire body.

The baby's coming, Peter thought, feeling himself almost dissociate from his very being. *Peter is coming.*

She screamed again and fluid poured out from between her legs. Her water had broken. Peter scuttled further away. The horror in his face was unmoving, unchangeable, unbreakable.

Martha writhed on the floor, screaming, next to the dead body of her old self. A surreal, nightmarish scene. The screams echoed through the cavern as the woman gave birth to the child she had conceived with her own son—a child blessed by Him, by his mother's Lord, by his mother's God—as Peter witnessed the horrid event.

He shook his head in denial. Sickened at the perversion before his eyes: this woman, who lay on the floor, hollering in the pangs of unholy birth.

After eternal minutes of screaming, there was silence. All that was left now was Mother, exhausted, on the floor, in a puddle of fluid. The white, ceremonial robe was stained with blood, and between her legs, still connected to his mother by a bloody umbilical cord that came out of her, was a baby boy, who soon cried in sudden peals, as if sensing the horror of his birth.

Still clawing at the floor from hurt, Martha turned her gaze toward the newborn. She regarded it with sweat on her brow and tears in her eyes, smiling as if it was the most beautiful thing she had ever seen. She hurried, grunting with pain, and took the baby in her arms.

"My baby," she whispered, almost inaudible among the creature's cries. "My beautiful boy."

(*There are still some preparations before Peter arrives.' That's what she said.*)

Peter had arrived.

"My Peter," she cooed. "Thank you, Lord. He's perfect. My perfect Peter."

Martha looked at her disowned son, who stared in an almost catatonic state, at the obscene display before his eyes.

"Now, it is the Lord's time." Martha looked exhausted, but made herself heard. "He will come for your son. He will take him. My offer to God to guarantee His awakening."

Martha created a small black blade from the substance that flowed out of the stone floor and used it to cut the umbilical cord. Then the tip turned red-hot, and she used this to cauterize it. Peter knew this would be the last separation she ever intended to have with her perfect son—her perfect Peter.

She stood and turned away.

"Wait!" Peter cried, weeping, angry. "You promised! You promised William would be spared! You said you never lied! You promised!"

"I did," she said matter-of-factly. "Your vision of the Dark Moonlit World—the Void, the place of endless pain and torment—that's what this world will become, but your son will be spared. He won't stay here. There's another Moonlit World, the paradise God came from, where He promised to take me and my baby. The Mother's blood in your son's veins holds power from the Mothers' Covenant. God will use it to fully awaken. Your boy will die here but be reborn there, free of pain and sorrow, as this world feeds God for all eternity. You should be thankful."

"No!" Peter shouted. "Take me! I have your blood! Use me to awaken your God and take William to that other world with you! Please! I'm begging you!"

She gave him a condescending smile. "Oh, you sad, dumb boy. God needs the last of my bloodline. Of her bloodline"—she motioned toward old Martha's corpse—"and that isn't you. You would've had your chance when you were sixteen, but you left me. You're irrelevant now. God has fulfilled His part, now he will feed on your son, and turn this world into his feeding ground. The cavern exit is sealed now. You can't escape. Embrace the truth. You can't fight God."

With that, she turned her back on Peter as a slit opened in thin air and expanded, letting in bright, silver-blue light.

Mother gasped with fascination, looking through the opening. "Oh, Peter, it's beautiful!" She gave her new baby a kiss on his forehead and stepped into the portal, which closed behind her, never to be seen again.

Stunned, speechless, Peter watched as the dim blue glow from the depths of the cavern grew in intensity as the ground shook. Something was moving, something was inching closer.

God was coming.

CHAPTER THIRTY-EIGHT

GOD

"Peter!" Nadine shouted, trying to shake him out of his near-catatonic state.

She'd found the door to the mental facility's boiler room unlocked, then the open floor grate, and climbed down into the cavern, running toward the blue light. She'd made it in time to witness everything from behind an outcropping rock. Knowing what Peter's mother was capable of, she been afraid to shoot at her. If she missed, Martha would see her and freeze her on the spot with a single word. She'd waited too long, though, she thought. She'd been too afraid.

The ground shook, and that blue light kept coming closer. Something massive approached from around the bend of the cavern.

"Peter! We need to find a way out of here!" He didn't react. She kept shaking him, calling his name. She slapped him in the face, and his pale zombie's countenance turned in her direction. She fixed her one-eyed gaze on him. "It's coming! If it takes William, it'll all be over! C'mon!"

"You heard Mother," Peter spoke in a dim, absent voice. "The exit is sealed. Mother never lies."

Nadine saw them now. Hundreds of appendages, each a strange combination of feelers, legs, and tentacles, glowing an intense silver-blue with black threads running throughout. Flexible as they crawled, but turning solid and carbon-black to cling to the walls of the cavern to drag something gargantuan behind them, just out of view.

No. She wouldn't have it. People were depending on her at Cunningham's. Peter had given up. She was all that was left now. She knew what needed to be done, but she wasn't sure she could. She kneeled in front of him, grabbed his face with both her hands. "Peter. I need you to listen to me! There are people at Cunningham's. Survivors. Jess, Chuck, Royce's family. Ray and the kids might still be alive!"

"I murdered Sylvia, made Barry fall into Freddie's trap," he said, his voice coming from the depths of a dark tunnel.

"I know."

"I'm a monster."

Nadine's breath caught. She tried to suppress the horror and hate boiling inside her. She'd felt this hatred when he took Elizabeth—or who she thought was named Elizabeth. Now, it surged again, remembering Peter had caused the death of their friends, and so many others.

Angie...

She tried to control it, knowing what was coming from the cavern was the end of the world. But she couldn't stop herself. Her fist flew at his face. Peter's head snapped to the side, almost falling over. He looked at her, more present, but still lost in his grief.

"What remains of our friends, Peter—of our town—is fighting to survive! That thing"—she pointed toward the end of the cavern, where more appendages clung to the walls and ceiling—"will feed on them... on our entire world! For all eternity! Not even death will come for any of us! If it gets William, every person we know, everyone in the world, will suffer forever!"

Peter stared at her, at first not grasping what she was saying, until he appeared to react to what she'd put in his hand. He looked down at the gun, then up at her. His head shook, an almost invisible movement. "No." He appeared to awake from a daydream. "No!"

"You heard what she said!" She knew she was asking him for an impossible thing, but it was the only way. "If that thing takes William, all of humanity is doomed. If he dies now, before it takes him, he dies in peace and humanity is saved."

"No," he repeated. "I can't. Everything I did... Everything I did was for him."

"I'm sorry, Peter." She took the gun from him. Without hesitation, she ran to the stone table on the altar, where William slept, peaceful, unaware of the horrors taking place. With tears in her eyes, Nadine pointed the gun at him. "I'm so sorry, sweetie! I'm so, so sorry!"

Something struck her face, knocked her to the ground. She dropped the handgun. When she looked up, she saw Peter picking up the gun.

"What the hell do you think you're doing?" he shouted.

"It's the only way!"

Peter stared at her as if she were insane. He raised the gun, pointed it at her, tears in a constant flow.

Nadine raised an arm in front of her face.

He kept the gun trained on her as the seconds ticked by, his face contorted, conflicted, horrified. Then he let his gun arm fall to his side.

"Every man, woman, and child!" Nadine shouted, bewildered that this wasn't getting through. "Children the same age as William! Younger! Royce's little girl! Barry's little boys! In endless torment to feed that thing!"

"I can't!"

"Peter, I love William!" Her voice broke. "I loved him from the first time you brought him to my house! I loved him calling me 'Auntie Deen'! But this is bigger than him, bigger than us!"

She could see it in his face. He knew she was right. He knew it, but didn't want to accept it. He couldn't let her do it. He couldn't let her kill his only son.

Another rumble drew their attention, and there it was, at last: God.

It filled the entire cavern, its legs dragging it forward, as tall as a four-story building, and just as wide. Its head, translucent, at times hard like a chitinous helmet, at times jiggling like a jellyfish. Beneath the surface, millions of swirling, glowing tentacle-like shapes swam and spiraled in liquid, along with small, blinking spheres resembling eyes. They gave the head its bright silver-blue glow. Surrounding it was a hard, glossy black substance, like crystal, reflecting the light. Black tendrils extended from it, solidifying at the appendages to grip and pull the creature forward, then softening, imitating the flexing and extending of muscle fibers.

It's beautiful. The thought crossed Nadine's mind in a microsecond, against her better judgment, but even now, aware she'd become paralyzed with fear, she was in awe at how terrible and beautiful this entity was. She could understand why someone might be spellbound into thinking it was a God.

Snapping out of her trance, she looked at William. She couldn't let it get the boy. As fast as she could, she turned to grab him off the table.

BLAM!

Peter stood there, pointing the gun at her.

He killed me. Did he...kill me? Something burned in her thigh. There was a tear in her pant leg. Blood. Only a flesh wound.

Peter gasped. He let the gun fall to the floor like it was red-hot. He regarded the weapon as if it were the first time he'd seen it and brought his hand up to cover his mouth, eyes open in genuine shock. His knees, his whole body quavered. "What have I done?" he berated himself. "Oh god, what have I done?"

"Pick up the gun! Move!" she ordered.

Peter scrambled for the gun, took it as if it were covered in shit, and he walked off the altar.

Nadine—William still in her arms—was about to follow him when she felt something touch her foot.

In a second, she was aware what was touching her foot was one of the creature's appendages.

She was also aware of everything.

She was aware of a million/billion/trillion realities where it existed, but only one where it belonged, not a physical reality, but a metaphysical one. It only had a physical body in this one because it was required. It had moved to another reality, seeking a mate, but had spent all its energy and gotten lost in this one, where it didn't exist before. She knew it was what we would consider the "male" of the species, which is why The Circle referred to it as "He". She knew it was young, only 13.7 billion years old. She knew it was scared. She knew the people who lived in the area long before the town was founded—natives known as the Tillamook—had mistaken its attempts to feed as the land itself wishing to remain untouched, and so it had remained dormant, barely sentient. She knew it didn't feed on suffering, like Martha Lange had stated, but powerful emotions. However, the strongest emotion it had felt had been from those people who had entered the cave in 1966 of the human calendar, and it had awakened it, though it was still weak. She knew the black threads were minuscule entities that had stuck to it as it traveled and kept a symbiotic relationship with it and could only live in the artificial reality it had created for them, unless they inhabited a physical body. She knew it feared and hated humanity and only wanted to leave this reality to return to its own, but it also found humanity an addictive source of energy, so it would keep them alive for sustenance for all eternity, feeding on them even from its own universe, like a remote stomach.

But...it would spare Nadine. She saw it as if it were already happening. A world of plenty. A version of this world where strife still existed, but it was fair strife. Where none starved, where conflict existed but was resolved through dialogue and fair compromise. A world where war did not exist, where she could be born again and have the life she'd always wanted. She knew freedom did not exist in any universe where sentient life had evolved, but this was as close to it as any sentient being could ever have. It even offered to give her back her sister, so they could live their lives in this new world.

All she needed to do was give it the boy.

The boy whose family it had imbued with a tiny fraction of its power, so it could grow, mature, evolve, become nutritious.

For a moment, Nadine couldn't move. She could feel the offer being made in her mind, over and over, little by little breaking down her defenses, her morals, her humanity.

Yes. Yes. Yes. Yes. Yes. YES!

"No!" she shouted and moved her legs away from the intrusive touch of the entity, and she kept running until she was off the altar.

The last image she'd seen, right before the appendage lost contact with her skin, was a nightmare landscape of torture and fear, and she knew this was what Peter had seen—what had driven him insane—its other "stomachs" from countless other worlds. She knew the truth now. She also knew she could never allow that to happen here.

She stumbled, fell beside Peter.

"You have to do it now! There's no time!"

He shook his head.

"I saw it! The fields with pillars of living bodies under the blue moon!"

He turned his perplexed eyes toward her.

"William can't survive!" She said this with earnest grief in her face. "He can't!"

Peter took a horrified glance at Nadine and looked at his son lying on the floor. His boy, his pride and joy, all he had left in the world. Then he looked at the approaching monstrosity. This elder god from places unknown. He remembered the fields of screaming people. Children. Babies. But his son. He couldn't, he simply couldn't. How could he ever do such a thing?

"I can't," he said, in a pleading, hopeless voice, looking at Nadine with desolate eyes. "I won't."

She placed her hand on his and spoke in a calm voice, but he could sense her anxiety, her urgency. "Think of the options. If William dies before that thing takes him, he will rest. He won't even feel it. It will be like he passed on in a dream, and humanity will be saved."

"You don't understand." Peter sobbed, sniffled like a kid. "I can't do it." Peter looked at his son lying on the floor. He looked like the most beautiful being in all creation.

Peter picked up the gun, held it with both hands and rested it between his knees. He looked down at it. He peered at his son again.

My boy.

He stood up. Tears and mucus streaming down his face, which was now red and contorted in an expression of unbearable anguish. Nadine's words sounded logical and right, but his parental instincts surpassed the concepts of logic and righteousness in every way.

Trembling hands brought the gun up, pointing at the boy who lay on the floor. So peaceful, unaware of the fate about to befall him.

I can't! I can't! God, help me! I have to, but I can't! Why me? Why my son? Why all of this?

He knew if he were to do such an unspeakable act and actually shoot his son, the next step would be to place the gun to his own head and pull the trigger. He would've saved the world, but it would've ended for him. If his son died, so would he.

Peter pointed the gun, his hand still trembling. He was sweating, sobbing, shaking his head in denial of the monstrous truth.

"I won't..."

He put the gun down. Fell to his knees beside Nadine.

"Listen to me, you fucking coward!" Nadine's tone shift caught him by surprise. "You are *not* a good person! Yeah, I know I said you were. You're not. Thousands have died today because you couldn't stay away from your mother. Callum, Sylvia, Barry, Bobby, Royce!" She choked back a sob. "Angie! You did that! You even killed Sylvia with your own hands, you asshole, but *now* you can't?"

"He's my son, Nadine!"

She swallowed hard, took in a ragged breath. "He's going to die, anyway!" He stared at her, his face a mask of horror. "That can't be changed! He will never wake up! When that thing touched me, I saw it! He can never wake up from this trance he's in! He's gone either way! It's a choice between condemning your remaining friends and the rest of the world or not! If you won't do it, I swear I'll wrestle that gun out of your hands and do it myself! Decide! Now!"

The creature was now crawling over the altar. They felt the tremor as the stone pillars and the stone tables crumbled as its weight crushed any resistance.

The cruel simplicity of things finally pierced the barriers in his mind. If William could never wake up, there wasn't much to ponder. Not a sentimental justification, but a cold, pragmatic one. Like murdering Sylvia but reversing the perspective from William to everyone else in the world. A simple choice: yes or no, black or white, day or night, life or death. It should've been clear since Nadine explained it the first time. He'd refused to listen. He didn't *want* to listen. Who would want to listen to the truth when the truth was so brutal?

Now he knew.

Sometimes, bad things happened to good people. He wasn't a good person, but his son was.

Peter raised his eyes, reddened from the salty tears blurring his vision. The colossal entity was close. The swirling threads in its massive head seemed almost eager, hungry. It was so close now. Time was running out.

He looked at his son, taking in his sleeping face for the last time. He pointed the gun at his head. His hands shook spasmodically. *Steady,* he thought. *I have to do it in one shot. I don't want my boy to suffer.* He was taking in deep, quivering gasps of air.

That demon was closer, its hundreds of appendages pulling it toward them, making the ground shake, its glow bathing them in cold blue light.

Peter lingered a moment longer on his son's face—his gaze almost a gentle caress—savoring every microsecond of life he could allow him. So beautiful. So much a little version of his dad. He wished he could see his son's green eyes one last time—one last reminder of the green he'd inherited from Jenny—but it was better like this, better if he didn't see.

"I love you, son... I'm so sorry."

Peter pressed the gun to the boy's forehead. He shuddered at the slight give of his skin against the muzzle. He closed his eyes and turned his head away. His finger began to squeeze the trigger. Then—

"Daddy—"

BLAM!

A gateway opened in the middle of the clearing in The Pines, at the center of the symbol Hitch and Tali had drawn on the ground. The gateway was similar to the one they'd crossed into the sacrificial chapel on the Second Night, but this one was larger, allowing more than one person to pass. On the other side, there was something that looked like a cavern of some kind. A blue light filled the entire space, as if the moon itself were coming toward them. Jess thought she could see two figures in the distance, apparently on their knees in front of the source of the light.

"Shit, we have no guns left." She regarded the knife in her hand.

"Weapons won't do you any good there, anyway," Hitch said, sitting in the wheelchair next to her. The symbol had been drawn around the wheelchair to make sure it wouldn't run over the lines as it rolled into the portal.

"Are you sure you want to go in there?" Jess asked.

Hitch nodded, placing a hand on the rucksack he'd gotten from Tali. "That thing and I have never seen each other face to face, but it knows me. I spent ninety years feeding it and got nothing but pain from it." He peered up at Ray, who was holding the wheelchair handles. "*You*, however, you don't have to do this. You should stay here with Giffen's children. They need you. Cunningham can push me there."

"You don't get to tell me what to do," Ray spat. "We might need to carry Royce and Nadine back, in whichever state they are, Chuck is old, and he's exhausted."

"Alright, let's go," Jess said.

They crossed over, their shoes and the wheels crackling on the wet floor of the cavern. They pushed forth as fast as they could. The tremor in the ground and all around them was undeniable, terrifying, making the whole of their humanity feel minuscule. Only a few feet from the entry point, they spotted Freddie Parham's corpse lying on the ground, in a patch of darkened earth that had soaked in his blood. They spared no more than a glance and a sigh for him as they pushed onward.

Soon, the figure they'd seen as the source of the blue light came into view. An all-encompassing form, crawling like an earthworm through the enormous cave toward two figures they recognized now as Nadine and Peter, and lying in Peter's arms, some other figure.

Royce? Jess thought with alarm. *No. Too small.*

Nadine turned her tear-soaked face toward them and gasped, noticing them, then regarded Hitch with apprehension.

Peter looked catatonic. He didn't even react to their presence. His face was an eerie shade of pale, a living corpse. Jess gasped when she spotted William lying in his arms, a bloody hole in the boy's temple.

"Help me pick them up!" Nadine said.

Jess and Ray were too busy staring at the monstrosity coming their way to hear her.

"Jess! Ray! Please!"

Shaking off some of her panic, Jess tried to pry the dead boy off Peter's hands, but he clung to him. He would not let him go. She looked at Ray. "Help me pull him to his feet. We have to get him out."

Ray regarded the dead boy, then the gun beside Peter. "Why should we?"

"What?"

"He murdered Sylvia in cold blood. Barry would be with us if it weren't for him. He clearly just shot his son."

"Ray! He's one of us. We're not leaving him here. He will answer for what he did, but we're not leaving him!"

He flashed her a begrudging glare but bent down and lifted Peter up by one arm. Nadine lifted from his other. He didn't so much stand up as was craned to a standing position, as if he were a human-sized doll, looking crucified between the two.

Jess gawked at the oncoming creature, grabbing the wheelchair handles from Ray. "Let's go. Right now!"

They shuffled away as fast as they could, putting some distance between them and the creature, passing Freddie's corpse for the last time. They stopped in front of the gateway.

"What about that thing?" Nadine said. "If it gets out of here—"

"It won't," Hitch said. "Go. All of you. Leave me here."

Nadine stared at Jess as if seeking approval, clearly not trusting the man who had murdered Callum and made Freddie murder Leroy.

Jess stopped pushing him, gave her a nod, turned to Hitch. "Good luck. This doesn't make us even, but I appreciate it."

He exhaled. "Remember the small grave I pointed out in The Pines? Nothing can make us even. Go." Before they took off, he reached out with a hand and grabbed Ray's arm tight.

Ray looked down at him with a confused sneer.

Hitch gave him an earnest look. "Christopher..."

Ray frowned, nonplussed.

"He was the love of my life. I did something unforgivable to keep him alive, and my reward was losing him. I deserved worse than death and that's what I got. You did *nothing* to deserve to lose Giffen."

Ray gulped, still bemused by what the man was doing.

"Nothing. I mean it. I'm sorry about my part in all this. I'm truly sorry." He felt strange realizing his voice had broken a bit while saying this, and his eyes felt watery. "You two deserve the life Christopher and I couldn't have back then. Never doubt that for a second."

Ray gave him an acknowledging nod, a teary smile, then disappeared through the gateway with the other two adults and the dead child.

On the other side, Tali broke the sigil as instructed, and the gateway closed.

Hitch turned the wheelchair around, watched the creature coming toward him.

The Ritual of the Four nights had been all about the creature, Uolmin, accumulating enough power to leave this plane. Each night feeding on both the electrical power of the town and the emotional turmoil of its people. The Fourth Night—the eternal night—would have started after the last sacrifice, the last of Martha Lange's bloodline, infused with Uolmin's incubated power. This would have given it the final boost it needed to not just escape this reality but tether it to itself so it could feed on it for eternity. Except Martha Lange's blood wasn't the only one with power.

He had tapped into Uolmin's power thousands of times. His blood would do as well. It wasn't as powerful as the Mother's, so it wouldn't allow Uolmin to create the tether. It would allow it to leave, though. That needed to happen. It wouldn't do to keep it here for another three hundred years, waiting for the next Martha Lange to come along and succeed.

Hitch reached into his pocket, pulled out his phone, searched the pictures he'd taken of the glyphs when talking to himself as Curling in the reality bubble. In particular, the glyph his old self had made sure he photographed.

He remembered what Curling had said: "*If things go badly, you can use this to send yourself to a reality bubble... You'll be dropped off a fair distance beyond those damned mountains. If you're injured, you can place yourself in a dormant state; let the reality bubble heal you as much as it can. You can still live a life.*"

"*I can't take a whole town of four thousand people into a reality bubble if things go sour,*" Hitch had answered then. "*I can only move one person.*"

I could still use this for myself, he thought selfishly, for a second. *Have my cake and eat it too.*

He could let Uolmin take his blood, take his pain, and just before dying, he could activate the glyph. Get himself far away from here, heal his wounds, live. Get a job, fall in love, get married, buy a home, get a golden retriever, vacation with his husband, have piña coladas by the beach, die an old man while his new love holds his hand.

Tempting…

Except, even now, another chance at life held no appeal for him. He'd already had a life with Christopher in a little cabin in the woods, with their pigs, their hens, and a warm fireplace to sit by. While it wasn't the life he could have today, they'd spent twenty-seven years together. Twenty-seven good years. It ended in tears, but don't all relationships? He'd held Christopher's hand as he died in their home, told him he loved him one last time before his eyes closed for good.

No. He knew coming here he had no intention of using the glyph on himself.

Uolmin was almost upon him.

He pulled out Tali's drawing block and the blood chalk out of the rucksack. He would only have one chance to get Curling's glyph right, a glyph he'd never drawn before.

He drew the larger symbol, then got to working on the sub-glyphs. "Time," he mumbled to himself. "Displacement. Physical state. Distance to subject. Damn, I don't know this one, an estimate, two miles? No, let's cast wide, just in case. Three miles. Dormant state. How long would be enough? Also, Time from event. This is the tricky one. If I choose negative time, can it reach back? If so, how long? Might work, though. Okay. Here goes nothing." He placed his hand on the glyph. The red lines glowed white on the paper, with a slight shimmer. He didn't know what this meant. Nothing he could do. It would either work or it wouldn't. He wouldn't be alive to find out, anyway.

Once done with this, he looked forward. The gigantic being was now about ten feet from him, its appendages clinging to the wheelchair.

"Yeah, I know," Hitch said. "You're pissed. We don't get everything we want all the time. You don't get the all-you-can-eat buffet. All you get is a two-hundred-year-old soul, overcooked, tough as a leather boot. But hey, look on the bright side, bud...you get to go home with a full stomach."

One of the tentacles circled around his torso, picked him up.

He sneered. "I hope it gives you the runs."

The creature pulled him through the film that covered its head and into the thick, liquid chaos inside. The light felt thick as it entered his eyes, his nose, and mouth. Soon, his body dissolved into millions of particles in the intensifying glow.

All that was left behind were the wheelchair, the rucksack, and the drawing block with the shimmering glyph.

Peter stared at his boy's bare feet. *What happened to his shoes?* He moved his gaze up the boy's legs. *So still, is he asleep?* His stomach, his chest. *I can't tell if he's breathing. Might be he's just breathing*

too slowly. His neck, then his face, his beautiful lips, his tiny nose. His closed eyes. *So, he* is *asleep, then*. There was something near his temple. Something was not so clear. He could see the individual hairs on his forehead, the little pores, the tiny hairs on his skin.

He wondered what was wrong. He didn't really see anything to contradict the thought the boy was only sleeping, save for that gut feeling that told him he was too still...and that blurry area near his temple. Blurry. Like his own brain was blocking out the sight to prevent him going insane from whatever it was hiding. Hysterical blindness. So, he focused on it, tried hard to see it. But why would he want to know what the blurry image was, when his own brain knew it wasn't good for him?

Because it's the truth, he thought, using an area of his mind independent from the one blocking his sight. *And sometimes the truth is horrible, unbearable, and unfair. Sometimes, bad things happen to good people.*

He had to know. He had to know the answer to a question, but even the question seemed to elude him, until he reached up, catching the thought in his mind like a mosquito buzzing around his head. What was the thought?

Did I kill my own son? Why would I ask that?

He tried harder to focus his eyes on the strange blur. It became clearer and clearer. First, he was able to see the edges, and noticed whatever this thing on his temple was, was shapeless and had no outlines. It was red, and it stretched into his hair. His vision's clarity continued to grow toward the center. Red, uneven, horrible.

And when he reached the center, he beheld the undeniable hole. It was red, black, and wet.

He had shot his son.

Time and space were flipped upside down and turned around. He perceived something like a roar, like a plane engine, all the way in the back of his head. Then another one on top of it, a little louder. Then another one. And another one. And another one. Raising the decibels to ear-shattering levels. Another one. Another one. Ten more. Ten million more.

He realized it was himself, screaming out of control, as he lay on his knees next to his son's body, surrounded by a large crowd of people. He sobbed, wailed all sorts of incoherent words that held no actual language to them.

He took long, asthmatic gasps for air, but the air had lost all oxygen. And when the air came out—

"OH GOD!"

—it was full of sorrow, grief, pain most crushing.

"Oh god! GOOOOD!"

His hand went out to his son. It hovered over him, one inch away, but it didn't touch him. Touching him would make him real. Touching him would make *it* real.

"He's dead! Oh-god-my-god-oh-no! My boy's dead!"

He grabbed William's hand and squeezed it tight, as he let out a moan saturated, infused, and overflowing with sorrow and hopelessness.

"I'm sorry! I—"

He moaned again.

"Please, forgive me!"

He hugged the boy close to his body. Staining his forehead with blood and diluting it with his tears.

"I love you! I'm sorry! I'm so sorry! Oh, God!"

He kissed his son's cheek and felt how quickly his face had gone cold and how his skin didn't react to his touch. He kept his face flat against the boy's chest, and he screamed with no control or shame.

And as he screamed, the earthquakes began.

The crowd around Peter screamed in terror. People held each other, looked around as the mountains moved to one side and the other, as if they were on a truck's flatbed on rocky terrain. A black-and-white Border Collie, perhaps the only surviving dog in town, barked madly at the chaos, running from one side of the clearing to the other. Trees fell, landslides ran down the mountains, the school buildings up the slope broke apart and were swallowed up by the earth, along with the creatures on the other side of the fence. A dark chasm opened all around them, and yet The Pines remained untouched. The land they were standing on shook, but the ground held as if the earth itself refused to split open and the trees refused to fall.

Peter, however, noticed nothing of this. All he could do was scream. Scream louder than the crowd. Scream almost to the point of forcing his soul to vacate his body, but not quite.

Royce stood on the edge of Lighthouse Rock, facing the town. The ground shook beneath him and the sea grew turbulent. He'd been able to escape the cell block by the skin of his teeth. Not unscathed, though. His breath came in ragged, wet gasps, and blood dripped from the wounds Freddie had inflicted and those he got while escaping the creatures in the building. He knew he wouldn't last much longer.

Now, in the shockingly bright light of the silvery-blue moon—despite the rain and the clouds streaking through the sky—Royce could see the Crescent Mountains and the town. Scattered fires flickered in the distance, likely to be extinguished by the downpour. His attention, however, was fixed on a tiny cluster of lights on the east side of town.

The Pines.

"Fancy seeing the only other YouTube celebrity in White Harbor here," a voice said from behind.

Royce turned to see Xavier Poe Kane, coming toward him, his steps unsteady on the shaky ground, his tiny LED flashlight poking out of his chest pocket, swaying this way and that.

He reached up with a hand and put the flashlight out. "That's better. I want to see the show *au naturel*."

"You know that means naked, right?" Royce said.

Xavier chuckled. "You wish."

"What are you doing here?"

"Becoming a legend, man. I walked here from the other side of the island. I was tossing a waterproof baggie into the ocean, far as I could. Figured the edge of the island marked the town limits and someone might one day find it."

"What was in the baggie?" Royce asked in a serene voice that didn't match the chaos around them.

"My cell phone. Videos of... Well, I think you're about to see."

Royce didn't ask any further questions.

They stared at the distance for a while, calm as if the earth and sea weren't shaking beneath their feet.

"Don't you got family in town?" Xavier asked.

Royce nodded. Pointed at the lights he was seeing in the distance.

Xavier squinted. "The Pines?"

He nodded again. "I know they're there. I've been following the flashlights since they appeared near Cunningham's, so I know it's them. I know they figured out where the safe place was."

"The Pines. Huh... Kinda makes sense, come to think of it."

They watched as the mountains moved with a life of their own. To their left, something colossal emerged from the ocean, shedding rocks and coral as cubic tons of water cascaded off its body. It rose, towering as high as the distant Crescent Mountains. The island's left side crumbled and sank, pulled by the water rushing into the void left by the creature, taking the criminal patient wing and the restored lighthouse with it, disappearing in a thunderous splash.

Royce and Xavier shielded their faces from the spray, a quiet understanding passing between them that soon the entire island would crumble into the ocean, dragging them along.

The creature's head rose higher, revealing a rounded form glowing bright blue, with countless swirling shapes inside. A mane of wriggling, translucent blue tentacles hung from it, and it supported its eel-like body on thicker versions of those tentacles. Black, vein-like structures swam through the appendages, like organic rebar, giving them support.

By the time the tentacle-like legs straightened and raised the body to its tallest position, it touched the clouds above.

"This is beautiful!" Xavier shouted, excited and in awe.

Royce didn't answer. He'd been overcome by terror as he watched the creature's body continue to rise in sequence from the ocean toward the town. In his mind, he did as he often did when he needed to stop himself from having an anxiety attack, and he recited the names of his daughter's dolls in alphabetical order.

Amelie...Ashlyn...Cecily...Felicity...

The entire western edge of the Crescent Mountains rose, shattered, and crumbled as the creature stood from under them. If there were still people in cars waiting for someone to help them cross the chasm near the Blue Overlook, they would be plummeting into the ocean right now, among metric tons of rock and earth.

"That's where my cabin was," Xavier said, as the first of the mountain peaks disintegrated.

From where they stood, it looked like a sequential detonation. Mountaintops cracked, exploded—sending dust and rocks and trees flying in the air—then fell apart as the ocean rushed in to fill the leftover chasm. One after the other, they broke to pieces as the unfathomable creature's body continued to shake an entire mountain range off its back. It was during this process they noticed the stony mountaintops locals used to refer to as The Horns were indeed horns, or fins, or vertebrae sticking out of the creature's back. They glowed an intense silver-blue.

Gwen-Gail the Gracious Girlie-Girl...

Along with the mountains, the town itself broke apart, taking buildings, cars and—they presumed—people with them. They could see eruptions of earth, like mud geysers, and bursts of fire as gas mains and tanks exploded, the sound reaching them only seconds later, like thunder after lightning.

Josefina...Kaya...

As the sequential destruction of White Harbor continued its path, it was now coming around to the part that made Royce's hair stand on end. The domino effect was coming down the eastern side of the mountain range, the explosions advancing toward the tiny spot where all of those lights danced, like the last bastion of life in a dying world.

"Please," Royce muttered. "Please, please, please, be safe!"

One hill crumbled, then another, then another, advancing toward the lower hills where The Pines were located, then—

Royce held his breath.

Keisha...Nanae the Nicest Nanny...

The next section of the creature's body rose, skirting The Pines, on the inner side of the mountain range, leaving the small patch of land completely intact, and—almost by magic—untouched by landslides or debris, connected to the mainland by a narrow piece of the lowest hills, where the survivors would be able to escape, or so he hoped.

"YEAH!" Royce shouted, ignoring the stabbing pain from all his assorted wounds, seeing the waving flashlights still shining through the dust and debris. "FUCK, YEAH!"

They could almost see the creature's entire body now.

Its long, eel-like form was covered in black, armored plating, with blue light shining between the segments, reflecting off the dark plates. Its head was a glowing, jellyfish-like mass atop leg-like tentacles. The tail, now rising from the ocean, was covered with glowing blue orbs in each armor-plated segment—which Royce recognized from his boat trip to the island. They were colossal, yet glowed with an eerie beauty. He realized they were likely the last thing he would ever see.

The tail rose out of the water, snaking, coming fast like a shark's fin, making water erupt into the air in a violent spray.

Rebecca...Rae-Rae... Susie-Q the Q-test... Wilhemina...

Xavier placed a hand on Royce's shoulder. "Looks like this is it, man. Any regrets before you go?"

Royce shook his head, pointed at the cluster of lights in The Pines, still visible just past the spray from the emerging tail. "My wife and my baby are fine. I know that. No regrets."

At this point, everything looked like it was in slow motion. To Royce's left, the creature rose out of the ocean and hovered in the air. Its tentacle legs went limp and dangled only a few feet off the tumultuous surface. It reminded him of one of those dancing paper and cloth dragons at Chinese New Year celebrations. To his right, the tail rose out of the water, skirting the island. Then, the entity flashed and disappeared into thin air as if it were made of mist, from the head to the tip of the tail, not before giving a powerful swing, sending an enormous wave rushing toward the island.

Zoey...

The inside of the wave flashed bright blue before the tail vanished from within it, leaving only the massive wall of water that devastated the remains of the mental facility, made the last half of the island break apart, and sent him and Xavier spinning into a watery grave, among rocks, earth, and chunks of the building.

EPILOGUE

THE BEGINNING IS THE END IS THE BEGINNING

1992

It was a beautiful day bathed in warm sunshine. The sky stretched forever in a cloudless, cerulean blue. Ray climbed back over the railing at the Blue Overlook with a beaming grin on his face. He raised a triumphant fist and let out a loud, "Woo-hoo! I did it!" right before his left foot caught on the guardrail and he went tumbling forward.

Barry put his arms out and caught him, and Ray clung to his T-shirt with both hands, stopping before he fell face-first onto the gravel. "Dude, watch it!" Barry said with sincere concern as he helped him to the other side.

"Whoops, sorry." Ray flashed a bashful grin as he regained his balance, one hand still clinging absentmindedly to the larger kid's shirt.

"Wasn't that the hand he was just using to hold his wiener while he peed?" Freddie asked, giving them a sideways grin with his head cocked and an eyebrow raised.

"Um…" Ray looked at his hand—a fistful of Barry's purple T-shirt clutched between his fingers—and immediately let go. "Oh, crap."

Barry blushed bright red, cleared his throat and took a discreet step back.

"I think that means you're officially engaged," Freddie said. "Brickhouse, as is custom, you mustn't wash that shirt, and wear it always, so Plus-One's penis germs will keep other potential suitors away. Make sure other people don't touch the shirt, though, or they'll become infected."

"Stop calling him Plus-One," Barry said.

"Stop calling me Plus-One," Ray said at the same time.

"They're talking in sync now!" Freddie turned back to look in mock-horror at the rest of the Vigilantes. "The penis germs are taking hold! No one is safe!"

Bobby, approaching him from behind, grabbed his head, and pushed it forward, mussing his hair. "C'mon, man, stop it. You're being gross!"

"Fine!" He pushed Bobby away and giggled like a hyena as he gave him the finger. "When we're all penis-germ zombies, remember I warned you!"—he pointed at Barry—"Patient zero! Right there!"

"Well, actually," Callum said, standing by the guardrail, giving an awkward push to his glasses, "it's not that rare to have another person wear their pheromones on a handkerchief or some other piece of clothing, like at social gatherings or balls, or bars, or nightclubs. The purpose is different, though. The musk is supposed to entice a potential mate."

Freddie motioned toward him. "He just used the words 'balls', 'musk', and 'entice' in a single breath...but *I'm* gross?"

Sylvia was now done crossing over the guardrail, herself having completed the ritual of pissing over the edge of the overlook with Nadine's assistance. "Well, it's done." She sounded happy to have gotten the damn thing over with. "Your stupid initiation ritual is complete."

"Yay!" Ray said, raising a hand for a high five. "Go, Team Asia!"

Sylvia stared at his hand, expressionless. "You're joking, right?"

"Oh." His smile vanished, and he wiped his hand on his pants.

Sylvia turned to Jess, who was sitting down on a large blanket they'd set on the gravel parking lot with a cooler and a picnic basket covered in punk band stickers. "Bastards of Young" by The Replacements playing on a silvery boombox. "Can we eat now?" her eyes shifted to Ray, then back. "Also, pass Ray his sandwich. Don't let his hands anywhere near the food."

Jess held up a pack of wet wipes. "I brought some baby wipes. Would that help?"

Again, Sylvia glanced at Ray, curled her lip, then turned back to Jess. "No."

"Alright, alright guys," Bobby said. "Can we get off Ray's penis-germ hands for a moment?"

"Bro, all I heard was 'can we get off Ray's penis?'" Leroy said, sitting on the left side of Jess's blanket.

"Please define 'get off,'" Royce added from her right. "Coz I don't know if you mean—"

Jess slapped him over the head with the pack of wet wipes.

"Ow!"

"Stop it." She then shoved a sandwich in his open mouth. "Here. Keep your mouth full so people don't keep sayin' you're a fuckin' dumbass."

"Ahm nawd a nuhmuss," he said while chewing.

Peter, who had kept chuckling throughout the entire exchange, poured himself some 7-Up.

Nadine took the next sandwich Jess held up with her hand and dropped next to him on a small cushion she'd brought for herself. "The level of maturity of our little group sure leaves a lot to be desired."

Leroy turned to his brother. "She's talking all mature-like now."

"She's a girl," Royce answered. "They do that right around the time they start bleeding out of the—"

Jess slapped him again.

"Ow! Shit! Sorry!"

Callum sat down. "Well, it's actually a known fact, biologically, females mature faster than males. That's why it's beneficial for males to be around them during pre-adolescence."

"What happened to 'no girls allowed' a year ago?" Royce asked.

Callum glanced at Sylvia and puffed his chest. "It takes a mature man to admit he was wrong."

"Oh, come on." Sylvia smiled. "You've always been one of the most mature boys I've met. Give yourself some credit."

Callum grinned with pride.

Freddie snatched a sandwich off Jess's hand and sat beside Bobby with half the sandwich clutched in his teeth.

Ray and Barry sat next. Jess passed them the baby wipes without saying a word. Barry passed Ray one, took one, and discreetly wiped at his shirt.

Jess glanced at Peter, who was still chuckling. "You're kinda quiet today, Petey-boy."

He ran his fingers over four tiny scabs on his forearm. Scabs left from the last time his Mother had violently grabbed his arm. "I'm just happy."

"Aw, Norman's about the get all corny on us," Freddie said.

Peter blushed.

Barry gave him a pat on the back with his large paw. "Don't listen to him. Go ahead, man."

"A year ago, I didn't have any friends. Now I have all of you. Guess I'm just thankful." He paused for a moment, surrounded by smiles. "Also, you're giving Ray a lot of crap about his penis germs, but nobody's pointing out Sylvia also pissed off the edge of the cliff and she hiked up her panties and didn't wipe."

Sylvia's jaw dropped.

Everyone stared in silence.

"Mad respect, Norman," Freddie said. "Mad respect."

Nadine was the first to break, 7-Up spraying out of her mouth as she burst out laughing, followed by Jess.

"That reminds me," Peter said. "Nadine and Jess didn't wipe either when they did it. Just walked around with a pee stain down their leggings, like it was nobody's business."

At that point, the entire group laughed in unison.

"Who the fuck are you and what did you do with innocent little Norman?" Royce asked.

They spent that afternoon laughing, eating sandwiches, drinking soda, listening to music, and capped it off at the Harrell theater with popcorn and *Pet Sematary Two*, which Bobby had warned them was an impressively shitty movie, with Edward Furlong destroying any career he might have had after *Terminator* 2. The author of the original novel it was based on had even asked for his name to be removed from the film.

It had been one hell of a fun day.

There was nothing better than popcorn and a shitty movie among friends.

2025

It was a rainy October afternoon, of the kind in which the world was defined in intermingling layers of gray, concealing the sun's face.

Peter sat in silence by the window of his room in Oregon State Hospital's psychiatric care unit. On the desk behind him, two mugs and a carafe of coffee sat untouched, the liquid likely stale and bitter by now. Every afternoon, before visiting hours, he brewed coffee, set two mugs, and waited by the window.

He sat. He stared. He never spoke.

Ray didn't work in Peter's unit, but he visited at least once a week, hoping his former friend would break his silence. It wasn't psychiatric mutism—Peter had made a conscious choice not to speak. In either case, Ray knew the coffee wasn't for him. It wasn't his visit he was waiting for.

He placed a hand on Peter's back, getting no reaction. "Alright, man. I'll see you next week." Peter's glazed-over eyes remained fixed on the trees outside. "I can't justify what you did, Peter, but I do forgive you. Maybe, one day, she will too. In the meantime, if you ever want to talk, I'm willing to listen."

Nothing.

"Uh, hey, Ray?"

For a second, he was startled, almost thinking Peter had spoken, but the voice had come from behind him, from the door. He turned to see Derek Espinoza, a charming, rather good-looking nurse who also worked at Oregon State. "Oh, hey Derek, what's up?"

"We're a little short-staffed in the ICU, and we were wondering if you could lend us a hand. Just an hour of your time?" He put his palms together. "Pretty-please?" He winked, giving him a huge smile.

Ray chuckled, tried not to blush. "Sure." He walked out of the room to join his colleague. He closed the door but cast one last glance at Peter through the door's observation window.

His phone rang. The caller ID read NADINE.

He glanced at Derek. "Hey, I really need to take this. Think you can spare me for a couple minutes?"

"No worries. We have a few transfers from Bay Area Hospital we need help with. They're not here yet. Should buy you, say, ten minutes?"

"You're the best."

"Oh, I know." Derek winked again, already walking away. "You gotta buy me a drink for each minute past that, though."

Ray smiled back, not sure how to react to his colleague's not-so-subtle advances. Once Derek was out of earshot, he picked up the call. Grinned. "*Bonjour, Mademoiselle Québec!*"

He could hear Nadine laugh on the other end. "You say that as if I can actually speak *any* French at all."

"Not a problem, coz that's literally the extent of mine. I learned only those words, specifically." He laughed. "How's Canada? Did you already try their world-renowned public health system?"

"Not yet, but I heard it's delicious. Poutine, though... Not really a fan, to be honest."

"Don't say that out loud. They hang you for that over there."

She chuckled. "I'm having a wonderful time. Right now, I'm sitting at this beautiful street cafe having a cup of coffee the size of a soup bowl."

"I'll pretend I'm not green with envy. Just kidding, I'm happy for you."

"How's Salem working out?"

"Three years later and I'm still getting used to the fact I've apparently *always* been from here."

There was an uncomfortable silence between them.

"Psychiatrists officially named it 'White Harbor syndrome' this year, did you hear? A psychiatric condition affecting survivors of the 2022 Oregon earthquake. Patients recall detailed memories of a town called White Harbor, where over four thousand people supposedly died, but there's no evidence the town ever existed—no rubble, no corpses, no records." He gasped, remembering something. "Oh! Right! This is new. Let me tell you this one!"

"I don't want to talk about White Harbor, Ray. I'm kind of trying to leave it behind, you know?"

"No, trust me. This is cool! Listen. Earlier this year, someone found a little air-tight bag with a phone in it—washed up on the shore. It belonged to Xavier Poe Kane. Remember him?"

"Sure."

"He was in the cavern!" He waited for Nadine's reaction but only got the street noise. "Sonofabitch actually recorded himself with that creature! The video made it online, and now paranormal freaks all over the world are losing it! There are Reddit threads, YouTube videos, dissecting every frame. Some insist it's a hoax, 'shitty CGI', but the true believers? They're all over it, talking about a government coverup, Xavier sightings, Xavier merch, video documentaries: 'Xavier: Rogue Area 51 official', 'My sister had Xavier's baby', shit like that. Guy's become like Big Foot."

She slurped some coffee. "Good for him."

"Alright, fine, Miss I'm-so-over-it. Back to me and Salem, then. Did you know I apparently grew up and went to school here? My siblings all remember growing up here. There are pictures! I recognize the pics themselves, but I know we didn't take them *in* Salem. There's even an old restaurant space in town which was supposed to be my parents' restaurant, and I inherited it from them. That's spooky, right? I mean, something rewrote our entire lives, and they couldn't even make us billionaires in the process."

"Look on the bright side"—she didn't match his jovial tone—"at least your siblings exist. No one remembers Angie. I never had a sister. Bobby, Royce, Sylvia, Cal, Barry, them and four thousand other people, never existed, and our lives were rewritten to accommodate everyone who died never existing."

"According to Lillian, Tracy's birth certificate doesn't show a father's name, like he was some deadbeat dad that didn't want his name included." He let out a cynical scoff. "Jesus, even reality-altering elder gods are racist. She's tried to find a legal way to fix this, but you can't register the name of someone who didn't exist as the father of your kid. Lillian says she's at least glad Tracy's too young, so this might not impact her as hard as it could. She still asks about him, though. A lot."

"I wouldn't have made it to the cavern without Royce. He helped save the world. He was also a wonderful dad. He deserved so much better."

Ray sighed.

"On that subject," she added, "how are Barry's kids?"

Ray flinched as if she'd poked him with a needle. "They're surprisingly okay. Growing up fast. They miss their dad, even if Barry's step-uncle claims to have never met him. He remembers Barry's dad, but says he never knew Logan Giffen had any children, so he was pretty shocked to have these two beautiful kids show up at his door. The adoption became official a year ago. Barry's cousin is officially their dad now. Pretty decent guy. One of his two kids is around their age, and they're getting along just fine. I visit them once or twice a month. I don't know how they grew that attached to me when they literally only met me for a couple days, but they always go nuts when they hear Guncle Ray is visiting."

"Well, you grew to love them, too."

"I did. I do." He let out a snort and smiled, then left a long silence, a vacant space for words he didn't have the heart to say.

"Hurts, right?" Nadine asked.

"I have no words for it... Danny's like a carbon copy of his dad, but little. Same face, same nose, pudgy fingers,"—he let out a ragged exhale—"got the same blue eyes, too. I look at him and...I miss him so much."

"I know." She sipped some more coffee. "Have you met any-one?"

Ray scrunched up his face as if he'd gotten a whiff of vomit. "I'm not interested in meeting anyone. I... I can't."

"It's been three years, Ray. He would've—"

"Don't." He was blunt and dry, the indignation in his voice intensifying with each sentence. "Don't give me that crap. He wouldn't have. He would've wanted to be alive and with me. He would've wanted us to raise those beautiful kids together. He suffered a lifetime of abuse, denial, self-hatred, longing. He deserved to be happy. Instead, he was erased from the world. My head isn't even close to a space in which I could attempt to... You know."

There was a long silence.

"Have you talked to Jess?" Nadine asked, swiftly changing the subject.

"Oh... yeah." He took a second to cool his head, gather his thoughts. "Cunningham's Capitol Hill was a hit. She and Chuck are doing great. They still share a place, but they're doing fine money-wise."

"Isn't Seattle like super expensive?"

"Yup, but Chuck had a pterodactyl's nest egg saved up. Last time we talked, Jess said she's probably gonna move in with this girl named... Sunshine? Brightlight? Radiance? Some hippy shit like that. I don't even remember. They started dating like two months ago."

"Two months? For real?"

"Deen, I've already gone to about four 'Jess-moving-in' parties in the last two years. First was Kiersten, then Nālani, Margarita, Hrafnhildr, and now... uh... Philips Incandescent Lightbulb, or whatever her name is. She isn't moving in with anyone."

Nadine let out an amused chuckle.

"She's happy, though. She's delegating a lot and taking time for herself. Takes care of Chuck but isn't afraid to just drop everything and go to some heavy metal festival in Germany, or whatever. Says she's trying to live enough for those she lost." He smiled. "All things considered, I'd say she's succeeding at that."

"I'm glad."

"So…" Ray looked from the hallway into Peter's room through the door's window. He remembered learning, a while back, windows in doors were known as 'Judas windows'. He wasn't sure if this applied to hospital doors, though. Peter continued to sit there—his back toward him—staring at nothing, two forlorn coffee mugs on the desk. "Are you planning to come visit him anytime soon?"

Nothing but street sounds for a few eternal seconds.

"I don't know," she finally said. "I'm kind of doing my own thing right now. I already signed up for a teaching job in Japan once I'm done with my contract here." As she said this, her tone brightened. "I'll be teaching English at a school in Nagoya! They have Legoland there, did you know?"

"Don't you teach history?"

"That's the cool thing! They don't care! I'm a native English speaker and a teacher. That's all they need. Can't wait to meet a bunch of new teenagers and adults all curious about my eye patch!"

"What do you tell them?"

"I change the story every time! Kinda like a 'Do you want to know how I got these scars?' thing. To my last group, I told them

I was blowing the candles on my birthday cake and a drunk friend thought it'd be funny to push my face into the cake, and a lit candle went into my eye."

"Jesus, lady!" He laughed, at the same time noticing how she was trying to move the conversation in a different direction. "Look, Nadine, I know… Well, we both know what he did. Jess and I were talking the other day. She said, during that last meeting at Clarendon, you said your absence would be Peter's greatest punishment. Is that what you're doing? Are you punishing him?"

No answer, just the sounds of indistinct chatter, passing cars, distant music.

"Every day he brews coffee, sets two mugs down and waits." She sighed in response. "Know what that's about?"

"He said…" She took a deep breath and let it out loudly. "He said once this was all over, we'd sit and talk over a cup of coffee. I don't know if I want that."

"Why?"

This time she took longer to respond, as if the words she was about to say brought up something too painful for her to put into words. "Do you remember how he always used to say his mother never lied?"

"Yes?"

"That night, at the cavern, when that thing touched me, I knew it was true. She never lied. She couldn't. But I realized *I* could… and I had to."

Ray wasn't sure he wanted to know what she meant by that. "If you ever change your mind…"

"Sure." The discomfort in her voice was palpable. "Maybe after Japan, we'll see. Maybe."

"Okay."

Another extended pause. People, vehicles, wind, life.

"It's been great talking to you again, Ray."

"Always nice to hear from you, Deen. I'm glad you're living it up. You deserve it."

Nadine took a quick pause. He would've thought she'd hung up already if it weren't for the background noise.

"You deserve to live, too. Don't forget that."

"Sure." His tone turned somber. "I gotta go. Take care."

"You too."

Ray burst into the ICU, a few minutes later than he'd promised. He'd made a quick stop at the restroom and locked himself in one of the stalls for five minutes until he'd regained his composure. He'd washed his face, dried it well and come help Derek and Carmelita—another nurse—who were already tending to three new arrivals.

"I'm so sorry," Ray said, out of breath. "Had to stop at the restroom on the way here."

"No worries." Derek gave him a hurried but charming smile. "That's five minutes. So, you owe me five drinks. Up to you if you want them in five separate outings."

He gave an awkward chuckle. He couldn't help but blush.

Nadine's words echoed in his head: "*You deserve to live, too. Don't forget that.*"

Derek motioned toward the patients in the beds. "Okay, each of us got one. You might want to start with that one over there. Won't give you much trouble. All three are coma patients."

"Who are these people?" Ray headed toward the bed furthest from the door, where one of the three patients lay, freshly moved to the bed but not plugged into any of the machinery or tubes, which meant they were in a coma, but considered stable.

"Transfers from Bay Area. They needed the beds and determined these three needed long-term care, so now they're ours."

"Huh. I really don't envy you. The reason I like the elderly is at least they're conscious and can wipe their own butts...half the time." He chuckled, flashed his own famously bright smile at Derek—even if it was a little forced—as he busied himself getting the EKG wire patches. "So, what happened to them?"

Derek pointed at his patient, a young woman of about twenty. "Car accident." He pointed at the man Carmelita was nearly done inserting an IV into. "Fell off a cliff, taking a selfie." Then he pointed at the one Ray was preparing to hook to the monitors. "Now, about your guy..."

Ray got a good look at the man at last. He was rail-thin—nearly emaciated—had his head shaved to accommodate for a bandage that covered his skull and came down over the left side of his face; the man had a five-o-clock shadow—which meant Ray would now have to shave him—his body was bandaged, his left arm and right leg were in Ilizarov frames with pins going into the skin, holding the bones straight.

"Your guy's something of a mystery," Derek continued.

Ray gave him a raised eyebrow.

"He hasn't been hospitalized long, actually. They found him lying naked on a beach two weeks ago near Seaside. No ID. Skull, arm, rib, and leg fractures. He was dehydrated, starved, comatose, but otherwise okay, even if it sounds weird calling *that* okay. He didn't even need intubation, breathed fine on his own."

Ray turned a frown at the man. He had the look of someone who had lost a significant amount of weight and was slowly coming back to a less critical one.

"He had no water in his lungs, so we know he didn't drown," Derek continued. "He was sunburned from lying in the sun for so long, but he didn't actually wash up there."

Ray's eyes found the man's right hand. While the man was thin, he could see he had large hands, thick fingers, hairy knuckles and arms. His heart skipped a beat.

Seaside...

"It was like the air opened up and just deposited him there."

Ray surveyed the patient's face, his closed eye, bandaged skull, no beard. *Because they shaved him... He has a five-o-clock shadow, though.* He took his hand, raised it a little, brought it close to have a better look.

"What are you doing?" Derek asked, puzzled.

The hand had scars in the knuckles—old scars—as if from the skin tearing from punching someone repeatedly. *That could mean anything. A boxer. A UFC fighter. A man with anger issues who punches walls.* Without letting go of the hand, Ray used his free hand to carefully turn the patient's head to one side, examined his neck. He found a long scar. *Like someone who was attacked with a T-Square when he was much younger, leaving a deep, straight cut.*

"How?" he muttered, afraid of others hearing the insanity forming in his mind.

A memory flew across his mind, unbidden. John Hitch, grabbing his arm at that cavern. He didn't know why his mind went there, perhaps mentioning that place during his conversation with Nadine. What he'd said: "*You two deserve the life Christopher and I couldn't have back then. Never doubt that for a second.*"

Deserve, Ray thought. *Deserve. Present tense.* "No." He shook his head. "No, no, I'm going crazy. You're not him. You're not him. You're—"

The man's thick fingers squeezed his hand.

Ray's heart stopped. He gawked at the hand. Its grip was firm. Not an involuntary twitch, or spontaneous muscular flexion. The man *was* holding his hand.

Gobsmacked, Ray swiveled his eyes at the man's face.

He was awake, his head turned toward him. He was looking straight at him. A bright, powder-blue eye opened wide with recognition and shock, moisture filling up the lower eyelid until a tear spilled over the brim and ran down the side of his face. That blue eye. That intensely blue eye.

"Ruh-h..." He tried to speak with a dry throat, lips trembling. His voice was coarse and flinty. "Ray?"

THE END

Map of White Harbor

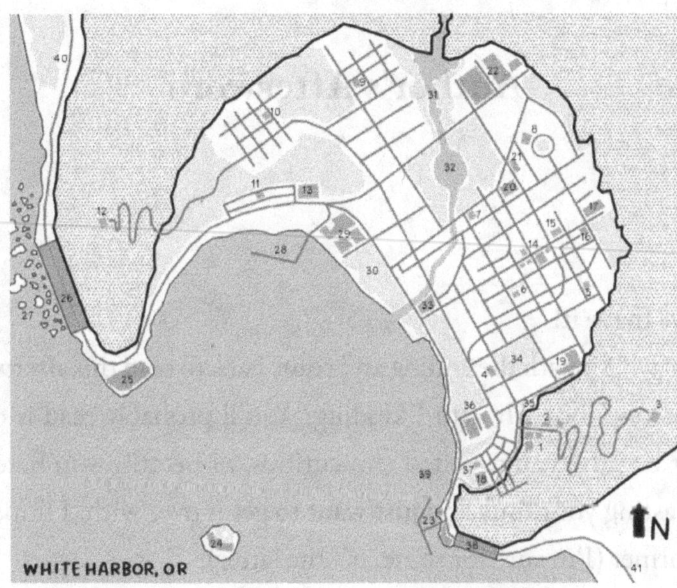

Residential:

1. Knox Family Home (Down), Vanek House (Up), Ben Curling's House (Left)
2. Stockman's Grocery (Left), Martha Lange's Home (Center), Bobby Novak's Home (Right)
3. Peter Lange's Mountain Home
4. Valencia Family Home
5. Nadine Schaefer's Home
6. "Christmas Lights" House
7. Callum Baker's Home
8. Barry Giffen's Home
9. Royce Howe's Home
10. Raymond Chang's Home
11. Chuck Cunningham's Home
12. Xavier Poe Kane's Home

Commercial

13. Holland's Gas Station
14. Lucas's Vet Clinic (Bottom-left), King's Korean Restaurant (Top-left), Merrill Yates's Pharmacy (Left-center), Harrell Movie Theater (Right-center), Esposito's Pizza (Right)
15. Cunningham's Bar & Restaurant
16. Callahan Inn
17. Harbor Grocers (Becker's)

Institutional / Infrastructure

18. Laura Garland Elementary / Middle School
19. Anne Summers High School
20. White Harbor Town Hall
21. Police Building
22. Clarendon Hospital
23. White Harbor Docks / Ferry
24. Lighthouse Rock Mental Health Facility

Landmarks

25. Blue Overlook
26. West Tunnel
27. Sheridan's Teeth
28. Seaside Marina
29. Seaside Amusement Park
30. Seaside Park
31. Pargin River
32. The Eye
33. King Street Market
34. Burkle Park
35. Etenia Creek
36. Lumenwood / Lumenwood Trailer Park
37. The Pines
38. East Tunnel
39. South Marshborough Ruins
40. West Road (To Gearhart, OR)
41. East Road (To Seaside, OR)

Author's Afterword

You've made it!

I'd say, "Sit with the ending and come back to read this afterword tomorrow," but who am I kidding? You'll probably read it now, either because you're elated and curious, or because you hate me for wasting your time and just want to get it over with. I hope it's the former (I'm sure for some, it's the latter).

Art is about interpretation, and you might have a different read of the story than I, and that's 100% valid, but my clinical anxiety demands I give you my take, which should not be seen as "the only truth" nor override your interpretation.

So, Barry died, then I revived him at the end. Let's unpack that. That's important. To some, this might be a cop-out or a fake-out, but halfway through book one, this ending was set in stone. To me, it's the realization of the entire theme of the story.

White Harbor—all three novels—is about trauma cycles, and either breaking those cycles or succumbing to them. The tag line since book one has been "There are events that sour a place, turn it into a hole in the world," and the question has been how do people get out of that hole and restore balance.

Nadine keeps caring about others but forgets about herself. Freddie keeps trying to "save" his family from their curse. Bobby is obsessed with "curing" Freddie. Barry keeps suppressing the fact he's gay. Ellis/Curling/Hitch, has spent a hundred years living with guilt, wanting to die, selfishly closed within himself. The whole town is in this cycle of tragedy and conformity, when they could just make an effort and get out. Peter makes excuses for his mother—his greatest abuser—no matter how bad she gets. Unbroken cycles all over the place.

So, how does that decide Barry's fate?

Think back to that scene in the Betrayal chapters when Barry is trying to find their reflection in the ocean, but it's blurry. Barry and Peter are mirror images of each other. They have many things in common but approach them in different manners.

Barry stumbles and falls a million times, but eventually breaks free from his cycles, even if he'd made every excuse to stay "safe" in his prison. He suffered probably the most out of all characters in the novels, but he broke his cycle, even if he had to literally give his life to save whom he loved most. Peter...he only fell deeper and deeper into that cycle, betraying his friends, siding with his abuser, culminating in him literally fucking his mother!

Barry could've succumbed like Peter did. Throughout the story, most characters who don't break their cycles either die or end up worse than they started. The ones who break their cycles are rewarded. Not all, but most, and they had to fight tooth and nail to break free. If I had killed Barry, it would've contradicted the entire theme of the story. It would've been just me beating down on a character for cruelty's sake. That his survival also let Ellis/Curling/Hitch have some redemption before dying—by giving him and Ray the life John and Christopher were denied—stays true to the theme.

So, Barry and Ray get to have a life outside White Harbor. Peter, he's physically outside White Harbor, but his mind and soul died there with his son. He's waiting for Nadine to come see him, when all she wants to do is leave everything behind—she's doing what he couldn't.

For all of you out there who've had to deal with trauma, addictions; familial, societal, religious, or gender expectations, remember, breaking your cycles is the hardest thing you'll ever do, but once you break them, you'll find it's worth it.

Acknowledgements

I think in my previous two books I've thanked everyone I had to thank, so go read those acknowledgements and multiply them by three. Thanks to all of you again, and to all the other wonderful people who've given me their support since the previous book.

I do want to highlight one supporter in particular, and that's author Xavier Poe Kane. Yes, he's real. He might not be a podcaster (at of this writing), and he might not be as kooky as his book counterpart, but Xavier is one hell of a talented author and a paranormal connoisseur. He's supported me since Book 1, knowing one of the characters in the book would be based on him. I just had no idea his character would enrich the story the way it did, lending it that final bit of mysticism, so White Harbor can continue existing in myth, though it vanished from memory. Go and read Xavier's stories. You will love them.

Xavier, I don't have enough words to thank you.

David-Jack Fletcher and Leeroy Cross James. Without you both, I don't think I'd be where I am right now. I'd still be writing, but you opened up the world to me in ways I couldn't have dreamed.

Jim Groves, Kiki Kirkpatrick, and Tanya Hagel, for giving me the authorization to put your lives in danger in my novel, and in two cases, ending them. Tanya in particular, thanks for being the big sister I never had.

Last but not least, as always, Jimmy. You are my world. Your staunch belief in me is something I'd never known in my life until you appeared in it twelve years ago this year. I can't imagine this happening in any other reality, so I am glad this is the one universe in which you and I crossed paths.

About the Author

Carlos E. Rivera is an IQFAF award-winning author, born and raised in Costa Rica, who has written and rewritten this bio too many times for comfort.

He'd describe himself as anxious and introverted, though he sometimes has to do the whole "acting like a human" thing on social media.

He grew up in the small town of Siquirres during the 80s and 90s, finding refuge in sci-fi, fantasy, drama, crime thrillers, and especially horror. Influenced by Stephen King, H.P. Lovecraft, Silent Hill, David Lynch, and Junji Ito, his writing blends these inspirations with his own experiences and folk stories, creating a unique, unsettling style.

He resides in Costa Rica with his husband, Jimmy, who deserves a "Ten Thousand Golden Retrievers" award for putting up with his level of weird and still loving him.

For updates, follow Carlos on social media: @carlosriveraauthor or visit his website at: criveraauthor.com